LOVE AND
OTHER GAMES
OF CHANCE

LOVE AND
OTHER GAMES
OF CHANCE

A NOVELTY

LEE SIEGEL

VIKING

VIKING
Published by the Penguin Group
Penguin Putnam Inc., 375 Hudson Street, New York, New York 10014, U.S.A.
Penguin Books Ltd, 80 Strand, London WC2R 0RL, England
Penguin Books Australia Ltd, 250 Camberwell Road, Camberwell, Victoria 3124, Australia
Penguin Books Canada Ltd, 10 Alcorn Avenue, Toronto, Ontario, Canada M4V 3B2
Penguin Books India (P) Ltd, 11 Community Centre, Panchsheel Park, New Delhi - 110 017, India
Penguin Books (N.Z.) Ltd, Cnr Rosedale and Airborne Roads, Albany, Auckland, New Zealand
Penguin Books (South Africa) (Pty) Ltd, 24 Sturdee Avenue, Rosebank, Johannesburg 2196,
South Africa

Penguin Books Ltd, Registered Offices: Harmondsworth, Middlesex, England

First published in 2003 by Viking Penguin, a member of Penguin Putnam Inc.

10 9 8 7 6 5 4 3 2 1

LIBRARY OF CONGRESS CATALOGING IN PUBLICATION DATA
Siegel, Lee, date.
    Love and other games of chance : a novelty / Lee Siegel.
       p.   cm.
    ISBN 0-670-89461-3
       1. Jewish men—fiction. 2. Birth fathers—Fiction. 3. Mountaineers—Fiction.
    4. Entertainers—Fiction. 5. Rogues and vagabonds—Fiction.   I. Title.
    PS3569.I377 L67 2003
    813'.54—dc21   2002029635

This book is printed on acid-free paper. ∞

Printed in the United States of America
Set in Dante MT
Designed by Nancy Resnick

For my sons
in the memory
of my father

LOVE AND
OTHER GAMES
OF CHANCE

DIRECTIONS

When, in May of 1991, I flew to Los Angeles to attend my father's funeral, there was sorrow but no remorse. Grief was tempered by a gladness that he had died suddenly, at home, of a heart attack while vigorously shaking a vodka martini, without ever suffering the humiliating infirmities and disgraceful decrepitude that would have been his lot were he still alive today.

Since, following rabbinical commentary on the counsel of Lemuel in the book of Proverbs, it is a Jewish custom to take strong drink upon returning home from the cemetery after the burial of a parent, my brother Robert and I were devoutly drunk in observance of that holy tradition. We took turns mixing memorial martinis and composing toasts in honor of our father, filial obsequies that had evolved through the grace of inebriation from an afternoon's solemn encomia into a loving nocturne of hilarious anecdotal recollections of the deceased. We were laughing when our mother entered the room.

Looking directly at me, she spoke with a sobering urgency. "I have something to tell you. Something important." I braced myself because whenever a woman says she has something important to tell me, it turns out to be bad news.

"I hope you won't be upset or angry," she proceeded uneasily, "that you won't feel deceived or betrayed in any way. I wanted to tell you a long time ago. But your father wouldn't have it. He didn't want you to know. Not ever. But now, now I can't help it. I feel I must tell you the truth."

"You really don't have to," I answered softly with a smile, trying to make it seem that I was letting her off some barbed hook of emotional obligation, while actually just hoping that I'd be spared whatever unpleasant reality she had in store for me. Not only do I consider truth egregiously inappropriate to funerals and times of mourning, I also believe that, at least in a Jewish home, it is a mother's primary obligation to love her son and, in accordance with that fundamental duty, to protect him from the truth, especially if it is in any way disagreeable. Truth is to be revealed by the father.

"I need to tell you," she answered.

The truth that my father had not wanted me to know was that he was not my father. My mother was my mother, my brother was my half brother, and the man whose burial I had just witnessed, and in whose memory I had become piously soused, had, my mother persisted in divulging, met and married her several months after my birth; he had legally adopted me and changed my name from Moshe Schlossberg to Lee Siegel. "I named you after Moses," my mother disclosed over the telephone several months later, "because he didn't know his real father either."

My mother's husband, I was eventually informed, had so genuinely considered me in every sense his first child that he performed for me the orthodox *pidayon ha-ben* ceremony, that patriarchal ritual that redeems a firstborn Jewish son from an obligation to dedicate his life to the service of the God of Israel. For that I remain grateful, since, quite adamantly, I do not believe in any god. But, although I am in no way a religious person and am entirely unencumbered by spiritual impulses, eschatological presumptions, or soteriological aspirations, I do believe in disposing of our dead respectfully. And I suppose that formal remembrance of the departed, if they are beloved, allows us to experience the sentimental as the sacramental. Memory has a potential to offer at least a faint taste of redemption. And thus I have, since 1991, faithfully gone to a synagogue each Yom Kippur—not to atone for anything, God forbid—but to recite *yizkor*. I have forced myself to endure the tedium of the liturgy just to mutter these words: "Remember with love the soul of my departed fathers whose lives I recall in this hour of remembrance. May their memory be a blessing." And twice a year, on May 4 and on June 21, I kindle a *yahrzeit* candle.

Literally millions of people were adopted in the United States during the 1940s, and, given American puritanical attitudes during that period toward both infertility and illegitimacy, it is not uncommon for many of us to discover only late in life that we were adopted. Psychologists and social workers specializing in this particular phenomenon explain that upon learning the truth of our nativity we typically go through an emotionally turbulent period in which we experience feelings of confusion, anger, mistrust, grief, and insecurity. Commonly there is an urge to reestablish our identities, and, as if the formation of the personality or psyche were significantly qualified by reproductive biology, we often search for our natural parents in belated attempts to become acquainted with them and earn their love. If the parent is deceased, the distraught adoptee, according to the diagnostic paradigm, frequently strives to reconstruct the life of the dead progenitor, to make of that mother or father a psychological shade to be posthumously known.

Anticipating, I suppose, that, in response to the sudden revelation, I might question who I am and, in that process, want or need to indulge in the clinically predicted self-therapeutic endeavor, my mother rather dramatically presented me with an old Sears & Roebuck cardboard boot box, in which, she alleged, there were papers that documented the true story of my true father's true life.

"His name was Isaac. Yes, Isaac Schlossberg," she revealed. "He was a showman. An entertainer. You know, in the amusement world. Fairs, carnivals, sideshows, vaudeville, cabarets, nightclubs, plays, movies, and that sort of thing. If you'd ask him what he did, he'd laugh. 'I'm a snake charmer,' or a 'sharpshooter,' 'magician,' 'mountain climber,' 'quick-change artist,' or any other wild thing. Sometimes he'd just smile his handsome smile and say, 'I'm a travelin' man.' And he was that to be sure. A wanderer—America, India, Europe, East and West, up and down, here and there."

Presumably it was a suddenly vivid memory of her long-ago lover, sentimentally incompatible with the grief that she was naturally feeling on the day of her husband's funeral, that brought a slight smile to the widow's tremulous lips. "He died in a mountaineering accident in the Himalayas in 1946. They didn't know exactly where or when, but I like to think that it might have been on top of Mt. Everest, on June 21, the longest, warmest, brightest day of the year. We weren't married, but, well . . ."

Hesitating, she looked into my eyes with abundant affection meaning, I think, to proclaim that my father was the first love of her life. And then, looking at Robert, she smiled a tender assurance that his father was the greatest love of her life. She looked back and forth at her sons, at a loss it seemed as to how to continue. Robert, a physician like his father, offered her a martini and a sedative.

"It might be meaningful for you, I think or at least hope, to look through these papers, to get to know a little bit about him," she muttered, her voice fading under the strain of the day's sorrow. While Robert, after pouring vodka over the ice in the shaker and splashing in three drops of vermouth, opened the olive jar and then the pill bottle, I, putting my arm around our mother's shoulders and kissing her on the forehead, whispered, "It's fine. It doesn't matter. It doesn't change anything, and, in that sense, it really doesn't mean anything."

Perhaps I am, in the depths of my soul, a profoundly superficial person because I felt neither anguish nor anger, neither confusion nor betrayal, and certainly no loss of identity over the admittedly very startling news. I was, however, even after I had sobered up, intrigued by the idea of learning something about this so-called showman whose semen had apparently contributed substantially to my existence.

In observance of the Jewish practice of sitting *shiva* in emulation of the seven days during which Joseph mourned for his father, Jacob, I didn't open the boot box until a week after the funeral. And then I took only a peek. There were a great number of large sheets of old newsprint neatly folded into uncut quartos, a curious game board, and a single antique bone die. It was not until I had returned home and settled back into the routine of my life that I quite lackadaisically began to examine the game and exhume the square sheets of cheap paper from the Sears & Roebuck carton, to unfold, confront, and finally read them. The papers were not stored in any particular order, but the game board, with its numbered squares, provided a designate model for arranging the correspondingly numbered blocks of writing.

One hundred squares form ten rows. Each square of the written game is composed of about two thousand words in black ink, hand-scrawled without paragraph indentation and small enough to be accommodated on one side of a single piece of newsprint measuring thirty-six inches by thirty-six inches, a size of wood-pulp paper used by some regional newspaper publishers during World War II. Each square is a discrete verbal block in a patchwork of autobiographical miscellany. Play begins on the fiery shores of the Dead Sea, the lowest place on earth, and the goal is to reach (by accident, probability, chance, luck, fate, some god, or whatever force it is that does or doesn't predicate the roll of the die) the chill summit of Mt. Everest, the highest spot on the world. Between the beginning and the end, players move geographically from the Wild West (rows 1 to 3), through the Mystic East (rows 4 to 6), to a Prime Meridian (rows 7 to 9), temporally from a remembered past to a gradually observed present in the Novel Antipodes (row 10). One moves sentimentally from love's beginning through its aspirations and almost to its realization (square 100).

Crisscrossing the board are twelve curling, twisting serpents of various lengths (one with two heads) and, likewise, eleven rigid ladders, each with a different number of rungs (and one, a folding stepladder, has its feet in two different squares). Youngsters of the period would have known the rules (although in my protected postwar American childhood the scaled serpents had been tamed and transmuted into "chutes," the benign, though slippery, slides of the playground). When a player, after casting the die, lands on a square that contains the foot of a ladder, he or she climbs up to whatever square, on whatever row, that ladder leads; when a player lands on a square wherein there is the head of a snake hungrily waiting for prey, he or she slides down to the square in which the snake's tail ends. The game of snakes and ladders provided Isaac Schlossberg with a definitive image, rooted in childhood memory, for a conceptual patterning of his experiences and structuring of his life. That structure takes the place of plot and the die provides the suspense.

It wasn't until several months after her husband's funeral that my mother told me more about my father. She had wanted to wait until I was familiar with the game. Norabelle Roth met Isaac Schlossberg in Honolulu: "I had just turned eighteen when Dad finally brought me and Mom over to live with him in the officers' quarters at Hickok Air Force Base. That was in 1944 and the war was still on. There was barbed wire all along Waikiki Beach, and air-raid drills all the time, but people were trying to have fun anyway. We'd go dancing every Sunday at the Royal Hawaiian. And that's where I met your father. He was juggling pineapples and coconuts in a hula show. And he was also making a little money by doing a magic act for private parties and entertaining in troop shows on the military bases. It was thrilling to dance with him. He said he had learned to rumba by charming cobras and I believed him. Yes, he was the charmer and I was the enchanted serpent, swaying as he swayed, bowing as he bowed, dipping with him, turning for him, rising and falling into his arms. Oh yes, he was a wonderful dancer, and he knew how to kiss a girl, too. You could tell that he had been around." My mother laughed affectionately over the memory. In subsequent conversations she spoke of things—love and death and adventure—that are the universal and eternal stuff of tales, the subject and theme of both literary masterpieces and fluffy romances.

They were in love and he planned to marry her, but he wanted to wait until after the war was over so that she might be betrothed to a real hero, not a war hero ("they we're a dime a dozen in '44 and '45") but a world-famous adventurer. His dream was to be the first man to conquer Mt. Everest and to do so on his own, to be the first player to reach square 100. After the war, with the ninety-five squares of his narrative game completed, Isaac Schlossberg, leaving the box of folded newsprint with his fiancée, went to India. The remaining squares, mailed to my mother from Sikkim, indicate that in June of 1946, disguised as a Buddhist pilgrim, he secretly entered Tibet without a permit to confront the highest mountain in the world. His body was never found. Had my father not perished, he would have gloriously descended from the heavenly summit to return to his beloved's earthly embrace.

While it became obvious, as I went through these literary remains of an unknown father, that, if the squares were read sequentially, the text could be followed as a chronological memoir, it also became evident that the narrative was not written any more as a book to be read in earnest than it was constructed as a game to be played frivolously, by hazard and caprice, climbing ladders and being swallowed by serpents according to tosses of the die. To play the game, it seems to me, is to become acquainted with the author in the same way we get to know a person in real life. We don't meet people at birth and follow them chronologically, moving through each and every square with them throughout their existence. By luck or chance or fate, as if by a shake of dice, we encounter people in one square of their life at one time in one place, and then we run into them again in another square at another time in another place, perhaps soon in a nearby square or row, or much later far up some ladder; we come to know that person better when we hear of their past, when the serpents of their memory reveal what has gone on before, even if that past is imagined or fabricated. A person's lies always reveal some truth about them. While we move quickly across some lives, we get stuck in others, going back and forth, up and down, over and over certain events and experiences. That different people know us in different ways and understand in us different characters is determined by which and how many of the squares of our life they happen to have landed in. We can play another person's game, but not our own. Our lives are necessarily lived sequentially from day to day, year to year, square to square, row by row, and there are no ladders by which to jump ahead, nor snakes to take us back and let us try again. And we never know the number of the square we're in at the time.

Ten years ago, after inheriting and then sporadically and randomly reading these squares, I played with the idea of editing them into a book and trying to get it published. The impulse would inevitably arise in me during yizkor on Yom Kippur. But none of the resolutions of the Days of Awe ever remain very long in the mind of one who does not believe in God. Nevertheless, from time to time I would imagine that, leaving filial sentiment aside, this textual oddity might merit publication on formal grounds as a literary curiosity and that it might, furthermore, be of some interest to aficionados of the amusement world or carnival, to variety or old-movie buffs, or to historians of popular culture. But I never quite got around to it.

The old Sears & Roebuck boot box, containing the game board, bone die, and the one hundred folded sheets of newsprint, stored away in the back of a closet, though occasionally pondered, would probably have remained in dark storage and cool neglect if it had not been for a letter that I received from my mother in April of 1998. Again there was a truth that she thought I needed to know. Again she said it: "I have something to tell you. Something important."

She wrote of a surprising letter she had received only the day before "out of the clear blue sky" from a complete stranger, a Dr. Li Shu Gah, research Tibetologist at Beijing's National Institute for the Cultural Study of Ethnic Minority Groups in the People's Republic of China. The letter was written as a result of that government scholar's having made a quite accidental and very startling discovery which he thought might be of interest to my mother. Officially delegated the task of filing and cataloguing a vast store of unpublished papers, letters, and other documents that had been seized in Tibet during the purge of September 1987 and deposited for inspection in the People's Archive of the National Institute, Dr. Li had recently chanced upon a letter dated July 22, 1986, and addressed to Lama Zabs-Dkar Khedrup Rinpoche in Lhasa, from his brother, Khram Nag Gyatso, a Sherpa living in Gangtok, a friend and former associate of Tenzing Norgay, the man who became world famous when he, together with Edmund Hillary, successfully reached the summit of Mt. Everest on May 29, 1952. Dr. Li probably would not have bothered to read all of what was clearly a personal missive without significant political ramifications, if he himself had not had his own particular interest in mountaineering, a preoccupation, he explained, responsible for his having studied the Tibetan language. "I was, at the age of twenty-eight, I am proud to say, a member of the Chinese expedition, led by Shi Chan-Chun in May of 1960, that accomplished the People's victory over the Mountain. And so, noticing the name of the heroic Tenzing Norgay in the letter, I could not help but read the document with considerable curiosity, an eagerness that suddenly on page two turned into outrage."

According to Dr. Li, Khram Nag Gyatso, after vehemently beseeching his brother never to divulge the story to anyone, confided that the esteemed Tenzing Norgay had confessed something "most terrible" to him in 1983: "I have something important to tell you. It is a dreadful secret, never to be repeated. I should not speak of it, but the burden of my silence has become too great. I must tell someone. I want you to know the truth." The celebrated Sherpa described to him the moment when just before noon he and Hillary first set foot on the summit of the dome of Everest: "We could clearly see the East Rongbuk Glacier. We could see as far as the Tibetan high plateau. It seemed as if we could see the entire world. Hillary was laughing with joy and shaking with exhilaration. I trembled in awe. I wept and the tears froze on my cheeks. Hillary's shouts, though muffled by his oxygen mask, were understandable: 'We've done it, Norgay! We've knocked the old bastard off!' Worried that our triumph might be a violation, I fell to my knees and began to dig into the snow with my hands to make a hole into which I might place an offering to the spirits of Chomolungma. I had brought the prayer-incised bone that you gave me for Her. I had not dug very deep when I felt something sticking up out of the ice beneath the softer surface of more recent snow. I signaled Hillary. He knelt down next to me as I shook the object to pry it loose. The ice cracked and it came free. I held it. An ice pick. It was old-fashioned, a kind we don't see anymore. On one side of the wooden handle there was engraved a ladder and around the handle, going in and out of the spaces between the rungs, there was a serpent. And on the butt of the handle there were initials: 'I.S.' I dropped the pick and there was a ghastly moment of silence. Suddenly Hillary picked up the thing that should not have been there and with all his might he threw it into the abysmal emptiness to the north of us. There was more silence. Then Hillary suddenly laughed and repeated himself: 'Yes, we've done it, Norgay! Yes, we've knocked the old bastard off!' By the time we reached Namche, the news had been transmitted by radio all over the world that Edmund Hillary had conquered Everest. And me too. We were the first. We were famous. We were heroes. And I.S., whoever he was, was dead. He was meant to be forgotten. There was no glory for him. It was no good to think about him. It would just confuse things. Soon, very soon, I began to wonder whether or not we really had found an ice pick on the summit, or whether fatigue, lack of oxygen, and the euphoria of the moment had prompted me to imagine it. Hillary and I never spoke of it."

Expressing profound shock over the incriminating story in Gyatso's letter, Dr. Li explained to my mother that the Tibetan court records as kept up until the liberation of feudal Tibet by the Chinese in 1950 were stored in a branch of his archive: "I was thus able to discover that, from July 1945 until April 1946, a man with the initials I.S., namely a certain Mr. Isaac Schlossberg, had repeatedly, but without success, petitioned the Dalai Lama for a permit to enter a closed Tibet and climb Mt. Everest by way of the North Col. The first few of these requests had been posted from the Royal Hawaiian Hotel in Honolulu. Several had been sent from the Tollygunge Players' Club in Calcutta. And the final one came from the Shangri-La Hotel in Gangtok. I wrote to the management of each of those establishments requesting any information that they might be able to unearth about an Isaac Schlossberg. But I received no replies. At that point I had, quite frankly, no expectations of discovering anything more. Several days ago, however, my nephew, an officer for the Bureau of Chinese Information Services and Tourist Development, visited me here at the Institute, having just returned from Honolulu, where, as a personal favor to me, he had done some research. He found an article in the Honolulu Star (December 21, 1945), which I enclose." In turn my mother sent it on to me. "Mr. Isaac Schlossberg, known to regulars at the Royal's Sunday Hula Show as Professor Leroy Lestrange, 'Magician, Mentalist, and Mesmerist,' has big plans for the new year. He says he's going to climb Mt. Everest! His fiancée and number one fan, Norabelle Roth, daughter of Brigadier General Gilbert Roth, says she knows that if any one can do it, he can, 'because he's a magician.' Good luck, Professor! And Aloha! We'll be waiting to hear all about it." Dr. Li commented on the article's photograph: "I presume that the young lady kissing the smiling man in question on the cheek is you."

Dr. Li's nephew had been able to identify Norabelle Roth as my mother through an announcement, in the same newspaper over a year later, of her marriage to a Dr. L. E. Siegel of Beverly Hills, California, an article that described her as the "former fiancée of the Royal Hawaiian Hotel entertainer Isaac Schlossberg, who was lost last year in a mountaineering accident in the Himalayas."

Dr. Li's letter went on to explain that, while his official duties precluded taking any action or making a formal announcement of the discovery, he felt constrained to inform my mother that, unless Khram Nag Gyatso was lying, or unless Tenzing Norgay had imagined the ice pick in some sort of high-altitude delirium, her former fiancé, and neither Sir Edmund Hillary nor Norgay, was the first person to successfully climb Mt. Everest. "It is, Madam, not as a government scholar but as a mountaineer that I feel a duty to report this matter to you. I would have wanted my wife to be informed of my success on Everest if I had not returned and if news of my victory had been covered up. My first son was born shortly after I climbed the great mountain. Had I been lost, I would have wanted him to know the truth."

Thus it was only a year ago, after receiving my mother's letter, containing as it did evidence that my unknown father was the first man to stand atop the highest peak in the world, that I recognized this book's historical significance and realized a responsibility to prepare the manuscript for publication so that the truth might be known.

—Lee Siegel

1	Call me Isaac. Years ago, when I was a child, I was known as Samoo, Samoo the Snake Boy. And although I've been called many things—Little Chief Magpie, Swami Balakrishna, Professor Solomon Serpentarius, Doctor Bungarus, and Leroy Lestrange, to

name a few—Samoo the Amazing Snake Boy of Hindustan, one of ten attractions in *Wyoming Willie's Wonders of the World* traveling spectacular, is the first identity I remember. I am displayed upon a table. The naked torso is a python's. Variegated scales form dusky reticulated patterns on a heavily sinuous, tapering double-S of a body. The head is human and the face is mine. Although my tongue is not forked, it darts as sharply as if it were, as if for the scent of prey, mate, or predator, the odor of food, sex, or death. The eyes roll wildly about in their sockets, and, because snake eyes are lidless, I try not to blink. A red bandana at the neck conceals the separation between snake and boy, and a thick hemp rope appears to secure me to the examination table beneath which mirrors, as long as they are clean and the angles are right, sustain the illusion. My father, none other than Wyoming Willie himself, watchful not to let those mirrors catch his legs in reflection, tugging my tail to stretch me out beyond the edge of the table, makes evident my size, a good six feet of hefty snake. As the torso retracts in resistance to his pull, he takes up a cane to poke the cold-blooded flesh. With each jab, the ophidian body flinches and flexes as the human face plays along with histrionic wincing and ghastly grimaces. When Wyoming Willie daringly extends a finger near the mouth, Samoo flicks his tongue, draws back his lips, hisses, and I snap fake fangs. But the wily showman is too quick for the feral Snake Boy. When Wyoming Willie says I'm deadly, you can believe that the crowd believes it. Everyone needs to be deceived and, provided it doesn't cost too much, wants to be fooled. That's what my father taught me, that and languages for the deception. "People began speaking," he'd say, "so that they could lie to each other. There's no civilization, not love, nor politics, nor religion, let alone entertainment, without lies. It's the lies that keep us free." I relished the game and ruse, the con and wonder. I liked playing the part of Samoo, and Kaleeya, my snake and body, my prop and pet, being by nature shy, didn't seem to mind having his head crammed down into the hole in the table and up against my chest. Snakes crave darkness. He and I were one in dime museums and odditoriums, pits and sideshows, all the string and kid shows. We played Dreamland, Wonder Mountain, Chutes, the Serpentine, Dante's down in San Diego, and Grossman's up in San Francisco. It was only in capitulation to our competition that my father, gradually succumbing to

Siegel's persistent urging, finally agreed to rent the kinetoscope and ten kine-tographs: "Buffalo Bill Meets Indians on the Warpath," "Firemen on Their Ladders," "Damayantee the Serpentine Danseuse," "Paris Cancan," "London Bridges Falling Down," "A Game of Chance," "The Merry Mountaineer," "Tiger Hunt," "Tunnel of Love," and "Bathing Beauties Behind the Bushes." It made sense: in one tent that held ten, one could see all ten for ten cents. The substantial popularity of the seductive new amusement made it difficult for my father to refuse Siegel's proposal to capture us on film. There was one reel of a hundred feet of film for each one of our exhibits, a thousand feet of cellulose nitrate that made for a ten-minute feature that sold out for its premiere projec-tion at Liplinger's on Mountain Way in Los Angeles. Because my first memory of myself is preserved in the reel of "Samoo the Amazing Snake Boy," I'm not sure whether I am remembering the moment or recalling the motion picture show, whether the film has sustained the memory or implanted it. "Watch this," Siegel said with uncontrollable glee as he turned the brass handle on the viewer faster and faster. My reptilian body was wiggling so quickly, my eyes rolling about so rapidly, my tongue darting and teeth snapping so briskly, all so very, very fast, that it made us laugh. "You see how funny that is? But watch this," Siegel declared as he slowed the crank down, slower and slower, and slowly my tongue was pushed out and sluggishly drawn back. Listless was the body on the table, lugubrious the swiveling eyes. "It's so sad, isn't it?" Siegel chuckled: "Look how sad it is! Life's amusing to the degree that it's accelerated, the faster the funnier. But slowed down, the funniest thing in the world be-comes woeful. And if you stop it dead still, the film burns up. There's a searing incandescent flash and you're gone forever!" I asked my father about it: "Being funny isn't the same as being happy, is it?" And he responded in practical terms: "Being funny pays better than being happy." Even though I knew it wasn't real, the slower Angel seemed to move along the high wire, the more frightened I became that she would fall. The more rapidly she bounced along it, the more reassured I was that the world could be a cheerful place. The most hilarious of all the moving pictures was of Kaleeya eating a chicken. Although it wasn't comedic as filmed, and not terribly funny when cranked up to top speed, any-one would have laughed when the handle was turned backwards: the lump in the snake's body, suddenly popping out of the fanged mouth, inflated into a chicken, and Kaleeya appeared to slither backwards, away from the bird as if in fear of it. "Does that mean that it's funny to go backwards?" I wondered. My father answered, "Only for chickens. For us it's bothersome to go backwards and thrilling to go forward, onward and upward. All the way to the top, to square one hundred! Climb the ladders and watch out for snakes in the grass." The exhortation was a reference to the game of snakes and ladders that he had given me for Purim. When I played it with Angel, I didn't care as much about making it to the top as I did about my token's landing in a square with hers. One day, while waiting for the show to start, after I had wiped the mirrors clean, slipped in my fangs, positioned Kaleeya, and taken my place, Angel approached the examination table upon which Samoo the Snake Boy was displayed. Very gently, a little nervously, she stroked the body of the snake from neck to tail tip, staring at it, and then she looked at my face. I was embarrassed, trembling under the table and breathing anxiously. As if the naked body that she touched really was my own, I could feel her finger tips upon it. *Ka-bamm! Ka-bamm!* Gunshots were the cue to begin the show. Having paid the price of admission, the audience, entranced by Wyoming Willie's boisterous ballyhoo, gathered on the platform in front of my ten-by-ten to gawk in astonishment: "Samoo the Snake Boy, dreadful duomorphic denizen of an Oriental Eden, dropped by surprise from a tree upon an unsuspecting me, wrapped his callous coils around my head so that I could not see—I swear to God Almighty, this is as true as true can be—and he twisted his terrible tail around my neck to choke me." Having quickly accelerated to top verbal speed, my father would then suddenly slam on the brakes, screech to a stop, a suspenseful silence, and then, when he had them where he wanted them, he'd start up again to take them on a wild ride. Depending on the constitution of the crowd, he could make a story as obscene or idyllic, heroic or comic, as they pleased; any tale could become a myth or joke, an allegory, farce, or true report. The lesson was that the facts of life don't mean a thing; it's words that make things what they are. "How did I escape from Samoo's coils? I'll be honest with you," he'd say, solemnly removing his Stetson to hold it over his heart. "In all modesty, ladies and gentlemen, it was neither skill nor any art of mine, no act of courage nor grace of God, that saved my life. That very day I had, just as I do each and every morning, dressed my hair with this." He held up the red tin: "Wyoming Willie's Wondrous Hair Pomade, my very own brilliantine, hand fabricated according to a secret Egyptian formula from the purest petrolata, finest fats, richest oils, marvelous minerals, rarest fragrances, and miraculous follicular medicaments, ingredients gathered on my travels up, down, and all around this wonder-full world. It will tame the wildest of hair. If not for this pomade I'd be dead today. When Samoo wrapped his fatal form around my head, his scales became coated with this glossine, and so unctuous is this unction that I slipped easily from his coils to bag the beast and look my best to boot, my hair still perfectly in place." And then he'd sell the grease, cheaply manufactured exclusively for him by Shmuel Grossman in Atlanta, for "only ten cents per precious ounce." It was guaranteed to make you more confident, more admired by men and desired by women. "If not, you'll get your money back." The tin itself was a pitch-piece memento emblazoned with a three-color portrait of me: "Samoo the Amazing Snake Boy, born in far-off Hindustan!" Wondering about the place from which Samoo came, a fantastically beautiful and dangerous land where deadly serpents danced, I thought that I might someday go there. I'm not sure whether audiences ever trusted the showman's claim that Samoo was born in the jungles of the East, but I do know that I never believed my father when he told me again and again that my life had begun at a holy place, the lowest spot on earth, the Dead Sea. Lots of the stories he told me were set there. It was there that the city of Sodom had flourished before our wrathful God destroyed it with terrible rains of fire, and there that the wife of Lot still stands as a pillar of salt. It was in the oasis of En-Gedi on the western shore of the Dead Sea that David hid from Saul, and there that in secrecy he made love to the wife of Uriah. And "once upon a time in En-Gedi, long, long ago," my father, sitting on the edge of my bed, began one night, "there was a teacher, one of the blessed Tannaim, and he had five sons, each one of whom he instructed to memorize one of the books of Moses. And when those sons, after they had left En-Gedi, each had sons of their own, they taught their sons to memorize a separate portion of the book that they themselves had committed to memory. Those sons, scattering around the world, in turn taught each of their sons a section of what they knew, and after several generations each of the hundred or so chapters of the Torah had been memorized by one of the descendants of the teacher of En-Gedi. And now I shall teach you, my only son, the single verse that was entrusted to me by my own father, Menachem ben Simcha: *Vatomer Sarah tzechok asah li Elohim kol-hashomea yitzachak-li.*" He translated it for me. "Sarah said, 'God made laughter for me so that whoever hears my laughter will laugh with me.'" After repeating it in Hebrew, he asked me to recite it. As soon as I had done so without error, my father smiled. "As long as everyone remembers what he is supposed to remember, the word of our God, the creator of all, will be kept alive, no matter how many scrolls and books may be burned by our enemies. Memory is our sustenance." He blew out the light and then, in the darkness of the boarding house room, kissed his son good night.

2 Yes, I was born, my father swore to Hashem, the Lord of All, in the deepest exposed depression on earth, in the oasis of En-Gedi on the saline shores of the Dead Sea, far below the dispassionate stars that glistened over a decomposing Ottoman Palestine on December 21 at the darkest hour in the middle of the darkest night of 1899. We were, he dared to claim with a straight face, on our way to Bethlehem, where he fancied destiny would have me born four days later. The trip was supposedly a detour on a great journey "up, down, and all around the world" undertaken by Wyoming Willie both to recruit "ten specimens of human strangeness as never before beheld by civilized mankind" for his Wonders of the World vagrant spectacular and to gather ingredients for his Wondrous Hair Pomade, the recipe for which he had gleaned from "an Egyptian pharmacological papyrus compiled in the Sixth Dynasty by the magician Dedi of Dedsneferu." The fabulous itinerary was detailed in a ten-cent, ten-page pitch book in which patrons, hungry for the exotic and incredible, could feast on juicy words about Wyoming Willie's amazing adventures in the lush Amazon, the barrens of Patagonia, the darkest jungles of Dahomey and the even darker forests of the Congo, the wastelands of Kamchatka, the dry sprawl of the Gobi, the Tibetan Himalayas, the Deccan of Hindustan, pharaonic Egypt, and biblical Palestine. In a supplement, my father, brazenly rendering perils, delights, misfortunes, and wonders, wrote of his further adventures in Bengal, Borneo, Madagascar, Hawaii, Tierra del Fuego, El Dorado, Tasmania, Nova Zembla, Suez, and Lapland. Even though it was the only account of my nativity that I had, I couldn't, no matter how hard I tried, believe it. I always knew it was false, not because of its preposterousness (since so many outlandish things are true), but quite simply because Wyoming Willie never told the truth. I assumed that he had never set foot in Asia, South America, Africa, the Pacific, or the Arctic. It was not that my father was devious. But truth bored him. It had never proved itself entertaining enough. He was irked by its brutal banality, lack of malleability, indifference to desire, its disregard for our fears and immunity to our control. "Truth," he said, "is the nemesis of love and religion, and an ally of oblivion." That my father earned our daily bread by telling tall tales condoned his prevarications. His stories weren't merely the pitch and patter for the shows. On the contrary, the exhibits were living proof that his lies were true. "Seeing is believing," he'd say with a shameless grin. "And vice versa!" "Hearing is believing," is what he meant. Never do I remember hearing his real name except when it was whispered as if it were some Cabalistic formula: "Avraham ben

Menachem—Abraham Schlossberg." While it's obvious that he was certainly from somewhere in western Russia, he swore, at least back when he was Wyoming Willie, that he had been born in Fort Laramie, Wyoming, in 1873. The sharpshooter claimed that after his pioneering parents had been murdered by No-Neck Nat's Invisible Mountain Gang, he had been found crawling about on all fours with a pack of wolves by Apache Indians who, naming him Laughing Eagle and raising him as one of their own, taught him to throw knives and tomahawks. He was pals with Geronimo. Even though my father surely knew that I surely knew that he had surely never even visited either Wyoming or Palestine, "you were born in the Holy Land," he'd swear to me in his western drawl as if I were just another gullible towner with twenty-five cents in my pocket. If I asked my mother about it, she'd take a long, slow, thoughtful puff on her perpetual Camel cigarette and refer me back to him: "If he says you were born in the valley of the Dead Sea, that's where you must have been born. He is your father, after all." Although my mother, as an obligatory capper, would never contradict her husband's fantastic fables, she was relatively, but not obsessively, truthful about herself, disclosing that she had been born in Volhynia in 1881 on the very day that Alexander II had died as the victim of a bomb thrown by a revolutionary. It was a significant moment for our people: the incumbent czar, determined to purge Mother Russia of Jews, officially schemed to exterminate one third, convert another third, and deport the rest. Luckily, if not by the grace of El Adon, my parents, so my mother confided, managed to arrive in New York in the winter of 1897. My father never spoke of the Jewish immigrant who had worked at a little ladder factory in Queens. It was as if Abraham Schlossberg had died on the first day of the twentieth century, the day that Wyoming Willie was born as a full-grown man, the afternoon that my father first performed with pistols, blades, and hatchets at Grossman's Music Hall in San Francisco. The insemination that resulted in the birth of that new persona occurred in the summer of 1898 at Madison Square Garden. Mendel Lansky had given Abraham and his wife tickets to the show. "Buffalo Bill's Wild West," Mendel had proclaimed, "*is* America." "Was I born in America?" I periodically and doggedly asked. "Where was I really born?" My father stubbornly reiterated the same story: "The Dead Sea, the lowest place on earth. There's nowhere to go but up from there, my son." He claimed that he and my mother had been in Palestine at the time in search of a certain species of snake that, as a defense when frightened, stiffens and straightens its body. The reptile instinctually lies to predators: "I am not a snake; I am a stick." And my father lied to me: "So Hashem showed Moses that when he grabbed the serpent by the tail, it became a staff in his hand. God was going to use that magic trick to redeem the Jews. But Pharaoh's magicians already knew the gag. They threw down their rods and the rods became serpents. They picked them up by their tails and the frightened snakes became rods again. I went to the Orient in search of that snake for an act I had in mind, the dramatic story of a magician-priest, a living descendent of Aaron." If my father really had been raised by wolves or Apaches he probably wouldn't have been so familiar with the Torah. The tale of the sacrifice of Isaac became the premise for a vaudeville performance some years later: "And Abraham, with his only son, Isaac, came to the land of Moriah, which God had told him of; and Abraham built an altar of wood, bound his son Isaac, and set him against the altar. And Abraham, in obedience to God, stretched forth his hand and took a knife to slay the son whom he didst truly love. And Abraham threw the knife toward Isaac and would have pierced his heart had not an angel of the Lord pushed aside the blade so that it entered the altar of wood near the flesh of Abraham's only son and harmed him not. Again Abraham, in devotion to the Lord of our fathers and deliverer of our children, tried to make the sacrifice, to cast another knife into his son, and again didst an angel of the Lord push aside the blade." As if protected by an angel of a merciful God no less than by a ruse, I took my place upon the altar, and a double-edged knife seemed to spin toward me, only to stick in the wood just above my head. Another appeared to stick near my cheek. Then the other cheek. That one was close! Two more, one to each side of the neck, then in between my arm and my chest, on one side and then the other. Then down the outsides of my legs. Then three more knives: between my ankles, my knees, and finally just below my crotch. My father used the trick wherein the thrower actually releases the knife backwards as his hand snaps behind his head and then fakes the forward toss in a quick motion as an identical knife pops out of the gimmicked backboard against which the seemingly endangered accomplice safely stands. On the stage at Grossman's in 1911, God revealed Himself in a loud voice with a Yiddish accent (not unlike that of Jake Grossman, but deeper and more grave): "Lay down thine knives, and neither do anything unto the lad: for now I know thou fearest God, seeing that thou hast not withheld thy son, thine only son, from Me." And then God, Lord of heaven and earth, commanded Abraham to take up the three torches of fire that had been prepared for the burnt offering and to juggle them. And Isaac joined his father, juggling three more flaming torches, and, lo, they were not burned for they were blessed by God. And it came to pass that Isaac, in the years that followed, didst journey far and didst juggle torches, swords, batons, pins, and balls for Canaanites, Philistines, and Gentiles in many lands, but mostly in California, Oregon, and Washington. And whenever I have had occasion to juggle, I think of my father's laughter. "We named you after Isaac," he said, "because, just like you, he was born on the shores of the Dead Sea and also because his name—your name, Yitzchak—means 'He will laugh.'" He'd say laughing, "Laugh, my son, and let others hear your laughter!" He told me the story of Jacob and of the dream in which there was a marvelous ladder that reached from the lowest place on earth to highest place in heaven, and he described the angels of God ascending and "they were laughing. The higher they'd climb, the harder and louder they'd laugh. From way up high, the earth looks a very funny place." The Pentateuch was a justification, if not a sanctification, of my father's lies: "Tatenui Foter himself composed the Torah and everybody knows it's nothing but fables. Our God loves good stories. Truth belongs to all people; it's not so special. But Jews were chosen to hear and retell a story that, even though it's not true, is truer than the truth because it was thought up by the Author of the world. You're a Jew; and to be a Jew means to love words and stories, to love listening to them and telling or writing them, and even being in them. Every Jew is a character in a story that began with Abraham and has yet to end." And so, just for the love of words, I, Yitzchak ben Avraham, even though I do not believe in God, am beginning a story within a story. Unlike my father or his God, however, I shall try to be truthful. It is a story about love and death and trying to have a good time anyway.

3 As Fatima el-Fatiha, Danseuse of the Desert, Mystic Mentaliste and Omniscient Oread, Clairsentient Reader of the Minds of Men, the Hearts of Women, and the Palms of Little Children, my mother wore a diaphanous yashmak over her nose and lower face that made her dark eyes premonitious and bewitching. Her costume for the act was the sort of garb in which one would imagine she must have been clad when Wyoming Willie, his hair well groomed and shiny, risked his life to rescue her from the harem tent of Eyada ibn Ajjueyn, the Despot of Damascus: sequined silk shulwaurs, a chupkun or chuddur, Oriental scarves and beaded shawls. She was bejeweled and bangled, heavy with charms and amulets, and the toes of her slippers were curled and bobbled of course. Bits of Arabic peppered her patter: *"Wa hyat Ullah* you shall find the love and wealth you seek. *Ullah gowwik! Bismillah!"* The performance started in the present as she read aloud words written in secret and concealed by some nervously volunteering innocent. And then the near future was apparently clear to a blindfolded Fatima as she wrote out a word or name in precise prediction of what another rube was about to think. And then there was the past: "You were born in Washington." "Your favorite flower? It's a rose!" "Your father's name was Gilbert." Her mastery of the manifold methods of mentalism (cold readings, lip and pencil reading, blindfolds, gaffed slates, swami gimmicks, faro boxes, center tears, billet switches, shills and stooges, leading questions and verbal ambiguities) and her innate skills (perfect timing, an inexhaustible memory, and the keenest powers of observation) served the actress. The themes were eternal: adventure, love, and death. Once you knew she knew your past, you trusted Fatima with all your heart, and paid her twenty-five cents to divine your destiny. "The future, that's the easy one," my mother said, smiling. "Just tell them what you know they want to hear. And I know exactly what you'd like to hear right now, my little lamb, *mein zeese nishumele,* my Isaac: I love you." She loved to tell me that she loved me. But I wanted to hear about the past and how it all began. I wanted to know the truth about Abraham Schlossberg. She held my hand. "Arriving in New York in the winter of 1897, we moved into a one-room apartment on Hester with your father's cousin, Mendel Lansky. He got your father a job at little stepladder factory that some Jews had opened in Queens. And about a year later, Mendel gave us tickets to the Buffalo Bill Wild West Show at Madison Square Garden." That she closed her eyes as she spoke made it seem that Fatima was revealing my origins not through memory but by some occult power. "When, in the center of the arena, the stallion reared, your father

19

grumbled, 'I hate horses.' Then Colonel William F. Buffalo Bill Cody, waving his wide-brimmed hat to the cheering crowd and smiling like only a shaygets can, bellowed with that foghorn voice of his: 'I now present, for your pleasure and edification, the Congress of Rough Riders of the World. Okay, Rough Riders, ride 'em!' The horsemen raced into and around the ring, cavorting and caracoling, galloping at full speed as the Buckaroo Band played 'The Star-Spangled Banner.' That was before it was the national anthem. There were hooting cowboys firing six-guns, then howling redskins with tomahawks, then gauchos with their bolos, and vaqueros twirling lassos. There were chasseurs and Ulans galore on lavishly caparisoned steeds, a band of Bedouins on their Arabians, a horde of Mongols on their stock ponies, and turbaned sepoys on their Bengal chargers. Every rider wore a native costume and brandished some exotic weapon. While the Buckaroo Band played what was supposed to be the native music of each land, Buffalo Bill, in the spotlight on the rostrum, was announcing each group, commenting rhapsodically on their respective equestrial customs, and introducing each of their leaders: 'And now, ladies and gentlemen, led by Prince Ivan Makharadze, former chief cavalry adviser to Czar Alexander the Third, the fierce, proud, and courageous Cossacks of the Don!' As the audience applauded, your father began to tremble, perspire, and breathe in harsh gasps as the veins swelled in his neck and his face turned borscht-red. The four Russian horsemen, sweeping into the arena, two of them mounted backwards on their horses, all of them with swords drawn and swinging as if to cut off Jewish heads, were shouting some gobbledygook that Buffalo Bill claimed was their chant of battle: '*Kakoe tomnoe volnenye v moey krove!*' When they somersaulted from their mounts to jump up and down in an idiotic manner, Buffalo Bill declared that it was a Cossack dance, 'the sight of which sends chills of terror up and down the spines of their enemies no less than it makes the hearts of their womenfolk throb with love.' Abraham was standing up and screaming in Russian, 'Die and rot in Gehenna, filthy dogs, Amalekites, Sodomites, degenerate sons of syphilitic whores,' and such obscenities that we would have been arrested if anyone had understood the language. The audience around us commanded Papa to sit down, but, paying no attention to them, he stood up on his seat to shake his fist. 'Maggots infesting the turds of pigs! You who killed Menachem and Milcah Schlossberg! You remember Reb Menachem! Even you cannot forget the wailing of your victims and their little Avi!' With tears streaming into his beard, he kicked at the man on the other side of him, who was trying to calm him. Spittle was spraying from his mouth with the invectives that melted from cold, hard Russian into molten Yiddish: '*Gai platz! Gai tren zich! Gai strasheh di vantzen!* Kaddish for Menachem and Milcah Schlossberg is always followed by curses on your vile heads. Three times a day I face Jerusalem to beseech the God of Abraham, Isaac, and Jacob for your punishment. You are not in Russia now. Here you are shit! Ha! Now the Lord Almighty will mete out justice for Israel. *Geharget zolstu veren!*' As the Russian horses continued to circle the arena and the Buckaroo Band played a cowboy version of the mazurka, the folks around us tried in vain to mollify Papa's outrageous display. All the sorrow and bitterness of the world seemed to be welling up in his heart to erupt in curses and tears. He cried out in Hebrew: 'O Lord God, remember me, and strengthen me, I pray to Thee, only this once, O God, that I may be avenged of the Philistines for my two eyes, my mother and father. Let me die with the Philistines as did Samson before me.' Madly bounding over the knees between his seat and the aisle and plunging into the crowd, he rushed frantically toward the faraway arena, possessed, his soul set on killing the Cossacks." Mother stopped to open a fresh pack of Camels, and, lighting one up, she took a deep, relaxing puff, and smiled. She had become addicted to nicotine from the many hours during which she practiced with the gaffed cigarettes to make it look like my father really was shooting them out of her mouth. She'd light one after another, fifty or sixty per practice session, inhale, blow out the smoke, inhale again, and *ka-bamm!* The bullet seemed to cut the cigarette in half. Then she'd slowly exhale a cloud of pure white smoke, and light another. She smoked hundreds a day. That she seemed to enjoy it when my father seemed to shoot at her with his Colt Peacemakers, and the pleasure he obviously took in seeming to do so, made it seem that they loved each other. They made up routines together, and I don't think they fought or argued very often. Perhaps this was because neither cared whether or not the other told the truth. Marriage was their entertainment. "I was terrified," my mother continued, "truly terrified. I couldn't see him. I didn't know what to do. I didn't dare move or try to follow him because, not speaking English then, I was afraid that I'd be lost. Sitting in my seat trembling and anxious, frightened that I would never find my way back to Mendel Lansky's apartment, I knew Abraham was going to try to murder the Cossacks, and assumed that he was the one who was going to die. As the Cossacks made their final circle of the arena, I desperately scanned the mob for some sign of him. It was as if he had been cast overboard from the deck of a ship into a dark tumultuous sea and carried away into oblivion. The United States Cavalry and a band of Indians in feathered warbonnets, shouting 'Geronimo,' howling as they entered from opposite sides of the stadium, began to reenact a frontier massacre over the sound of gunshot, Indian war cries, and the Buckaroo Band playing 'The Star-Spangled Banner' again. Searching for your father was hopeless because the audience had stood up to applaud the entrance of Buffalo Bill. I was sobbing as he shot the chief of the Indians, cut off his hair, and then, waving what I assume was a wig in the air, thundered, 'This scalp for Custer!' As the cheering audience sat down, I remained standing with only the faintest hope of spotting my husband. The next act was two acrobatic clowns with a ladder which one climbed and the other held precariously. The high ladder, with a clown atop it, swayed this way and that way, almost falling, and the audience roared with laughter as I cried, 'Avraham, Avraham ben Menachem, come back to me! Help me!' I was certain that I would never see him again." She stopped to light another Camel and smiled a smile complex in the many emotions that it seemed to reconcile, then laughed, then frowned fleetingly, exhaled, shook her head, took another puff, and finished the yarn: "He came back to me beaming with delight, and, grabbing my hand, he pulled me forcibly to the dressing room of the Cossacks who were not Cossacks at all, but Russian Jews who had shaved their beards and put together some Ukrainian costumes! Prince Ivan Makharadze was none other than Jacob Tsadock Grossman from Papa's village, and the other three Cossack horsemen were Jacob's younger brothers, Beryl, Hayim, and Shmuel. They had been in heder with your father. He was delirious with excitement and joy: 'My dear Mrs. Schlossberg'—that's what he called me in those days, even when we were alone, even in the most intimate of moments—'we are going to get out of that little apartment of Mendel's and travel in great open spaces. We are going to see America! Up, down, and all around the country. North and South, East and West—the Wild West! Grossman is going to get me a job with the one and only Buffalo Bill. He's sure he can do it. He might have been nothing but a luftmensch in Russia, but he's a groyser-macher now! He's a prince!' He laughed loudly, the loudest he had laughed since we arrived in America. He removed his yarmulke and waved it in the air the way Buffalo Bill had flourished his Stetson: 'Okay, Abraham and Sarah Schlossberg, ride 'em!'"

4 "Buffalo Bill was a shmuck," Jake Grossman said with a laugh when I saw him in his room at the Merry Medusa Hotel in Greenwich in 1924, the year he exhibited twenty-one American Indians as "The Last of the Wild Redskins" in Moscow, Berlin, Rome, Paris, and London. Like all showmen, Jake was sentimentally compelled to reminisce, cutting up jackpots to cook up the past. "As soon as I said that your father was a Jew, Buffalo Bill was eager to hire him as a bookkeeper in the Office of Wild West Accounts. Just as he believed that Cossacks were born to ride horses backwards, so Yids, according to Buffalo Bill, were chosen to manage money. I had become a Cossack because that's what Buffalo Bill needed me to be. In 1895, some Wild West booking agents had traveled to Russia to recruit Cossack horsemen for an upcoming Rough Riders of the World Congress. Jobless and not one to wait for the coming of Messiach, I had, at that time, taken to hawking things: mezuzahs, yarmulkes, a shtrayml if I could get my hands on one, and used books in Yiddish, Russian, Polish, German, and occasionally a Hebrew Bible or Siddur. I had a little cart that I'd set up in the morning on this corner or that to wait, if not for a customer or a miracle, at least for a passing friend who might stop to shmooze, to tell me some bad news or a good joke. One morning on Zhidi Street a foreigner approached me and, in the worst Russian I had ever heard, asked if I knew of any Cossacks who might be available to go to America. Sure, I said, and I'd be happy to send some to his hotel, the fancy-shmancy Chlopicki Palace. My three brothers and I shaved our beards and overnight Getsle Kopitsky the tailor made some Ukrainian costumes for us. We were hired with no questions asked. Although we didn't know much about horses, for a way out of Russia and the promise of sixty dollars a month in America, we figured we could learn. I found a Russian book for us to study on the ship, an edition of *Filosofiia i praktika izkusstva verkhovoi ezdy,* Prince Ivan Makharadze's monograph on the philosophy and practice of horsemanship, and I figured it must be good because it was in a very used condition and it smelled of horse shit. You can learn to do anything in the world if your life depends on it and if you can read." Jake paused to ask if I wanted vodka. After drinking to the memory of my father and pouring a second shot for both of us, he resumed the tale. "Our act was so convincing that even your father was fooled. Threatening to kill all of us, he was just about to assault me with his bare hands when I yelled out to him, 'Avraham ben Menachem, my friend, it's me, Yaakov Tsadock!'" Jake laughed and his eyes closed. "So, I got him a job in the show. Because we didn't want Buffalo Bill to know that we weren't really

Cossacks, we'd have to sneak into your parents' tent on Shabbis to light the candles. We had to work on Saturday, but what the hell, we thought, we're in America now and earning big money. You can be a good Jew without keeping all the mitzvoth. Only the commandment that forbids us to bow down before another god is absolute. The rest are only important, according to the Talmud, to the degree that they make life better. That's what your father always said. You could hardly keep kosher on the road with the Wild West show, and, of course, there was no mikvah. But your father said that it didn't matter, and that even if Sarah and Shmuel's wife, Leah, were to let their hair grow and discard their kerchiefs, it would not offend God. 'They are beautiful,' he smiled, 'and, according to *Zohar*, beauty is purity in heaven.' Because your father was the son of a rebbe, and because his Hebrew was so good, we took his opinions on Jewish matters seriously. But, you know, I don't know how much he really knew. His talent was languages. Your father could speak Hebrew like a Baal Koray and Russian like one of the slavophile Black Hundreds. He knew Polish and German as well. And, after just a few months with the Wild West show, he could speak English like an American cowboy or a British gentleman, accents and all. And this God-given ability changed the course of Abraham's life. In no more than six months, as unbelievable as it seems, he could converse in most of the tongues that were used by the people who worked for the show: Chinese, Sioux, Apache, Spanish, French, Hawaiian, Arabic, Greek, Hungarian, Italian, German, and God only knows what else." As a child I had felt victimized by my father's linguaphilia: although I never went to a real school, I was constrained to devote two hours a day to a curriculum that consisted entirely of languages. He wanted me to know ten languages and to read ten books in each one of them. "The same thing could happen here," my father said, "that is happening in Russia. It has always happened—in France, Spain, England, Germany, Poland, everywhere we have gone. By being chosen and blessed, we have been cursed and dispersed. We might have to flee from America next. Where can we go? Tierra del Fuego, Iceland, Borneo, China, Tibet, India? The more languages you know, the more places you can go and live, the more truths you can hear and lies you can tell. The more languages you know, the more free you can be." In order to justify promoting my father from accountant to chief translator, Jake explained over a third vodka, "Buffalo Bill theorized that Jews were even more proficient at languages than at bookkeeping because all the languages of the world had evolved out the language of Eden in the 'old Jew Bible. The Hebes,' he said, 'are the watchmen of Babel.' As an interpreter, Abraham became friends with people who only knew their native languages, who weren't able to speak with anyone who was not of their own nationality. Choctaw Charlie, who needed to learn English if he was going to become a

24

main attraction, offered to teach Abraham knife and tomahawk throwing in re-turn for language lessons. Charlie learned English and Abraham learned to throw. Abraham, in a similar deal, learned everything there is to know about rifles and pistols, snap shooting, trick fire, quick draw, and blind shot, from a Frenchman who billed himself as the Count of Monte Pistole. He was teaching me and my brothers English too, right up until we quit the show. We had to leave when Buffalo Bill asked us to do a special performance of Cossack songs and dances for the Russian ambassador in Washington. The kazatski was more difficult to fake than Cossack riding since we didn't have a book on dancing. Shmuel and Leah moved to Atlanta and started a business, the little factory where he made that hair schmaltz for your father. Beryl and I pooled our savings, went out to San Francisco, and leased a run-down little theater, not performing ourselves anymore, but booking acts and managing. We made enough to renovate the place by renting it out each Sunday to the Grand Metropolitan Ecclesiarch of the Pentecostal Church of the Outpouring of the Latter Day Rain of Love. They'd come with their burlap bags of rattlers, copperheads, and cottonmouths, and their flasks of strychnine and arsenic, and act meshugeh in the name of the Lord. And Hayim? That's another story." Jake claimed that when he heard my father had quit the Wild West, he had invited him to come to San Francisco. "It made Buffalo Bill angry when your father left, not because he cared about your father, but because he knew he had a real star in Sarah. More vodka? Yes, let's have a few more drops. *L'chayim!* All the women who came to the show with their husbands began as seamstresses, laundresses, or in concessions. And then, if Buffalo Bill decided they had the theatrical talent and moral fortitude, they could be promoted into the victims of bandits and Indians. Sarah had the talent all right. It wasn't long before she was being kidnapped each night by Geronimo himself in 'Attack on a Settler's Cabin.' But Buffalo Bill, insisting that 'Jews can't shoot straight,' wouldn't allow Abraham to perform the gun and knife act he had developed. And so your father quit. Nobody lasted very long. Abraham had saved up all the cash he needed to buy a pair of Colt pistols, a Marlin rifle, a set of throwing knives, and a costume—buckskins, a Stetson hat, black leather gloves and boots. Dressed as an Indian squaw, Sarah called herself 'Deer Heart, the Apache Maiden.' Abraham would fast-draw, spin his pistols, and shoot an Indian-head nickel out of her hand and a Camel out of her mouth. And you'd swear it was real. When you were just a baby, she'd hold you in her arms for the act. There's something about an infant in mortal danger that has a way of thrilling people. That's what gave Abraham the idea for your solo debut as 'Little Chief Magpie the Half-Breed Papoose and his Baby Rattle.' Your tiny face striped with war paint, wearing a chamois diaper, and Indian beads around your neck, there you were, cute as cute could be with a real live rattler in your Pawnee wicker crib. 'And the suckling child shall play,' I said over the loudspeaker in a voice that I tried to make sound like that of Elohim, 'at the burrow of the asp.' Your mother had taken out the fangs by teasing it with a burlap bag and then, as soon as that sidewinder bit down, yanking on the cloth. With its teeth removed, it was safe for Sarah to dig into the snake's jaw with a knitting needle and get the poison sacs. That terrified toothless snake rattled faster and hissed louder than ever. The more harmless a creature is, the more menacing it'll try to be. Customers were always willing to pay a dime to see the amazing baby who cooed and giggled in the face of death. Abraham stopped the act, however, in fear that you might be kidnapped when the Grand Metropolitan Ecclesiarch of the Pentecostal Church, after seeing the show, declared that the Lord had chosen you. That's when your father decided to go on the road. But I don't think his heart was ever really in the ten-in-one, in that *Wyoming Willie's Wonders of the World* business. And vaudeville didn't seem to satisfy him either. And neither did the motion pictures. But then, seeing that airplane doing loops over the Durbar of Delhi in Chula Vista, he suddenly knew what he really wanted to do with his life. He said that he had been born to fly." It seemed a reasonable moment for me to ask Jake where he thought I had been born. Startled by the question, he coughed, took another sip of vodka, and answered in all seriousness: "The Dead Sea, the lowest place on earth. That's what your father told me." When I said that I didn't believe it, Jake only laughed. "Why not? Anything is possible. *Nor Got vaist!*"

5

Wyoming Willie's Wonders of the World was filmed in Los Angeles in 1906 by Joseph Siegel, whom my father had met aboard the steamer that delivered them to Ellis Island. They occasionally played pinochle and drank pekoe together at a landsmanshaft on Eighth Street. Having been a slapstick skomorokhi in the Ukraine, touring for several seasons with the celebrated Stavrogins, Siegel had the skill, experience, and connections to begin the twentieth century on Second Avenue as a performer in New York's efflorescent Yiddish theater. Although initially enjoying some popularity in stock shmendrick roles at the Muhntik-Duhnershtik Playhouse, by 1903 the clown had outraged and alienated the Ashkenazi theatrical community with the production of a play that he himself had proudly written and directed: *Mitn Gruhbn Finger.* This disastrous musical adaptation of the biblical story of Onan set in turn-of-the-century Brownsville (featuring Gershom Greenspan as Judah, the patriarch who curses his son for masturbating) was, in both content and presentation, so puerile, coarse, and tasteless that a review in *Yiddishes Tageblatt* noted: "One fears that Gentiles might attend, thereby giving them reasonable justification for any anti-Jewish sentiments that they might harbor." An undaunted Siegel, hired as a flat painter at the newly founded American Phunograph Motion Picture Company, showed up at work each day in an orange mop-wig and red-rubber-ball nose, making stupid faces and doing pratfalls. As a result of his antics, he was cast as the lead in Phunograph's *The Merry Mountain Man.* His zany performance in the successful one-reeler earned him sufficient eminence in nickelodeon circles so that, after Phunograph went bankrupt in 1905, Siegel was able to wheedle a group of prosperous Jewish businessmen into purchasing Phunograph's equipment and sending him with it to California to make a moving picture. When one of the investors, Shlomo Rothstein, who had been mystically moved some years earlier by Edison's motion pictures of Buffalo Bill's Wild West, insisted that "we want cowboys and Indians," Siegel reassuringly boasted that he was a "close amigo of the infamous gunslinger and Indian scout, Wyoming Willie." The notice in *Moving Picture World* of Siegel's directorial debut, *Wyoming Willie's Wonders of the World,* was immensely more flattering than the review of his play in the *Tageblatt:* "There is novelty and fine trick film in this effective motion picture about carnival life. The show is well worth taking the kids to see. They'll surely enjoy the Oriental Snake Boy and the darling little angel of a tightrope walker. The strong man was not believable, but the Siamese twins were quite an unusual treat both as a medical curiosity and as comics. That these characters are real people, not actors, is both the charm of this motion picture and its biggest flaw." While Siegel was thrilled with the judgment, my father was rankled by the accusation that we were "real people." In any case, the public received the motion picture enthusiastically enough to satisfy Siegel's investors, despite Rothstein's diffident grumbling that there were no horses and only one cowboy. In between each of the ten reels of film, a tinted lantern title slide was projected to announce the name and nationality of each artist: Wyoming Willie the Magnificent Marksman (United States of America), Fatima el-Fatiha the Clairsentient Danseuse of the Desert (Arabia), Angel the Acrobatic Alpine Aerialist (Switzerland), Yellow Yeti the Hirsute Himalayan Snowman (Tibet), Adam Adamantine the Strongest Man in the World (Circassia), Lady Lucy Lovelace the World's Ugliest Woman (England), Oorangoo the Headhunting Wild Man (Borneo), Miranda the Mysterious Mermaid (Nova Zembla), and Foo & Ling the Hermaphroditic Siamese Twins (China). And then there was me, Samoo the Amazing Snake Boy (India). Our live ten-in-one was never as well appreciated as the motion picture. Sideshow was big work for little money. We were mostly doing still dates in towns up and down the West Coast, from Chula Vista to Blaine and back again without advance work, playing more often in grange halls, barns, or field tents than in theaters, and relying more on the sales of pomade and the fees for Fatima's private prognosticatory consultations than on admissions. The popular reception of Siegel's film, however, led to a booking at Dante's. It was low-end vaudeville to be sure, but vaudeville nonetheless. Although we weren't hooked into the big-time national-trust circuits, it was a good roll and a jump up a row from the midway. When Wyoming Willie boasted of the Dante's run, Siegel glowered to pronounce theater dead and beamed to announce the motion picture as drama's apotheosis: "Forget vaudeville and remember the future! The great Glansic has left vaudeville for motion pictures, and young Jock Newhouse, the same thing; and Sarah Bernhardt too. Listen, brudder, I've got a guy with some money, a real knacker named Rothstein, who's dying to start a company to handle not only production, but distribution and exhibition as well. He loved you in my picture because he loves cowboys. I don't know why, but this Galitsianer is completely meshugeh about everything Wild West. He wears cowboy boots to shul! It's a chance to strike it rich. You, the cowboy hero, and me, the director, trying to bring a little amusement, excitement, and joy into the American people's generally miserable lives. When folks of all ages in all nations see Wyoming Willie in my motion picture masterpieces for the masses, shooting your guns, throwing your knives, roping buffalos, breaking broncos, scalping Indians, and catching outlaws, you will be the Wild West. Move over, Buffalo Bill! Crank that projection machine! Here comes Wyoming Willie! This magical amusement promises eternal life. When Abraham Schlossberg is waiting in the darkness of his grave for Messiach, Wyoming Willie will still be fast-drawing his six-guns in halls around the world for millions of cheering people. Wyoming Willie will live on in my motion pictures." My most vivid childhood memories of my father, like those of myself, flicker in darkness. They are the black, gray, and white square images of motion picture that I must have watched a hundred times. Wyoming Willie is dressed to kill in fringed buckskin, with three eagle feathers in the Stetson that had replaced Abraham Schlossberg's yarmulke at the beginning of the century. Shining are the mother-of-pearl grips on the silver-plated Colt .45-caliber six-guns in their black leather holsters; black too are the soft high boots. Willie reaches with his left hand for the bone grip of the knife holstered over his right shoulder, and then with his right hand for the pol- ished oak handle of the tomahawk over his left shoulder. He throws the two at once, and the weapons, crisscrossing in midair, appear to stick in the board on either side of the face of Deer Heart, the Indian maiden. Simultaneously fast- drawing both pistols and silently firing, he shoots the bead and-feather baubles from her earlobes. You can only imagine the deafening *ka-bamm! ka-bamm!* There's a shiny black braided whip, coiled up like a serpent and fixed to his belt behind the right holster. With one quick snap of it, the cigarette between the Indian maiden's lips is cut in half and it looks like the whip has really done it. Wyoming Willie takes off his hat and his thick black hair gleams bright with pomade. As closed eyes encourage memory to project the motion picture in a darkness from which I sense I come and into which I imagine I shall someday return, I can fathom the silence of that blackness and then hear in it my father pitching on the bally platform. At first faint and then louder and louder still, fabulous lies echo from his grave in Hollywood's Hebron Cemetery. He speaks of the murder of parents (not peasants slaughtered by pogromshiks in the steppes of Russia, but homesteaders gunned down by outlaws in the Badlands of America), of being raised by wolves until the Apaches found him near Crazy Woman Creek. Once upon a time there was a five-year-old white child, adopted by the redskins, waiting in a pit that he himself had dug, camouflaged with sticks and leaves, and baited with a live rabbit. When an eagle swept down upon that prey, the child reached through the cover and grabbed the predator's fierce talons. "That was no ordinary eagle, my friends, but she, the pure-white heavenly raptor the Indians call Matanka. As higher and higher she soared, I clung to her for dearest life. We flew all day above the clouds, all night amidst the stars, and at dawn landed on a lofty peak where her nest was made." There were two golden eggs that hatched that day, and my father dares in this mem- ory to claim that he watched over the hatchlings while Matanka hunted for their food. Once the eaglets were strong enough to fly, wily Willie, clinging to

Matanka, descended from the mountain peak, and ever after that his avian brothers flew over him to lead him to quarry whenever he hunted. Matanka watched over them from the heights and the wolves of his infancy, remembering him, protected him. "That'll be the first reel of the motion picture," Siegel exclaimed. "You couldn't do that on a stage! There will be ten reels. Or a hundred! In one Geronimo appeals to you, the only paleface he trusts, to go to Washington and speak to President McKinley on behalf of his people. We can get Geronimo to play himself. The Army rents him out for exhibition as long as there's a bond put up insuring his return to Fort De Leon. He's played lots of Wild West shows, but hasn't been in the movies yet. He's a natural and the two of you would make a great team. In another reel you could capture the Dalton Gang. Emmett Dalton, just out of the Kansas State Penitentiary, is here in Los Angeles hoping to make motion pictures about the outlaw way of life. I talked to him about it. Not a bad guy for a bad guy. Let's not forget about love: you could have a shoot out with No-Neck Nat over some gorgeous frontier koorve. Love, death, and adventure, and of course, a little humor too. We'll have it all. *The Ballad of Wyoming Willie: True Story of an American Cowboy!*" My father adamantly refused, earnestly explaining to Siegel that, as a performer, he required the physical presence of his audience, that he could act only in response to the fears and desires of his spectators as he sensed them. Mother told me a secret: "He cannot be a cowboy in motion pictures because (and he won't admit this to anyone, so don't tell him that I told you) he is afraid, deathly afraid, more afraid than of anything else in the world, of horses." The real truth, I suspect, was that he so loved words that he didn't see any point in performing without being able to talk and, of course, to lie. I believe that he was far more afraid of silences and truths than he was of horses.

6 When the sharpshooter fired charged words, spieling the bally bravura and cantillated come-on, sly melodies and seductive syncopations enchanted the ear, beguiled the brain, and rustled the hand of many a towner deep into a pocket for twenty-five American cents. The traveling show was a ten-act mystery play, an allegorical elucidation of the rampant sentiments that make us who we imagine ourselves to be. He counted ten of them: love, sorrow, mirth, fear, disgust, courage, anger, wonder, pity, serenity. Ten-in-one, "all for just a quarter." The low-pitched pitch was high-toned overture, and as it played, it was my job to mix and mill around, an unnoticed kid eavesdropping on marks for little bits of comment or conversation to serve Fatima's clairvoyance. A name or place perhaps, almost anything uttered in the crowd could pay off. What might seem the least significant of references could yield the most inexplicably profound of prognostications. Tip turning, fast talking, and slow walking up and down the banner line, Wyoming Willie, fetching in buckskins and a spruce black Stetson with three eagle feathers in the swanky snakeskin band, would pause, as reverentially as if he himself were inveigled by her mystic mien, to point out the painted portrait of my mother. He'd remove his hat to show off the sheen of slicked-back pomaded hair. "I must, in all honesty, and to be fair, warn you, ladies and gentlemen, that if you have any secrets, anything on your mind or in your heart that should not be known, then do not look into the eyes of Fatima el-Fatiha. For if your glances so much as meet, she'll know it all, everything about you, things you've kept from others or even from yourself. The lady of the East witnesses the past and knows just what you're thinking now, each desire, hope, and fear bound up with every thought. She can, I swear it's true, see and hear what's in the future too, yes, all that is in store for you. But do you want or dare to know? She often talks of love, not to mention adventure and faraway lands. I've also heard her speak of fortunes yet to be made or lost. Sometimes there are whispers about death and what comes after, and what the departed have to say to those of us they've left behind. Fatima knows the roll of the die before it's tossed. Do you dare to know the truth? If so, then ask. But let me caution you once again, my friends, Fatima, unique amongst the women of the world, never, ever, ever lies." Mother could do a cold reading as well as any Gypsy and it was to her advantage that people back then trusted Arabs more than Gypsies. After no more than four sessions with Madame Luvni, an aged Hungarian Tsigani fortune-teller in San Francisco, during which she pretended to believe in occult Gypsy powers, my mother had mastered the act, had learned how to set up the mitt camp and play it out with cards, bells, candles, crystals, blindfolds, or just her wits, dark eyes, and graceful fingers. She reflected that the reason it was mostly women who came to her or visited Gypsies was that "men don't really want to know the truth, though they'll swear they do." By listening to my father's spiels and reading his pitch books, I was introduced to the magic power of words. El Adon, I was told, had created the world with words alone. I got a percentage of whatever I brought in by selling our ten-cent autographed souvenir pamphlets. Lady customers seemed especially tantalized by the one about my mother, the lurid tales of Fatima's experiences as a concubine in the harem of Eyada ibn Ajjueyn, the Despot of Damascus. Women asked as much about her past as they did about their own futures, curious to know how many men had held her in their arms. What were her lovers like? What were the colors of their bodies? The tongues they spoke? Were they cruel or tender, gentle or rough? Did they ever bind or thrash her, or force her to do shameful things? They'd ask about pessaries, aphrodisiacs, erotic postures, and ways to win, keep, or curb the affections of a man. The mentalist served them whatever fantasy, no matter how orgiastic or innocent, profligate or sentimental, that she sensed they needed to hear. Every Shabbis the Mohammedan dupatta that Fatima el-Fatiha wore to gaze into the innocent eyes of hopeful clients was turned into a Jewish platoke covering the head of Sarah Schlossberg. After whispering blessings with her hands over her eyes, she would gesture magically to spread the hallowed incandescence about the boarding house room, tent, railcar, or wherever else we were. *"Baruch ata Adonai,"* she began and my father always gazed at her with a wine-spiked longing, the sparkling ardor of which was apparent even to a child. And inevitably on the Sabbath, if I didn't fall asleep before it happened, I could hear muffled moans and soft sonorous sighs. Even though I did not know exactly why they made those sounds or just what they were doing, I understood that it was what they were supposed to do and what God wanted from them on the holy night of rest. My mother recounted our genesis: "Hashem made us in His own image, in the image of Himself He created us, commanding men and women to love each other, and He gave us dominion over the earth." It ended with Hebrew recitation: *"Va-yehi erev, va-yehi voker, Yom ha-shishi."* With no less art than that with which she played Fatima, the Mystic Moslem Mentaliste, mother acted the part of Sarah, the Devoted Jewish Wife who, at the age of fourteen, one night many years ago beneath a wedding canopy in the Pale of Settlement, had been consecrated as a bride in accordance with the laws of Moses and Israel. The marriage broker had introduced him as Avraham ben Menachem. The marriage contract was solemnly recited and duly signed. It did not take so long after the wedding for the woman to begin to love the man. Under my mother's direction and with herself as the star, Shabbis was an ancient drama about the beginning of the world, the dénouement of which was a reading from the Song of Songs: "Like an apple tree among the trees of the forest is my beloved among men. In his shadow I long to sit, and his fruit is sweet to my taste. He brings me to the house of wine and looks at me with love." Jake Grossman remembered celebrating the holy night of the week with us: "She was a great actress," he repeated with a generous smile and, after offering me another vodka, continued his meandering, affectionate reminiscence. "Buffalo Bill knew right off that he had a real star in Sarah. While the Indians yelped, dancing ecstatically around her (and everybody was damn sure she'd be raped, scalped, and dismembered, if Buffalo Bill didn't show up soon), Sarah's screams curdled the blood of the whole audience, made every man, woman, and child fear for her life and, even more so, for her virtue. No one could shriek with such convincing horror as your mother. And Buffalo Bill made good use of that talent by promoting her into his leading female victim. In 'The American Fireman' she wailed that hair-raising howl of hers in a window high up in a building front. As the firefighters fought their way through smoke and flames, up the perilously tall ladders, to redeem her from the merciless blaze, everyone in the audience would be shouting, 'Hurry! Hurry! For God's sake, save the woman!' When Buffalo Bill needed a female snake charmer to dance with a few pythons wrapped and writhing around her arms, neck, and waist for his production of 'An Oriental Dream,' both of his regular exotic dancers, Bertha Blanchette and Lulu Larue, were too afraid of snakes to take the role. And so your mother got the part. She was so convincing as an East Indian, and comfortable enough with snakes that, in 'The Attack of the Thugs,' her shoulders again draped with a large constrictor, she played a Hindu high priestess ordering votaries to fetch the blood of white men to slake the thirst of the goddess Kali. She was always good in religious parts. She was, above all else, an actress, and religion is all dramatics. It's make-believe. That's how it makes people believe. I adored Sarah in all the parts she played in Siegel's motion picture, Torah. The movie was farshtinkener as far as I was concerned. I always thought Siegel was a putz, and he was a drug fiend by the time he started the picture. But Sarah was perfect as the priestess of Baal in the Pesach episode. She made you want to worship to the Golden Calf. But she was best of all as the Shulamite at your father's table each Friday night. It made you want to take our religion seriously, to actually believe that it is holy for a man and woman to love each other, and even to believe that we, men and women, really are created in the image of Elohim and that we really do have dominion over the earth. Why not? Anything is possible!" Jake poured more vodka, scratched his ear, drank up, and continued: "Abraham loved Sarah with all his heart. When she was all dolled up as the Apache maiden in leather, fur, and feathers, leaning against the fake tree on the stage at our theater, and he threw those knives and tomahawks and they just missed her, and then when he drew his pistols and shot those cigarettes, one after another, out of her mouth, you believed she really was in danger. It made your heart pound and your breath stop. Abraham understood what people wanted. And he loved to give it to them. His shows were about dangerous love." That was, I think, true, even before we started playing vaudeville, back in the days of the ten-in-one. The women in the show, Fatima of the Desert, Lucy Lovelace the World's Ugliest Woman, Miranda the Mermaid, and Ling, the female half of the married hermaphroditic Siamese twins, provided the audience with cryptic symbols of love and revealing incarnations of feminine sex. There was, furthermore, an insinuation that any man who dressed his hair with Wyoming Willie's Wondrous Pomade stood a damn better chance than other men of having what he wanted when it came to women. Even Angel, the little girl in white lace who climbed the high ladder to walk the wire, was acting in a love story. She was an image of a sylphic innocence that vows to carnally transform itself in time into the most profoundly voluptuous of all human experiences. I can still see the child across the Sabbath dinner table from me. When I allow myself that memory, I hear my mother's voice: "Love is as strong as death itself. Ardent love is as severe as the grave; its flashes are of fire, a flame of the Lord." But in my most vivid recollection of Angel, she is high above me, on the tightrope, dancing across the sky.

7 Higher and higher Angel climbed the hundred rungs. The ladder was love and desire was a serpent. At circuses, fairs, and carnivals, Angel performed an outside free show to lure crowds from a distance. It was difficult to resist the vision of a child in the sky with a white lace umbrella, hard not to worry that she might slip, and impossible not to watch for it, desiring just a bit of what you feared. At the same time, she made you imagine that if you looked away, if you did not concentrate upon her, she would surely fall. Her life was in your eyes. "Angel, the Alpine Aerialist of Aargau, learned as a toddler to walk along cables stretched high over the deep gorges between Swiss mountain peaks," Wyoming Willie'd announce. "That was the only way she could get to school." And then, picking up the Marlin semiautomatic blowback-action carbine from the rack, he'd release the trigger lock, and wait for the little girl on the wire to reach the pole atop which there was a white globe. When she lifted it above her head, Wyoming Willie fired, and it was blown to smithereens. It snowed flakes of glass. My father insisted that he didn't have to use a blank and have Angel break the fragile gaffed globe, that he could have really done the stunt. "But then it wouldn't be a show," the showman smiled. So too the marksman swore that he could have loaded his silver-plated Colt Peacemakers with real bullets to blast asunder the balls and plates that I subsequently pitched into the air, but he used low-choke stunt shot by convention: a .44/40 W.C.F. short cartridge with a thin paper bullet that dropped off the shot charge as soon as it left the muzzle; the charge itself was a short-range load of about twenty-five grains of black powder and an ounce of special Colonel Cody's no. 20 chilled show shot. Given a five-to-ten-foot spread at a range of ten to twenty yards, this ammunition would have made anyone who aimed in the general direction of the target a very sharp sharpshooter. *Ka-bamm! Ka-bamm! Ka-bamm!* Once Angel had descended the ladder, rushed to my father, and jumped up into his arms to give him a kiss on the cheek, the showman would flash his bright white teeth and drawl, "Now, my sweet Angel, it's time for you to give these good people a chance to see wonders like they've never seen before." Wyoming Willie would fire a few shots in the air and bleat a cowboy holler, and the eager crowd would push and shove to purchase tickets from Angel while they lasted. No one suspected that in addition to being a tightrope walker, the little girl was a shortchange artist. The dainty equilibrist enticed a curious throng to the opening of Siegel's motion picture show and got us a story in the *Los Angeles Examiner* by walking a cable stretched high across Mountain Way from the roof of Liplinger's Theatre to the eaves of the Western Union Building without a net or mechanic. In the motion picture she ascends the ladder as easily and gracefully as if the satin wings sewn to her sleeves were the true seraphic appendages of heaven. So high up that you cannot see the wire, Angel's white lace costume blends into the clouds behind her so that she almost disappears. Often I would dream of her dancing on the wire, slowly, so slowly. Still sometimes the dream returns and Angel smiles there. I remember: "Let's play hide-and-seek," she said and I hid from her beneath a draped table upon which my father had set display jars of punks pickled in formaldehyde, including a five-legged goat fetus, a two-headed garter snake, a bouncer that was supposed to be a shrunken head with its lips and eyelids sewn shut from Borneo, and a horse brain that was labeled "Brain of a Criminal." Unable to find me, Angel shouted, "Okay, come out. I don't like this game anymore. Let's play something else." She often insisted on snakes and ladders because she thought she was better at it than I. Whenever our tokens landed together in the same square, I thought of the Shabbis sounds, those intimations of adult delights beyond childhood imagination. The game board, with its Oriental-style border, gave my father the idea for an exhibition. Dressed as an East Indian child fakir named Swami Balakrishna, I played a flute in a pit of serpents as Angel climbed a ladder of sharp swords above me. I had a dozen snakes in my collection by then. By sewing horse hairs as eyebrows into the scales above the eyes of my listless sand boa, my mother turned a rather dull snake into a spectacular wonder. Together with Angel's mother, Tivya, my mother did the sewing for the show. Angel's true name was Devora, and her father, Yellow Yeti the Hirsute Snowman, was really Zev Mocher Rabinowitz from not the Himalayan peaks but a razed shtetl near the Baltic Sea. Neither Zev nor Tivya spoke much English or had much talent. They were in the amusement business only through a realization of the financial potential of their only child's abundant gifts. She was born with perfect balance, without a fear of heights or the slightest shyness, a natural acrobat and tumbler who had, they recalled, danced as early as she had walked. Although Jake Grossman, who first brought us together, had given the Rabinowitzes work only as an obligatory favor to fellow immigrant Jews, he instantly recognized little Devora's extraordinary talent and billed her as the Breathtaking Balancing Baby of Babylon in the first show that he and his brother Beryl produced in San Francisco. So that Zev and Tivya could have something to do in the business, he encouraged them to develop the conventional Girl-into-Gorilla carny act in which a scantily clad but respectably demure lady in a cage magically turns into a ferocious gorilla who then wildly pounds his chest and brutishly shakes the bars of his jail. As an act that had mythic appeal and yet required no skill, it was an appropriate number for Angel's parents. They might have continued to present it after joining our ten-in-one if it had not been for the accident. Tivya Rabinowitz lost her left leg as a result of being run over by a Peerless automobile driven by Consuela Heimenhoff, a wealthy San Francisco socialite who, in remorse over her reckless driving, gave Mrs. Rabinowitz two thousand dollars and the right shoes of ten pairs of elegantly handmade Italian shoes. By the grace of losing her leg, Tivya became the Marvelous Miranda in a rather realistic mermaid costume. It was my father's idea. Initially Zev played Captain Shnorrer Shturluson, an Icelandic fisherman who had netted and married the mermaid. But because he was shy without a costume in which to hide, Zev beseeched my father to let him back into the gorilla suit. It was tempting since it was hard to pass Zev's Yiddish off as Icelandic (it didn't matter that Tivya didn't speak English since she performed under water) but, my father insisted, "A gorilla is a zoo attraction, Zev Mocher, not a Wonder of the World." And so the gorilla outfit was bleached and fluffed; shaggy blond hair was glued over the black leather chest, and the head was weirdly elongated. Zev Rabinowitz, whose breath always smelled of herring and whose eyes were ever moist with woe, was transformed into the fantastic Yellow Yeti. An article in *Life* magazine had been the inspiration. My father read it aloud to us over a Sabbath meal: "Major L. A. Wheedle, renowned adventurer, mountaineer, and mesmerist, will return to Tibet this year in search of a strange creature the Lamas call Yeti. At the end of the last century, when explorers had to disguise themselves as Buddhist pilgrims in order to enter the forbidden kingdom, Major Wheedle discovered large footprints in the snow leading up toward the range of peaks that includes the unconquerable pyramid of Everest, the highest mountain on earth. These tracks are alleged to mark the trail of giant hairy men who inhabit the icy heights of the eternal snows of the lofty Himalayas." There was photographic documentation of monstrous footprints. "Imagine exhibiting one of them!" father exclaimed as he stared purposefully at his friend Zev Rabinowitz. In Joseph Siegel's ten-reeler, against a backdrop of painted mountain peaks, amidst obviously fake boulders, with snow flakes of soap flurrying thick, Wyoming Willie tracks the beast. Willie doesn't notice what the audience sees: Yeti darting here and there on those enormous hairy feet of his, hiding, peeking, running from behind one boulder to another. He should have known better than to pounce on Wyoming Willie! The weird creature's wrestled to the ground and our triumphant hero, his hair as neat as before the brawl, ties up the Abominable Snowman and puts him in a crate addressed to "Wyoming Willie, Wyoming, U.S.A." Tivya worked a little harder than her husband: human from the waist up and scaly fish from hips to tail fin, she had to hold her breath as she bobbed around in the glass tank. It was the hoochiest of our vignettes. Audiences either hoped or feared that the seaweed over her ample undulant breasts might dislodge and float away. As little children, Angel and I had bathed in the tank. Naturally, we couldn't help inspecting each other's nakedness with sly glances, peeking at wonders of an unexplored world, as my mother and Tivya, speaking to each other in Yiddish of things that we did not care about, dried and warmed us. We had already descried that sweet smell was addictive and soft touch dangerous. On the road we often had to sleep in the same bed. The funambulist and the snake boy fell in what we did not yet really know, but sensed perhaps, was love. Although we never talked about it then, we both figured we'd work the ten-in-one forever and be together always. We were a good team; she was not afraid of heights and I was not indisposed to snakes. Seeing children without the terrors that most people naturally have, my father explained, encourages those people to think, and pay to see it demonstrated, that their fears were learned and not innate, and thus might be undone and overcome. Angel and I proved it to them and to each other. Every woman whom I have in any way ever loved has in some sense dangerously embodied Angel, unknowingly climbing ladders of Jacob and making the heart of Isaac beat with each footstep. Each one, whether vividly or faintly, has appeared dancing on heavenly ropes. I have feared that any woman I love might fall. And, at the same time, each one has allowed me, to some degree, to believe that fear, whether of death or of life, might be overcome. The marks upon us of first love are indelible.

8 It was flimflam consecrated by delight, bamboozlement's epiphany, our show with its false fronts, hyperboles, and tarradiddle. Vending wonder, big diversions with little fibs, my father loved to play the game, cog the die, and thimblerig the ear, offering up the pleasure of an afternoon's deception. He reveled in verbal gaffs and linguistic trepans, in humbug's capacity to redeem any soul with a quarter from the indifference of real life and prevalence of real death. "Lying to save your skin or make a buck—that's no fun," Wyoming Willie philosophized. "Dissembling for the pleasure of the feint, a lie for lying's sake—that's the art." To be fair, he smiled on the bally just enough to insinuate that everything he swore to just might be a joke. "They're from the heights, they're from the depths, from the Mystic East and the Wild West. From faraway India, there's Samoo, the snake with a head of a boy, or the boy with the body of a snake? That's for you to decide, my friends. And Marvelous Miranda the Mermaid: Is she a fish with the upper body of a woman, or a woman with the lower body of a fish? See for yourself! But let me forewarn the particularly proper or modest amongst you: there are no clothes to hide the bare beauty of Miranda. And speaking of beauty, right inside, right beside the mermaid, you'll meet Lady Lucy Lovelace, the World's Ugliest Woman. Although she's the most hideous damsel on the earth, she has not, you'll soon discover, been unloved by gentlemen. You'll hear of her many paramours and innumerable romantic escapades. Ladies should be warned not to leave their husbands alone with her. And speaking of love, that most noble and sublime of human sentiments, that funny feeling of being one with an other, as Adam and Eve were before our almighty God split them asunder, come in, my friends, and see the perfect lovers, the man and woman who are truly one. Prince and Princess Yoo: Foo the groom and Ling the bride, Siamese twins and man and wife." They were fake. All of them, including me. Even though there were plenty of performers with true deformities looking for work in show business (bearded women, lobster boys, legless wonders, lots of giants and tons of midgets), my father wouldn't hire them. He scorned real freaks, not at all as human beings, but as performers and most of all as employees: "Freaks are prima donnas. A genuine alligator man, bona fide penguin boy, true rubber man, real pinhead, or authentic Siamese twins will make demands that a Shakespearean actor wouldn't dare. There will be orders on how they're to be displayed and billed. They'll insist on beefsteak and first-class coaches. Freaks are congenital ham chewers and self-centered scene stealers. They think they're different from everybody else. I want actors, people who seem other than what they are. It should be fake to be real in this business." Although Tivya Rabinowitz, after the loss of her leg, might have been considered a freak, we never thought of her as such and never exhibited her as anything other than the beautiful submarine nymph of Nova Zembla. A half girl, an authentic human torso, had once pleaded with my father to hire her after her own ten-in-one went bust and her husband, Lee the Lobster, ran off with Countess Prekrasnova, the Russian Regurgitatrix. She called herself Flora and painted pictures of flowers while holding the paint brush in her mouth. "It makes no sense," my father told her. "I mean, if you didn't have arms and you painted with your mouth, that would be good. But you don't have legs. So why aren't you holding the brush in your hand?" His criticism hurt her feelings, but later we heard that things had worked out well enough for Flora, that she went on to earn a substantial living and some renown as a prostitute catering to wealthy clients with special tastes in San Francisco. Beneath Miranda's banner, Wyoming Willie made his pitch: "While the Hebrews believe that mermaids are the descendants of the Egyptians who drowned in the Red Sea, the Greeks contend that they are the offspring of aqueous Aphrodite, the glorious goddess of love herself." A convincingly gaffed baby, "the stillborn daughter of Miranda and an Icelandic seaman," was displayed in a jar of formaldehyde next to the mermaid tank. It was actually a large Pacific salmon from the waist down and a small shaved monkey from the waist up. Just as all our freaks were fakes, so too our pickled punks (except the fetal goat, two-headed snake, and horse brain) were bouncers fabricated of India rubber, ceresine, and ader wax. Lucy was deft at fashioning them, and she was a master makeup artist too. Though hardly unattractive without cosmetics, Lucy used wax, greasepaint, powders, pencils, creams, and cakes to create, on the plain canvas of her face, the hideously distorted, blotched, and bristled mug with porcine snout, saurian eyes, and donkey lips that people handsomely paid to behold. She was even uglier than Zizi Praline, the "World's Ugliest Woman" in Buffalo Bill's Wild West Show. Lucy had left her apprenticeship at Broadway's Palace Theatre in the costume and makeup shop to be with the man she loved, George Washington, a handsome Negro who played the part of Oorangoo in our show. A fine dancer (the turkey trot, grizzly bear, and mongoose march) and a reader too (Shakespeare, the Bible, and Variety), George claimed he had auditioned for us to get away from doing East Coast coon shows, hoping that carny might be his stepping-stone to Shakespearean theater. Why, some wondered, did he insist on working in disguise? Rumor had it that Lucy and George had fled New York because they were wanted by the law, that her husband, Broadway actor Morris Fitzmorris, had caught them in flagrante delicto and pulled a gun and that George, in defense of himself and his beloved Lucy, had killed the irate thespian. "Have any of those Pinkerton beagles been sniffing around here today?" George would often ask. And just as a joke, Foo and Ling Yoo, who were neither siblings (let alone conjoined) nor married (since both were men), would inform George with straight faces that they thought they had spotted a bounty hunter in the crowd. Ling, who was really named Lee Kwong Yee, and Foo, a.k.a. Phoebus Fong, had initially been hired in San Francisco to cook, launder, and shine our shoes and boots. Discovering (when George spilled the beans on them in revenge for the pranks they played on him) that most of the meals they had prepared for us had contained some amount of pork or lard, my father cursed them to Gehenna and would certainly have fired them if they hadn't had five weeks left in their one-year contract. But there was no way that my father would let them near the kitchen again, and so, inspired by the success of both Barnum's world-famous Chang and Eng and the East Indian hermaphrodite Swamee Ardhanaree Ishvaree Haree, who had earned fame and fortune displaying two complementary sets of genitalia in London, Paris, Berlin, and Moscow, my father came up with the idea of hermaphroditic Siamese twins who were man and wife. Wyoming Willie proudly proclaimed their marvelousness: "In China they have a system as sacred to them as biblical enjoinders are to you and me, one laid down by old Confucius, wherein parents negotiate the marriages of their offspring. The mother and father of Foo and Ling, realizing that they would never find mates for this boy and girl, born as they were joined at the waist, deemed it just that they be wed unto each other. Amongst Mandarins in olden China, brother-sister marriage was not abjured. So see today a husband and wife who are literally and truly, spiritually and physically, one and undivided. And let them be an inspiration to us all!" Of all the freaks on the circuit, my father particularly disliked midgets. "They think they're big shots. The smaller they are, the bigger their heads." He especially disdained Bachnele Poopik, a thirty-three-inch-tall Litvak who infuriated my father by performing routines wearing a putty hook nose, fake payes, and a dirty shtrayml, earning a living by encouraging Gentiles to laugh at him as he sang songs about moneygrubbing. Sometimes on the road, he'd come around on a Friday just before sunset knowing that even though my father detested him, my mother would insist that as Jews we couldn't refuse him a glass of Sabbath wine and a morsel of braided challa. He never failed to greet me with "Isaac, how you've grown!" He had a reputation as a ladies' man, a libertine and seducer. Women, for some reason, couldn't resist him. It was hard to imagine, but that's what I had overheard my parents say. My father suspected that he might have enjoyed illicit relations with Lucy and my mother feared that he might have seduced Tivya as well. Midgets were huge in 1905. The biggest smash on the circuit that year had been *Colonel William W. Wee's Wild West Weeview* in which a hundred midgets on Shetland ponies reenacted the Battle of the Little Bighorn. In hopes of cashing in on Colonel Wee's success, Angel and I were presented in the spring of 1906 as the Duke and Duchess of Darlington, the Majestic Midgets of Manchester. Lucy fixed my mustache and goatee and mother tailored a little tuxedo for me. With a top hat on my head, a monocle over my eye, a Blaine Havana in my mouth, and a brandy snifter in my hand, I toasted Angel as "Her Royal Lowness." With full round breasts and ripe red lips, in her small sequined gown and tiny tiara, she curtseyed cutely as I took regal bows. Our banner proclaimed "True Love." The performance ended with a kiss, each one of which made me wish it wasn't all just make-believe. I yearned to grow up and be tall, to have slick hair and a sweet smell, to smoke cigars and drink strong drink, to kiss an Angel whose breasts were really real, whose lips were really flush, and maybe to do with her what parents did on holy Sabbath nights once they thought the children were asleep.

9 "Love and death," my father said with a dead serious smile, "that's what we're selling, and all the drama they inspire." The pitch books that he anonymously authored were full of high romance: "Fatima el-Fatiha, beloved of Bedouins and Legionnaires, houri of Hafeez the Hashshash of al-Hamamaham, snake dancer and masseuse in the casbah of Casimir the Cunning, darling doxy of the Despot of Damascus, was given the power of clairsentience by the angel Zadkiel, the Mystic Eye through which she envisioned her rescue by Wyoming Willie a full month before it happened. She knew that it was her redeemer even before he rode that starry night of Ramadan into the Arab camp, galloping to where she waited outside the tent to swoop down, pick her up, and race off across the sands with her safely in his arms." The back page of the booklet advertised Wyoming Willie's Wondrous Hair Pomade as "the choice of Sheiks and Caliphs." As Fatima the mystic medium theatrically represented a transcendental feminine gnosis, Angel incarnated virgin grace, Lady Lovelace inner beauty, and Miranda the Mermaid was an allegorical personification of female longing in the face of passionate love's ineluctable obstacles: "She was found curled up upon a rock jutting out of the sea near the wind-whipped Nova Zemblan coast, combing her hair and humming a haunting hymn, waiting long and anxiously for the ship that would deliver her beloved seaman. She stays beneath the water now because there, and only there, she cannot see, in the heart-shaped mirror she holds, the copious tears she sheds for love." Her pitch pamphlet, like all of them, culminated with a pomade promotion ("the choice of Commodores and Admirals"), tying the mermaid's tale in with well-groomed hair and eternal love. Just as the women in the show were intended to conjure up sundry facets of Woman, so the men were components of Man. I suppose Samoo was meant to represent something innately dangerous in us, aberrant tendencies and deadly instincts, a cold-bloodedness that we, in becoming full-fledged human beings, have hidden from others and denied to ourselves. Adam Adamantine was introduced, in contrast, as a specimen of our antediluvian perfection. The part of "the one and only Circassian Strong Man" was played, over the years of the ten-in-one, by many men. I don't remember any one them in particular. They looked pretty much the same: tall, muscular, clean-shaven and fair-skinned, with blue eyes and golden hair. They were invariably named Matthew, Mark, Luke, or John. The act required some physical beauty (enhanced in any case by Lucy's brush), but hardly any talent (compensated for by Wyoming Willie's patter). Mother and Tivya cut Adam's costume of pastel-colored silks scant enough to reveal ample portions of brawny Circassian flesh. Anyone who had ever been to a sideshow, fair, dime museum, or an odditorium, had surely seen a Circassian Beauty, a woman of the purest of the Caucasian tribes. Now was their chance to behold one of the male masters of those stunning women, the one and only survivor of that autochthonous race. His pitch book outlined in convincingly scientific language a theory (attributed to a Herr Doktor Adolf von Lügner, Professor of Eugenic Teleology at the University of Nuremberg) that human beings descended from a perfect God-made man and woman, an unblemished race from a mountain kingdom near the Black Sea that had degenerated, losing their beauty, strength, and innocence as they spread out across the globe, compromising their purity with random mating. Archaeologists from the University of Nuremberg had, furthermore, scientifically identified Circassia as "the land called Eden in the Bible. The area is overgrown with apple trees and rife with serpents. The skeletal remains of a man missing a rib were excavated to the east of Circassia." Wyoming Willie assured people of it with a straight face: "This Adam is as Father Adam in Eden before the Fall. Pure as pure can be. Behold the perfection!" Based on a premise that human language established its original vocabularies in mimicries of natural noises, uttered in physical response to pain and pleasure because of an innate physiological need to vocally release pressured feelings caused by love, sorrow, mirth, fear, disgust, courage, anger, wonder, pity, and serenity, my father created the Circassian language out of sounds that imitated the wind in trees, birds at sunset, barking dogs, and howling wolves. Circassian was a complex juxtaposition of metrical moans and whistles, clicking teeth, sharp intakes of breath, sucking and kissing noises, and highly inflected whimpers and wahoos. Adam had to memorize his lines: *"Oooo een-een wheeeee. Eeen oooo-ooo whee noo. Oooo koo-oo nush-nisssss krrraw tisk-skit-tsit noo. Eeen nush-nush plee-plee-o wee, eeoo dee-oo nushteee hmmm sooo-o ooo?"* Wyoming Willie, apologizing for not being able to capture all the subtleties and nuances of the original, translated for the crowd: "I am happy to see you. I am happy you see me. I am a lonely man without a woman from my tribe. Can you find a woman for me, one who is perfect and whose love is pure?" Adam would interrupt: *"Baba-moooh ja, wee-haaa chhh chhh! Unnn boooo, whooo-o whee, aay noo na ku-kuku koo hnnn. Hnnn? Weeenoo tzik-tziks!"* Wyoming Willie almost seemed to blush: "No, I'm sorry, Adam, I'm afraid I can't translate that, not with women and children present. Such words are not for Christian ears." Isolated in his innocence from other human beings in this degenerate world of ours, Adam often spoke of love: *"Nush-too tzokist ooo woo!"* You didn't need to know what it meant to feel that it somehow summed it all up. Oorangoo, the dark headhunter and cannibal from the steamy jungles of Borneo, was a descendant of Cain. In Siegel's motion picture of the ten-in-one, Oorangoo, eyes rolling about, wearing a grass skirt and ornamental strings of bones, proudly displayed his collection of shrunken heads and trephined skulls. Dancing in ecstatic frenzy and gnashing his teeth, the savage menacingly jiggled a spear in the air. Although Siegel had wanted him to bite off the head of a chicken, George Washington refused to compromise his theatrical dignity by playing the geek. Instead he pretended to mesmerize the bird, and then to make it do an aboriginal dance of death. Hairs too fine to be seen by the camera, tangled around the chicken's claws, made the bird jump about in a frantic attempt to get them off. Just as George was in love with Lucy the ordinary person, Oorangoo was in love with Lady Lucy Lovelace, the World's Ugliest Woman, but so (according to the pamphlet) was Yeti. And Ling, the female half of the married hermaphroditic Siamese twins, was suspicious (so the spiel went) that her husband, Foo, was also sweet on Lucy. Lady Lucy Lovelace proved true the falsehood that beauty is in the eye of the beholder. Her pitch book told of torrid love affairs with great European composers, painters, poets, and military leaders, with such beaus as "the Marquis de Talleyrand-Fourchette, dapper French spendthrift and bon vivant; Count Boniface de la Mettrie, Swiss balloonist and wit; and the Earl of Wankton-on-the-Marsh, who needs no introduction, and who, incidentally, dresses his hair with Wyoming Willie's Patented Pomade." She had also had a passionate adventure with the Nawab of Nagpur. There were even subtly insinuating innuendoes about Theodore Roosevelt. When in real life the rumor went around that Lucy had had a liaison with Bachnele Poopik during the San Diego fair, George went crazy. "Had it pleas'd heaven to try me with affliction, had he rain'd all kinds of sores and shames upon my head," he ranted, "I should have found in some part of my soul a drop of patience; but, alas, to make me a fixed figure for the time of scorn to point his slow, unmoving finger at!" Because he frequently began to weep in the middle of his act, my father had to speak to him. "Maybe you should take a rest, George. It doesn't work. The crowd is standing there in front of you, thrilled with the terror that you might think one of them looks tasty and, just as I'm explaining how you shrink heads, you start quoting Shakespeare, burst into tears, and sob like a baby. It undermines the power of your performance as the Wild Man of Borneo." In time, solaced by Lucy's embraces and vows of fidelity, George, as eager as anyone to believe the lies of those we love, was able to regain his composure and make Oorangoo better than ever. A true thespian, he used the anger that had been aroused by the Lithuanian Jewish midget, allowing it to be heard in his howls and growls and seen in the ferocious shaking of his spear and the gnashing of his teeth. His dance became a ritual preparation for the sacrifice of the little Jew to the simian gods of Borneo. My father shook his head: "Why must love make us so crazy?" George continued to warn every new Adam Adamantine to stay away from Lucy. He even cautioned Zev Mocher Rabinowitz, who in turn just shrugged his shoulders and mumbled, "That's ridiculous. I'm a married man, and in any case, my friend, she isn't even Jewish." George also kept his eye on both Lee Kwong Yee and Phoebus Fong, but particularly on Fong because Fong as Foo, the male half of the married Siamese twins, flirted with Lady Lovelace in the act. It was, of course, only a gag, the setup for the comedy skit that I remember from the motion picture: man and woman, joined at the waist since birth, have a quarrel when the wife half catches her husband half ogling the World's Ugliest Woman. The jealous Madame Ling is slapping the henpecked Master Foo as he crosses his heart, gesticulating oaths that he's been faithful, that there's never been any hanky-panky between him and Lady Lovelace. But Mrs. Yoo keeps clobbering Mr. Yoo, whose attempt to escape then brings them both to the ground in a conjoined pratfall. But Foo Yoo knows how to end the lovers' quarrel: hidden in the pocket of his half of their Chinese silk brocade robe is a flask of schnapps which he drinks down in one big gulp. His angry wife, Ling Yoo, soon sweetly drunk, hiccoughs, forgives him, and they kiss. People roared with laughter during the first showing at Liplinger's. My father had to explain it to me: "Married people feel like that, stuck to one another. Because they've got different desires and needs and impulses, they are, to the degree that they're attached to each other, bound to fall and get hurt. Folks see themselves in Foo and Ling. They see the folly of love." It still didn't make sense. "Then why would they laugh?" I asked. "Shouldn't they cry?" Wyoming Willie sighed. "People in the audience at a theater laugh over the very things in the show that make them weep when they're at home and all alone. That's why they come to the show. And why we do it. Anything to make life a little more bearable."

10 Although I knew entertaining stories about death, I did not become conscious of the reality upon which they were commentaries until 1909, the year that Geronimo the Indian, Kaleeya the serpent, and Tivya Rabinowitz the mermaid died. Before then death was essentially a thematic undercurrent in *Wyoming Willie's Wonders of the World* spectacular: Fatima had the power to see spectral shadows in its darkness and to hear eerie murmurs in its silence; climbing the high ladder to walk the rope, Angel was forever and exquisitely one breathtakingly precarious step away from the fall into its abyss; Wyoming Willie's set-and-holders (whether I or Deer Heart) faced oblivion with each bullet fired, risked life with every knife or tomahawk thrown. People eagerly paid twenty-five cents to witness the Reaper bamboozled by Wyoming Willie's sure aim, Angel's graceful balance, and Fatima's penetrating knowledge. Death was a carny chaser and blowoff, that extra added attraction out back, behind a last curtain, an amusement man's ploy to move people along and make room for a new crowd of innocents. Wyoming Willie dropped his face into his hands and wept when the Western Union boy brought the news that Geronimo had died of pneumonia at Fort De Leon. My parents had known Geronimo during the Indian's yearlong stint with Buffalo Bill's Wild West. In matinee and evening performances of "Attack on a Settler's Cabin," my mother would scream her incredible caterwaul as the infamous Apache Wildcat rode his pinto pony at full gallop toward her, swooped down to pick her up, and then raced out of the arena with her howling in his grip. With a nostalgic smile, Mother reminisced that she had always felt safe in his arms "except, of course, when he had been drinking." Buffalo Bill had assigned my father not only to translate and interpret for Geronimo but to teach him English too. The Indian, however, refused to learn, or perhaps merely pretended that he did not know, the "cruel language." It was my father's increasing fluency in the tender Chiricahua dialect of Apache that allowed for the development of the odd rapport between the Jew and the Indian. When, in that language (so my father claimed), he recounted memories of the brutal pogroms that had spread fanwise over the upturned anguished faces of victims from Kiev to Odessa, Geronimo, keenly appreciative of the affinities of those Cossack atrocities with the nefarious crimes committed by the United States Army, declared in Apache that he wanted to learn not Hebrew (because he scorned the Bible, that wicked batch of words that had vindicated the iniquities of white men) but Yiddish, the tongue of a tyrannized people. *"Oych mir a leben?"* Geronimo (if one is to believe my father) always used to say as he mounted his pinto pony to ride into the arena of the Wild West. "This you call a living?" Taking particular delight in a Purimspiel as paraphrased into Chiricahua by his immigrant interpreter, Geronimo cast President Teddy Roosevelt as King Ahasueros, Brigadier General Nelson A. Miles as Haman, and himself as Mordecai. The three eagle feathers in my father's Stetson and the Apache leather dress that was Deer Heart's costume were gifts from the infamous renegade warrior whom my father eulogized with reverent solemnity: "Geronimo understood history as dramatic arrangements of meaningless events into meaningful plots in which real human beings become the dramatis personae as heroes, villains, clowns, or extras. To weave his epic adventure story and make a lasting legend of a fleeting life, Geronimo knew exactly when to fight and when to surrender, then when to escape, take flight, return and ambush, to slay or spare, to surrender once more, and then escape again. Although Apaches had never used tomahawks, and had given up arrows and spears for rifles before he was born, Geronimo purchased some cheap feathered hatchets crafted by Quahadi Comanche women on an Oklahoma reservation. By carving his autograph on the handles of those props and including a photograph with the same signature, he sold them at fairs, carnivals, and Wild West revues for three times what he had paid the Quahadi women for them. Each one had a story: with this one he had scalped five Mexicans at El Cabron in revenge for the slaughter of his parents; with this one he defended himself against ten of Miles's cavalrymen at Canyon de los Embudos; another had been used to mete out justice to a band of ranchers who had raped an Apache squaw. His autograph authenticated hundreds of 'Geronimo's War Bonnet's,' and each one of them sold for no less than twenty-five U.S. dollars. He reenacted, time and time again, 'Geronimo's Last Buffalo Hunt' for ranch shows, circuses, and national fairs. Once you saw him, all dressed up in his Apache warrior's costume, shoot a buffalo and skin it, you couldn't help but love him." I cried over my dear snake a good deal more than my father had wept over the Apache, and I saved his last exuviae. Kaleeya was, after all, my body. He died of star gazer's disease, an illness to which pythons are particularly susceptible. It starts with convulsions, tremors of the skull, and a mechanical, slow opening and closing of the jaws. And then the final symptom, a sure sign of death—the serpent points its snout straight up and holds it so for a long time, as if staring transfixed at the stars, as if beckoned by them or seeing in their heavenly arrangement some terrible portent. When Lucy asked me for the limp reptilian corpse, saying that she'd "take care of it," I thought it was to console me, that she would perform some redemptive funerary rite of disposal. But instead, she chopped off Kaleeya's head and gaffed the body with the waxen head of a human doll. Coiling up the fabricated monster in a large glass vessel of formaldehyde, she sold it for twenty-five dollars. It ended up on permanent display at Worden and Worden's Museum of Marvelous Monstrosities in Philadelphia as "the Late Samoo the Snake Boy." As if Worden and Worden actually believed in mermaids, they had the audacity to inquire about the remains of Miranda immediately after her death in the cold December of that same dolorous year. That Tivya Rabinowitz drowned in her exhibition tank was strange, since she had become quite adept at holding her breath as she bobbed about underwater. Given that she had recently been suffering from a ringing in her ears ("the din of lighthouse bells," she had said, "and crashing ocean waves"), the doctor attributed the drowning to an anemia of the brain which in turn, he explained, could have been caused by "hemorrhage, or a want of energy in the action of the heart, or an irritation of the vagus nerve, whether by thrombosis or embolism, excessive alcohol intake, or the sudden advent of a strong emotion." I had found Tivya in the tank, seen the squinted eyes, and the mouth gaping in a silent scream, the neck and arms swollen, pulpy, and dappled. Miranda the Marvelous Mermaid's body was so bloated that my father and the Adam Adamantine at the time had to cut the fish costume loose from her hips and leg. White wet flesh was stamped with the blue blur of swollen lips and gray of bloodless nipples, with the purple smear and twist of the scar of amputation next to the soggy black wisp of pubic hair. And I was ashamed of myself for looking at her there. Black too, and all the more so in contrast to the stern whiteness of dead flesh, were the snakes of soaked, coiled, and twisted hair lying still upon the inanimate face of Tivya Rabinowitz. Angel and I were swept away by Lucy, who then held the stunned little girl in her arms as I, not knowing what to do, kept repeating, "It'll be okay. I know she'll be all right," even though I knew it would not be so, and that this was not another show. Consuela Heimenhoff brought a hundred red roses to the funeral. Zev Rabinowitz could not find any relief from the devastating grief. The sight of the depressed Abominable Snowman, slumped down on the exhibition platform with his elongated hairy head drooping forward in sorrow, occasionally whimpering, other times moaning, was so pathetic that my father kept him on the payroll only on condition that he did not perform. Angel no longer bathed with me and she no longer took pleasure in the high rope. I never ever saw a trace of tears on Angel's pale cheeks and I heard her cry only once: it was while we were playing hide-and-seek in a rooming house in Sacramento and she was in a closet; I pretended not to know where to find her. Wrapping his arms around my father, Zev kissed him on both cheeks and then sobbed as he said good-bye to my mother and me. A sister in Maine would take care of his daughter and his brother-in-law there would give him a job at his kosher shellfish factory, slipcasting lacquer lobster and crab shells and filling them with gefilte fish. As a going-away present, I gave Angel the game of snakes and ladders that we had played together, hoping that, whenever she might roll the die, she would remember me. My mother kissed her and told her to take good care of herself. My father kissed her and added, "And take care of your father too." As the train snaked its way out of Union Station, I cried as I had done only the day Kaleeya died. That was a long time ago, that year when I became aware of the bleak reality of our inevitable mortality. Since then I have found a certain succor in cultivating memories of the loved ones who have disappeared from the game.

|11| That *Wyoming Willie's Wonders of the World* spectacular ten-in-one spectacle, after the loss of the Rabinowitzes, had only seven wonders made my father speculate and wonder. It was one of ten lame excuses invoked to disband the troupe. The stint at Dante's and the booking with Grossman, as savory servings of vaudevillian banquet, stimulated my father's hunger for a fuller feast, theatrical spreads more tasteful than anything dished up on the salty midway breadline. Working solely with his wife and son as an independent trio would obviate obligations to temperamental Siamese twins, a wildly jealous Man of Borneo, and an almost pretty Ugliest Woman in the World. Much to Wyoming Willie's relief, Lucy and George Washington were happy to be fired. George Washington had long yearned to abandon the role of the savage Oorangoo in order to consecrate his dramaturgical endowments on the altar of Thespis. Where George and Lucy had been content to say good-bye, Lee Kwong Yee and Phoebus Fong beseeched my father to retain them in any capacity, if not performing, then cooking, sewing, cleaning, or even just keeping us company. In a mishmash of Chinese and English, my father tried to convince them that he could no longer afford to pay them for their services as Foo and Ling Yoo. Undaunted, they pledged to remain with us unsalaried, and might have done so had they not believed that my mother actually had some clairvoyant powers. "The Chinese are congenitally credulous when it comes to prognostications," my mother noted, and then, in order to redeem us from the uncomfortable predicament of having two yellow roustabouts tagging along with us, Fatima el-Fatiha did a reading in the Chinese style with dice, coins, and a tortoise shell. With closed eyes she persuasively proclaimed that they would soon own and operate a restaurant in San Francisco called the Palace of the Jade Buddha. Lee would marry a woman from Shanghai with very tiny feet and Phoebus would be wed to a lady from Peking with a very big coffer of gold. Both were destined, furthermore and certainly, to father many sons. Thus Foo and Ling Yoo took leave from us to catch an overnight train to San Francisco on rails undoubtedly laid down by their very own fathers and uncles. As a farewell memento of their glorious days in show business, Wyoming Willie presented each of them with a tin of souvenir brilliantine. The red cans of opalescent grease, festooned with the portrait of Samoo the Amazing Snake Boy, were, he assured the Chinamen with ballyboard enthusiasm and earnestness, certain to become valuable. There weren't many left and the pomade would never again be available because Shmuel Grossman's cosmetic factory in Atlanta had been burned down

51

by Ku Klux Klansmen. "The Gentiles in American Georgia," Shmuel had written in a solicitation of financial assistance, "make the Cossacks in Russian Georgia seem like throngs of angels." The factory's substantial store of petrolatum and mineral oil, the basic ingredients of Wyoming Willie's Wondrous Pomade, had nourished a tossed torch into an inferno. Shmuel and his wife, Leah, fled Atlanta to take up residency in St. Petersburg, Florida, a destination chosen off a map of the South for no other reason than because Shmuel vaguely remembered hearing as a child in Russia his father saying something about a grand synagogue in a city of that name. The Atlanta fire convinced the Grossmans to conceal their Jewishness. The distinctly daitshmerish Yiddish accents that characterized their speech, however, made posing as Germans their only credible ethnic option. By introducing himself as Herr Peter von Groß-engel to a Mr. Melkart, manager of the St. Petersburg Sunshine Bank, and informing the banker that, before coming to the land of freedom, he had been superintendent of Dachau's Zoologischer Garten, Shmuel was able to sway the capitalist into lending him funds to open a pet shop—Saint Pete's Pets. Shmuel had always liked animals. This choice of national identity had seemed like a good idea in 1910, when Germans were as admired as Teutons. The bank manager authorized Shmuel's business loan on a conviction that Germans were innately intelligent, industrious, and idealistic. But in 1914 the esteemed Aryan had become the excoriated Hun. While both Jews and Germans were generally distrusted as "hyphenated Americans," it became even worse to be German than it was to be Jewish as rotogravure images of German atrocities in Europe began to appear in American newspapers. Pretzels and sauerkraut were officially banned throughout Florida. And in St. Petersburg, after an outbreak of German measles, the mayor reported that the town was teeming with German spies. He decreed that all the books in the public library by authors with German names were to be burned at an Americans-for-America-for-Americans demonstration. As the folks of St. Petersburg were not particularly zealous in their intellectual pursuits, their municipal library was a modest one; the great bonfire that had been organized for their anti-German rally amounted to only a piddling, smoky, and entirely anticlimactic smoldering of no more than ten volumes. In dire need of something more spectacular to feed the brighter, hotter flames of nationalistic ardor that burned within their hearts, the citizens marched en masse to the shop owned by the only Germans in town, namely Peter von Großengel and his wife, Isolde. As the patriots shouted such inspirational slogans as "Hang the Hun" and "Kill the Kraut," a public-spirited Mrs. Melkart valiantly cast a brick through the glass window front of Saint Pete's Pets. When a terrified Shmuel and Leah emerged with their hands trembling in the air above their heads, Mr. Melkart, with Yankee valor, commanded his three sons to storm the pet shop, and they obeyed with all the spunk and gumption of diehard doughboys. Once inside enemy territory, the lads threw open the cage doors to liberate the captives of the Huns, freeing all the animals except the fish, two garter snakes, and a lone dachshund. As a German, the frightened dog was taken prisoner along with Shmuel and Leah who, during questioning at the Sunshine State Council of Justice, explained that they were not really Germans at all, but Russian Jews. This was not much better than being German, since the mayor, the chief of police, and Mr. Melkart had all been privy to recent government documents regarding the Jewish Menace: Jews were taking grievous economic advantage of true Americans as they plotted to establish their own nation of Zion. They would betray Uncle Sam just as they had double-crossed Jesus Christ. That Shmuel confessed to establishing residency in Florida under a false identity provided ample grounds to arrest both him and Leah. Tried and convicted under the United States of America Espionage and Sedition Act, Shmuel was sentenced to ten years in the Ponce de Leon Maximum Security Prison in Miami and Leah to the same term at the Betsy Ross Women's Penitentiary in Odessa. The dachshund, after a brief internment in the St. Petersburg SPCA, was executed in the pound's gas chamber in an apotropaic rite designed to keep the Kaiser out of Florida. Although I had listened to many a telling of my father's myriad renditions of the tragic tale, I did not meet Shmuel Grossman until years later in Jake Grossman's hotel room in Greenwich, just outside London, where Shmuel, after his release from prison, had come to attend a rally of the International Communist Party. Leon Trotsky was scheduled to speak to representatives from Europe, the Americas, Africa, and Asia. Jake disclosed that after only a few months of incarceration, prison officials, customarily opening correspondence received by inmates, discovered a letter written to Shmuel by Trotsky, who was residing in New York at the time. Shmuel was subsequently placed in solitary confinement, where he was to remain for the duration of his ten-year sentence for conspiring to overthrow the United States government. The ex-convict was still alone; released several years before her husband, Leah Grossman was living in Miami with an Irishman who, while employed as a guard at the Betsy Ross facility, had fathered a child by her. When Jake told Shmuel that I was Abraham Schlossberg's son, he stared at me in proctorial silence. "I remember your father fondly," he finally conceded. "I recall the evening he bounded into our dressing room at the Garden cursing in Russian and threatening to kill all four of us with his bare hands. And I remember him as a boy in heder. He knew more Hebrew than the melamed. During lessons, sitting behind me, he'd risk a smacking by whispering the Hebrew words that I didn't know or couldn't remember. Abraham always did everything he could to help. He sent money when the factory burned down." I told my father's old friend that, all these years later, I still had a tin of the pomade that he had manufactured in Atlanta and that, although I never used it to dress my hair, I took it everywhere with me and would, now and again, twist off the top and sniff it. "I can smell my father in it," I said. "It's the scent of my childhood." The melancholy Communist softly confessed that he was tempted to find some gratification "in imagining that something I did a long time ago, could still today, and perhaps even tomorrow, give someone else a little bit of pleasure. But actually my former wife deserves the credit for the aroma. It was she who selected the special ingredient: Finkelman's Industrial Fragrance No. 11. They just don't make smells like they used to."

12 Jehu, zealous captain of the Israelite army, the most skillful archer in Samaria, whose arrows had pierced the heart of Jehoram, vanquished the priests of Baal, and decimated the house of Ahab, appeared on stage at Dante's in the number three spot, following Maddie Mahoney, the Irish farmer's daughter whose trained geese danced the Siamsa Beirte in 2/4 hornpipe time, and preceding a song and dance by a tall and lean Tubs Shortman, who used burned cork on his face even though as a full-blooded Negro he was quite dusky enough to do minstrel routines without it. As Jehu, my father was coldhearted, intimating that marksmanship, no less than prophecy, requires a restraint of feeling. As Jezebel, my mother was enraptured, insinuating that heathen cults, no less than honky-tonks, encourage unbridled eruptions of emotion and an abandonment of moral restrictions. While the idolatrous queen shimmied before a graven image of lust, my father, appearing to release one arrow after another at his moving target, took credit for piercing the flapping flowing folds of a homemade Phoenician costume. Pinned to the wall by ten arrows, the beautiful Jezebel could dance no more. The prophets of Elijah, no less than officers of the Gray Society, Christian ministers, and suffragettes, hated sexy dancing as much as the votaries of Baal and the habitués of burleycue loved it. That there was the sound of barking dogs when the music stopped and the curtain fell would have been ominous to those who knew the biblical narrative. It was, however, not the yelping of the ravenous hounds of Jezreel backstage but Larry Lafitte's poodles yapping in anticipation of their immanent appearance on the boards in the number five spot. With hand gestures Lafitte cued the canine thespians from the wings through a portrayal of bohemian life in Paris. Dressed in apache dance costumes, cigarettes glued to their lips, the dogs were billed as "direct from the Folly's Barjeer." At my father's exit, Pierre, the star of the tab, beret cocked to the side, growled and barked at the future King of Israel. "Jehu and Jezebel" was one of the several vignettes that my father had been developing in a repertoire of vaud skits, "Great Sharpshooters of the Bible." It had been initially inspired by the popular reception of our "Abraham and Isaac" as played at Grossman's in 1911. It was for the dénouement of that routine, in which Isaac and Abraham juggled flaming torches for the burnt offering unto the Lord, that I had learned the moves, the take-aways and side-by-sides, steals and feeds, spins and balances, passes and breaks. As Isaac I did a four-torch fountain, but David had to master a more difficult and yet less impressive five-ball cascade in order to stay true to the haftorah passage in which the young psalmist "choseth him five smooth stones of a brook and didst put them in his shepherd's bag." Though the juggling was real, the shot was fake. I palmed the shiny stone ball and, as the sling strap snapped, let it fall back into the rustic chamois satchel as the misdirected eyes of the audience followed the invisible stone, as surely as if it were real, through the air to the forehead of Goliath. Hearing the crack of the impact and then seeing the head of the Philistine swivel around on the neck like a clown head in a shooting gallery, the audience wailed with laughter. I seemed to shoot five bull's-eyes. The last one knocked the big head off the giant torso. Goliath hopped in circles around the stage like a decapitated chicken and spiraled into an exit. Because the voice of Ola Namnlösa, the acromegalic Swede inside the Goliath suit, was inappropriately high-pitched, my father spoke for him, bellowing the menacing words of the terrible giant of Gath from behind a curtain: "Haha! Behold this youth from Bethlehem, puniest child of all the runts of Israel! Come hither, little boy, so that I can feed your flesh to the birds of the air and the beasts of the field." Laughing back and brazenly accepting the challenge to battle, I recited the moral of the routine: "You come to me with sword, spear, shield, and armor, O Goliath, whilst I stand before you armed only with the name of the Lord. All this assembly shall know that the Lord saveth not with sword and spear, but with love for those who trust in Him and have faith in His name." Even though Ola couldn't speak his part convincingly, he did an adequate job of spinning the fake head when he heard the gong that was supposed to be the sound of a stone striking his pate. He was almost seven feet tall without the mannequin head, which, placed on the shoulders of his costume and topped with a plumed helmet, made him well over eight feet tall. Because my father didn't consider the giant a freak but just a very, very, very tall man, he didn't have to compromise his vow never to work with teratoids. Ola had, in fact, played freak shows, dressing as a groom to pose with Catherine the Little, a Russian midget in a bridal gown. The exhibit appealed to the prurient imaginations of sideshow audiences, evoking fantasies of bizarre nuptial intimacies that aroused a laughter expressive of amusement, titillation, awe, fear, and disgust all at once. Ola's real wife, Skadi, who was almost as tall as the giant, had received repeated invitations both to exhibit herself as an Amazon and to play the squaw Wampanoag, the red-skinned wife of Colonel William W. Wee in his Wild West Weeview. She had demurely and consistently refused, insisting that she had no interest in show business, that she was quite content to dedicate her life to Christ and to sewing all the very big clothes and cooking all the very big dinners for her very big husband. As a parishioner of the Pentecostal Church of the Outpouring of the Latter Day Rain of Love, she had zealously handled rattlesnakes and enthusiastically read the Bible. The latter activity lead to a persistent pestering of her husband to point out to my father the flagrant discrepancies between our portrayal of David and Goliath and the one she had so assiduously studied in First Samuel. The fact that none of the "Great Sharpshooters of the Bible" skits were very faithful to Scripture did not concern me at all as a vaudevillian, but I could not help but think a bit about it as a boy preparing to be a bar mitzvah. Which, I had to ask myself, was I to take more seriously: entertainment or religion, vaudeville or Judaism? That question was answered during the bar mitzvah ceremony itself, when, after the recitation of the second Torah blessing, my father recited the *Baruch shepetarani:* "Blessed is He who now frees me from all responsibility for my son's future actions." Having been a Jew only for the sake of my father, I, upon hearing those words, suddenly felt free not to take Judaism, God, or his six hundred and thirteen demanding commandments seriously. Now I could eat ham, bacon, and pork and, if I so wished, bow down before the gods of heathens. Just recently, despite my aversion to religion, I found myself in a synagogue in Honolulu reciting the words *"yizkor Elohim nishmat"* for Avraham ben Menachem Schlossberg. The formal remembrance of him, bringing tears to my eyes, detonated a volley of explosive images: pitching pomade, loading stunt shells, fast-drawing a Colt six-gun, snapping a bullwhip, lighting a Blaine Havana with a vesuvian, fixing the faux-diamond studs in the buttonholes of his white silk shirt, turning the propeller to start the engine of the airplane, kissing my mother on the cheek, and laughing. "Blessed art Thou, Lord our God, God of our fathers, of Abraham, Isaac, and Jacob," I was automatically muttering, "Who rememberest the good deeds of our fathers, and our father's fathers, and Who will redeem our children, and our children's children," when, all of a sudden, I couldn't help but laugh. I had remembered the earnest expression on my father's face as he ballied hard to convince authorities in Stockton that I, his eleven-year-old son, was, in reality, his sixty-one-year-old father. In an effort to enforce California's child labor laws, three policemen, accompanied by a pastor and an officer of the SPCC, had raided the Chutes, arrested us, and threatened to turn me over to the Good Templar Juvenile Shelter if my father did not take me off the vaudeville stage and enroll me in a proper school. Wyoming Willie used the occasion as an opportunity to work a scam by performing a skit he had been developing for us. "Tell the judge the story, Pop. Tell him the truth," my father said to test my proficiency in the humbugological arts. "Calm down, son," I said and rolled the spiel to turn the tip. "Yes sir, it's unbelievable, but the story was in all the papers back then. You could have read about it in any of the medical journals. It happened in the summer of '86, the year of the great drought when the vast skies over the Wyoming range country were laced with heavy smoke from the ceaseless grass fires. The sweltering nights grumbled with thunder. I don't even remember the lightning striking, and I didn't wake up again until winter. I came to in an army hospital in Laramie where, I was told, Cheyenne Indians had brought me." I paused for a reaction, trying to discern if there was any hope of making the judge believe us or if we were entertaining him to the degree that he wouldn't care whether the yarn was true or not. Uncertain, I backtracked, remarked that I had been born in 1849, related a few vivid details of my exploits as a Union cavalry man, only to work my way back up to the lightning bolt, the colossal shock of which had, quite amazingly and to the utter bafflement of medical science, completely reversed the aging process in my body: "I didn't realize that anything about me had changed for a while. But after a few months I started to notice little things that made me aware that something strange was going on. While my son, Willie here, was becoming naturally older, I was—and I know it's unbelievable—getting physically younger. My hair got thicker and darker and my eyesight began to improve. Well, Judge, it's gone on like that ever since. I stopped shaving and lost the hair under my arms and on my chest about two years ago. My voice has gotten higher and my cheeks rosier. I reckon I'll look like a baby in another seven or eight years." Pretending to be my son and holding his hands heavenward, my father cried out to me: "Papa! Papa! How will it end?" And then, without the slightest fear of appearing to be an idiot or liar, a con man or madman, he buried his forlorn face in his hands and went all the way: "When my father becomes an infant, must I find some woman who can suckle him and into whose womb he can be placed at death? And within her, shall the fetus shrink into an embryo until, nine months later, that woman unites with a man who takes my father's seed back into his loins? And what if I were to be that man?" My father always insisted that if a showman was good enough, he could convince anyone of anything, no matter how preposterous. But this one was just too much. I remember the woeful look on my father's face when the judge in Stockton said, glowering, "That's the most ridiculous, outlandish, and crazy cock-and-bull story that I have ever, in my thirty-three years on the bench and my sixty-nine years on this earth, heard." My father blustered defensively, "I swear before God Almighty that it is true. This child is my father! That is the truth, the whole truth, and nothing but the truth!" And like Pilate unto Jesus, the judge laughed in the showman's face. "What in the hell is truth?"

13 Because the Paradisio was a stag house, ever likely to be raided, I suspected they wouldn't sell a ticket to a fourteen-year-old. So I mixed gum mastic with ether to put on a beard that, together with an old straw katy, faded Levi Strauss field overalls, Sears & Roebuck boots, and dirty fingernails, made me look just the sort of Northwest joskin who'd nervously creep into such a slab on a Saturday afternoon in heated hopes of seeing a little leg and shoulder and lots of spicy jiggle and shimmy. Because the Paradisio was a burlesque house, and a blue one at that, I suspected my parents wouldn't condone the notion of my going, since, now that we were supposedly vaudeville, working the business on the Rungman Circuit, we were expected to spurn burlesquers. While we were artists doing highfalutin biblical vignettes, they were common buskers pandering to the petty depravities of lonesome souls. Thus I announced my plan to spend the day at the Seattle zoo, visiting the reptile house, where, the advert claimed, they had a two-headed king snake. From my father I had learned to lie well enough to lie to him. The Paradisio had booked Bachnele Poopik that week but, since the midget was not being billed under the name by which I remembered him, I wouldn't have realized that it was the diminutive comedian from our past if I had not overheard my father's harangue. "Little Hymie Horowitz, the Hilarious Hebe of Hebron, playing the Paradisio, that honky-tonk and hook shop, this week is (can you believe it?) none other than the despicable, intolerable (may God forgive me for even saying the name!) Bachnele Poopik!" Without looking away from the mirror in which she was being transformed into Jezebel, who, according to Second Kings, "painted her eyes and adorned her hair to face Jehu," my mother tried to calm the sharpshooting bowman of Tyre. "You're too hard on him. Please be kinder. After all, he is a midget. Try to have some compassion, my dearest one. Did not Hashem, the Lord our God, say to Moses, 'Your little ones, them I will bring in and they shall know the land which I have promised'?" My father, setting down the quiver that had been embroidered with the Shema, stopped his wife. His guffaw was corroded by acidic ill temper. "Little ones! Ha! That's children, not midgets." Fixing the turquoise bijou into the lobe of her ear, mother smiled as if she knew what she was talking about. "In the Gemara no less an authority than Rav Ashi himself argues that the Torah passage refers specifically to midgets and dwarfs." Biblical midrash aside, I wanted to see him. My adolescent curiosity was aroused by the fact that, though my father loathed him, all women seemed to feel an irrepressible and uncanny affection for him. At that age I imagined that it might be possible to know what women desire in a man, not the obvious, stated things, but the secret, real things. Out in front of the Paradisio, before the matinee, doing his bit to entice passersby into buying a ticket, Little Hymie Horowitz, dressed as a Hasid (his beard as fake as mine), was trying to evoke laughter with wisecracks about midgets and jokes about Jews: "Ya betta git your ticket qvick, vhile dey last. Dey're so cheap dat all my relatives—yeah, every Yid in Seattle— vill be buying dem up to peddle dem for tvice de price." After a contortionist did an ocarina solo in a variety of seemingly impossible postures, there was a giant who, with arms outstretched, held two tall ladders upon which petite twin chorines in flesh-colored tights climbed up and down, performing acrobatic feats as a fat man in blackface played a banjo. After an ample-figured soubrette in a scant Greco-Roman tunic, costarring with a trained white duck named Moby, did a parody of "Leda and the Swan," and just before the intermission in the second-to-headliner spot, Bachnele danced out into the lights singing his heart out. "Little Hymie is my name, Hymie Horowitz! Isn't it a shame? I stayed too long in de shvitz! Do you see what I became? I shrunk right up, shrunk up bit by bits. Yes, I'm Hymie Horowitz!" In a tattered kapuhte and battered shtrayml, with crumbs in his pointed beard, the midget leered at the audience over large spectacles crookedly perched on a putty hook nose. With his hands behind his back he danced a buffoonish schottische. His comic monologue focused on the sexual implications and complications of a midget's marriage to a woman who was twice his size. Six-foot-two rhymed with Jew as he once again broke into song: "Yes, my vife is tall! Mrs. Sarah Horowitz! But if you tink I'm small, you should see her . . . ears." The audience laughed over the hackneyed vaud rhetorical turn and every racy innuendo. Collective laughter assured each member of the audience that his murkiest musings did not isolate him from others. On the contrary, his little lusts bound him to those around him. The audience actually stood and whistled as the midget danced offstage singing, "Little Hymie is my name, Hymie Horowitz! I hope you're glad you came! I hope you liked my skits." At intermission, a house-butcher in pinstriped gabardine flogged candy, balloons, sheet music, and titillation: "Gentlemen, I am proud to announce that the headliner this afternoon at Seattle's world-famous Paradisio is the one and only dainty darling of the Deccan, Little India! Yesiree, just arrived from Old Calcutta via Paree, France, London, England, and New York City, New York, where her Oriental shimmy shook Broadway like an earthquake. And for your edification we have a book for sale, a humdinger of a translation as unexpurgated as it is unabashed, of a French *biographie de boudoir*, entitled *Les Amours Fantastiques de la Belle Mademoiselle Petite India*, in which you'll discover ten of the sauciest stories ever written and ten French exposures *photographiques* of Little India herself that could make a midwife or a maharaja blush. Nothing is left to the imagination." As the headliner, Little India was the ninth act, appearing just before the Sarah Bernhardt impersonator reciting Thisbe's lines from *A Midsummer's Night Dream;* thus it was a man pretending to be a woman pretending to be a man pretending to be a woman to say: "Most brisky juvenal and eke most lovely Jew, I'll meet thee at Ninny's tomb." And she appeared right after an aging but zaftig as ever Trixie Cocotte, whose tight corset, beaded gown, and tough swagger highlighted all the sauce and raunch in her repertoire of burley hymns: "Tickle My Fancy," "Under My Ladder," and "Snake in the Grass." Miss Cocotte was preceded by Macstro Mentula Loquenza, a ventriloquist from Quintana Roo, who carried on a conversation about life and love with a prominently animated bulge in the front of his trousers that sang a blithe ditty which, from the favorable response of the male members of the audience, apparently put into words what they imagined their own genitalia would melodically express if such things were possible anywhere but on a burlesque stage. Finally Little India was introduced. She was much more petite, delicate, and graceful than I could have imagined a cooch dancer at the Paradisio would be. An Oriental dress exposed a bare midriff that was seemingly possessed by ancient spirits, flexed by the primal pitipatation of native drums, twisted by the whine of strange strings and eerie whispers of bamboo flutes, pulsed by trills and tremors of the East. Carnal undulations radiated up the torso from the naked stomach and out through the tendrilous arms into outstretched fingers, and simultaneously down into the pelvis to churn and distill into a sway of thighs and swoon of calves. Clouds of sound and melodic mists swathed her as she floated in arabesques with wafting veils flourishing about her, faster and faster to the mesmeric beat and drone, and every muscle of the delirious body flexed in syncopated transport as she unveiled a mystic rapture with arms reached out to heaven. Then she stopped. Dead still. A plaintive flute called out. Lights dimmed and drums hushed. Slowly her arms lowered and hands joined over her heart. Slowly, so slowly, a naked leg emerged through the purple silk of her skirt to expose itself from foot almost to waist. The limb reached in a long step to the right, stretched, paused with purpose, and then darted back to obscure itself once more within the cloth. Then the left leg imitated the teasings of the right. As the drums returned to quicken and ruffle the tempo of the score, the nautch girl's arms began to twist about in an independent dance above her head. Eyes closed, fingers spread, tongue darted, and the abdomen, glistening with sweat, flexed all the more, inviting eyes to act for fingers and gaze for touch. Hands were clasped together as if each were trying to restrain the other. She bit her lip, rolled her eyes, and gasped for breath. One hand broke loose to reach for her jeweled breast and, as the men in the audience couldn't help but holler for more, so much more, her hair, as if in response to the howling, fell loose and long. Someone lobbed a large pink rose onto the stage. She didn't pick it up, but paced around it as an animal would do in instinctual response to an unknown intruder in its lair. Falling to her knees then, she circled it, curious, desirous and yet cautious, almost afraid. Suddenly she poked it, gazed again, then snatched it up. Rising to her feet, she sniffed the flower, held it to her breast, grazed it up her neck, touched it to her cheek, and recommenced the dance. Breathing the inebriating fragrances of the floral offering, delicately she kissed it as if it were the mouth of an angel. And then, all at once, music and dance ceased and the stage was still and midnight dark save for the moonbeam spot upon her. The hall was silent. Little India threw the rose back into the audience. But before you could see to which lucky man it fell, the calcium light was extinguished and there was a potent pall of blinding darkness. It made you want to visit India. When the houselights went on again, she returned to the bare stage to take a dramatic bow before the ecstatically applauding audience of bewitched men. I whistled, clapped, and stamped my feet with them. After the program, I waited anxiously for her inevitable entrance into the illegal beer hall that adjoined the theater, the rowdy smoking room where, before, between, and after the shows, song-and-dance men in blackface tended bar and costumed soubrettes hustled drinks, hawked dances, and made false promises. I had recognized her the moment she had appeared on stage, and, despite my fake beard and the four years of separation, she recognized me too. "Isaac," she laughed with surprise, and I, struggling to smile under the burden of adolescent longing, answered: "Angel."

14 "Wyoming Willie was finished," Jake Grossman sighed: "By the time your father was on the vaudeville circuit, a cowboy act was, first and foremost, a song-and-dance number. A showbiz cowpoke had to heel-and-toe and two-step, play the harmonica, banjo, spoons, and Jew's harp. But most of all he had to croon. Wyoming Willie could shoot a gun like Buffalo Bill, throw a knife like Choctaw Charlie, and snap a whip like Lash Labitte, but *a Caruso vas er nisht.* He couldn't carry a tune if his life depended on it, and in vaud, a cowboy who couldn't sing just wasn't, as far as paying audiences were concerned, a cowboy. So Abraham Schlossberg cast himself as an English thespian, to act like an actor, figuring that that particular character could play any part that came along. Wyoming Willie changed his name to William Shakesberg, his birthplace from Laramie, Wyoming, to Greenwich, England, his accent from cow puncher to British gent, his duds from buckskins to tails, and his hat from Stetson to bowler." Indulging himself in the wistful pleasures of sentimentality, the amiable entrepreneur was not quite resigned to allowing the departed to be entirely gone. He poured vodka for me, himself, and his brother Shmuel. "I still miss my friend from the faraway Pale of Settlement, dear Avraham ben Menachem. *Uhlevashuhlem!* I could never understand the berserk obsession with airplanes. If God wanted us to fly, don't you think he would have given us wings just like He gave His angels?" Shmuel interrupted: "Stop talking nonsense. There is no God, and you know it as well as I do!" Jake smiled. "Communists don't believe in Hashem or Messiach." Shmuel defended himself: "How can any Jew believe in God anymore, my brother? Hasn't our history demonstrated his conspicuous absence? But, at the same time, I would understand if you believed in Ashmedai, the Evil One, for the power of wickedness is evident all around us. He has plenty of priests even without a church." Apparently amused by the sermon, Jake chuckled. "The brothers Grossman are a theatrical family. We got our start playing Cossacks in the Buffalo Bill show. After that, for me as a manager, and for Beryl as an agent, theater became a matter of business, show business. For the revolutionary here, politics is the drama, the eternal tragedy. And our Hayim, for him love has always been the play, the universal slapstick comedy. The bedroom has been his theater and the bed his stage." I had met Hayim Grossman at my bar mitzvah celebration in San Francisco. He was a traveling man with no fixed profession and all the women at the party, young and old, married or not, seemed to remark at least once that evening on his good looks, his sparkling azure eyes and confident smile. In giggles and whispers there was gossip about the reputed enormity of his penis that would include a joke insinuating that his brother Jake's was the opposite. After the ceremony, with family and guests all a little drunk and very mirthful, the women mixing freely with the men in a defiance of orthodoxy, a circle for a huset dance was formed. Whenever the klezmorim, on fiddle, viola, cimbalom, and zongura, slowed down even a little bit, my father threw coins to them, exuberantly calling out, "Faster! Faster!" Hayim, spinning around in the center of the circle like a human dreidel on one leg and then the other, seemed to rise from the floor. Everyone cheered, laughed, and clapped their hands. The women and girls blushed at the sight of the fringes flying about his waist. A few had gone home. Some, including my mother, father, and the Lanskys, who had come all the way from New York for the occasion, had fallen asleep with their heads cradled on arms folded on the long table. Still drinking in a candlelit corner, Beryl and Jake were talking show-business business. Taking me outside, offering a puff on his Blaine cigar and a sip of his schnapps, Hayim readjusted my yarmulke, congratulated me on the day, and insisted on giving me his own version of *Pirke Aboth* (*the Wisdom of Our Fathers*): "Now that you're a bar mitzvah, you can—praise be to God!—start fucking girls. Fuck as many of them as you can, Jews and Gentiles alike. Fuck them as often as you can. This is the very foundation of our faith, the first mitzvah in the Torah, the holy commandment that Elohim gave to Adam. It's why you're circumcised, as a reminder. Today you are a bar mitzvah, so now it is your obligation. 'Fuck Eve,' the Creator commanded the first man. That's what it says in the Torah. And Hashem commanded Abraham to fuck Sarah and Hagar, Isaac to fuck Rebecca and Keturah, and Jacob to fuck Rachel and Leah, and the rest is history, our history! Jews were chosen by God to fuck. Praise be the Lord to whom all praise is due!" The repeated utterance of "fuck" shocked me, not because of its meaning but because I thought of it, like "Christ," as a Gentile word, a sound as out of place in a Jewish mouth as pork. Christians said things like "I fucked her, fuck you and fuck me, fuck up and fuck off, fuck my luck and fuck a duck," and God only knows what else. But Jews said "shtoop" or sometimes "yents." The high Hebrew "letanot ahavim," the phrase God Himself had used for shtooping, wasn't to be voiced, according to my father, until the coming of Meshiach. "Mishkav" and "ziun" were as unutterable as the Tetragrammaton. In English we might say "sleep with" or "make love to," or "bang" or "screw" to be a little dirty. In my language lessons, my father had not shied away from verbs for this activity. I could speak of it in French (*baiser, tringler,* or *tremper le biscuit*), German (*in die Muschel rotzen, die Sichel putzen,* or *einen kleinen Käfer ins Ohr blasen*), Spanish (*chingar* or *chamuscar el horno*), Latin (*coitare* or *tractare tui cucumem*), Zemblan (*pezup* or *lindagoú pu fugelep*), not to mention Italian (*sbattere* or *trambare*), Russian (*trakhat 'sya*), Arabic, and the vocabularies and idioms of other languages since forgotten. But the English "fuck" was, I thought, a thou-shalt-not word for Jews. Although occasionally falling into temptation and saying it silently to myself or whispering it when no one was around, I never uttered it out loud with anyone listening until I was eighteen years old. And then it was murmured in disappointment, sadness, and anger, not whispered in hope, lust, or love. In retrospect it was probably more because of vaudeville than because of Judaism that "fuck" was forbidden to me. If that sound slipped from the lips of a performer in a vaudeville theater, even just once, there was sure to be a heavy fine; twice and you got the boot; three times and you could be barred from the circuit. Poodle trainer Larry Lafitte was blackballed by Rungman for using the outlawed word three times in one run-on sentence: "Fuck you, you little fucker," he shouted at Pierre, the perky top dog of his canine troupe. "What the fuck do you think you're doing?" The punishment seemed excessive, since the word was not being used to refer to sexual intercourse; the syllable was merely an invective intensifier in a curse that Lafitte could not repress when Pierre failed to perform a diligently rehearsed showcase trick. A volunteer from the audience had been instructed to pick a card from a well-shuffled deck, show it to the audience, and return it to the pack. Sniffing was the only skill that Pierre required to locate the forced queen that had been wrapped and stored in bacon strips for a week. But Pierre had been entirely disinterested in the smell of bacon, distracted as he was by the scent of the heat of a female Pomeranian that had urinated on the stage after her tightrope performance in a chaser the night before. Lafitte was replaced as the opener on the bill by an up-and-coming animal impersonator named Al Alighieri, Jr., who, in a suit of curly fur, played a poodle, scratching for fleas, barking at the audience, sniffing the stage, and fetching a ball thrown by a chimpanzee in a fedora and smoking jacket. While Alighieri's poodle routine was, by all accounts, lackluster, his subsequent laughing hyena impersonation at the Novelty in Los Angeles in 1913 was praised in a *Variety* review as "gut-bustingly hilarious!" In general, animal acts, inevitably slated in either the opening or closing spot on a bill due to their limited popularity with adult audiences, were disdained by troupers. Since snake charmer was one of my various roles, however, I could not help but feel a fellowship with both Larry Lafitte and Al Alighieri, Jr. I always most appreciated the very acts that other performers most disparaged, not only animal acts but plate and barrel spinning, handcuff and ladder acts; I admired clay modelers, whistlers, yodelers, contortionists, Indian club tossers, sword swallowers, regurgitators, and quick-change artists. My father liked Alighieri, not for his talent, but because, like my father, he was a White Rat. As such they had marched together on the picket line outside Dreamland when the Rats called a strike against the Universal

Amusement Syndicate. The protest met with a harsh reprisal from management: any vaudevillian identified as a White Rat was denied future booking. In order to feed, clothe, and house his wife and child, my father resorted to working for the Cony-Dew-White Chautauqua System. A resurrected Wyoming Willie delivered an inspirational sermon entitled "The Great American Ladder." This uplifting lecture on the wholesome habits of the American cowboy had been written especially for him by one of the pioneers of Chautauqua, the Reverend Conway Conwell, "World-Renowned Theologian, Geographer, Economist, and Lecturer." "We respect women and horses," my father was told to say. "We keep our rifles and our thoughts clean, work hard all day and say our prayers at night." A sharpshooting demonstration gave dramatic bite to a stirring polemic on the relationship between morality and the God-given American right to bear arms. Much to his shame, my father had to borrow money from his cousin, Mendel Lansky, when it became morally impossible for him to endure Chautauqua. He quit in disgust upon hearing a talk, "American Money Belongs to Americans," delivered on a warm summer afternoon in Sacramento by none other than Conway Conwell himself: "The takeover of the American economy by the nefarious Jew has already begun, my friends. You cannot rely on a strange name or hook nose to know who or where he is, what he is doing and why," the preacher had warned the caucus of Caucasian Christian Americans. "Many of them look just like you and me. Yes, many a Judas, Shylock, and Hymie has changed his name to Tom, or Dick, or Harry. Any Mr. Washington, Jefferson, or Lincoln could be a Lipschitz, Goldberg, or Dreyfus." My father lamented, "I don't know how we're going to survive." His wife put her hand on his shoulder, smiling as she leaned over to kiss the top of his head. "Ringling, Barnum, Bailey, and Bannerjee are auditioning performers for a very big show." The patriarch recoiled in horror. "Circus? Never! We are actors! We are artists, my beloved, not clowns!"

15 It was, in my assessment of how things happen to happen in my novel life, by chance that our paths occasionally intersected during the two years since I had seen her at the Paradisio. In her aerial view of the topography of the game, it was by luck that we landed on the same square every once in a while. I wondered if, beyond chance or luck, there might be such a thing as fate in matters of love. That was a winsome notion, she mused, as sweet and appealing as the idea was bitter and appalling that destiny dictated the conditions of death as well. I hadn't seen Angel Rabinowitz for over a month and had been having the kinds of dreams about her that wake a young man up. I counted on her being in Chula Vista, the first stop on the West Coast route card for the Durbar of Delhi, "the most magnificent spectacle ever assembled for the amazement of mankind," coproduced by Ringling Bros. and Barnum & Bailey in cooperation with the Bannerjee Brothers Menagerie. Literally thousands of performers were being hired through the regional circuits for an extravaganza that was bigger than all of Big Bee's other biggest biggests, including Nero's Roman Circus, Herod's Hippodrome, and Cleopatra's Carnival. The pay was so good that it didn't take much for my mother to convince my father that, despite his scorn for circus and horror of horses, we could not afford to turn down the deal cut for us by Beryl Grossman. I became Swami Balakrishna, Prince of Snake Charmers; my mother was Maharanee Mayadevee, the Mystic Mentaliste of Mysore; and my father, as the Commandant of the British Imperial Arsenal, manned the Colonial Shooting Gallery. While we were stock players, Angel was a star. Her appearance in the sky just before midnight was a climax to the pleasures of each day. Tungsten and naphtha flared and flourished with the rataplan and roll of snare drums and trumpets in an annunciation of her sidereal dance. Ten beams of light converged on her platform perch high above the crowd. She could have performed cabulot jumps, somersaults, hoop or snake walks, a hair spin or the ladder of death, but instead she simply danced. Although this nocturnal epiphany, the aerial arabesques of her languorous Oriental ballet across the wire in nimble sways and bows, bends and turns, all rallentando, without a pole, was far more tricky than an acrobatic stunt walk, the congregation of circus goers was less flabbergasted than moved by the beauty of it. And because she made it seem so natural and effortless, no one feared for her. That's where she got them with something unexpected: in the center of the wire, in the midst of a pirouette, she'd fake an accidental slip to shake the earthlings out of the dream into which she herself had lulled them. The gaping mouths of upturned faces gasped in unison. As rehearsed, Angel, barely catching the wire, hung suspensefully precarious in the night. I could hear heartbeats and muffled orisons in the anticipatory silence into which the throng had been thrown by the shock of her close call. Slowly, without panic, she began a beat back, swinging to and fro from the hips to build up the momentum with which to birdnest the wire. Regaining her footing, she took a bow as everyone on earth applauded, whistled, and cheered. And then she danced with ease the rest of the way along the wire. Orchestral brass, wind, and string chanted loud laudation and fantastic fireworks (fizzing serpents, lady fingers, and whiz-bangs), all in time to the musical grand finale, exploded in the sky around the angelic daredevil in a pyrotechnical liturgy. It was holy assumption, a vision of the triumph of beauty over death, the heavenly over the grave. On opening night I happened to be standing in a spot that put the full moon directly behind Angel as she hung from the wire in beatific silhouette, suspended before the luminous lunar face that seemed to gaze at her. Angel would finish the night, each night, eight extravagantly thrilling hours after the show began with the Grand March through the streets. The parade dazzled and seduced, dragging residents to the admissions booths outside the fairground gates. No one could resist the raucously rolling orchestmelochor or the calliope screeching cacophonous quasi-Oriental tunes as it chugged along, swathed in the black smoke and white steam that it exhaled in pants and wheezes. Elephants dominated both the street parade and the Spec; bulls and queens in long-mount, styling for the gawking masses, trumpeted in obeisance to the whitewashed Heema, the "Sacred Albino Elephant of Elephanta," her tusks gold-leafed and bejeweled. In the ornate howdah on Heema's back, waving a golden goad as if it were a scepter, sat Ganesh Bannerjee, billed as "His Holiness, High Priest Shankar, Pope of Patna." Most of the Indians, however, were not really Indian, but local talent, as were most of the animals: Texas shorthorns and California heifers, festooned with feathers and bells, played the parts of Brahma bulls and holy cows; palfreys, dobbins, and nags were caparisoned into chargers and prancers. Even goats and sheep were booked as extravaganza extras. As an agent for my snakes, I earned ten cents per reptile per day, and I had now more than twenty in my collection. Everyone was in the Grand March: jugglers, pongers, stilt walkers, pole perchers, antipodists, benders, unicyclists, globe walkers, and rolla-bollers; wazirs, fakirs, dervishes, and votaries of Mother Kali, Gurkhas and sepoys, black-skinned slaves and pale zenana girls, the Light Brigade, and Bengal Lancers. The fabulous Equestriennes of the Royal Harem of the Nawab of Nagpur were circus bareback riders in dusky tights that made it seem that there was naked Oriental skin to be seen through translucent blue pajamas. On their tanbarks and rosinbacks, riding ringstock and liberties, reining through flip-flaps and dosidos, they caracoled in fantasies of a faraway voluptuous realm where pleasure was a way of life. The dream was fortified by each float, car, and wagon with sunburst wheels, all flowered and feathered, carved and painted with exotic tableaus and depictions of heathen gods and demons. Tigers snarled as grinning tamers, with poppered lash whips cracking, waved. There were bears, monkeys, camels, and ten harnessed ostriches that no one seemed to know or care were not native to the Orient. My snakes, displayed in glass cages, drawn on a wagon in the parade prior to their installation in my booth inside the fairground, were advertised as "The Deadliest Vipers, Asps, Cobras, and Kraits of the East." I was on display with Jesus Estafar, a Mexican a few years older than myself who, wearing a loincloth and turban, posed as a fakir on a bed of nails. His little brother, Jaime, doing the Amazing Snake Boy of Hindustan routine under the name of Ramoo, was installed in the tent next across the way. With a large Burmese python named Kaleeya Junior, I made a little extra cash by allowing anyone who had the inclination, courage, and nickel, to pet him. To fulfill expectations aroused by my banner ("Famous Indian Rope Mystery"), I did variations on a cut-and-restored rope routine, using an egg bag to transform the three pieces of rope into three garter snakes that were, in turn and with a sleight, turned into a longer corn snake that was, in turn, turned back into the original length of rope. The performance seemed to amaze Jesus Estafar far more than it did any of the circus goers who stopped to see or pet my python or buy one of the anoles that I promised would change colors when pinned by the threads that were their leashes to a bright shirt or coat. From where we were stationed I could see the turning of the towering Everest Ferris Wheel and hear the eccentric, endlessly repeated music of the one-hundred-key Ophidion Karezzaphone hidden within the Samsara Carousel. Not faraway, in a region of the fairground named the Bombay Bazaar, the Mystic Mentaliste of Mysore was vending fortunes. Just outside the bazaar, handsome in his colonial pith helmet, officer's regalia, jodhpur breeches, and shiny spurred boots, my father, in front of the Imperial Rifle Gallery, in a polished British military accent, challenged Yankees. With both rifle and pistol, left- or right-handed, blindfolded or hanging upside down, backwards with a mirror to take his aim or bending over to shoot from in between his legs, he'd demonstrate how easy it was to hit the cast-iron mechanical targets of tigers, rhinos, cobras, thugs, mutineers, mythic monsters, and pagan idols. Taking the dare to impress their kids, win a swag for their girls, or merely vaunt American adroitness, the rubes discovered that it wasn't quite as easy as the British crack shot made it seem. Again, again, and again, they'd lay down a quarter and take up a weapon until they ran out of money, admitted defeat, or stopped having fun. It was humiliating for William Shakesberg to be operating a shooting gallery in a traveling circus; but we needed the money, more of it than ever after what occurred during the first afternoon of the Durbar, something that changed my father's life forever. He was turning the tip for the gallery, displaying the Lee Enfield with which he claimed to have brought down a man-eating tiger in the jungles of Bengal, when his thrill-packed spiel was interrupted by a hum in the sky that became louder and louder, rising into the roaring din of gasoline engines overhead. As moving shadows were cast in circles and figure-eights on the fairground, everyone looked heavenward, shading their eyes with their hands as if in salute, to see the maneuvers of two Curtiss Eagles. To inspire young American men to volunteer for service with the Allies in the war in Europe, the promoters of the Durbar had invited three French aviators from the Lafayette Escadrille to do a demonstration of stunt flying. It seemed a miracle that the man standing on the wing of one of the planes did not fall to earth even when that plane went into a dive and came around in a loop. As the second plane, with a rope ladder dangling from one of its wing tips, overtook the first, the man on the wing grabbed hold of the last rung of the ladder and deftly climbed up from the one plane to the other. It so moved my father that he could barely finish his spiel, scarcely aim his rifle, and hardly concentrate on managing the gallery. He was possessed. He had to fly and needed an airplane, resolving to become the world's premier aerial show marksman. After two weeks of his unrelenting pestering, one of the pilots, triplets named Faucon, finally agreed to take my father aboard. But the Gallic aviator adamantly refused the showman's desperate demands for a second ride. A diplomatic Beryl Grossman had to intervene with the management of the Durbar of Delhi and the deputies of the San Diego sheriff's office to save my father's job and keep him out of jail. The Faucon brothers complained that Monsieur Shakesberg, holding them at gunpoint, had threatened to shoot them if they didn't take him flying again, something, they explained, that was out of the question given his behavior during his first flight. "'Ee is crazy," one Faucon observed, as another shook his head in disapproval and a third testified, "''Igher, 'igher,' 'ee was shouting all zee time. When I tried to land, 'ee grabbed me by zee neck and started choking me, screaming like a maniac, 'No, not down! Up! Fly up, up, 'igher, 'igher! I want to go aaaaaaall zee way up!'"

16

"I'll teach you to walk," a luminous Angel, palms softly on my cheeks, promised. "I'll show you how to dance on the high rope. And what do think I want in return, my darling Isaac? You'll never guess. A serpent! Yes, I want one of your snakes for my audition next week. Beryl Grossman arranged it: legit theater, the part of Cleopatra! Isn't it wonderful? So please, Isaac, give me an asp to place against my breast at the climax of my Egyptian dance of love and death, a sweet snake, though, bright and beautiful, one that I can trust not to really bite me. I must get the part: 'Come thou mortal wretch, with thy sharp teeth this knot intrinsic of life at once untie. O poor venomous fool . . .' I don't want to play burlesque anymore. And I'll never do a circus act again. No more hair hangs, web crawls, or ladder spins. I'm sick of the mud. I don't like crumb boxes, boil-ups, hay eaters, or caged cats. I want to have my own dressing room in a real theater, with a velvet tête-à-tête, a three-way mirror, a globe of the world, a tiger-skin rug, and a little white poodle who licks my fingers. So, please, my darling Isaac, give me a snake, one that looks dangerous but won't really bite the Queen of Egypt." I explained to Angel that if she'd wear the same underclothes for a week and sleep on the same pillow, and then give me the lingerie and pillowcase, I'd put a snake in the case with her garments for a few days. "And then, no matter how dangerous it might have been, the creature will be tame with you, crawling into your hand for warmth and sleeping between your breasts at night." She simpered, "Does that work with men and boys? Can I tame a wild boy?" "Yes," I answered, leaning close to her to re-savor a fragrance from years before, when, as children on the road with the *Wonders of the World,* we slept sometimes in the same bed. The bouquet of the sheets had so subdued and transported Samoo the Amazing Snake Boy that, when she left my side to use the pan or crawl in with her mother and father, I'd take her pillow in my arms, push my face into its softness, breathe and feel the scent dissolving me. Lithe hands fell from the flush of my face as she stepped back, smiling coquettishly. The crimson ribbons in her hair were like the flames of the fire that did not consume the bush on Mt. Horeb. I resolved to offer my scarlet king to Cleopatra, a docile two-footer, stunningly scaled with glistening tar-black, blood-red, and sun-yellow bands. Only the order of its colors distinguishes the species from the venomous coral harlequin: "Feel no dread when black meets red; but red's by yellow on a deadly fellow." The behaviors of the lethal creature and the benign are the same until it's too late. "And something else," Angel pleaded. "I want you to teach me French. Will you? Please promise. After

71

the war's over I'm going to France. You do still know the languages your father made you study, I hope. I felt so sorry for you back then, when he forced you to learn all those strange words. But now I want to know them. I'll teach you to walk, and you'll teach me to speak. That's fair. I can already say my name. Bachnele taught me. Listen: *Bonjour Monsieur, je m'appelle Angélique, Maîtresse de la Corde.* It sounds so beautiful, doesn't it? Not like our homely Yiddish: *Huhb es in drerd.* I love everything French: champagne, eau de cologne, eau-de-vie, the pas de deux, petit fours, French cuffs, French lace, French poodles, and the French horn. Of course I love the great Monsieur Blondin because he strolled along a hemp rope over Niagara Falls, playing a violin sonata of his own composition that was so beautiful it surely would have made people weep if only they would have been able to hear it over the roar of the cataracts. I love Napoleon because he was kind to Jews and the Eiffel Tower because it's so tall. I want to rig a cable from its girders all the way to the Arc de Triomphe, and dance across it, gazing down upon the City of Light. I want to be a star in the sky over Paris and a gem down below in the Folies-Bergère. I want to dance, not to titillate cowboys, farmers, miners, and day laborers, but to beguile cavaliers, connoisseurs, artists, and statesmen, all in tuxedos with their mistresses in satin gowns. I want to wear French clothes and be beautiful like those women. I want to drink champagne for breakfast. Have you ever tasted champagne?" I lied, said I had, and then told the truth, said that she was perfectly beautiful without a French gown, without any adornment at all. "So, my darling Isaac, will you give me a snake, a friendly one that will love me always? And will you teach me French so I that can understand beautiful words and say sweet things?" *"Mais oui, Angélique, ma jolie funambuliste, un ange qui reste à jamais dans mon cœur, pour toi . . ."* A warm finger touched my lips to silence me. "I'm sure that means you will. Good. I'll learn French tomorrow. But now, come with me." She giggled as naughtily as she had done when we were children, when she splashed me in the bath, when her token landed on a ladder square or mine on a snake, and when we stood in front of the distorting mirrors at the Chutes, first the convex one that made us squat and fat and then the concave one that made us tall and lean. "Come on. You carry the ladder and the pole, the long pole, and that over there, the small case, and I'll bring my rope and the bag. Come, come quickly. I'm going to teach you to walk." Because she had played many of the burley houses and honky-tonks that had been established near the Mexican border in case performers had to flee the country on the spur of a bad moment, she knew the lay of Chula Vista, and one Monday in May, a dark day for the Durbar, she took me to a deserted clearing beyond the orange groves, well over a mile from the fairgrounds. Her rope, unraveled and stretched out by us between two majestic eucalyptus trees with sumptuously peeling bark, was tied and clamped on one end to one of the tree trunks. At the rope's other end there was a spliced eye that she fixed by a tarnbuckle over a hoist hook. As she explained the rigging of the obseclungs, stakes, guy wires, and two caval-lettis, I helped with the pulley block to stretch the rope so tight that I supposed that it would snap. "Hemp," she said, smiling proudly, "wonderful hemp, so supple, strong, natural, and alive. Each and every rope, all walkers swear, has a soul. The more you walk it, revealing yourself to it, the more it discloses itself to you. The rope must trust you. And you it. Rope rolls more than wire cable, but it's more pure and it gratifies the naked sole. Though I wear snakeskin slip-pers for the wire, my foot is always bare for rope. Take off your shoes, Isaac, and your shirt too. Now you're going to walk." After stripping away the blue Oriental tunic that belonged to the Durbar's wardrobe unit to bare her own creamy lace under-chemise, Angel stood comfortingly close to me. Even though the rope was not more than five feet above the ground, it frightened me. I had no confidence in it or myself. "Trust me, darling. Don't be afraid. You don't need any sense of balance at all. The pole has the balance. And you don't need any skill either. Nature has the skill. Go on, up the ladder, one foot on the rope and, here, take the pole." The flexible pole, telescoped out to a length of some forty feet, was weighted on its ends. "Now hold it horizontal. See the line that marks the center? It should stay between your hands, lined up with the center of your body, yes, pointing toward your belly button. Lower, a little lower. Yes, now step up and line up the line with the rope. Do it! Go on, Isaac, do it now! Don't be afraid. Step up quickly. You won't fall." I was, to my utter astonishment, balanced on the rope and she was applauding me. "As long as the tips of the pole are lower than the rope, as long as that line is over and parallel to the rope, you cannot fall because your center of gravity is under the rope. Since nature thinks you're already below the rope, suspended from it, it can't make you fall off of it. So walk, my darling Isaac. Yes, walk." As I began to move, I couldn't help but laugh with relief, then again louder with an illusory sense of power, and then louder still with a delusory intimation of glory. Bathing in an ether scented with the citrus perfumes of the nearby groves, I was in a newfound heaven, and Angel, without a balancing pole, joining me there, sauntered with perfect grace and sublime ease toward me from the end toward which I was slowly heading. "You can't fall. We could be walking a rope stretched between the peaks of the highest mountains in the world and you wouldn't fall." Beginning then to walk backwards, and whispering, "Come to me. Don't be afraid," she rested against the eucalyptus tree and waited. Slowly I walked until I was leaning up against her. The pole was pressed in between us, just below our waists, as, unafraid, I kissed her. The eager opening of her mouth so startled me that I let go. Unbalanced, I tumbled to earth. Rolling over on the ground, feeling the sharp pain in my shoulder, sprained from my attempt to break the fall, I tried not to divulge how much it hurt for fear that she might descend and stop laughing. I wanted to remain on my back on the earth gazing up at her with the expanse of eucalyptus behind her, the branches and leaves of the two trees touching, and behind them the immaculate blue light of a boundless firmament. "That was to introduce you to the rope, to show you the view from up above," she remarked as she effortlessly skipped back and forth above me, daring to close her eyes now and then, "and to encourage you not to be afraid. But I want you to know the true feeling too, the exhilaration of a real walk. We'll do it slowly, gradually shortening the balancing pole and lightening the weights until its tips are even with the rope, and then just above it, shorter and lighter, until finally there is no pole at all and the balance and the skill are yours. And then, bit by bit and step by step, we'll raise the rope, higher and higher, and you and I will dance together way above the earth, on the border of heaven, without poles, nets, or mechanics, without any thoughts of ever falling. We'll do that together someday, yes, someday when I have a snake and can speak French. Someday. But it can't be done until . . ."—she paused with the perfect theatrical timing to create the desired seductively sentimental effect— "until you're not afraid to die." Swinging down from the rope in an acrobatic turn and landing next to me, dropping to her knees and bending over me, her hair around my face, she closed her eyes, parted her lips, and gave her hands rein to reach, search, and linger. I made love to a woman for the first time in my life, and right afterwards I told three lies: I said that, no, it was not the first time for me; and I said that, yes, I would love her, only her, forever. And then I said that I was not afraid to die.

17 "The Angel of Death," Bachnele Poopik read, "that smote the firstborn in the land of Egypt, passed over the dwellings which were marked on their doorposts with the blood of the Passover." He laughed heartily. "I love this part, when our God shows those shmucks who's the boss." The midget had organized the meal for the Pesach that fell during the Durbar of Delhi's Los Angeles run. Although it was almost as much an opprobrium for my father to attend a seder hosted by the licentious Litvak as it was for him to work in a circus, Mother prevailed by imploring her husband to put his devotion to the Creator above his disdain for one of that Creator's little creations. Despite an escalating disinterest in God, Israel, and the Messiah, my considerable adoration of Angel made me eager to celebrate with her the advent of the season in which the voice of the turtle is heard in the land and the fig tree puts forth her green fruit. I read the megillah for the Pesach, the Song of Songs which is Solomon's, not for Israel, but for Angel. Comparing my beloved to a company of horses in Pharaoh's chariots, I rehearsed soft whispers: "Thy cheeks are comely with rows of jewels, thy neck with chains of gold." I made sure that I was at her side as we gathered around the makeshift table in the canvas tent that was illuminated with kerosene lamps and flickering candles and decorated with lily bouquets and bunches of California grapes. Sweet wine was ready to be consumed in memory of both oppression and redemption. Tsipora Gotlober had slaved over the preparations for the feast, koshering the dishes, roasting the eggs, and concocting the charoset. My father was seated next to Joseph Siegel, with whom he had been reunited when the director coincidentally passed by the shooting gallery in the Durbar a few days earlier. Even though they were not Jewish, Bachnele had invited George Washington, the former Wild Man of Borneo, who had been cast as Tamburlaine for the Durbar's Grand March, and his beloved Lucy. The midget had a soft heart for old acquaintants. And George was eager to participate in preparation for his upcoming role as Shylock in Gershom Greenspan's road show production of *The Merchant of Venice* in which all the actors (including the great Tubs Shortman as Bassanio) were Negroes in whiteface. Abe and Lucy weren't the only Gentiles present. Beryl Grossman came with his bride, a demure girl from Canton named Hui-jin, whom he had recently won from her father in a poker game in Sacramento. Since the girl didn't know a word of English, Beryl had hoped that my father, acting as an interpreter, would help him convey some of his more delicate connubial expectations to her. "There are no Chinese words for that," my father told Beryl after listening to his friend's con-

fidential whispers. Bachnele had also invited the octogenarian Choctaw Charlie, who was performing in the Durbar's "Indians East and West: Who's the
Best?" production in which he demonstrated the superiority of American Indians to Indian Indians in a knife throwing contest against an Irishman in brown
makeup and a white turban. It was hard to tell whether it was politeness, senil-
ity, wit, or ignorance that inspired Charlie to make a Passover toast to Jews as
"the lost tribe of the Pawnee nation. Pawnees and Jews are brothers: both love
tobacco and women with big breasts; both hate the white man and Wild West
shows." The Gentile presence at the seder was more than compensated for by
the festive zeal of Tsipora Gotlober, who, with a faded shaytl on her head and
a reverential smile on her lips, hummed "Da-da-yay-nu" as she served the meal.
Her husband, Moshe, using the name Antelope Andy, was garbed and coifed
like Colonel Cody each day to replace Buffalo Bill who had declined the invitation to stage his famous "Sepoy Mutiny" for the Durbar of Delhi. Since a seder
requires children to justify telling the same old story once again, it was
serendipitous that the Gotlobers had three of them, two boys (Jackrabbit Jake
and Jackrabbit Joe) and a little girl named Bunny who was just old enough to
manage the Four Questions. Our diminutive leader, holding his yarmulke in
place as he leaned his head all the way back to down the first glass of wine,
heartily smacked his lips and grinned with joy. "Blessed indeed is the fruit of
the vine." Angel adored Bachnele. "Without him," she had told me, "I
wouldn't have anyone. He's kind. He loved my mother and so he tries his best
to look after me." After Zev Mocher Rabinowitz, Angel's father, froze to death
in a cold-storage locker at the kosher shellfish factory in Maine, the girl had
been without protection until Bachnele happened to find her castaway on
Coney Island. We went around the table, taking turns at reading from the Haggadah. "V'hi she-amdah la-avotaynu v'lanu," my father recited, and then my
mother, for the sake of the Gentiles, switched to English: "He brought us from
the depths to the heights, from darkness to light, from sorrow to joy. Let us
then sing unto Him a new song: Hallelujah." Feeling blessed to be sitting next
to Angel, my leg pressing against hers under the table, I listened to her read
praises of a deity who was supposedly "permitting us to enjoy this festive day
together." After the washing of hands, a taste of parsley dipped in salt water,
and a breaking of matzah, little Bunny Gotlober, with substantial prompting
from her mother, recited the "Ma nishtana halaila hazeh?" I thought of answers
just for Angel: "Why is tonight different from all other nights? Because on all
other nights I am separated from you, while on this night I shall kiss you with
the kisses of my mouth, stay you with flagons, comfort you with apples, and lie
between your breasts as a bundle of myrrh." I was Pesach's rasha, the wicked
child in the text who denies God, who would not hesitate to renounce the

Lord's sanctifications for the sake of a girl's moist lips. Bunny had wet her pants and was crying. Her father insisted on changing her just when it was my turn to read. "And Moses told Aaron what the Lord had commanded: 'Take thy rod, and stretch out thy hand over the waters of Egypt, and there shall be blood throughout the land of Egypt.'" With the announcement of each of the ten plagues, epitomized by Bachnele as "God's ten-in-one," we sprinkled droplets of wine into our plates, where they became blood. Show people understand transubstantiation. When it was George's turn to read a passage in which Moses, in the name of God, cries out, "Let my people go," the actor, doing his best to imitate a Yiddish accent, interpolated into the Haggadah Shylock's entire "If you prick us, do vee not bleed? If you tickle us—*oy vay!* — do vee not laugh?" monologue. Lucy, Choctaw Charlie, Hui-jin Grossman, and the children applauded. Bachnele Poopik sniggered. "George, bubee, you're getting the Hebe shtick down pretty good. I got to admit it. I'll coach you if you coach me. I'm opening a shvarzter number at the Oasis next month. I'll be the only midget in burley doing classical coon material. Well, maybe not the only one, but certainly the only Lithuanian Jewish midget doing female impersonation in blackface. I'm Mammy Minny Mite, maidservant to Mrs. Tom Thumb. I'm gonna sing, 'Dat Wee Liddle Man o' Mine Has Got Sometin' Big an' Fine.'" Bachnele loved burlesque, preferred it to vaudeville, even to legit theater and motion pictures. "I'm at home in the mud," he boasted, "I glory in smut and whirligig." As Mrs. Gotlober, assisted by Angel and my mother, served the stewed chicken, Bachnele continued in delight, "I love the gags and jokes, but most of all, I love the dames in flesh-colored tights, big shikses with big tsitskes and big toochises." Abruptly standing, my father shouted at his host, "There are children present." Frowning, and pausing rather overdramatically, Bachnele responded with a softly spoken, plaintive query: "Why do you hate me so much, Abraham, my friend?" Before my father could answer, George had piped in with the booming voice of theater: "Hath not the midget eyes? Hands, organs, senses, affections, passions? Is the little one not fed with the same food, hurt with the same weapons, subject to the same diseases, and healed by the same means as thee?" Again Lucy, Charlie, Hui-jin, and the children applauded and my father sat down. After the meal, Jackrabbit Jake and Jackrabbit Joe obeyed Antelope Andy's paternal directive to open the entry flap to the tent just in case Elijah happened to be at the Santa Culebra Fairgrounds in Los Angeles that spring night to announce the coming of the Messiah to the Durbar of Delhi. Joe Siegel, who had been uncharacteristically restrained throughout the evening, rose and, over the fourth cup of wine, made an extraordinary declaration with all of the solemnity and grandiloquence that one would have expected from Elijah himself: "My friends gathered here to thank, praise, and glorify the Lord our God, Who performed these wonders for our ancestors in days of old, I wish to speak to you of the Almighty's dedication to a perpetuation of the drama that we have recounted here tonight." The motion picture director, after purposefully noting that "megillah," the Hebrew word for "scroll," could also be translated as "reel" ("as in motion picture *reel*"), announced that Yahweh, appearing to him in a dream, had commanded him to make a motion picture of the Torah. It would have fifty-two celluloid megillahs, one of which would, corresponding to each week's Torah reading for Jews, be shown at Saturday matinees in movie houses all around the country. Thus the Jewish Sabbath would be integrated into American life. After one year, beginning on Simchat Torah, the movie would be shown again from the beginning, and again each year thereafter until the coming of the Messiah. Although everybody certainly realized that Siegel had gone completely mad, most were nevertheless flattered by his casting for the story that we had just read from the Haggadah: my father was Moses and Beryl was Aaron; Tsipora was Tsipora, and her sons, Jackrabbit Jake and Jackrabbit Joe, would play Gershom and Eliezer. Antelope Andy would be as good a Jethro on the screen as he was a Buffalo Bill in the arena. George had the part of Amalek and Lucy was ordained to do makeup ("We'll need a lot of beards"). I'd be one of the Egyptian magicians who turned a staff into a serpent; Angel would be beautiful as Miriam the prophetess, dancing on a rope with her timbrel; and my mother would be a vampish high priestess of Baal, swaying and bowing before the Golden Calf. Choctaw Charlie and Hui-jin Grossman had minor roles as Hebrew slaves, and Bunny would cry in the wilderness. "And Pharaoh," Siegel smiled proudly, "shall be played by the one and only Bachnele Poopik." Raising a final cup of wine, the motion picture director concluded the seder with a Hebrew toast: *"L'shana ha-ba'a bi-Chollyvood!"*

To 86

18 "I'll teach you to speak," I reiterated with impassioned palms restrained in their caress of obliging cheeks, "and, yes, I've brought the serpent for Cleopatra's breast." Reaching fearlessly into the black velvet pouch with the red silk drawstrings, with delight shimmering in the ethereal azure of seraphic eyes and smiles dancing on the rose pink of devilish lips, the would-be Queen of Egypt held up the would-be deadly asp, the serpentine "baby that sucks the nurse to sleep." Angel giggled over the dainty flick of the bifid tongue against the soft skin of her neck, chin, and cheek. The banded scarlet king slid through her fingers, around her wrists, across her palms, soothed by the scent that had become familiar during the days and nights of being curled up in a pillowcase with her intimate under-linens. Scaled rings of red, black, and yellow were lovely and frightening in their sly mimicry of the markings of the venomous coral. Just as Abraham Schlossberg, the persecuted Jew from the Russian Pale of Settlement, disguised as Wyoming Willie, had the audacity on the bally platform to recount shoot-outs with the likes of No-Neck Nat Norton, so the vulnerable scarlet, masquerading as a deadly snake, works a scam to keep predators at bay. Humbug is survival. I replaced the mimic in my modest collection with the real thing, a hot coral harlequin with two grooved fangs. There is an incomparable thrill in the seduction of a treacherous creature. I learned the ways in which the warmth of my fingertips, steadiness of my hands, and sureness of my movements could ease a deadly being. Once you can fake fearlessness, there's no need to be afraid. Because Angel named her snake Antony, it was appropriately theatrical to call mine Caesar. Just as Angel, in order to teach me to walk the tightrope, had started me with the long, flexible, weighted balancing pole so that I could get the feeling of the walk prior to a mastery of the skills required to actually walk on my own, so I decided to begin her French lessons by having her memorize words she did not understand, allowing her the taste of French on her tongue before she knew what she was saying: *"Amour, seigneur souverain des dieux autant que des hommes, des serpents autant que des anges, devant qui tout disparaît, jusqu'à la raison, tu sais combien mon cœur te vénère, lui qui fait tant de sacrifices sanguinaires."* She wanted to learn the French for "I want" and, no sooner had I said *"Je désire"* than she made a list of one hundred nouns and infinitives for me to translate into French and for her to memorize. If she whispered *"Je désire Isaac,"* unfamiliar words displayed familiar power. We alternated between the language and the rope, playing and struggling like infants to learn to walk and speak. *"Je désire parler,"* she said and I, *"Je désire marcher."* She revealed the fundamental principles of her art: "With half your weight on one side of the rope and the other half on the other side, feel a vertical line through the center of your body, drawn from the spot where the rope is gripped by your foot, straight up through your groin, gut, and heart, into your skull, right between the eyes. In the pit of your stomach, halfway between the sole of your foot and the top of your head, cross the vertical with a horizontal, establishing these lines as the diameters of an infinite set of concentric circles. The circumference of one touches the ground below you and, above you, has its zenith at a spot in the sky from which you must feel you are invisibly suspended. The circumference of a larger circle encompasses the earth. Another contains the sun. And then there are the stars. Always look along the rope, beyond where it's tied to where it's pointing, to the horizon where heaven and earth touch. No matter how high or low your rope is rigged, you're suspended halfway between heaven and earth. As the earth pulls you down with gravity, heaven will hold you up with levity." She stopped to ask if I understood. "Yes," I answered as eagerness pulled me toward her. "The lesson's not over," she laughed, pushing my hand away. "Pay attention. You'll feel the bounce in even the tightest rope or wire. Take pleasure in the ways in which it responds to you and, in so doing, asks for your response. Respond to its responses to your responses to its responses. The walker gives life to the rope, just as the rope does to the walker. The cavallettis steady the rope, but it will still shake. When it does, as if angrily trying to throw you off, or if it trembles as if afraid that it might lose you in a fall, never, despite your natural impulse, try to force it to be still. It will become calm as you do, and it will reveal your grace to you, but only after it has completely exposed your awkwardness, impatience, and fear." When she hesitated, I again tried to touch her and again was thwarted: "Oh, I want you too, my darling. *Oui, oui, je désire Isaac!* Friday night we'll be together. My audition is Friday morning. I need time to practice with Antony. I don't want him to be afraid." When I arrived at nine o'clock on the Sabbath night for our secret assignation, the sight of Angel—the expression on her lips, the distance in her eyes, and the posture in which she was slumped on the bed—was reminiscent of the little girl whose mother had drowned. "I didn't get the part," she mumbled without looking at me. The scarlet snake, listlessly coiled in her lap, seemed to have absorbed her despondency. "The casting agent said that my portrayal of the Queen of Egypt was 'too suggestive, unwholesome, and downright blue. You must understand, young lady,' he continued condescendingly, 'that we are producing Shakespeare expressly in order to provide folks out here with high-class, edifying, and enlightening family entertainment.' He said that the way I danced with the snake, the way my arms and legs moved, even the way that my eyes opened and closed, would 'arouse men, embarrass ladies, and disturb children.' I was so furious that I grabbed Antony out of the bag, pointed his head at the agent, and cried out, 'Bite him, O asp of the Nile, sting our vile foe.' I chased the wretch, screaming for help, around the theater, and because everyone was afraid of Antony, no one dared to try to stop me. I left before the police arrived." I couldn't help but laugh over her evocation of the attack of Antony and Cleopatra on an ignoble Octavius. Angel scolded. "It's not funny!" Apologizing, I tried to convey how very sorry I was that she didn't get the part. But at the same time I appreciated the casting agent's evaluation. He was right. She was, just in her presence, despite herself, even if she had auditioned in a Salvation Army uniform and had genuflected rather than danced, too carnal for family theater. Her mere glance was voluptuous. Had Jesus been blessed enough to witness her *danse du ventre* at the Paradisio, Christianity would have been a fertility cult with its church at Sybaris and its Holy Communion an orgiastic feast in which the bread was Angel's flesh and the wine her kiss. Aching for my newfound pleasure, I tried to get my arm around her waist, hoping she'd allow me to comfort her. She pushed me back. "No, no, please, not now. I don't feel like it." Although I understood that it was uncomfortable for her to give herself over to the very sexuality that was apparently preventing the advancement of her career as a legitimate actress, it was nevertheless impossible for me not be disgruntled by rejection. Sensing my disappointment, she asked for patience: "It's not that I don't want you. I enjoy holding you in my arms, and being held by you. I take pleasure in you and more of it in the feeling that I am giving pleasure to you. With most men, it's not like that. Most of the time after I'm with a man I try to go to the mikva. It's not easy, of course, to find a real mikva when you're on the road. Bachnele once told me that, according to the Talmud, any body of natural water, the ocean, a lake, a pond, or spring, can be a mikva. But I don't feel I have to bathe after I've been with you." My heart was pounding ferociously, my stomach churning tumultuously, my brain shuddering recklessly, over this sudden unbearably shocking revelation of promiscuity. I imagined armies of men, young and old, drunken and dirty, circus roustabouts and burley house riffraff, and not only Jews, but the uncircumcised as well: Negroes, Mexicans, Chinamen, Apaches, Pygmies, and wild men of Borneo, all lining up to defile my beloved. While the nonchalant confession of profligacy anguished me, it did not revulse me; on the contrary, and to my utter confusion and dismay, it made me, in my jealousy, desire Angel all the more fiercely. I longed to give my whisper, breath, kiss, and embrace the opportunity to eradicate the traces of other men. Again I tried to touch her, and again I was checked: "No, please, Isaac, not now." Rising from my seat next to her on the bed to turn my back on her, I tucked in the shirttails that had come out of my trousers and adjusted the suspenders that I had borrowed from my father. "But don't go," she said wearily, "don't leave me just yet. Please. We'll do something else. I want to show you something." After handing Antony to me, she produced from her wardrobe trunk the going-away present that I had given her when she left for Maine with her father years before, the game of snakes and ladders that my father had given me for Purim years before that. "I've kept it all this time. It's been so long since we've played. Let's play it now, just like when we were children on the road." Although I recognized the eleven ladders (one of them a folding stepladder) and the twelve snakes (one of them two-headed) crisscrossing the faded board from my childhood, nostalgia was not strong enough to make me want to play. "It's a stupid game for little kids, Angel. There's no skill involved. It's all just chance." She laughed, a very slight laugh, but very welcome, nonetheless, as the first of the evening. "That's why I like it. I would hate to play one of those games like chess that are all skill; it's not fair, the better player is always sure to win. So, what's the point and where's the fun? I like snakes and ladders because playing it is like living a life. It's nothing more or less than luck." Indulging her, I threw the die, rolled a snake eye, and moved into square 1. She rolled a four and climbed right up to 82. It didn't take long for her to win the game, whereupon she laughed a second time. The feeling that the victory gave her, a sense that she wasn't so unlucky after all that Friday, so distracted her from disappointment that she took my hand in hers and touched it to her cheek. I set the scarlet snake on the game board. The boardinghouse bed was magically transformed into a golden burnished barge, with purple sails and silver oars, burning hot on the cool waters of the Nile.

19 Averting his head as if abashed, the scarlet king seemed to sense that the Queen of Egypt no longer needed him. Since she could not be Cleopatra, the discouraged Angel resigned herself to accepting high rope and low cooch as her lot, at least until the war in Europe ended and she had enough cash for passage to Paris. She trusted that they weren't afraid of sexy women in France. At each stop on the Durbar's tour she'd dance for the extra money at burley houses or honky-tonks in matinees and on Monday nights which were dark for the Durbar. Reluctantly she consented to let me accompany her to the Breakers on one of those nights, to ride the two trolleys and three buses that it took to get from the lot in Santa Culebra to that dance club on the pier in Santa Monica. To the clack of castanets, a trill of guitars, and shouts of *Olé!*, serape'd caballeros, a Franciscan monk, and a bandito or two strolled into the taverna where a melancholy Angelita was beautiful in the florally embroidered mantilla that would spread like wings when she began to dance the habanera hechizita. From the back of the hall, across the dance floor and onto the stage, swaggered the mysterious hero in a black cape, black sombrero, and black boots. A black mask concealed his face. "Who," one was supposed to wonder as he extended his hand to the sultry señorita in invitation to dance, "can this hombre be? And why the mask?" They began dancing slowly at first, then faster and faster, down from the stage and onto the floor, and every soul at the Breakers was entranced by the rhythmic sways and turns. In the climax of the dance, the rogue leaned his heroína back across his knee to kiss her, and then the dramatic surprise: suddenly Angelita ripped off the inamorato's mask and I, in unison with every member of the audience, gasped. Beneath the black mask was a white skull, the face of death. With a scream the lights went out. And when they came on again, brighter than before, everyone squinted as they applauded Angel and the young man who was billed as El Grito. With the black mask of the lover in one hand and the white mask of death in the other, he took a bow. I didn't speak to Angel on the first of the buses back to Santa Culebra. On the second bus she asked me what was wrong and I said, "Nothing." Aboard the third I confessed my jealousy and she said nothing. On the first trolley she spoke again: "You're being ridiculous. El Grito would never really kiss me. It's acting. He only performs at the Breakers to get customers, rich old men willing to pay for the embraces of poor young boys. He'll go with a woman if she offers him enough, but he prefers the men." Angel was so insulted and infuriated by my rude but obvious question ("And you, Angel? Do you sometimes sell yourself to them?") that again, on the second and final trolley back to the fairgrounds, she neither spoke to me nor looked in my direction. I couldn't watch her on the wire that night. I was jealous of the men in the crowd who would gaze up at Angel in the sky, jealous of all the men who had ever been with her, and of those who were yet to be. Despite what Angel said, I remained leery of El Grito. I did not at the time really believe that there could be men who would actually chose to make love to a man rather than a woman. Assuring me that there were no Jewish homosexuals, my father had maintained that the ludicrous practice in question had originated and developed in Bulgarian Christian monasteries as a consolation for those who, as a consequence of their deluded acceptance of Jesus as the Messiah, had renounced the covenant of marriage. Still I could not imagine that any man, no matter how zealously devout a Christian, could see Angel walk a rope, dance a floor, or even just move across a room, and not yearn to discover with eyes and fingertips the nakedness beneath her costume. I so wanted that nakedness to divulge itself to me alone that I was jealous even of the mirrors that had enjoyed it. Just the thought of her nakedness aroused and enraptured me, but in the rapture there was inevitably a touch of sadness and a trace of fear. Bareness and death had revealed their covert alliance to me when I witnessed the scaling of the mermaid's costume from the bloated body of the drowned woman. I remembered the inanimate body of Tivya Rabinowitz as I gazed at her daughter sleeping naked on the white sheets after making love. When Angel casually told me that Nathan Nister, the photographer whom Joseph Siegel had hired to film his *Torah,* had offered to pay her to pose for him at his studio, I knew that she would be naked, and that in the photographs she would be as white and still as her mother had been in death. I asked her not to do it. "I need money," she insisted, "I need it for Paris. Are you jealous of Nister too?" "No," I claimed, although I was. "No," I maintained again (although again I was) when she accused me of being jealous of the flying Faucon brothers who had taken her for a ride in their plane. I feared that she might sleep, or even fall in love, with one or more of the indistinguishable triplets; after all, they were French. I called them "Les Frères Faux-Cons" and hoped they'd crash. But it would have to be all three of them at once; if just one or two died, Angel would probably mistake the sympathy she'd naturally feel for the one or two survivors as love and then offer her warmest embraces as tender condolences. I was sex-crazed and love-mad. The only solace for my condition was in the knowledge that I was I was not alone. I recognized my erotic lunacy as the theme in a Durbar of Delhi production, "Suttee! Death Ritual of the Widows of Hindustan." At the climax of a nautch number, after dancing around an ornately garbed and decorated mannequin that was supposed to be the corpse of a maharaja, ten chorines in Oriental pajamas lay down next to the dressed-up dummy, and two harem guards with oiled chests and billowing purple satin pantaloons, after doing a short fire-eating routine, faked setting the funeral pile ablaze. Strips of red, orange, and yellow tissue paper, blown upward by concealed fans, were supposed to pass for crematory fire. "The wealthiest of wealthy princes in India," the pitch professor explained, "is apt to ensure the fidelity of his young wives and mistresses after his own death by decreeing that, reclining upon his pyre as upon a marriage bed, they shall be cremated with him and in death shall accompany him to Hindu heaven where they shall continue to delight in connubial dalliance for all eternity. The combination of jealousy, lust, and superstition so rife in India truly makes the men there mad." I imagined that, except for the superstition, I would feel at home in that strange Eastern land, sane amongst love's madmen, able to cope with the overwhelming and disarming feelings that Angel had aroused in me. Like a maharaja I wanted to dally with my beloved for all eternity. I wanted Angel to love me enough to die for me and before that final death, to die a thousand deaths with me, consumed together by sexual fire. The amorous customs and erotic manners of India made sense to me, at least as I had learned about them in the Durbar of Delhi and before that at the Paradisio in Seattle when Angel danced. The spieler that afternoon, hoping to sneak a blue show past the police, suffragettes, clergymen, and representatives of the decency leagues, had lectured on etymology, anthropology, and theology: "The word 'coochie' comes into English parlance from the old Hindustani 'kuch.' Although the closest English translation of the word is 'dance,' it means much more than that. It insinuates divine veneration, supplication, glorification, oblation, and more. The hallowed 'kuch' to be presented for your edification today by Little India herself has since ancient times been the headliner in a mystical fertility rite performed in devotion to the hoary idols of India. The ineffable 'kuch,' when danced in actual Oriental sanctum sanctorums, culminates in sacramental copulation. The heathen Hindu believes that sexual intercourse, like coochie itself, is a pious act of worship." That, at that time, explained why Ganesh Bannerjee marched so unabashedly each day, sometimes twice or even three times, always smiling cheerfully, to one of the lineup wagons that had been set up by the Durbar's layout men at the very back of the lot. Within these impromptu brothels, towner girls, admitted gratis to the fairgrounds through the service gate, were given mattresses at lunchtime upon which, Jesus Estafar revealed to me in giggled whispers, they'd "take on all comers for only a dollar a throw. They do it less for the money than for the glory of being a part of the Durbar of Delhi. They are happy and proud to be in show business even if it must be so far behind the scenes." Hiding amidst piled bales of hay, Jesus and I spied on the traffic to and from the wagons, snickering over who appeared, how often, and in what way: repeatedly and proudly, like Ganesh Bannerjee, or only once and wearily, like Choctaw Charlie. Clowns, acrobats, cage boys, riggers, candy butchers, and trapeze fliers all lined up for midday romance. Almost as regular, but not nearly as cheerful, as Bannerjee was Al Alighieri, Jr., the renowned animal impersonator who was working the Durbar in a comedy routine that lampooned "Leona Wilder and Her Ferocious Felines," an *en férocité* act that played the center ring of the main tent. In imitation of a Bengal tiger, Alighieri scrambled around a cage on all fours in a yellow-and-black-striped cat suit, chased by a clown who, dressed vaguely like Miss Wilder, snapped a whip and fired a pistol in the air. One day while Alighieri was inside the trailer with one of the town girls, Ganesh Bannerjee, waiting his turn outside, became extremely impatient. His amatory eagerness reached such a pitch that he began to pound on the door, shouting, "Hurry up! Stop hogging her!" As if possessed by the wildcat that he played, the animal impersonator, a tiger insulted by being called a pig, perhaps, sprang snarling from the lineup wagon to ferociously pounce, scratching and biting, upon the merry mahout. Lot hands pulled Alighieri off Bannerjee and dragged him away. A wounded but chipper mahout promptly entered the trailer, quickly took his one-dollar Holy Communion, and then emerged with a smile to skip off in time to bathe, whitewash, and festoon his elephant in preparation for the afternoon's Grand March. I attributed the Hindu's joie de vivre to his religious background. That evening, when, after her rope dance, we met in her room, I asked Angel if she wouldn't rather come with me to India than go to Paris by herself. "In India," I told her, "they say that lovemaking is religious." She laughed at the suggestion: "Oh, but in Paris they say that lovemaking is fun."

20 It was a clairvoyant's dream come true, an unpredictable apparition that allowed chance to masquerade as destiny. The client supposed that she was a stranger to the mentalist who knew so many things about her. After impulsively investing fifty cents to pass through the green velvet curtain into the tent of the Mystic Mentaliste of Mysore, the heiress to the Heimenhoff hosiery fortune sat down at the table across from the Oriental telepathist and necromancer. Mildly embarrassed by the frivolity that had spontaneously allowed her to consult a circus performer about her destiny, she demurely laughed at herself. Whereas Consuela Heimenhoff had not the slightest recollection of Sarah Schlossberg, Maharanee Mayadevee remembered the San Francisco socialite very well indeed. Lightheartedly the impeccably attired and subtly perfumed woman remarked that she didn't actually put much credence in such fanciful things as "Ouija boards, Tarot cards, poltergeists, and spirit rappings. But I'm not a total cynic either. I do believe in God, of course, and there are such things as intuition and animal magnetism. And sometimes, especially in dreams, some people do have certain telepathic experiences that can't be explained by science. In India there are fakirs who can do all sorts of things that, quite natural for them, seem utterly supernatural to us. Are you really from India? Father used to go tiger hunting in Bengal . . ." Suddenly realizing that she was doing all the talking in a session for which she had paid a half dollar to listen, Miss Heimenhoff checked herself: "So, Madame Mayadevee, what can you tell me about myself? Please don't talk about money, politics, or religion. Get to the fun. You know, love and that sort of thing." By convention the mentalist began by baiting the trap with flattery as deft hands manipulated the decoys, her cards, crystals, and coins. Meaningless gestures seemed meaningful as she ambled in whispers, spiced with nonsense syllables passed off as old Hindustani, through easy ambiguities and predictable predictions that put the quarry at vulnerable ease. Extending steady hands, palms upward, the psychometrist encouraged her client to place her own hands, palms lined with legible ciphers, down lightly upon them. Ready and set, Mayadevee closed her eyes, aimed, waited, and then suddenly quailed as if beholding something startling in the ectoplasmic shimmerings to which her powers made her privy: "There is an automobile, a shiny new motorcar. And you are at the wheel, laughing and having a fine time." The heiress shook her head, entirely unimpressed since she had given up driving years before. "No, I don't think so. But I do realize that there are bound to be some little mistakes in these sorts of endeavors. In any case, my dear, I don't want to hear about automobiles, but of gentlemen with sparkling eyes and daring smiles. Tell me about love." The intensification of my mother's concentration was visible around her still firmly closed eyelids: "No, the automobile is clear. It's a Peerless and it's speeding toward us. You're younger than now." After an eerie moment of silence, the psychic, shivering histrionically, went in for the kill: "The motorcar screeches to a stop. I hear a scream. I see blood splattered on the front fender. There's a young woman." Hesitating, Mayadevee allowed the conjured image to come into focus and the scream to echo in a now trembling Consuela Heimenhoff's memory. "The woman approaches, hobbling with difficulty on a crutch. She has only one leg. Yes, the left leg is missing. She reaches out." "Oh God, my God!" the socialite gasped as she pulled her hands back for her flushed face to fall into. Over her snared customer's muted sobs the pythoness continued: "She wants to speak. She beckons. She's mutters a single word: 'con . . .' I can barely hear it: 'con . . .' No, it's a name: 'Con . . . Consuela.'" The innocent casualty of credulity, eyes wild with wonder, straightened up in her seat: "Yes! Consuela Heimenhoff! That's my name! I am Consuela Heimenhoff!" Anxiously she begged the mentalist to ask the woman if she knew how truly and deeply sorry she was for what had happened. Her cries were plaintive: "Please forgive me, Mrs. Rabinowitz. I was just learning how to drive. Did you ever try to drive an automobile, Mrs. Rabinowitz? It's not that easy. Do you forgive me?" The seeress was serenely silent while the heiress desperately babbled: "Are you there, Mrs. Rabinowitz? Please, answer me. Are you there?" Opening her eyes, Maharanee Mayadevee began the blowoff and the setup for a subsequent and more expensive spirit manifestation. A calmness in her voice simultaneously comforted and teased: "The spirit seemed eager to converse with you, but something suddenly made her withdraw. She is gone." The harried heiress beseeched the composed clairvoyant to recontact the one-legged ghost: "Tomorrow. Come to my home tomorrow. She'll feel more comfortable there. It's more peaceful without any blaring bands or calliopes. And it doesn't smell like elephants, sawdust, and cotton candy. A circus is really no place for a wandering spirit." Miss Heimenhoff promised to pay Maharanee Mayadevee one hundred dollars if she could conjure up the specter once more in the drawing room of her Pacific Heights mansion. It was unusual for my mother to push her clairsentience routine so dramatically beyond the nebulous border that separates entertainment from fraud. "At first," she explained to my father that evening as we sat waiting for dinner to be served at the Palace of the Jade Buddha, "I was acting simply out of the delight of knowing enough about Consuela Heimenhoff to do a spectacularly miraculous reading. Then, as I recalled Tivya's suffering over the loss of that leg, I reflected on the fact that this very wealthy lady could have done so much more for the Rabinowitzes, not only for Tivya, but for poor Zev and little Angel too. I was acting, I confess—and may Hashem forgive me!—out of a wish for reprisal. But then the poor creature wept so pitifully as she muttered her pathetic expressions of remorse that it was impossible not to feel sorry for her. And that's why I'm going to see her tomorrow. I want to comfort her, to let her hear Tivya forgive her so that she can forgive herself. I'm confident that Tivya would want me to do that. And Hashem too." Mother was interrupted by Lee Kwon Yee and Phoebus Fong, who set out the dishes on our table, petulantly complaining that they had not yet found the brides and riches that had been promised to them. My father asked if they were certain that there was no pork in the kreplach. "No, not pork," Lee said, glowering as Phoebus grinned. "Sweet-and-sour horse." The next night my father and I ate kasha varnishkes at the more reliably kosher Ale Zibn Glikn Delicatessen before taking a stroll together along the waterfront. Reflections of a swollen moon shimmered like elusive smiles in the dark chill waters of the bay as we walked back to the rooming house to wait for the clairvoyant to return from the Heimenhoff estate. She didn't arrive until midnight. "It was beautiful," she remarked with a vaguely shy smile as she put on the copper kettle for her nightly cup of Hillcastle Assam tea. She lit a Camel, took a puff, and then extinguished it to begin her account of the séance: "Perhaps it was wrong, a little dishonest, maybe even a touch immoral, but not wicked. After all, I made her happy. I helped her. And that's good, isn't it?" After she had finished her tea, relit her cigarette, and smoked it to the end, she staged a reenactment of the evening's metapsychical manifestation. Her eyelids closed as her hands rose in the air. The revenant's voice, tempered by the distinctively bittersweet Yiddish accent of an immigrant Jewish woman praying in English, was unmistakably that of Tivya Rabinowitz: "Thank you, Miss Heimenhoff, for all of those right shoes. And the roses for my funeral were very nice. I want you to believe that I am not angry with you. I have not come to torment you or take revenge. There is no need for me to forgive you because I never blamed you. It was an accident. It was bad luck. Here you don't think about how many legs you have. So, you are probably wondering, why have I come? It is because of a sorrow that persists in clouding my spirit. It hinders my soul from merging into the pure splendor and infinite light of the divine. I come to ask you to ease this sadness. You have the power to help me. Please listen. I had a daughter who was born with perfect balance and grace, a beautiful little girl who danced as early as she walked. I fear for my lovely Devora, roaming alone now in a world that is so often cruel. I ache with thoughts of the anguish that my passing must surely have caused her. And now that her father is here, what has happened to her there? What will happen to her? If you will promise to find her and help her if she needs help, then, and only then, can I rest. Only when I am assured that someone is looking after my orphan child will I be able to allow my spirit to be dissolved into the joy of eternity. There can be no peace until I know that my daughter is safe. Help me. Help her. Please . . ." Tivya Rabinowitz's voice ebbed into silence and my mother opened her eyes and smiled as her own voice declared that "it wasn't really a lie or a swindle. After all, if there were such a thing as ghosts, if Tivya really could speak, I'm sure that's exactly what she would have said." My mother was genuinely concerned about Angel: "Circus, burlesque, and honky-tonk is no life for a young Jewish girl. And Nister, Siegel's photographer, has been taking pictures of her. Probably naked! This kind of thing can lead to prostitution. I did just what her mother would have wanted me to do. The thirty-six tzaddikim themselves would surely bless and sanctify my act." She smiled so proudly that I believed that she believed that fraud could be a holy mitzvah and pious demonstration of moral righteousness. Mother further explained that the performance, absolving as it did the heiress of her guilt, made Consuela Heimenhoff so happy that she gave the medium not merely the contracted one-hundred-dollar fee but a thousand dollars with the promise of an additional thousand if the clairvoyant could locate young Devora Rabinowitz. A week later Angel accompanied the Mystic Mentaliste of Mysore to the Heimenhoff estate for tea. The following Shabbis, after the blessings over the candles, wine, and bread, Sarah Schlossberg gave her husband a gift of two thousand dollars. I left the rooming house both to visit Angel and so that my mother and father might be alone and free to heed Rabbi Eleazar's admonition in *Zohar*: "A man and woman should enjoy physical intimacy on the Sabbath with an understanding that their pleasure on that night is a participation in the joyous union of the Holy One with his Bride and Indwelling, the Shekhinah." On Monday morning my father sent a purchase-order down payment of two thousand dollars by Western Union wire to the Curtiss aeronautics factory in San Diego for an Eagle biplane, which, upon delivery, he christened *Amuriel* after the Hebrew Angel of Love.

21 The forgotten truth is that when President Woodrow Wilson declared war on Germany on the first day of April in 1917, no one believed it. Assuming that it was but a droll April Fools' Day prank, America laughed. The *Los Angeles Examiner* epitomized the declaration as "the first significant display of executive zaniness since President McKinley brought down the house at the Inaugural Dinner of the Pan-American Exposition in Buffalo by putting a Whoopee Cushion on the seat of the unsuspecting Mexican President Porfirio Díaz." *Movie Life* applauded the President's knack for comedy: "Our nation needs to laugh in the face of the gloom that threatens us from abroad. Let us never forget that, as much as it is the land of liberty, America is also the funniest nation in the world." It was not until several days later, on Easter Sunday, that President Wilson, informed by top-level advisers and intelligence officers that Americans thought he had been pulling the country's leg, had to declare war on Germany once more. The news was as sweet to my father's ears as it was to those of Colonel Charles Bladud, commanding officer of the Santa Monica base of the United States Army Air Service. While I was happily a year too young for the draft, my father was unhappily a year too old to enlist. But the colonel offered him a job as civilian instructor of aerial marksmanship. Colonel Bladud, who believed that great wars were meant to be fought in the "heavens, the battleground of the gods," had met my father two years earlier in San Diego at the Durbar of Delhi, where he had tried his hand and eye at the Imperial Shooting Gallery. "Aren't you Wyoming Willie?" Colonel Bladud, confessing to having once paid to see our ten-in-one, inquired. "I used to use your pomade, just the kind of brilliantine American army pilots are going to need to keep their hair neat in an open cockpit." Colonel Bladud had appealed to my father to bring his technical expertise to the realization of a patriotic project: a mobile shooting gallery that would afford American boys the opportunity to fire the regulation U.S. M-17 .30-caliber Winchester rifles that would be issued to them once they were finally given the opportunity to "kick the Kaiser's keester." Three pulleys, driven by ½-horsepower motors, moving German U-boats below, Fokkers above, and tanks behind the parade of cast-iron infantrymen in between, offered fairground customers the thrill and glory of the Front. Colonel Bladud took the rig (gimmicked so that the little Huns fell under fire despite the shooter's aim) on a tour of the western states in a campaign to arouse public support for Republican and military opposition to President Wilson's policy of neutrality. We'd run into him every once in while at a fair, circus, or parade. Prior to the United States' entry into the war, my father, in order to keep up with his payments on the Curtiss Eagle, took leave from vaudeville to perform aerial exhibitions over stadiums, fairgrounds, racetracks, and barnyards. Just as when Angel walked the high wire, I could sense that deep down in the heart of each member of the crowd there was a secret wish for death, the hope of witnessing a crash. But because they were good people, they didn't *really* want that; they only *almost* wanted it, craving rather, as a compromise, a narrow escape or close call, just a scary little brush with death and then a happy ending. My father gave it to them by flying under telephone or telegraph wires with a black hood over his head that allowed them the wonder of believing that he could not really see where he was going. The extensive American tour of the Faucon brothers had made looping the loop an expected cliché in the rhetoric of stunt flying. Crowds loved it when my father did it blindfolded, almost touching the ground upside down at the bottom of the loop. He'd demonstrate it after the exhilarating Kegel-Bakakt maneuver, a half-roll at the top of a steep climb in which the controls were abruptly reversed so that the elevators functioned as rudders and the rudders as elevators, and the Grafenberg pass, a vertical climb into a midair stop, then a slide, tail first and backwards, into a last-minute recovery just above the ground. But the real money was in rides. People would pay fifty cents a minute to fly, and, although they'd swear that they wouldn't stay up more than a dollar's worth, once in the sky they wouldn't want to ever land. Women begged their husbands, and kids their parents, to let them ascend with my father again and again for more dips and rolls. For a climax, the Eagle soared straight up, faster and faster, higher and higher, and then suddenly the motor was turned off and in silence the plane dove, nose first, toward the earth. Just when, thrilled, you feared the worst, the pilot eased the responsive body of *Amuriel* into a perfect dead-stick landing. But my father wanted more than money out of aviation. Having heard above the howl of the Cobra engine the beckoning of seraphic songs from the highest heavens, he had his heart set on beating the altitude record that, on the verge of our entry into war, had been set by Baron Frederick von Grafenberg. My father's eye was on an invisible mark in the sky at 29,028 feet, the Royal Geographical Society's official estimate of the highest spot on earth, the summit of Mt. Everest. To reach that goal, he needed more horsepower, less oxygen intake, a lighter body, and reinforced wings. Until he could save up the money for all of that, he was demonstrating just how crack a marksman could be from the cockpit of a biplane. Even upside down and shooting blanks, he'd never miss a single one of the pumpkins, watermelons, or whatever other large seasonal fruit or vegetable was fixed atop the line of poles that I would have planted for the show. One after the other they were blown to smithereens as the topsy-turvy Eagle passed between them and the grandstands. And even if I had stood out in the open, no one in the crowd could have taken their eyes off the plane to notice me throwing the toggle switches to fire the charges that made the fresh produce explode so grandiosely. While cheering audiences were standing to applaud the aviator, his wife inevitably closed her eyes, shook her head, and whispered, *"Mi she-gemalcha kol tov . . ."* She sighed with both dread and resignation. My generally fearless and carefree mother had been upset by a dream in which she heard the explosion, saw the flames, and smelled the black smoke gushing from the wreckage. Not believing in the prognosticatory powers of Maharanee Mayade-vee or Fatima el-Fatiha, my father took Sarah Schlossberg's hand in his, smiled, and gently chided, "It is, even in dreams or crystal balls, you know as well as I do, impossible to see the future. By its nature, the future is yet to be deter-mined. Anything can happen. Nothing is fated." Because he had, in the dream, been alone in the plane, she didn't worry as long as he had passengers with him. With my father at the stick, Angel and I were in back, crammed snug and warmly together, her upon my lap, our bodies vibrating to the hurly-burly of the moiling engine. Bracing wires, stretched diagonally between the struts of the wings, whistled as we gained velocity, the faster the louder. At top speed, they'd scream. It was for her that I dared to do the stunt. She asked it of me, coaxing with a beguiling smile: "At least if we die, it will be together." It was billed as "The Flight of Hermes and Aphrodite." White togas billowing in the sky at fifty miles per hour concealed the belts to which our safety cables were hooked. Our sandals too had unseen latches that fit the rigging on the upper wing, and from a distance you couldn't tell that we were wearing the skin-colored tights that almost kept us warm. Once we stood, as long as our legs were straight and our knees and hips locked, we were secure even in a dive, even when we looped and soared up to disappear into a cloud. A pure unfath-omable whiteness was all there was. Then suddenly, outside the cloud, Angel reappeared with arms outstretched as if she were really flying. At each over-night stop my father would find a hotel or rooming house near whatever air-strip had hangar space for barnstormers and rent two rooms, one for us and one for her. No sooner had we gone to bed than, in sweet paternal sympathy and the silent complicity of men, he would pretend to be asleep (one would have expected a professional performer to fake a better snore than his) so that I, with-out the embarrassment of explanation, might tiptoe to the room where Angel waited. With her head resting on my shoulder I confessed that, no matter how many times we did it, I was always still a little anxious. She laughed at me. "No, not that," I said, "I mean 'Hermes and Aphrodite.' I mean standing on the wing." In the darkness of a strange rented room she spoke of falling out of the sky: "Every wire walker has heard the soft, seductive sound that claims to be the voice of earth. She invites you to step off the rope or wing for her, to trust her and fall into her arms, to abandon heaven for her sake. But if ever she tries to speak to you, don't listen. Don't bend your knees, release the cables, or close your eyes. It is not earth but death, disguising its voice with love." During the San Francisco runs Angel stayed in Pacific Heights with Consuela Heimenhoff. Standing on the runway after we had finished the show, she spoke to my father as if she needed his permission: "Please, if you don't mind, fly back without me. I want to stay a little longer with Consuela. She's giving a party for me this weekend. I'll take the train back to Los Angeles next week in time for the seder. I want to celebrate Pesach with you and with my dear Bachnele." The week without her seemed interminable. Greeting her with open arms as she disembarked from the overnight train at Union Station, I was relieved that she agreed to spend the morning and early afternoon with me in a room in one of the little traveler's rest lodges behind the station. That year, the year that America went to war in Europe and Passover fell on April Fools' Day, our seder was held at the swanky hacienda that the suddenly prosperous Joseph Siegel was renting in the Almeja Canyon. When, just before sunset, Angel and I arrived, Bachnele, rushing to greet her, reached up to embrace her. When she bent over to kiss him on the forehead, he smiled affectionately. "I missed you, my little darling." He then remarked on how much I had grown since he had seen me last. Cutting the nonliturgical chatter short, Siegel directed everyone to the table. "O Lord Our God, King of the Universe," Rabbi Solomon Brodsky, who presided over Hollywood's first synagogue, Temple Beth Ziun, began. "We have gathered here on this festive evening to give thanks to Thee for inflicting the ten plagues upon Egypt, for parting the Red Sea, for smiting the armies of Pharaoh, for giving us manna in the wilderness, for favoring us with Thy Torah, and most recently—because every generation must discover anew the meaning of freedom, redemption, and love—for providing our host, Joseph Siegel, with the financing to make Thy motion picture."

22 The waters of the Red Sea were never parted and the armies of Pharaoh never drowned. Before the Israelites could be delivered from Egypt, after the first three reels of Exodus, *Torah* was canceled. Though *Picture Play* blamed it on sex and *Movie Life* on drugs, the actual reason for the abandonment of *Torah* was neither moral nor legal. It was financial. Rothstein and Liplinger, cofounders of Eagle Pictures and principal investors in *Torah,* straining under Siegel's progressively increasing budget, would, even without the scandal, have had to terminate the project at some point soon to avoid bankruptcy. "It's not just me you're ruining, you Philistines," an infuriated Siegel screamed at his producers, "This is the Creator's picture!" It had started out well enough; the budget for the creation of the world was modest, and it really didn't cost Eagle very much to depict life in the Garden of Eden. That the reel was shot in a single day meant that Adam and Eve were paid only five dollars each. At ten cents per foot of snake, I received a dollar for the use of Kaleeya Junior who, stimulated by the heat of the mercury-vapor kliegs, did a fine job as the tempting serpent. Although Siegel was not very extravagant with Abraham, Isaac, and Jacob, he had, by the time his forefathers had become slaves in Egypt, lost his mind, or at least that part of the mind responsible for thinking about such mundane things as money. Discovering that D. W. Griffith was building Babylon on Sunset Boulevard, Siegel began to construct Egypt less than a block away. When the plaster parapets of the Palace of Belshazzar rose to three hundred feet, those of the Palace of Pharaoh at Pithom rose to three hundred three. Imagining that he was in some sort of biblical agon with Griffith, that the two productions, *Intolerance* and *Torah,* represented a contest between Gentiles and Jews, the director was committed to sparing no expense. Because most of the locally available horses, those that hadn't been shipped to Europe for a real war, had already been leased to Griffith for the Persian and Babylonian cavalries, Siegel rented more costly camels and elephants from Bannerjee Brothers. The director also bought a goat from Ganesh Bannerjee, named him Yentsele, and, leading him on a leash, took him everywhere he went. "I love this goat!" Siegel would say, beaming as he fed the animal a Lucky Strike cigarette or gave him a swig of Rasputin vodka from a silver flask. "He's the son I've never had." Maintaining that Yahweh Himself had ordained the motion picture whenever his investors brought up the subject of the budget, Siegel, refusing to discuss such ignoble matters, would quote Scripture. "Remember the words of the prophet in the wilderness: 'There shall be a light in the darkness, the still shall move, and the people shall behold the glory of Israel before their eyes.'" The director imagined himself to be a Kohayn in a religion for which motion picture theaters were the tabernacles and movie screens the curtains of the ark. Although I played both Jacob and Esau in Genesis, I had only a minor part in Exodus, appearing in the mere ten feet of film that it took for me, as Pharaoh's chief magician, to transform a staff into a serpent. Ten of my snakes were in the scene, and I was paid fifty cents each. My entire collection would have had the opportunity to participate in the plague of serpents that afflicted the Israelites in the desert near the Dead Sea if the motion picture had not been canceled prior to the filming of Leviticus, Numbers, and Deuteronomy. And I was scheduled to play the part of Joshua. In the final reel of the fifty-two episodes of *Torah*, I would stand atop Mt. Nebo (represented by Mt. Baldy in the San Bernardino Mountains) beside an aged Moses (played by my father), who would grandly point his staff toward Hollywood in the distance. The end title would declare: "The Promised Land!" Although my father's only genuine interest in the film was in flying his plane for the aerial sequences over Death Valley (*Amuriel* had, in the desert dusk, with a setting sun behind her, been beautiful as the Angel of Death passing over Egypt), he did an adequate job in his portrayal of both a blind Isaac and a wide-eyed Moses ordering Pharaoh (played by Bachnele Poopik) to let God's chosen people go. Because the film was silent, it didn't really matter what the actors said; but when Bachnele addressed the patriarch as "Moyshe Kapoyer" and responded to the Lord's demand with *"Azoy zuhgt men tsu an Pharaoh?"* it so infuriated my father that he walked off the set. A critic from *Movie Life* was particularly bothered by the casting of Pharaoh: "It typifies the utter inanity and absurdity of the biblical serial as a whole." Siegel dismissed the criticism on the grounds that a goy couldn't be expected to understand that Pharaoh was played by a midget to make a comic character of him, "all the more terrible to the degree that he is funny." To that end, and characteristic of his idiosyncratic genius, Siegel directed Lucy to paint a pimple on the end of little Pharaoh's big nose for the sixth plague, when God caused boils to break forth on man and beast in Egypt. "A sore near the mouth is disgusting and makes a character repugnant," Siegel explained to the makeup artist, "a sore near the eye is sad and arouses sympathy. But the same sore on the nose makes a character comic. Long after audiences have forgotten the Persian army of Griffith's Cyrus, they will remember the pimple on my Pharaoh's shnazzola." Contrary to that assumption, audiences tried to forget as much as they could of what they saw in the initial episodes of the biblical epic that were shown on consecutive Saturdays at the flickers. Presented as "The Authentic Recreation of Holy History, Starring Hundreds of Genuine Hebrews as Their Ancestors," the one-reelers were shown along with the capers of the Keystone Kops, sundry adventures of Bronco Billy, Porky Pig cartoons, and Movietone footage from the Front. All across America audiences hissed the Hebrew heroes. They laughed when Lot's wife was turned into a pillar of salt. Although uninspired by the religious themes, unmoved by the suffering of the Israelites, and unimpressed by the expensive elephants and camels, audiences were, however, because of the scandal, pruriently eager to see those episodes of *Torah* in which Carmen Zambra appeared. She played Eve, Lilith, the wives of both Lot and Potiphar, as well as Hagar and Tzipora. The director was, after all, in love with her. That it made the headlines of the *Los Angeles Examiner* meant that more people read about Siegel's sexual escapades and drug indulgences that day than they did about the heavy losses suffered by American forces at Champs-Labitte: "Joe Siegel, writer and director of Hollywood's rendition of the Bible, was arrested yesterday on the set of Pharaoh's court for statutory rape. Following allegations made by the mother of the director's sixteen-year-old ingenue, Carmen Zambra, police raided Siegel's office. While Siegel, a Jew, contended that he had every reason to believe that the girl was at least twenty years old, he was harder pressed to come up with an explanation for the large quantities of cocaine, morphine, and marijuana found in his possession. The Bible has had plenty of problems. Throughout the country, theaters exhibiting the one-reel weekly segments have been picketed by church groups and women's clubs. D. W. Griffith, famed director of *Birth of a Nation,* when asked whether or not Siegel's arrest would have any impact on current efforts to establish an enforceable morality code for the motion picture industry, said, 'Who's Siegel?'" The Christian protest of *Torah* alluded to in the article occurred after only a few weeks of production. Reverend Conway Conwell together with Curtis Custer, the Grand Ecclesiarch of the Pentecostal Church of the Outpouring of the Latter Day Rain of Love, delivering sermons and publishing pamphlets on the corrupting power of motion pictures, rallied substantial support for a pan-Christian boycott of movies produced, directed, or written by Jews. They never failed to report that Siegel had hired some twenty-five male and female prostitutes as well as a score of dancers from the Breakers at the Santa Monica pier as extras for the orgy that, according to Siegel's cinematic midrash, caused Yahweh to lay waste to Sodom and Gomorrah. Whereas Siegel considered the scene a moral castigation of immorality, church leaders deemed it blasphemously pornographic. When they arrived with police in an endeavor to terminate further production, Siegel, greeting them from the parapets of Pithom, shouted through his megaphone, "It's the Bible. Go home and read your fuckin' Bibles. If you've got a problem with what's in the book, take it up with God. He wrote that smut, not me!" Siegel had hired Rabbi Solomon Brodsky of Temple Beth Ziun as a technical adviser on the film to guarantee that it remained true to the original and "would please God if He were ever to have the opportunity to see it." His faithfulness to the narrative did not, however, prevent him from expanding such episodes as the orgy in Sodom or expunging others. Because of the hard luck he had in the Yiddish theater with *Mitn Gruhbn Finger,* he omitted the story of Onan entirely from the film, conceding that "nobody really wants to see some jerk jack off. That's why God doesn't allow Jews to do it." Although Rabbi Brodsky firmly agreed on that particular point of halakah, his affiliation with Siegel was temporary. After being offered the part of Jethro in the second reel of Exodus, and accepting it on the condition that he did not have to film on Saturdays, the rabbi was fired when Siegel discovered that Rabbi Brodsky was also playing Judas Iscariot in the Judean segment of *Intolerance.* Siegel would not forgive Brodsky for working with Griffith even after the venerable rabbi perjured himself on Siegel's behalf by giving testimony in court—and swearing on a Bible, no less—that the director was "a man of the highest moral caliber who does not eat pork or shellfish, let alone take drugs." Perhaps the inclusion of the New Testament in the court's Bible made it easier for the rabbi to lie. The charges of statutory rape were dropped when Carmen Zambra testified that the woman claiming to be her mother was actually only a stepmother who had, herself, had an affair with Siegel. Tears filled the jurors' eyes when the young actress sobbed on the stand, "I love Joe with all my heart. That's why I told him I was twenty-two years old. Since he's such a law-abiding and God-fearing man, I worried that he wouldn't allow himself to love me if he knew my real age." Within hours of his release from jail, Siegel began to shoot the story of Jacob and Esau, filming night and day to catch up with the schedule. I was comfortable enough as Jacob, but the black lamb's wool that was glued to my body with spirit gum so that I could also play Esau made me itch like the devil. Irritated by my complaint, Siegel shook his finger at me. "God does not save us from suffering, but through suffering. So stop scratching and kvetching! Let us all try to be a little more cheerful about our afflictions."

	"Sex, love, violence, death, adventure, deliverance," Joseph Siegel,
23	enthroned upon the canvas director's chair, proclaimed. "Our story has it all. It's God's own spiel." With the devotion of the sofer who solemnly inscribes the word of the Creator on parch-

ment, the director was piously rendering it on cellulose nitrate. He'd ceremo-
niously lift the mouth of the megaphone to his lips as if it were a shofar to blast
a blessing: "*Baruch ata Adonai, Elohenu melech ha-olam.* Blessed art Thou, O Lord
our God, who hast commanded us to make Thy movie." Although I supposed
that Siegel believed it, my father said it was the cocaine talking, embellishing
what the morphine allowed him to imagine. The director's pharmacological
proclivities were unabashed: "Cocaine is for comedy," he explained to me.
"Life's a high-speed flickering flicker, all celerity and zany mirth. Everything is
funny. Cocaine's a ladder." A frown eclipsed a bright grin. "But, alas, it must be
granted, the happiness can become a kind of sad one." A smile reappeared
from behind the darkly passing grimace. "Morphine, on the other hand, is
melodrama. Life's melancholy. Morphine's a serpent, beautiful and deadly. 'In
much wisdom is much grief; and he that increaseth knowledge increaseth sorrow.' But, it must be admitted, the sadness can be sublime; there's an uncanny
enchantment to it." It must have been cocaine that shaped his recension of the
story of Jacob. Since Jacob and Esau were twins, the idea of having a single actor play both parts seemed reasonable. And that I would be paid only one
salary as both the sons of Isaac seemed at least an acknowledgment of the
budgetary restraints that Liplinger and Rothstein were trying to impose upon
the prodigal director. But the casting had deeper exegetical ramifications: Jacob
and Esau were, in the dualistic Siegelian midrash, representatives of two sides
of the Eternal Jew. As Jacob, one half of that mythic wanderer, I was smooth-
skinned and clean-shaven, a mollycoddled mama's boy who wore an apron and
loved to cook and tidy up the tent. My other half, Esau, was hairy-chested and
broad-shouldered, a two-fisted and hot-blooded he-man, a rough-hewn chip off
the old patriarchal block who wore bearskins and loved to brawl and hunt.
When, as Esau, I arrived home, tired and hungry after a rough day of ravaging
Hittite women and beating up the enemies of Yahweh, I found myself, as Jacob, at the stove, preparing gefilte fish with chrain, chicken soup with mandeln,
and kugel. A rash and ravenous Esau traded his birthright to cunning Jacob for
a kosher meal. Maybe that could have made sense; but once our father had sent
me (as Esau) out hunting, and our mother convinced me (as Jacob) to disguise
myself with black lamb's wool and spirit gum as me (Esau) so that I (Jacob)

might receive my father's blessing, the narrative, unless the moviegoer was well versed in Torah, was confusing. Isaac mistook Jacob for Esau as he was supposed to. But, unfortunately, so did the audience; they were as much in the dark as the blind son of Abraham. And then, when Rebecca urged Jacob to flee to Mesopotamia and hide in the home of her brother Laban, the confusion was further compounded by Siegel's casting. Angel, through the cosmetological artistry of Lucy, played both of Laban's daughters, the beautiful Rachel and her more homely sister Leah; thus it was supposed to make sense when Jacob mistook Leah for Rachel in bed. Angel, in blackface, also played both Leah's beautiful maid Zilpa and Rachel's homely handmaid Bilhah. As if that weren't confounding enough, Angel also had bit parts as Esau's three wives, Adah, Aholibamah, and Bashemath. At one point during the filming of a love scene with Angel, I had to ask, "Who am I? Who is she? Who are we supposed to be?" Siegel laughed through his megaphone. "Life, now as for our forefathers, is all farcical vexation. Love is ever fraught with mistaken identities. Don't fuss over the details. Just act like you're in love. Give her a kiss. I'll figure out who you are when I edit." In watching the reel I knew that I was Jacob and Angel was Rachel: as he reached for her, she leaned into him, her head tilting across the tilt of his, as lips opened to opening lips and arms enfolded and focus softened. "Here's where it gets good," Siegel yelled out in the darkness of the projection room. "Watch this!" There was an abrupt cut to a shot of Yentsele, Siegel's pet billy goat, mounting a nonplused nanny goat. Gripping her neck tightly in his teeth, eyes blazing and nostrils flaring, he pumped furiously at her from behind. "Do you get it?" Siegel roared with glee. "They're playing the goats in Laban's herd that Jacob was breeding during his years of labor, and at the same time they're representing what Jacob and Rachel are doing—shtooping their brains out! Yentsele is quite an actor, a born star! Look at those soulful eyes and that rakish goatee." Yentsele was a one-trick pony, or rather a one-act goat— the only thing he ever did on the screen was copulate, not only in Laban's herd but also in Noah's ark. Had *Torah* not been canceled, Yentsele would have had the opportunity to play the more psychologically complicated role of the scapegoat in Leviticus, bearing all the sins of Israel upon his head. "Noah's Ark" had caused the first of the scandals that made *Torah* so notorious. Though the episode enjoyed some acceptance for its realistic depiction of animal husbandry in the Midwestern farm belt, it had been confiscated by police in almost every urban center where exhibitors were rash enough to show it. Following a title in which God commanded Noah to bring forth from the ark "every beast, fowl, and thing that creepeth upon the earth, that they may breed abundantly, be fruitful, and multiply," there was substantial footage of the great Yentsele coupling with an ingenue she-goat. The scene lasted longer than the flood.

Siegel fought the California confiscations of Genesis 8–9 in the court on moral grounds ("It's in the Bible, it's natural, and it is God's will"), and the publicity that such hearings provided for the project had significant commercial value. Siegel viewed himself as a prophet, if not a messiah, in motion picture making, not only in terms of his aesthetic sensibilities and religious vision, but also in matters of technique. While Edison and Griffith were trying to figure out how to bring sound to the movies, he had patented an "esterograph" that would supposedly generate a variety of synchronized biblical smells, every fragrance, he claimed, "from goat turds to bundles of myrrh." Siegel used established cinematic tricks (stop-frame animation, split-screen superimposition, mirrors and mattes) to film Jacob's dream of angels ascending and descending the ladders that connected heaven and earth, but he broke new technical ground in special effects for the descent of the angel of God who wrestled with Jacob and named him Israel. An actor dressed in billowing white robes and with large feathered wings attached to his back would be suspended from my father's Curtiss Eagle, and a camera, mounted on the belly of the biplane, would capture the angel from above as he flew over Death Valley in search of Jacob. That footage would be interspliced with film taken after the angel had been dropped from the sky with a parachute. As the aircraft followed the heavenly being, the camera, focusing on him as he fell to earth, would keep the parachute out of the frame. Because it might be hazardous to be that angel of the Lord, none of the actors, extras, or crew members, despite the rumored three-dollar-a-day bonus, auditioned for the part. I rescued Siegel with the perfect angel: Jesus Estafar, who had remained in contact with me since the Durbar of Delhi and who, in hopes of becoming a movie actor, had grown a little mustache and taken carioca lessons. At first Siegel had been hesitant to cast a Gentile as Yahweh's envoy, but the fact that Jesus would do the perilous aerial stunt work for a mere dollar (plus lunch and bus fare) changed a mind that was continually being pressured to economize. Because Jesus injured his leg in the landing, it was the angel, rather than the patriarch, who subsequently limped with a dislocated thigh. Nothing seemed to work in *Torah*. Money was running out and salaries were cut. When actors and crew started to quit to join Griffith or seek honest work, Siegel, shouting irately through his megaphone, compared them to the children of Israel camped on the shores of the Red Sea who, when they saw the approaching armies of Pharaoh, doubted Moses and the Lord and wailed that it would have been better to have remained slaves in Egypt. Like Moses holding out his staff, Siegel extended a swagger stick to beseech them to have faith in the Torah and *Torah,* in Him and in him. But there was no miracle—the motion picture was canceled. Angel shrugged her soft shoulders as her shepherdess's robe fell to the floor. "I was leaving anyway. Didn't I tell you? I'm moving to San Francisco. Consuela has invited me to live with her. I'm going to have French lessons. Are you sure I didn't tell you? I meant to tell you." Less stunned by the announcement than by the casualness with which it was made, I barked, "What about us?" The question seemed to make no sense to her. "What do you mean? We don't have to stop loving each other just because I'm a few hundred miles away." She alluded to Jacob's seven-year separation from Rachel: "And it seemed unto Jacob but a few days because of the love he had for her." Grieved by the thought of the loss, I muttered the Gentile expletive aloud for the first time, snarled it not in lust or love but in disappointment and anger; the obscene word for lovemaking seemed appropriate since separation from Angel would make sexual longing an anguish and humiliation. "Stop that," she scolded. "It's not over. I still love you. We'll still see each other. It's what's best for me. If you really love me, it's what you'd want for me." Alone with her in the darkness that night, holding her desperately in my arms, I imagined that we might really feast on mandrakes together, that I really was Israel and that she was the Mesopotamian maiden: "When Jacob saw Rachel he kissed her, for Rachel was beautiful and well favored. And then Jacob lifted up his voice and he wept."

24 The house was on the corner of First and Samuel, a block from cliffs that have faced a winsome sea with adamant indifference for a million years. My father put a down payment on the Santa Monica property because it was less than a half an hour's bicycle ride away from the airfield and because the address seemed auspicious. Turning the living room of the house into a séance salon, my mother called herself Madame Endor after the woman who, in the book of First Samuel, was visited in the night by a disguised and desperate Saul. When he entreated her to divine the spirit of Samuel, the ghost of that priestly judge rose from the earth to reveal to the distraught king of Israel that, because of his failure to execute Yahweh's wrath upon Amalek, he and his army would be slaughtered by the Philistines. So that our fighting boys might fare better in battle than the sons of Saul, Colonel Bladud of the United States Army Air Service had employed my father to train fledgling Yankee fighter pilots in aeronautic marksmanship. His squadron, the "Sharpshooting Seraphim of Santa Monica," consisted of ten men and five Curtiss Jennies until two of the planes collided in midair over the Santa Culebra fairground during a Fourth of July demonstration of American aviational prowess that had been meant to inspire enlistment in the U.S. Aero-Bombardment Corps. Despite the unfortunate accident, in which four of the pilots died, the government continued the training program that provided my father with money, gasoline, bullets, and so much air time that we rarely saw him during the daylight hours. Never a morning went by, however, that he did not buzz the house to drop a rose from the sky for his wife. He believed that nine out of ten times, given suitable wind conditions, the floral missile hit the front yard. The truth was that he was rarely on target. When a rose landed on the roof, in the street, or next door, his wife, greeting him when he came home in the evening, would lovingly lie to him: "Another bull's-eye today, my dear." She gathered up the petals of the fragrant roses that always fell apart up under the impact of their plummet to earth to put them in a crystal bowl in her salon, a stage she set with gimmicked candles, crystalline globes, dusty books, and a large painting of archangels, dominations, and cherubim, all garishly rendered in the bally banner style. Fatima and Mayadevee had been laid to rest together with Deer Heart and Jezebel in a battered trunk of old costumes. The Great War was great for people in the necromancy business: lots of customers were as eager as Saul to contact the dead. Auguries sold like hotcakes. This wasn't hokey Gypsy palmistry, mindless midway mind reading, or fly-by-night fortune-telling; Madame Endor provided high-class mediumistic services by appointment to sophisticated clients. Mother had perfected spirit writing and table raising; she had mastered the manipulation of floating body parts, icy hands, apports, spectral sparks, and ectoplasmic shimmerings. She worked assembly seances from a spirit cabinet, the black velvet curtain doors of which reached from floor to ceiling. For those exhibitions, my father, wearing tails and speaking in the English accent he had developed for the Imperial Shooting Gallery, played a vigilant guardian, protecting Madame Endor from the specters she divined, watching out for dybbuks, diakkas, and malevolents, always ready to snap the medium out of her mystic trance if the cunning spirits lured her perilously too far into the beyond. I played the dead. The geometrical geomantic designs on the ceiling concealed the seams of the trapdoor into my upstairs bedroom. When the curtain was drawn, I'd open the hidden hatch to descend the padded black ladder into the spirit cabinet. To prepare the costume paint and makeup, I'd mix calcium sulfide with banana oil and damar varnish, and burn magnesium wire over the concoction shortly before the show to intensify the numinous luminosity. Séances were always held at night. Once participants had gathered and signed a document acknowledging that Madame Endor could not be held responsible for any possible emotional or intellectual side effects of the séance, my father would seat them and bolt the door with an ominous thud. Candlelight flickered moodily on the dark walls as a volunteer was directed to bind my mother's hands with hemp to the steel bolt in the solid, securely braced upright beam in front of her. Her feet were lashed to steel floor rings. All the knots were coated with red sealing wax. It would be as impossible for spirits to abduct the medium as it would be for her to fake any of the phenomena that were to follow. On a table inside the cabinet, well out of Madame Endor's reach, were the props: a tambourine, horn, bell, burning candle, and glass of water. No sooner had my father pulled the curtain over the front of the cabinet than the tambourine began to rattle, the horn to howl, and the bell to clang. The trembling of glass in the chandelier, rattling chains, and plaintive moans made it seem that the tuxedoed watchman was concerned for Madame Endor's safety when he suddenly pulled the curtain back: the medium was still securely bound; the instruments were in place; the candle had been blown out; the water glass was empty; and the audience was amazed. Ever since she had first raised Tivya Rabinowitz from the dead for Consuela Heimenhoff, mother acted out spiritualistic performances with a moral conviction that they provided a therapeutic service to the bereaved. She was helping, not cheating, people, even if she did have to hoodwink them in order to do so. Black-veiled in mourning, a wealthy Mrs. Hortense Hubbard, who had lost a son on the battlefield at Champs-Labitte, found consolation when I, face and hands dappled with luminous powder and wearing a tattered military uniform, emerged from the cabinet to glow in the shadows. Bandages obscured my features. For twenty-five dollars (which my father had the nerve to swear would buy gas masks, playing cards, and brilliantine for our boys in Europe), the grieving woman was given the opportunity to tell her son one last time how much she loved him. I assured her that I had not suffered. I had died instantly and my death had not been in vain: "Before Jerry threw that doggone grenade of his, I had taken out over twenty of Kaiser Bill's machine-gun nests. Single-handedly I held off the Huns while my battalion circled around behind and sent them to hell. In giving my life, dear mother, I saved over two hundred doughboys. I've been decorated in heaven. God is on our side." Although I studied the newspapers each day for patter, I had to be able to improvise. Not every client wanted to communicate with victims of war, and I never knew ahead of time whose ghost I might have to be. Even Al Alighieri, Jr., probably the greatest animal impersonator of the twentieth century, couldn't have been more convincing than I when no less a social luminary than the director of the Los Angeles Christian Ladies' Hooverization League, Alice Vanderbilt-Coffin, contacted her deceased Pekinese. From within the cabinet, as a glowing doglike shape appeared to move across the ceiling, I barked pure canine delight to eloquently reassure her, no less than I had the woman who had lost a son at Champs-Labitte, that all was well in heaven. "I love you, Cuddles!" Miss Vanderbilt-Coffin cried out in what seemed like love's most genuine anguish. When, after taking a moment to regain her composure and dry her tears, she asked Madame Endor if she might have a chat with Teddy Roosevelt, the clairvoyant reminded her that the former president was not quite yet deceased. "Oh well," she sighed. "What about Jesus Christ? He's dead and I wouldn't mind having a word or two with Him." Rescuing me from having to be the Nazarene, Mother suddenly opened her eyes, stood up, and raised the lights: "It is over. That holy name dispels the spirits. We cannot continue." By the time the cabinet curtain was drawn back, I had ascended the padded ladder, shut the trapdoor, and slumped down on my bed. Missing Angel and aching for her embrace, I worried that she might be seeing other fellows. More and more frequently visiting our house, Jesus Estafar assumed that tales of his sexual escapades would somehow cheer me up. I never believed a word of what he said, as it seemed very unlikely that he really had made love to Theda Bara, Gloria Swanson, and Mary Pickford, let alone to both Lilian and Dorothy Gish at the same time. Certainly they could have done better than a Mexican teenager whose only entertainment credits consisted of playing the part of an Indian fakir on a bed of nails in a circus sideshow and being suspended from an airplane in white robes over Death Valley. When his stories failed to cure me of love's malaise, he offered to introduce me to a thirteen-year-old girl who, he said, would happily have sex with anybody. The idea would have been repugnant to me even if I had not been in love with Angel. One day, despite my explicit and repeated expressions of disinterest in the girl, he brought her to my room. "Snakes!" she exclaimed, trembling with the fascination, a sentimentally titillating commingling of fear and attraction, that serpents often inspire. While she inspected the collection, I took Jesus into the hallway, shut the door behind us, and demanded that he take her away. "I don't want her here. I have a girl. I'm in love with Angel." When, grinning, he asked if I didn't suspect that my sweetheart had other lovers in San Francisco, I grabbed him by the neck and might have choked him to death if he had not been able, despite my stranglehold, to apologize and promise to leave with the girl. When we returned to the room she was naked and leaning over the terrarium in which Caesar, my hot harlequin coral, was hiding his head under a coil of his body. She turned to ask if we had any beer. Assuring us that he could get some from his father, Jesus left us. By the time he returned, the girl and I had gotten dressed. After the three of us had shared a bottle of warm Cerveza Endiablado ("Pancho Villa's favorite") in awkward silence, Jesus took her away. Though I wouldn't recognize her face if my life depended on it, I do vividly recall her pubic hair, so unusually fleecy and golden, and her nipples, so surprisingly large and pale. It was my first vision of naked Gentile flesh. Some months later I asked Jesus her name. "I don't know," he shrugged, "I always just called her 'mi cordera.' She was sweet. I was kind of sad when she left. Her mother married a shoe salesman who took them back East. I miss her sometimes." On the evening of the day that the girl had been in my room, my mother, after our observance of the Havdalah ceremony of separation, casually mentioned that Consuela Heimenhoff had written to announce that she was coming to Los Angeles because she urgently needed to speak with Tivya Rabinowitz once more. Maharanee Mayadevee had to be brought out of moth balls. I asked if Angel would be coming along. Mother hesitated, smiled, and then said, "Yes and no."

25 "No," Devora Rabinowitz said to Consuela Heimenhoff, she would not come, since she did not believe in ghosts. "Yes," Angel wrote to Sarah Schlossberg, she would come so that a drowned mermaid could be conjured up. It was not that Angel and my mother were callous enough as swindlers to laugh behind a dupe's back or profit unduly from chicanery. No, the hoax was meant to please and benefit the hoaxee. Since moving into the Pacific Heights estate, Angel had become fond of the socialite. "In a funny way," she confessed, "I love her." Perhaps the more we love someone, the more prone we are, intentionally or not, to mislead them. During the séance, it occurred to me that perhaps Consuela Heimenhoff actually knew that her mystic medium was an actress and that the revenant was none other than Devora. It's possible that she did not believe in sciomancy, spirit materialization, astral guides, or necromantic shades, and was merely playing along, deceiving them by pretending to be deceived. Perhaps it was merely for her own amusement or because she did not wish to embarrass the con artists by ruining the show. It's hard to know where truth begins and where it ends. My mother, as well as my father, I realized, must have known the truth about me and Angel because it was assumed that she would sleep in my room and that, like the Amazing Snake Boy and little Alpine Aerialist of the good old days, we would share a bed. Prior to her arrival, I had vowed not to allow myself to broach the topic of fidelity, to pretend that my love was not insistent, possessive, or in any way restrictive. I was already well enough aware of the perversities of affection to understand that the more I demanded, the less I'd have. True or not, I ached to hear her say, "No, there haven't been any others. Not a single kiss. *Je désire Isaac, lui seulement! Mon maître des serpents.*" No sooner had my father left for the airfield than my mother began to rehearse Angel's cues and lines with her and to practice the accent and tone of voice that would make daughter sound like mother, the quick like the dead. The painting of the Jewish angels in the seance salon was covered with a faded banner portrait of Maharanee Mayadevee. The resurrected spirit rapper recruited me to pose as Swami Balakrishna, less a character than a set piece providing Oriental ambiance. There was no seductivity in the nakedness that was fleetingly displayed as Angel changed. After she had pulled on black tights, slippers, and gloves, I painted her mother's death-worn one-legged shape on her with luminescent compound. Straining to refrain from asking her about other men, I asked if she felt guilty about flimflamming a woman who had already been tricked into supporting her. Adjusting a wig that had been seasoned with phosphorescent dust, she assured me that "Consuela loves this sort of thing. The supernatural is a refuge from a tedium of teas, garden parties, and charity functions. It's entertainment and religion. Your mother says that my mother would approve." As I knelt before her, waving the bright fizzling magnesium near the chemicals on her torso, I wondered whether Angel's insouciance was sham, whether it was emotionally strenuous to play the part of her deceased mother. After she had daubed parts of my body that I couldn't reach with dark pancake, I wrapped the loincloth and turban that I'd wear as I sat cross-legged at the seance with Kaleeya Junior around my neck. In addition to bringing two trig bluestockings from San Francisco and three philanthropic parvenus from Los Angeles, Consuela Heimenhoff had invited Major L. A. Wheedle, an expert on mesmerism and director of the Pan-American Institute for the Scientific Investigation of the Incredible. As the major was an anthropologist, a geographer, and the leader of three expeditions to Himalayan Asia to capture the elusive Abominable Snowman, his interest in the event was essentially scientific. My mother was not intimidated by Wheedle, since scientists, with their vain trust in their own rationality and powers of observation, are the easiest fools to fool. Once the guests were seated, the curtain was drawn over the spirit cabinet and the lights were dimmed. The audience was instructed to be still and silent as Mayadevee hummed deep unearthly syllables: *"Divya tivya ooo divya divya tivya hey livya givya tivya hmmmmm!"* As the crystal baubles of the chandelier above the gathering began to jingle, the curtain over the spirit cabinet rustled slightly. There was a whimper, and, one at a time, ten gimmicked candles were extinguished as if by the force of some otherworldly pneuma. The curtain shook fitfully and there was muted moan. It was gravely dark and cryptically silent. "Tivya," Maharanee Mayadevee whispered, "Have you come?" Silence. She repeated it three times: "Tivya! Tivya! Tivya!" With each utterance, one of the tapers, as if in answer to the call, was magically reignited. Approaching the cabinet, the necromancer's guardian boldly drew back the curtain to reveal a revenant balanced on a single glowing leg. The shimmering incandescence of spindly arms, a gaunt torso, and wispy mane defied the shadows. Deep black pits were haunting eyes in a starkly glowing face. The spirit guide signaled Consuela Heimenhoff to address the wraith directly. "Is that you, Mrs. Rabinowitz?" Miss Heimenhoff asked the drowned Jewess, and, nodding in silence, the subtle phantasm hopped forward. "You look a lot like your daughter," the socialite remarked politely to the ghost. "Thank you for coming, Mrs. Rabinowitz. I'm so pleased you could be here. I'm terribly sorry to bother you, but I do need to ask you about something. The Great War, Maharanee Mayadevee assures me, will be over soon—thank goodness for that—and your dear Devora, whom I have come to love as my own child, wants to go to Paris. Although it seems to me nothing but a young girl's romantic fancy, I do want to make her happy. But I'm afraid to send her off by herself. The place is teeming with demi-mondaines, mountebanks, cancan dancers, lesbians, surrealists, opium addicts, absinthe drinkers, pornographers, and Communists." Suddenly realizing that, as usual, she was doing all the blabbing when time with the dead was so precious, she checked herself, took a deep breath, and got down to business: "I think it would be best for her to remain with me in San Francisco. I've introduced her to some very nice young gentlemen. One of them, only twenty-six years old and already a physician, has fallen in love with her. Dr. Church is not of the Hebrew persuasion, I'm afraid, but he doesn't mind that Devora is. He hopes to marry her. She could have such a charmed life with him. I don't know what to do. What do you want for your daughter?" Silently swaying from side to side, finally, in a soft voice, tinged with a Yiddish accent, the one-legged apparition spoke: "Tell me about my child. Please, speak more of her." Consuela answered: "She's beautiful. She's kind. She laughs with such sweetness. She's very intelligent. She's learning French. She's brought so much joy into my household. I don't want to let her go. I want her near me always." I wished that the real ghost of Tivya Rabinowitz really could have heard the tender testimony. "Let her go," the conjured eidolon said, sighing: "Let her go to Paris when the war is over. But there's something else I desire for her with all my heart. It is my dream that she will star in a motion picture, that she will play the part of Cleopatra. Do you promise that you will help our child, that you will see that she plays the Queen of the Nile and goes to Paris? If you can promise that, I can finally rest in peace, dissolved into the infinite ether and absorbed into the holy joy of eternity. Can you promise?" Gripped and transported by the drama, Consuela cried out, "Yes, I promise! I promise!" As if those words were magical incantation, the spirit instantly disappeared (when Angel turned her back, upon which there was not a trace of calcium sulfide, to us), and simultaneously the three gaffed candles that provided the only light in the room were extinguished. Then all the lights were slowly raised and everyone could see that the cabinet was empty. "Wasn't my mother wonderful?" Angel, already out of her black tights and wrapped in a white satin robe, asked as I arrived in the bedroom to change out of my turban and loincloth. Once the thoroughly beguiled guests were gone, we went downstairs to celebrate the performance. "I've brought French champagne from Consuela's cellar, Château d'Amour," Angel announced and, after my father had eagerly popped the cork and filled four glasses, proposed a toast to Consuela Heimenhoff. "And to the memory of Tivya Rabinowitz," my mother added. "I didn't charge them for the show," she said, as if that exonerated them from the mendaciousness of the evening. In fact, not having to pay for the seance only further assured the heiress, as well as

109

Major Wheedle and the other guests, that the materialization must have been real. At midnight, Angel announced that she had to be up early in the morning to catch the first train to San Francisco in order to arrive back in Pacific Heights before Consuela. I followed her up the stairs to my room, and as she disrobed I could not restrain myself from asking about Church. "Oh," she said, yawning and sliding naked into bed, "he's sweet enough, but he doesn't want me to go to Paris. He says there's a syphilis epidemic there. But if you really love someone, you want them to have what they want, no matter what. And you want me to go Paris, don't you, Isaac?" I said yes even though I didn't mean it, and pushed close to her under the covers. "We can't," she whispered, kissed my cheek, and uttered the words that Rachel had used to prevent Laban from finding the gods she had hidden beneath the camel saddle upon which she sat: "The custom of the lonely days of women is upon me." I explained that it didn't matter, since I was not constrained by any of the mitzvoth attributed to a god that I knew did not exist. "I love eating pork chops, pig's feet, ham hocks, and bacon." I invoked talmudic rhetoric: "Levitical interdictions do not prohibit a Jewish woman from intercourse with a man during her menstruation, but only an observant Jewish male from making love to an impure woman. And I can assure you that I am in no way observant." By the time I woke up, she was gone. That morning, by the light of day, I discovered smudges of blood on my sheets, on my right hand, genitals, and the inside of my leg. And that evening, by the darkness of night, I saw remains of luminous paint, a hand print on the wall, and finger marks on the pillow and on my shoulder and thigh. The eerie mediumistic incandescence was unnerving. I felt that I had had contact with the dead. Angel's mortality was as blatant when she was in my arms as it was when she walked the high wire without a net, mechanic, or pole. That's what made her so beautiful. The orphaned rope dancer, I imagined, had made some sort of pact with the Angel of Death. The next time I saw her was at a funeral.

26 "Buffalo Bill was a shmuck," Jake Grossman said with a sigh when I saw him in Denver at *Buffalo Bill's Last Roundup,* the funeral extravaganza that was Big Bee's most spectacular spectacular since the Durbar of Delhi. "Colonel William Frederick Buffalo Bill Cody" the *Los Angeles Examiner* had reported, "is watching the sands in life's hourglass run out as he listens to the dreadful din of the hoof beats of the pale horse upon which the Grim Reaper is galloping toward Denver for a showdown." That the death of the legendary frontiersman was pre-announced in newspapers across the country gave producers, managers, and agents an opportunity to get to work well in advance of Cody's last curtain call, booking performers, scheduling acts, shipping in rides and animals, manufacturing souvenirs, taking bids on the concessions, and launching an advertising campaign that would attract many thousands of customers to ceremonially weep over a man whom they had never met. "You'll Cry! You'll Laugh!" publicity posters promised, "You'll Never Forget Being a Member of the Most Thrill Packed Funeral in History." It was guaranteed to "put the *fun* back in *funeral.*" When the buffalo hunter finally died, American, Allied, and enemy troops on the battlefields of Europe simultaneously stopped fighting, removed their helmets, bowed their heads in silence, and took a solemn moment to honor Buffalo Bill Cody. The minute of truce was followed by war cries from the trenches: "Three Cheers for Buffalo Bill! Hip-hip-hooray! Huzza-huzza!" and *"Vive Guillaume Bison! Vive la gloire cowboyesque!"* and *"Ein hoch auf Büffel Wilhelm, möge er ewig leben!"* President Wilson, declaring a national day of mourning, announced that Congress had reserved a plot for the American hero to the right of President McKinley's grave in Arlington National Cemetery. There was no way, however, that the patriotic Republican mayor of Denver, William Cowper, was going to give the American scout's body to the quasi-liberal Democratic president. Cowper announced to the public that it was too great a risk to national security to transport the dead plainsman to the capital, given top-secret intelligence reports of both a German plot to steal Buffalo Bill and take him to Berlin and a Bolshevik scheme to blow up the great American. In quick response to that news, federal troops were dispatched to Denver to guard Buffalo Bill as he lay in state and to accompany him in the Grand Parade, his procession on the horse-drawn caisson that had been sumptuously decorated with buckskin, fur, chamois, bone, horn, and feathers in high rococo Wild West style. The parade included stage coaches, wagon trains, and floats, Pony Express riders, Indians on their paints, and Bedouins on their Arabians, Cossacks, sepoys,

Bengal Lancers, the Equestriennes of the Royal Harem of Delhi, and, on Shetland ponies, the midget Rough Riders from *Colonel William W. Wee's Wild West
Weeview*. The mourning masses struggled not to let bereavement get in the
way of a good time, as they listened to the Buckaroo Band play Wild West re-
quiems in the grandstand by which the pall procession passed. Cody's favorite
song, "The Star-Spangled Banner," was played every hour on the hour. Combing the crowd of spectators, Pinkerton agents spotted the Reverend Fred
Schlangeleiter, a Lutheran clergyman and organist who had just arrived from
Philadelphia to play the accompaniment for Diva Falla Pia Algolagnia, the Cal-
abrian Canary, singing *"Non e questo un morire, Immortal Buffalo Gulielmo, ma un
passar anzi tempo a l'altra vita."* The reverend was arrested on suspicion of being a German agent and a key player in the Kaiser's alleged plot to undermine
American morale by body-snatching Colonel Cody. Kaiser Wilhelm and President Wilson weren't the only ones with their eyes on the earthly remains of
Buffalo Bill. Keenly aware of the economic, political, theatrical, and sentimental value of the cadaver, Mayor Cowper arranged for twenty tons of concrete
to be poured over the celebrity's grave to ensure that no one tried to abscond
with Denver's premier civic asset. While the concrete hardened, the federal
troops were joined in protective vigil by armed guards from local chapters of
the Elks, Lions, and Eagle Scouts. Those who had been with the scout, watching him play a game of solitaire at the time of his death—his sister Julia and his
wife Lulu, Johnny "the Kid" Baker and Chief Laughing Eagle—each declared
that Colonel Cody, who had neglected to request a burial site in his last will
and testament, had revealed his wishes to them individually. Julia Cody insisted
that her dead brother, "ever since he was just a little tike, had dreamed of being
buried in Snake County, Iowa, where we were born." A poker-faced Johnny
Baker argued for Cody, Wyoming, on the grounds that the Chamber of Com-
merce of the hamlet formerly known as Goshen had changed not only the
name of the town but that of its hotel, railway stop, drinking saloon, and general store, to Cody in 1890 on the assumption that the colonel would be buried
there as he swore he would be at the dedication of the "Buffalo Bill Cody Barber Shop." Chief Laughing Eagle informed reporters that "Pahaska wanted his
corpse to be put on a platform on the open plains like an Apache brave so that
his flesh could be eaten by eagles." Mrs. Lulu Cody (from whom the colonel
had repeatedly tried, without success, to get a divorce) asserted that her late
husband's wishes, whatever they might have been, were irrelevant: "His will
names me as sole beneficiary, entitled to all of his earthly possessions. And
since he was broke as a result of investing all of our money into making those
stupid movies about himself, 'earthly possessions' refers only and specifically
to his body and the wardrobe with which he so preposterously clothed it. His

body is my body, and I'm taking it to St. Louis." The states of Kansas, Nebraska, and New York were also making claims for the flesh of the plainsman, but Wyoming put up the biggest fight of all. The governor of that state issued a declaration of war on the state of Colorado. Resigned to the realization that he had little hope of getting the body for himself, President Wilson intervened, informing the citizens of both states that he could not sanction fighting between states while the nation as a whole needed all able-bodied men, and all available arms and munitions, to wage the greater war for democracy overseas. Most of the feuds over Bill cooled with the reading of a will that, other than bequeathing his possessions to the wife he so disliked, expressed, in dramatic terms that invoked both the apostles of Christ and the Founding Fathers of America, one last wish: "that there be a monument erected, a statue of me, three hundred and five feet high, the exact height of the Statue of Liberty and the same weight (thirty-one tons of copper for the skin, one hundred twenty-five tons of steel for the pylon and framework, and twenty-seven thousand tons of concrete for the foundation), and like that other monument in style, design, and feeling. Instead of robes, I shall be wearing my signature outfit and a Stetson, the brim of which should be thirty feet in diameter. And instead of a torch, I shall hold aloft a sixty-eight-foot-long Winchester carbine rifle into the barrel of which the descendants of my devoted fans may crawl for centuries to come." That the estate provided no funds for the erection of the monument did not daunt Mayor Cowper. Passionately he appealed to the red-blooded boys of America to raise the millions of dollars needed to make Buffalo Bill's dream come true: "Surely you'll be eager to go from door to door collecting money from Americans who want to keep the free spirit of the Wild West alive forever. In addition, if every kid in America would set aside just a penny or two a day out of their candy money for one year, we'll be ready to start building the Buffalo Bill Memorial before you know it." Cowper vowed to allocate an undisclosed portion of the profits from *Buffalo Bill's Last Roundup* to the memorial fund. Those profits were substantial. The funereal fair drew more customers than the Durbar of Delhi, the Pan-American Exposition, President Wilson's inauguration, and even Buffalo Bill's own Rough Riders of the World Congress of 1915 put together. Laborers, vendors, concessionaires, attraction managers, performers, and pickpockets earned top dollar. Pay was sufficient for my mother to be able to convince my father to leave his beloved airplane behind in the hangar in Santa Monica and take us by train to Denver. Wyoming Willie once again shot glass balls out of the sky and Camels out of the lips of Deer Heart. In order to play Big Chief Magpie, I added a defanged rattler to my snake collection. Choctaw Charlie, now claiming to be one hundred years old, in war paint and chief's regalia, chanted Indian dirges while I waved the rattling snakes in the air above my feathered headdress, improvising what was billed as "the Arapaho serpent dance for braves who have died in battle." Authentic Indians, if they came on horseback in native costumes and rode in the Grand Parade, were given free admission, a dollar a day, and a souvenir bottle of Buffalo Bill Bonded Bourbon. The pageant was a reunion for veterans of carnival, circus, burlesque, and vaudeville. Characters from every square of the game of my life, cashing in on the funeral, reappeared. Jake, Beryl, and Hayim Grossman, all three bemoaning the absence of Shmuel, recreated their Cossack equestrial display. "I hadn't been on a horse or spoken Russian for a long time," Jake chuckled eight years later in London. "My toochis and tongue were sore for a week." Al Alighieri, Jr., with his new wife as the rump, impersonated Imsak, Buffalo Bill's favorite Arabian stallion. Larry Lafitte's poodles, dressed as Indians and cavalrymen, with Pierre as Buffalo Bill, performed a canine rendition of the massacre at Wounded Knee. We bumped into Zizi Praline, Bertha Blanchette, Lulu Larue, Trixie Cocotte, and Leona Wilder the Lion Tamer. Bachnele Poopik was nowhere to be seen since he was hidden inside the Geronimo Automaton that, for twenty-five cents, took on challengers at checkers. Antelope Andy and nine other Buffalo Bill look-alikes (all of whom had been unsuccessfully sued by Cody for impersonating him) were available to shake hands with mourning fans. George Washington, given the pay, condescended to be "The World's Greatest Negro Buffalo Bill." Siegel and Nister were filming the funeral for Movietone. Yes, everyone was there, including one whom I had not expected. I was utterly startled by the sudden vision of her dancing across the sky, the white lace of her costume blending into the clouds behind her. At that distance she could have been the child whom I had so often watched moving in grace and beauty upon the high wire. She lifted the globe above her head. Wyoming Willie fired his rifle and it felt as if my heart had been blown to smithereens.

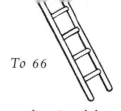

27 At the bottom of the ladder I waited for the descending Angel that I might confess how terribly I had missed her over the last month and ask when we could be alone together. "I'm staying at the old Palace Hotel with Consuela," she said. "It's difficult to get away, especially at night. I want to, of course, but it's awkward. Where's your exhibit? I'll try to visit you there tomorrow." Dressed in my Big Chief Magpie costume and holding a frightened fangless snake, I welcomed her to my "Authentic Indian Wigwam," where, during a distressingly brief conversation, it became clear why Angel was in Denver. She had appealed to Consuela to bring her to the gala funeral under the pretext of wanting her dear guardian to see her on the high wire. It would appear coincidental that they would run into Joseph Siegel and that he, after being introduced to the San Francisco hosiery heiress, would casually mention that he had recently consulted a fortune-teller who had told him that he would someday make a motion picture about Cleopatra. Confessing that he doubted the clairvoyant really had any mystical powers because he didn't see any possibility of ever being able to raise the money for such a big project, he added, "But if I did, I'd want to cast Devora as the Egyptian Queen. She's a great actress. If the anti-Semites hadn't nixed *Torah*, Angel would be bigger than Bernhardt." With the bait in the water, Consuela bit once more. That evening, unable to endure being in the same town with my beloved without seeing her, I went to the posh Denver Palace that had just been renamed the Buffalo Billtmore. Asking at the desk for a Miss Consuela Heimenhoff, I was informed that she was unavailable to callers. I didn't know what to do with myself and don't know where I was heading when, over all the chatter and a band playing "There's a Hoedown in Heaven Tonight," I heard a shout from across the lobby: "Hey, Schlossberg! Over here!" There, nested in a large green leather armchair, was a beaming Bachnele Poopik in a tuxedo, waving his arm in an invitation for me to join him. After his customary "Isaac, how you've grown!" I seated myself across from him and began with a sigh: "I'm so in love with Angel." "Yeah, I love her too," he interrupted. "That's why I'm so happy for her. She's going to play Cleopatra in the Siegel movie, and as soon as the war's over she's going to Paris. All her dreams are coming true." As cheerful as I was miserable, he was waiting for his current paramour, "a great celebrity," he boasted, to join him. They were dining at the swanky Colorado Corral, the Denver eatery that had just been renamed the Buffalo Billbecue. "Oh, yes, I remember the first time I was in love," Bachnele consoled me. "I was just a boy in Lutzk. Like the friends of Job, the people in our village wondered what sin my father must have committed to deserve a midget for a son. My parents were so ashamed of me that they wouldn't let me be called to the Torah as a bar mitzvah. So I ran away. But how was a boy alone to survive? All my life people had laughed at me and I figured there must be some money in it. I could do somersaults and sing dirty songs. I'd travel from shtetl to shtetl, and for a laugh people would toss a kopeck or two. To entertain is to survive, whether you're Sarah Bernhardt or a Litvak midget Hebe. One day the tax collector for the ghetto in Troki, seeing me performing in the street, had such a laugh that he decided to take me home to entertain at his precious daughter's fifteenth birthday celebration. Her name was Khozi Kokusi. She was tall and beautiful, with golden Baltic hair and the pinkest cheeks in the world. She clapped her hands and giggled with delight as I sang comic Lithuanian dainos in her honor. She begged her father to keep me, 'that we may laugh every day, Papa.' The idea appealed to the man's grandiosity. The Grand Duke Witold had a jester, a Jewish midget, always at his side, and what was good enough for the grand duke was good enough for Mr. Kokusi. So I got a little bed, a lot of food, and even some cash for amusing the family and being Khozi's playmate. One day, two of her girlfriends came to the house. Rummaging in an old chest, they found one of Khozi's childhood dresses and, just for fun, decided to make a little girl of me. Because it was my duty and pleasure to entertain Khozi, I let them undress me. They snickered at the sight of my naked body: "Oh, because he's so small," one of them squealed, "it looks so big!" Wearing a lace-trimmed dress, I danced and in a high-pitched voice sang about a maiden who, in love for the first time, has been jilted by her beau. It was a melancholy number and I put my whole heart into it. After her friends left, Khozi helped me change. No sooner had she pulled the dress over my head than she took me in her arms, more like a doll or pet puppy than a man at first. But then, as she held me close to her, I could feel her breathing become heavier. Then she was kissing me. And then she was naked and her kisses were more uncontrollably fervent. What could I do? The only thing I could do! And the next thing I knew, I was in love. And I told her so, and she told me that she loved me too, and we both agreed that it would be forever. It was a great love, that first love, all the more powerfully passionate because it was a secret. Who would suspect that a beautiful and rich (not to mention tall) young girl of pure Lithuanian stock could be in love with a dirty little Yid? First love! So terrible, so sweet, and so silly. Even though, deep down, you know it won't last, you struggle with all your might not to admit that to yourself. Years later you look back on it and laugh, realizing that it was really nothing. Maybe it was just the shtooping. But at the time it was the love that the poets say moves the planets and the stars. I know it's hard to believe, but you'll look back on your love for Angel like that. You'll laugh at yourself someday. You'll laugh at love." When the woman with whom Bachnele Poopik was dining that evening, his latest love, gorgeously attired in a black chiffon gown with a black satin collar and marten fur trim, appeared, the midget slipped down out of the large chair, took her hand to kiss it in a genteel manner, and introduced me: "My darling, this is Isaac Schlossberg, Abraham and Sarah Schlossberg's boy. Isaac, may I present none other than Zizi Praline, the one and only World's Ugliest Woman as certified by the State of New York, former star attraction of Buffalo Bill's Wild West Sideshow." She extended her hand, in a gesture that invited me to kiss it as Bachnele had just done. I was struck by the beauty of the fingers, by the softness and fragrance of the skin. She was, one had to admit, quite hideous; the drooping jowls, twisted chin, and flattened nose were grotesque, but, strangely, not repulsive. Like her hands, her eyes were beautiful, generously blue and sparkling with uncanny delight. As she seated herself in the leather armchair, Bachnele remained standing like a courtier in service to a queen. "Of course I remember the Schlossbergs," she said in a enchantingly melodic voice as the distorted flaps of lip twisted into a recognizable smile: "How is your father? And Sarah? Are they here in Denver? I'd love to see them again. Those were wonderful times. We had a lot of fun. Is your father still as good-looking as ever? I think it was because he was so handsome that Buffalo Bill didn't let him perform. Some folks said it was because he was needed as an interpreter. But I think Bill was jealous of his good looks. When he overheard Orillia Dooling telling me that she thought Abraham Schlossberg was the prettiest fella she'd ever seen, Buffalo Bill fined her twenty dollars for immoral behavior. Although the colonel had a big reputation as a lady's man, I don't think he cared much about being intimate with women. He never once tried to seduce me. Like most men who love animals, he was puritanical, more interested in riding horses than making love. He had sex appeal all right, but it was for public consumption. It took your breath away to see him canter around the arena on a horse. The two creatures, man and animal, were one. All the girls fell in love with him, all except Lulu, that wife of his. Yes, I think his reputation as a lover was mostly flapdoodle and fizgig. He strictly forbade mashing, which he defined as consorting with members of the audience, and he prohibited any dalliance between unmarried members of the show. If you were caught hanky-pankying on the lot, you had your choice: leave the Wild West, pay a big fine, or let Buffalo Bill whip you with a cat-o'-nine-tails." As she continued her reminiscence of love in the Wild West, Bachnele gazed adoringly at her. Suddenly I couldn't hear what she was saying over what seemed like the deafening sound of my heart pounding as if trying to get out of my chest. I saw them across the lobby, sparkling in their evening attire as they walked toward the stairs to the grand ballroom, newly named the Buffalo

Billroom: Angel with Consuela Heimenhoff, Joseph Siegel, and a young man I did not recognize. Without excusing myself, I jumped up, zigzagged forcibly through the throng of hotel guests who were so festively mourning the demise of Buffalo Bill, and reached the foot of the stairs before them. Seemingly embarrassed by my sudden appearance, Angel nevertheless condescended to introduce me: "This is Isaac Schlossberg. I told you about him. He was Samoo the Amazing Snake Boy of Hindustan. Isaac, this is Miss Consuela Heimenhoff, my guardian angel and closest friend in the whole world. And this is Dr. Church from San Francisco. And I believe you know the famous Hollywood director, Joseph Siegel." No doubt afraid that I might ruin her scam, she excused us for a moment to have a word with me: "Please, Isaac, don't make a scene. We'll be together next month. I'll be in Los Angeles to start shooting *Cleopatra*. Please, darling. I promise we'll have lots of time together then. *Je t'aime, mon chéri*. And if you love me too, you'll leave me alone." She kissed me lightly on the cheek and rejoined her party. Overwhelmed with disappointment, I didn't know what to do and don't remember what I did. But I do recall wishing that I had had the spirit to storm the ballroom, grab Angel in my arms, draw a six-shooter to stop Doc Church from trying to rescue her, and carry her, kicking and squealing, out of the Palace. I would lift her onto the back of my black Arabian and gallop off with her into the darkness. Soon she'd surrender, and at midnight I'd pitch camp, build a fire, and lay out a warm Indian-blanket bedroll. We'd make love on the prairie, beneath the canopy of stars, clinging to each other, unaware of any separation between man and woman, lover and beloved, human being and angel, at least until dawn, when a rising sun would attempt to illuminate real things once more.

28 "What *Torah* might have done for religious devotion," a cocainized Siegel fanfaronaded, "*Cleopatra* will accomplish for romantic love. Imagine a celluloid epiphany—beauty, truth, love, death, good, evil, political intrigue . . ." "And safe driving," an augustly smiling Consuela Heimenhoff interpolated. "Don't forget automobile safety, my darling." As the financier of the extravagant epic, the lingerie heiress insisted that the motion picture, dedicated as it was to the memory of Tivya Rabinowitz, serve to remind humanity to drive with caution and courtesy. "Automobiles are not so different than chariots," she reflected. "Pedestrians in ancient Alexandria were no less vulnerable than they are today." The movie would include a chariot race in which the charioteers would indicate turns and stops with appropriate hand signals, keep to the right-hand side of the track to avoid oncoming traffic, and, halting their horses at all SISTE signs along the racecourse, look both ways and give the right-of-way to people on foot. As aesthetically ludicrous as this may have sounded, Siegel had no choice but to agree to the heiress's conditions, since no one interested in making a profit would, after *Torah,* have been frivolous enough to invest in a Joseph Siegel film. While the director needed Heimenhoff to make another movie, so she depended on him to fulfill the last wish of the ghost of Tivya Rabinowitz "that our Angel will star in a motion picture, playing the part of Cleopatra." From D. W. Griffith the socialite purchased the Roman chariots, costumes, and props that had been used in the Judean sequences of *Intolerance.* She commissioned Monsieur Alcibiade Couvade, the renowned Parisian couturier credited with inventing the brassiere, to Egyptianize and alter for Angel the Babylonian wardrobe that had been worn by Princess Beloved in the Griffith epic. Swathed in shimmering silken veils of violet voile and delicately draped with retiary roses and glistening gossamers, the carny soubrette became the Macedonian ruler of Egypt. Sheer sapphirine chiffons, clinging tulles, and trailing taffetas were finely filigreed with mystic symbols and Circean signs. The costumes, seeming to delight in contact with such vital, supple flesh, covered her body paradoxically, making her seem more naked than nudity could have done. Clothes ardently promised what they coyly concealed. "This is made of byssus," Angel explained, holding up the diaphanous robe that would be worn in the suicide scene, "the linen Egyptians used to wrap their mummies. The one I'm wearing now is the gown in which I'll greet Antony in Egypt." Embroidered constellations of silver stars, shimmering against a skintight night of dark-blue Damascene damask, augured love's conquests. Urging me to touch gently flexed curves of stomach, buttock, and thigh, all caressed by a soft, thin fabric of sky, a nubile Cleopatra placed my palm over the embroidered moon that ornamented her breast. "There is gold," the actress recited, "and here my bluest veins to kiss; a hand that kings have lipp'd, and trembled kissing." With her cheek resting against my chest after lovemaking, she used her improving French to sleepily whisper things that no one would dare say loudly, wide awake, or in a mother tongue: *"Moi, Cléopâtre, la femme la plus parfaite et la plus désirable qui ait jamais existé, être unique et mystérieuse! Pour me posséder, les serpents veulent être anges . . . pour eux, je ne suis dangereuse qu'en rêve."* And then in sleep, I sensed, she dreamed the queen's dreams: sphinxes, pyramids, a Nile barge with perfumed purple sails and silver oars, a woven wicker basket of ripe figs, and a corpse wrapped in white byssus. The movie, like life itself, was essentially plotless. Audiences were presumed to know the story, if not Shakespeare's version, then their own. Using the same device of the multiple casting of individual actors that had made *Torah* so unintelligible, Siegel had Angel play not only Cleopatra but also Ptolemy, her brutal brother and incestuous husband, her first sexual partner and first political enemy. A morphinized Siegel revealed the meaning of it: "Cleopatra's first love is Cleopatra. It's the same for everybody. The first time we're in love, it's with ourselves. Just like the first time we have sex: it's usually jacking off." I appeared twice in the film, once for eight seconds as an awkwardly foppish Gnaeus Pompey, and once for eleven seconds as one of the many prisoners of war who were, for the sake of the queen's amusement, given one night of lovemaking with her, only to be decapitated at dawn by a loincloth-clad and skin-oiled George Washington, Cleopatra's Nubian slave and master over her harem of boys and men. The largest male role in the film was that of Cleopatra's mascot, the Goat of Mendes, played by Yentsele. Although there did not seem to be any reason for Yentsele to appear in almost every scene, the doped director confidently justified it: "He's a symbol. In ancient Egypt, the goat represented love, fertility, immortality, and that kind of thing. And, in any case, I'm a Capricorn. Goats are lucky for me. Speaking of animals, we need to get a viper from Bannerjee for the suicide scene." I suggested to Siegel that if he was interested in authenticity, we'd need a cobra: "Cleopatra wouldn't have used a viper. It's too hideous a death. Because the venom effects the blood, the victim foams at the mouth, vomits, urinates, and defecates uncontrollably; the flesh becomes bloated as it turns blue and then a dark purplish green. But the poison of the cobra goes right to the nerves. The victim feels drunk, becomes pale and languid, and drifts into a coma; there is a suspension of thought and feeling, a perfect peace and then, by and by, a quiet death." Bannerjee, who had supplied the director with camels, a tame tiger, and a magnificent elephant named Frederick, also provided the recommended hooded serpent, removing not only its fangs and poison sacs but all of its teeth, just for good measure. Ever since my bar mitzvah ceremony, when Mendel Lansky had given me Vladmir Yesnovitch's magnificent monograph, *Thanatophidia Indica,* I had wanted to handle a cobra. The first live one I had ever seen was in the reptile house at the Seattle zoo, the same day I had gone to the Paradisio and landed by chance on a square in which Angel was Little India. As I watched the keeper taunt the snake with a stick, witnessed the majestic spreading of the scaled hood, emblazoned with a cryptic cipher, beguiled by the lithe sway of the dance, I felt an odd tug, a yearning to someday go to India and see real snake charmers playing with king cobras. And that same day, as I watched Little India on the stage at the Paradisio, I had been no less bewitched. Angel seemed to know the cobra's dance. "Bachnele came up with the idea for the nautch girl routine when I first went on the road with him," Angel had revealed. "He said that there was something about an East Indian woman that fascinates men out West." Bachnele begged Siegel to let him play Caesar in the film. "No," the director snapped, "you ruined *Torah.* Every review pointed out the ridiculousness of a midget portraying Pharaoh." Bachnele protested: "I could stand on a ladder." When a scoffing Siegel repeated his no even more adamantly, Bachnele cried out, *"Et tu, Brute?"* Gershom Greenspan landed that part and Jesus Estafar was Antony. My Mexican pal changed his name for the occasion to Valentine Rudolfo and subsequently, but unsuccessfully, sued a certain Rodolfo Guglielmi, who had, also for the sake of a movie career, changed his name to Rudolph Valentino at about the same time. Angel decided to change her name too, from Devora Rabinowitz to Dévoré Rabbin. But when I pointed out to her that in French that meant the "eaten rabbi," she further modified it, following my suggestion, to Dévoué Rabonnir. For tactical reasons it was only possible to be alone with my angelic Dévoué during the days when Siegel was shooting the little footage that didn't include her. We'd rendezvous on the occasional afternoon in my room in the house on the corner of First and Samuel. At night she stayed with the protective Consuela in their suite at Hollywood's Garden of Osiris. In fear of the influenza epidemic, Miss Heimenhoff had insisted that her personal physician, Dr. Church, accompany them from San Francisco to Los Angeles. He was handsome, adroit, intelligent, witty, composed, and financially secure. In other words, he was despicable. But at least he didn't speak French and was, much to my satisfaction, beginning to annoy Angel by persistently insisting that she not go to Paris. When, as she rose from my bed to dress, I asked her if the doctor had ever examined her, she scolded me, and I interpreted her outburst of indignation as a ploy to avoid answering the question and, as such, as a confession that she had, indeed, been intimate with the Gentile. When I sarcastically inquired as to whether or not he was circumcised, she left the room, slamming the door behind her. Contrary to natural impulse, I did not run after her to beg forgiveness and vow eternal love. "Ignorant of ourselves," I remembered, "we beg often our own harms, which the wise powers deny us for our good." I didn't see her again for several days, not until the filming of the climax. I was on the set with the cobra that would take the life of the most desirable woman who had ever lived, the mysterious being for whose sake angels would gladly surrender their wings and gods their immortality. With eyes languorously opening and closing and moist lips trembling, a fearless Cleopatra caressed the snake, kissed a spreading hood, and rose for the dance of death. The beauty before me, like the love within me, was too vicious to endure. Walking off the set, I did not see the scene until the premiere at Liplinger's. I watched Angel, sitting several rows in front of me, between Siegel and Heimenhoff, watching herself as Dévoué Rabonnir play Cleopatra. I thought her death would be the end. But then suddenly Octavius appeared. Gloating over the body of my beloved, he raised his sword triumphantly and there was a title: "A sacrifice to the gods of Rome! Hail, Augustus Caesar! Long live the Roman Empire!" The audience gasped as the sword swiped down across Yentsele's neck and the scapegoat's head rolled across the black and white linoleum squares that were supposed to pass for marble. Close up, there was more surprise than terror in the goat's eyes. Blood streaming from the mouth and neck formed a puddle around the severed head. One eye blinked as if some portion of the brain was still alive. "The End."

	The Great War ended, to my chagrin. The treaty signed by the
29	delegates of the German and Allied governments broke my heart,
	as the Armistice, reuniting so many lovers, separated me from
	mine. When Angel left for the very place whence homesick Amer-

ican boys were returning to the arms of their sweethearts, I was wounded and
maimed, a casualty of first love. Peace was irksome for my whole family. Séances
went out of fashion as fewer American deaths overseas meant fewer spirits
needing to be contacted by the folks back home. Siegel, however, promised my
mother the part of Betsy Ross in his proposed epic *America!,* a movie that he
was confident would do for democracy what *Torah* ("if it weren't for the big-
ots") might have done for religion and what *Cleopatra* ("if it weren't for the
bluenoses") might have done for love. Even though the epic Egyptian romance
had been a complete bust, Consuela Heimenhoff was happy to invest in yet another Siegel oeuvre, for it did, much to Miss Heimenhoff's gratification, win an
honorary service award from the California State Bureau of Licensing's Division for the Driving of Motorized Vehicles. After filming the decapitation of his
pet, Siegel, preparing the offering of that "male goat without blemish" in strict
adherence to the Levitical directives, had presumed that the sacrifice of
Yentsele, "whom I loved no less than Abraham loved Isaac," would move the
Lord of Israel to answer his ardent prayers for box office redemption. "But at
least God has given me you," Siegel, according to Angel, had said in proposal of
marriage to Consuela Heimenhoff: "You are my balm in Gilead." The end of
the war was as much of a blow to my father as it was to my mother and to me.
Without a government paycheck for training Yankee Eagles in aeronautic
marksmanship, my father had to take agricultural work, using *Amuriel* to spray
citrus groves with a poison that, developed for use on German infantrymen,
proved lethal to American fruit flies. He needed cash to remodel his Curtiss Eagle, to lighten its body and lower the oxygen intake ratio on the Cobra engine,
so that *Amuriel,* the mechanical Angel of Love, could set the world's altitude
record. In hopes of seeing Angel, I flew along with him up to Camp Corvus in
Santa Chingada, near San Francisco, for a military memorial ceremony being
held for those "valiant sons of California" who had sacrificed their lives for
America. My father had been invited to deliver a eulogy for his squadron of
students, all ten of whom had perished during the war. None of them had ever
actually left California: the six who had survived the four who had died when
their Curtiss Jennies collided over the Santa Culebra fairground went down together. My father had been training them in deflection shooting, using a ma-

chine gun mounted on the starboard side of the fuselage, when intelligence reports revealed that the Germans were testing a synchronized interrupter gear that connected gun and engine so that bullets could be fired straight ahead through the propeller without striking the blades. Without consulting my father, Colonel Bladud, looking for a simpler approach to forward fire, calculated that, given the rotational velocity of his Jennies' propellers and the firing speed of his Vickers machine guns, no more than one out of ten bullets would hit the propeller, and that these could be deflected by mounting steel protector plates on the props' jeopardized areas. Climbing into the cockpit of the Jenny to test his hypothesis, Colonel Bladud curled a finger gently around the trigger of the machine gun, stared through the translucent circle of spinning propeller into the pile of hay bales against the wall of the hangar that was his target, and squeezed. Hopeful that soon they would be blasting Fokkers out of European skies through the propellers of their own Jennies, the six aviators watched in avid anticipation. When Bladud, after firing a full round of deafening artillery, rose up in the cockpit, fanning the smoke of gunfire from his eyes, he had the empirical results of the test: six out of the six patriotic pilots were dead, their uniformed bodies riddled with ricocheted bullets. In a letter published in *Liberty Bell,* the commander of the United Army Air Service praised the boys for their heroism and reassured Colonel Bladud that the Army in no way held him responsible for the tragedy. "You had the guts to take a risk," the commander wrote from Washington just a month before the Armistice: "Even though it didn't turn out as well as it could have, we can't get discouraged. We've got be willing to take risks if we're going to vanquish the diabolical Hun. Taking risks has made America what it is." Without mentioning Colonel Bladud's ballistics experiment in the eulogy, my father used his old-time bally skills to bring tears to the eyes and goose bumps to the flesh of his audience. Not having seen Angel for over a month, I was antsy to get to the Heimenhoff estate, and my father insisted on coming with me. After a brief detainment in the mansion's reception hall, an elderly Negro butler informed us that, although we could not be presently received, we were "cordially invited to join Miss Heimenhoff, Miss Rabonnir, and Mr. Siegel at eight o'clock at the Coit Theater for a public lecture to be followed by supper at the Explorers' Club." They arrived in a black-and-yellow Lincoln Brougham driven by Miss Heimenhoff, whom Siegel had cured of autophobia. Leaping out of the vehicle from his place in the front seat next to his fiancée, the director threw his arms around my father and kissed him on both cheeks. My rival in love, Dr. Church, emerging from the back, held out his hand as if Angel needed help getting out of a car. The shimmering silk of her stocking, exposed as her foot touched the pavement, closed my eyes and opened the gates of memory. I watched my hands slowly rolling the hosiery down her leg from the thigh, and then the other stocking, and then, when she said my name, my eyes opened and I saw the newly bobbed hair, a fringe of gingery gold from under the rim of her cinnamon cloche hat, fox fur around her neck, and her face, the rosy cheeks that, without rouge but flush with love, had rested against my chest, and the glistening lips that, without lipstick but wet with kisses, had whispered sweet words that I longed to hear again and again. Ushering us into the theater, Consuela seated Siegel and Angel on either side of herself, Church next to Angel, my father next to him, and me on the end. Hardly able to pay attention to the lecture, I persistently leaned forward for the sight of Angel's shoes and ankles extending out from under the creamy lace trim of her beige satin dress. Glances gave license to elaborations of the amorous curbside reverie and transport: slowly I lifted the lace above her knees, up to the slender waist, to use my teeth to undo the bow of pink ribbon on pure white underlinens as hands caressed supple thighs. My eyes were closed when the lecturer, recounting his adventures in Himalayan kingdoms, pointed to the greatly enlarged photographs of the footprints of the Abominable Snowman that he had published some years before in *Life* magazine. Consuela Heimenhoff, a donor to the speaker's Yeti Research Fund, had been proud to introduce him: "It gives me great pleasure to present the world-renowned scholar, explorer, and mesmerist, Major L. A. Wheedle, director of the Pan-American Institute for the Scientific Investigation of the Incredible, comptroller of the International Society of Animal Magnetists, field commander of the Eagle Scouts, and adventure editor of *Boys' Life* magazine!" Touring the country to raise money for another expedition to the Himalayas, Major Wheedle presented evidence for the existence of a hairy primate "known as *Pilogigantopedopithecus* to scientists, Yeti to the Lamas of Tibet, Berti to the Sherpas of Nepal, and Abominable Snowman to the layman." I didn't get a moment to talk to Angel until the reception at the Explorers' Club. And then it was furtive. Apologizing with a frown that it was impossible for us to be alone later that night, then promising with a hasty smile to meet me outside the western gate of Camp Corvus early the next morning, she warned me that she'd have to be back in Pacific Heights by twilight. As my father had ceremonial obligations to the deceased throughout the day, I counted on taking Angel to the transportable hut in which my father and I were housed, a plywood and corrugated sheet-metal box furnished with a bunk bed, equipped with a Bible, and decorated with a framed photograph of Woodrow Wilson. The eyes of the president of the United States followed me up the ladder into the top bunk where the lithe aerialist lay naked. The United States Army Air Service Marching Band, playing "The Star-Spangled Banner" loudly for the deafened dead, provided a gallant beat and triumphant rhythm for young bodies alive and electrified with desire. Military blankets, like tangled banners waving in midmorning's pearly light, were kicked away and fell to the floor, exposing our nakedness to the president. With syncopated breath, staccato groan and simper, the soft sighs of gobbling mouths, closed eyes reopening full of bright stars and pleasure's first gleaming; with loins flaunting desire, and hands scaling yearning ramparts of flesh as if in perilous fight as love-aching limbs so proudly were flailed like broad stripes, all twisted and wet, with sweet sweat so gallantly streaming; I saw the moist socket's red glare and heard the bombs bursting in her hair as muffled whispers—"I love you"—gave proof through the day that our hearts were still there. Then the band played "Oh To Be Remembered" and Angel urged me to descend the ladder and fetch the bottle of champagne from her bag. Waiting until the pop of the cork, with her head resting on her hands as she looked down at me from the bunk, she said it: "I'm leaving for Paris tomorrow, Isaac. I'll miss you. I'm taking that game of snakes and ladders with me, the one you gave me when I left for Maine. Remember? It always makes me think of you. Let's try not to be sad. Pour the champagne. Château d'Amour. And I know what that means now. Let's drink to first love. But please, Isaac, don't make it difficult. Let's drink to the future, too, to the true love that each of us, somewhere, someday, will surely find." I didn't shed a tear until three days later. I was alone in my room. I smiled when I thought about it: Dévoué Rabonnir had landed on a square in which there was a tall ladder and she was ascending it with her usual grace, climbing all the way up to Paris where she would understand all the beautiful words that would be whispered to her in French. I was in a different square, and suddenly I cried out. A snake had bitten me and the venom burned. I groaned and doubled over in fear that I was about to die.

30 The serpent was no metaphor, nor the venom love. I had been caught by surprise. The diminutive harlequin was so diffident by nature that if I'd drop a live mouse into his cage, he'd hide his head beneath his own coiled body as if the prey were predatory. I had to kill the mice for Caesar. Seemingly soothed by the warmth of my hand, he had always allowed me handle him. It must have been a lingering scent of mouse that triggered the strike. True instincts are uncontrollable. With a snap of the stunning crimson and yellow head, he bit into the skin between the thumb and forefinger of my left hand. Then releasing, whipping and writhing open-mouthed out of my grip, splattered with the eruptions of blood, he fell to the floor and disappeared beneath my bed. As if flaring fires of venom had cauterized the punctures from within, the blood flow stopped as the swelling bruise and bleeding gums began. I don't remember screaming. There was the slow opening of a curtain behind which Samoo the Amazing Snake Boy of Hindustan S'd his way through a humid jungle, lushly overgrown with lavishly fragrant flowers that glistened with silvery mists and golden honeys. Then I remember vomiting and seeing a series of tournequets tied at intervals up my arm. Turning my head, I saw Cleopatra on a burnished throne, an undulating cobra sucking at her naked breast, its flexing jaws concealing the nipple. She smiled languidly as she exposed the other breast to offer a taste of the milk that began to drip from it, and I might have drunk if I had not started vomiting again. My skull seemed about to explode and I heard incomprehensible languages spoken by people whose faces I couldn't discern through the film over my eyes. The full moon behind Angel on the taut hemp rope made a silhouette of the dancing figure as she sang, *"Pour me posséder, les serpents veulent être anges . . ."* Tightly gripping fingers were stretching my arms above my head, tugging on them, then forcing them back down to my sides, then pulling again, and at the same time large hands were compressing my chest and releasing in rapid succession. Madame Endor was crying and Little India laughing. I distinguish what I imagine to have experienced inside my stupor from what I imagine to have happened in the outside world by presuming that the painful was real and that pleasures were dreamed. Consciousness was nausea, vertigo, acidic tears, burning muscles, frozen joints, blistered gums, crusted nostrils, gasping for breath and choking on it. The delirium, all golden glow and soothing softness, was where Angel waited to breathe her warm spirit into me. In a few days, I was awake and sitting up in bed. Though a Jewish doctor attributed my revival to ammonia, strychnine, and atropine, Ganesh Bannerjee, who had rushed to my bedside as soon as he heard about the bite, credited it to arcane Hindu incantations that he had murmured into my ear. When my mother ascribed the cure to her prayers and the application of bankis, my father said with a sigh, "We were just lucky." It didn't please me that Bannerjee had trapped and killed Caesar, but I understood that the slaughter of the serpent had served to console my parents, as if the sacrifice of the assailant had some magical power to revive the victim. One day during my recuperation, Bannerjee had to flee our house in fear of Joseph Siegel, who assaulted the Indian for having betrayed him by permitting his animals to work in D. W. Griffith's new picture, *The Idol Dancer.* With the director in pursuit (and my parents yelling, "Stop!"), Bannerjee shot up the stairs to take refuge in my room. As Siegel pounded on the locked door, screaming, "Let me in, you dirty little sepoy *gazlinr!*," I opened the trapdoor and lowered the black padded ladder so that Bannerjee could descend into our séance room and make his escape from there. When I finally unlocked my door for the raving Siegel, after looking in my closet and under the bed, he asked where the Hindu animal trainer was. "What Hindu animal trainer?" I asked in return. No doubt wondering whether or not his habitual intake of cocaine, morphine, marijuana, and alcohol might have allowed him to hallucinate a confrontation with Ganesh Bannerjee, the director looked puzzled. "Well, whatever. It's *nisht aheen, nisht ahear,*" he exclaimed, laughed, and explained that, in any case, he had come about *America!* My father, in dire need of money to finish the rebuilding of his plane, agreed (on the condition that he did not have to appear on horseback) to be President George Washington. I was offered the part of young George, the boy who roamed the Virginia woods, surveyed the Shenandoah Valley, and fell in love with a girl named Martha. "We need to get started right away," the director said. "I've got to finish the movie by Pesach. That's when I promised Consuela that we'd go Paris. She misses the girl. And we're going to get married on the top of the Eiffel Tower." Since I was not afraid of horses, I had to appear on horseback in almost every scene to compensate for the fact that General Washington never did. Siegel had hired the equestrienne Carmen Zambra to manage the horses in the film. I remembered her from both *Torah* and the Durbar of Delhi, in which she had portrayed Mumtaz Mahal, Indian Queen of Bareback Riders. Both because of the scandalous statutory rape trial and because it was in his professional interest to marry Consuela Heimenhoff, Siegel had supposedly terminated his intimacy with the girl. But the breakup had been amicable enough for her to work for him. Carmen didn't hear me enter the stable. As she curried the flanks of the massive roan, the strong strokes of her arm, radiating down her back, made her buttocks (the naked curve and cleavage of which were imaginable through the cling of the Sears & Roebuck blue denim work overalls) churn.

The horse's muscles twitched under the brush. I felt a spontaneous impulse to approach her from behind, press my stomach against her back, reach around her waist, clasp my hands together, and kiss her softly on the neck, just to see what she'd do and how I'd feel. Instead I just said, "Hello." Lackadaisically turning, she looked me up and down. "Oh, yeah, young George Washington, the boy who never lied. I'm supposed to give you riding lessons." Turning back to the horse, she brushed and curried as she talked: "I heard a snake bit you a couple of weeks ago. At least you're still alive. If you work with animals, you've got to take the risk of getting hurt. My Joe's with the heiress now, and they're going to get married. So what? Sure it hurt. But, like I said, you've got to take the risk. I heard your girl's gone to Paris. Joe told me. Was she your first? I don't mean just sex. I mean love, too. Was she your first love?" Apparently uninterested in my answer, Carmen continued: "Joe was my first and so I thought it would be hard to let him go. But it wasn't. I cried for about ten minutes. But that was that. I don't have any regrets. A girl's first love should be an older man. Now I'm kinda curious about younger fellas, boys more my own age. What do you think? I mean about first love? What kind of girls do you like?" She turned around to face me again. "I don't know," I muttered and awkwardly fabricated an excuse to leave the stable: "I promised my father I'd be at the airstrip. Would you like to come flying with us sometime?" She said no, that she was afraid of heights, and then asked what frightened me. "Nothing," I said, and she laughed. "Everybody's afraid of something. What about snakes? And are you afraid of girls?" She had begun to unbutton her red-and-black-striped shirt before I could answer. While making love to her, I closed my eyes and allowed myself to imagine that she was Angel. But then, frightened by my success, afraid that for the rest of my life any woman whom I might embrace would be only my first love, I opened my eyes to gaze at the naked girl beneath me and whisper, "Carmen, Carmen." That her eyes remained closed, that there were tears on her cheeks, and that she did not make a sound, made me suspect that she was allowing herself to pretend that I was Siegel. There was, I sensed, still something going on between them, and I suppose that it was to make him jealous that she later told him about us. He warned me not to do it again. "If it's pussy you want, just tell me. I've got lots for you. Not low-class koorves, you understand, but movie actresses! Jewish or Gentile, milchig or fleishig, whatever you want, but just keep that eager little putz of yours away from Carmen. What kind of women do you like?" I said it again: "I don't know." After falling in love with Martha there was nothing more for young George Washington to do in *America!* It was my father's turn to be the father of our country. For the first time in my life I was bored. Perhaps it because of the boredom and because I couldn't think of anything else I wanted to do that I quite impulsively decided to go to India. I had thought about it before and had earned enough money as George Washington to pay for passage. I reckoned that the exuberant Bannerjee, whose life I had recently saved and who thought that he had also saved mine, could arrange for me to be welcomed in his homeland. Much to my surprise, my mother and father, though well aware of how much they'd miss me, put up no opposition. It was time for me to leave home. When my mother produced the birth certificate that I needed for a passport, I asked my father why it indicated that I had been born in Los Angeles, when he had always claimed that I was born on the shores of the Dead Sea. "We had to forge a fake certificate," he solemnly swore, "to get you into the country." He accompanied me to the San Pedro dock, where he kissed me on both cheeks and told me to "try to have a few laughs." I had kissed my mother good-bye outside the house on First and Samuel, where she cried the sweet tears of maternal affection. Soon after I had left, she wrote a letter that must have traveled, at least part of the way, by air, because it was waiting for me at the Bannerjee house when I arrived in Calcutta a month later. In it my mother informed me that, in an attempt to set the world's altitude record, my father's plane had fallen back to earth. Avraham ben Menachem Schlossberg had perished, and no one, except the deceased aviator himself, knew whether or not he had been successful in ascending higher than any other human being before him. My grief was slowly tempered by a gradual gladness that at least he had gone down with his beloved *Amuriel,* the way I try to imagine he would have wanted to go, without ever having to suffer the humiliating infirmities and disgraceful decrepitude that would inescapably have been his lot were he still alive today.

31	Unaware that rolls of dice and sea would someday return me to the volcanic islands in the middle of nowhere, where right now I write this, I had no inclination to linger long enough in Honolulu to make a square of it at the time.

The only recollected passengers aboard the sugar freighter from San Pedro are the family from Alaska and Morris Mendelssohn (whom I probably would have forgotten if I hadn't run into him again here on the beach), now Merry Moe of Maui, crooning emcee at the Royal Hawaiian Luau Lollapalooza each Sunday and cantor at Temple Beth Aloha on Saturdays. He had introduced himself to me on the forecastle of the *Alexandria*'s upper deck as "the grandson of Felix Mendelssohn, the great composer, great-grandson of Moses Mendelssohn, the great philosopher, great-great-grandson of Israel Mendelssohn, the great Cabalist, great-great-great-grandson of Hermes Mendelssohn, the great alchemist, and so on all the way back to Canaan." He was Hawaii-bound to manifest a genetically destined genius by learning to play the ukulele and accomplishing for that instrument and its repertoire what his forefathers had done for their own respective obsessions. Inspiration to perpetuate the Mendelssohn legacy had come in consultation with the clairvoyant Madame Endor of Santa Monica. She had divined that he'd cash in on his inherited grandfather's musical talent on a tropical isle. I spent time on deck with the Littler family from Alaska, a father and mother with their son, Larry. Examining young Larry, who had been shot in the head with a Luger at the battle of Champs-Labitte, doctors had declared it too risky to attempt removal of the bullet which had rendered the doughboy blind and deaf. Larry's senses of touch, smell, and taste were, however, perfectly intact, "and he's bright as a button," Mom gloated. They were taking him to a clement Hawaii with its fragrant flowers and sweet pineapples. "We're hopin' to find him a Polynesian wahine with a grass skirt around plump hips and a floral lei over big soft boobs," Dad said, winking: "and she's gotta be able to cook. We reckon there are lots of ugly girls without much to say who'd jump at the chance of gettin' hitched to a feller who can't see or hear, particularly one who's a decorated veteran of the United States Infantry. And we've got plenty of money to sweeten the pot." For someone who had no idea of where he was, when it was, who he was with, or why it was so dark and quiet, Larry was remarkably merry. "You got nothing to complain about so long as you got your health," he'd snicker. He loved to eat, drink, and smoke, and talking also greatly pleased him. "As I was saying," he'd begin, and, with no knowledge of who might be listening, he'd usually talk about sex, reminiscing blithely over

amorous wartime adventures with French demimondaines, and enthusiastically delineating how he would proceed when and if God answered his prayers
for an opportunity to get back to them. He loved to tell dirty jokes even though
the punch lines would invariably cause him to laugh so powerfully that he'd
convulse. Tears rolled down his cheeks as he struggled to subdue the spasms
and catch his breath. He'd always recover, dry his eyes with his sleeve, and ask,
"Do you get it?" Death made him chortle as uproariously as sex. Reminiscing
lightheartedly over hand-to-hand combat with German soldiers, he'd tell just
what he'd do, and how he'd do it, if and when God gave him the chance to return to battle. One afternoon, a day out of Honolulu, Mr. Littler took me
aside. "It would be a mighty big favor to me, if you'd sit with our boy for a little while so the missus and I can be alone in our cabin, if you get my drift. We
thought we'd be able to do it with him in the room since he can't see or hear.
But, no, it's just too darn distractin' because he talks all the time. And my wife
fears that God might suddenly answer her prayers and our boy will recover his
eyesight and see us doin' it." Once I had consented, the father instructed me to
"reach over and poke him every once in a while, particularly if he stops talkin'.
If you go too long without touchin' him, he'll think he's alone. And when he
thinks he's alone he begins, as the Bible calls it, 'breakin' wind.' And if you
don't poke him as soon as those gassers start, then my boy is damn sure he's
alone. And that's when he starts, if you'll pardon my French, jackin' off. That's
why we need to find a girl for him: masturbation's bad for mental health." As
long as I remembered to poke Larry, I enjoyed his company. The same cannot
be said for Mr. S——, a disagreeable character with whom I was constrained to
share a cabin on the steamer to Canton. Although imposingly intelligent and
strikingly handsome, he was a heartless person, the first truly wicked creature
I had ever met. Just as I refuse to write about the great influenza epidemic that
killed Tsipora Gotlober and more than one Adam Adamantine, I refuse to
write about this individual, who, on several occasions later in my life, again
tried to trespass this book. I have barred him from our game because he will
not play by the rules. The unpleasantness of being cooped up with Mr. S——
was, however, mitigated by the delight of an unexpected encounter between
Canton and Singapore. We were aboard a nine-thousand-ton liner originally
named the *Siegfried* but rechristened the S.S. *Buffalo Bill* after being captured
from the Germans in 1918. Although she could barely manage thirteen knots,
she was strong enough to carry as many passengers as there are mitzvoth in the
Torah. As a third-class passenger I would not have met the first-class traveler
had it not been for my developing appreciation of alcoholic beverages. I was
drinking vodka highballs in the men's saloon, where "Caucasian gentlemen of
all classes may commingle for refreshment," when I heard the barman ask,

"Champagne, Professor Yesnovitch?" Unable to restrain my excitement, I took the liberty of introducing myself to the renowned herpetologist whose *Thantophidia Indica* had meant more to me than any Bible. Grasping my left hand in his right and raising it toward his eyes, he inspected the scar through a smudged pince-nez and frowned. *"Micrurus elegans?"* Whereas I had imagined the author of my favorite book to be lean and serious, he was in reality large and jocose. Over drinks, I amused him with tales of Samoo the Amazing Snake Boy of Hindustan, and he in turn entertained me with an account of Huang-ting Ching buns in Shanghai: "Stuffed with cobra testicles and spiced with ginger, licorice, and cassia, they are always steamed, never fried. My host, a mandarin of subtle tastes, having extolled the aphrodisiac properties of the delectable dumplings, advised limiting myself to three. He recalled witnessing the spontaneous combustion of a Buddhist monk in Peking who had consumed no more than five. Two of my host's host of concubines were introduced as he excused himself so, he said, that I might empirically assay the potency of the amorous appetizers. Although the Oriental attributed the felicitous results of my experimentation to the dumplings, I was, as a scientist, inclined to credit the nubile Celestials who subsequently assisted me in a similar testing of *Panax quinquefolium* infused with a distillation of cobra venom. The Chinese avouch the erotogenic qualities of deadly substances." On the day we docked in Singapore, Professor Yesnovitch graciously provided me with a letter of introduction to a Dr. Anthony McCloud of Bengal: "Less interested in the venereal potentials of venom than in it's toxicity, the doctor detests snakes. He is, nevertheless, a dear man." I embarked for Calcutta aboard the *Aphrodite,* a forty-year-old merchant ship built for the Indian trade in Greenwich with one funnel, two masts, and a groaning iron hull. With no more than six of us in Christian class, most of the passengers, being Chinese or Malays, were confined to the Oriental hold. On the first night out, no sooner had an irascible tropical gale stormed the Strait of Malacca than Captain Plato Boeotion cheerfully challenged me to a game of pool in the smoking cabin. Aiming a moving cue ball at rolling target balls when you can hardly keep your balance (let alone your dinner down) on a ship that seems pitched in battle against bellicose troops of waves is a challenge. Enormous oceanic battering rams pummeled the vessel on all fronts. While a sudden shower of sea spray sharply rattled the window like machine-gun fire, a brutal blow to the bow so powerfully pitched the boat that, just as I dropped my cue to stay afoot by catching hold of the table, all of the remaining balls were tipped into the corner pocket. "You win," the mariner laughed as I vomited into a receptacle provided for that purpose. "Let's drink to victory. It's not who wins the game that matters, as I always say, but who buys the drinks. That's my philosophy. Well, not my whole philosophy, not my big one, which is made of many interrelated little philosophies. By the way, hope you don't mind my asking, but what's your philosophy?" Too seasick to accept the whiskey that he poured for me, I had to confess to not having one. "You've got to have a philosophy. That's what I always say. But I'm Greek and I'm not called Plato for nothing. Listen, young feller, you've got to get yourself a philosophy before we dock in India because in the Orient you especially need a good philosophy to make any sense of things. Are you sure you don't want a whiskey?" I had to excuse myself and go to my cabin, where I could lie down in the dark. By morning the sea was calmer and I was sufficiently recovered to go out on deck and look out across an expanse of moody ocean. "It's not who goes to bed sick that matters, as I always say," the captain chuckled as he joined me for a breath of air, "but who it is that wakes up well. That's my philosophy. Speaking of which, have you come up with your philosophy yet?" I had to admit that I hadn't. "I'd suggest that you start with one that's already been worked out and proved to be true." I promised to adopt his philosophy as my own, whatever it was, and to live my life by it. "No, no, mine is far too complicated for a beginner." I asked if he might suggest one suitable for a novice, perhaps something Greek. "Well, as Heraclitus always used to say," he began enthusiastically, "all is change and only change is real. The universe is in constant flux and everything is continuously passing away. That's Heraclitus' philosophy. How do you like it? It could come in mighty handy in India, at least until you can come up with a better one of your own."

32 India was chthonic theater: the overture was a snake show. Ships, boats, and barges were galleries around a proscenial dock as an invisible curtain opened and a harsh sweep of searing wind, fetid and fragrant, wiped across my face. There was a voluminous swell in the raucous roar and stevedoric anthem of the jetties and piers: pandemonial moans, hapless laughter, coolies' complaints, captains' commands, scoldings, curses, a crash, grind, and hectic clitter-clatter. Suddenly rising above it was the sharp *rat-a-tat-tat* rataplan of the hourglass-shaped snare that ferociously dancing Shiva plays. His throat, engorged with azure poisons and garlanded with laughing skulls, was necklaced with gaping-mouthed, fanged, and hissing serpents. Snakes, the god's armlets, bracelets, and anklets too, his sacred thread, belt, and bowstring, were writhing entwined as scaly tendrils in his wild matted locks. The rattling timbal had evoked his likeness in a rumpled canopy of swollen, ash-colored clouds that teased a tired earth with promises and threats of storms. Drum-snared and trance-formed, I was on the verge of a new life, eager, awed, hopeful, and afraid. Agitating the perfumes of India (masala, sandalwood, gasoline, feces, ganja, flower garlands, and tropical sicknesses), the heat was hallucinatory. The stage below was set with bamboo baskets, an open box of amulets, bundled herbs, bottled potions, a brass bowl of milk, and a clay chillum. An orange turban was wrapped around the wobbling head of the hero, gray-bearded like a mendicant. He was costumed in a black lungi and shirtless, adorned with necklaces of snake vertebrae and rosaries of beads that were the eyes of god, all magic signs of a camaraderie with the Lord of Serpents. There was a jewel, dark as a clot of blood, in the snakeman's ring. Squatting before the baskets with feet firmly flat, the enchanter took up the instrumental badge of his trade: a gourd with two reeded flutes fixed in it with black beeswax, encrusted with glistening pieces of mirror, cowrie shells, coins, and broken bits of bangle. Swaying in reptilian turns and bows to the primordial music, its hypnotic drone all whine and moan, the charmer's eyes, set close and open wide with ecstatic gaze, met mine, lingered momentarily, and then grazed on. A supporting actor with silver earrings and a black turban rattled Shiva's drum. The melodious score, infinitely repetitious of and in itself, echoed sex. The sky reeked of it; the earth creaked with it; the sea swelled with it. India burned with sex. And helplessly I ached with it. When one of the snake-wallah's hands left the holes on the instrument to flip back the top of the largest basket, the boy removed the sinuously august python with its doglike head, its scaled skin emblazoned with grayish-black-outlined diamonds and stripes of buff, a lugubrious king, fearless and languid. The snake charmer looked up at me on the bulwark of the *Aphrodite* and shouted, "This esnake, Ajgar from Rishikesh. Big junglee! Very estrong. Very wise one." And he took up the tune again, slowing to let it capture the undulant movements of the majestic serpent. There was a gray jester to the king: "This esnake, Domuhi. Two heads, one each end, this and that." Tying the creature into a knot and rolling it on the ground, the charmer laughed. "No knowing which way going. And you, Saab?" Another basket lid was knocked off, and another, and, as the vertiginous music recommenced, hooded lovers rose and fell in time. "This esnake, Nag," the snake charmer grandly announced and then introduced the more dreadfully and exquisitely lethal female: "This esnake, Nagin. Husband, wife. Very poison. Very beauty!" And the stunning snakes danced to the arresting drone of the *bin* with mythic grace, necks fanned anger-wide into spectacle-marked hoods that augured pain, delirium, and death. Provoked by the charmer's hand, they struck, missed and hissed, and took up again the dance. Intrepidly the snakeman held them up in splendid adoration: "Nag and Nagin are remembering everything. I let go. Then they are telling and telling other esnakes in junglee if this feringhee man is giving the good baksheesh. If yes or no, they will esay. If you are giving to Shankarji's esnakes, you are the esafe man, never bitten. Never! But if no, then big esnake trouble in this India. India is esnake." I threw down all the coins I had from Honolulu, Canton, and Singapore. Over the snake charmer's laughter, I heard the shout: "Is that Mr. Isaac?" The man, wearing a striped linen jacket, boater hat, bleached dhoti, and leather sandals, waved excitedly. "Is it you?" hollered Kumar Bannerjee. At the behest of his younger brother, Ganesh, he welcomed me to India. The snake charmers packed up, counted their money, lit their chillums, returned the snakes to their baskets, and suspended those coffers with hemp ties from bamboo poles across their shoulders. They disappeared into the dockyard jungle of cranes, crabs, erectors, dredgers, and bins of jute, saltpeter, indigo, and tea. Suddenly and apprehensively wondering why I had come, I made my way down the gangway to tentatively place my foot on Indian ground. Captain Boeotion waved good-bye as Kumar Bannerjee hollered hello: *Svagatam!* Welcome to India! Welcome to Bengal! Welcome to Calcutta! Welcome to everywhere!" Bearers dealt with my trunk and bag while the beaming babu coerced me into the grimy seat of the rickety rickshaw of a scrawny, barefoot, old human animal who wheezed, coughed, and drenched himself in sweat as he struggled to haul us into urchin-pariah-beggar-leper-scoundrel-clamorous streets, steaming, stinking, and strident. "Calcutta," my host smiled proudly. "Paris of the East. Yes, just like Paris. But no Eiffel Tower as yet." The former capital was, he boasted, the city of Kali, the bloodthirsty goddess whose ears are ornamented with dead infants, whose neck is garlanded with human heads, and whose loins are girdled with severed arms. Her terrible visage, he promised, would become beautiful to me once I made Calcutta home: "In her ghoulish screeching you will hear the sweetest songs. Once you give yourself to her and love her, you will never feel fear or sadness." He laughed again. "Only delight!" That delight was insinuated by the girls and women of the bustee, balancing clay pots and burlap bales upon their heads, with perfect posture and graceful gait, wrapped in red, green, and blue saris, with golden earthy ochre skin, naughty smiles and curious eyes, naked bellies and feet, jingling jewelry on ears, necks, arms, ankles, and toes. Every sense was electrified. Head and heart, like sky and earth, were spinning, and Mr. Bannerjee never stopped talking. "The home of the illustrious Bannerjee brothers is your home, Mr. Isaac, and you may stay forever." There were four of them: Ganesh Bannerjee, who represented Bannerjee Brothers International Menagerie in America; Nagendra Bannerjee, who as a consequence of a persistent participation in the National Noncooperation Cooperative spent most of his time "caged up like an animal" in jail; Albert Francis Charles Augustus Emmanuel Bannerjee, the youngest, a taxidermist; and my host, the eldest brother, Kumar Bannerjee, who reminded me of Jake Grossman even on that first day, several months before he said, "Buffalo Bill was a *bahenchuth.*" I guessed the word was Bengali for "shmuck." The Wild West showman had apparently advertised in the Calcutta newspapers for sepoy cavalrymen to appear in his Rough Riders of the World Congress of 1896. "I was twenty-one years old at the time and damn great at taming and training horses, women, and other wild creatures." After being signed, Kumar Bannerjee was subsequently canceled when Buffalo Bill "was advised by Yehudi accountants to save some money by putting turbans on Apaches. It's just as well," an ever cheerful Kumar said, laughing. "My late, great father, retiring from his veterinary practice that very year to start the then 'Bannerjee & Sons Magnificent Menagerie' under the patronage of His Highness the Maharaja of Diwanasthan, needed my assistance (it wasn't called '& Sons' for nothing)." As soon as we arrived at the family villa off Chitpur Road, before I met the other members of the household, Bannerjee handed me the letter from my mother. Watching me read it, he softly asked what was wrong. When I said, "Nothing," he knew it was something and took me to a room that he said would be mine as long as I wanted it, "or even much longer." He left me alone, absolutely alone, more alone than I had ever been. Sitting on the edge of my new bed, I looked at the garish print on the wall, a portrait of the bucolic god Krishna dancing amidst serpents with the heads of girls, charming those winsome mistresses of Kaleeya with his flute. I could hear women's voices in nearby rooms, and I wondered what had prompted me to come to India. I supposed it was chance, a roll of the die, a snake eye. I reread the letter and waited for tears. Nothing. I read it again and still my eyes were dry. I got up to rummage in my trunk for the tin of Wyoming Willie's Wondrous Hair Pomade, slowly twisted off the lid, and smelled it. And right now, twenty years later, as I write this, I stop to open the same olfactory kaleidoscope, and again I smell the *Wonders of the World* variety show that was my childhood: my father's sandalwood shaving lotion, my mother's eau de lavande, the heady scents of polished leather, oiled wood, wet fur and feathers, sweat and doniker fumes, a smoky smolder of paper and elm leaves, Camel cigarettes, Blaine Havanas, gunpowder, mothballs, Macassar and mechanic's oil, fumes of lye, burning sugar, and madder, miasmic vapors of kerosene, formaldehyde, and spirit gum, of jujubes, taffies, butterscotch, falernum, and the Sabbath's chicken stewed with carrots, leeks, parsnips, and lots of pepper (and, smelling it, I taste it, hear Hebrew blessings, and see a cosmogonic flicker of twin white tapers). Amidst shifting scents, blending and separating in wild memory's effluvial patterns, I smell Angel's wet hair as she rises above me in the bath, and then the talc sprinkled on her belly, under her arms, and between her legs, all the soft folds and recesses of her body. I smell the aroma of her whispers: "I'm sorry, Isaac. I loved your father with all my heart. I'll miss him." I still see him on the bally board and hear the echo of his voice: "See Samoo the Amazing Snake Boy of Hindustan! Is he a boy with the body of snake, or a snake with the head of boy? That's for you to decide, my friends." Having been transported by the mystic power of Finkelman's Industrial Fragrance No. 11, I close the tin right now, here in Honolulu, just as I did years ago in Calcutta, and as I have done everywhere I have ever been. I close it tightly so that no memory can escape from it. Removing my father's token from the game board and folding up my mother's letter, I then closed my eyes, lay back, and recited the words that Avraham ben Menachem had asked me to remember for him and for his ancestors: *"Tzechok asah li Elohim kol-hashomea yitzachak-li.* God made laughter for me so that whoever shall hear my laughter will laugh with me." And then, I just now remember, I wept myself to sleep.

From 10

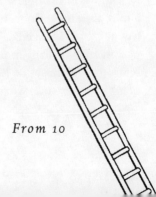

33

"This is the season of the serpent," Dr. Anthony McCloud, surgeon major of His Majesty's Bengal Army, professor emeritus of toxicology at Hooghly Medical College, warden (ret.) of Dum Dum Hospital and Asylum for Native Women, grand satrap (ex officio) of the Herpetological Society of Belfast, and president of the Royal Asiatic Croquet Sodality of Calcutta, grumbled as with considerable purpose he positioned a hefty pinch of Macouba No. 7 on the maculated skin between his left thumb and trembling forefinger: "The heat invigorates them and makes them petulant." He sniffed the pulverized tobacco into his right nostril. "Death flourishes"—his monocle fell from his eye as he blew a fantastically paroxysmal midsentence sneeze—"in summer. When the rains come, the devils creep out of their flooded burrows to bask in intermittent sun." After resneezing only a tad less exuberantly, he sighed in recovery. "That's when one steps on them, only to be bitten and die. Welcome, my boy, to the land of the serpent." Replacing his monocle to continue reading the letter of introduction, he gave his left hand shelter in the pocket of his striped trousers. "Professor Yesnovitch explains that you are somewhat of an ophidiophile. Not I, sir! No, I execrate the envenomating worm, so aptly cursed by God to crawl upon his belly consuming dust. I would send them, the fanged cobra, krait, adder, and viper, one and all, slithering into the Patala hell from whence they have come, and seal the entries to their burrows behind them, would it not, alas, but serve an increase in the population of the no less loathsome and all the more devastating *Rattus rattus*." Intent upon my participation in his serological research, he provided little opportunity to decline his offer of employment. "Whether you were sent by the one true God who watches over the Empire, or were delivered to my door by recalcitrant fate or merry chance, I do not know nor presume to conjecture. Whiskey?" He produced two black pellets from a snakeskin purse out of his paisley waistcoat pocket, dropped one in each drink, and stirred. "Opium. It's the only thing to prevent diarrhea and tropical melancholia." Folding up Yesnovitch's letter, he placed it in the breast pocket of his plaid jacket. "Vladimir is intriguing," the physician remarked on the verge of snorting up another dose of sternutatory snuff. After typhoonically sneezing, he gulped down his opiated dram, blotted his sweaty pate with the very handkerchief into which he had emptied his nose, and then recounted the history of his friendship with the enigmatic Russian professor, which had begun at a Durbar held in Delhi during McCloud's first year in India. As he spoke I looked beyond him, through louvered windows, across a jaffrey-shaded verandah into a garden, where I counted eight European women lounging in cane basket chairs beneath brightly colored tarpaulin umbrellas. A tympanic roll of nasal thunder brought my attention back to McCloud, whose right eye had focused fiercely on my face. A scrubby Scottish brow twitched above a fogged monocle: "With your assistance, Mr. Schlossberg, I shall hopefully find a polyvalent serum efficient against all species of the venomous herpetofauna of Greater Bengal. Whiskey?" Having decided on my way to India to decide nothing there, to give chance a chance and follow the rolls of unseen dice, I put up no resistance. "Opium," he noted, dropping another analgesic bullet into each of our shot glasses. "It's the only thing to prevent constipation and Oriental hebetude." As the result of a mild stroke, blamed on Calcutta's satanically conflagrant summers, the right half of his face perpetually smiled as the left half frowned. The visage suggested that Dr. McCloud, his monocle over his right eye, was pleased by what he saw before him while saddened by something within. His drooping left shoulder, mildly maladroit left arm, and slightly sluggish left leg gave an impression, more comic than sinister, that the enthusiastic right side of the body had taken charge of the left, pulling it along as he circumambulated his disorderly desk in the cluttered study where he had received me on my initial visit to the South Calcutta government estate. Pointing to the portrait that hung not quite straight between two jackal-head trophies on a wall striatedly stained with evidence of the floods of monsoons past, the doctor introduced his wife, an almost handsome lady despite a jutting Anglo-Saxon jaw, who had died of fever the previous year. When he enjoined me to walk around the room in order to determine whether or not her gaze would follow me, I, assuming that he subscribed to the aesthetic theory that such a quality is a characteristic of true art, complied and, out of courtesy, claimed that, yes, her blue eyes had observed my every move. "Oh," he sighed as the chipper right half of his face synchronized with the left in frown, "I thought it just for me. It hasn't worked with other visitors, nor any of the servants, not even with Pythia." But the right cheek perked up forthwith: "It seems that Celeste approves of you and will watch over you during your stay. In your bedroom you'll be pleased to behold a portrait of her identical to this one except for the color of the dinner dress." The gown in the study was pink, the one in my room, I would discover, blue; purple in the dining room, yellow in the card room, and green in the library, all pastel except the red one in Pythia's bedroom. In the original, from which the other six had been copied, hanging on the wall of Dr. McCloud's bedroom, Mrs. McCloud was clothed in bridal white. As my new employer, pouring another dram for each of us and once more dissolving a tarry pill in each ("It's the only thing to prevent flatulence and Asiatic fugue"), extolled the connubial virtues of his late spouse, I again looked out the window at the women whose veil-swirled sun hats in muted hues of crocus, hyacinth, wisteria, and lilac, were efflorescent garden blossoms fluttering in the sweet breezes of an idle laughter. "You will have a room, meals, a modest stipend, complimentary medical treatment, and a houcca-burdar to polish your shoes, serve your tiffin, and, most importantly, to assist you with the snakes. It's his duty to catch the rats for them to eat. Though he's not at all honest—no one out here is—he has a good heart and will neither betray you nor cause you any physical harm. Call him Ishmael. Unless you're particularly squeamish and are put off by disease, deformity, hunger, poverty, violence, corruption, mosquitos, vermin, and infernal weather, you'll find life rather pleasant in Calcutta. There's a croquet party here each Sunday after church and the Shakespeare Society meets on Wednesday evenings at Harmony Hall. At the Tollygunge Players' Club one can count on decent whiskey, a fair game of whist, fantan, or snooker, lots of news from Europe, and more than enough Calcutta gossip. In case you're equestrially inclined, the Gymkhana Club has a weekly chukker of polo and a monthly jackal hunt. My horses are never to be ridden. They're kept strictly for serum production. There's a dinner dance every other Saturday night at Charnock House, but the men far outnumber the women. Speaking of which, I must warn you to stay away from native rumjennies. Syphilis is rife in both Sonagacchi and Chinatown." As McCloud paused to inhale another noseful of snuff, I, glancing out the window, saw the women rising to disperse with amicable hugs. Mrs. McCloud soberly stared at me from between the grinning jackal heads as her husband, after three noteworthy sneezes, related that on assignment from His Royal Majesty's Commission on Death by Poisons in the Colonies he had arrived in Calcutta in 1915, the very year, I reflected, that I had been Swami Balakrishna, Prince of Snake Charmers, for the Durbar of Delhi in California. The women in the garden had disappeared by the time Dr. McCloud escorted me across the verandah with its empty planter's chairs and longsleevers. We headed for the laboratory, a converted storeroom adjoining the stable and kennel. Sunlight from its only window was obscured by an antique thermantidote encased in moldy moist tatties that did little to dispel the odor of serpents. There were nearly fifty of them in pine boxes with grimy glass tops, and even more of them pickled in formaldehyde. Both the quick and dead were labeled with their vernacular native names as well as their Linnaean designations; size, weight, habitat, prevalence, and toxicity had all been meticulously recorded. I could hear both the frantic yapping of dogs and a weary whinnying of the six former polo ponies that were regularly injected by Dr. McCloud with varied venoms to which they would slowly build up immunities. In order to breed the puppies that were methodically inoculated and envenomated to test the effectiveness of the sera, there was a retired jackal hunter, a surly male named Krishnakukkur, and nine restless females collectively referred to as the Gopis. The number was meant to ensure that at least one bitch would always be in heat, one always pregnant, and at least one nursing a litter. Uninoculated puppies were used to measure toxicity, on the basis of the amount of time it took for them to die after being bitten at the age of one month and the approximate weight of one stone. It would be my job to milk the serpents of their venom by gland compression, massage, and cannulation, to identify new snakes, to weigh, measure, and sex them, and to introduce the puppies into the snake boxes, time mortality, and monitor rates of venom regeneration. McCloud would teach me the methods for both the gross and microscopic examination, analysis, and evaluation of venom samples. "The Saperas supply the snakes. Though they are supposed to come on a regular basis, you can't count on them. In a few days I'll take you to Mayapur, their village up north, near Chandernagore." He was not surprised to hear that I had seen some of them performing at the docks: "Yes, of course, they're always there when a foreign ship comes in, counting on an innocent white sahib to offer a gratuity for their show. But that's not the only way the Sapera earns his bowl of rice. They sell snakeroot and bezoar stones to cure snakebite, and amulets and mantras to prevent them; there's a market for python skins; and frightened babus are damn sure to call the sampwallah when there's a snake loose in the house. The snake charmer, as clever as he is unscrupulous, collects his fee for catching a snake that he himself has slyly planted in the bungalow. One hears that one can hire a snake charmer to have someone murdered. They make it look like an accidental bite. And they have a reputation for being able to charm women no less than cobras with that flute of theirs. Whiskey?" Returning to the house for drink, we were greeted on the verandah by one of the women whom I had seen in the garden. "My daughter, Miss Pythia McCloud," the doctor announced. "My dear, this is Mr. Schlossberg. He shall be residing with us for a while." When I ventured a polite handshake, she stepped back. "We don't do that here," she said with a demure smile as if to begin to teach me the rules of a game of social propriety as played in the colony. Like a songbird silenced and paralyzed in fascination by a serpent, I stared mute and motionless at the beautiful girl. It was, in my assessment of how things happen to happen in my novel life, by chance that our paths had intersected. It would become her view of the game that past lives had something to do with love.

To 15

34 Like Oriental Muses, the four wives and five unmarried sisters of the Bannerjee brothers, although I had never even seen them during the week in which I was a guest in their home, piteously wailed over my good-bye. In the shadow of the huge taxidermied elephant in the magnificently dilapidated villa's central courtyard that was garishly embellished with painted carvings of Hindu gods, they huddled weeping at the venerable feet of Mother Bannerjee, who tenderly caressed them to ease the sorrow that they, out of Oriental etiquette, were constrained to demonstrate over the announcement of the departure of a total stranger. "My blessed mother would surely wish you Godspeed with adamantine nuggets of profoundest sagacity," Kumar noted with filial solemnity, "but, alas, upon the passing of my father, because we, her sons in selfish sorrow, would not permit her to immolate her good self on the funeral pyre of her late lord, she took a renunciatory vow of silence. She has not spoken for the last two years. Not a peep! Nor, furthermore, has she worn even one item of jewelry, nor eaten a single bite of food during the same period of mourning. Not one grain of rice! Allowing herself no worldly pleasures, she is immersed in the beatific bliss of a constant contemplation of her late great mate, Shri Shri Shri Bippin Phineas Bannerjee, D.V.M. Such is true love. May we all be fortunate enough to know even the paltriest pittance of such sacred love during our respective fleeting sojourns on this illusory plane of phenomenal existence." Though the ample rolls of doughy flesh hanging down from her arms and chin and squeezing out from under the tight bottom of her white choli and over the even tighter waist top of her white sari suggested to me that Mata Bannerjee was sneaking food, to her sons the chubbiness was a sign of the miraculously nourishing power of divine love. Kumar consoled the weeping women with promises that I would visit often. "This is your home whether you are here or not," Kumar and Albert announced in unison, adding that they spoke for Nagendra and Ganesh as well. "Our sorrow over your absence will at least be compensated for by the arrival of yet another illustrious American sent to us by our Ganesh, who continually provides us with foreign guests to dotingly love. We are shortly expecting no less a luminary than Miss Leona Wilder from the United States of America, a lion tamer of the highest caliber who wishes to endow her act with the Oriental flair and exotic flourish that is all the rage in Paris these days. Arriving any day now to acquire Bengal tigers from none other than us and to collect costumes and props from the bountiful bazaars of Calcutta, she will perform at the illustrious Folies-Bergère de Paris, scantily clad and thoroughly bare-bosomed in the chic French fashion, cracking her whip to bay the beasts that will vie ferociously and romantically with one another for her love and slabs of fresh meat. Ganesh has testified that Miss Wilder's breasts, putting as they do the sinus lobes on the forehead of Indra's own elephant to shame, with the support of our wild cats, promise to garner her world fame and fabulous fortune." As Ganesh Bannerjee represented the menagerie abroad, touring with its animals and booking them in stage, fair, circus shows, as well as in motion pictures, so Nagendra was in charge of the beasts at home. I didn't meet him for a while after my arrival in India, however, since he had just been arrested for a show that he had staged in the Maidan: the corgi wearing a crown was too obviously and seditiously a lampoon of the Prince of Wales, who had arrived in India a few weeks earlier. Though it was indicated that Rufus Isaacs (the Jewish viceroy of India), as well as Sir Edwin Montagu, Lord Chelmsford, and Justice Rowlatt, were also played by dogs, people were in disagreement as to which dog (the Oxford sheepdog, Yorkshire terrier, Sussex spaniel, and Shropshire setter) was which imperial figure. By anointing the corgi with the drippings of a dhole bitch in heat, Nagendra had provided the Indian public with the satiric spectacle of the British male canines attempting to mount the Prince of Wales. A herd of imported whiteface Hampshire Downs sheep (each in a different symbolic hat: pith helmet, busby, campaign cap, top hat, bowler, and shako) represented various political, mercantile, cultural, military, and religious functionaries of Raj rule in India. These animal actors were, for the amusement of the public, and to the fury of British officials, harassed by a wily little Nilgiri langur in a loincloth who must have represented Gandhi. A bear in a Lenin cap was supposedly the Communist leader Shripat Amrit Dange, and the Bengal tiger was most definitely Subhas Chandra Bose. And holy cows were the masses of India. "Nagendra's political activities are costing the Bannerjee Menagerie," Kumar complained despite the apparent prosperity of the family business. "At least we can boast that he once had the honor of sharing a cell with the Mahatma. What can we do? A brother is a brother." Bannerjee Brothers leased horses, camels, and elephants locally for wedding celebrations. On the international market, they provided sportsmen with trained otters for fishing, trained cheetahs for hunting, and trained hawks for falconry. To wealthy collectors they sold such exotic creatures as hoolocks, caracals, binturongs, flying foxes, pangolins, and dugongs. There were rhino horns and pizzles for the Chinese; tiger, leopard, and cheetah furs for the French; bear and lion skin rugs for Germans; and elephant-leg standing ashtrays for anyone who could afford one. Albert Bannerjee was responsible for the colossal stuffed pachyderm in the courtyard. Although not much older than myself, Albert was already an accomplished professional who had, he boasted, been "a child prodigy at taxidermy. I stuffed my first bird, a Himalayan kingfisher, when I was only three years old." He refused to let me leave without a guided tour of his workshop. "By the time I was ten I had stuffed fish, frogs, lizards, snakes, turtles, squirrels, rabbits, mice, two cats, and the collector's cocker. I was, I must confess if you'll but pardon my jactation, born to stuff and mount. My God-given talent came to the attention of Professor B. J. P. Basu, who arranged for a show of my work at the Bangabassi Academy Gallery of Fine Art, the Louvre of Calcutta, an exhibition of sculptures in flesh, fur, and feather that attracted the enthusiastic attention of aesthetes from around the world, including no less a luminary than our own Maharaja of Diwanasthan, who was soon to go into mourning over the death of Bill, his favorite elephant, a magnificent animal who led the Durbar of Delhi in 1902. When Bill died, the Maharaja, remembering my exhibition favorably, had an inspired idea: he would spare no expense to send me to London to perfect my skills by studying the philosophy and practice of stuffing and mounting at the Royal Academy of Taxidermical Arts and Sciences so that I could stuff Bill as beautifully and regally as he deserved. He would, furthermore, keep his beloved pet frozen in a cave in holy Badrinath, high in the Himalayas, until I returned to Calcutta." As the ebullient preparator continued to extol his own genius, I looked at the array of bones, pelts, and skulls on the workbenches. I lingered over the red-velvet-lined jewelry boxes of white porcelain teeth and glinting glass eyes of many hues and varied sizes, until Albert eagerly pulled me toward an enormous open-mouthed crocodile yet to be fit with those sharp teeth and lustrous eyes. "I am preparing this fellow for the upcoming British Empire Exhibition at Wankton-in-the-Marsh, where the muggar will be displayed next to the seventy-five pounds of jewelry that was found in his stomach." Albert's ultimate aspiration was for taxidermy to be recognized as a fine art and for him to be acclaimed as the Rabindranath Tagore of that art. "Professor Basu has written to the trustees of the Nobel Foundation in Sweden to encourage them to institute a long-overdue prize for taxidermy." He explained that he would use the money from that prize to serve humanity by building an All-India Institute of Taxidermy: "Looking at stuffed creatures makes people feel all the more alive, thus more happy, and therefore better human beings." I surveyed the fantastic array of equipment and supplies: skinning knives, bone cutters, fleshing blades, and claw hammers, jars of sulphonated neat's-foot oil, arsenite, borax, and carbolic acid, and a dark terrarium teeming with the ravenous beetles that were used to clean the flesh from the bones of his subjects. "Come and behold a wonder!" Bannerjee beamed as he took my hand to lead me to a table on which there was a mounted mongoose facing a cobra with its head raised and hood spread. "Watch this," he said as he flipped a switch that made the cobra sway. The mongoose's mouth opened and closed and a concealed music box resounded with the very tune that I had heard the snake charmers play at the dock. "This is the future of the art. Someday, instead of cremating or burying deceased loved ones, people will have them mounted, mechanically animated, and equipped with hidden phonograph machines. The dead will speak of love. They'll roll their eyes, clap their hands, and laugh with joy! That is my humble dream, that taxidermy delivers mankind from the prick and sting of death." After more than two hours in his studio, I insisted, with an apologetic promise to return, that I really did need to be excused. "I am grieved," Albert Bannerjee sighed, "that you are leaving. As an expression of great sorrow and of the deep friendship that has grown up between us during the last hour or so, I have a gift for you." He presented me with a stuffed dwarf hyena that had been rigged with a sound box so that squeezing the animal's rib cage produced what was supposed to be a laughing sound. "Whenever you feel sad, just give him a hug and he'll laugh for you, and that will make you laugh in turn. As long as you can hear the laughter of the hyena, you will be happy and thus a better human being." Kumar and Albert waved good-bye as the tonga driven by Ishmael carried me, my trunk, and hyena out of Black Town. That heated night, my first in the McCloud home, thinking of my father and of Angel, I became gloomy and felt so lonely that, not knowing what else to do, I resorted to squeezing the hyena. It did not, as Albert had promised, cheer me up. It seemed to be laughing at me, and at all of us who presume to imagine that laughter, or anything else, can provide any solace over the loss of loved ones.

35	Pythia McCloud in a yellow day dress, poised in half of the S-shaped tête-à-tête beneath the portrait of her mother in a yellow evening gown, without looking up from her book as I entered the card room, asked if I knew Latin.

"Had I known that the most sensational passages in literature would always be in Latin," she sighed, "I wouldn't have studied Italian at school." Seating myself in the empty curve of the S, I translated the Latinized portions of Giacomo Algolagnia's *Fisiologia e igiene dell'amore animale*: "First ejaculation occurs when the phallus of the bull rhinoceros, measuring up to a meter in length, is no more than an inch inside the vaginal canal. Violent seminal eruptions recommence every few minutes for several hours until the membrum virile has been buried to the capulus. Since complete penetration lifts the male entirely off the ground, the female must ultimately bear the entire weight of her paramour on her back." The text reverted to a less clinical Italian after detumescence: "*La rinocerontessa alle donzelle il volto volge repente, pallida d'amabile terror.*" "Charming," she declared as she rose from the sofa. "The sexual life of beasts is so marvelously unencumbered by pretense, intention, sentiment, and rhetoric; in short, it is unetiolated by love." Hesitating at the door, she turned with an afterthought: "Animals enjoy coition more than human beings because they are incapable of lying." The next morning, on my way to the laboratory, when I encountered Pythia in the garden reading, she pointed out a monkey on the roof of the main house. "That the poor dear's rump is so swollen suggests that, although she's no doubt already been mounted by numerous beaus in the last few days, she's looking for a fresh one to help her through the end of oestrus." She hesitated. "Oh, I'm terribly sorry. I don't mean to keep you from your work. Daddy would be frightfully upset if I turned out to be a distraction. Good-bye, Mr. Schlossberg." Although I wished to linger in conversation, she gave me no choice but to continue on to the laboratory, where Ishmael was dropping rodent-dinners into the snake cages. The day was dedicated to an inventory of McCloud's serpents and a review of research methodologies. I noted that while *Bungarus fascinatus,* a large (seven-foot seven-inch) and stunning serpent with its bright rings of variegated imbricate scales disposed in oblique rows, was only moderately deadly (with a toxicity label of "37:04:22:01," indicating that an envenomated test puppy had taken thirty-seven days, four hours, twenty-two minutes, and one second to expire), *Echis yesnovitchii,* though a puny (nine-inch) snake, unremarkable in appearance (with its drab grayish-brown carinated scales), was ominously lethal ("00.00.00.18"). "Very, very death," Ishmael said, grinning, and exhaled. After serving fried hilsa fish and rice for lunch in the lab, he explained that it was procedural to retire in the hot afternoons and to return at sundown to work for an hour or so before dinner. Alone in my room, watched by both Celeste McCloud on the wall and the stuffed hyena in the corner, I wondered why I was in India, and felt that I should have gone to France, where I could have been with Angel. I lifted the diaphanous mosquito net to crawl, fully dressed, into my bed in hopes that, despite the contumacious caw of the crows outside my shuttered window, I might escape the humid Bengal heat by falling asleep. Hearing the doorknob turn, I looked up. Pythia McCloud was standing in the entry to my room. Jumping out of bed, I confessed the delight that the unexpected visit afforded me. "I thought I should come during siesta," she said graciously, "when I wouldn't be disturbing your work, to resume our unfinished discussion of langurs. I'm fascinated by them, and by the animal kingdom in general. When a fit young male langur arrives for the first time in her territory, the female will approach him with curiosity. She circles him like this." She walked around me. "And then, she boldly confronts him, taking his paw in hers, like this." Pythia grasped my hand and, to my utter astonishment, lifted her skirt. "And she places it upon her deliquescent pudendum, a greeting that arouses him greatly." As a guest in the McCloud residence, I felt that it would have been rude by British conventions, if not simian standards, to resist. But, dumbfounded and embarrassed by the girl's headlong display of ardor, I laughed uneasily and, as if my hand were not actually between her legs, jabbered pleasantries: "How nice to see you again, Miss McCloud. Yes, I do want to learn about monkeys as well as snakes. I'm honored by the opportunity to work for your father." Paying no attention to my inane chatter, she, with a pleasant expression on her face and an affable tone in her voice, continued the lecture on the mating rituals of *Presbytus lascivis*: "The female then places the male's paw against his nose, like this, offering him the scent of her passion. Once he has smelled it, he quite naturally wishes to sniff for himself the tumid region that has so bewitchingly fragranced his fingers. Since animals are not encumbered by garments, she does not need to unbutton his trousers like this." Beneath the tutelary gaze of her mother in a blue evening gown, Pythia, after brusquely pulling down my trousers, turned to balance herself with her hand on my small writing table and, with spread legs and arched lower back, continued: "When the female presents her rump to him, like this, the male monkey, unlike his human counterpart, never pauses to think about it. In obedience to natural instinct, he mounts her from behind and grandly gives her all he's got." When it was over, she pulled her dress back down from around her waist, turned to me, and smiled. "And then our female scampers off to rejoin the herd and find another mate. There is no languor for a langur after lovemaking." With that, Pythia vanished. During supper there was no acknowledgment in word, gesture, nor even in glance of what had transpired that afternoon. She retired from the dining room when her father, after consuming a substantial serving of jackfruit jelly trifle, invited me to his study for a whiskey. "She read zoology and Italian at school," he said proudly, "and won the Lord Kitchener Prize for her senior essay 'Flights of Fancy: Reflections on the Aerobatic Courtship Displays of the Brahminy Kite.'" Ritually dissolving the customary pellet of opium in our drinks, he noted, "It's the only thing to prevent insomnia and monsoonal moramentia." I didn't see his daughter again until two days later, when, after her father had gone to call on the Maharaja of Diwanasthan, she appeared in my room, again after lunch, to announce that for tigers, "as for all the big cats and indeed most of the carnivores of the Indian subcontinent, copulation is a rough and raucous affair, and much more time-consuming than that of langurs." She had begun to remove her clothing. "Once the tigress has presented a swollen vulva to the male, he is compelled to inspect it with his nose, whereupon she turns to smell his hindquarters. Excuse me, Mr. Schlossberg, would you mind undressing?" I nervously complied, as she, stark naked, lifted the netting over my bed. "After each tiger has been sufficiently inspired by the aroma of the other," Pythia continued, "the female will tacitly turn, extending her forelegs so that they are resting completely on the ground, like this, while her hind legs are spread and slightly bent, like this, to facilitate the deepest possible penetration with a minimum of effort and imagination on the part of the male. If I had a tail, it would, at this point, be raised and averted." The address on feline mating manners continued even after I was inside her: "The male tiger's climax is so paroxysmal that the pleasure is experienced with pain. Then, as if in retaliation, he bites her neck. This infuriates the tigress, so much so that, immediately upon disengaging from her, the male cat must run for his life." Sapped, I fell over on to the bed and, wet with perspiration from the heat of India, Pythia, and love, I reached to caress her neck with trembling fingers that she had said she wished were clawed. "Am I supposed to run away now?" I asked. "I hope not, because I'd like to talk to you. And I'd like to kiss you." Rising from the bed, she put on her cream-colored bandeau and matching bloomers. "Tigers neither kiss nor talk," she declared. "Indian bears do, however, often loll about after congress and rub their muzzles up against each other, drooling and making bubbling sounds in a manner that might be considered a sort of ursine osculation. But even bears do not talk." Just as she had done after we had behaved as monkeys (and as she was to do on the subsequent afternoon after we were mongooses), she left my room as soon as she had dressed. The next day (after having been a jackal), I did my best to block a prompt escape: "Please don't go. Or let me come with you. I'd like to go for a walk, to spend some time together, and to learn more about you." She laughed. "Why would you want to know any more than you can ascertain with your nose? The smell of a creature's sex reveals far more than anything spoken." I begged to differ: "But I do want to hear what you have to say, not only about animals, but about yourself, about your feelings." "Why?" she asked with what seemed genuine puzzlement as she put on her pastel pumps. As she stood before my mirror, replacing the pins in her gloriously golden hair, I answered sincerely: "Because you are beautiful and obviously very intelligent. Because you won the Lord Kitchener Essay Prize at school. And, well, just because I'm attracted to you, not only physically as an animal, but mentally and emotionally as a human being. I'm sorry, but I don't want to just bite and lick you, and mount you from behind. I want to look at you, talk to you, and take a ride with you into the town, perhaps have dinner at the Great Eastern, or go dancing on Saturday night at Charnock House, and then stroll along the Hooghly arm in arm when the moon is full. That's what men and women who are attracted to each other do." Instead of heading for the door as I feared, she walked toward the bed as I hoped. "The human male," she informed me, "takes the female's hand in his and lifts it politely to his lips to demurely kiss it and says something charming." I did what she described. "Thank you, Pythia, human behavior means a great deal to me." She continued: "And then, emboldened by being allowed to kiss her hand, the male slowly, cautiously, and unlike like other mammalian carnivores, moves his face toward hers. Without growling or biting, he places his lips gently against hers in hopes that her lips will open slightly to invite him closer still." I did so. "And then," she laughed, "the human female, to arouse, tease, torment, and make the male primate love her with all his heart, pretends to be offended by the advance. Suddenly pushing him back, like this, she asks: 'Do you imagine that I am a girl of easy virtue?'" I didn't know what to say. "Answer me, Mr. Schlossberg! Do you suppose that you can have your way with me? Do you dare to come into my father's home, accept his hospitality, and then seduce his daughter unbeknownst to him and against her better judgment?" I was speechless as she, in a simulation of hominid sexual ritual, rose and tromped out of my room, slamming the door behind her.

36 "Once upon a time," Dr. McCloud began, beside me on the tiger-skin-upholstered backseat of the open Peerless that the Maharaja of Diwanasthan had provided for our journey to the snake charmer's settlement, "there was an itinerant sadhu who had re-nounced this world and performed obsequies for himself in order to incarnate Shiva. As the embodiment of that Lord of Serpents, with filthy matted locks, tiger-skin-loincloth clad, toting a damaru and a skull-topped staff, he had, by means of strenuous austerities in Himalayan caves and relentless ganja smok-ing, accrued fantastic magical powers. When, coming to the door of a farmer named Bolon, he begged a meal and a bed, the householder swore that he had neither to spare: 'This year my crops didn't grow, nothing edible, only a few hard loki gourds. And there is no room under my roof, for I have as many chil-dren as Dhritarashtra—one daughter and a hundred sons. Not really, but when you're responsible for feeding eleven children, ten sons might as well be a hun-dred.' It was a pack of prevarications: his harvest had been a rich one that sea-son, and he didn't have a single son (although, as a result of his persistent efforts to produce one, his wife had given birth to three daughters). Everything he said was false." Dr. McCloud interrupted the story in order to order Krishna, the Maharaja's chauffeur, to stop the car so that he could have a snort of snuff. After a colossal sneeze and a soothing swig of opiated brandy from a silver flask, he signaled Krishna on. "Everything, as I was saying, that the farmer Bolon told the mendicant was fictitious. And lying to holy men is as egregious a sin to these superstitious souls as blasphemy is to those of us who worship the one true God. Having overheard the fabrications, Bolon's wife was ashamed of her husband's transgression, and, well aware that denying alms to god men is as perilous as lying to them, she feared the sadhu's wrath. Late that night, while the farmer slept, the woman took rice and hilsa fish to the Ananta cave where her husband had suggested the renouncer might find shelter. Mak-ing obeisance to the holy man and placing the eleemosynary food at his feet, she confessed her husband's perfidy: 'Our crops were plentiful this year. We have not one daughter, but three, and, I'm sad to say, not a single son.' The hi-erophant appraised the situation: 'He who lies to sadhus is consigned in death to the Mitthaloka, the Hell of Liars. And, as the sins of a husband, far more than any of his good deeds, infect the wife, she is condemned to follow him to that infernal realm where nothing at all can be believed.' When, breaking un-der the burden of her grief, the woman wept, the sadhu, comforting her with an arm around her waist, disclosed a means to redeem both her husband and

151

herself: 'Each lie must be transformed into a truth.' For the sake of their salvation, the mendicant set the plan in motion by embracing the woman who, in
turn, offered her flesh as lustral alms to Shiva. Following his esoteric counsel,
the reverent wife, on each of three successive nights, faithfully brought one of
her vestal daughters to the Ananta cave that they might likewise consecrate
themselves as piacular offerings to the omnipotent miracle worker and, by receiving his seminal unction, exculpate their father. By the next year all the
farmer's lies had, alas, come true: he had ten sons and only one daughter (his
wife gave birth to one son, and his daughters, two of whom died in childbirth,
had each given birth to triplet boys); and thus there was no room beneath his
roof for guests. The wandering holy man, with a spell preventing the growth
of Bolon's crops, had also made it come true that he had no food to spare. Only
inedible loki gourds had grown. Thus were the farmer and his wife redeemed
from the Hell of Liars." As Dr. McCloud told the tale, I gazed at the voluptuous
Bengal delta, patchwork-mantled with rice paddies, trimmed with banana yellow, mango orange, and flameflower crimson. Palm, bamboo, and banyan
shaded tanks of rainwater where holy cows languorously quenched eternal
thirst and laughing women blithely bathed in bright saris. Dung patties with
the handprints of those women dried on whitewashed walls of mud. The doctor told me that Lingnath the snake charmer had told him the story that he was
telling me: "The farmer was both heartbroken over the death of his two
daughters and distraught that he would have to beg for food like a sadhu.
Squatting outside his door and hearing the pitiful cries of ten hungry babies,
Bolon decided to try to make some use of the hard loki gourds: after drilling a
hole in each end of one of them and securing two wooden pipes, each fitted
with a bamboo reed, into one end of the gourd, he had a musical instrument—
the first *bin*. No sooner had he begun to blow upon it than his famished infants,
soothed by the sound, ceased crying. As he repeated the improvised tune, milk
began to flow from the breasts of his wife and surviving daughter, who, enraptured by the music, smiled at the cooing babies cradled in their arms. While
Bolon, afraid of breaking the spell, played on, cobras appeared from their burrows: first the females, who, charmed by the gourd pipe, began to sway in
delirious dance. And then the males came to join the cotillion of their enchanted mates." With a rain-insinuating grumble of gloomily gathering clouds,
Krishna pressed his foot on the accelerator of the Peerless and the story sped
up. McCloud explained that when Bolon's neighbors, drawn in curiosity by the
strange music, came to the farmer's house, they were so amazed by the spectacle of serpents dancing to the melody of a gourd-flute that they cheered,
shabashed, and threw coins in appreciation of the marvelous show. Counting
the money that he had inadvertently earned, a delighted Bolon made an offer-

ing of the milk from the breasts of his wife and daughter to the snakes in gratitude for their performance. He decided to give up farming and become a snake charmer. And in time, his ten sons, having heard the music of the *bin* from infancy, and having been raised with the serpents that Bolon kept in round baskets, followed in their father's footsteps, traveling throughout the countryside and charming snakes everywhere they went. Each son, settling in a different part of India, raised his sons to be snake handlers in turn. Just as we reached the settlement, Dr. McCloud concluded: "And that is the origin of the Sapera caste." Breaking under a burden of supernal grief, the clouds fitfully rained. Krishna opened an umbrella to shelter us as Lingnath, the charmer in the black lungi whose performance I had seen upon arrival in India, emerging from his palm-thatched dwelling, welcomed us to Mayapur with a gregarious smile. Following him into the darkness of the humid hut, we were directed to seat ourselves on charpoys and forced by civility to drink extravagantly sweet tea from clay tumblers. Although I could not yet understand any Bengali or Hindustani, it was obvious that Dr. McCloud, in a mixture of the two (seasoned with the occasional English expletive), was berating the charmer for not having brought any snakes to Alipore recently. With a gleeful grinful of betel-stained teeth, Lingnath produced an irascibly writhing viper from a burlap bag. He gripped it behind the jaws with one hand and stretched out the tail with the other. "Maarchiti," the charmer cheerfully announced. "Big death esnake." A haggling Dr. McCloud finally handed over the rupees. "The unscrupulous tatterdemalion demanded double because the snake is gravid." As soon as the rain eased up we were taken outside, where Lingnath began to play the *bin* with all the abandon of the legendary Bolon. A boy performed in a woman's clothes: the nautch girl's arms twisted about in an independent dance above his head; as if trying to restrain each other, hands were clasped together; he bit his lip, rolled his eyes, and gasped for breath. Another boy, playing a drum for the dancer in accompaniment to Lingnath, began to sing a song (*"Sapere bin baja de re to calungi tere sath"*) that McCloud simultaneously translated: "O snake charmer, play your *bin* for me and I'll walk away with you, abandoning my husband and forgetting all my children. Those dancing cobras are, I now know, the women you've seduced with strange melodies." Though the women of Mayapur, peering through openings in curtains and gaps in fences, were invisible, I could hear them laughing at the sight of us as the skies again began to darken. We sought shelter from the brazen downpour beneath the charmer's roof, where McCloud agreed to stay for a meal of rice and hilsa fish. Afterwards, an unidentified girl, who had been crouching in a penumbral corner of the hut, her face covered by the end of her sari, ochre like a mendicant's, was ordered to clean up. As she obediently reached in solemn silence for the banana leaf upon which my food had been served, I noticed that her wrists were tattooed with indigo serpent bracelets, the hooded heads of which adorned the back of each darkly delicate hand. She wore neither anklets nor rings on her toes. A torrential persistence of rain coerced Dr. McCloud to accept Lingnath's invitation to spend the night. We slept amidst baskets of snakes, watched over by graven idols installed in cobwebbed crannies in the walls. While Lingnath, McCloud, and I slept on charpoys, the two women were curled up on a single mat at the far end of the hovel. Despite the exorbitant din of monsoon on the thatch and the duet loudly snored in staccato by our host and the doctor, I could, several times during that long night, faintly hear one of the women moaning. Believing that it was the girl with the snake tattoos, I envisioned wildness in a bright smile and the ache of passion's transport in storm-cloud-dark eyes. Back in the back of the Peerless in the sunny morning, returning to Calcutta with our deadly maarchiti, I asked McCloud about her. "It's an Oriental melodrama." He yawned. "Nagini's her name, Lingnath's daughter. Three years ago, when she was barely fourteen, her parents arranged for her to marry a ne'er-do-well snake man from Assam. In less than a year, the girl was back home and disgraced because, shortly after the wedding, the boy's father died of snakebite. Then, a month or so later, his mother was brutally disfigured at the stove by the explosion of a kerosene can. A brother subsequently hung himself, and after another few months Nagini gave birth to a monstrously malformed baby boy who died within hours. A few days after that, her husband disappeared, supposedly nabbed by a crocodile while performing ablutions in the Brahmaputra. Folks say that Nagini's bad luck, that associating with her, brings misfortune. She was born under the sign of Shani and some suspect that she's a churel, a witch of sorts. Certain that they'll never find another man to marry the girl, her mother tried to sell her to a bawd in Sonagacchi. But Lingnath, in an uncharacteristic display of morality, wouldn't allow it. I suspect that, despite his low station, idolatrous religious propensities, and congenital scurrilousness, he must, in his own way, feel as much protective affection for Nagini as I do for Pythia. Love, I suppose, is no different for them than it is for us."

37

"*Maarchiti* (Bengali) = *Lundchoos* (Hindi) = *Ophiophagus scala* (Latin [*Than. Ind.* 4:27]); [Eng.?]," my first herpetological label read: "☠ (α-Bungarotoxin). ♀ (Parturient). + Mayapur (Candernagore District, Bengal). 37" x 3". 1.78 kg. Brownish gray w/ ovate grayish-brown-edged white spots; oblong anteriorily convergent umber markings on crown. Ventrals (egg-whitish) 159; subcaudals (tar-blackish) 38. Scales imbricate & boldly keeled. Nostrils small, round, & upward. Dentition: solenoglyphous (fangs long & mobile). Ruthlessly active & fiercely aggressive. Canine introduced [3:15 p.m.] >> in immediate response, specimen twisted into double coil. Fricative hissing produced by scraping together prominent carinated scales. Struck after 18 secs. with sudden dart from a distance of over 1'. Victim instantly immobilized. Venom chewed into musculature (42 secs.); released, retreated, and again twisted into a double coil as if to strike again (or to observe the death of the intruder?). Canine convulsed violently while whimpering softly. Bile regurgitated & blood excreted as viper retreated. † TX = 00:00:03:22. [7/4/21]. Venom fully replenished (—jss) [7/10/21]. 16 eggs, 4 unfertilized slugs [7/22/21]; 12 hatched. All eggs, slugs, & live neonates consumed by mother (7/24/21)." On the verge of a pachydermical snort of Macouba, Dr. McCloud proceeded with my tutorial in the techniques of venom cannulation: "Only through the power and grace of hatred," he, noticing a slight trembling of my fingers on the neck of the snake, reflected, "will fear be dispelled." Then, after trumpeting a mammoth sneeze, he enjoined me to look to the mongoose for inspiration: "Awe is perilous, fascination disastrous. As long as you grant the serpent beauty . . ." The advice was interrupted by the tumultuous entry of a hurry-scurry Ishmael. "Dr. Saab and Mastar Isaac! Come for one incredible unbelievable! It is a here and now!" The astounding thing was brought to us by Colonel Francis Coffin-White (ret.), a government deputized tiger catcher and author of *Man-Eaters I've Eaten*. The hunter's beak of a nose, pointed jaw, and fluffy fair forelock made him look like a caricature of himself. Joined by an enthusiastic Pythia and several staggering servants, McCloud and I stared in astonishment at the tethered creature that Coffin-White kept at bay with a pigstick. The shikari's heronlike legs were profusely scratched as a result of wearing khaki shorts in the jungle, and his face was scorched scarlet from going hatless beneath a mercilessly mocking Indian sun. As is typical of predators, his eyes were set close together. "I didn't know where else to take the devil," the tiger hunter, proud of his cowering, panting catch, explained. "I didn't even consider the zoo, as I regard all zoos as prisons. Killing animals, I believe, grants them far more dignity than caging them up. In any case, I reckoned that you, sir, might take some scientific interest in the creature and even have some use for it in your toxicological experiments. Quite a remarkable specimen, don't you think? Of course we've all heard of them—Amala, Kamala, Mowgli, and the rest—but I never thought I'd see one in the wild, let alone get the chance to stalk and bag one." The filthy creature in question, now growling, baring its teeth, and tugging against its leash in a fearful attempt at ferocity, was a human being. "Isn't he wonderful," Pythia exclaimed, clapping her hands in delight. "Oh, Father, do let's keep him. Please! I'm confident that we can tame him, and in time, once he's wormed, deloused, bathed, coifed, toilet-trained, walking upright, wearing clothes, and eating cooked food with cutlery, he can dine with us, and eventually, once we've taught him to speak, he can entertain us with reminiscences of life as a wild animal in the jungle." After being hosed off and muzzled by Ishmael, the feral lad was installed in the kennel. Sniffing the air and glancing anxiously about, he growled menacingly at an unimpressed Krishnakukkur. Ishmael asked if he should give the boy a live rat, chicken, or spare puppy to eat, a meal to make him feel at home. "No," McCloud answered, "we must show him that he does not need to kill in order to survive. That awareness is the beginning of civilization." That evening, over water-buffalo steak and kidney pie, Coffin-White told us how he had discovered the creature: "From the restless behavior of a mature male that I had spotted from my machan circling his ladies protectively in the brush in the ringal forest near Rakshapur, I knew that there was a young rogue prowling nearby. But I wondered why I couldn't find any pugmarks to substantiate his presence." Pythia impatiently interrupted to bring up the question of a name for the boy: "I, for one, am rather partial to Tarzan." Coffin-White objected: "This is India, Miss McCloud, not bloody Africa, thank God." We took turns around the table trying to come up with a name for the feral adolescent: Brutus (Coffin-White), Remus (Pythia), Cain (Dr. McCloud), and Oorangoo (me). Nobody liked anybody's suggestion but their own. I could hear the nameless creature howling in the distance as the contest continued: Romulus, Kaspar, Legion, Puss-in-Boots, Geronimo, Narsingh, and then it was Pythia's turn again: "What about Grrrr? I imagine that's what his mother must have called him." Her father insisted that since it was our duty to teach him to speak as a human being, "we ought not permit his presence to reduce us to making animal sounds." Although it is an Indian servant's duty not to have any ideas, Ishmael, in the midst of serving McCloud a shimmying mound of blancmange, made a suggestion: "Mansur," he said, Arabic for "Victor," a princely Mohammedan name that was misunderstood by Pythia. Assuming that he had said "Man, sir," she cried out her approval: "Yes, Man! How delightfully allegorical and intriguingly anthroposophical! Yes, oh yes! Let us make Mann (with two *n*'s so it's not too obvious) his surname and christen him with the Christian name Hugh." And so Mr. Hugh Mann, Esq., now that he had a name, was ready to be domesticated, then trained, socialized, and then civilized. During an educational process that would recapitulate the history of human development from a savage Neolithic period to the present, it would be possible, through a scientific observation of the creature's progress, to augment human understanding of human nature and its evolution. It was my job to make the label for his cage: "Tiger Boy = *Homo ferus* = *Vyaghrapurush* (Skt.) = *Rakshajan* (Beng.) = Mann, Hugh (family). ♂. + Rakshapur (Diwanasthan Dist., Beng.). Age: 14 ± 1 yr. Ht.: 5'8". Wt.: 63.37 kg. Cranial capacity: 1537 cc (est.). Hair: black & matted. Eyes: hypermetropic (brown). Complexion: ruddy. Nostrils: small, ovate. Dentition: heterodontic (brutal halitosis). Penis: 12.4 cm (flac.). Diurnal lethargy (rocks back & forth on hands & knees); nocturnally nervous & active. Growls, whines, grunts, & periodically bares teeth to make hissing sounds. Seeks darkness (covers eyes with paw-hands). Afraid of fire. Urinates haphazardly, defecates spontaneously (then sniffs it); masturbates frequently, urgently, & fearfully. Cooked meat (goat) introduced: timidly sniffed it, circled it, growled, ate it in corner. Morose (over the waning of the moon?) & hyperflatulent (7/25/21)." McCloud asked me to keep a daily record of his behavior. "There is so much for us to learn from him," he said, sneezed, and elaborated, "even more than he has to learn from us. Is the mind a tabula rasa? What is congenital and what is instilled? Is morality innate? Is reason learned? What about hatred and love? Which emotions are naturally ours, independent of the influence other human beings? Can we empirically test the doctrine of Original Sin? What is the origin of language? What separates us from the beasts and gives us dominion over them? What is human nature? On what rung of the great ladder of mentation does he, having lived in the wild, stand, and how many rungs higher can we, having introduced him to civilization, encourage him to climb. Does he have intent, consciousness, or a capacity for reflection? Can he joke or lie?" Over opiated whiskey in McCloud's study that first night, Coffin-White hypothesized: "The story is always the same. A village woman, in the jungle scavenging for berries, nuts, or firewood, is carrying a baby. When a tiger suddenly appears and roars, the terrified mother drops her child and runs for dear life. Bounding after her, the cat pounces and devours the poor jennie. If the tiger is a male, the baby is dessert. But if it's a female, and if she herself has recently given birth, she cannot help but respond to infantile whimpering. Instinctually she gently clamps the critter in her deadly jaws to carry it by the neck back to her den, where she cuddles it up with her other cubs, and offers it the teat. If the Lord God condones survival and temperamental Atropos does not interfere, the child becomes a member of the family and from the tigers learns to be wild." Waiting for Pythia to come to my room as promised with a subtle nod of the head during the passing of walnuts and claret, I wondered what she'd be that night: a civet, sloth bear, pangolin, crocodile, maarchiti, or what? Beginning to undress the moment she arrived, she spoke of Hugh, asking how long I thought it would take to make him one of us. "The pubic hair and descended testicles," she noted with a scientific tone, "indicate that he must be at least thirteen. I'd guess fourteen or fifteen. What do you think? Do you suppose that he's ever copulated with a tigress? One might assume so, for animals begin to attempt reproduction as soon as they are physically capable of the act. But, on the other hand, all beasts must be innately and instinctually driven for the sake of collective survival to mate only with members of the same species. Thus, while deep down he must surely desire a human mate, his upbringing in the wild must have instilled in him impulses to copulate with felines. Poor dear, that must be terribly confusing." When she asked that we be feral foundlings that night, imagining that we were raised by tigers in the jungle and completely uncivilized, I was at least gratified that we would be human beings for a change. It was the first time I made love with her face-to-face. She snarled on top of me and then hissed beneath me. She scratched my chest, neck, and shoulders. With menacing passion, her eyes flared and her lips pulled back to bare sharp teeth as she savagely growled. I answered her in a softer growl that she was unaware was jungle talk for "I love you."

38 "Croquet," Dr. McCloud proclaimed, "is one of the most civilized of ludic activities. While profoundly aggressive, requiring ferocity and cunning in the execution of roquets and croquets, it is also singularly polite, demanding delicacy and amenity in ticing and the bestowal of bisques. Hostility must be well tempered by etiquette." In the All-Empire handicap at Wankton-in-the-Marsh in 1897, a callow Anthony Mc-Cloud had, so the matured version reported, vanquished the reigning Oxbridge champion, Charles Lutwidge Dodgson, the English mathematician whose Latin monograph on the history, philosophy, and psychology of croquet remains the game's vulgate: "After Dodgson played blue coyly to the sinistral boundary, I responded intrepidly with red, progressed strategically to a four back on an ironic two-ball break, and triumphantly ended the battle with a chilling triple peel." On the grass, armed with a cherrywood mallet and focusing one good eye on his pilot ball, the physician cut a fine figure in the white moleskin suit that he wore exclusively for croquet. Unlike his other trousers, all of which had zippered or buttoned flies over a foot long so that his belt could buckle above his paunch, the white croquet slacks, worn well under the belly, required only a three-inch fly. Once word of the feral foundling spread, Sunday croquet meets at the Alipore estate were by invitation only. Everyone in Calcutta was eager to see the amazing Tiger Boy of Rakshapur with their own curious eyes. Kumar Bannerjee, though totally inept with a mallet, was welcomed as a guest by Dr. McCloud in hopes that, given his years of experience as the director of a menagerie, he would have practical advice on training our human beast. Bannerjee was escorted by Tara Tigresse, a.k.a. Leona Wilder, who had just arrived in Calcutta from the United States. The extravagantly eyelashed circus performer appalled McCloud with both a request to purchase the boy for her act and a flagrant use of such vulgar American croquet terms as "dead ball, danger ball, and hot ball." He had to admit, however, that she was not a bad player and did have a way with the creature. Entering the cage and pacing catlike around him on all fours, she growled to him in tones ranging from fierce to kittenish. And he responded in kind as if grateful to have an animal to talk to. On her second Sunday visit, the buxom felinophile confidently removed Hugh's muzzle, moved the leash from his neck to his wrist, and, using her whip to direct him, pranced him around the garden to the applause of delighted guests. She adamantly disagreed with Bannerjee that a Tesla Electromatic Neckband would be the most expedient means of taming: "Like most young male cats, he will, I am confident, in response to edible and tactile treats,

be most efficiently broken and controlled by applied affection." She did, however, after several embarrassing moments on the croquet court, concede that
the collar might facilitate curtailing defecation in public. High-voltage shocks
to the neck each time he emptied his bowels in the presence of visitors soon
taught the Tiger Boy to indicate his bodily needs to whoever held the electrified leash so that he might be led into the bushes. With décolletage shimmying
like Ishmael's homemade blancmange, Tara rewarded successes in his lessons
with lumps of sugar; playfully petting and, scratching his head, neck, and back,
she'd meow and purr her approval. "The creatures we train," Tara reflected,
"are simultaneously training us, teaching us what we need to do to teach them
to do what we want them to do." Although he did learn by an alternation of
electroshock and affection to defecate in the bushes, to turn his back to others
when squatting to urinate, and not to masturbate in the presence of European
ladies, he persisted in stripping off any clothes that were put on him except a
homburg hat that he had swiped off the head of the Maharaja of Diwanasthan.
It had startled the provincial potentate when, let off the leash, the Tiger Boy
scrambled toward him on all fours to leap up and grab the imported felt crown.
It would have been unseemly for a gentleman of his stature to retrieve his hat
from the poor boy, who was not yet advanced enough in his humanity to understand the notion of possession. Arriving in the Peerless that had taken us to
Mayapur, the Maharaja, his physician's only competition on the croquet court,
wore a vermilion silk khurta, gold-filigreed trousers, jeweled pansy-purple velvet slippers with curled toes, and the homburg, which in its incongruity looked
as absurd on him as it subsequently did upon the naked savage. The Maharaja
had brought his guru, Shri Karnaghee, who was eager to test a Vedantic hypothesis that, being unspoiled by human interaction and untainted by intellec-
tion, the boy would naturally have "a profound awareness of the mysterious
Brahman, that ineffable absolute beyond all qualities and dualities, the one true
reality that unfortunately and inevitably becomes obscured by language, ideas,
and other such mundane things." Hugh growled at the holy man who, sitting
in lotus posture before him with closed eyes, repeatedly hummed the mystic
syllable "Aum." Hearing of it, and fearing that the heathen swami would take
possession of the hapless creature's soul, Father Theophilus Fitzwilly of the
Episcopal Diocese of Ballygunge hurried to the estate from church the very
next Sunday and, after beating the guru at croquet, made plans to baptize the
Tiger Boy. My favorite visitor and, more significantly, Hugh's as well did not
come on Sundays; Shulamite Levi was delivered each Saturday by Krishna in
the Peerless, brought under the sponsorship of the Maharaja of Diwanasthan
from the Ananga Ranga Club, a cabaret-cum-brothel in Sonagachi. She was
paid as a research assistant in a scientific project that promised to shed consid-

erable light on the true nature of human sexuality, on sexual behavior unrestricted by cultural norms and social mores. When French Jesuit anti-Semites in Algeria urged Moslems to wage jihad against Jews, Miss Levi had fled, crossing North Africa disguised as a man to board a boat in Suez bound for India, where she hoped to find refuge in the home of a brother who was prospering as a senior accountant for the Hillcastle Tea Company. Upon arrival in Calcutta, however, she discovered that her brother had died of malaria and that, of the various jobs that were available to her there, prostitution (since she was white, relatively pretty, and could sing and dance a bit) would be the most lucrative. Because I had been deputed to keep the research journal on Hugh's progress, and because I understood French, she was to report to me after each experimental session on the mattress in the kennel, which, subsequent to his initiation into human sexual activity, became his regular bed: *"Pour un homme il n'est pas trop bête. Comme la plupart de mes clients il y va direct, sans préliminaires, et il éjacule très vite; mais c'est un brave garçon avec beaucoup de potentiel."* Sex did a lot for the feral boy: he learned to say yes in French, English, Bengali, and Hindustani, stopped masturbating almost entirely, and began to distinguish Saturdays from the other days of the week. That it was the only day on which he would allow himself to be dressed suggested that he perhaps wanted to please Miss Levi or that he took pleasure himself in being undressed by her. I made a note of that in the notebook that documented the first five months (7/28/21–12/24/21) of Hugh Mann's socialization: "Howls during the dead of night (7/28). Resists haircut & bites barber (8/2). Symptoms of *dementia ex separatione* are manifest (8/7). Will take lumps of sugar from Shula, Tara, Pythia, & even strange women, but not from men, not even McCloud, Ishmael, or me. Does he distinguish between the sexes by sight, sound, or smell (8/9)? Human interaction still a disagreeable novelty. In sunlight pants heavily with tongue hanging out (8/17). Shakes lock on meat safe & tries to force open door (8/27). Frightened by sound of gun (9/2). No impulse to clean himself after bowel movements & resists being washed by Ishmael (9/3). Some standing, but essentially all movement is on all fours (9/11). Growls at me; bites Ishmael; cowers in the presence of McCloud (9/12). He's taken to whiskey & will do almost anything for it. Jabbers in what seems a parody of human speech (9/17). Allows me to pet him & hold his hand. No longer caged, fettered, or muzzled (9/19). Seeks water pitcher rather than puddles when thirsty; licks hands after eating (9/20). Steals eggs from pantry (9/26). Sleeps on bed, but tears apart down pillow (10/1). Has begun to clean himself after defecating (10/2). Screams unremittingly during enemation treatments prescribed for melancholia (10/3). Tries to eat homburg hat (10/9). Purrs while staring at the full moon (10/14). Drinks an entire pitcher of buttermilk without taking a breath; repeats same with beer; points to whiskey bottle (10/15). Has taken a fancy to my stuffed hyena, hugs it & tries to prevent me from it taking back (10/20). Has mastered some sense of cause & effect through squeezing hyena (10/21). Enjoys being allowed into laboratory & watches in fascination as cobras kill puppies (10/22). Laughs for first time when he makes stuffed hyena laugh (10/23). Cries for first time (cause unknown); sobbing continues intermittently throughout the night (10/24). Squeezes dead puppy (presumably to make it laugh) (10/25). Disrupts croquet match by chasing ball & scampering off with it (11/2). Hides in lantana bushes; prowls close to the wall sniffing the air (11/3). Sleeps in pantry. Sits in corner of study staring at portrait of Mrs. McCloud (11/4). Squatting awkwardly in a chair, has started eating dinner with us; will not wait for grace to be said or use cutlery; tries to take food under the table (11/7). Shula reports that he likes to suck her breasts (*'pas comme un amant, plus comme un infant'*) & that he inevitably falls asleep while doing so (11/21). Howls so menacingly in church in Ballygunge that he has to be taken outside & given whiskey (12/3). Walks upright without being urged to do so (12/5). Steals a pair of my trousers from the clothesline & dresses himself in them (12/7). Accepts a shirt from me & wears it tied around his head; smiles at the sight of himself in the mirror (something that has previously terrified him) (12/9). Licks Pythia's hand after dinner (12/12). Circumambulates Christmas tree with considerable curiosity; sniffs wrapped packages beneath it (12/20). No longer afraid of fire; stares transfixed at burning Christmas candles (12/21). Picked chameli & genda flowers in the garden & offered them to Shula; waving good-bye as the Peerless drove off with her, Hugh smiled ever so slightly (12/24)."

39 "May it please your Lordship and you, gentlemen of the jury," the advocate general, Melech Goldman, began. "I detail you to hear the circumstances which have led to this prosecution and the evidence upon which it shall be supported. As the inexorable prosecutor for the public, with an ungracious duty to state the law and facts without any considerations save universal justice and the public good, I call upon you to affirm the guilt of the native defendant, Sapera Lingnath Meghdar, a Gypsy snake charmer residing in Mayapur, Chandernagore District, Bengal, who is duly charged with being an instrument of culpable homicide amounting to murder as defined in section 209 of the Indian Penal Code. It will be irrefutably demonstrated that, by introducing a deadly krait, *Bungarus caeruleus,* known to the natives of Bengal as Dhomun Chiti, into the Tollygunge home of the late Mr. Godfrey Sassoon, on the twenty-third day of August, 1921, the defendant did purposefully cause the death of Mr. Sassoon with the malicious intention of producing such bodily injury as he, a snake charmer well versed in ophidian toxicology, knew with certainty to be amply sufficient in the ordinary course of nature to be fatal." Not relying on English to understand the prosecutor, Nagini broke into tears. As the snake charmer's daughter covered her face with the end of her sari, Pythia wrapped a comforting arm around the girl's trembling shoulders. The unventilated chamber was chokingly sultry despite the labors of two elderly look-alike punkah-wallahs who, naked except for grubby military-green turbans and matching loincloths, stood on the raised, teetering platform in the shadowy back recesses of the dilapidated hall. They pulled the hemp ropes in, let them go to sweep the air, tugged and released again, rhythmically and with imperturbable longanimity. I fixed my gaze on Nagini and Pythia to spare my eyes the sight of Lingnath, whose slumped posture and woefully frightened expression were too pitiful to bear. Immediately after the arrest, Nagini had come to Alipore in hopes that Dr. McCloud, the only gora-sahib she knew, might be able to help. The first time I saw her face, like the last, it was drenched with tears. From that night on, at McCloud's invitation, she stayed in the estate's servants' quarters. Although McCloud deemed all snake charmers "caitiffs, bezonians, and badmashes," and Lingnath, in particular, a "pilfering scoundrel and precious rascal," he was strangely amused by them, and actually (but not admittedly) liked them. During the several years during which he had been purchasing snakes from Lingnath, he had been charmed by the man, moved by the irrepressible exuberance with which, until now, he had endured a miserable life. The softhearted scientist could not help but take

163

Nagini in and hire a lawyer to defend her father. That the barrister engaged by McCloud was Menachem Goldman, the identical twin brother of Melech Goldman, the prosecutor, must surely have confused the jurors in what was already a muddled case. The Goldman twins, indistinguishable in their legal gowns, although dearly beloved to, and inseparable from, each other outside the courtroom, were the most contentiously competitive of adversaries at the bar. Although testimony made the courtroom seem like the Mitthaloka, the Hell of Liars, one thing, agreed upon by both the Goldman twins, was true: Mrs. Sassoon, née Fiona Hastings of Blessingham, had admitted Lingnath into the courtyard of her home on the occasion of Nag Panchmi. The magistrate called for a description of that Hindu holiday for the sake of any jurors who might not be familiar with the tradition. "It is the festival of serpents," Melech began, "celebrated on the fifth day of the bright half of Shravan. With cobras ensconced in their cane baskets, snake charmers use the occasion to solicit alms and gratuities by going from house to house. When they play hypnotic tunes on flutes to make their serpents spread their hoods and sway in what appears to be a dance, native women, prey to pagan superstition, worship the creatures, offering milk, rice, flowers, and incense to the snakes and money to their masters, fearing that, if they do not do so, they will be susceptible to vengeful snakebite in the coming year. It is, it may be noted, not unusual during this season for our own more enlightened ladies to occasionally admit charmers into their homes out of curiosity, for the sake of amusement, or, as was the case when the accused was permitted into the Sassoon household, to offer charity to an unfortunate member of one of India's oppressed lower classes by allowing the knave to earn a few paise at her expense." Menachem objected that the prosecution was using the invitation to describe the festival to incriminate the accused with insinuation. With his brother's objection sustained, an undaunted Melech turned the court's attention back to the details of the crime at hand, arguing that, after being cordially and charitably admitted into a place where a person of his low station really had no right to be, the snake charmer, dazzled and fascinated by the mere sight of such a genteel lady as Mrs. Sassoon, became obsessed with her. "He imagined that he might seduce her. These mountebanks ever suppose that their flutes have a power over women no less than over snakes. With obscene hope, he did repeatedly visit the house. Deluded by lust, he presumed that marriage to Mr. Sassoon was Mrs. Sassoon's only cause to reject his advances. Thus he released the krait that killed Mr. Sassoon." Menachem had a different story to tell: "This so-called genteel lady, the court will learn through the corroborated testimony of servants, neighbors, members of the Tollygunge Players' Club, as well as from the trustworthy mouth of no less an observer than Reverend Theophilus Fitzwilly of the Episcopal Diocese of

Ballygunge, had a perverse penchant for clandestine intimate relations with native men—madaris, malis, dhobis, bangis, chamars, and baloo-wallahs. The lower the caste and the darker the skin, the more they have been desirable to Mrs. Sassoon." When Melech objected, noting that Lingnath, and not the British widow, was on trial, Menachem counterobjected to remind the court that the district superintendent of police, having discovered during his investigation a ruby ring formerly belonging to Mrs. Sassoon in Lingnath's Mayapur home, had with good reason suspected that Mrs. Sassoon had hired the snake charmer to kill her husband. Melech counter-counterobjected to further remind the court that Mrs. Sassoon had been found innocent of that crime in a separate trial two weeks earlier. It was Menachem's turn: "Let not a miscarriage of justice that occurred in another court be permitted to reduplicate itself here. Testimony can have left no doubt in any intelligent, fair, and honest mind that this poor, uneducated man, unguided by Christian moral values and Occidental ethical codes, under the sway of a woman whom he admired and respected as a representative of the loftiest principles of Empire, acted unwillfully. Yes, he surrendered to her sexual advances. But he had neither the fortitude nor courage to refuse the behests of such a high-ranked personage. And yes, bewitched by her, he did consent to plant a snake in her husband's study. But in repentance he returned to the home, as has been testified by eyewitnesses, to retrieve the krait and confess his misdemeanor. But Mr. Sassoon refused to admit him. And, also attested to by witnesses, he returned again on the following day, the day that Mr. Sassoon was bitten, offering to cure the victim of the snakebite. Once again, audience was denied, and on that occasion it was Mrs. Sassoon who sent the snake handler away. Although he may have been used as a murder weapon, Lingnath Meghdar is not himself the murderer." The magistrate called for the sworn testimony of the accused to be translated for the jury by the recorder: "Yes, I kissed Memsahib and touched her too. I was bad. I couldn't help myself. She asked very nicely, and gave me a beautiful ring for visiting her, playing *bin* music, and making her happy when her husband was in Delhi. But that is all. No murder. I don't know why Memsahib is saying these things. I don't even keep kraits. When I heard that Sahib had been bitten, I went to give a cure. I have herbs and roots and some bezoar stones that sometimes work. Please don't punish me. Be nice to me. I am India. Help me." The prosecution urged the gentlemen of the jury "to see through the flimsy veil of rhetorical subtlety and legal sophistry with which the defense, my learned colleague and esteemed brother, has so craftily endeavored to shield the defendant from prosecution." After a brief summation by the recorder, the jury retired to consider their verdict. Fifteen minutes later, Lingnath was declared guilty. Menachem Goldman then attempted to minimize sentencing: "We have a mandate to administer Hindu law to the Hindus and Moslem law to the Moslems whilst maintaining a parity instituted by English Common Law. In light of this responsibility, may the court note that Indian legal literature, in its discussion of the use of serpents as homicidal instruments, prescribes an appropriate punishment. I read from the *Code of Gentoo Laws*: 'If a man throws into another person's house a serpent whose bite or sting is mortal, this is *shahesh,* a crime for which the magistrate shall fine him five hundred *puns* of cowries and require him to throw away the snake with his own hand.'" On the twenty-third of December, 1921, the Colonial court proved harsher than its native antecedent: "Sapera Lingnath Meghdar of Mayapur, you are sentenced to be imprisoned in the Cellular Gaol of Port Blair on South Andaman Island for a term of one hundred years." Dr. McCloud, Pythia, Nagini, and I returned to Alipore in silence.

40 Hoping to distract Nagini from sorrow, Pythia bought gifts for her: Chanderi and Maheshwari saris, each one matched with a new choli, silver ear and toe rings, jingling anklets and glimmering glass bangles. As the bearded Moslem bangle-wallah snapped each one to check for flaws before slipping it over her tattooed hands, the snake charmer's daughter protested that, as a sonless widow, she should not wear fine clothes or jewelry nor in any other way try to make herself beautiful. Pythia laughed: "You cannot help but be beautiful, my dear, with or without ornamentation." I remember the first time I was alone with the girl. One night (it must have been three in the morning because Pythia had left me at least an hour earlier), unable to sleep (remembering my father, missing my mother, thinking about Angel, and still wondering why I had come to India), I went downstairs to the study for a shot of soporific brandy. Slowly I turned the globe to see from far away the Dead Sea and the Russian Pale of Settlement, New York and California, Europe and the Pacific. I placed my finger over Paris, where Angel was, and then I had another drink. Noticing McCloud's telescope in the corner, I wondered if it might be powerful enough for me to see the constellations Serpens and Ophiuchus. Taking the instrument out onto the verandah, I aimed it eastward toward Antares, visible that night to the naked eye in a vitrean post-monsoon sky. Moving across the heavens, I was slowly passing Scorpius when the faint sound of anklets startled me. Barefoot and wearing a cream-white sari, Nagini was staring at me. Motioning for her to approach, I pronounced the English word ("tele-scope") and stepped back that she might have a look. "Telescope," she said and, wrapping her fingers tentatively around the slender brass tube, leaned to the eyepiece. As if searching for some particular constellation in the dark expanse, guiding the scope across the firmament, she suddenly stopped and held it still. When she stepped back, stood upright, and looked up into the sky as if to match what had been magnified with what her eyes could see, I peered into the telescope to find out what that was: nothing save the infinite darkness and inexhaustible emptiness of an endless universe. She was gone by the time I turned to her. I asked Pythia about her. "She's very shy," my lover said, "but I think that she's spied on us when we've been making love, put an ear to the door or looked through a keyhole, not out of some prurient voyeuristic impulse or for any devious purpose, but out of a natural curiosity. She's as intrigued as any of us are by the ways in which other people love. She suppressed her modesty enough in order to ask, albeit with some embarrassment, about it, and about us. She asked about you." Pythia laughed, took my hand in hers, and, saying that she had told the girl I was "an absolute beast," pulled me along with her, late at night, across the garden, into the kennel and onto the mattress that had formerly been the feral boy's bed. Hugh had displayed sufficient signs of progress to be transferred into the house and installed in a pantry that was converted to suit his peculiar propensities and particular needs. Krishnakukkur and the Gopis seemed unimpressed by our imitation of canine copulation and I was embarrassed. When, several nights later, in the presence of the six ponies in the adjoining stable, I asked if we might embrace face-to-face, Pythia was adamant: "These horses must, like Houyhnhnms, have a rather low opinion of human beings and must laugh at our eccentricities and follies. When they were polo ponies, they surely must have wondered why these bipeds in silly hats and ridiculous jodhpurs sat upon their backs in order to race about smacking a little ball with a mallet. And they must think it strange that my father repeatedly injects something into their rumps with a hypodermic needle and then uses the same to suck out their blood. They would be certain of our imbecility if they were to now see us doing, in the way that you suggest, what should be done with hooves on my back, whilst biting my mane and whinnying." A few nights later, after convincing me to take her to the laboratory, she asked me to tell her about the sexual behavior of cobras, and, although I suspected that she probably knew more about it than I did, I complied: "They don't mate during molting when they are blind because of the fluid between the old and new skin over their eyes. But, after sloughing, the male eagerly seeks out a female, using his bifid tongue to locate her. He follows her scent until, smelling him, she stops and waits. Upon his arrival, she uncoils, stretches out, and lies inert while he rubs his chin along her back, up and down her body from head to tail." "Show me," Pythia whispered, and I was Samoo the Snake Boy of Hindustan once more. Immediately after it was over, she gleefully jumped up. "Come here. I want to examine your venom under the microscope." As commanded, I prepared a slide, adjusted the light, and focused the lenses. Naked, she stood over the binocular instrument through which her father and I examined poisons and antitoxins each day. "Look at them wiggling about," she squealed: "They're like little snakes. And they're so frantic. They look confused, lost, even desperate. And there are so many of them! When Mr. Acton, my biology teacher at school in Darjeeling, told us that there are enough spermatozoa in one spoonful of semen to populate all of India, I found it hard to swallow, reckoning that it would have to be a very large spoon indeed!" Turning from the microscope to face me, caught up in the thrill of reproductive biology, she wrapped my lab coat around her shoulders to continue her scientific disquisition: "With so much sperm and an ability to ejaculate regularly, men cannot be held responsible for the fact that human beings have the lowest reproductive rate of all the animals. No, if left to the male, there would be many millions more of us. Women control the population. While the female baboon in estrus flaunts her gloriously swollen vulva to make it quite clear to the entire community that she is sexually receptive, the human female rarely has the freedom or opportunity to do likewise. It is precisely that behavior that promotes the highest possible birthrate among baboons and other primates. Beholding the flaring female genitalia, so moistly tumescent and brilliantly colored, all the males, as you can well imagine, go into an absolute tizzy. Collectively the mature males then mount younger males in the presence of the ready object of their desire to demonstrate what they can do for her. She is naturally drawn to the most powerful one as attested to by the most impressive pelvic thrusts. This manner of courtship has the additional advantage of providing young males with sexual education, something sadly missing from our society. Unlike the boys of our species, they have the opportunity to learn early in life techniques that will serve them as lovers when they have the maturity and strength to win back the females from the older baboons who mounted them in their youth. It's all very sane, practical, and enviable, don't you think?" Unable to answer seriously, I sighed, politely smiled, and told her that I couldn't help but love her. "That reminds me," she answered quite seriously, removing my lab coat to change into her own clothes. "Please don't say that you love me while we're doing it. It distracts me. It ruins it. Say you love me afterwards. I like it then; it's sweet. It attests to the fact that we've not done anything improper. But while we're doing it, I rather enjoy the thought that I am doing something wild. Baboons snarl and shriek during intercourse." She was not herself one to often utter the words in question. I heard them from her lips for the first time on Christmas Eve of 1921. She said it in the library both to her father and to me, adding a "Merry Christmas," and then, in Bengali, she told Nagini that she loved her as well, and then, as she lit the Christmas candles, Pythia went so far as to announce that she loved "all God's creatures. That's the point of Christmas, isn't it?" Despite my disbelief in the God of my fathers, the flames brought back ancient words (*Baruch ata Adonai, Elohenu melech ha-olam . . . ve-tzivanu le-hadlik ner shel Chanuka*), as a mirthful McCloud, after a glorious sneeze, sang, *"Adeste, fideles, laeti triumphantes; venite, venite in Bethlehem."* Facing Mecca and muttering prayers (*"la ilaha illa Allah"*), Ishmael had slaughtered a goose that was braised with Kashmiri cashews and stuffed with buffalo sausage and jackfruit for the Christian feast. In the spirit of the holy night, McCloud invited him and Nagini, as well as his own khansama, Ishmael's elderly father, Ibrahim, to join us for dinner. After the meal, we retired to the card room, where gifts were presented to the servants: McCloud gave Ibrahim a blue silk cummerbund and, on my behalf, an identical one to Ishmael; Pythia gave Nagini a nose ring studded with a sparkling little ruby. At ten o'clock, when Dr. McCloud and Pythia, having bid us a joyous Christmas, left for church, Ishmael salaamed good night and dragged his decrepit, yawning father off to bed. The snake charmer's daughter, dressed in a new red sari and green choli, her new nose ring in place, sat still in the tête-à-tête beneath the portrait of Celeste McCloud, who stared at us staring at each other in awkward silence. Hugh, who had been crouching under the game table since dinner, emerging to grovel about the room on all fours, approached Nagini and sniffed her feet. I poured a glass of port, took a sip, and then offered the glass to her. She shook her head no, rose, placed her hands together in a polite namaskar, and left the room. I would have liked her to linger. I downed the port, switched to whiskey, and slumped into the sofa upon which she had been sitting. Her sorrow both intimidated and attracted me. Still on his knees, Hugh crawled toward me and, as I patted him on the head, smiled contentedly. Much to my astonishment, he suddenly stood up, walked erect to the door, shut it, and turned the key in the lock. With a perfectly human gait he walked back and, seating himself in the empty half of the sofa, crossed his legs and spoke: "Pardon me, Mr. Schlossberg—or do you mind if I call you Isaac?— I've been keeping an eye on you ever since I got here, and you seem the sort of chap whom one can trust. As McCloud's your meal ticket no less than he's mine, I presume that we might collaborate. How do you think I'm doing so far? Be honest with me. It's not an easy role to play for such an extended period. It's already been five months. It was a snap at first, just acting like an animal, and it won't be all that difficult to behave as a fully civilized human being. But it's this transitional phase that's problematic. You know, maintaining consistency of character while growing and developing. Mind if I help myself to a whiskey? Here's to you, and merry Christmas! Listen, I need someone on the inside who can tell me what they are saying about me when I'm not around. That will enable me to know what to do and when. It's got to be played just right. Imagine what they'd do if they caught on! Can I count on you? You might wonder what's in it for you. Well, for one thing, it could be a spot of fun."

	"She's a man-eater, as beautiful and vicious as any being that has
41	ever stalked the earth, five hundred untamable pounds of striped
	grace," Tara said to McCloud. "Francis trapped her near Chander-

nagore, where she's been terrorizing villagers for the last few months. Mohini, she's called. Eight kills documented and another ten reported. Just as you, Dr. McCloud, have dedicated yourself to limiting death by snakebite in the Colonies, so Colonel Coffin-White aspires to put an end to death by tiger in India. The wild boy is the key. We'll take him with us to Bannerjee's, where we're keeping Mohini, and introduce him into her cage. Having been raised as a tiger, he'll know how to behave with her, establishing himself with purrs, growls, and snarls, with postures, passes, and other feline signals. Hopefully she'll not suspect he's human and, as captives, they'll naturally communicate with each other, commiserating as it were. They might even become intimate—she's ready for oestrus, making her both all the more dangerous to us and all the more vulnerable to one she imagines to be a young male. In any case, he'll get to know her, understand her, and then, in time, when, back here with you, he learns to speak English, he'll be able to explain something that has always baffled tiger hunters, trainers, and poachers: What makes a cat turn man-eater? Human flesh is not normally an item on a tiger's menu. Other than the brains, it's too salty and lean, not nearly as juicy sweet and lusciously gamy as ghooral, tahr, or buffalo. Are they born man-eaters or do they learn it, either alone, out of necessity, or from other homivorous cats, watching the kill as cubs and getting a share in the fruits of it? We need the boy to find out." Dr. McCloud was tempted by the idea. Certain that Hugh did not stand a chance of survival in Mohini's cage, I argued against Tara's proposal: "The boy has come to exhibit too many human characteristics in his behavior for fraternization with a wild animal. He has, furthermore, since beginning to bathe and enjoy British cuisine and whiskey, lost the jungle smell. It would, in my opinion, thus amount to culpable homicide by negligence if he were to be admitted into the cage of the man-eater of Chandernagore." That Menachem Goldman, visiting regularly to consult with McCloud about the appeals that were being made on behalf of Lingnath Megdhar, agreed with me saved Hugh's life. While I presumed that the adolescent would be grateful for the redemption, he privately laughed over the incident, remarking that "since I've been able to so easily dupe scientists, theologians, and animal trainers, convincing them that I really was raised by tigers, perhaps I would have been able to fool a tiger too. That would have been a sure test of my talents." Hugh had taken over the journal documenting his humanization, dictating to me whenever he found an opportunity for us to be alone: "Hugh Mann's humanity resides in, and will by reclaimed by the grace of, his mouth, rectum, and phallus. Advantage of the fact that his most significant advances toward civilization have been made through amorous interaction with Shulamite Levi should be taken into account. It would be interesting to provide him with other specimens of the human female from the Ananga Ranga Club, Chinese, Malay, and Indian girls as well as European ones; this would enable us to determine whether race, as a subcategory of species, is, in the service of survival and evolution, instinctually and preferentially perceived, and whether or not it is natural for the races to interbreed." He paused to ask if I'd get him a packet of cigarettes: "American if you can manage it. Not being able to smoke has been the most difficult part of being uncivilized." One afternoon in the laboratory, after each of us had lit a cigarette, he told me what he claimed was the true story of his life: "I wasn't, obviously, really raised in the jungle, but on the estate of no less a hegemonic luminary than Lord Blessingham. I was called Puru, short for Purushottam, which means 'the Highest of Men.' My great-grandfather on my father's side was chief bearer to Warren Hastings, and since my great-grandmother was the governor-general's bibi, it is hardly unlikely that there's Hastings blood in my veins. That would account for both my British wit and Anglo-Saxon nose. My father, poor fellow, having all the nose and none of the wit, formerly served the Empire as Lord Blessingham's khansamah. Born on the very same day as his lordship's son, Jonathan, I was raised with the young aristocrat, my duty as servant in the manor being to amuse the lad. I was his indentured playmate. We dined together, and because he was always, even in infancy, afraid to be alone, I slept in his room. By sitting in obedient attendance during his lessons with a staff of tutors, I was exposed to philosophy, theology, history, and could even, in a pinch, recite a bit of Latin: 'Fallite fallentes: in laqueos quos posuere, cadent.' That we were the best of chums made it a sad day for me when young Blessingham was sent to England for schooling at Westminster, all the sadder that in his absence I was reduced to dining with my father and brothers in the servants' quarters, and sadly sadder still that I was assigned the daily cleaning of horse shit off his lordship's riding boots and the polishing of the same. I owe my deliverance from servitude to Mahatma Gandhi. When, on the first day of April of 1919, the wily rascal called upon Indians to suspend all labor in protest of the unjust and subversive Rowlatt Acts, my father obsequiously asked Lord Blessingham for permission not to work that week in support of the Independence Movement's protest. After being promptly and severely thwacked by his lordship with a riding crop made from the scrotum of a rhinoceros, Babaji was dismissed from service, banished with his wife and sons to the bustee, where pulling a rickshaw would be the only means of survival. Perhaps I'm just finicky, but the pestilential squalor of the slum is not my cup of tea. So while my father and brothers became beasts of burden, I took to hanging around with kangali boys who know how to survive by wit and cunning, hustling on Bentinck Street by day, scrounging around Lower Chitpore Road at night, and learning from the older chentais in Chor Bazaar how to steal food from a stall, pick a babu's pocket, and nab the purse of a burra-sahib. I made offerings, one tenth of all I stole, to Muldev, patron deity of swindlers, for the sake of divine assistance in what I anticipated would be a prosperous life of crime. One day, after snatching a package of sweets out of the basket of a memsahib who was shopping at Mairadanga, and then disappearing instantly into the crush of Barabazar, I took refuge in Muldev's shrine. The plunder was wrapped in an English-language newspaper, which I read as I ate: 'Wolf Boy to Be Taken to America. Professor Kaspar Worden of the Worden and Worden Institute of Philadelphia will be escorting a small Indian wild boy to Pennsylvania this week for scientific study.' The pathetic creature, discovered living in a wolf's den by herdsmen near Maiwana, had been taken for lockup to Allahabad, where, according to the newspaper report, barking and growling, he tried to bite both prisoners and guards. International religious, academic, and medical interest in the wolf boy became keen as news of his discovery spread. With an undisclosed sum of money, Professor Worden won the bid for the feral child's guardianship against competing offers from representatives of distinguished research institutions in London, Paris, and Moscow. The newspaper article quoted the professor: 'The native orphan should enable us to determine the nature of human nature. And, during our research, I will do everything in my power to make sure that the wolf boy is happy in Philadelphia.' I looked up at the face of Muldev, and the idol winked at me. It was obvious. All I had to do was pretend that I had been raised by wild animals and some scientist would soon be dedicating himself to making me happy. And here I am! Except for the electrified neckband, it's been rather amusing. The food's not bad, the whiskey's good, and Shula is a sweet-heart. But where is it going? What will happen when McCloud believes I'm fully civilized? Will he turn me out? The doctor already seems to be losing his interest in me. He's back to the snakes. Even the Sunday visitors seem more ea-ger to play croquet than to see me. And there hasn't been a word about me in the press lately. A natural appreciation of comfort, good food, drink, tobacco, and sex with Shula, has perhaps encouraged me to become a bit too civilized a bit too quickly. I've got to reinvigorate the plot and move the game along. Not much is happening at the moment." Hugh fell silent, crouching down animal-like, when Pythia suddenly entered the laboratory to bring me a letter that had just arrived from America. "It's from my mother," I muttered in recognition of the handwriting as I opened it, anxiously as always because whenever my mother wrote to me it was to tell me that someone had died. This time, much to my relief, it was only the demise of the very aged Pierre, Larry Lafitte's retired poodle. She also informed me that she had sold the house on First and Samuel and was moving in with the Grossmans in San Francisco. Since Pythia had never shown any interest in my background, I was surprised when she asked, as I folded up the letter, about my mother and father. "I was born," I told her, "at the lowest spot on earth, on the barren shores of the Dead Sea, on December 21, at the darkest hour of the darkest night of 1899. My parents were on their way to Bethlehem." Hugh purred and Pythia yawned. A few weeks later, Shree Karnaghee showed up, as he did each month on the occasion of a new moon, to chants mantras over the Tiger Boy that would protect him from Father Fitzwilly's efforts to make a Christian of him. No sooner had the guru settled down into the lotus posture than Hugh, much to Karnaghee's amazement, looking him straight in the eyes, distinctly uttered, *"Kamo marash cheti samsare 'sminn asare parinatitarale ye dve 'rtha eva vaktavye samprate."* The astounded guru leapt to his feet and, bounding toward the card room to find us, was shouting: "Ram! Ram! It is Sanskrit! He has spoken! He knows Sanskrit!" What, of course, everyone wanted to know, had he said? The flabbergasted spiritual preceptor, excitedly repeating the words, apologized: "Being Sanskrit it cannot be translated into lesser tongues without losing much of the nectarous wisdom informing each and every syllable of the original. Nevertheless in vulgar English it conveys something like: 'Love and death: in this world, so transient and without essence, these two things alone are worthy of being spoken about.'"

42. "Eight hundred years ago, the Holy Roman Emperor, Frederick II of Hohenstaufen, sponsored a linguistic experiment on twenty-four infants born out of wedlock," the Maharaja of Diwanasthan informed us before stepping up to the red ball to begin the first Alipore Sunday croquet match of 1922. "Bidding wet-nurses to suckle and bathe the children without prattling or speaking any words in their presence, he was determined to determine what language they would naturally speak. Hebrew, Latin, Greek, or German? The emperor despaired over what seemed the meaningless babbling of the toddlers. They grew up without ever being able to speak to anyone but themselves. I would propose that our amazing Tiger Boy's recent and eloquent articulation in Sanskrit suggests that the presumed nonsense uttered by the subjects to each other in Frederick's experiment was, in fact, Sanskrit, unintelligible and unidentifiable to the monarch because of a want of Indian pandits in his court." After successfully passing through the first two wickets and positioning his ball near the right boundary (an attempt to tempt McCloud into a foul), the Maharaja continued: "All human beings would naturally come to speak Sanskrit if not discouraged from doing so by the imposed learning of degenerate languages." Dr. McCloud, after a snort of Macouba and a full-bodied sneeze, a shot of opiated whiskey and a wholehearted sigh, placed his blue in position to croquet his opponent's ball, and rebutted: "Isn't it possible, Your Highness, scientifically speaking, that, now that the boy, climbing ever higher on the ladder of mentation, is confronted on the current rung by the Sisyphean task of language mastery, the lobes of the brain that are responsible for speech have been activated and, thus stimulated, have released from the penetralia of memory a phrase (a series of sounds that he himself does not comprehend) heard in infancy before whatever traumatic mishap resulted in his being separated from his human parents and raised by tigers." "No, no, no," Shree Karnaghee, accustomed as a guru to knowing everything, objected: "You are both equally misconceived, if I must say so myself. The boy is obviously a Brahmin by birth, for every Brahmin is born with a knowledge of Sanskrit as acquired through rigorous study undertaken in previous lives, during which the student has, by virtue of diligent lucubrations and observances of chastity, assured his future birth as a Brahmin." Infuriated by everything the Hindu holy man said, Father Fitzwilly harangued from the sidelines: "No! This is the work of Satan, the voice of evil, the language of iniquity. The boy is possessed." His wife, Constance, tried to calm her ruffled man of the cloth: "Theo, my dear, could it not be an instance of glossolalia, not so much the work of the devil as of our very own Holy Ghost?" Colonel Francis Coffin-White, with Tara nodding her agreement at his side, attempted to put things into perspective: "Let us be honest with ourselves and admit that the little brute's only linguistic capability is mimicry. He has no doubt merely parroted a phrase that he heard spoken by some village priest while he was prowling around one night near some heathen jungle shrine." Pythia was cynical: "Could it not be that Hugh, as he so often does, just happened to blabber some bibble-babble in no particular language and with no meaning whatsoever, and that the syllables that just happened to bubble out just happened to make some sort of sense in a language that just happened to be known by Shree Karnaghee?" Menachem Goldman spoke as a lawyer: "Arguing that we have heard false testimony, I would postulate that the holy man's story, being as preposterous as any Hindu myth, has been fabricated to convince us of the validity of his absurd belief in reincarnation. Were there other witnesses?" Even Ishmael had an explanation: "Maybe the boy was drunk." I was confident in my own understanding of the event, since I had, in compliance with Hugh's request, purchased for him (in addition to American cigarettes) a copy of William William-Monier's *A Modern Missionary's Guide and Grammar to the Sanskrit Language with Selected Phrases for Every Occasion, Adapted from Both Christian and Hindoo Scripture.* That Hugh, despite repeated enticements of whiskey, did not speak again soon, was confidently interpreted by Karnaghee: "In the spiritual history of India, silence, if it is in Sanskrit, is considered the most perfect articulation of wisdom. Like God, he is speaking without saying anything, and saying everything without speaking. And in Sanskrit what he is not saying surpasses in sapience anything that may be voiced in a mundane tongue." Just as people were favoring the skeptical explanation of Menachem Goldman, it happened again, this time in the presence not only of Karnaghee, but also of Dr. McCloud, Mr. Goldman, Pythia, the Maharaja, Shulamite Levi, and myself. *"Dvayi vrittir askmakam murdhni va,"* he, with closed eyes and a convincingly peaceful smile on his lips, recited, *"sarvaloka shiryate vana eva va."* Again commenting on the incapacity of English to capture the multivalent and sublime semantic subtleties of the Sanskrit, the awed guru translated: "There are two alternatives in life: to whither away in desolate depths or shine on the summit of the world." Everyone was amazed. Explanations were revised. Discussion was heated. Hugh soon took me aside: "I've only got a few more of those silly Sanskrit platitudes memorized, and I need to move along to the next act. I could use a little bit of help. Look at this." He showed me an advertisement from the morning's *Bengal Statesman* for a public lecture that was to be given on Thursday evening at Harmony Hall by a Major L. A. Wheedle, "Director of the Pan-American Institute for the Scientific Investigation of the Incredible, world-renowned scientist, mesmerist, and explorer, just arrived in Calcutta en route to Nepal to capture the elusive Abominable Snowman." I told Hugh that I had been present at a fund-raising lecture he had delivered in San Francisco. Hugh got to the point: "Mesmerist! That's the key. Animal magnetism! All you have to do is attend the lecture. Try to convince McCloud to go along. At the end of the presentation, ask Wheedle about mesmerism. Let him blather on about it, as he surely will, long enough to impress the audience with his expertise. And then focus your inquiry: 'Would a person suffering from amnesia be able to recall their past under hypnosis? Can a person in such a trance remember forgotten experiences from early childhood? And if a person has forgotten a formerly learned language, would that person be able to speak it while hypnotized?' You get the idea. He'll pontificate, no doubt, extol the powers of hypnosis, and boast of his own skills. That's when you say this: 'Perhaps, sir, you have heard the legend of Romulus and Remus, the history of Kaspar Hauser of Nuremberg, and the accounts of the Pig Boy of Kronstat, the Chicken Girl of Bellingham, the Wolf Girls of Midnapore, and, most recently, the Tiger Boy of Rakshapur? Surely these children of the forest, reared by wild animals in isolation from human contact, must be of some interest to you as director of an institute dedicated to the investigation of incredible and unusual phenomena. I wonder whether or not the inducement of a hypnotic trance might enable us to solve the manifold mysteries that surround the boy, to answer such questions as: Who were his true parents? At what age, and under what conditions, was he adopted by tigers? and, most beguiling of all: Why does he speak Sanskrit on occasion and no other language whatsoever? The answers to these specific questions about our specimen of *Homo ferus* would surely answer much larger questions about the true nature of *Homo sapiens*.'" Perhaps it was because I imagined how amused Wyoming Willie and Maharanee Mayadevee would have been by Hugh Mann that I went along with it. I was hardly able to pay any more attention to the lecture in Calcutta than I was when I first heard it in San Francisco. As Wheedle recounted his adventures, pointing to enlarged photographs of footprints of the Abominable Snowman, I leaned forward in my seat to look down the row at Pythia, seated on the far side of her father, and, seeing her little shoes and delicate ankles, I thought of Angel, closed my eyes, and reached for the loosely tied bow of pink ribbon on white underlinens. My eyes opened by applause, I raised my hand. After the same questions about the Abominable Snowman that had been asked at Coit Theatre, I got the floor and delivered my lines. I had Wheedle in the palm of Hugh's hand and Dr. McCloud was squeezed in next to him. "Oh yes," the lecturer answered with scientific certitude, "hypnosis could solve this case, taking the boy back to reveal the truth." Major Wheedle and Dr. Mc-

Cloud shook hands. The scientists were eager to begin the experiment. The next day, growling slightly and crouching down a bit as he always did around male strangers, Hugh was installed on the divan, close to the chair in which Wheedle seated himself. Behind the hypnotist there was a seat from which Karnaghee would translate to and from Sanskrit. And lined up against the bookshelf walls were chairs for the spectators: Dr. McCloud, Pythia, the Maharaja, Tara, Coffin-White, Kumar and Albert Bannerjee, Maithun Wadsworth Tagore, both Goldmans, the Fitzwillys, and others too, including me. When Wheedle asked for the jillmills to be closed to darken the room, Ishmael obeyed. Then lighting a white candle, the experimenter held it in his left hand in front of his subject's face, gesturally inviting the boy to stare at it as he passed his right hand in wide and graceful sweeps all around Hugh, staring all the while through the flickering flame into his eyes: "Notice now that your eyelids are getting heavy, very heavy, heavier"—and Karnaghee translated simultaneously, "guru, gariyas, garishtha"—"yes, your eyelids are getting heavier, more and more tired, heavier, so heavy that they are beginning to blink. Don't struggle. Relax. Let your eyelids close, tighter, tighter, heavier and heavier, and relax, deeper, go deeper, deeper, deeper relaxed, heavier, heavier. With each breath you are going deeper, deeper, and deeper relaxed. A numb, heavy feeling is moving up, up, up from your toes and feet, up your legs, your thighs, deeper. Heavier, deeper, deep, deep sleep." Because Karnaghee, having fallen asleep himself, had stopped translating into Sanskrit for Hugh, he had to be awakened with a swift kick from McCloud. "You want to go deeper, deeper, farther and farther back, back, long ago." Wheedle was counting backwards from a hundred, interspersing the numbers with repeated deeper's: ". . . forty-five, forty-four, forty-three, yes, deeper, farther, all the way back, back to a time before there were any tigers, back to your very first memory. What do you see? What do you hear? Can you tell us?" Hugh's head nodded in a languorously prolonged "yes." Then slowly he opened his eyes, and slowly, so slowly, he parted his lips to speak.

	Confident that through the powers of hypnosis he had trans-
43	ported the wild boy of Alipore back in time, into a childhood
	memory preceding whatever it was that had separated him from
	his parents (an event sufficiently traumatic to precipitate both

acute aphasia and chronic amnesia), Major Wheedle proceeded with questions
aimed at establishing the true history of the foundling. The boy had no recollection of his natural parents: "My mother died shortly after I was born, and
then my father ran away." Everyone was naturally surprised that it was stated
in perfect English. His earliest memory was a sunny one of lolling lazily beside
a stream on a summer afternoon: "I'm looking at a shiny green, gold-speckled,
chrysalis nestled in the curve of leaf. It begins to tremble, throb, shake, split,
and now something's squeezing out of it. A butterfly! Yes, a yellow-and-black
striped nymph struggling to unfold crumpled wings, unbend cramped and
crinkled legs, and I hear Aunt Elizabeth's voice in the distance. She's calling out
for me, 'Warren! Warren!' She's searching for me: 'Where are you, Warren?'
But I don't answer. I want to stay and witness the first flight of the reborn creature. I don't care what else happens." It seemed reasonable to assume that Aunt
Elizabeth was some kindly cantonment memsahib who, before the tiger got
him, had adopted the orphaned native, and that her guardianship undoubtedly
accounted for both his British name and his quite extraordinary command of
English. Becoming gravely empathetic, Major Wheedle rested his hand reassuringly on the boy's arm to ask the important question: "And is that when you
saw the tiger? When you were in the jungle, by the river? When Aunt Elizabeth
couldn't find you?" The suspense in the room was broken by Hugh's sudden
laughter. "Good Lord, or course not! I didn't see a tiger until I came to India."
Wheedle was as confused as anyone present. "The stream is not in India?" the
puzzled major inquired and an animated Hugh laughed again. "No, no, it was
Blessingham stream near Churchill. The wildest beast one might encounter
there would probably be a hedgehog or a field mouse. I didn't see my first tiger,
not a live or uncaged one, until the Company sent me upriver to Kasimbazar."
Wheedle, now at a complete loss as to what was happening, trying to compose
himself and maintain control, tentatively inquired as to whether or not his subject happened to know his full name and the date and place of his birth: "Well, of
course! Do you take me for some sort of cretin? I was born on the sixth day of
December, 1732, in Daylesford, Oxfordshire. And my name, sir, as if you didn't
know, is Warren Hastings." The audience gasped. Could we, everyone was dying to know, really somehow be in communication with Warren Hastings, *the*

Warren Hastings, architect of the Empire? A nonplused hypnotist looked to McCloud as if he might have a rational explanation of the incredible scene. The room was silent. "I've heard of such occurrences," the major finally said, "but never believed in them myself. It appears, much to my astonishment, that we've gone very far back indeed, not into the childhood of this pitiful lad, but into a previous childhood, that of a transmigrating soul. Oh dear! I suppose I'd better bring him out of it." Despite gasps of "no," Wheedle, counting forward ("forty-one, forty-two, forty-three") and interspersing the numbers with "you are waking up, wide awake, awake, refreshed, awake, aware," brought Hugh back. The Tiger Boy growled softly, slumped his shoulders, and timidly glanced around the room at the amazed faces. Wheedle was perspiring, clearing his throat, and trying to say something that made sense: "I've never experienced anything like it. Something very extraordinary has transpired here today." Everyone was flabbergasted except me, for in addition to the William William-Monier's Sanskrit phrase book, I had provided Hugh with a copy of Sir Alfred Aspton's epistolary biography of Warren Hastings. A flurried McCloud, taking a triple shot of opiated whiskey, insisted that Wheedle move into the house so that the two of them could continue the mesmeric experiments. I couldn't believe that anybody believed it, but, as my father and mother used to point out, people like to believe preposterous things. *The Bengal Statesman* reported the story: "Major L. A. Wheedle of the United States of America is conducting experiments here in Calcutta, using hypnosis to scientifically document the empirical reality of the ancient Hindu religious doctrine of transmigration of souls." Major Wheedle, having postponed his search for the Abominable Snowman to devote all his time and energy to hypnotizing Hugh, convinced Dr. McCloud that, working together, they had a good chance, with the publication of their research findings, of earning a Nobel Prize for their breakthrough in the eschatological sciences. Succumbing to temptation, McCloud felt his interests in herpetology, antivenins, and even croquet beginning to wane. "The development of an antitoxin would certainly reduce the number of deaths by snakebite in Bengal," he remarked as he stirred a black pellet into Wheedle's whiskey snifter, "but our experiments, demonstrating the fate of the soul after death, will benefit not merely the native population of Bengal, but all of humanity." The voice of Warren Hastings had an even more profound effect upon Reverend Theophilus Fitzwilly; becoming utterly convinced of the validity of metempsychosis, a doctrine absolutely irreconcilable with Christian metaphysical dogma, the pious cleric removed his Episcopal collar and donned the ochre robe of a Hindu acolyte. Much to the annoyance of his wife, the Bishop of Bengal, and the more devout members of his congregation, he became a disciple of the guru Shree Karnaghee, who renamed the convert

Swami Madananda. Out of the hypnotic state, the adolescent foundling became all the more insensate, regressing into his animality, and never speaking a word. But once the jillmills in the library were closed and the white taper lit, once Major Wheedle was counting backwards, the curtain would rise on an amazing drama in three acts, three incredible stories of the three previous lives of the amazing Tiger Boy. Hugh's most recent past life, we discovered in the next hypnosis session, accounted for his apparent knowledge of Sanskrit: born in the village of Shantivihar, near Kasimbazar in north Bengal in 1858 and named Shankara Sharma by his Brahmin parents, he spoke a rather refined Bengali spiced in the pedantic panditic style with Sanskrit terminology. After the session, I listened to Dr. McCloud paraphrasing in English the Bengali speech, made under hypnosis, for Wheedle: "My life, except for the beautiful Rani (first a joy and then a heartbreak, but always a blessing), has not been so unusual an existence for a man of my varna, endeavoring as I have always done to represent my station by fulfilling all the duties that are incumbent upon a Brahmin. After investiture, I dutifully worshipped my spiritual preceptor's lotus feet, collecting kusha grass for the rituals, abstaining from all sense pleasures, and reciting the Veda with diligence. Upon completion of my education, I returned to the home of my beloved parents, who had arranged for my marriage to a virgin Brahmin girl who was sweet of tongue and relatively free of moles, freckles, and other unseemly bodily blemishes. In the very year that the great Victoria became empress of India, there was a smallpox epidemic in our village that, despite my most ardent sacrifices and relentless recitations, took my parents and my bride from me. In sorrow I repaired to the jungle to live an ascetic life of meditation. One day, while gathering roots and fruits for my daily repast, I heard crying, a whimpering so touchingly plaintive that I could not, despite my vows of detachment, resist the temptation to investigate. I found her in a dense patch of ringals: my little Rani, all by herself, trembling, afraid and hungry—a baby tiger. As soon as I picked her up, she licked my face, and, when I held her in my arms, she purred. I carried her back to my hut, gave her milk, and she slept that night cuddled up next to me on the charpoy. I raised her as my own child, my only child, loving her with all my heart. I believe that Rani believed that she was a human being, so much so that she adopted my own vegetarian diet and listened attentively each morning as I recited the Gayatri mantra. The villagers and forest dwellers were astounded to see such an absolutely docile tiger. Every father of a girl knows that inevitably the day will come for the ceremony of kanyadhan, of giving the daughter away in marriage. And though it may bring tears to the eyes, it must be. And so I accepted it when the man from America, having heard of the incredible tame tiger of the Shantivihar forest, arrived, proposing to take her away with him. I was relieved that he did not ask for a dowry. She was a talented girl, my beloved Rani, and went on to earn fame and fortune in America in what they call 'Vedaville.' Though she was as sweet and gentle as any pussycat at home, when she pretended to be a wild on stage, her ferocious roar made everyone believe that she was a man-eater. I was proud of her and happy, so happy until, one day not long ago, I encountered a young farmer on the road, taking his vegetables to sell in Kasimbazar. He spit at me and cursed. 'How do you dare to greet a Brahmin so disrespectfully?' I asked, not out of anger at the lad, but out of fear for him, out of a concern over the terrible misfortune that such misbehavior would bring him in his next life. He sneered at me: 'I cannot treat you otherwise, you who are responsible for the death of my father!' Much to my despair, I then learned from him that his father had been eaten by a tiger, Rani's mother. Returning to her lair only to discover that her cub was missing, she became infuriated and so brokenhearted that she would take any risk to try to find her baby. Having smelled a human being (my own scent!) where she had left the cub, she prowled around the villages in her search, her anger displacing all fear of people and turning her into a man-eater. Unfortunately she ate eight villagers including the young farmer's father. The government shikhari duly shot and killed the man-eating mother. So, you see, I am responsible for the death of that poor creature, who was rightfully fulfilling her dharma as a mother and a tiger, as well as for the deaths of those eight villagers. In remorse, I have called upon the spiritual preceptor with whom I lived as a brahmachari in childhood, and confessed the whole story to him. He says that, because I let my emotions get the better of my judgment when I heard those cries, I am destined in my next life to be stolen as an infant from a human mother by a tiger and to be raised in the jungle as a wild animal. I accept my destiny. The joy that Rani gave me in the past amply compensates for the misery that awaits me in the future."

44 "Deeper and deeper, down, down, farther and farther back," Major Wheedle repeated, waving his hypnotic hands in circles over the limp adolescent body, coaxing the transmigrating soul back into his previous incarnation. The last memory was a blinding flash and deafening *ka-bamm!* of gunfire. And then nothing. "Farther back, just a little farther," the hypnotist urged, steadfastly guiding the unmoored soul into safe anchorage. "Where are you? Who are you?" As Hugh opened his eyes, a stranger looked at us and looked strange. His name was Kholo Mehtar, a pariah whose merest glance was polluting. And his onus in that life, in between being Warren Hastings and Shankara Sharma, had been to clean British latrines. Karnaghee offered a cosmological English gloss on the pathetic Bengali story: "For his wanton extirpation of the innocents of the Rohillas, for mercilessly tormenting Raja Chait Singh, for turning the lush garden that was Oudh into the miserable desert that is the United Provinces, for molesting begums and torturing natives who did not submit to his imperial governance, Mr. Warren Hastings, following his corporeal death in 1818, was reborn as this miserable bangi, lower than Ishmael and Ibrahim, lower than a mahar, chamar, or dhobi, the very lowest of the lowliest lowlies, thus conclusively demonstrating the cosmic justice of the immutable laws of karma as elucidated in the eternal Veda. But what, we must objectively determine, did this abject chandala do to become a venerable Brahmin like my own good self? What extraordinary act of righteousness could have justified such a leap of station?" Kholo's Bengali was too difficult for me to follow. It was teeming with "vulgarities appropriate only to the toilets he himself emptied and cleaned," Pythia said as, later that night, she began to undress. Removing the black pins from her blond hair, and shaking her head to loosen her curls, she apologized that she could not literally translate the posthumous report, but promised that she would at least convey the content of the tale: "I won't try to capture the disgusting tone of it. I wonder how on earth Daddy translated it for Major Wheedle. Daddy never says things like 'fuck,' and our Kholo relentlessly used such words as *'chodh,' 'bahenchuth'* and *'madarchuth,' 'chuth,' 'lavda,'* and *'gaand'*—'fuck, motherfucker and sisterfucker, cunt, cock, and asshole.' I'm going to skip those parts, if you'll pardon me, but that kind of talk puts me out of the mood for sexual intercourse. Especially 'fuck.'" Discarding her lustrous peach sateen bloomers, Pythia crawled into the bed next to me to tell me a bowdlerized version of the story of Kholo Mehtar and the Sepoy Rebellion: "In May of 1857, a coolie at Dum-Dum asked a sepoy named Pashupati Acharya for a sip of water from his lota. Acharya explained that, as a Brahmin, sharing his bowl with a low-caste person would be polluting. Here Kholo's mouth so gushed with filth that I must sanitize extensively. The pariah uttered obscenities and laughed at the Brahmin: 'I wouldn't worry about being defiled by me! You're going to lose your caste purity altogether! The British are going to make you eat beef! Yes, haven't you heard? The cartridges for the new Enfields are greased with cow fat, and you'll have to bite them to load them!' Pashupati Acharya went crazy with rage. Brandishing a loaded musket, he marched straight to the bungalow of a Colonel Harding and commanded the commander to appear: 'Come out here, you blank-blank blank madarchuth (oh, do excuse me, Isaac), I'm going to kill you. Then I'm going to (you know) your blank-blank wife in the blank.' I think I'll just skip over the blanks or I'll be here all night. Appearing on the verandah to determine the source of the commotion (and there were some obscene words about Mrs. Harding at this point), the colonel promptly ordered his sepoy attendants to shoot the madman. But they refused because he was a Brahmin and harming a Brahmin is the gravest sin that a Hindu can commit, even graver than letting cow fat touch your lips. But when Pashupati Acharya fired at Harding and the bullet hit the gora-sahib in the thigh, one of the sepoys, a Mohammedan, leapt onto the Brahmin from behind and wrestled him to the ground. Acharya was immediately imprisoned, tried the next day, and condemned to be executed at the end of the week." When I reached over to caress Pythia, she stopped me. "No, let me finish. You must be patient. You're always in such a hurry. I haven't come to the important part yet, to what Kholo Mehtar did to become reborn as Shankara Sharma. Kholo was Colonel Harding's bangi, the lowest of the servants in the household, the one who cleans the toilets. Going to perform that duty, unaware that his master was using the commode at that moment, Kholo, pushing the door in with some force, quite accidentally knocked that door into the wounded thigh of the colonel. In fury, with a pain that screamed to be inflicted on another, Harding thrashed his servant, shoved him to the ground, kicked him, and then, for good measure, proclaimed a punishment: 'This week you will not only wash my latrine, but you will also clean up the shit and piss of the prisoners in our jail, the cells of which are not equipped with toilets of any kind. That, my nigger Hercules, should teach you a lesson!' Lots of filthy language, of course, during this part of the story. Be that as it may, the next day Kholo, carrying a lantern, rag, and bucket, was admitted into the windowless, toiletless cell in which Pashupati Acharya was solitarily confined to await execution. 'Sub lal hogea hai,' the sepoy said to the bangi, 'everything will become red. The blood of the feringhis will flood India. Have you not seen the chapattis?' Urging Kholo to take part in the mutiny, he assured him that he could become one of the greatest heroes in India's history: 'All you have to do is give me your turban and loincloth. I'll adopt your obsequious posture, downtrodden gait, and then walk out of here to join the loyal men of the Native 44th Artillery for the attack on Meerut and then on to Delhi. As my liberator, you'll be responsible for our victory. When, coming to get me for the execution, they discover that I am actually you, they'll ask for an explanation. Just tell them that you were too intoxicated on bhang and opium to remember what happened. Then they'll let you go.' Kholo confessed to Major Wheedle that it was not so much to support the rebellion that he agreed to do what the mutineer had ordered as it was because he realized that if the execution were carried out, his master, Colonel Harding, would be responsible for the death of a Brahmin and would, thus, be punished in his next life, condemned to the lowest of low births, even lower than his own: 'And because it is my duty to serve my master, colonel-sahib, I did what the criminal told me to do.' The two gora-log guards, arriving at the jail to escort the prisoner to his place before the firing squad, immediately gagged Kholo and blindfolded him with a black hood so that he was neither recognized nor given an opportunity to identify himself. He probably would have been shot even if he had not been silenced since Colonel Harding, the only person other than himself or Pashupati Acharya who knew who he was, had gone to Hooghly and been hospitalized there because the wound to his thigh had become quite perilously infected. Kholo didn't live long enough to find out whether or not he actually ever became one of the greatest heroes in India's history. It's a rather melancholy story. But sad stories, unlike foul language, do sometimes make me a bit amorous. Okay, Isaac, I'm ready now. Yes, we can make love now." Karnaghee had climaxed the Bengali version of the story with an English proclamation that "with a flash and *ka-bamm!* of gunfire, the chandala became a Brahmin. The lowest was transformed into the highest; fecal matter was transmuted into gold." After Wheedle had brought Hugh back to consciousness, we had our customary late-night opiated whiskey (the "only thing to prevent insomnia and Indian indoluria," Dr. McCloud said, yawning). Hugh guzzled his dram in the corner while the rest of us mixed. It was the first time I had met Nagendra Bannerjee, just out of jail (thanks to the clever lawyering of Menachem Goldman), and brought as a guest to the hypnosis session by his brothers Albert and Kumar. "If only Mahatma Gandhi had been around at the time," Kumar sighed sympathetically, "he could have helped poor Kholo." Dr. McCloud subsequently offended Kumar by referring to Gandhi as that "bandy-legged, trouble-making little cotton spinner who hates sex, science, and us." Nagendra, on the other hand, a former Gandhian and active activist in the Calcutta Noncooperation Cooperative, was amused by the characterization. During his most recent stint in jail, after reading a pamphlet by Leon Trotsky, he had, he announced, become disenchanted with Gandhi, and violently opposed to his ideology of nonviolence. "Violence is man's only hope for peace." Tara and Coffin-White agreed with Nagendra, noting that the social behavior of wild animals in the jungle proved Gandhi's strategies unnatural. Coffin-White added that the great religions of the world, while disagreeing on the specifics of dietary and sexual restrictions, unanimously extolled aggression. "Our gods," Nagendra boasted, "Shiva, Vishnu, Durga, and the rest, are far more violent than yours." Coffin-White begged to differ: "At Jericho our God smote not only the men, women, and children just as your gods might have done, but our God killed the cows as well, and that's something your gods would never have the gumption to do." Escorted by Nagini, Pythia, bored by political and religious debate, left for bed where she'd linger before joining me in my room once all the guests had gone and her father had retired. While waiting for her, I reread the letter I had received from my mother that day. As usual she had written to tell me about people who had died: this time it was both Jackrabbit Jake Gotlober and Skadi Namnlösa. I couldn't help but wonder if Skadi, given her participation in the rites of the Pentecostal Church of the Outpouring of the Latter Day Rain of Love, had died of snakebite. But, while mother didn't reveal the cause of either death, she did mention that Hayim Grossman had asked her to marry him. In the otherwise quiet house, I could faintly hear laughter from the pantry downstairs. Although it was obvious that Hugh was squeezing my hyena and laughing along with it, I wasn't sure which laugh was his and which was the hyena's.

45

"The highest place on earth, crown of the Great Goddess Chomolungma, Holy Mother of the World," a salivating Major Wheedle said as he stabbed a pork sausage that, the instant its skin was pierced, spit hot fat onto the gray beard resting on his Sears & Roebuck dining dickie. "There's nothing in the world hotter than a hot sausage," he earnestly remarked as if it were true, and then, blowing on the dribbling morsel of stuffed intestine on the tines of his fork, turned back to Mt. Everest: "It's where the Yeti breeds, protected from humankind by the insurmountable heights, by cold, wind, ice, stone, and the vaporous thinness of the heavenly air. It's there that I'll capture one of the elusive creatures. My plan is top secret, so don't whisper a word of it. Intelligence reports indicate that the Soviets are putting an expedition together, and we wouldn't want the Communists to bag a Yeti before we do." He lowered his voice as if the ears of Bolshevik spies might be pressed to the walls of the adjoining room. In her purple dinner gown, Celeste McCloud seemed to be eavesdropping. "I'm going to disguise myself as one of them with golden fur, huge fake paws, a pointed hairy head, and, of course, very, very big feet, and then, I'll lure one to me by prancing about suggestively on the slopes of Rongbuk Valley, which, my friend Lama Kushog Doubtub Gylatsap avows, is the Yeti mating ground." With his blue silk Christmas cummerbund sagging loosely around his waist, Ishmael, sneering in barely concealed disgust at the pork that he was constrained to serve to infidels, and listening in hardly hidden disapprobation to the adventurer's screed, yawned as he shuffled around the table with his tray. Hugh was wolfing the sausages down like an animal as Wheedle explained that, just as the Tibetans are well aware of the existence of Yetis, so too they are certain of the reality of the transmigration of selves from one body to another in a series of karmicly determined lives. "The perspicacious lamas," he peremptorily assured us, "would not be in the slightest bit surprised by what has come out of the Tiger Boy's trances. They rely on such posthumous revelations to determine their leadership. The soul of the deceased reincarnates forty-nine days after death." In the midst of Wheedle's elucidation of Tibetan eschatology, Hugh, on his eighth sausage, suddenly broke wind. "No, no, my boy," Dr. McCloud gently chided, "human beings don't do that at table. Sausages do, alas, give all people, no matter how civilized, gas. But it is a mark of our humanity that we learn to restrain ourselves until we have a moment alone. I'm sure that Warren Hastings never passed gas during supper in the company of a young lady." Pythia, who had not taken a single bite of her sausage, asked Major Wheedle if he thought Hugh had any idea of who Warren Hastings was, any consciousness or memory of what he had experienced while mesmerized. "It is very unlikely," the major answered between bites and swallows. "His present mind moves aside during trance to let the mind of the former governor-general, the Brahmin, or the toilet cleaner take over those areas of the brain that think and speak. It was as if he were dispatched to another room in the lodge of consciousness. But we are only on the frontier of our research with hypnosis as a tool to excavate the mind for the remains of previous lives. The only thing like it that I've previously experienced firsthand was a spirit speaking from beyond the grave that I once witnessed in California. I was taken to a séance conducted by an Indian medium. As a scientist and a Hegelian to boot, I am bent on being objective, logical, even skeptical and yet, of course, open-minded. Since the world of spiritualistic phenomena is rife with quacks and charlatans, metapsychical claims must be investigated with scientific probity. I saw the glowing spirit of that revenant in California with my own eyes, heard her unearthly voice with my own ears, and, both before and after the conjuration, I methodically examined the spirit cabinet in which she so mysteriously made her appearance. I can attest that it was all quite real. And I am no less convinced of the authenticity of the testimony of Warren Hastings from the mouth of this pathetic creature." Hugh farted again, whereupon Dr. McCloud asked me to take him for a walk in the fresh air. Once outside the Tiger Boy asked if I'd mind getting more cigarettes for him as well as a few books: *The Origin of Species, Tarzan, Civilization and Its Discontents*, and *The Story of Doctor Doolittle*. Later, after everyone had retired, while waiting in bed for Pythia, I wondered whether she'd want us to be Yetis that night. I decided that if so, I'd tell her Wheedle had confided in me, in greater detail than he supposed suitable for the ears of a young lady, that during intercourse the Abominable Snowman lies on top of the Abominable Snowwoman, facing her in embrace. Much to my surprise, however, I didn't have to lie: Pythia did not want to pretend that were Abominable Snowlovers that night. She had stranger things in mind. "If you could make love as anybody in history," she asked as she rolled off the first of her silk stockings, "incarnating that person's soul, feeling just what he (or she, for that matter) felt, physically and emotionally, during intercourse, who would that be?" As she slipped out of her slip, I easily answered: "Antony. Antony making love to Cleopatra." Standing unself-consciously naked before me and, as usual, ignoring my answer to her question, she told me with a straight face that she suspected that she had been Elizabeth Barrett Browning in a previous life. Sex might help her confirm it. "Sex," she explained, "which Elizabeth herself described as 'that strain of passion which devours the flesh in a sacrament of souls,' when you give yourself over to it completely, dissolving in it, letting your pleasure become its pleasure, a bliss in which you merely participate, is very much like hypnotic trance. Thought is suspended, individuality disintegrated, boundaries between lives obliterated. It is thus during intercourse, just as during mesmeric transports, that one can remember and experience past lives." As she crawled into the bed, I asked if the Brownings faced each other during sex. She ignored my question: "I loved Elizabeth's poems at a very early age, even before I could understand them, and I always found them easy to memorize. I won the Lancashire League of Ladies Elocution Award in my first year at school for a recitation of her sonnet: 'Straightway I was aware how a mystic shape did move behind me, and pulled me backward by the hair; and a voice said in mastery while I strove, "Guess now who holds thee?" "Death," I said, but there the silver answer rang: "Not Death, but Love."'" I told her it was beautiful and she thanked me as if she had herself really authored it. During lovemaking she whispered "Robert" and at the dénouement of it cried out, "I love thee with the breath, smiles, tears, of all my life! And, if God choose, I shall but love thee better after death." I was very pleased the girl I loved had told me for the second time that she loved me as well, even though I knew it was not Pythia McCloud speaking to Isaac Schlossberg, but Elizabeth Barrett baring her soul to Robert Browning. As she slipped back into her slip, she reflected on the past: "Elizabeth died on the twenty-ninth of June, 1861 and I was born on the eighth of February, 1903. So the important question remains: 'Who was I during the missing forty-two years?' Major Wheedle has explained that the Tibetans, who follow the transmigrations of their lamas from body to body, from life to life, hold that the soul wanders in something called the Bardo for forty-nine days between death and rebirth. Thus I was, in my last life, born on the eighteenth of August, 1861, and died on the twenty-first of December, the darkest night of the year, 1902. I must find someone with those exact vital statistics." The next night after dinner, when we had adjourned to the card room for port, Pythia pleaded for Wheedle to hypnotize her, to take her back, all the way back, into the Barrett home on Wimpole Street in London. She went under almost immediately. I knew that she was not faking it, for had she been putting on a show, we would certainly have heard a few *Sonnets from the Portuguese*. Wheedle did take her back to England, not to London, however, but to the country house in Lancashire where the McClouds had lived before the physician had been dispatched to India. Seeing a rooster mounting a hen in the yard, Pythia cried, "Mummy! The naughty cock is killing the hen." An amused Celeste McCloud had eased her daughter's fears: "No, my darling Pythia, they're just making little chicks. I'm sure you'll do the same one day. Our hen, despite her squawking, is not so displeased as it seems by what the rooster's doing." An awakened Pythia was eager to hear about her former life. Naturally disappointed, she complained that Wheedle had not taken her farther back. He defended himself: "Such returns as we have witnessed with Shankara Sharma, Kholo Mehtar, and Warren Hastings are extremely rare and cannot be expected." She asked him to try it on me: "See how far back you can take Isaac." I didn't want to be hypnotized, but Pythia made me particularly vulnerable to her whim by tenderly saying that "perhaps you'll turn out to be Robert Browning. Wouldn't that be beautiful?" With Pythia, Dr. McCloud, Celeste, Ishmael, Ibrahim, Nagini, and Hugh staring at me, I took my place on the couch after dinner, looked through the candlelight into Major Wheedle's eyes, and listened: "Your eyelids are getting heavy, heavier," and, as he counted backwards, "forty-six, forty-five, forty-four," I had a very pleasant feeling, faint at first, a vague sensation that it was not simply me reclining there, not merely Isaac Schlossberg, nor anyone else in particular, gazing at the flickering flame and hearing Major Wheedle's voice. ". . . Thirty-three, thirty-two. You're going down, down, deeper, farther, back, back." There was no transmigrating soul, but it was, I imagined, as if (". . . twenty-six, twenty-five") life itself were perceiving itself through my senses, that something formless, persistent, and separate from any individual was appreciating itself through me. There was an odd feeling that when I have died, this same whatever-it-is will see and hear and feel what I am missing in the world, will have and be this feeling, taking my place, not missing my absence, but being what I no longer am. "Twenty-one, twenty, nineteen." Eyelids opening and closing ("deeper, farther") and torso twisting ("back, back"), arms waving ("deeper"), Cleopatra danced in grace with a red-, yellow-, and black-banded serpent and Angel's voice drowned out numbers in song: *"Amour, seigneur souverain des dieux autant que des hommes, des serpents autant que des anges, devant qui tout disparaît."* "Eighteen." The snake was wrapped around her neck, its tail entwining her left arm, its head clasped in the right hand that drew it toward her face, letting the bifid tongue flick to smell the soft skin of Angel's cheek. The Queen of Egypt danced with ancient languor upon the shimmering deck of a gold-burnished barge with purple sails and silver oars, burning hot on the cool waters of the Nile.

To 67

46 Despite the drastic changes in decor that had been made during the one hundred fifty years or so since he had been there, Warren Hastings recognized the library of the Alipore home. "Where's the hookah?" he asked the moment Hugh's heavy eyelids became light enough to open. "And who the devil is that frightful woman in the painting? Oh Pinkie, you've always had such queer tastes in ladies. I recall with great amusement, some pleasure, and only a spot of pain, that week I spent here with you when Marion thought I was on the budgerow. Remember? You had all those naughty nautchees from Sonagacchi here to entertain us. You and I really are rather heterosexual, at least for Englishmen. We did have a spot of fun, didn't we? And I needed a laugh before Oudh. That was where the trouble broke out and subsequently festered and suppurated. I assume that the Indian press, seizing upon an excuse to defame me, kept Calcutta well informed of the trial. 'High crimes and misdemeanors' my arse! As you yourself were constant witness, I discharged the trust that had been reposed in me by the directors of the Company according to the principles upon which that hallowed institution was founded. And, as governor-general of Bengal, I acted ever and always on behalf of the Empire, striving to maintain the ideals of civilization that it has proffered to all mankind. I performed as a loyal servant to the King, unaware as I was at the time that His Majesty was incurably insane. I do hope, dear Pinkie, that you did not believe a word of the malicious indictments. Everything charged about the Rohillas, the opium monopoly, the Nobkissen diamonds, and the royal family of Oudh was a distortion of truth. And truth, as you well know, has always been my banner. I swear to you as my lifelong friend that neither I nor any of my military or mercantile agents, nor indeed any other British gentlemen known to me, did ever, in any way, molest the begums of Oudh. Do you believe me, Pinkie?" That Wheedle answered yes reassured the former governor-general within the body of the native adolescent: "Women fainted and had to be carried out of Westminster Hall when Burke's bombast so got the better of him that he described to the court how I had supposedly publicly stripped the begums naked and ordered the nipples of their breasts put in clefts of bamboo, and torn off. This was Burke's licentious fantasy, not my actual deed nor inclination. This is not to gainsay that there was violence, and a spot of torture too, but only as much as was necessary to maintain order, peace, justice, and liberty in the Orient. Yes, the eunuchs of the Oudh zenana were flogged. But that is, and always has been, the Hindu way of dealing with such scoundrels. My governance, if it was to be effective, was necessarily executed in an Asiatic fashion. As the Hindu is a spunkless poltroon even with his testicles, imagine how much more recreant he is without them. It took so little torture to encourage the begums' craven eunuchs to sing the pretty song of where the treasury was that I'd hardly deign to call it torture. No, it was more of a cajoling, accomplished, it is true, with Gentoo scourge and thumbscrew, but only to the extent that was legitimately necessary for the greater good of preserving the East India Company and defending the British Empire. But let me get to the point. I'll be candid with you for I do know that I can trust you, Pinkie. You never breathed a word about that week here, or about the pregnancy of the khansamah's wife, my sweetly wanton bibi. I wonder what's happened to the bastard. Who knows or cares? The point is that I need to confide in you once more. I suppose you are aware of the financial setback that the impeachment proceedings caused me. I have a debt of almost two hundred thousand pounds. For the moment I shall be able manage for they cannot legally take Daylesford from me, and the Company has agreed to give me my pension retroactive to 1785, as well as an interest-free loan of fifty thousand pounds to be invested with interest in Company bonds, as if such money could compensate for the humiliation of the trial. Now, Pinkie, here's the situation. I have some money saved from dabbling in the opium trade, profits from personal business dealings that really had nothing to do with the Company or the Crown. But if the government were to become aware of these assets, they would certainly be seized to pay off my debts. And then, if anything were to happen to me, my dear Marion would become destitute. Since the court has not allowed me to make financial provision for her or to provide inheritance to an estate, I have sequestered this revenue so that my beloved wife, provided that she remains faithful to my memory, may be taken care of when I am gone. She herself does not know about this. Women cannot be trusted to keep silent, even when it serves their own interests. That's why I need you, Pinkie. Upon my death, you, unless you die before me, must take responsibility for my fortune, disbursing it discreetly as a trust to keep Marion as comfortable as possible. There is quite enough to make you, for your services and loyalty in the matter, comfortable as well. I've buried it by the Blessingham brook, near Churchill, a spot where I idled away many an hour of my lonely childhood. I'll have to show you the exact location. Will you come with me? Will you help me?" When Wheedle and McCloud answered, in perfect unison, "Yes," Warren Hastings closed his eyes. A protracted silence was finally broken by McCloud: "Whiskey, anyone?" We retired to the card room for strong drink over which awe gave way to excitement. Pythia was telling the Goldmans about the discovery that she had formerly been Elizabeth Barrett Browning, and about her quest to ascertain who she had been between the eighteenth of August, 1861, and the twenty-first of December, 1902: "I've sent notices to be published as queries in newspapers in London, Torquay, Bath, Wankton, Hope's End, Florence, Pisa, Venice, Paris, Lisbon, Jamaica, and Florida, everywhere there's an Elizabeth Barrett Browning connection, either physical or literary. It's terribly exciting. My ayah, Nagini, you know, the murderer's daughter, assures me that she remembers her past life. She was a devadasi in Puri, where she danced and sang each night for Lord Jagannath. Let me call for her, let's have her sing one of the sacred songs tonight. And, please, whichever one of you is Menachem Goldman, do tell her that you're hopeful about the appeal. She misses her father terribly, and worries about him." When she went to fetch Nagini, I asked the Goldmans what they thought of the hypnotic session. One (I'm not sure which) said, "Warren Hastings was a shmuck." Tara and Francis Coffin-White were circling the room to make sure that everyone understood that they were invited to the forthcoming celebration of their wedding at Diwanasthan Palace. I tried to get McCloud's attention in order to inform him that Maarnath the snake charmer had come that afternoon with a pair of king cobras, a male and a female. But the physician was too absorbed in conversation with the hypnotist to take notice. "I've been thinking about the money," I overhead him say to Wheedle, and Wheedle answered McCloud, "Yes, so have I. I don't mean the money per se, not the cash as mere lucre, but rather the revenue as proof that this boy really does contain the reincarnated self of Warren Hastings. If, under hypnosis, he could lead us to that buried treasure, there would be no doubt at all that we are in contact with the deceased statesman. We could dedicate the funds to support further metempsychotic research. Together with the embursement that we shall probably receive from the Nobel Foundation, it should go a long way." McCloud was concerned: "But if the money isn't there, will it disprove anything? Hastings could have, during his lifetime, actually already taken Pinkie (whoever he was) to the site. Pinkie and Mrs. Hastings may well have already spent it." Wheedle proposed that he would contact Hastings directly during the next mesmeric session in order to determine whether or not he had already shown Pinkie where the money was buried. Hugh was squatting in the corner like an animal. Maithun Wadsworth Tagore, handsome in his clean white pajama and khurta, with his long ringlets of shiny black hair and oiled mustache, introducing himself to me, remarked that he had been inspired by the session: "I'm a director of motion picture films, and I want to make a movie of this." Interested to learn that I had formerly acted in motion pictures, Tagore was then ecstatic to discover that they had been directed by Joseph Siegel. "The master!" he exclaimed. "The great Siegel, so misunderstood as an artist in America! It is my humble aspiration to become the Bengali Joseph Siegel." His enthusiasm for Siegel's work was so great that he asked me to play the part of the young Warren Hastings in the film. With the clinking of a dessert spoon against a whiskey glass Pythia seized our attention to announce that her ayah would sing for us: "Nagini may be my dutiful servant by circumstance, but she is my beloved friend by feeling and perhaps by bonds forged in past lives, during one of which she was a devadasi. Because she is by nature demure, I have, for your pleasure, had to exercise my prerogative as her mistress to command her to sing for you a song that she once sang for the Lord of the Universe." The ruby-studded nose ring, cerulean bangles, and silver earrings glistened stunningly and the pastel-blue Chanderi sari made her seem as soft as sky. With serpent-tattooed hands poised palm to palm in a gesture of devotion, eyes lowered in modesty, she softly hummed the melody and then slowly began to sing, and though she sang softy, so softly, each note pierced the heart. If you closed your eyes, you might think she really was a devadasi. "*Virahashokar vishishtah . . . ,*" she sang, and later that night Pythia translated the famous idolatrous Sanskrit hymn, holy words transmitted from one lover to another, eager to be passed along, sung to beloved after beloved, again and again: "Exquisite is the pain of separation. When I am apart from you, you are everywhere: all shadows are cast by you and every rustle of leaves is your whisper; I smell your cheek in the blossoms I pick in pretense that they come from you, taste your lips in mead drunk to ease the anguish of a heart cockled by your absence, and I feel the warmth of your neck and shoulder in the bough I clutch to keep from falling. Exquisite is the pain . . ." Pythia hesitated. "Or something like that. It doesn't really matter, does it? All love songs, no matter how eloquent or crude, ornamented or plain, in whatever language they are sung, say essentially the same thing. All love stories have but one meaning."

47 "His Highness the Maharaja of Diwanasthan regally requests the honour of your presence at the marriage ceremonial to be consummated by Colonel Francis Coffin-White and Miss Tara Tigresse at noon on Saturday, the first of April, at Diwanasthan Palace for libational, gustatorial, terpeschoreal, and philharmoneal celebrations of the hallowed hymeneal ritual." The palace was an eighteenth-century reconstruction of a Gothic castle in ruins, purchased and disassembled in Wanktonshire, England, in 1899, and then shipped to India for reassembly in Diwanasthan. An accidental switch in the chaos of the Hooghly dockyard of two shipments of opium for two containers of sandstone, ashlar, iron, and oak (the materials for three garderobes, two oubliettes, a turret, and the castle's portcullis) had necessitated some architectural modifications. The Maharaja was curious to see whether or not the Tiger Boy might recognize Wankton Castle, since it had formerly stood not far from Churchill, where he had played as a child two hundred years earlier. With a homburg on his head, Hugh, dressed up for his first social event outside the Alipore compound, did, as he sniffed the walls with apparent olfactory curiosity, seem to recognize something. Shulamite Levi, who had been invited to accompany the feral boy in order to encourage him to behave as humanly as possible during the ceremony, turned to me: "*Les aromes des pipis anciens lui plaisant beaucoup.*" Guests were greeted at the arched entrance to the castle's inner ward by the Maharaja himself, gorgeously garbed in a gold-embroidered apricot silk brocade flared knee coat and rusty-rose skintight leggings, and dandily draped with hefty necklaces of white, pink, and black pearls. And especially for the nuptial feast, he had chosen, out of his vast collection of headgear, to crown himself with his precious Geronimo's warbonnet (authenticated by the autograph of the Apache Wildcat himself). "Welcome to a jubilee of love," he repeated as each guest filed past to namaskar him. When it was her turn to greet the ruler of Diwanasthan, Mother Bannerjee burst into tears, fell to her knees, and kissed his curly-toed, cobra-skin royal slippers. Lifting her up with the help of his brothers, Kumar, after assuring His Majesty that his mother's obeisant prostration expressed an affection felt for him by the entire family, including his late father, added: "This day is made even more joyous for us by the fact that it marks the end of a two-year ascetical vow of silence and fasting undertaken by our blessed mother in holy memory of our venerable father. She spoke for the first time this morning." What, the Maharaja and everyone in the line within hearing distance naturally wondered, had been her first words? "Rasogoola," Kumar announced, referring to the sweetest of Bengali sweets, so sweet that they almost sear the tongue. "She said that she hoped Your Highness would be serving rasogoola." Matajee did have ample opportunity to devour the confections, waddling throughout the day from table to table in room after room in search of them, with her daughters and daughters-in-law, their faces covered with the ends of their saris, following her like chicks trying, in fear of raptors, to huddle under a hen. The Bannerjees were even more convivial than usual, celebrating not only the wedding, the end of their mother's austerities, and the release of Nagendra from jail, but also a visit by Ganesh, making a stopover on the way to Ulan Bator, where he would purchase two two-humped Bactrian camels for the Bannerjee Brothers Magnificent Menagerie. After grandiloquent greetings, there were tender condolences over the death of my father. "Camels," my friend from California sighed, "are so much safer than airplanes. Bactrians, a rarity in American circuses and shows, in contrast to the one-humped dromedary, are good-natured and mild-mannered. Thus everyone loves to sit between their humps. And when it comes to romance, they are never testy like mononubblous Arabians. Yes, in matters and manners of love, they are most civilized. Our newly wedded couple would do well to look unto the Bactrian camel for inspiration in their conjugal life." At this point, catching what was being said out of the corner of her delicate ear, Pythia, stunning in her pink fichu gown, turned away from Kumar, with whom she had been discussing reincarnation, to listen to Ganesh. Nagini stood by her in a white Maheshwari sari and daffodil-yellow silk choli. A Mr. Hillcastle, who apparently knew Pythia quite well, sidled in between her and me to hear Ganesh's account of true love: "When a Bactrian female comes into heat, her beaus peaceably, without any of the spitting and nipping that one would expect from the one-humper, line up single file and, on a first-come-first-serve basis, in an orderly, polite, and yet most amorous manner, mount her. When finished, each paramour, courteously giving way to the next, humbly and happily proceeds to the end of the line, where he patiently awaits another turn at his ladylove's rump." "Charming!" Hillcastle said. "Don't you think so, Pythia, my dear?" I walked away before she could answer. Since Tara had been residing in the Bannerjee home, it was Kumar's duty, as the oldest male member of the household, to give her away. The ceremony, held in the castle bailey, was performed by Father Theophilus Fitzwilly, a.k.a. Swami Madananda, who, though having renounced his formerly fervent Christian faith to become a Hindu, was still licensed by the Episcopal Church and the colonial government of Bengal to solemnize marriages. After the bride and groom had sworn to love, honor, and protect each other in this and any future lives in which they might be reunited, there was a six-gun salute, and then, only a few minutes later, rose petals rained from the heavens courtesy of the Royal Air Postal Service of Greater Bengal. Folk performers entertained in the inner quadrangle: as his cobras swayed in time to the *bin,* Maarnath told love stories about Nag and Nagin, and a baloo-wallah prodded a chained white bear, costumed as a feringhee bride, into a kuch dance. Introducing himself as "a one and only Professor Wonderful," and trying his best to perform what he thought was European magic, a man dressed in what he presumably imagined was British formal attire produced a chicken (which had unfortunately suffocated to death during its long wait in the load) from a top hat. Then the hijras, eunuchs dressed unconvincingly as women, hoisting up their filthy saris and crooning lewd songs, made a loud and lurid mockery of love. I searched for Pythia and Nagini to escort them to the refectory, where dinner was promised to be served as soon as the Maharaja finished making the last of his longiloquent toasts to bride, groom, and "above all to true love, the great love which transcends the restrictions of family, class, race, order, kingdom, species, genus, and phylum." After he had publicly presented Tara with a ruby bracelet by Cartier and Francis with a Peacemaker pistol by Winchester, the bride and groom were invited to speak. Her plush bosom heaving with bliss, Tara addressed the party of guests, most of whom were complete strangers to her: "Just as, after years spent in cages with leopards, jaguars, panthers, pumas, and lions, I decided to become exclusively a tiger woman, so after being with men of many families, classes, races, kingdoms (and so forth as explained by His Majesty), I've decided to become an exclusively Coffin-White woman, and to lionize him above all others." After polite applause abated, Francis was urged to speak. He stood up but couldn't say a word. Trembling with stage fright, he looked to Dr. McCloud with an expression that begged for salvation. After rescuing the terrified tiger hunter by joining him on the dais to extol his courage as a slayer of savage beasts, McCloud invited his daughter to entertain the bridal couple and their guests with the poetry of Elizabeth Barrett Browning: "How do I love thee? Let me count the ways," she began and, by the time she got to "I love thee purely," I needed to look for the castle commode. Shula, holding Hugh's hand, in the line for it before me, informed me that *"Il y a beaucoup d'hommes içi qui sont bien connus à l'Ananga Ranga."* After dinner there was dancing to the music of Les Lapins Chauds, a jazz quartet composed of three young Calcutta marwaris and their Chinese friend. Wearing black dinner jackets and made up in blackface, they played ragtime fox-trots. First to take the floor, the frisky bride navigated her jittery groom around the room to "Runnin' wild, lost control, I'm in love, lost my soul." While dancing with Pythia, I gazed over her shoulder at Nagini, who seemed saddened by the merriment she watched the merrymakers trying to make. Cutting in, Hillcastle took Pythia from my arms, and Maithun Tagore bumped his way through dancing couples to join me on the floor, where he informed me that he'd soon be ready "to start shooting Warren Hastings." A sitar, tabla, and harmonium ensemble had given Les Lapins Chauds a break. Dr. McCloud suggested to Pythia and me that we ask the Maharaja if we could see some of his collections: "Collectors love to show off things that most people don't care to look at." Happily escorting us to the vaulted chamber, formerly the chapel of Wankton Castle, where his collection of mounted animals, mostly the work of Albert Bannerjee, was on display, the Maharaja proudly pointed to the sumptuously caparisoned taxidermied pachyderm with its raised trunk trumpeting silence: "The great Bill, the one and only Bill, magnificent leader of the Grand March in the Durbar of Delhi in 1902, a raja of the jungle, a true friend, faithful servant, and winner of the International Elephant Derby in Lucknow in 1899." Following Bill, as if in parade, were the assembled skeletons of two smaller elephants. "This grand lady is Lucy, Bill's devoted maharani. She was ill during the Durbar, and died just afterwards. She had a mammoth heart. And this skeleton is her younger companion, Bill's other mistress, the demure Mumtaz, who became his principal after Lucy was gone, lovingly doing her best to solace her beloved." Pythia lingered by the elephants as I followed the Maharaja, past the stuffed crocodiles, bears, spotted linsangs, and a lone rhino missing both a horn and a scrotum, toward the stairs that led to the donjon, where he kept his collections of board games, hats, eggs, mirrors, and erotic miniatures, when we were suddenly arrested by Pythia's cry: "Oh my God! It's me! It's me!" The Maharaja was startled. "Surely she means, 'It is I'?" he whispered as we turned back to determine the cause of the ungrammatical outburst. "Look!" Pythia, quite beside herself with excitement, shouted, pointing to the plaque at the forefeet of the skeleton: "Look! 'Lucy: b. 1861, d. 1902.' I never thought I'd find myself here! Don't you see? Look at the dates! It's me! I was Lucy in my former life!" After being silenced by the deep breaths she needed to recover her composure, she finally commented, "One can only wonder why Elizabeth Barrett became an elephant in India. And what on earth could Lucy have possibly done to be reborn as a doctor's daughter in Lancashire?"

48 "Bill was most adroit at using his trunk to arouse and please me," Pythia, eager to see Lucy's bones again, reported during the drive to Diwanasthan: "I imagine it so vividly that it must be memory. He was in musth, the gland between his ear and eye exuding an oily treacle of ichor that stained his face with love. Tenderly intertwining his trunk with mine, he was ever careful that the magnificent tusks that kept other bulls at bay did not hurt me. During lovemaking, Bill never clung to me, but merely placed his forefeet lightly on my back so that he wouldn't lose balance. When it was over, as he trumpeted triumphantly, his little tail would twirl about in happiness. That the mahout separated us after mating made me subject to bouts of amorous melancholy. Mumtaz would inevitably console me by rubbing up against me or teasing me into good humor by prankishly spraying me with a trunkful of water. I know that she too has been Bill's lover, but amongst elephant cows that's accepted. After all, he loves us very differently." Pythia was in many ways romantic but in no way sentimental. As we approached Diwanasthan, I asked after the bereft Nagini, and Pythia responded nonchalantly: "Her father's imprisonment is weighing heavily on her. The harder she struggles to be cheerful, the more easily she breaks into tears. She's lonely, but not interested in any of the men who've tried to seduce her: not Ishmael because he's a Moslem, not Maarnath because he's her cousin, and not Krishna because he's married. Other servants have also tried to have their way with her, but as a snake charmer's girl, she looks down on people who obey orders. Still, like all of us, she needs and deserves physical intimacy, pleasure, and relief. I think that magician at the wedding, the funny fellow who called himself Professor Wonderful, might be right for her. He's a young low-caste Hindu bachelor, an entertainer, and he seemed rather sweet. I've invited him to perform a little gilli-gilli show on Sunday for the croquet crowd in hopes that the two of them might hit it off." Our arrival at the steps to the castle ended talk of Nagini. Receiving us in the gaddi room, His affable Highness, wearing a campaign hat that he claimed had protected the head of Clive from bullets during the sack of Chandernagore, was lolling on a marble throne that he alleged had once "given respite to the sovereign buttocks of the Holy Roman Emperor, Frederick II of Hohenstaufen." His beard, parted in the middle of his chin, swept outwards and up into two twisted points and his mustache was hardly thick enough to cover an irrepressible smile. "This was not the castle upon which my heart had been set, but, alas, I had to settle for it when that monarchical duffer, King Humbert of Italy, refused to sell the Castel del Monte in

Apulia, which had been designed and inhabited by Frederick. All I could get out of Humbert was this throne." Eager to visit the castle's former chapel, where, amidst the Maharaja's collection of taxidermy, the skeleton of Lucy stood adoringly behind her stuffed beloved, Pythia beseeched the Maharaja to reveal all he knew about the dead pachyderm. "It was an arranged marriage. When I purchased the nubile cow for Bill from the dissolute Nawob of Nagpur, she was temperamental, frisky, and rather wild, but, chained to her, Bill led her around the curtilage and taught her to parade. Love tamed her. The wedding of Coffin-White and Miss Tara was, since Christians have such a meager appreciation of pomp, pale in comparison to the Hindu nuptial festivities of Bill and Lucy. Surrounded by musicians, boys with silver platters overflowing with sweets and savories, girls laden with bells and bangles, and elephant cows adorned with silks and jewels, the magnificent Bill, draped in gold brocades, his tusks studded with diamonds and rubies, arrived at the stable where Lucy, covered with blankets of marigolds, her face painted with vermilion, her legs and feet with turmeric, and her ears with sandalwood paste, waited for him to lead her in the seven steps around the sacred matrimonial fire. Bill loved to see his bride caparisoned for parade. After he passed away, I stopped keeping elephants. Ganesh Bannerjee took the ones I had left, a bull named Frederick and his three cows, to America, sold the girls to Barnum & Bailey, and leased Frederick to the United States Republican Party so that Charles Hughes could ride him in the campaign against Woodrow Wilson for the presidency in 1916. Although the Republicans blamed Frederick for Wilson's victory, the undaunted elephant, with Bannerjee as his agent, went on to star in several motion pictures in Hollywood, including one about Cleopatra. The Queen of the Nile rode up on his back." Staring dreamily at the bodily remains of her former self, and deaf to talk of other elephants, Pythia asked if she might be alone with Lucy. In gracious compliance with her wishes, the Maharaja gestured for me to follow him. As we began to ascend the stairs to the donjon, I could hear Pythia reciting a poem to Lucy that they had written in their shared previous life: "Most like a monumental statue set in everlasting watch and moveless woe, the skull's eyelids are not wet: If she could but weep, she could arise and go." The Maharaja showed me his collection of collections: hats and headgear (a busby, a coxcomb, a conical dunce's hat, and a crown of thorns, fezes, fedoras, toques, sombreros, pith helmets, a yarmulke, and a Stetson); eggs great and small (of birds, lizards, snakes, and a platypus, and one he swore to be an unborn cockatrice); hand mirrors that had belonged to such historical celebrities as Cleopatra, Vatsyayana, and Vlad the Impaler. And then the board games: pachisi, plopitin, elephant dominoes, aeropuzzle, l'attaque, table croquet, bagatell, Brahmin blotto, ludo, Wee Wankle's Wedding, Flip the Kipper, and many a set of snakes and ladders. When I told him that I had had the game as a child but had given it away to a friend, it piqued his interest: "What a shame! I would have purchased it from you. Do you play?" I said yes, but dismissed the game as not much of a challenge. He shook his head in disapproval. "You obviously haven't been initiated. It is a subtle and fascinating game from the playing of which one may come to understand many things about the world and about oneself. Permit me to teach you the secrets of snakes and ladders. Yes, return in six days and we'll play." He led me into one of several antechambers to the donjon where he kept his sexological collection. "This *Kamasutra,* the holy Hindu bible of marital manners with hand-painted miniatures illustrating the sixty-four possible postures in which to experience true love, was commissioned by Akbar the Great." He opened it. A delicate girl astride a turbaned raja in the illustration looked, I mused, like Nagini. "But don't think I'm just an antiquarian. I have a collection of more modern erotica: photography, not a very extensive collection but a personal one, showing a convergence of my tastes in women with my tastes in art." There were four sets of four sets of four naked Indian women, each representing a different genus within a traditional aesthetic taxonomy: the Snake Girl, Tiger Girl, Cow Girl, and Elephant Girl. Which was which would be known to the connoisseur by their respective ornaments, postures, and the backdrops against which they were posed. There were three sets of three sets of postcards from Paris: a trinity of nudes who were meant to be the Graces in one grouping, the Fates in another, and the Furies in yet another. "I don't appreciate photographs of naked women if there are men in the picture, if anyone's being spanked, or if the girls are making either silly faces or obscene gestures. I like only beautiful photographs of beautiful women. Like this one." Could it have been a sudden shriek of my heart that startled him into dropping the photograph? Picking it up with trembling fingers, I was ashamed of myself for feeling what I felt. It was signed "Nister" and it was Angel with a snake held close to her naked breast. In the open byssus robe that she had worn in *Cleopatra,* reclining with seductive languor on a divan in front of a drop painted with a sphinx, she seemed overexposed. "You know her?" His Highness asked and I didn't answer. In the car on the way back to Alipore, with the sepia image of Angel overwhelming me, I was hardly listening to Pythia's prattle about a dead elephant and transmigrating poetess, until suddenly I was startled to realize that what she was saying indicated that she would soon be leaving India and me: "Yes, I've got to convince Daddy to let me stop in Italy on the way back to England. I need to go to the Villa La Scala where Elizabeth died in order to try to discover why on earth she became an elephant. Since she was so very thin and small, perhaps she wished to be much larger and becoming an elephant was her wish coming literally true." I interrupted. "You're leaving Calcutta?"

But she didn't let me stop her. "Yes, of course. But here's the exciting part. I was troubled by the fact that Robert Browning couldn't have been Bill since the poet didn't die, despite his vows to join his beloved after death, until 1889, twenty-eight years after Elizabeth's demise. And Bill was born in 1860. Here's the unbelievable part: according to her memorial plaque, Mumtaz was born in 1890. Don't you understand? She was probably Robert Browning!" I tried again: "You're leaving Calcutta?" Pythia was surprised that I was surprised: "Yes, of course. Haven't you heard Daddy talking about it? He and Wheedle are taking Hugh to England to dig up the Hastings fortune and continue their research. We're giving up the house. Oh, don't look so pathetically sad! We won't be leaving for over a month." Although I was confident that I would be as able to cope with the departure of Pythia as I had been with the loss of Angel, I was troubled by a host of uncertainties: "What should I do now? What's going to happen to my life? What about the snakes? And what about Nagini? What will become of her?" Before we arrived back at the estate, Pythia asked me to accompany her in a few days back to Diwanasthan for a visit to Shree Karnaghee's ashram. "I need his help. I've got a lot of questions. These discoveries about my past lives have taken all my attention. But I don't think it's healthy to just dwell on the past. It's important to think about the future too. Don't you agree? That's why I need to consult Guru-ji. As an expert on karma, he should be able to advise me on how to determine my destiny. Don't you ever wonder what you did in a past life that brought you to me? Wouldn't you like to arrange what you'll do and who you'll love in future incarnations? After the last three lives, as nice as they've been, I think I'd enjoy being a man for change, handsome, physically fit, intelligent, witty, wealthy, and of course very accomplished, although I'm not yet sure in what. It's so terribly difficult to decide what to do with a life."

49 "He knows the truth, the real truth, the cosmic one," Pythia said of Guru Shree Karnaghee: "Understanding the mysterious metaphysical mechanisms of karma as he does, he'll be able to advise me on how to determine my next birth, influencing the qualities of that incarnation and dictating the opportunities of that future existence." She had asked me to accompany her to Karnaghee's ashram because of gossip concerning his attempts to molest women who had turned to him for spiritual counsel. It was not that she held the alleged moral infraction against him: "Higher spiritual wisdom and lower carnal lust, as apposite sensibilities of two discrete planes of existence, are not necessarily incompatible in a single human being, composed as we are of both the eternal and the temporal. While he is privy in his incorporeal self to a sublime wisdom, it is no contradiction that, just as his body must perish, so too it must be subject to the instinct to sexually perpetuate the species. That the transcendental and immanent converge so perfectly in him, each without displacing the other, is indicative of an ontological accomplishment." He had been born Karna Dayal in 1861 (the year, I realized with some amusement, that Elizabeth Barrett Browning died), the son of a Sanskrit pandit at the since-defunct Kathamitya Academy for Brahmin Boys. Once the schoolteacher had convinced the current Maharaja's father to subsidize his son's higher education, the young man was sent to America to study at Harvard Divinity School. That *v* is pronounced *w* in Bengali English caused some confusion: an eager Dayal found himself in Washington, D.C., at Howard University, enrolled in a theological seminary with the missionary mandate of "Training Colored Men for the Ministry." Although fellow students were quite hospitably willing to consider the Indian Hindu an honorary Negro Christian, the haughty Brahmin quit Howard after one semester. Hearing that there was another divinity college with a similar name in Cambridge, Massachusetts, he went there only to be denied admission. Disgusted with America, he returned to India and, through the influence of his father, was given the cushy job of student spiritual custodian at Kathamitya. The foreign experience, however, wasn't a total bust: in a Washington beer saloon and billiard parlor, during his term at Howard, he met and struck up a friendship with a young and charismatic fellow Aryan named Conway Conwell, himself a theology student at Bob Roberts Baptist Seminary. The two remained in contact with each other by mail, and when Reverend Conwell's first book, *He's Not Called God for Nothing,* became an international best-seller that made its author rich and famous, it inspired Dayal to become a guru and write a holy scripture of his own in English. Dropping "Dayal" from his name (which to many an Indian ear might suggest a scribe or accountant) and adding "ghee" (the word for the clarified butter that is so important in Hindu ritual and cuisine) augmented his sanctity. Although Karnaghee's book, *It's Not Called Brahman for Nothing,* did not sell very well, it did establish him as a holy man in the environs of Diwanasthan: when a blind beggar there, while rummaging through a trash bin, happened to pick up a copy of the book, he suddenly regained his eyesight. The only explanation that anyone could come up with was that Karnaghee's book had effected a miracle. In addition to the man cured of his blindness and the recently converted Father Fitzwilly, the guru's following included the Maharaja of Diwanasthan (a disciple out of respect to his father's committed patronage of Dayal's father) and, by royal decree, the Maharaja's few subjects and servants. Most of the disciples were women: Mother Bannerjee and her daughters and daughters-in-law in India, and in San Francisco, by correspondence and occasionally by telepathy, no less than a dozen members of the Ladies' Chapter of the Golden Gate Metasophical Society. The American women had been fascinated by his evangelic pamphlets on "The Ancient Hindu Philosophy of Pantheism," a teaching to which he had actually and ironically been formally exposed in America. Leaving Washington in 1882 in search of Harvard Divinity School, Dayal got lost in Massachusetts. Going into a bar in Concord to ask for directions, he was offered a drink by a passionately extroverted poet named Walt. Upon discovering that Dayal was from India, the boozer invited him to come along to the home of the essayist Ralph Waldo Emerson who, he explained to the Hindu, was highly enamored of India. According to Winslow Putnam, Emerson's authorized biographer, Dayal insisted on going for a walk in the woods with Emerson. After Emerson had talked to him about pantheism, Dayal, not one to be philosophically outdone, recited all the Sanskrit homilies that his father had forced him to memorize in childhood. He continued the recitation even after it began to rain. A week later, the Transcendentalist died of pneumonia, and Dayal was subsequently referred to by Putnam and other friends of the belletrist as "the Hindu who killed Emerson." The Maharaja had spared little expense to build the hermitage for that Hindu, not so much for Karnaghee as for himself: an ashram lends dignity and prestige to a kingdom. And so His Highness made sure it was impressive. There was a cave for meditation, cast in plaster to look like a natural formation; the garden bloomed year-round with silk crepe flowers imported from Paris; and, as a monument to the Gandhian ideal of nonviolence, there was a sharp-toothed tiger lying gently down to doze with a wide-eyed deer. Both animals had been stuffed, mounted, and posed by Albert Bannerjee. On the day we visited the ashram, Swami Madananda could be heard chanting "Aum" from within the darkness of the cave. Malis were dusting off the animals and perfuming the flowers as we were received into the Holy Hall of Hindu Happiness by the guru. Although he was swamped with demands for epistolary and telepathic counsel from his acolytes in San Francisco, he was more than happy to receive Pythia. Getting right to the point, she explained that she was dead set on determining her next life: "I've decided that, in my subsequent incarnation, I want to be the president of the United States of America and win the Nobel Prize for Peace like Woodrow Wilson." The guru solemnly elucidated the complexity of it. He needed detailed information, including the exact time (to the second) and place (longitude and latitude) of her birth, a full genealogy, a list of moles, freckles, and other bodily markings, and all phrenological details. As he read her palm to himself, he informed her that "every rebirth, according to the strictest and most immutable laws of karma, includes both punishment and reward. Thus you must perform certain tasks and behave in specific ways, to be delineated by my humble self, in which a balance of merits and demerits are precisely accrued, so that you will be born in the United States as a man with an attractive personality, nimble mind, high moral sense, and other such qualities befitting an American statesman." The guru promised that once he had the data, he would make all the necessary astrological and metempsychological calculations, and report the results of his cosmic research in Alipore when he came for croquet. He arrived with the Maharaja, who, at the request of Pythia, had also brought with him Professor Wonderful. After McCloud had beaten the Maharaja at croquet but before the hypnosis session (during which Warren Hastings assured Pinkie that, yes, he knew exactly where the fortune was buried, and was certain that no one could have already found it), the magician performed for us as we, lolling in the cool of the verandah, drank gin and quinine water. That night, after all the guests had left and McCloud had gone to bed, when Pythia, shimmering with affectionate smiles, appeared in my room, she said we didn't have to pretend to be animals or poets or anything else, that we could be anything or anyone I wanted us to be (or even just ourselves), and that she would do that for me because she had a very big favor to ask of me. "You know," I confessed, "that I have never been able to refuse you anything. So consider it done. Tell me about Nagini and the magician. Did they take to each other?" But Pythia didn't care to talk about the snake charmer's daughter. She reclined naked on the bed next to me, lying in the opposite direction from me, touching my cheek playfully with her toe, and teasingly massaging my cold feet with warm hands through the bedcover. At first I couldn't understand why she was so uncharacteristically putting so much effort into being seductive; but then, what she wanted turned out to be a very, very big favor indeed. Consultation with Karnaghee that afternoon had revealed exactly what needed to be done in order for her to become the president of the United States of America in her next life: "If I do everything Guru-ji has told me to do, I will be born at 5:49 P.M. on January 16, 1964, in Los Angeles, California, and will, forty-four years later, in November of the year 2008, be elected as the forty-fourth president of the United States. And I will be the first Negro to hold that office!" Congratulating her on the victory, I became the first person to kiss the toes of the future commander in chief. Pulling her foot back, sitting up, and covering her breasts with the bleached bed sheet, she looked me straight in the eyes: "But you have to help me. In order for that to happen I have to die at exactly 12:30 P.M. on the twenty-second of November, 1963, at 32°47' north latitude and 96°48' west longitude, which is in America, a city in Texas called Dallas. Now here's the problem: I can't commit suicide because, according Guru-ji, that would cause a punitive fallback very far down the karmic ladder. I'd be reborn, he said, as a lemming. They have a rich sex life, but they are destined from birth to commit suicide by jumping off high cliffs. It's not only a painful death; it causes them to come back in a even lower state. That's why I need you. You must come to Texas on that day, forty-one years from now, and find me. I'll be staying in the best room at whatever hotel in Dallas is the most expensive in 1963. Don't let me know where you are or establish any contact with me, because that could make you a suspect in the murder, and also I might become fainthearted and try to talk you out of it, my resolve weakened by a frivolous impulse to remain in a sixty-one-year-old body. My lives are in your hands." Sitting up, I took her shoulders firmly in my hands, and told her to be quiet. "Pythia, you're losing your mind. Don't you hear what you're saying? This is nonsense. First of all, I would never kill anyone. Second of all, even if I weren't averse to murder, I would never kill *you*. I love you. Don't you understand? I love you!" Angered by the uncooperative response, she rose from the bed to gather up her clothes. "If you really loved me, you'd kill me," she said in exasperation as she pulled on her frock. She turned back to me from the doorway. "But even if you don't love me enough to murder me, you should at least be willing to do it for your country."

50 "I am the Wonderful," the magician in formal dinner wear (the spiffiness of which was somewhat compromised by bare feet) proclaimed as he tipped a topee to make a splendacious theatrical bow to his esteemed audience sahibishly installed on longsleevers in the tenuous shade of the cluttered verandah, where Ishmael and Ibrahim, in ever-increasingly soiled blue silk cummerbunds, served gin with a quinine water to protect us from the malaria that was devastating the bustee. "Professor Wonderful! Indrajalin extraordinaire, meaning in an English 'the magician,' like my father before me, his father before, and his before him and his, entirely all the way back. This gloriful day is giving me a pleasure for giving you a pleasure of the lip-smacking amazement-cum-amusement with ten displayings of the Indian miraculosity, each and every being the discoverment by one and more of my most wonderful progenitors. Please be a bear with me and take your time. But enough prolix and on with the great patter. Long ago I am making a greatest debut in magicality at the tender age with a performing of feats for a one and only Great Whydini, the greatest great magician of Great Britain, who was traveling in India to behold the magic of an Orient. On my occasion, he was judging a First International All-India Calcutta Junior Division Amateur Conjuring Contest. Being superior to other judges, the great one was damn nuts about me. It was to study his great how-to-do-great-magic books that I mastered an English language. Furthermore, for his magical humor I was telling the rollicking jokes nonstop in the Oxford English: 'Every magician in your own bonnie braes of Britain is producing the rabbit from one hat. But in the India there are no rabbits except the hares, and no top hats except the topees. Thus I am miraculously producing that same from this same.' And that moment, I am producing a hair, not a hare, but a hair from the hat. Is everyone understanding? A hair! H-a-i-r. A Great Whydini himself was so riproarious that he was rolling humble-tumble from a judge's chair with hilarious hahahas and amples of repetitious 'the magic boy is a greatest wonderful.' Just when he was thinking he has seen the all, I was dazzling beyond belief by actually producing a hare, not a hair, but a hare. A hare! Does everybody understand? A hare! H-a-r-e." And then the magician did, in fact, produce a dazed Himalayan rufous-tailed hare from the Minto topee, a symbol of British Raj rule, that he had shown to be empty. Gesturing for our perfunctory applause to ease up, he informed us that that magic was really "a nothing," since many people have already seen magicians pull rabbits from hats. "But, I am asking, who has watched the magician pulling the hat out of a rabbit?" And as he asked it, it appeared that he was, indeed, removing something from the rectal cavity of the hare. The animal thrashed about in the magician's grip, wriggling with understandable discomfort as the object was dislodged from its colon. It was a sort of floppy beret of black-and-white-checkered silk that was subsequently purchased by the Maharaja for his hat collection. "That is a nothing!" Professor Wonderful proclaimed as he began to delineate the fabulous feats of his forbears. He concocted a lineage of magicians whose secrets he had inherited. At the Durbar of Delhi of 1902, he swore, his father had caught with his teeth a bullet fired at his face, as the son would soon demonstrate for us if Francis Coffin-White would be so kind as to shoot him. And if Pythia would be so gracious as to bind him with hemp ropes and iron chains, he would demonstrate an escape that his grandfather had shown the begums of Oudh as a subtle way of assuring them it was possible to squirm out of whatever strictures, literal, legal, or economic, were placed upon them by the Warren Hastings administration. When that name was uttered, everybody simultaneously looked at Hugh for a reaction. That there was none, and that he was not paying the slightest bit of attention to the magic show was scientifically explained by Major Wheedle: "Animals, for whom all experience is real life, can be terrified or pleased, but neither amazed nor amused, by the surprising. Hugh still lacks the human rationality needed to be fooled by the magician." It was difficult for me to concentrate on the show or enjoy it because of my anxiety over the McClouds' departure from India, which would deprive me of both a lover and a livelihood. All of the tricks as performed by Professor Wonderful's ascendants (and as about to be demonstrated by him) had had some sort of contextual message and significance. His performance of the transformation of a rope into a snake and that snake back into a rope (the same routine that I, as Swami Balakrishna, had done at the Chula Vista Durbar) had had special meaning when performed by his great-grandfather for the Nawob of Nagpur, since Nagpur (which means "Snaketown") had been formerly known as Rajjunagar ("Ropeville"). And there was a deeper mystical meaning, as Karnaghee insisted on explaining, for the Nawob who, though a Mohammedan, had been an adherent of the Advaita School of Vedanta, a philosophy maintaining that phenomenal existence is completely illusory. The epistemological and metaphysical discourses of the tradition often used, we were informed, the snake-rope metaphor to warn of the dangers of mistaking empirical reality for a more real reality. Karnaghee recited a text, first in Sanskrit and then in English, noting that much of its wisdom had been sacrificed in the process of translation: "Just as a man who, thinking a snake is a rope, grabs it and thus dies, and just as a man who, thinking a rope is a snake, runs away and is thus a laughingstock, so the man who thinks that this world as perceived by the senses is real will both die and be the butt of laughter." Professor Wonderful, though probably annoyed by the erudite interruption, politely thanked Karnaghee for "an eternal wisdom," only to impatiently add, "But a show must go on!" We were up to his great-grandfather's father, who, as demonstrated before our very eyes, took one of the snakes that had been a rope and seemed to kill it by enthusiastically crushing its head under his bare foot. Since my recent work with Indian snakes had made me privy to the knowledge that members of the *Heterodon* genus of Serpentes will, when threatened, play dead by flipping over, going limp, and letting their tongues dangle out of their open mouths, I was not surprised that the dead snake could be resurrected. But, according to the magician, when Shah Jahan had seen his great-great-grandfather do the routine at "the grand opening of a Taj Mahal," he had been deeply moved, assured that if a serpent could return from the dead, the same might be possible for his late beloved Mumtaz Mahal. Before him, another father in the fanciful long line of Wonderfuls had demonstrated mind reading for Akbar, who wanted "to know the what that was on his subjects' minds." He had even compromised the magician's sacred vow of secrecy to teach the great mogul how to guess what number between one and ten one of his subjects might be thinking of. That magician's great-grandfather had performed for Lakshmanasena, the last Hindu king of Bengal. Whereas the living Professor Wonderful's vanish of rice and coins didn't impress his audience very much, Lakshmanasena's courtiers found the disappearances ominous, viewing the trick as a magically prophetic warning that the end of the kingdom was at hand. Love was the theme hundreds of years earlier, when Pandit Adbhuta ("Meaning 'Professor Wonderful' in Sanskrit," Karnaghee interjected) performed for King Chandragupta and his teacher, none other than Vatsyayana Mallanaga, author of the *Kamasutra*: the solid and seemingly seamless metal rings, one gold and one silver, that when rubbed gently together and lightly blown upon with puckered lips became interlinked and were shown to be inseparable, we were told, represented the amorous bonding of a man and a woman. There was an elaborate story about how, because of conflicting obligations and duties, they were separated, as illustrated by the unlinking of the rings. But then, through the magic power of love, the rings were relinked and handed out to the audience for inspection. "They will never be apart again. The love is an eternal!" It was the first time I saw Nagini laugh. Covering her mouth with the end of her sari as she did so, she seemed to be laughing for the first time in her life. Another of the magician's ancestral predecessors had done the mango tree trick for Vikramaditya thousands of years ago as a way of advising the legendary king not to rely on warfare to build his kingdom, but to encourage agriculture. "There is power," we were told and shown, "in fruit!" Finally it was time for the most wonderful wonder of all time, the climax of the show,

"Buried Alive!" His earliest known ancestor had performed it for Prince Rama and his brothers in Ayodhya. In preparation for it, at the beginning of the afternoon, Ishmael and Ibrahim had been ordered to dig a grave within viewing range of the verandah. The magician unveiled a wooden coffin, its lid inscribed "R.I.P. Professor Wonderful," and after inviting me and Wheedle forward to inspect it, he asked us in a voice loud enough for all to hear that we "nail it tight most securely" once he was inside it. Before taking his place in the coffin, Professor Wonderful, with an irrepressible smile thanking us all for watching his show, asked us to reconvene: "Right here, exactly three weeks from this today, neither a more nor a less, at this same hour, with one purpose to digging me up and out of my premature grave and finding me, to a greatest amazement-cum-amusement, entirely one hundred and one percent alive and as happy and healthy as a day I was born." Once Wheedle and I had nailed down the lid of his coffin, Ishmael and Ibrahim used ropes to lower the magician into his grave. "Carefully, please," we could hear from within the box. "Do not drop me at all." Nagini looked almost as worried as Pythia looked amused when the coffin disappeared into the earth. Everyone rose from their seats on the verandah to approach the grave site as the servants replaced the dirt that had been taken out of the earth. Major Wheedle wanted to explain things: "I can't figure out how he linked and unlinked those rings, but at least I understand this one. The fakirs of India have long been known to be adept at self-hypnosis. They are able to put themselves into trances in which they reduce the rate of heartbeat, breathing, and metabolism to such an extreme that three weeks is, in that hyp-noyogic state, physiologically no longer than three minutes is to us. It's really quite easy if one knows self-hypnosis and yoga." Ishmael used the back of his shovel to pat down the ground over the inhumed body of the magician. Dr. McCloud suggested that someone might plant a cross to mark the spot so we'd remember where to dig him up three weeks later. There was a long silence during which everybody, not knowing what to say, stared down at the ground. In order to provide some sort of closure to the show, I clapped my hands. The others joined in with their applause as if the buried man might have been able to hear it.

51 *Transmigration: A True Story!* was one proposed title for the motion picture. There were others. *Tiger Boy: A True Story!, The English-man, the Outcaste, and the Brahmin: A True Story!, Former Lives of a Feral Foundling: A True Story!,* and *The Jungle Book: A True Story!* Since all of them included the phrase *A True Story!,* it seemed reasonable to call the film just that, even though no one particularly liked it. But, much to the relief of both the director, Maithun Wadsworth Tagore, and the producer, the Maharaja of Diwanasthan, settling on it meant that the expensive-to-rent motion picture camera could start rolling. It amused the Maharaja to have become a movie mogul and it gratified him to believe Tagore's prophecy that Twentieth Century–Tiger Studio Productions would establish Diwanasthan as the Hollywood of India. That the Maharaja consented to let Tagore direct was generous, since by his own admission Tagore had never actually directed nor even been involved in any way in the making of a motion picture. "But," he insisted, "I have seen every one of them that has ever been shown in Calcutta, and a member of my family won the Nobel Prize." He further argued that his art background prepared him for the cinematic undertaking: after matriculating from the Kathamitya Academy, he had studied painting and sculpture at the Aurangzeb College of Art in Jihadpur, where in his third year he was runner-up for the coveted Majnun Prize for his laconic essay "The Nude in Islamic Sculpture." He had developed an interest in theater as "moving sculpture" and, through the influence of his second cousin, the Nobel laureate, had been given the opportunity to direct *Ramyo ar Zhulyeti* for the Shakespeare Society at Harmony House's bimonthly Bengali Amateur Night. In order to accommodate the tastes of Indian audiences, the ending of the English-language original had been changed into a happy one with, as a grand musical finale, a Hindu marriage ceremony performed for the adolescent lovers with the blessings of their fully reconciled parents. "Shakespeare would surely wish that he could have thought of that one," Tagore had mused. According to his own testimony, it was after seeing Joseph Siegel's epic *Cleopatra* that Tagore decided that he had been karmicly determined to direct motion pictures. He had a conviction it was his destiny to pioneer this new art form that was so quickly taking Calcutta by storm. The most popular Indian film at the time was a hand-tinted one-reeler called *Hastomoithun* (Bengali for "masturbation") that had been produced and distributed by the Bengal Royal Society for Mental and Moral Health. Another picture, made in Bombay, *Lord Krishna,* was hailed in the press as "the longest film ever made by anyone in any country in the history of the

world." Censors confiscated *The Great Bonfire of Foreign Clothes* before it could enjoy the popularity it deserved; Mahatma Gandhi had made his film debut in it by burning a homburg, a pair of oxfords, a formal dinner jacket, an ascot tie, a checkered waistcoat, golf pants, and a kilt, in the Maidan as a tribute to Tilak and a protest against something. Tagore promised the Maharaja that *A True Story!* would have all the spirituality of *Lord Krishna* ("and more"), all the swadeshi political idealism of *The Great Bonfire of Foreign Clothes* ("and much more"), and all the eroticism of *Hastomoithun* ("and much, much more"). There were three reels at the heart of the picture: one depicting Warren Hastings, the heartless colonialist; another, Kholo, the abject latrine cleaner; and the third, Shankara Sharma, the pious Brahmin. Each reel was prefaced by the same feet of film in which the feral boy was being hypnotized; and each concluded with the same footage of him coming out of his trance. The film opened with the capture of the Tiger Boy and, even though it was supposedly a true story, ended with Hugh rejecting civilization to lead a happier and healthier bucolic life in the jungle with the animals. With a large lethargic python wrapped around his shoulders, the wild child sat upon the taxidermied Bill's back to smile and wave happily through the camera lens to the audience in the closing shot. Jiggling the camera gave the impression that perhaps Bill was still alive. Tagore had planned on having Hugh play himself in the picture, a touch that might have helped the film to live up to its title, but the uncooperative creature was adamantly unwilling to remove even his homburg, let alone his pants to prance around the jungle naked prior to captivity. The director was, however, able to find a boy in Chor Bazaar named Haramjada who was quite happy to do anything for money. After jumping up and down naked in the room in Wankton Castle that had been decorated as the jungle, he improvised Hugh's savagery by dramatically moving his bowels, after which there was a heated philosophical discussion between Maithun and the Maharaja on the relationship between propriety and realism in the arts. Holding that the scene was "realistic and convincing of the barbarity of Man in the natural state," Maithun wanted to keep it in. But the Maharaja, with the purse for the budget on his side, cogently argued that "we will have ample opportunity to show fecal matter in the scenes of Kholo the bangi cleaning the commode of Colonel Harding." Ibrahim had just the perpetually humiliated demeanor to make him perfect for the part. Because, however, he considered himself far too elevated in the Hindu social hierarchy to actually clean real excrement out of Harding's toilet, artificial turds were fashioned by Albert Bannerjee. Nagendra Bannerjee, given his political proclivities, was more than eager to the play the zealous sepoy mutineer Pashupati Acharya and brought a fiery passion and ideological conviction to the role that, unfortunately, didn't come across on the screen. He looked nervous. Francis Coffin-White, on the other hand, did an adequate job as Colonel Harding, even though he was really very nervous. He had not wanted to appear in the film, but his bride gave him no choice: "There is no need to suffer stage fright since there is no stage. In France, furthermore, we shall be dedicating our lives to show business. So you'd better get used to it. You won't be doing too much big-game hunting in Paris." She coerced her already henpecked husband to surrender to Tagore's artistic genius, demanding as it did that he also play the entrepreneur who bought Rani the tiger from Shankara Sharma, Clive in a sequence with young Warren Hastings, and himself in the opening of the film, stalking and capturing the Tiger Boy. Maithun noted that the technical term for this device of casting a single actor to play multiple roles was "the Siegel technique. And the fact that one man plays Harding, Clive, the Talent Agent, and Coffin-White underscores the point that all colonialists are essentially personifications of the same horrid thing." That Maithun himself played the part of Major Wheedle, and that during the hypnosis scenes he stared into the camera, hypnotically waving his hands at the audience, suggested that a director must hypnotize the viewers of his films. "Film is religion," Tagore said Siegel had once said in an interview in *Movie Watch,* and he elaborated in his own interview in *Filmi Chokh Rakha:* "Going to the movie theater is like going to a shrine, synagogue, church, or mosque. Or at least it should be." Shree Karnaghee, having deigned to take the part of Shankara Sharma, informed the *Filmi Chokh Rakha* reporter that, as an actor no less than as a holy man, he would do all he could do "to facilitate the enlightenment and liberation of all sentient beings and other moviegoers." Mohini, the man-eater, again using the Siegel technique, was cast as both the killer mother of the cub taken by Sharma and Rani, that cub grown up. Baby Rani was played by a stuffed alley cat painted with stripes by Albert Bannerjee for the scene in which Sharma had to cuddle the cub. Actors were willing to work with Mohini because she was heavily sedated at all times with opium, the drug that had facilitated her capture. Coffin-White had tied up a buffalo in the jungle as bait to lure the predator. That the buffalo's skin had been smeared with opium, some of which was absorbed into the blood stream of the prey, made being ripped to pieces by a tiger slightly less horrible than it might have been for a sober buffalo. After attacking the tethered beast, tearing out its throat, and devouring it, Mohini, under the influence of the sedative, fell asleep and was snoring by the time Francis loaded her into a palanquin cage, which was carried by native bearers to the Bannerjee house. Ishmael played both the farmer who cursed Sharma because of his father's death by tiger and a native peon whom I, as Warren Hastings, had to thwack with a pizzle. Maarnath played a snake charmer. A shot of his cobras menacingly looking at me as I walked haughtily by was portentous: India would have its revenge on the colonialists. This was further emphasized by closeups of the eyes (with my reflections in them) of Mohini, Bill, and a few other animals, live and taxidermied, from the Bannerjee menagerie. The Bannerjee women, playing the courtesans of Oudh, ran in all directions as I entered the palace to face Mother Bannerjee, the high begum. She happily noted that since the film was silent she would have been able to play the part even if her vowed period of silence had not ended. I was to rape a Bengal village girl as played by Nagini. "Look at her lustfully, just as Warren Hastings would have done," Maithun shouted through a megaphone (even though he was standing only a few feet away from me). "She is India and you are the Crown. That's why you want to fuck her! You want her to fight back so that you can subdue her. And then, when you have forcefully penetrated her, you want India to surrender to you, to feel rapture, the perverse pleasure of rape. It's a parable, not to mention an allegory." The assault was staged in Diwanasthan's shrine of Manasa, the Bengali goddess of serpents. Tagore directed Nagini, costumed in a torn peasant's sari, to tremble as she looked at me: "You're afraid of the foreign beast!" There was a closeup of her face, eyes wide with terror, her snake-tattooed hands on her flush cheeks, and the shadow of Warren Hastings fell over her. "Look at the white devil! He's going to rape you!" It frightened me that, as she stared at me, she actually looked afraid. "Now when I give you the cue, as Isaac approaches you, I want to hear the most bloodcurdling scream you can scream, a shriek so terrible that it breaks through the silence of the motion picture theater." My shadow moved toward her, loomed, and engulfed her in its darkness. And, as directed, Nagini screamed.

To 28

52 "Kill the snakes," Dr. McCloud, after a snuff-sneeze so elephantine that he practically lost his balance, commanded. "Execute every last one of the slithering satanic serpents. We don't want any of them getting out and biting some poor soul. Do it as soon as possible. We're sailing Saturday on the *Queen Mab*. Colonel and Mrs. Coffin-White, with their tigers, Mohini the man-eater and her mate, Shere Khan, just purchased by the newlyweds from the Bannerjees, will be on board with us until Marseilles. Pythia's set on stopping in Italy, but Wheedle and I feel that the sooner we can get Hastings back to Britain, the better. And I don't dare let my daughter travel on her own. Italian men are animals. The antivenin research has been officially suspended until the Royal Commission on Death by Poisons in the Colonies can, or cares to, find someone who is daft enough to resume the work. Because there's so much for me to do in preparation for the journey, I'm counting on you to exterminate the snakes, the rats, and the dogs as well. Don't worry about the horses. The chamars will come for them next week and take care of the slaughtering. The laboratory, kennel, and stable must be emptied, cleaned, and put in order for the arrival of Dr. Adderson, who will be taking over the estate to conduct research here for the Royal Academy of the Psychoneurological Arts and Sciences under the local sponsorship of the Royal Bengal Society for Mental and Moral Health. You can remain here at least until Adderson arrives. Oh, yes, by the way, do remember to dig up that magician buried in the garden. Sunday at three o'clock. I don't know if you've made any plans, but Adderson may want you to stay around a bit longer in order to orient him to the Orient. He's a bachelor like yourself and it's his first time out. I've written a letter recommending you to his service. Even though you're a hopeless croquet player, you're good with the snakes and the natives, and, I must admit, I've grown rather partial to you, and, just between us as men, I suspect that my daughter may well have taken a bit of a fancy to you yourself. If you ever have an opportunity to visit England, do call on us. It would be pleasant if our paths were to cross again by a stroke of luck. Whiskey?" As he dissolved the pellets of opium in our drinks, he sighed. "Opium, it's the only thing to prevent—how do I describe it?—the loneliness. Yes, that's it." He then supervised the careful packing of the seven portraits of his beloved wife. Watching Ishmael crate up the telescope, microscope, globe, and croquet equipment, I suddenly became concerned that my hyena might accidentally be boxed and shipped to England. Seeking out Hugh to retrieve it from him, I discovered that he had given it to Shula, "to cheer her up in my absence. Like that animal, she, when squeezed, though feeling nothing, automatically makes sounds of pleasure. I suppose that's why the hideous thing tickled her fancy. I still really don't know whether she knows that I'm just pretending to be wild, or if she actually believes that I was raised by tigers. I suspect that she doesn't care, that she is perhaps amused by her feral loverboy and that whether he's real or not is quite irrelevant. I must thank you, by the way, for the books, the cigarettes, and, most of all, for your complicity. You really have been a chum. Do a favor for me, will you? Just one more. Make a last offering for me at the shrine of Muldev, something (anything) stolen. If you ever have the opportunity to come to England, do call on me. I'll be staging the adventures of Hugh Mann, Act Two, 'Jerusalem in England's Green and Pleasant Land.'" I paced my room anxiously that Friday night, waiting, waiting for Pythia, waiting to blind my eyes with the splendor of nakedness and suffocate in fragrant golden hair, waiting to drown in the honeyed wetness of her mouth and be burned at the stake of her love, all for the last time. On the eve of her departure, the anguish of waiting defined itself as love, a terrible love. I felt that I loved her more than I had ever loved her, even more than I had loved Angel, more than I would ever love another girl again. Still she didn't come. It must have been three in morning. Although I had, during my residence in Alipore, been forbidden for caution's sake to make love with her in her room, I was unable to endure waiting any longer. Dressing, I made my way down the dark hallway to softly knock on the door. Nothing. Again, a little louder, and, then a little louder still. She cracked the door slightly. "Shhhhh. Go back to bed. I'll be there soon. I'm with Nagini. She needs to talk to me. She's very forlorn." I stood by the door of my room so that I could kiss her the moment she crossed the threshold, cover her mouth with my lips before she had a chance to say a word, to talk about animals, reincarnation, or anything else. During lovemaking, I only stopped kissing her to whisper, "I love you." Because she did not respond, refusing me the "I love you too" that I so needed to ease the pain of losing her (even though the whispers would have served to increase the very pain they would soothe), I said it again, a little louder. Nothing. Again, a little louder, and then a little louder still. All I could do was to imagine that her moaning expressed the sentiment. I translated the sighs of sex into an ardent love song: "Exquisite is the pain of separation. When I am apart from you, you will then be everywhere." After lovemaking, I was so saddened by the understanding that it had been for the last time that tears welled up in my eyes. Imagining that they might move her, I blinked to force them out and down my cheeks. I turned to look at her so that she would see them. Again I whispered it: "I love you." Taking the edge of the sheet to blot the tears for me, she offered condolences. "Though melancholy is common in the higher animals after intercourse, the lower creatures are never happier. The greater the intelligence of the lover, the greater the sadness of love. That's one of the reasons I have been so fascinated with the erotic customs of the animal kingdom. The more meager their intellectual and reflective capabilities, the greater their capacity for sexual bliss. The most amorously enviable of all animals is, I would argue, the Gangetic snaketrout: the male attaches his mouth to the body of the female and begins to suck nourishment out of her, right through her skin, in a sort of cannibalistic kiss. As he does so, an enzyme developed in the female's blood during egg production begins to work on his system, progressively dissolving the male, first his fins, his big eyes, then his little brain, the gills, and so on. All that is dissolved is processed into a potent spermatozootropic jelly. In the climax of intercourse, he is no more than a gooey, pulsating, sperm-exuding blob on her body, completely fused with her, experiencing that state of blissful, fecund oneness that all lovers yearn for and yet fail, owing to their higher state of evolution and consciousness, to attain." I considered it rather sad that the male had do die during lovemaking in order to enjoy such fulfillment. "Oh, but of course, like all of us, he is reborn. That's the part I like about transmigration, the realization that death is our opportunity to experience life in an entirely new way. Hindu eschatology is so charmingly cheerful. That's why I believe in it so wholeheartedly. By the way, the female snaketrout is relished as a gastronomic delicacy and aphrodisiac by the tribals of Bengal. I was one many lives ago." Her speech had dried my tears. She smiled. "Feeling better, I hope. Don't be sad. I do love you." Because it was almost dawn, she dressed hurriedly. Stopping at the door, she turned to say good-bye. "And I did mean it. You know, the part about 'I love you.'" When, on the pier, as Mr. Hillcastle took Pythia's hand in his and gently kissed it and then looked up at her face, I could see that tears were forming in his eyes just as they had in mine the night before. What I had suspected at the wedding, that she had probably made him pretend to be a lion, tiger, skunk, rooster, and maybe even a Gangetic snaketrout, seemed a certainty. Much to my surprise, the jealousy that had so affected first love, so agitated my innocent affection for Angel, was now only very slightly felt. As he stood next to me waving good-bye to them—Dr. McCloud, Pythia, Major Wheedle, the Tiger Boy, Francis Coffin-White, Tara Tigresse, and a drunkard who was apparently mistaking us for people he knew, all leaning against the railing of the bridge deck to wave back to us—I sensed that Hillcastle was not as fortunate as I, that, because of jealousy, he detested me in a suspicion that I too had roared, growled, barked, meowed, purred, clucked, bleated, and cock-a-doodle-dooed with love for the future president of the United States. Nagini was standing at what she no doubt considered an appropriate distance from us, not waving, but with hands pressed together in a reverential namaskar, and there were tears in her

217

eyes too. Shree Karnaghee, as detached as holy men are supposed to be from the joys and sorrows of this world, used the occasion to utter a few wise words: "Let mankind learn from this. The dockyard is like life itself: the boats come in and the boats go out!" The ship had already blown its mighty horns and was pulling away from the dock when, after being delayed by a punctured tire on the Peerless that had been transporting them to the pier, Les Chauds Lapins arrived to play the jazz that would make a gala celebration of the departure. Even though the boat that carried the intended audience had almost disappeared into the farthest reaches of the harbor, they unpacked their instruments and performed as planned: "Toot, toot, Tootsie, goo'bye, toot, toot, Tootsie, don't cry." Gathering clouds auguring the beginning of the monsoon made everyone anxious to find shelter before the certain storm, but the band played happily on: "Kiss me, Tootsie, and then, do it o-ver a-again. Toot, toot, Tootsie, goo'bye, toot, toot, Tootsie, don't cry." On the way back from Alipore, Nagini asked me what the song meant. Although I was in full agreement with Pythia's contention that "all love songs, no matter how eloquent or crude, in whatever language they are sung, say essentially the same thing," I did my best, despite the limitations of my rudimentary command of Bengali, to translate: *"Tut, tut, Tutsi, shonaa, arken donaa, taataa baai baai-baai, daao chumu daao! Tut, tut, Tutsi, aabaar chumu chaai, aabaar chumu chaai. Tut, tut, Tutsi, shonaa."*

| 53 | The cadaverous mansion, cere silent, pall dark, emptied of all words and light, reeking of hurried abandonment, was drenched by the nocturnal gush and spew of monsoon clouds grumbling in an unfathomable pitch of heated heavens. The ferociously |

drunken god Indra, splitting open the engorged coils of the serpent Vritra with spears of lightning, had, any lore-abiding snake charmer would tell you, released these rains. Rather than intrude upon the strange vacancy of the house, we sat still wet after the dash from the gate on the stone floor of the verandah, leaning against the wall with legs outstretched, staring into the darkness through a curtain of water hung and drawn by the overflow of eaves-drains strained by the brazen storm. We did not speak. Since she had already said that she would miss Pythia (and I had said, yes, I would too), and since she had already, several times, asked me to talk to Menachem Goldman about her father's appeal (and I had said yes, yes, I would) there was nothing left to say or ask. I wondered if the silence was as awkward for Nagini as it was for me. It was a speechlessness of interrogative stirrings: What now? Right now? And tomorrow? And, then, after that? What next? For me? For anyone? Because of the way in which the blue Banarsi shawl that Pythia had given her was draped, I couldn't see the white flowers entwined with the black snake of braid or the expression on her face, but the smell of jasmine aroused a vision of dark doe eyes. There was a sudden realization that I did not really miss Pythia, that I did love and certainly desire her but was not, for some reason, at all grieved that she was gone. Love refuses to make sense. It lies to us and sometimes tries to trick us into believing that if it cannot be forever, it might as well be over. The rain evoked a memory: we were somewhere in the north, on tour in the early days of the ten-in-one, and we had just started a game of snakes and ladders, when suddenly Angel said, "Let's play hide-and-seek instead. Shut your eyes. I'll hide." I could remember the heady smell of the hallways of the old boarding-house in which I searched for her, the trill of the rain on the windows, and the hatch of time-yellowed lace curtains hanging limp over the wet panes of glass, but I could not for the life of me remember finding Angel. In that memory she was lost forever. I asked in my childish Bengali: "Is there a game in India: one child hides and the other, after closing his eyes and counting from one to ten, looks for the one who has hidden? Do you play that here?" "*Shikharkhel*," she said, "the hunting game." Then, just to see what she'd do, I shut my eyes and began the count: "*Ek, dhui, teen . . .*" Opening my eyes at "*dosh*," I was amazed that the snake girl had disappeared. I would have suspected that someone who believed in ghosts would have been afraid to enter the house alone. By memory I made my way though the darkness to the buttery, where, feeling for remains of candles in drawers and cabinets, I finally touched one, took it, lit it, and began the hunt. "Here I come, ready or not!" She would be upstairs, I guessed, in the place in the house most familiar to her, yes, hiding in the room that had been Pythia's. If I was right, I decided, I'd take it as a sign that I was meant to find her. "Finders keepers, losers weepers," I said loudly enough for her to hear as I entered the bedroom. By the little light remaining to the candle stub, I looked around, noticing the dark rectangle on the bare wall where a portrait of Celeste McCloud had recently been hanging, and took account of the remains of a former life: a bed stripped of its bedding, a dressing table devoid of all that Pythia had once used to make herself all the more beautiful, a wicker chair with a broken leg, and the large armoire in which I hoped that Nagini was hiding and waiting to be found. "No, she's not in here," I said aloud in English, as, blowing out the candle, I opened and shut the door loudly without leaving the room. I moved quietly along the wall to the dressing alcove, where I stood as hushed, still, and watchful as any tiger hunter in his blind. After a minute, during which I suspected that I might have been wrong, the slowly opening door of the armoire faintly creaked. A silhouette circled the room to glide to rest at the open window, from which the girl looked out at the persistent downpour. "Nagini," I whispered as, standing behind her, I placed my hands upon her shoulders. That she did not flinch implied that she had known I was there and expected my touch. Ever so lightly I kissed the back of her head, coercing my arms to wrap around her, timidly kissed her again, behind the ear, then the neck, and again the whispered name: "Nagini." She did not move nor make a sound. There was no resistance when I turned her around. She let me lead her to the bed. Nakedness was covered by darkness and feelings so hidden by her silence that I had to modulate the sound of the storm into the moans and whispers that I yearned for. When, in the morning, I woke up covered by her blue shawl, the rain had stopped and she was gone. Ishmael, saluting me as I descended the stairs to look for her, informed me that my "last cup of chai" was ready, that this was good-bye, that he and Ibrahim were going back to their village, unless, of course, I'd double their meager pay and let them move into the main house at least until the new doctor-sahib arrived. On the condition that they'd wash their cummerbunds, I consented and gave them my old room. I had grown fond of Ishmael, and, lucky for him, I had saved up some cash. In addition to news of people who had died, my mother's letters always contained a bank draft, money left to me in my father's will and sent in installments to prevent me from squandering it in one lump sum. When Ishmael demanded extra rupees to have the cummerbunds cleaned, I agreed to that as well and asked if he had seen Nagini. No, he claimed, but he had seen Maar-nath outside on the verandah waiting to help us get rid of the dogs and snakes. Maarnath the snake-wallah also asked if he could move into the house with his family, and, sure, I said, why not? They could occupy the guest room that had been Major Wheedle's. The profoundly empty house soon became frivolously full. Maithun Wadsworth Tagore, trailed by the street urchin Haramjada, came to tell me the true story of how *A True Story!* had been confiscated by the po-lice and banned by the censors. While Tagore railed against colonial injustice, the little ne'er-do-well who had played Hugh Mann in the film explored the house on his own. When the boy reappeared to announce his decision to move into Dr. McCloud's suite, Tagore urged me to allow it: "Think of the poor or-phan as a representative of all the Indians who have been oppressed by the colonial institutions that this estate represents. This is your opportunity to do something for India." I installed myself in the room that had been Pythia's. Re-turning there in the afternoon of the day following my first night there, I found that sheets and pillows had been brought and the bed had been made. There was a vase of fragrant chemeli, a bowl of ripe mangoes, and a clay pot of clean water. Nagini's saris, cholis, and shawls were neatly folded on a shelf in the ar-moire. As Maarnath and I loaded the snakes into large burlap bags, he promised that he would release them outside the city, far away, back into the jungle. A re-port that week in *The Bengal Statesman* made me suspicious: "Mr. Harold Swan, director of Hubbard and Sassoon Industries of Calcutta and Rangoon, Ltd., died instantaneously in the garden of his Alipore home yesterday as the result of being bitten by a maarchiti, a species of poisonous reptile rarely found in re-gions populated by human beings. This is the latest mortality in a series of snakebites reported in the area this week. Residents are advised to be on the lookout for venomous serpents during the remainder of snakebite season." The chamars took the six retired polo ponies and Ibrahim shooed and kicked the dogs to freedom. Ishmael stacked the daily-arriving boxes and crates, ad-dressed to Dr. Adderson, in the empty kennel. I played at being master of the mansion. Lying in bed with my bibi on a Sunday, refuged from the heat of af-ternoon, I stroked Nagini's lushly unbound hair as she explained the red stone on a black string around her neck: her father had given it to her before they took him away. It was a snake-gem, she said: premsamp snakes burrow for them and swallow them up; after being in the reptile's stomach for a while, they will, when regurgitated, glow bright in the night and in so doing will at-tract frogs. The serpent devours the frogs and reswallows the stone. In the best Bengali I could muster, I tried to tell her that she herself was a radiant snake-gem, dazzling me by night, and that just for the sight of her I would gladly be swallowed up by a premsamp, the viper that is love. Frowning, she reminded me to talk to Goldman about Lingnath's appeal. We were interrupted by shouts from outside: "Hallo, hallo. Anybody house?" I recognized the voice. "Where is the everybody? Finally is it the three weeks for the amazement. Hallo! What is a going on?" Ashamed that I had indeed completely forgotten about the magician who had been buried in the garden, I leaned out the window to tell him to come in, that I'd be right down. Clearly upset and dressed like the day he was buried, he was pacing the vestibule as I descended the staircase in my pajama pants. "Where is the everybody I am wondering nonstop during the waiting for some last twenty minutes of the timely digging up of Professor Wonderful. Finally I am arriving for the explanatories and apologies." He complained that he had been counting on the success of the "Buried Alive Miracle" to get him the publicity he needed for a decent booking. Ever since coming to Calcutta from the countryside, he had earned practically nothing and was forced by penury to sleep in the colonnades of Chowringhee like a beggar or a holy man. To make amends for not digging up his coffin, I impulsively invited him to move into the house with the rest of us. His smile was exuberant. "Why not?" He took my former room. Exactly seven days after becoming my lover, Nagini, sitting on the edge of our bed when I woke up, handed me a small packet of carefully wrapped red paper that was secured with black string. She left the room before I could open it. It contained, much to my bafflement, a tuft of soft, dark hair. When I asked Maarnath, as a member of her caste, what the gift might mean, he, with some amusement, explained that it was a custom among some of the Sapera women. This was what courtesans did for the maharajas who engaged them in their harems; likewise when a snake-charmer girl takes a lover who is not her husband, she offers her pubic hair to the man as a promissory token that she will be his, at least for a little while. "It is a not-marriage marriage," he said. "Pubic hair means love."

54 "Call me Isaac," I said when the Maharaja called me Mr. Schlossberg. He smiled. "Are you ready to play, Isaac?" He had been waiting to teach me. "Snakes and ladders, I like to imagine, by making sense of a senseless past as it orders memory into squares, episodes, and scenes, offers a heavenly glimpse of earthly patterns. The game stimulates a sense of direction." Accepting the Maharaja's invitation to initiate me into the subtleties of play, I returned to Diwanasthan, the ten-square-mile kingdom ruled by a ruler whose only subjects, other than a motley troupe of ten inherited servants aimlessly shuffling about in the castle's shadows, were the toothless old man who, after having supposedly being cured of blindness by Karnaghee's book, managed a customerless chai and biscuit stall outside the castle gate, a crone who was the self-appointed priestess of the Manasa shrine at the border crossing into Diwanasthan, and, stationed in a makeshift hut, fabricated at that checkpoint from the leftovers of the castle's reconstruction, Diwanasthan's chief of police, a blind man who claimed to have lost his sight by the strain to his eyes of reading the very book by Karnaghee that had healed the eyes of his compatriot. Although Diwanasthan's only crops were loki gourds and cannabis, its birdlife, thanks to all the unsold biscuits that the teawallah tossed out each day, included (in addition to the usual marauding mynahs and crows, and cruising kites and hawks) babblers, bulbuls, lovebirds, cuckoos, and a seagull who had curiously abandoned the sea. The Maharaja, wearing the checkered beret that Professor Wonderful had magically pulled out of a rabbit, was eager to show me his entire collection of snakes and ladders games and was ready to play. "I have the most extensive collection in the world, so complete, spanning so many centuries and so many lands, that every other collector of the game is mad with envy. The Jebtsundamba Khutuktu of Mongolia, author of *How to Win at Snakes and Ladders,* himself the most recent winner of the snakes and ladders championship held every ten years in Petropavlovsk, has challenged me to a match, with my collection going to him if he wins, and if I win, his collection of Buddhist manuscripts are the stakes. Why would I risk it? Lots of people own Buddhist manuscripts. Libraries are full of them. But who on earth has over one hundred sets of snakes and ladders? There can, in any case, not really be a champion, but only a winner and loser of this game or that. The more you play, the more you win and the more you lose. The only champion is he or she who has played the most games. And no one knows who that might be. It could someday be you. My wives play among themselves every day upon arising, and whichever one among them wins that morning earns a place in my chamber that night and plays it with me before going to bed." I had learned from Dr. McCloud that the Maharaja's first wife, a delicate woman, had died some twenty years earlier while giving birth to a thirteen-pound Yuvaraja, Prince Frederick of Diwanasthan, "still rotund and residing in Oxford, England, where he formerly read theology and now plays croquet, drinks pink gin, and, one hears, enjoys homosexual relations with intellectuals, foxhunters, and clergymen." There were, McCloud continued, more than ten wives in the "collection of consolatrices, including a Jewess from Cochin, a Mohammedan girl from Kabul, a Roman Catholic from Goa, an ex–Buddhist nun from Sikkim, and a Protestant debutante from Philadelphia." The collection of women, sequestered in the zenana within the castle keep, was, unlike his games, eggs, hats, mirrors, erotica, and mounted animals, never displayed. Since the sight of them was forbidden to all but the Maharaja himself, Dr. McCloud had been blindfolded each time he had been called to treat one of the royal paramours. "Not only am I not permitted to see their bodies during examinations, I am forbidden to hear their voices, and I am made to wear a nose clip so that I cannot smell them. His Highness describes the symptoms as he takes my hand in his to guide it to whatever afflicted part of whichever unwell girl's anatomy. Gynecological examinations are, of course, easy enough in the dark, but other diagnoses can be problematic. It is fortunate indeed that surgery has, thus far, never been required. Sometimes in the harem room I hear muffled giggles in the background, the jingling of jewelry, and the rolling of dice." As we, on our way to the donjon, passed by Bill, Lucy, and Mumtaz, the Maharaja patted the bull elephant's hind leg. "Nothing gave me more pleasure in my youth than riding each Sunday around my kingdom upon his back. As I'd turn to gaze at the Maharani, so splendid in full royal regalia, Bill would turn his head to look at his beloved beauty in full festive dress and bearing the howdah in which my lady rode. I felt for Bill, and he for me, in the joys and sorrows that came and went with love. He mourned no less for Lucy than I did for my own queen. That's the bit about love I hate, you know, the part where the one you love dies." Lucy's bones were a reminder of Pythia. I imagined her, as I followed the Maharaja into the darkness of the spiral stone staircase, on the deck of the *Queen Mab,* saline gusts tousling her hair, stinging her cheeks, and filling her lungs. I wondered if she missed me and what I meant to her. "Here we are," the Maharaja said, beaming as he headed for the ladder against the wall of floor-to-ceiling drawers from which he began to produce box after box from his unrivaled collection: "Snakes and ladders, kismet, mokshapata, gyan chaupar, golokdham, nagapasha: the great aleatory game of divination and delusion, knowledge and ignorance, liberation and entrapment, virtue and vice, hope and fear, and all the other ups and downs of life. Is it by chance or luck that we win, by probability, fate, or destiny that we lose? A little bit of each, or none at all? Your guess is as good as mine. The oldest known set, purloined from Indian soil at Mohenjo Daro for display in the Ashmolean Museum in Oxford, has unnumbered stone squares that for play must be assembled as a puzzle, using the engraved snakes and ladders as a guide. It was certainly played in India over forty thousand years ago, in Neolithic times; but, since the squares, snakes, and ladders were merely etched into the earth with a stick during that period, there are no archaeological remains. That a ladder that was recently discovered during excavations of the city of Ur indicates that this vatic divertissement was very popular among the fun-loving Sumerians. It was a strictly hieratic game in Mesopotamia; Hammurabi played it daily and based his code upon it. And in Egypt, that rascal, young Amenhotep IV, consolidated his kingdom by winning a game of it against the priests of Amon. In more modern times, players of renown have included Frederick II of Hohenstaufen, Suleiman the Impotent, Akbar the Great, William Shakespeare, King Humbert, Vladimir Ilyich Lenin, and your very own president, Woodrow Wilson. The oldest set in my collection is this Buddhist one from Rongbuk Monastery in Tibet. The die is human bone, reputedly a relic, the finger with which the Buddha touched the earth upon attaining his enlightenment. Look at how many snakes are etched on the linked palm leaves. It's almost impossible to make it to the end, get off the board, and attain nirvana. But if you do, you never have to play again. Nirvana means you win. The game is over forever. No more fun nor boredom, no more hope, danger, joy, sorrow, no more snakes and no more ladders. So what's the point? Raising that question is, I suppose, the point of that otherwise pointedly pointless game. Here's a Vaishnava version on birch bark with its three hundred and thirty-three squares. The ladders are as perilous as the snakes and the snakes as helpful as the ladders. By rising too high and moving too fast, you can overshoot Vishnu's heaven. Nirvana means you lose. Here's a fine example of an ophidiomantic board. There are no snakes painted on it, just ladders; that's because real living snakes were used, set upon the board to coil, twist, and squirm about at will. You'd never know until a snake head came to rest just which square might be dangerous. Our Lord Shiva, a known cheater at dice, so loved the game that when it was his turn to create the world he, for his own amusement, designed it as a game of snakes and ladders. Here's one with Shiva at the top, a different form of him in each of the ten squares of the last row, beneath which the game's divided into three regions of three rows each: the first region includes the three rows of hell, that of liars, serpents, and mirrors; the second includes three rows of sky, that of birds, of clouds, and of angels; and in the third realm, our gods and goddesses are hierarchically enthroned. Compare that one to this Italian version purchased from King Humbert that has three regions: Inferno, Purgatorio, and Paradisio! This puritanical English edition, with all its serpents being satanic tempters, is a kind of pilgrim's progress: the first roll, no matter how low or high, locates you in the City of Destruction; but here, in square 4, the Bible is a ladder up to Golgotha, and then, if you pray (so the directions say) you might make it to the ladder which was used to retrieve the body of Christ from the cross. Now, let's find a board for today's game. What year were you born? 1899? Yes, yes, good, I do have an edition from that year. And that's what we should use to make the game prognosticatory for you. Open the box. It's a hundred-square Victorian version, typical of the turn of the century, with twelve snakes, one of them bicephalous, and eleven ladders, one folded open into two." I recognized it. "Come along into the playing room, out this door, down the hall, up the stairs, and watch your head; down the ramp and watch your step, through this door, and here we are. Ready? Serious players don't begin at the beginning. Rather we divine where in our lives we are at the moment of each return to play. My token is taken like this. Holding it in my hand, I wave it over the board. I shut my eyes and, the moment it feels right, I let it go: one, two, three, four, four and a half . . . Yes! Now! Haha! There, you see, I'm on square sixty. Now it's your turn. When, at the end of the last century, the game was relegated to children, an important rule was omitted, and with it much of the fun. The finesse is in the pass. At any time, depending on how you assess the odds, read the portents, or on the basis of how lucky you feel, or just on intuition, according to this rule, you can pass, skip your turn, thereby giving whatever probability you faced to your opponent. But you cannot pass if you are passed to. In that case you must roll. Pick up your pawn with the understanding that it has become you and you, it. Shut your eyes. Around and around. Drop yourself into the game which is your life whenever you're ready. There you are, right on forty-seven and it's your turn. Do you pass? No? Then roll!" I took the die in hand, blew on it to warm it up, and tossed it. Snake eye! "Forty-eight," the Maharaja exclaimed. "A ladder of hope leading to a serpent of disappointment!" I was swallowed up, returned to the beginning, the first square on the board and lowest place on earth.

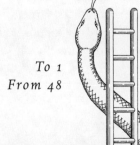

To 1

From 48

	"Professor Solomon Serpentarius's Oriental Oddities and Indian
55	Incredibilities: ten amazing curiosities collected during an argonautian quest up, down, and all around the Indian subcontinent, into its thickest jungles, over it's highest Himalayan peaks, and

across its most barren Deccan deserts, in search of the most mysterious mysteries and wonderful wonderments of Hindustan." That's how I'd begin once I had assembled a troupe of performers to take to England where lots of people with a few shillings in their pockets, familiar with reports of the strangeness of the land they had colonized, would be eager and willing to pay the price of beholding exotic things. The vision had come to me with the snake eye that landed me, by way of a ladder, on a snake that took me back to the beginning. Looking at my token on square 1 again, it seemed to me that, by fate, luck, destiny, or chance, it was meant to be. Like a snake charmer or a maharaja, I'd do what my father before me had done. I took a whiff of Wyoming Willie's Wondrous Hair Pomade for inspiration. "India! Nubile nautchees and beautiful bayaderes, cunning cunchunees and ravishing ramjanees, schooled from earliest childhood in the amatory arts and erotic sciences, are, with their seductive songs and daring dances, mistresses of hallowed secrets for seducing any man or god. Scantily dressed and darkly beautiful, the priestesses of carnality, with their Asiatic agility and pagan grace, have rarely been seen unsequestered from the zenanas of the Orient. One of them, however, the ravishing Ratiranee, having been freed by me from bonds that tied her to the funeral pyre of a wanton maharaja, is here in England, safe, sound, and ready to dance for your enjoyment." I planned to find Ratiranee at the Ananga Ranga Club in Sonagacchi. Nagini would be a more ethereal display of Oriental womanhood: "As a child she was sold to the priests of Juggernaut, her body and soul consecrated in heathen marriage rites to the graven idol. Each night, until I rescued her, she would, in the smoky sanctum sanctorum of the jungle shrine, sing ancient love songs to that grotesque divinity. Once you hear her sing those stirring amatory odes, if any one among you can claim ever to have heard a sweeter voice, your money will be refunded." Then I'd move from the theme of love to that of death, dwelling upon the perils of the exotic colony to introduce the fearless Maarnath: "See deadly cobras sway in hypnotic dance and trance to the sound of the Oriental flute. The charmer shall take up serpents and, let us pray, not be harmed." I'd solemnly swear that right inside and ready for inspection was the strangest teratoid that ever slithered a course upon the earth: "Samoo the Amazing Snake Man: Is he a snake with the head of a man, or a man with the body of a snake? That'll be for you to decide as you watch him wiggle and squirm, trying to bite me with his deadly fangs." Ishmael, who would surely be happy to give up servitude and India for show business and global peregrination, could play the part. I even had the pitch cards to show him as a young Snake Boy on exhibition in California. I figured a feral child would be expected and counted on casting Haramjada, since he had already played the part in *A True Story!* He'd also be the boy who, in my presentation of the ancient Indian Rope Mystery, would be dismembered at the top of a freestanding length of hemp, and then be resurrected in a wicker basket by a sinister thaumaturge whom I had no doubt Professor Wonderful would be delighted to impersonate. Requiring religious representatives and routines to fulfill the British audience's expectations of the wonders of India, I planned to ask Karnaghee to help me find a yogic contortionist and a fakir to lie upon a bed of nails, stick pins in his flesh, and put on whatever other displays of self-mutilation that his religion had codified as outward signs of inward grace as instituted by Shiva Mahadeva. Kumar Bannerjee, I trusted, could provide me with a bear and handler, and I knew I could count on Albert Bannerjee to fashion an assortment of pickled punks, not the usual two-headed chicken or run-of-the-mill five-legged sheep, but more mythic specimens such as a basilisk, cockatrice, embryonic griffin, wivern, or hippocampus. Nothing from India would be too strange. When, over dinner in the Alipore mansion, I presented my scheme to my tenants, Ishmael, Haramjada, Maarnath, and Professor Wonderful, they argued in their enthusiasm as to who among them would be the greatest star. Nestled in my arms that night, Nagini whispered that she was afraid of leaving India, but that she would do whatever I wanted if I helped with her father's legal appeal. I kissed the hoods of the serpents tattooed on each of her hands, moved my lips along their coils, around her wrists, and up her arms, following the scent of coriander, cumin, and cardamom. Her body was a garden of spices. My own body, so lacking in the color and aroma of Sapera flesh, embarrassed me. Nagini had been shocked by the sight of circumcision: how had I injured it? she wondered, and my Bengali was hardly fluent enough to explain the method and meaning of the Jewish and Mohammedan tradition. But once I conveyed to her that the mutilation, like her tattoos, was intentional, she allowed herself to be amused by it: "Turban always off," she giggled, "always looking, always loving." I taught Nagini to say the English words "I love you." She helped me carry the boxes that continued to arrive for Dr. Adderson to the laboratory because Ishmael, now that he considered himself an entertainer and world traveler, had stopped working. Even though he did absolutely nothing all day except smoke ganja, he insisted on being paid, and I complied just to avoid an argument. More money arrived in a letter from my mother that informed me that she and Hayim were taking a train to Florida to appeal to the warden of the Ponce de Leon Penitentiary to transfer Shmuel Grossman from solitary confinement to a communal cellblock. She also mentioned that Phoebus Fong had died of food poisoning and that Lee Kwong Yee had returned to China to join either the Communist Party or the Kuomintang. Haramjada happily offered to escort me to Sonagacchi, the streets of which had been his home since birth. His mother, one of the thousands of prostitutes of the quarter, had died, he said, of "love disease." Professor Wonderful insisted on accompanying us to the Ananga Ranga Club. "It is the great nonstop dream of my own to behold the woman dancing naked. It will be your advantageous to enjoy my India expertise on what girl is a best nautch for our great show." Squeezed in between the urchin and the magician in the rickshaw in which we were slowly hauled into the red-light district, I listened to Professor Wonderful's story: "I am not really a son of the magician. That is not the lie, but a patter. The real name I am is Pharphika, not the magician of a birth and caste, no sir, but one kisan farmer son who at the tender age beholded the wandering gilli-gilli jadugar with the diving duck, a basket trick, cups and the balls, eating and disgorging the stones, tongue cutting, decapitation, and other wonderful what-have-yous. I was so one hundred and one percent amazing that I decided beyond shadows of the doubt that I am the great magician when I am the man. I studied a night and day great books of a Great Whydini." It wasn't a very exciting story, but it had a rather touching point: because he was not a member of the magician's hereditary caste, he could not marry a magician's daughter; and because he had renounced his own social duties and run away from home, he couldn't marry a farmer's daughter either. "So I am seeking the nonproblem woman for the great love." He prayed that she would be dancing naked at the Ananga Ranga Club that night. "If so, I will love her for a forever." Amidst the bodies so hotly pushing their rude and wayward ways through the narrow cluttered lanes of Sonagacchi, cursing, coughing, spitting, laughing, and arguing, there were the pimps who, spotting us, fought each other for turns at grabbing hold of our rickshaw and shouting, "You want to fuck my daughter, beautiful virgin girl and best fuck in Calcutta. No? My sister? Mother? You like old woman? No, you fuck little boy? No? Okay, I fuck you cheap. Yes?" Boisterous whores, leaning out of the windows overhead, jeered, cackled, and screeched coarse solicitations. When one of them spat betel onto Professor Wonderful's head, he took it in good cheer: "They say it is a luck when the crow is shitting on a head. Maybe this is a one and the same." Once the lathi-armed guards at the door to the Ananga Ranga Club, wrestlers dressed and painted as the monkey god Hanuman, understood that Haramjada was a Sonagacchi boy, they trusted his testimony that I was neither with the British police nor the Royal Bengal Society for Mental and Moral Health. The boy went through the perfunctory ritual of haggling over the price of admission into the hot black hole of a room that reeked of hashish, opium, tobacco, rum, kerosene, and fried fish. In the dark crowd of shape-shifting silhouettes of men I thought I saw Mr. Hillcastle at a nearby table. But it was difficult to be sure of anything in Sonagacchi. We ordered rum from a young girl whose just budding breasts, their nipples brightly rouged, were visible through her sheer shawl; another provocatively alluring girl, not much older, juggled three mangoes on the brightly lit stage as she sang a racy song about seasonal fruits. I didn't understand the lyric's Bengali obscenities that were so explicitly indicated by the desperate cheers and drunken laughter of lonely men. We had arrived in time to see Shulamite Levi's show. Billed as Brigitte La Bombinette of the "Folly Burger de French," she wore a cancan dress to sing, *"Tut, tut, Tutsie, salut! Hélas! Tut, tut, Tutsie, ne pleure pas! Embrasse-moi, Tutsie, alors, et puis refais-le encore! Tut, tut, Tutsie, salut!"* As the only European in the review, she commanded a higher price for admission to her backstage room than did the other girls. Stage presentations were mere bally pitch for the performances awaiting high rollers inside. Opening the door, she didn't seem startled to see me, Professor Wonderful, and Haramjada standing there. Very little surprises a prostitute. When I explained that we hadn't come as customers, but because I hoped for her assistance in finding someone to come with us to England and perform there as a nautch girl, she laughed. *"Elle est trouvée, mon petit baratineur. C'est moi!"* Arriving the next morning at Alipore with all of her belongings (one valise, two hatboxes, and my stuffed hyena), she moved into the house with us, installing herself in the pantry, where it had previously been her job to provide the wild Tiger Boy with human intimacy.

56 "Yogi Shamboo Baba, Tantric Mahasiddha of Banaras, having attained superhuman prowess through innumerable years of austerities, mortifications, meditations, metabreathilizations, and yogic postures, can cut off his own head with a sword, at which point that head, nestled in his lap, proceeds to mutter mantras, chant hymns, and give wise counsel," Shree Karnaghee had sworn when promising to bring the sadhu to Alipore. Though I have always found it hard to believe anything that religious people say, I wanted to keep an open mind as I sought out Oriental religious routines for my proposed traveling sideshow. I mused that if the fakir really could do anything like that, I would teach the severed head the words to "Toot, Toot, Tootsie, Goo'bye." Karnaghee further avowed that the yogi could walk on water and through walls, levitate, fly, and make himself "as big as an elephant, as small as a mouse, or even smaller. He can also make himself disappear. Completely invisible! I have seen it with my own eyes!" When Karnaghee brought the sadhu, with his filthy matted locks, tiger-skin loincloth, damaru drum, and a skull-topped staff, to the house on a Sunday afternoon, I asked to see the self-decapitation, only to be informed that it would require several months of esoteric tantric exercises to prepare. Asking to see him levitate, I was told it couldn't be done in the rainy season. Enlarging, shrinking, and disappearing, furthermore, relied on particularly auspicious planetary configurations. Suspecting my skepticism, Karnaghee confided: "Shamboo Baba can actually do all those things anytime and anywhere, without any preparation, but he does not do so in the presence of strangers because too often, experience has taught him, too many people, particularly foreigners, are so amazed by the miracles that they begin to worship him as a god for the wrong reason, for his magical powers rather than for the lofty spirituality that is the true basis of his divinity and only incidentally the source of his ability to do such trivial things as flying, walking through walls, and disappearing." What, I naturally wanted to know, could he do right now? The yogic adept demonstrated that he could indeed arrest his pulse and hold his breath for over a minute. If that wasn't enough to prove that he was a living god, he proclaimed that he could swallow live snakes and regurgitate them, still living, at will and on command. But most amazing of all, he could, Karnaghee swore as the yogic adept wobbled his head affirmatively, lift a twenty-pound stone with his penis. Unfortunately he couldn't demonstrate that extraordinary feat at the moment because the wonder-working appendage was sore, specifically "rope-burned from penilely pulling a bullock cart one furlong." The pulse stopping and breath holding didn't seem very theatrically promising, but the penis number and the snake-vomiting routine might, I surmised, be entertaining on a British stage. "Yogi Shamboo Baba will take the West by storm," Karnaghee promised as he handed me the contract that he had drawn up on behalf of the sadhu: "He can do everything that your Jesus Christ ever did and more! Upon seeing his miracles, every Christian will want to be a Hindu." Although I could not in good faith sign the document, which demanded top billing and more money per performance than Sarah Bernhardt had ever been paid, I did agree that, if he really could lift a stone with his penis, I'd take him to England and provide room and board there. Karnaghee agreed to it and Yogi Shamboo Baba moved in, not into the house but onto it, making a place for himself on the roof. "He will not require a bed," Karnaghee informed me, "in that he sleeps standing on one leg." The claim that he could make himself invisible gave me the idea for an Invisible Man routine. It promised publicity: once we were in England, after reporting to Scotland Yard's Bureau of Missing Persons that our Invisible Man from India had been kidnapped and we had received a ransom note, I'd announce it to the press. Kumar Bannerjee did, as requested, bring a bear and handler, a drunkard named Ballatadas and a likewise inebriated albino brown bear, Shakuntala, that he claimed was a polar bear. I recognized the animal from the Coffin-White wedding, where she had danced the kuch. I allowed them to move into what had once been the library, at least until Shakuntala sobered up enough for me to verify Bannerjee's testimony that she could walk a slackrope. With nine of the ten acts I needed, I thought about the girl who had juggled the mangoes at the Ananga Ranga Club, wondering whether she might juggle something more interesting, like live snakes. Cobras would be impressive. But before I found my tenth incredibility, Dr. Adderson arrived, earlier than expected, in Alipore. An infuriated voice had awakened me: "Schlossberg! Mr. Schlossberg! Where on earth are you? What is going on here?" Wrapping a sheet around myself, I hurried down the stairs to welcome him to the government estate. "Who in the hell are all of these creatures, and what, more significantly, are they doing in my house?" The stocky man with short black hair, a neat mustache, bright white teeth, and quick eyes, dressed in a corduroy Norfolk suit that was too heavy for India, was blatantly hardhearted: "Get these brown blighters out of my house now!" Once I had apologetically promised that I would do so as soon as I had the opportunity to get dressed, he composed himself sufficiently for formal introduction. I would have left Alipore with the rest of them if Adderson hadn't announced that he had, at the recommendation of Dr. McCloud, arranged for me to receive a rather generous government payment for one month of orientational service. Despite the bank drafts that I periodically received from my mother, I needed money to take my new family to England. I convinced Maarnath to take Ballatadas and Shakuntala to Mayapur with him, promising that once arrangements for passage to England had been made, I'd send for them. Because I still felt guilty about forgetting to exhume Professor Wonderful, I rented a room for the magician at the Asvapna Lodge. After timidly asking for permission to invite Shulamite Levi to stay with him there, Professor Wonderful bowed his head to shyly confide, "I am thinking that the Miss Levi might be the great number one tootsie for me." I didn't have to evict Yogi Shamboo Baba, since he never came down from the roof, where, supposedly deep in meditation, he, like my Invisible Man, would probably not be noticed. I had to persuade Adderson to let Ibrahim, Ishmael, and Haramjada stay on as servants by telling three lies: they are hardworking; they are trustworthy; and they come free with the house. I then had to pay them. Although Haramjada resented having to pretend to be a servant, he did so after I convinced him to consider it acting in a dramatic role: "Sweeping and cleaning up can, with the right attitude, be show business." And Nagini, I informed Adderson, in introducing her, couldn't leave without me because she was my wife: "Well, not really my wife in the strictest legal sense of the term, but the mate that a man, after a while out here, requires no less than gin, quinine, and opium." Nagini did in fact serve me as an Indian spouse, washing, shampooing, and shaving me, and singing to me like a devadasi to her lord when I could not sleep: "*Ebar jeney shune namio saabdhaney . . .*" No man, even if he was aware that it might not be sincere, that such attention came from training and duty rather than from impulse or desire, could have resisted or refused it and not pretended that it was love. It amused Nagini that Dr. Adderson called her Mrs. Schlossberg. As my crew moved out, his moved in: there were two assistants, Mr. Higgins and Miss Wiggins, both nurses (the former psychiatric, the latter surgical), who could have passed for brother and sister (both had berry-red blotches on equally pale skin and humidity-frizzled carrotine hair parted down the middle); and there was the black-bearded Mr. Singh, Dr. Adderson's armed guard, wearing a crimson turban, a black military uniform representing no identifiable army, and perfectly polished jodhpur boots, who never said anything but looked at everything. He methodically inspected every drawer and cupboard, looked through every window, behind every door and curtain, and under every piece of furniture. The Sikh was not the sort of man one would dare to cross. When he snatched a cigarette out of my mouth as I was about to light it, Adderson informed me that there would be no smoking or consumption of alcoholic beverages in his house, a rule that increased the agitation I was feeling from not having had any opium since McCloud's departure. I was, however, permitted to smoke on the verandah. Adderson approached me there after our first din-

233

ner together: "Look, Schlossberg," he said in a tone meant to familiarize us, "the expulsion of those natives from the premises may, I realize, have seemed somewhat rude, but there's a lot at stake. We must be very careful. The work we're doing here must be kept absolutely confidential. McCloud avows that I can trust you. And so I shall. But do understand that if word gets out about my research, it could bring the humanitarians down on us, and there's nothing more nasty than an irate humanitarian." For his sake, I repeated, with only slight emendation, the words that McCloud had used to welcome me to India: "Unless you are particularly squeamish and put off by disease, hunger, poverty, violence, corruption, mosquitos, vermin, infernal weather, and poisonous snakes, you'll find life rather pleasant in Calcutta, a city relatively free of humanitarianism." The nature of Adderson's research was insinuated by the activity in the house over the next few days: each of the six stalls in the stable was contained by raised walls and a locked door of steel bars, and furnished with a metal bed with bolts by which its future occupant could be restrained. The laboratory was transformed into a surgery, the operating table fixed with a prominent metal headrest; and the kennel, newly lined with shelves, became a storeroom. Ishmael and Ibrahim, once I had threatened to stop paying them, diffidently agreed to help me help Adderson, Higgins, and Wiggins unpack the boxes that had arrived during the previous weeks: strange electrical devices, a vast array of surgical instruments, and innumerable jars. I had volunteered to assist in hopes of finding some morphine. As Ishmael uncrated a shipment of glass containers and handed them to me, I lined them up on an empty shelf. To my untrained eye the contents would have been indistinguishable if it had not been for the neatly written labels: "Brain of a Woman (Insane)"; "Brain of a Negro (Rapist)"; "Brain of a Communist (Russian)"; "Brain of a Murderer (Electrocuted)"; "Brain of a Spy (German)"; "Brain of a Prostitute (Syphilitic)"; "Brain of a Clown (Suicide)"; "Brain of a Criminal (Jew)."

	"We've been doing psychosurgery for over forty thousand years,"
57	Dr. Adderson explained as he unpacked his surgical instruments:
	"Archaeologists have unearthed a multitude of skulls with holes
	bored in them, ample evidence that trepanning was used to re-

lease demonic spirits from the heads of Neolithic sociopaths. The cave surgeons didn't have humanitarians interfering with their work. Of course now
we know that incubi, succubi, and the like are not beings, but neurophysiological malfunctions. A treatment that works, even though the understanding of
the dynamics of therapeutic action may be erroneous, is nevertheless an effective therapy." Higgins and Wiggins did not seem to be paying attention as they
uncrated electrical apparatuses: tesla and faradic coils, a diathermy machine,
an ultraviolet germicidal radiation lamp, and other fantastic contraptions. Dr.
Adderson was elucidating medieval antecedents to his research: "A prelate of
the Church, one Theophrastus Microbius of Apulia, was engaged in alchemi-
cal experimentation in secret collaboration with Hermes Mendelssohn, when
an accidental explosion in his laboratory sent a bar of lead that he had hoped to
transmute into gold, flying with great force into the center of his forehead.
Court surgeons, amazed that the alchemist could have survived the blast and
the blatant presence of a foreign object in his brain, concluded that any attempt
to remove the metal from his cranium could result in death. That the bar remained, for the remainder of the priest's life, protruding from his head not
only made it impossible for him to wear a clerical hat, but also substantially
transformed his personality. Although memory, intelligence, and physical coordination remained entirely unaffected, Theophrastus had lost all knowledge
of Latin. It was logical to conclude that the lead bar had destroyed that portion
of the brain in which Latin is stored. When it also became apparent to the
prelature of Apulia that the priest had lost all faith in God, there was scholastic
debate on the relationship between a knowledge of Latin and a knowledge of
God. That theological disputation, however, became merely academic in light
of a subsequent observation that the man with the lead in his head had also
lost all inclination to restrain desire or anger, to put into check gluttony, lust,
or aggression. After gaining over two hundred pounds, he was arrested, tried,
and found guilty of the rape and murder of thirty-seven nuns, members of
an Adamite order, the Sisters of Sordino. By order of Frederick II of Hohenstaufen, Theophrastus Microbius was imprisoned in the dungeon of the Castel
del Monte, where theologians, casuists, physicians, and barber-surgeons, given
the opportunity to examine the corpulent criminal, concluded that the lead

bar in his head should be removed. Theophrastus died during the operation. Though the findings about religious faith are obsolete, the implicit recognition of a neuroanatomical and psychophysiological relationship between aggression, desire, and language mastery is apt." Unpacking and shelving medications as he spoke, I noticed a label: "Liquor Morphinae Sulphatis." Since the doctor was so thoroughly absorbed in his lecture on the history of psychosurgery, I assumed that he would not notice a vial or two of the anesthetic sedative slipping into my pocket. "Now let us jump forward to certain events that occurred here in India," Adderson persisted. "In 1857, a Captain Harding of the Bengal Lancers fired his pistol in self-defense at the head of drunken sepoy who assaulted him with a pigstick. The mutineer fell into a coma. Surgeons removed the bullet from the mutineer's frontal lobe in hopes of restoring the consciousness of the rebel sufficiently enough for him to stand trial, be judged, and executed. The trial, however, never came to pass, for, upon recovery, the native, entirely repentant and proclaiming himself a devoted vassal of the queen, the captain, and all other representatives of the Crown, pleaded to be admitted into penitential servitude in the Harding home, where Mrs. Harding soon declared him 'the dearest, meekest, most gentle man in the colony.'" Dr. Adderson's historical account of psychosurgery in India had taken him up to 1889: "The Nawab of Nagpur was mounted in the hunting howdah on the back of his elephant when a ferocious tiger, suddenly bounding out of the underbrush, leapt up to attack him. With regal sangfroid, the Nawab, firing a Lee Enfield at the man-eater, struck the beast right between the eyes. Falling to the ground, the tiger whimpered, rolled over, and trembled. In order to put the wild cat out of its misery, the noble Nawab climbed down from his elephant, drew his pistol, aimed it at the wounded creature's head, and fired. The gun did not go off. By the time a beater had brought fresh ammunition and the Nawab had loaded the pistol, the tiger had inched its way forward to lick the hunter's silk slippers. The cat's eyes met those of the Nawab who suddenly recognized in them an extraordinary gentleness and heartrending docility. With its striped tail wagging, the tiger purred and rolled over onto its back to be petted on the chest. The hole in the head of the formerly ferocious feline was bandaged with a finely embroidered silk scarf and the Nawab's new pet followed him everywhere, slept at the foot of his bed, and played like a kitten with his seventeen children. A report of this strange transformation, published by a Dr. Bippin Bannerjee in the *Journal of the Asian Academy of Veterinary Psychiatry*, came to the attention of Frederick Golz, an amateur veterinary surgeon in the picturesque Bavarian township of Dachau, and so stimulated his curiosity that he began to experiment with the surgical ablation of canine neocortices. In a research paper with the whimsical Latin title *Cave Cerebrum Canis* (unpublished but widely circulated in German medical circles), he reported that six ferocious Alsatian guard dogs, after removal of the temporal lobes of their brains, became markedly more submissive and affectionate. This data inspired the father of modern psychosurgery, Dr. Gottlieb Burkhardt, director of the Aargau Asylum for the Insane, to ablate portions of the temporal and frontal cortices of the brains of six human patients, all schizophrenics with violent tendencies. Like Golz's dogs, Gottlieb's human beings became gentler and more affectionate. Detailed study of the benefits of the surgery were, however, unfortunately curtailed when, after news was leaked to the scientific press that five of the patients had died (three from surgical complications, one from suicide, and one shot while trying to escape from the asylum), medical authorities, pressured by humanitarians, censured Gottlieb. Since then experimental psychosurgery has been sadly restricted to animal subjects. I myself have, in my research during the past year, confirmed the findings of Bannerjee, Golz, and Gottlieb with operations on pigs, goats, langurs, and several Himalayan bears." As he spoke, I, contemplating the specimen jars containing the human brains that I had previously shelved, was startled to notice, as I turned to examine more closely the brain of the Jewish criminal, the reflection of my face on the glass of the jar. I adjusted the position in which I was standing to provide myself with the amusing illusion that I was looking at my own brain in my seemingly translucent head. Unpacking a box of bandages and sponges, the doctor continued: "My own interest in this promising area of medicine was aroused about two years ago on the occasion of being invited to the St. Tutinus Hospital in Blackpool to participate as a consultant in the examination of a patient with a brain injury. Since survivors of severe cerebral trauma who show no signs of loss in intellect, memory, or motor skills are relatively rare, I was delighted with the opportunity. The patient, a professional stage magician, had attempted a stunt in which he claimed that he would catch with his teeth a bullet fired at his head by a volunteer from the audience. Through some sort of mix-up in backstage magical preparations or a failure of the apparatus, however, he caught the bullet with his brain rather than his teeth. After recovery from the surgical removal of the foreign object, the only symptoms of brain damage were the development of a tic and a loss of the ability to lie." As Mr. Singh polished and oiled his Luger, the doctor went on to explain that it was an empirical certainty that the human personality can be modified by neurosurgery that had inspired him to devote his talents entirely to research in the area. Because experimentation on human subjects was too controversial in Europe, he had applied to the Royal Academy of Psychoneurological Arts and Sciences in London (arguing that "we've got to do this before the Soviets beat us to it") to station him in Calcutta and provide him with the assistants, equipment, and facilities necessary to conduct research on human beings, "not just any human beings, but natives provided through the cooperation of the Royal Bengal Society for Mental and Moral Health; not just any natives, but inmates from Indian prisons, convicted of heinous felonies, criminals who would be executed if their sentencing had not been so delimited by the noblesse oblige of English Common Law. The six of them, who will be arriving shortly, have all been convicted of murder, and each one of them is entirely lacking in conscience and in any inclination to control desire or anger. That, as pathological liars, all claim to be innocent, demonstrates their unrepentance. By cauterizing or excising certain portions of their brains, identified in advance by electrical stimulation, we shall reorganize the hierarchy of neurological processes within the cerebral cortex so that these men will be incapable of lying, sexual assault, or acts of aggression. Thus our work here, as begun over forty thousand years ago, promises to transform the criminals, miscreants, and sinners of this world into honest, gentle, and civilized souls. My goal is simply to make the world a better place. For this I hope to be awarded a Nobel Prize." Two days later, six prisoners in straitjackets, shackled to prevent them from walking, were delivered from the dock where they had arrived from South Andaman Island, unloaded from the back of a truck and carried in palanquin cages by coolies to the stable, where they were secured to their respective beds under the watchful eye and drawn pistol of Mr. Singh. Black cotton bags over their heads were fixed around their necks with rope. Dr. Adderson announced over a dinner of sausages that the operating room should be sterilized in the morning in preparation for an operation to take place the following day. "Which one is first?" Wiggins wondered aloud. "The worst of the lot," Adderson answered, "a man who, here in Calcutta, ruthlessly murdered a Mr. Godfrey Sassoon, coincidentally a schoolmate of mine at Westminster and a bit of a chum back then. The devil, who also raped Mrs. Sassoon, was a snake charmer."

58 While planning the snake charmer's salvation in the small room in the Asvapna Lodge, I had the idea that Shulamite Levi could seduce and then drug Dr. Adderson to get him out of the way. Much to the relief of Professor Wonderful, Shula said that she could not do it, not because she was not willing, but because she was certain that the doctor was a homosexual. It was, she noted, her métier to assay the amorous proclivities of men. But, as committed as any of us to the great escape, she suggested an alternative: Gopal, the mango juggler at the Ananga Ranga Club, the beautiful boy whom I had mistaken for a girl, because he loved Shula and because she would promise that I would take him to England with us, could deal with Adderson. Professor Wonderful was thrilled with our plan, gratified by the idea that all the work he had put into his Buried Alive illusion would finally pay off. Ishmael would report the noises and, together with Ibrahim, dig the grave exactly where they had previously dug it for the magician. He would insist with Islamic zealousness on the immediate burial of the body. Maarnath would supply the snakes and Haramjada would release them. Yogi Shamboo Baba had initially been hesitant to reveal to me the secret of pulse stopping; but once I explained the end to which the miracle would be put, he cheerfully disclosed that one merely had to place rubber balls in one's armpits and squeeze down on them to cut off circulation. "But the secret of stone lifting with penis," he said quite adamantly, "that I shall never reveal." Ballatadas and Shakuntala were the lookouts and Nagini was our audience. I doubt that any spectator in a theater has ever been as thrilled, delighted, and moved by any performance as she was by our *Snake Charmer's Deliverance*. My part was not easy, since my lines exceeded the limits of my fluency in Bengali. As the only one of us allowed into the stable where the prisoners were confined, it fell upon me to explain to Lingnath in that language what we were doing and exactly what he must do and when he must do it. Because I didn't have a key to his cell, I'd have to whisper the instructions through the bars. Although worried that the prisoners on either side of him would be able to hear and might, when their gags were removed for occasional nonintravenous meals, reveal what we had done, I kept hope that as fellow convicted murderers they would be sympathetic enough and sufficiently entertained by our performance to keep their mouths shut. As I rehearsed my lines, Nagini corrected my mistakes and laughed over them as well. And then she cried a little, "for happiness," she softly said in English. To ensure the success of the show, and honoring Hugh Mann's request, I went to the shrine of Muldev, Lord of the Mitthaloka and tutelary deity of scoundrels and thieves. Since offerings to him had to be things stolen, I swiped the brain of the Jew from its jar, replacing it with the brain of a horse that I was able to purchase for twenty-one annas from the slaughterer who had taken away Dr. McCloud's venom-immune polo ponies. The offerings having been made, the lines memorized, the cues rehearsed, and the stage set, the curtain went up. Enter Gopal, his eyelids dark with kohl, his lips moist and red with betel, his feet bare, and his delicate hands holding a basket of ripe mangos. Singing a Bengali love song, an overture of sorts as he meandered toward the house, he stopped at the gate. Dr. Adderson, Higgins, and Wiggins were preparing the surgery for the first experimental operation, boiling the instruments and sponges, washing down the walls with carbolic acid, setting up the lights and screens, when I arrived to inform the surgeon that there was a boy at the gate with mangoes for him, "a welcoming gift from Lord Krishna," I said he had said, "offered with prayers for the success of all endeavors undertaken by the occupants of the estate." "Tell him to go away," the impatient Adderson automatically responded. But Shulamite Levi had been right about him: when I added that he was the most amazingly beautiful boy that I had ever in my life seen, the physician looked up, wiped the perspiration from his brow, took a deep breath, and removed his rubber gloves. "Well, I suppose it would be undiplomatic to offend the natives." After instructing Higgins and Wiggins to continue sanitization, he followed me to the gate. Gopal's smile was as irresistible to Adderson as Nagini's tears were to me. "What's he saying?" Adderson asked and I answered according to the script: "He says that for the mangoes to bring you the blessings that he hopes you will enjoy, he must humbly feed them to you with his own fingers." Opening the gate, the surgeon beckoned the boy in and led him to the house. I had previously injected the mangoes with morphia sulfate and was somewhat concerned that my roughly estimated dosage might kill him. Adderson's absence for the next two days was explained to Higgins, Wiggins, and Singh by Ibrahim: "Doctor Saab is very diarrhea. He is demanding: 'Do not disturb.'" That was Ishmael's cue to inform Higgins, Wiggins, and Singh that just then, while cleaning the storeroom, he had heard some "great commotions" in the stable, and that he was very frightened that one of the prisoner-patients may have broken free from his restraints and was trying to break down the door to his cell. I heard Mr. Singh, as he drew his Luger, speak for the first time: "Follow me." We obeyed, and as, with great caution, we peered into each of the six cells, Haramjada took his cue to release the serpents in the hallway that, connecting the storeroom, stable, and surgery, provided us with our only way out. "False alarm," Singh, seemingly disappointed that he hadn't gotten the opportunity to shoot anyone, grumbled as he returned his revolver to its meticulously polished black holster. "Back to work."

No sooner had she opened the door than nurse Wiggins screamed and leapt back into the scrawny arms of Higgins, who, seeing what she had seen, matched her scream with one of his own. The spectacle of nearly forty serpents, a dozen of them king cobras with hoods spread, hissing and S-ing into the room toward us, was impressive. Seeing Singh redraw his gun, I cried, "Don't shoot! If you kill one of them, the others will go into a frenzy and start striking and we'll all die." The most fearless of men, I have discovered, are more frightened than anyone else of God, venereal disease, and snakes. Warning everyone to stand very still, I informed them that these were the snakes that McCloud had used in his antivenin experiments, that all of them were very deadly, and that "obviously they have returned to the place they consider home." From the terrified tone in Higgins's voice as he asked "What should we do?" I knew that our show was going to be a smash. "Don't panic," I repeated, knowing that that command always intensifies fear. "Isn't one of the prisoners a snake charmer? That's what Adderson said. He's our only hope. Does anyone have a key to his cell?" Mr. Singh, as I knew very well, did, and when he acknowledged it I recommended that he release the serpent handler, who could then be commanded to capture the snakes, adding, "shoot the devil if he disobeys or tries to get away. He's our only hope." As amenable to me as he would have been to Adderson, as obedient as men with guns in military uniforms love to be, he complied. Released from his shackles and straitjacket, with his gag and blindfold removed, Lingnath, with Singh's Luger aimed at his head during the entire scene, gave a virtuoso performance, intrepidly grabbing each of the snakes by the tail and putting them, one at a time, into a burlap bag. The snake charmer stole from that bag, unnoticed by his audience, the two rubber balls which, when placed in his armpits and squeezed upon, would allow him to arrest his pulse like a yogi. Remembering that he needed to be bitten for the show to work, he stuck his hand back into the bag, wiggled it around, and then, pulling it back out, showed his audience a gush of blood. He fell down and, just like the heterodonic serpent in Professor Wonderful's magic show, flipped over, thrashed about, went limp, opened his mouth, and let his tongue hang out. After rushing to secure the bag of snakes with a rope, I knelt by the snake charmer and lifted his hand by the wrist to check for his pulse. Pronouncing him dead, I asked Higgins and Wiggins, as professional nurses, to confirm it. Yes, no breath, no pulse. "He's dead," said Wiggins, and Higgins added, "Dr. Adderson will be furious. Human subjects for experimental surgery are very costly." Covering Lingnath's body with a sterile sheet from the shelf, I recited my next line: "Better this criminal than us. It was a close call." Ishmael and Ibrahim started digging the grave immediately. I explained to Higgins, who was very worried that Adderson would want to inspect the body himself, that, according to Mohammedan law, the body had to be buried at once. "If we ask these pious men to compromise that sacred injunction, we'll have the local Moslems, a group more violent than even the humanitarians, at our throats." My moment of dramatic glory came with the eulogy, a monologue delivered as Ishmael and Ibrahim shoveled dirt over the coffin that had previously contained Professor Wonderful. This time Singh had nailed it shut. "O Lord," I began, "this man, whom we bury here today, was a heathen and a sinner. But we count upon Your omniscience to acknowledge that he gave his life so that we, Your humble servants, might continue to dedicate ourselves to a great experiment that promises to make Your world a better place. Have mercy upon him. Amen." While Mr. Higgins and Mr. Singh both had tears in their eyes, a less sentimental Miss Wiggins commented that she doubted God would have any mercy for a snake charmer convicted of rape and murder. Mr. Singh informed the Christian that even if her God was too narrow-minded to forgive the murderer who had saved our lives, Sat Kartar, the True Creator and Great Giver, would release him from bondage in this world. Miss Wiggins turned to Mr. Higgins to say, "I hate India." And *"Jai Hind!"* I cheered in the little room at the Asvapna Lodge as the cork popped out of one of the three bottles of Château d'Amour that Shula had stolen from the bar at the Ananga Ranga Club. It was the first time any of them except Shula had ever tasted the effervescent wine. And they loved it. It made Lingnath weep with joy. Yogi Shamboo Baba, standing on one leg in the corner of the overcrowded room, suddenly said, "It would have been much more impressive if, instead of stopping his pulse, our snake charmer had lifted a twenty-pound stone with his penis." We laughed, toasted to our triumph, and opened the other two bottles of champagne, and Nagini joined Gopal in singing the Bengali love song that he had sung outside the gate to the Alipore estate. Lingnath and Maarnath took up the tune on the gourd flutes with which they had charmed so many deadly serpents. Under the spell of the music, Shakuntala began to dance. And it was the most charming performance of a jig that one could ever have expected from a bear, particularly one who was drunk on champagne.

From 39

59

"Dig up the body! I need the brain," Adderson ordered, but Ishmael and Ibrahim refused ("because they are Mohammedans," I explained). Adderson, unmoved by religious orthodoxy, fired them. Removing his filthy blue cummerbund to throw it on the ground, Ibrahim muttered, *"Bokaachodaa,"* which I diplomatically translated as "Thank you, kind master," even though it means "You stupid fuck." The old servant, his son confided in me, wanted to leave anyway. "The excitement of show business and gravedigging is too much for his heart. He wants to retire to our village to devote himself to prayer and await for deliverance into Paradise, where Allah gives deceased Mussulmen the rigor, vigor, and opportunity for daily carnal connection with hosts of houris." Ishmael escorted his father away and Haramjada, in fear of Adderson, went with them. Shortly after their departure, the doctor, emerging from the storeroom in a rage, accused them of black magic: "Satanic tantric necromancers! The Jew's brain has been stolen and replaced with that of a horse, as if I, a neurosurgeon, wouldn't notice. They use human body parts in their orgiastic rites. They eat them! Now I understand the cause of my delirium the other day. The devils put some potion in my tea to get me out of the way while they conducted their nefarious business. That's the real reason they wouldn't exhume the body. They have no doubt stolen certain vital organs from it. We must dig it up at once. If it's not too late, I want that brain. Where's Wiggins? Where's Higgins? Where's Singh? Find them, Mr. Schlossberg, and fetch the shovels." Aware that once the grave was undug and Adderson found no body there, I'd be in jeopardy, I improvised my own escape. "I'm sorry, Dr. Adderson, I was just about to tell you, there's an emergency, news from my mother. My father's dying. I know you'll understand. He has a brain tumor. I'm leaving tonight on a freighter in hopes that I can make it back to California in time." His stern demeanor softened. After a speechless moment, he approached to wrap his arm around my shoulder. "I am terribly sorry, young man. My own father, I must tell you, died of the same horrible affliction when I was just a boy. A gummatic tumor of the frontal lobe was responsible for progressive psychic changes, bouts of lachrymose emotionality that would inevitably culminate in maniacal excitement and acts of aggression against his immediate family. It was that tragedy in my life that inspired me to become a neurosurgeon. If there is anything I can do, please tell me. Come, let us go for a walk in the garden and talk." The conversation was not about what he might be able to do for me, however, but about how I could help him: "Do you know where I might locate that native boy, the one with the mangoes? He's disappeared. In the short time since my arrival in India, I feel that a friendship has begun to develop between us, and thus I take the liberty of confiding in you. I'm a bachelor and, given the demands of my research, there is little prospect of my ever having a family of my own. Love and domestic affection have always been foreign to me. That's why I must find the boy. I hope to adopt him and show him the sort of paternal affection of which I was deprived by a brain tumor. Before losing consciousness, as the smiling child was gazing into my eyes and feeding me morsels of mango, I felt stirrings, longings, and hopes, an intricate conglomeration of startling sensations and strange emotions that can only, for want of a better word, be called 'love.' Do you know where he is?" Informing the surgeon that there was that week a great festival being celebrated in Puri for Jagannath, the Lord of the Universe, I suggested that, as an ardent devotee of Krishna, the boy had probably made the pilgrimage. As one always sympathetic with amorous anguish, I told him the sort of lie that lovers love to hear, assuring him that the beautiful boy would certainly return to the estate. And, of course, he allowed himself to believe the preposterous words of consolation and, like all lovers, wanted to talk about love: "That I have, in my life, been such a stranger to love is indeed an irony, since I have, in fact, dedicated myself to extensive research on the neurological aspects of the sentiment. Animal subjects are hardly appropriate for research on the neurophysiological dynamics of love, and, as you know, human subjects are difficult to acquire. Autopsies have given us ample data to suggest that an erosion of limbic tissue in the septal and thalamic regions of the brain in combination with injuries to, or a pathological degeneration of, medial insula and the cingulate cortex, result in a complete incapacity to love. My hypothesis, based on that data, is that controlled electrical stimulation, as might be provided by a Golz bipolar intracranial electrode for faradic current, of those areas of the brain could excite, enhance, and sustain feelings of love. The problem is in implanting the electrode without killing the potential lover. My idea, and I plan to test it on one of our patients, is to surgically embed a cathode in the appropriate cranial fissure, and then to conduct experimentation by introducing an anode into the nasal passages of the subject. With currents beginning at five milliamperes and gradually increased to sixty milliamperes or even higher, if the patient can endure it, we should be able to make one of our heartless murderers fall in love. The question is, with whom? In order to prove the effectiveness of the faradic stimulation, it must be a woman for whom my subject could not under normal circumstances possibly feel any attraction. I need a truly hideous woman. I'd like to find the world's ugliest woman." When I apologetically interrupted to explain that I really did need to excuse myself in order to pack and prepare for my journey, he insisted that Mrs. Schlossberg and I join him, Higgins, Wiggins, and Singh for "a last cup of tea as a little bon voyage party. They've grown almost as fond of you as I have." As Nagini and I sat with Higgins, Wiggins, and Adderson over tea and cucumber sandwiches on the verandah, I suddenly noticed, much to my panic, that Mr. Singh was directing two coolies, whom he must have just brought in for the job, to dig up the grave in which the snake charmer's body was not buried. "We really do have to leave, now, right now," I said, abruptly standing, picking up my valise, and directing Nagini to follow suit. As the workers dug deeper, Adderson stood outside the gate to wave good-bye to us. When the rickshaw stopped at the Bannerjee house on Chitpore Road in Black Town, suddenly imagining Adderson's surprised expression over the empty grave, I could not help but clap my hands in applause for Professor Wonderful's Buried Alive illusion. Professor Solomon Serpentarius's Indian Incredibilities and Oriental Oddities waited in hiding as Kumar Bannerjee did his generous best to arrange passage for us to England. During the five weeks it took to find a ship that would accept all of us, Nagini, glorying in the deliverance of her father, beamed with the very power that had so poignantly generated her gloom. Before giving up India for me, she said, she needed to visit Kali at the Dakshineshwar shrine to make an offering in supplication of her blessings and protection. Nagini pulled me through the crowd, agitated with devotion, hope, and fear, to the sacrificial pit. The gleaming blade swiped down across the neck of the goat, and the wide black eyes of dog, crow, and human devotees of the goddess watched the head roll across the concrete trough. There was more surprise than terror in the goat's eyes. One eye blinked as if some portion of the brain was still alive. I recollected the promise, made by Kumar Bannerjee on my first day in Calcutta, that by the grace of Kali, I might be delivered from fear and sadness: "In her ghoulish screeching you will hear the sweetest love songs." As we returned from Kali's home, Nagini revealed that, in order to be safe in absence from Calcutta, she had installed the goddess in her heart. I could see the gaping blood-smeared mouth of the bloodthirsty goddess as Nagini leaned forward to kiss me, and in making love after our return from the temple that morning, I was sacrificed to the divinity within her. We were awakened by the knocking on the door: "You have a visitor," Mother Bannerjee cheerfully announced: "I shall serve sweets so that everyone is happy." Nagini and I rose, dressed, and went to the courtyard where he was waiting in the shadow of the stuffed elephant. The visitor, a snake charmer from Assam named Bolondas, was Nagini's husband and he wanted her back. Maarnath had told him where to find her. When I asked if he really cared about her, he sneered: "Bokaachodaa." His feelings were clearly none of my business. Nagini insisted on going with him, "just to talk," she said and promised to return by nightfall. Mother Bannerjee, arriving in the courtyard with rasogoolas just as they left, immediately sensing how upset I was, insisted that the sweets would make me feel better. I ate one and the sweetness made me sick. I took refuge in the room where I had spent my first night in India, slumping down on the bed below the garish print of Krishna playing his flute for the snake-bodied girls dancing around him. I was swallowed by a serpent of memory and transported back into a dark square: it rained that night in August of 1922, the Hindu month of Shravan, when she hid from me where she was sure that I'd be sure to find her and lose myself in our desire. A circling silhouette glided to rest at an open window from which she looked out at the nocturnal downpour. "Nagini," I whispered as, standing behind her, I placed my hands upon her shoulders. Each moment of love, reliant on the pleasures of recollecting, cleansing, and polishing feelings from the past, is threatened by the darkness that lies ahead. I remembered: the first sight of indigo snake tattoos on delicate hands; the first faint sound of sigh and muffled murmur; the first smell of jasmine blossoms falling from unbound hair as from a tree bough shaken by summer wind; the first taste of tears on warm cheeks; and the first time she dared to touch me. The more urgently we sense that we are coming to the bitter end of a love story, the more vividly we are aware of what we imagine to have been a sweet beginning.

From 40

60 "I am guilty: I stole the brain of the Jewish criminal and snatched the body of the Hindu snake charmer," I confessed in a letter to Menachem Goldman in which I enclosed both the money and the information he would need to defend Ishmael, Ibrahim, and Haramjada against the charges of theft and witchcraft brought against them by Dr. Adderson, who had traced the men to Ibrahim's ancestral village. It would also dispel any suspicions, should they ever arise, that Lingnath might still be alive. Kumar Bannerjee promised that he would not deliver the confession until I had left Calcutta and was out of the reach of the law. Without a snake-bodied man and a feral child, my ten-in-one was two wonders short, but everyone had an idea as to what to do about that. The ever-inebriated Ballatadas would find a monkey to replace Ishmael so that we could display a python with the head of a langur, and a wolf to replace Haramjada so that instead of a feral boy raised by wolves in the jungle, I could exhibit a tame wolf raised by boys in the city. Professor Wonderful suggested invisible replacements to create the Invisible Family: "Father Invisible, Mother Invisible, and the Baby Invisible! Curious question: Who is a least invisible? Humorous answer: Baby Invisible because he is just a little invisible! Do you get a joke? It is the great one! Perfect for a patter." Shula brought a tribal girl named Kamadhenuka whose mother, being unable to find a husband for her, had taken financial advantage of her anatomical peculiarity (she had six breasts, eight if you counted the nipple in each armpit) by selling her to a brothel. That she was famous in Sonagacchi and was one of the most popular girls at the Ananga Ranga Club led Shula to suppose that she would appeal to British audiences: *"Cet oiseau vraiment rare va faire des ravages en Angleterre. Les Anglais, qui sont si refoulés, ont toujours un faible pour les choses bizarres qui se passent au baisodrome."* That Shula had already promised the girl fame, fortune, and the amorous adulation of gentlemen abroad made it impossible to turn her away. Karnaghee arrived at the Bannerjee home weeping. Startled and touched by the sight of tears on the cheeks of man esteemed for his detachment and venerated for having transcended such mundane dualities as joy and sorrow, I tried to console him with avowals that my departure would not terminate our friendship, that I would return to India someday. "Why would I cry over you?" he asked. "My tears are formally shed in respect for my royal patron and his queens. The Maharaja of Diwanasthan is dead. Long live the king! And British officials have besmirched our tradition. At the funeral proceedings, whilst I myself was piously reciting holy Sanskrit shlokas on the subject of the illusory nature of death, the queens of Diwanasthan were arrested for attempting to offer their bodies as oblations upon the funeral pyre of their lord, to perform the great sacrifice that is love, and thereby to bestow one billion and one of years of bliss on the Maharaja. Thus I am sad. But as Bhagavad-Gita says, 'Sarvameghe rupyantarasthah: every cloud has a silver lining.' Just as in life, so too here today there is good news with the bad." Smiling as he dried the tears that had rained from the silver-lined clouds in his ethereal brain, he gave me the "good news": "I am going with you to England. My sapience, holiness, purity, and the like will invest your show with dignity. I shall be all the rage in England as the British have a soft spot for wisdom. Yogi Shamboo Baba and I will make an excellent team, he providing exposure to the practical side of Indian spirituality with breathtaking demonstrations of yogic postures, pulse stopping, reptile regurgitation, levitation, and penile feats, whilst I provide the theoretical side with recitations of Sanskrit homilies and irrefutable philosophical discourses on the illusory nature of reality. My disciple, Swami Madananda, will manage the ashram in my absence in case spiritual needs arise in Diwanasthan. As I understand that three reserved berths, given the arrest of the Moslem lowlies, are empty, I shall be amply accommodated." Aware that protest would not be heard, that any effort to prevent his coming would be considered illusory, and thus resigned to having the guru's company, I figured that I might be able to turn what he considered the splendor of the manifestation of wisdom in his presence into a passable act if he'd let me teach him a few of the techniques of mentalism that I had learned from my mother: how to handle billets and envelopes, do a switch and a pass, read through a blindfold, and use a swami gimmick. I wished that those tricks might have enabled me to read the mind of Nagini. Since the afternoon she had spent with her husband, her melancholy had returned. She refused to talk about it. Like the rest of my Indian Incredibilities, she had been instructed to be on board the *Aphrodite* by noon. Professor Wonderful, more exuberant than ever, arrived well ahead of time with Shula, the beautiful Gopal, and a shyly smiling, eyes-averted Kamadhenuka, whose shalwar kameez concealed the celebrated octomammae. Ballatadas and Shakuntala, both drunk, arrived with Maarnath, who informed me that Nagini would be along soon: "There is a small delay for big family business." That Guru Karnaghee and Yogi Shamboo Baba had more luggage than anyone else belied their claim of having renounced all worldly possessions. The Bannerjee men had come to wave good-bye. The women, Kumar told me, were at home weeping and wailing over our departure. As a good-bye present, Albert brought me his latest masterpiece, a table lamp, the base of which was adorned with two entwined cobras. When the electric current was turned on, not only did the lightbulb shine but the snakes undulated in a rhythm that was meant to be copulatory. "The English are wild about unusual table lamps," he said with the authority that came with having attended taxidermy college in London. "These lamps, once I set up my factory, will be all the rage in Britain. I have chosen you, my friend, to introduce this item to the public there, and eventually, to distribute them to retailers on behalf of Bannerjee Brothers International. To pave your way, I have sent an exact duplicate to Buckingham Palace for King George and Queen Mary. Between the royal family and yourself, I am confident that a market will be established." Albert confessed to a sadness over the death of his patron, the Maharaja of Diwanasthan: "I had hoped to be able to stuff, preserve, and mount him atop his magnificent Bill. I believe that he would have appreciated such a memorial tribute. But the authorities prevented it, insisting upon a cremation. Censorship is as rife in taxidermy as it is in cinema!" Recognizing me, and happy to welcome me back onto the *Aphrodite,* Captain Boeotion asked if I had developed my own philosophy yet. Although eager to lift anchor, he was philosophical about it when I ignored his question and made my plea that we wait for Nagini. Sympathetic to my anxiety, he reflected, "Better to wait a little than to be sorry a lot, as I always say, and false hopes are better than no hopes at all. That's my philosophy." As my Incredibilities and Oddities explored the ship, bickering over berth rights, my eyes, scanning the dockyard jungle of cranes, crabs, and dredgers, strained in desperate search of Nagini amidst the labored throng of wharf-wallahs. That the Bannerjees had been waving good-bye for over half an hour inspired Karnaghee, who appeared beside me at the railing: "This is exactly like life itself! You see the posted notice there: 'Departure 1300.' And yet the clock indicates a quarter to two and the boat is still here. The ignorant are confused and confusion leads to anxiety. At the first level of wisdom, a man thinks that either the notice, the clock, or the boat is illusory. But at the highest level of wisdom, a man understands that all three are illusory, that there is in reality no time, no boat, and no place to go." Overhearing him, Captain Boeotion was delighted: "That's quite a philosophy you've got there!" Karnaghee was beginning to explain Indian philosophy to the captain when I suddenly spotted Lingnath's orange turban, gray beard, and black lungi in the distance. He was running (something snake charmers rarely do) toward the boat. "Where is she?" I yelled to him even before he had made his way to the ladder that provided a way up to the deck, where standing before me, panting and struggling to catch his breath, he finally spoke: "Nagini big problem. Husband obligation. Not coming. My India, marriage is marriage. Also I am estaying with wife and esnakes. Nagini esaying namaskars for Mastar Isaac and prem which is love and big esadness." In a Bengali that was probably no better than his English, I told him that I wouldn't leave without her, that I was going with him to get her, to take her with me or to stay in India with her. I told him that I wanted to be with her forever. He shook his head woefully: "No, no, Nagini Assam going with husband man. Must. Mastar Isaac England going. Memory is forever estaying. Every other going." Yelling "No!" as he climbed down the ladder, I continued in English because it mattered less that he understood what I was saying than that I say it: "Tell her that I will wait for her, that I will send money to bring her. Tell her that I will love her forever." Karnaghee tried to quiet me: "You are making a fool of yourself. Love is the greatest illusion of all, greater than life itself." Hearing my shouting, Shula appeared. "Calme-toi et oublie le cafard. L'amour est un mélo, triste mais amusant. Les larmes des amants plaqués séchent vite au soleil inévitable d'une nouvelle allumeuse." Professor Wonderful also tried to cheer me up: "The English women are having the soft spot for the showbiz-wallahs, especially from the America." Maarnath, speaking as a snake charmer, consoled: "Our women are no good, except for us." The Bannerjees were still waving good-bye as the engines of the Aphrodite awakened with a groan. Joining them, Lingnath, on the proscenial stage where he had opened the show by making serpents dance for me upon my arrival in India, once again took up his gourd flute. The melody evoked a vision of the cobras tattooed on Nagini's wrists and hands dancing to the tune. The snake charmer's traditional anthem, the hypnotic drone of ancient India, gradually gave way to another music, modern, jazzy, and familiar, as the Aphrodite, with the bold blow of her whistle, leaned away from the dock in a rolling turn out into the harbor; in the thrill of setting out to sea, Captain Boeotion broke into exuberant song: "Tooot, toot, Toootsee, andeeoooh! Tooot, toot, Toootsee, meen klehs! Fee-lee-seh-meh Tootsie keh-toh-the, ksana-kahn-do-os-toh-the! Tooot, toot, Toootsee, andeeoooh!"

| 61 | As he stalked the rolling white cue ball that haphazardly bumped the brightly striped and solids in harmony with the pitch of the sea, Captain Plato Boeotion again asked if I had developed my own philosophy. I confessed that I was still using that of Heracli-|

tus. Sinking the 4-ball in a corner as the *Aphrodite* heeled the 6 and the 10 into a side pocket, he began: "Well, if Heraclitus is right, if all is change, his philosophy isn't right if it doesn't change. Right? In other words, Heraclitus was right when we talked about him the first time, but now here we are on the *Aphrodite* again talking about the same philosophy. Nothing has changed. Heraclitus's philosophy is correct when you look at the world close up and momentarily. But from a distance and in the long run, the truth is different: nothing changes and change is illusory; the universe is in constant stasis and nothing ever really passes away. That's my philosophy. It's all at Omou Pan. The Ineffable, the Invisible, the Inconceivable," he remarked as my 3 rolled into a corner pouch. "Absolute Being," he continued as he shot the 2 in behind the 8 and then, with the cooperation of the Indian Ocean, cleared the table before I had a turn. "Or, to make a long story short, eternity. I win," the seafaring philosopher said and laughed. "Let's drink!" Eager to expound, Captain Boeotion repeated the cryptic phrase "Omou Pan" as he poured us each a whiskey. "It's Greek for all-at-once. It's where all is change and nothing changes. It's where Heraclitus is right for being wrong and wrong for being right." He explained that Omou Pan was a phallic rock rising up out of the very center of the clear water of a lagoon contained by a perfectly circular and entirely unpopulated coral reef known as Snake Atoll, the westernmost bit of land in the Gilbert and Ellice Islands Crown Colony. "The tip and center of the rock marks the exact spot, to the degree, minute, and second, where the Equator and the International Date Line cross." Putting philosophy into action, he explained, he would go there alone after Bombay, where the *Aphrodite* was due to be scrapped and her captain was scheduled to be retired. "It is a point in space in which there is no time and therefore a point in time in which there is no space, both a time in space and a space in time in which there is no point. Are you following me?" he asked, noting that "philosophy can be difficult to understand, especially if you're not Greek." His scheme was to sail to Snake Atoll, swim out to the rock, and at either midnight, high noon, dusk, or dawn ("I'll try all four"), stand upon it, "straddling the Equator, simultaneously in the Northern and Southern hemispheres, in winter and summer (not to mention fall and spring) at once, and, at the same time, spanning the Date Line, existing yesterday and tomorrow at once, experiencing the eternal moment in which all the moments that constitute time are present in each instant and all space is convergent in the pinpoint upon which I stand, encompassing the globe, the point that is the center of the center of the infinite circumference of the universe." Listening to the disquisition, Shree Karnaghee shook his head ambiguously. When Captain Boeotion had discovered that the Indian philosopher had been booked in the Oriental Hold, he immediately promoted the guru to the status of "honorary Caucasian" and moved him up to White Class so that the two metaphysicians could regularly discuss the presence of both the eternal in the temporal and the infinite in the finite. Karnaghee, who was more than eager to expound upon "the Ineffable, the Invisible, and the Inconceivable," begged to differ with the Greek philosopher over Omou Pan, arguing that the "point in space in which there is no time" was actually in India, "if not everywhere else, given its illusory nature." As Boeotion and Karnaghee each considered himself the champion of a hallowed philosophical tradition, the Western and Eastern, respectively, there was a lot at stake in their debate. Truth was being determined. Hearing the news, so casually mentioned in passing, that this was the *Aphrodite*'s last voyage moved me: as she rocked me to sleep each night, I felt that I felt her nautical melancholy, sensed that in her taut nerves of rope, cable, and guy there was a sense that the end was at hand. The sad bow of her prow, anxious flapping of her canvas, pained creaking of her keel and timbers, and lugubrious groan of her engines seemed woeful expressions of resignation as the *Aphrodite* carried us toward Bombay. I shared a cabin with Shula not out of choice but from the necessity dictated by the segregation of the ship's quarters into White and Oriental. Informed of these arrangements, Professor Wonderful politely and plaintively begged me "to please, sir, not sleep with a woman I am loving with the whole heart." No less tormented than the magician by separation from Shula was Ballatadas by separation from Shakuntala, who, as an albino, had been booked in White Class and lodged in our cabin. That Shula and I had a chaperone, even if it was a bear, comforted Wonderful. Though I did not ever sleep with Shulamite Levi, I did several times awaken to discover company in my berth. A snoring Shakuntala, perhaps dreaming she was in a Himalayan cave during the mating season, was holding me snugly in her arms. It was hard not to feel a bit of fondness for the animal in bed with me as I recalled Pythia's words: "Indian bears do often loll about, rubbing their muzzles up against each other, drooling and making bubbling sounds in a manner that might be considered a sort of ursine osculation." Although I liked Shakuntala, I was afraid of falling victim to the blow that she might, if piqued or offended, mete out with a powerful round-arm swing of her sharp-clawed forepaw. And so not only did I not throw her out of bed, I also pretended not to be annoyed when she urinated and defecated on the floor of our cabin. An intrepid Shula, however, scolding and cursing (*"Merde alors! J'ai jamais vu une emmerdeuse comme cette ourse! Je l'emmerde!"*), had the nerve to slap Shakuntala, who, though growling menacingly, never struck back. Shula really gave Shakuntala a thrashing when, hearing terrible screams of laughter, she rushed to our cabin only to catch the inebriated bear mauling the stuffed hyena. But despite the destruction of the hyena and the mess on the floor, Shula no less than I felt an affection for the creature, and she was as upset as I when Shakuntala was kidnapped in Port Said. Waiting there to reboard the *Laocoon,* the ship on which passage from Bombay to Greenwich had been arranged for us in advance by Captain Boeotion, I was sitting with Shula and Professor Wonderful, drinking absinthe at an outdoor café in the European settlement. Somali, Abyssinian, and Arab street vendors hawked ostrich eggs, elephant tusks, rhinoceros horns, hippopotamus scrota, and sawfish saws. As Shula gave a French lesson to Professor Wonderful, I started a letter to my mother, to be mailed from Suez, in which I could not resist the temptation to lie: "I have just visited the place of my birth, the Dead Sea, the lowest place on earth." That's when we were startled by the loud wailing of Ballatadas: "My Shakuntala is gone! Taken from me! Perhaps murdered! Perhaps raped! Oh, Lord Ram, help us as the bears helped you!" Because he had left her tied to a pole outside an arak shop into which he had gone to buy liquor, he blamed himself for the abduction. The bear handler refused to reboard the *Laocoon* and leave Port Said. "I am nothing without her," he cried. Karnaghee advised that we all heed the words of the Ramayana, a text that thousands of years ago had cautioned people against becoming overly attached to bears. We waved good-bye to a weeping Ballatadas. Built in 1908 for the Hillcastle Oriental Steam Navigation Company, the *Laocoon* was a fifteen-thousand-ton vessel with one funnel, two masts, a triple screw, and accommodations for a hundred "high-class" passengers and five hundred "low-class" travelers. Booking my Incredibilities and Oddities in "low-class" berths, I treated myself to an expensively pleasant cabin with easy access to an open gallery that was furnished with comfortable leather divans and long Chinese cane chairs from which one could stare out to sea. Just as I lost my Incredible Ursine Funambulist in Port Said, I would also lose my Incredible Androgynous Juggler during our two-day stay in Trieste. A former Russian prince, mistaking him for a girl, as I had once done, asked for his hand in marriage. A Fabergé ring for the hand in question was bait to trap the heart of the beautiful Gopal. Although I was initially concerned about what would happen when, in an attempt to consummate the marriage, the prince realized that his bride was a boy, Shula assured me that that very discovery had been made many times at the Ananga Ranga Club and that there had never been any complaints. Much to my surprise and delight, Professor Vladimir Yesnovitch boarded the *Laocoon* at Port Said. After inspecting the scar on my hand again, he listened with a curious smile to my account of my work with Dr. McCloud. We were drinking a bottle of champagne that the herpetologist had ordered to celebrate our reunion when the irate captain of the *Laocoon* arrived in the bar to berate me: he held me responsible for the fact that Maarnath's snakes had escaped from their baskets and that, in terror, all lower-class passengers were pleading to be let off the ship as soon as possible and demanding to be refunded the cost of their passage. Professor Yesnovitch calmly and genially convinced the captain that the snakes were benign, that they had been devenomed and defanged, and that in any case, given their fear of human beings, the serpents would certainly not come out from wherever they were hiding to pester any of the passengers. The captain, Yesnovitch further suggested, could tell the voyagers that the majority of reptiles in question were sea snakes and so would have slithered overboard into their natural habitat. For the sake of a good night's sleep, the travelers would, I added, be eager to believe it. The captain was relieved that, as unlikely as it seemed, they did. Maarnath suggested to me that, since I had lost my bear act and he had lost his snakes, he could get a bear costume in England and play Shakuntala's part in my review. "Or, if such an outfit is not available in my size," he reflected, "we could simply explain that the Invisible Family owns an invisible bear and lots of invisible snakes. Invisibility will make the deadly snakes all the more frightening." Without informing me that Trieste was his destination, Professor Yesnovitch did not reboard the *Laocoon*. As we were tugged by tugs up the Thames, I ran into Karnaghee in the ship's baggage and cargo claim cabin. "Just about now," he observed, "Captain Boeotion is probably approaching the Pacific island where he imagines that he will experience all space and all time, Absolute Being, his Omou Pan, what we Indian sages more correctly call Brahman. Who knows, given the illusory nature of our existence, what we will experience at our destination!"

62 "Buffalo Bill was a shmuck." Jake Grossman laughed when I saw him in his room at the Merry Medusa Hotel in Greenwich, the year that he exhibited twenty-one American Indians as "The Last of the Wild Redskins" in Moscow, Berlin, Rome, Paris, and London. After greeting me with a happy kiss on the forehead and then offering solemn condolences over the death of my father, he held my hands in his and smiled as I told him how delighted I had been to see his name on the poster for the revue. "I went straight to the box office where I was told you'd be here." After pouring us each a vodka, he confessed that he'd rather be staying at the Dorchester, "but they don't take in wild Indians there. This hekdish gave me the top two floors exclusively for the redskins." Like all showmen, Jake was sentimentally compelled to reminisce about the past and to report on the present successes and failures of people in the business. He spoke lovingly of my parents. "But I don't know why your father hated Bachnele Poopik so much. The midget's here in London doing variety. He and that poor schlimazel of a giant, Ola, formed a song-and-dance comedy team, the Bigger Brothers. That little Litvak adored your mother. But who didn't! I loved to watch her do our bentshen-licht on Shabbis. Hayim tells me that he's going to marry her. You'll be my nephew! And Shmuel's too. He's out of jail, you know, and here in London. Come tomorrow morning and see him. And in the afternoon, come with us to the show. We've got an exhibit of Indian costumes, musical instruments, and weapons where folks can buy baskets, blankets, peace pipes, Indian tobacco and pemmican, as well as pitch cards and pamphlets, and they can get their pictures taken with authentic savages from the Wild West. We dress the shmoes up like cavalrymen, cowboys, pioneers, gamblers, outlaws, whatever, and I've got Nathan Nister, Siegel's old pal, taking the photographs. Very profitable. We've even got a stuffed horse, all painted up and decorated with feathers like a real Indian pony, for the more daring rubes to pose on. Then there's the show itself, an irresistible mishmash of Indian love songs, war dances, children's games, and primitive religious rituals. After the show, everybody gets to shake hands with a real Indian, and ask him questions about his heathen ways. That's when we sell the souvenirs. In France they'd pay to touch the redskins and hold the papoose we've brought along. One of my Indians, that little pisher's pa, who calls himself Chief Crazy Dog, boasts of being the brave who killed Custer at the Little Bighorn. He describes how the American general fell to his knees, sobbing and begging for mercy, trying to save his own neck by offering Crazy Dog rifles, bourbon, white women, and silver dollars. Then he shows them a blond shaytl that he swears to Wakantanka is Custer's scalp. I had brought along an extra added attraction, a little number called 'My Father, Pancho Villa: The True Story of the Mexican Robin Hood.' In Moscow, billed as the 'Last Son of the Late Father of the Next Revolution,' he was a bigger hit than the Indians. Just a week or so before I left on this tour, Pancho Villa got killed and the press made a big deal out of it, turning that ganef into a hero. Heroism is big business. That's why it was hard to resist when that south-of-the-border schlemiel, your old pal Valentine Rudolfo, shows up with the idea for the Villa tab. He's not much of an actor, but he's a Mexican, and he's got the right dedication because he thinks that men in show business can get all the yentsing they want. Supported by the Bolsheviks, he stayed on in Russia touring his one-man show and trying to shtoop Commie dames. Because that routine was such a success, one of my Indians, a chutzpenik named Laughing Eagle, now suddenly claims that he's the illegitimate son of Geronimo and wants me to give him a speaking role, to promote him from tom-tom playing and calumet smoking to doing for Geronimo what Rudolfo did for Pancho Villa. It's a stupid idea, but lots of stupid ideas turn out to be good ideas in the entertainment business. But of course he wants to be paid a big salary and that's not in the cards. The only reason I'm making any money on this tour, given the expense of traipsing all over Europe with these shtunks, is that I got them from the Bureau of Indian Affairs by putting up a bond of a hundred bucks per brave, fifty a piece for the four squaws, and twenty-five for the papoose. And I get the money back when I return them to the reservation. I had to promise, however, that I wouldn't let them act in any staged battles because the secretary of the interior believes that that would turn them wild again and encourage them to scalp white men and rape white women. 'Once a savage always a savage,' he told me. 'There's no taming them.' Let's have a vodka." I asked if he had any news of Angel. "The Rabinowitz kid?" he smiled happily: "Oh, yeah, she's doing great. I saw her last month, during the Paris leg of my *Wild Redskins Revue*. She was working in a show at the Folies-Bergère called *L'Amour en Folie*, a spectacle with thirty of the prettiest tabs I've ever seen. She's dancing in a few of them and starring in one of them, '*La Herse Infernale*,' in which she's costumed as an angel with big feather wings, bare bristen, and a skimpy bit of lacy stuff meant to be a cloud covering her knish and that cute little tooches of hers. She dances across a tightrope over a pit of fire, the flames of which seem to be reaching up to consume her. It's an artsy-fartsy number and the French are meshugeh over art. She did just fine. It's not easy getting hired by the Folies-Bergère. But she was lucky. Just when she arrived in Paris, America was all the rage because of the war, and they were auditioning dames for a show called *Les Demoiselles du Far West*. She got the part of a cowgirl named Kitty Hawk." I wanted to find out if she was with a man, if she was in love. Jake, discreetly claiming that he was in the dark about her personal life, suggested that I ask Bachnele: "He's always been kind of a father to her. He goes over to Paris every once in a while to see her. Come for Shabbis with me tonight in Whitechapel. Bachnele might be there." I claimed that I had to get back to my friends. In explaining who they were, I told him about India and about my idea for the Professor Solomon Serpentarius show, not that I had a ten-in-one after the loss of my bear, snakes, snake-bodied man, juggler, and devadasi. "So let me get this straight," Jake said. "You got two hookers, one of whom has a few extra tsitskes, a snake charmer with no snakes, an amateur magician, some frimer who lifts rocks with his schlong, and a Hindu philosoputz who can't really do anything at all." I had to admit it: that's exactly what I had. Pouring us each another vodka, he said he'd think about my situation and try to come up with something: "There's nothing I wouldn't do for the son of Abraham and Sarah Schlossberg." I had a gift for Jake, the Indian souvenir given to me by Albert Bannerjee. He opened it, plugged it in, and turned it on, and beneath its bright bulb the stuffed mechanical cobras began their undulous copulation. "Just what I needed," Jake sighed. "Just what I always wanted. Yeah, come back tomorrow. I'll try to figure out something for you. But I don't think I can do much for your Indians." Walking from the tram station through a gray English drizzle, I missed the more exuberant rains of India. And always associated in my heart with those downpours was the snake charmer's daughter. When I finally arrived at the rooming house where I had rented four rooms (one for myself, one for Shula and Wonderful, one for Kamadhenuka and Maarnath, and another for my yogi and guru), I could smell the food. Shula, who did not know anything about cooking, had found a Jewish market and, to celebrate the Sabbath, had bought two challot, three bottles of kosher wine, and four pots of daffina, the Sephardic equivalent of the cholent of my childhood, a comforting stew of rice, potatoes, eggs, and beef. My Oddities and Incredibilities were crowded into the small square room that the Jewess shared with the Hindu magician. After reciting blessings with her hands over her eyes, Shulamite Levi gestured to spread the hallowed incandescence around us. *"Baruch ata Adonai,"* she began as Professor Wonderful gazed lovingly at her smiling face and waving hands. In Bengali for the sake of this motley family, she explained that we were celebrating the day that the Creator had formed us in His own likeness and commanded us to love each other and accept dominion over the earth. Recalling the words of my father, I uttered them by heart: *"Va-yehi erev, va-yehi voker, Yom ha-shishi."* Karnaghee proclaimed that he would consent to drink the wine and eat the meat normally forbidden to him as a Hindu holy man as a "dramatic expression of my humble acknowledgment of your barbaric religious rites." Professor Wonderful excitedly announced that he had an idea: since there were only six attractions left in our ten-in-one, he proposed that Mr. Invisible and Mrs. Invisible should, in addition to their newly acquired invisible bear and invisible snakes, have two children instead of just one, a boy and girl, "invisible twins and the invisible tiger to boot. Everybody worldwide is associating the India with a tiger. It could be the smash." He then made a second announcement: he wished to convert to Judaism because of the "deliciosity of your Yehudi food and the wine as atasted to by this fine fare but also far more because of a greatest love of the Miss Shula. Yes I will be the wonderful Jew!" After dinner, lying in bed, cold and alone in the darkness of that holy night, hearing through flimsy walls the muffled murmurs and wistful whimpers of love, I remembered other darknesses and entered them in search of Nagini, Pythia, and Angel. I would have settled for a few hours with Carmen Zambra or the nameless young girl whom Jesus Estafar, before he was Valentine Rudolfo or the son of Pancho Villa, had brought to my room in Santa Monica. I wished that I might suddenly discover that Mrs. Invisible was illicitly there in bed with me, and that she, although married and invisible, was impassioned and most beautiful. Unable to find her, or any of the others, I then ached for strangers, for the bodies of loving women, real but unseen because they were hidden in the shadows of squares that lay ahead, squares of the game in which, sooner or later, luck or chance or fate might or might not place me.

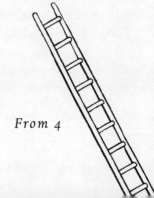

From 4

63

"How would you like to be the son of Buffalo Bill?" Jake Grossman, pouring us each a vodka, asked with his customarily generous grin. "Big Chief Laughing Putz's constant pestering that I feature him as Geronimo's son gave me the idea. I'll let him do the shtick if he performs it with you. The illegitimate sons of Geronimo and Buffalo Bill together, telling the true stories of their famous fathers' exploits and real adventures in the American Wild West! He'll do some tomahawk and knife throwing and you'll do some sharpshooting. The idea's based on a true story. After a pow-wow with Geronimo in Wyoming in 1897, Buffalo Bill actually wrote to President McKinley, to inform him that he, leading his Rough Riders, together with Geronimo, followed by his Apache renegades, were ready to make a surprise attack on the Spanish occupational forces in Cuba. You'll explain to the audience that Geronimo, that red-blooded American redskin, was damn eager to scalp those Spaniards for the United States: 'But we had a little problem because pride is a virtue amongst the Indians. Geronimo wanted to lead the attack on Cuba himself with me and the Rough Riders riding behind him and his native warriors.' Then Geronimo cuts in: 'Geronimo great leader, win many big battles and take many scalps. I do Ghost Dance and Great Spirit speaks: "O Goyahkla! Kill Spaniards! Capture Cuba for United States of America! Geronimo must lead attack on Cuba and then on Philippines."' Then you say that, no, you're going to be the leader. The two of you argue until you make the suggestion: 'Let's settle this the Wild West way.' The music starts (tom-toms and a military march), the stage is set, and you explain that the Apache Wildcat, with his knives, tomahawks, and bow, and you, the Great Plainsman, with your Colt Peacemakers and Winchester fifteen-shot repeater rifle, had a shooting contest to determine who would lead the capture of Cuba. We'll put on a display of shooting and throwing that will thrill the Brits right out of their seats. Neither of you misses a single target, moving or still, and it looks like a tie. The stage, strewn with broken glass and shards of clay, is hazed in gun smoke. As Geronimo stretches his bow, taking aim to fire an arrow at a stuffed buffalo that's speeding on a track across the back of the stage, a boy in a Western Union uniform enters: 'Telegram! Telegram for Buffalo Bill and Geronimo!' Because the Indian is illiterate, you sign for it, take it, and read out loud: 'Dear Bill and Geri. Stop. Thanks for offer. Stop. No. Stop. Am trying to prevent war in Cuba. Stop. Your friend and fan. Stop. William "Bill" McKinley, President of the United States. Stop.' Then Geronimo says with great purpose and gravity: 'President is Great Chief. He know peace better than war!' The two of you then turn solemnly to the audience, hold hands, and just before you take your bow, you say with all the majesty you can muster, 'Yes, my brave friend, if only all men knew that! Peace *is* greater than war!' Curtain. It's got true history, great men pitted against each other in competition, patriotism, colorful costumes, deadly weapons, and a profound message with a potential to put an end to man's inhumanity to man. What more could anyone ask for?" I said I liked it. "It gives me naches," he smiled, "to be able to do a favor for the son of Abraham and Sarah Schlossberg. When your parents and I were working the Wild West show, Buffalo Bill actually staged an attack on Cuba by his Rough Riders and a band of Indians, portraying himself winning the Spanish-American War single-handedly. He had lost all sense of the distinction between real events in history and imagined events in his arena." Jake sent me to Kopitsky and Sons, Ltd., a posh four-story haberdashery on Wimpole Street, owned and managed by Getsle Kopitsky, a friend of the Grossmans' and Schlossbergs' from the dark days of the Pale of Settlement. After reminiscing about being in heder with my father ("Abraham knew Hebrew like I know tailoring!"), Getsle personally supervised the costuming of Buffalo Bill, dressing me in a fringed deerskin coat, beaded chamois gloves, blue worsted military breeches, a lavender broadcloth dress shirt, and a Carlsbad-style Stetson hat with an eagle feather in the snakeskin band. I ordered a pair of black leather boots from Sears & Roebuck in America and I've kept the box in which they arrived, using it to store my tin of Wyoming Willie's Wondrous Hair Pomade, Kaleeya's last sloughed skin, the pitch book (*Les Amours Fantastique de la Belle Mademoiselle Petite India*) with Angel's picture in it that I had bought at the Paradisio, the red packet of Nagini's pubic hair, and now, these pages, these squares of the game. Getsle's brother, David, the premier shaytel maker in London, provided a wig of long fair curls as well as the Indian scout's signature mustache and goatee. "*Gloib mir!*" Jake exclaimed, "you look just like the shmuck himself! You could actually be his son! Laughing Eagle, you know, has already started telling everyone that he really is Geronimo's son, not even illegitimate. He attacked his brother Laughing Wolf, the basket weaver, with a knife for telling people that their father's name was Laughing Horse and that they were not Apaches, but Navahos. It's funny," Jake frowned. "I've never seen either Laughing Eagle or Laughing Wolf laugh." Sharing a dressing room with the somber Laughing Eagle, watching him apply his warpaint with all the purpose of a real warrior preparing for real battle, I remembered the affection with which my father reminisced about the man whose son the Indian was playing. But Laughing Eagle always ignored me, never speaking to me offstage unless I asked him a direct question, in which case he'd answer as laconically as possible. It so troubled me that I finally confronted him, asking point-blank why he disliked me. He adjusted his war bonnet. "You're a white man and I'm an Indian. Don't take it personally." Despite the animosity, I couldn't help feeling a little sad when, after a month of performing with him, I had to say good-bye. The European tour of "The Last of the Wild Redskins" was over, and Jake, in order to get his deposits back from the Bureau of Indian Affairs, had to take Laughing Eagle and his tribe back to the reservation. And I felt more than a little sad to say good-bye to Jake. I never saw him again. The ridiculous tableau that he had composed for me had proved so popular that, with the showman's encouragement and suggestions, I decided to try to develop and tour it, substituting Maarnath for Laughing Eagle, figuring that if Buffalo Bill could successfully cast American Indians as Indian Indians in his shows, I could do the opposite in mine. Maarnath didn't really understand the point of the performance or why I didn't want Kamadhenuka, with whom he had fallen in love, to display her amazing supernumerary breasts to the audience. His instincts as an entertainer, I realized, were not entirely wrong. Since the tab would probably be improved by a female character, I created Matanka "Wild Mattie" Hickok, the beautiful half-breed daughter of a Texas lawman and an Apache squaw, with whom both Buffalo Bill and Geronimo were in love. It was over her, and not over Cuba, that they would be pitted against each other. A woman would give new power and meaning to the competition between the valiant heroes of the West. I cast Shulamite Levi in the silent part of Wild Mattie. Her fiancé and my magician, Professor Wonderful, designed illusions: after Geronimo threw a tomahawk at me, which I caught in my bare hand, I fired my Peacemaker six-gun and he seemed to catch the bullet presumed to come from its barrel in his teeth. It was only under the unrelenting pressure from everyone in my little troupe that I finally agreed to the illusion that Professor Wonderful was most eager to stage: because the match was tied, both of us hitting all the targets, Buffalo Bill and Geronimo figured out a way that both of them could have her. They decided to put Matanka Hickok in a box and saw her in half. But then there was the argument as to which one of us got which half of her, with all the hackneyed quick-fire one-liners about the pros and cons of the lower and upper halves of a woman. To settle the dispute, each of the halves of the box were covered with an American flag and mixed up behind our backs. Demonstrating the civility that comes with being civilized, I let Geronimo chose his half of the boxed half-a-woman first. Through Professor Wonderful's conjurational ingenuity and prestidigitatory prowess, once the boxes were selected, undraped, and opened, out of the one I had a chosen an entire Shula, having quick-changed into the outfit of pure white pioneer woman, emerged and took my hand in hers. At the same time, Kamadhenuka, costumed in fringed buckskins as a whole Apache squaw, hopped out of her half of the gaffed box and took

Geronimo's hand. As Shula and I do-si-do'd offstage in one direction, the Indian couple war-danced off in the other. "The True Story of Buffalo Bill and Geronimo in Love as Portrayed by their Real-Life Sons" ran in variety theaters throughout England for over a year, thanks to Bachnele Poopik, who, after the success of the Bigger Brothers at the Royal Command Variety Performance at the London Hippodrome on December 21, 1922, had substantial clout with British booking agents. I was happy to be earning a living and to have found regular work for Shula, Wonderful, Kamadhenuka, and Maarnath, who, despite his love for Kamadhenuka, was dutifully sending money to his wife and children in Mayapur. I had been initially concerned about my responsibility to the two Hindu holy men whom I had imported to England, but much to my relief, Guru Karnaghee and Yogi Shamboo Baba were delighted to be released from any obligation to my nonexistent ten-in-one. Having found their way to the Uxbridge Theosophical Society in search of a vegetarian meal, they were cordially received as spiritual ambassadors from the Mystic East and were subsequently offered accommodations so that the guru could deliver lectures on nonviolence, pantheism, and the illusory nature of phenomenal existence, while the sadhu demonstrated the power of yoga by stopping his pulse and lifting a variety of heavy objects with his penis. During that first year in England, I fell in love more passionately and obsessively, more pleasurably and tormentingly, than I had imagined possible. Her name was Billie Custis, yes, *the* Billie Custis, the then world-famous British aviatrix who held the international altitude record for female fliers until it was broken by Amelia Earhart.

64 "Let me thrill you," the aviatrix said. "Let me take your breath away, transport you beyond supposed limits to where fear feels like delight, eternity seems real, and, in the exquisite intensity of the moment, you don't care about anything in the world below."

It began backstage, the night after my first performance as Buffalo Bill's illegitimate son in London. Introducing her as "the Sarah Bernhardt of aviation," Jake Grossman announced with a sly wink that the celebrity had come just to meet me. I could hardly turn down the stunning woman's invitation to join her for a late-night bite to eat. While navigating her snazzy Stutz Runabout at perilously high speeds to Hounslow, careening around turns and barely missing everything in her way, she calmly explained why she had wanted to make my acquaintance. My heart was pounding wildly as, while hanging on for dear life, it became apparent that our encounter resulted from a case of mistaken identity. She had wanted to meet the son of another Buffalo Bill. In 1903, an inventor from Texas named Samuel Cody, no relation to William Frederick Cody, fled to England in order to avoid prosecution for fraud in the United States. In dire need of funds to subsidize experiments with man-lifting kites and aileroned gliders, Samuel Cody decided in 1904 to capitalize on his surname and nationality by costuming himself as the genuine Buffalo Bill Cody, complete with signature goatee and mustache. On a lecture tour of Great Britain, he thrilled audiences with firsthand accounts of buffalo hunts, battles with savage Indians, and love affairs with illustrious ladies whose names he could not, as a gentleman, disclose. He enjoyed sufficient success portraying the American plainsman to accrue the capital required to become, in May of 1908, the first man in Britain to successfully make a powered flight, a journey of one hundred eighty feet that lasted for sixteen thrilling seconds. By the end of that year, his wife, Isabel, became the first woman to fly in a plane over England's green and pleasant land. Billie Custis, then a twelve-year-old girl, watching the event from the saddle of her roan jumper, was instantly certain that it was her destiny to fly. She was able to forsake horses and foxhunting for airplanes and aviation in 1919, when the long-dreamed-of opportunity to purchase her first airplane, a Sopwith Cub, presented itself. The end of the war had put a glut of planes on the market; you could get a Jenny, Sopwith, or Blériot for about five hundred quid. Billy had hoped to fly her Cub to the O.K. Corral, the Cody farm in Lancashire, to meet the inspirational aviators in person, but before she had the occasion to do so, Samuel and Isabel crashed their Cody Canary into Preston Cathedral, an accident that caused the death of the fliers, the destruction of the cathedral's bell tower, and an outburst of protest against nonmilitary aviation from church groups and historical societies. "And so, because I never had the opportunity to meet them," Billie said as we sped through the gates of Hounslow airstrip, "I wanted to at least meet you." Although realizing that I might be ruining my chances for further association with the adventuress, her eyes as blue as the sky she loved and her skin as white as its clouds, I felt I ought to confess a truth that would, in any case, come out sooner or later. I revealed that I was merely playing the part of the illegitimate son of the true Buffalo Bill, who was not an aviator, and that I was not really the son, legitimate or otherwise, of either the genuine Buffalo Bill or the fake Buffalo Bill whom she was confusing with the real Buffalo Bill. Billie slammed on the brakes of the Stutz and, as we skidded sideways into a dramatic stop, turned to me in shock: "What?" I tried to compensate for not being who she wanted me to be. "But it is, in any case, a great pleasure for me to meet the renowned Billie Custis. For, you see, I'm no stranger to aviation and I have long been an admirer of yours. My real father, Abraham Schlossberg, was a stunt flier in America during the war, and I often flew with him." Being the legitimate son of my father turned out to be even better than being the illegitimate son of any Buffalo Bill. Having read his obituary in *Wings* magazine, Billie knew more about my father's aeronautic accomplishments than I did. "I flew for the first time the very week of his crash," she said, as if that had some significance. "He was one of my heroes. That must be why I was destined to meet you. Pilots crash only if they're fated to die just as people become lovers only if it's meant to be." Everything she learned about me affirmed a ridiculous conviction that fate had seated me in her American Stutz Runabout: she planned to fly the following year to Calcutta, where, she soon learned, I had been the previous year, and to make a stop en route at the Dead Sea, where, I told her, I had been born. "There are just too many coincidences," she said, "for it to be coincidental that we've met." It was midnight by the time we arrived at the hangar where she had taken me to show me her new plane. "The Sopwith was like my first pony, small, gentle, easy to handle, good to learn on, but hardly capable of leading the hunt or winning a race," she commented as she demonstrated her startling strength by pulling back the enormous door of the cavernous hangar. She aimed her torch at an all-metal German Junkers F-13, a low-winged, cantilevered monoplane. The wing construction, she explained, was meant to reduce the risk of fatal injury in a crash; being first to hit the ground, the wings would absorb much of the initial shock of impact with the earth. The plane had been customized: behind the leather pilot and copilot seats, the four original passenger seats had been replaced by a fixed bed with fringed silk pillows and a fox-fur comforter; the cabin was upholstered in burgundy velvet and fitted with rosewood cabinets with brass locks; and there were white lace curtains over the windows. There was a medallion, the image of a female saint, on the control panel, above the altimeter. "This is my home," she said with obvious satisfaction, "my true home. Only in this cabin do I truly experience pleasure." She opened a jar of grouse confit to make a sandwich on dark bread, served with a sweet onion relish and a wine that numbed my mouth. "Do you like it? It's Vin Mariani, a Bordeaux in which Peruvian coca leaves have been soaked for no less than a year. I have to fly to France to get it. Most of the ace French aviators drink it to stay alert and curb the appetite during long flights. It's an acquired taste, but, once you acquire it, you hardly want to drink anything else." Although, as we finished the shared sandwich, I intimated sex in the air, I was too intimidated by this remarkable woman to dare, despite desire, to attempt to instigate any intimacy. Thus, awkwardly, unsure of what to do or say, I asked if she knew when the first meal on an airplane had been served, precisely the sort of thing that she wrote about in her occasional aviation column in *Twentieth-Century Girl* magazine. "Obviously lots of French cuisine was consumed in balloons over Paris in the last century," she said. "But the first real meal served on a heavier-than-air, motor-powered airplane was prepared by Chef Dmitri Raskolnikov, recipient of La Bedaine d'Or, Russia's highest culinary honor, awarded to him for preparing the poisoned buns that were used in the final attempt to kill Rasputin. The revolutionary Sikorsky Grand, the first four-engine ship ever built, flown under the command of a former cavalry officer named Makharadze, included such luxuries as a washroom with a bidet and a bathtub filled with champagne for the occasion, Oriental divans, and a Persian carpet. On the first leg of the voyage, after leaving Moscow for Minsk on April 1, 1915, the passengers, belted to the railing on the plane's exterior observation balcony, shot geese, duck, and the occasional crane out of the sky beneath them. The carcasses were then collected by beaters in pursuant automobiles and delivered to Chef Raskolnikov in Minsk, where he prepared various dishes with the birds for consumption on the flight's continuation to Kiev. The experience proved so exhilarating to the aristocratic passengers that, tossing modesty, propriety, empty champagne bottles, and more than a few expensive articles of clothing to the wind, they indulged in an orgiastic party that, from the descriptive logbook of Captain Makharadze, set an as yet unbroken world record for high-altitude debauchery." Appreciating the direction in which the conversation was going, I asked if that was the first time people had enjoyed sexual relations in an airplane. "No," she answered with complete authority: "That began in 1913 with the invention of the automatic pilot. Aerial intercourse, however, was in those days necessarily rushed and not terribly satisfying until longer airtime was possible. But lovemaking in the sky had, in any case, taken place many years earlier. In June of 1784, Comte Boniface de la Mettrie, as he himself recorded in his *Journal Intime,* took off from Grenoble in a Montgolfière with a young milkmaid named Mademoiselle Lunarde who, quite understandably, was unable to resist the comte's invitation to become the first woman to fly in a hot-air balloon. Succumbing to the thrill of the heights, she also became the first girl to lose her virginity in the sky, at an altitude of eight thousand feet above the earth." In order to keep the conversation on sex, still nervously harboring hopes that some earthy intimacy with the beguiling aviatrix might be on the horizon, and stimulated by the vin-de-coca, I asked if she thought her idol, Isabel Cody, had ever made love to her husband, the fake Buffalo Bill, in their airplane, adding that "maybe they were doing it when they crashed into the cathedral." "Isabel Cody is not my idol," she responded. "An inspiration, yes, but Maggie Kempe is the pilot I most admire. Taking off solo in a Farman biplane from this very airstrip on July 22, 1911, she set a record by becoming the first woman ever to die in a crash. If we fly long and daringly enough, with enough abandon, we will crash. It's how we're supposed to die. At the same time, it must be remembered, the thrill of flying is not so much in flying as it is in not crashing, not crashing *this time.* The ecstasy is in the discovery of destiny. Your father would understand what I'm saying. That we'll never know how high he went, whether he broke the altitude record or not, doesn't matter. He saw the altimeter. He knew the truth." Hesitating, she looked at me more intently than she had all evening: "Are you, because of your father's death, afraid to fly?" When I told her the truth, that I really didn't know, she said that she wanted to take me up right then, in the middle of the night. "I need to know whether or not you're afraid." And then the aviatrix said it: "Let me thrill you."

65 A cough or two here and there in the darkness of the otherwise silent hall, *shhhhh*, and then the *tap-tap-tap* of an invisible bandleader's baton. Music! *Da-da-daa*. Curtain. *Da-da-dee*. Spotlight! *Da-da-dooooo* and, yes, oh yes, out they dance, dance, dee-dance, a *rap-a-tap-tap*, a *la-dee-dee-da*, a *hoop-dee-ho-dee-hoo*, and a *hi-dee-hi-dee-ho*, oh, ho-ho, oh, yes, yessiree, it's the one and only big-time Bigger Brothers, the cross-talking and back-chatting midget and giant in matching dinner jackets, top hats, and canes, high stepping, low shuffling, hopping, hoofing, tapping, turning, goofball and off-the-wall, all in unison to the rollicking tune of the catchy theme song: "Big and small! We got it all, 'cause we're the Brothers Biggerrrrrr!" Fun-lovers cheered with the silly thrill of beholding with their own eyes, on a Friday night in London's New Oxford Theatre, the zany duo from the United States of America who became celebrities by making King George laugh uproariously during the Royal Command Variety Performance of 1921 at the London Hippodrome. Even a demure Queen Mary snickered over the buffomantic antics of the signature routine in which the dapper dapperling and the colossal colossus argue as to which Bigger brother's bigger. What was funny enough for the king and queen a few years earlier was manifestly no less hilarious for their subjects the night that I was there. The crowd guffawed exuberantly when the slow-witted, clodhopping giant was slyly tricked into admitting that, yep, his cunning little mean-spirited brother must be the bigger of the two since he was indeed "a little Bigger." The troupers knew how to concoct and serve up just what was hungered for in the refuge from the gloom of quotidian reality. Delivered from great tedia and little miseries, the throng was terribly tickled by the unrelenting verbal and physical assault of the baritone midget upon the giant with the high-pitched voice. While the conventional banana peel provided its surefire explosion of laughter, the acrobatic panache with which the little Bigger tripped the much, much bigger Bigger in the midst of black-bottom dancing was just plain knockdown funny. Ola Namnlösa had perfectly perfected the slapstick pratfall. Everyone, in the back of minds amused upfront, had to wonder each and every time if he might really be injured and unable to get up this time. According to expectation, a quick Bachnele pulled the chair out from under Ola when the clumsy giant tried to sit. And then, after the fall, when he tried to seat himself again, there was the hilarious hoot of the whoopee cushion. Then there was the good-old "let's-shake-hands-and-make-up" gag that, when the electrical hand-buzzer goes off, so amuses young and old alike. The pretext for this abuse came early in the routine with Bachnele's high-spirited low-toned solo, "Laughter in the Mirror," a ditty that was the setup for a proud proclamation that "my big brother can laugh at himself, and that's the mark of a real sense of humor, the humor that makes life worth living." But the giant did not laugh along with the audience during his ordeal any more than Jesus laughed with Pilate's soldiers when they laughed at him in his crown of thorns. The overgrown buffoon, quite blatantly emotionally injured by the deprecatory jibes and physically pained by the hard falls, became sadder and sadder until, in the dénouement of the act, after a final violent pratfall from which, utterly defeated and shamed, he no longer had the resilience to rise up, he sobbed his solo, "Nobody Loves a Big Loser." Just when the agony became too flagrant for laughter, Bachnele wrapped his little arm around his brother's big shoulders and, after kissing him affectionately on the forehead, sang "Who Couldn't Love a Fella with a Heart as Big as Yours?" With perfect timing and an impeccable sense of spectatorial vulnerabilities, Bachnele bestowed upon his teary-eyed audience the license to indulge themselves in the sumptuous, though ephemeral, pleasures of sentimentality. He understood the ways in which sentimentality allows us to compensate for our innate heartlessness. The comeback climax was spectacular: although the rigging for the trick was elaborate, the overwhelming response that it inevitably evoked would have been worth the trouble to any real entertainer. "Let me take you home, big brother," the lilliputian Bigger said as he, to the amazement of one and all, picked his Brobdingnagian sibling up and, as if the giant weighed no more than a down pillow, kicking his heels together in the air, danced offstage with him in his arms. To the exuberant applause and unrestrained cheering of enthralled variety buffs, the Bigger Brothers heel-and-toed back on stage to sing their merry theme song: "Big and small! We got it all, 'cause we're the Brothers Biggerrrrrr!" And "Bravo!" I said as I entered Bachnele's dressing room. "Isaac," he exclaimed with delight upon seeing me for the first time since Buffalo Bill's funeral in Denver, "how you've grown! Kiss me, bubee. Ola, you remember the Schlossberg kid!" Yes, the giant, who was removing the rouge from his cheeks with cold cream, acknowledged. "He used to knock my head off. I was Goliath and he was David. It was a stupid routine, but religious folks appreciated the way it brought the Bible to life." While Ola declined Bachnele's invitation for a late supper as his club, I eagerly accepted the same. "But," Ola said as we left, "I'll see you later at Harmony House." There was nothing about the unmarked entrance to the club on the narrow lane not far from Trafalgar Square that intimated the intimidating formal elegance of the reception hall. Bachnele was welcomed by a steward ("Good evening, Mr. Bigger, sir, your table is ready") who fitted me with the tie and jacket that were required for admission to the dining room with its plush green carpets, dark wood-panel walls, and painted portraits of notable members dating back to the seventeenth century. I had never seen more silverware on a table set for two. "Good evening, Mr. Bigger, sir," the waiter said with a slight bow. "Will you be having your customary *après-théâtre* repast this evening?" Bachnele nodded an unarticulated "of course" appended with a voiced: "And the same for the young gentleman, President Wilson's nephew from America." The waiter verified the order: "Two mixed grills with a double portion of bacon and a bottle of Château Ségla 1900. Glentossel while you wait." No sooner had the server turned from the table than Bachnele whispered, "The extra bacon's so that they don't suspect we're Yids. This place once turned Disraeli away." Throughout dinner, gentlemen at neighboring tables would look in our direction, and if they were lucky enough to catch Bachnele's eye, they'd raise a glass and nod a greeting to the little big celebrity. I was impressed not only with his big success, but with how little it had changed him. The Bachnele Poopik of my childhood, so detested by my father, whispered from across the table, "What do I care about these knackers? And I don't care about the moolah either. But, I'm telling you, once you've played for the king and queen, you get more pussy than you can handle. I'm not kidding. You wouldn't believe it. I've shtooped royalty." The waiter brought our whiskey, and after gulping it down he told me how the act had come about: "Ola's wife, Skadi, remember her? Six feet five inches tall! She died, bitten by a rattlesnake while practicing that meshugeh religion of hers. So I'm at the funeral and I'm looking at Ola and he's crying like I've never seen anybody cry before. The tears are flowing out of his eyes like piss out of the pecker of a kid just waking up in the morning. Seeing a giant sob like that is so heartbreaking that I say to myself, 'If I can get this shmuck to do this on a stage, we could make a million bucks.'" After our dinners had been set before us and our wineglasses filled, Bachnele reminded me to eat my bacon just in case anyone might be thinking I looked Jewish. "So," he continued, "he needs work and I make him a partner and we're playing the West Coast circuit. I'm in San Francisco, eating Chinese one night at the Jade Palace, and who should walk in but Gershom Greenspan, who, it turns out, has become a groyser-macher booking agent. He sees me, comes straight to my table, and tells me he needs a midget. He's booking acts for Europe and, he explains, King George of England, a patron of variety and music hall, is fuckin' nuts about midgets. All monarchs seem to adore midgets. Queen Victoria couldn't get enough of Colonel Tom Thumb. So, on the condition that I promise that our act isn't too dirty, Greenspan signs me and Ola, and arranges for an audition here in London for the Royal Command Variety Performance. And the rest is history." Waving to get the waiter's attention, Bachnele asked for more bacon and another bottle of wine. With the pop of a cork, I got to the point: "I'd like your help." I told him about

India, my failed ten-in-one, and about my run as Buffalo Bill's illegitimate son in Jake Grossman's "Last of the Wild Redskins." "Since Jake left," I explained, "I've developed the routine, adding a female love-interest. But it's tough getting a booking. I think it's got potential and I was hoping that you might be able to arrange an audition." He laughed and slapped the table hard with his little hand. "This proves it! There must be a God! It can't be just coincidence! This morning Eddie Burke, an agent and a real shnorrer, calls on me to ask if I know anybody with an act. 'Somebody new, something different, something very American,' he says, 'as soon as possible,' for a variety show playing the Olympia in Blackpool, to replace the New Jersey Jollies. The Jollies were an American husband-and-wife comedy team until last week, when Mrs. Jolly murdered Mr. Jolly with an ax after catching him being a little too jolly with one of the Merry Muses of Middlesex, a variety girlie dance troupe. You can meet Burke tomorrow and be onstage by Shabbis." When I asked if he didn't want to see the routine before recommending me, he laughed. "If Greenspan had actually seen the Brothers Bigger, he probably wouldn't have signed us. But he was desperate for a midget for the king. And this putz Burke needs an American act right away. What could be more American than Buffalo Bill? Break a leg, bubee." At around midnight, as we finished the last of the wine, Bachnele invited me to accompany him to "his other club. Hastings House. All the bigwigs go there. Buffalo Bill was a guest there every time he came to England. He took Geronimo there. It's London's best heizel." I asked the meaning of the unfamiliar Yiddish word. "A shandhoiz, you know, a whorehouse," Bachnele cheerfully answered. "In principle they don't let Yids in there either, but unlike this dive, they make exceptions. They never turned Disraeli away!" I declined the invitation, as I was eager to get to Hounslow. The woman who held the world altitude record for female fliers had by then become my lover.

66 The goddess of memory, the mother of the Muses eternally on Mt. Olympus in Macedonia, appeared twice nightly on the stage of the Olympia Variety Theatre in Blackpool. That's where I had my first vision of the divine Mnemosyne zaftigly incarnated by Mimi Navis. After a brief stint with a spirit cabinet at the beginning of her career, Mimi had developed the mnemonic act and had been performing it for as long as anyone in show business could recall. Having played the good-ol'-daysian halls, the Pav, Pal, and Prom, the old soldierette remembered the very first *ta-ra-ra-boom-de-ay* in human history. She had recently recruited from pub-cabaret nine high-kicking-long-legged singsongstresses whom she coquettishly clad in cutie-pie chitons as scant and diaphanous as censorship would allow, and christened them the Merry Muses of Middlesex. Watched over by the matriarchal immortal in her stately white Doric peplos, enthroned like the Apollonian oracle at Delphi upon a tripod over an omphalos wherein an Edison Professional Electric Smoke-and-Fog machine generated classical Graeco-variety ambiance, the Olympian demigoddesses chorus-lined, quickstepped, pigeon-winged, and chip-chippity-chirped such long-forgotten songs as "Love Is Just a Memory." Taking a synchronized rolling bow, each with a rosily naked knee pertly bent, they fell into line as Mr. Eddie Burke himself, the boss (producer, agent, and moral counselor), filling in for the bungler he had just fired on the spot for being too soused to play the prof in a scholar's black gown and tasseled mortarboard, pushed a library cart of stacked books onto the stage. After introducing himself as L. L. Lexington, Professor of Comparative Prosody and Theoretical Phonology at the University of Oxford and Warden Emeritus of Pontius Pilate Library, the enormously fat Mr. Burke announced that he had been officially solicited to authenticate each of the nine tomes before him as identical copies of the genuine *Oxford English Dictionary* (second shorter domestic edition), and that "Madame Mnemosyne has memorized, word for word, the entire text, all 2,516 pages of fine print from the indefinite article 'a' all the way to 'zymurgy,' that definitely defined English word for 'the art and science of fermentation.'" Obeying, like school girls their master, Lexington's instructions to pick up a copy of the authoritative lexicon, the prancing muses caroled, "All the Words in Here Can't Say How Much I Love You." Then, as they followed the professorial directive to randomly distribute the nine dictionaries to volunteering hands-up spectators, the proctor roll-called: "Calliope, the Muse of epics and prolix; Clio, history and fiction; Erato, love poetry and pornosophy; Euterpe, doggerel and anagram; Melpomene, tragedy and the daily news; Polyhymnia, prayers and curses; Terpsichore, cabaret and striptease; Thalia, comedy and jokes; and Urania, astrology and urology!" The audience would laugh at each joke and applaud each girl. Professor Lexington instructed the audience members holding dictionaries to open them and select any word, no matter how "obscure, archaic, technical, or bizarre," and, when called upon, to yell it out. With a perfect word-for-word recitation of each challenging definition, Mnemosyne demonstrated that she had indeed memorized every one of the 176,983 entries in the dictionary. The initial time I saw the act, when the first book holder shouted "mystacal," I was amply impressed and mildly amused with Mnemosyne's "resembling a mustache." "Smouse" was next. "Slang," she said, "a Jew." Although "lotophagi" and "metensomatosis" seemed recondite to many, any amateur etymologist would know precisely what they meant. The same, however, could not be said of "furfur." Although it was not surprising that "snaketrout" was some sort of ichthyic creature, it was quite remarkable that Mnemosyne recalled the parenthetical Linnaean cognomen (*Salvelinus gravis*). Some of the words seemed pieces of cake to the erudite but were, in fact, hard nuts to crack (like "highlow"); many others were the other way around. The charm and appeal of the routine was that it highlighted the audience's comedic sensibilities, not merely allowing them to laugh at the jokes onstage but to be funny themselves. For the sake of that sweet pleasure volunteers rummaged for words that were laughable in sound (like "flapdoodle" or "fizgig"), in sense (like "pizzle" and "titubation"), or in the ways in which the venerable *Oxford English Dictionary* seemed tricked into making decent, by their presence between its hallowed covers, verbal indecencies: "prepuce" and "clitoris" were as popular as the vocables that sounded illicit but weren't ("fucus" and "prickmadam" were always sure to get a laugh). On my first night with the show, still not able to figure out how the words were forced, and suspecting that volunteers were cued or stooges, I was startled when merry Melpomene gave one of the nine dictionaries to my darling Billie, who had flown in from Hounslow to surprise me for the occasion. When it was her turn, she called out, "'Love.' Can you tell us what 'l-o-v-e' means?" There were snickers in the audience during Mnemosyne's hesitation, a feigned struggle to remember the definition. The goddess closed her eyes to answer: "Page 1171, column two, between 'lovage, an unbelliferous herb used as domestic remedy,' and 'loveapple, the fruit of the tomato.' 'Love' is defined as 'that state of feeling with regard to a person which arises from the recognition of attractive qualities, or from sympathy, and manifests itself in warm affection, attachment, and desire for proximity. In religious use, applied to the paternal benevolence and affection of God, the affectionate devotion due to God from His creatures, and to the affection of one created being to another thence arising.'"

I was nervous that night. My new act, "Buffalo Bill and Geronimo in Love," went on right before Mnemosyne and immediately after "The Dance of Salami," a parody of *Salomé* in which veteran female impersonator Wilkie Wilde did a ventriloquy tab, dancing with the head of John the Baptist on a silver platter. The severed head told predictable jokes ("She told Herod that she wanted to get a-head") sang the obvious songs ("I've Got No-Body But You), and smoked a cigarette. It wasn't a very hard act for "Buffalo Bill and Geronimo in Love" to follow. In replacing the Jollies, we were constrained by their time allotment of a mere six minutes. Previewing the routine, Burke cut both Buffalo Bill's monologue on "Wild Western Love" and Geronimo's "Mating Prayer with Tom-toms." The producer had shaken his head solemnly: "Get right to the action, the shooting and the knife throwing. That's what folks want to see. Nobody likes just a lot of words. I'll give the background, explaining that you're both in love with the half-breed maiden and are holding a shooting contest to determine who gets her." Professor Wonderful was very proudly pleased when Eddie Burke said he especially liked it when the two halves of one woman turned into two whole women. Burke congratulated us: "It's got a profound message about love and it affirms the need for a preservation of the purity of the races." Although initially disappointed that she was still not given the opportunity to display her amazing eight breasts to the audience, Kamadhenuka was ultimately content to be in show business and very happy to be matched on stage with her beloved Maarnath. After the show, I apologized to Billie for the vulgarity of the revue. Rather than trying to say something polite as many a girlfriend might have done, my aviatrix agreed: "Yes, it was the most vulgar, pathetic, puerile, and meaningless display of human folly that I've ever had the misfortune to witness. Can't you come up with something better to do with your life?" Because I couldn't, I stayed with the show. Thankfully the British public was easier to please than my beloved. We worked for Burke, playing the combine circuit for almost a year, during which time I'd never know when Billie would show up for a rendezvous. She liked to surprise me. Making love in the cabin of the Junkers F-13, her body on automatic pilot, was earthly foreplay for empyrean flight, carnal intimations of the exhilarating aerial acceleration and full-throttled roaring soaring that precipitated the detumescence of her soul. She was, I sometimes sensed during intimacy, making love only to the part of me that preserved in body and spirit the man who had flown higher than her and, for the sake of altitude, had crashed to earth and been consumed by flames. "You don't understand," she'd sometimes say, "but your father would." Then she'd lower the nose of the plane and, as we began to fall from the sky, ask if I was afraid. "No," I'd lie and hope she wouldn't kill us. Billie was trying to frighten me, something she inevitably did when, all of sudden, she'd have one of her terrible bouts of jealousy. "Don't lie to me," she'd warn, kill the engine, and let the plane fall into a perilous dive. "Tell me the truth! Tell me what's going on between you and that Jewish whore." Nothing. "What about those dancing floozies? Which Muse amuses you the most? What's going on with them?" Nothing. "What do you do on the road, after the shows. What happens in those dirty little flophouse rooms where you stay?" Nothing. "I won't start the engine until you tell me." "Nothing," I'd swear: "Nothing. I love you. I love only you." I'd repeat it again and again until I heard the 220-horsepower Kegel-Benz radial engine start and saw sky again as she allowed the ailerons to lift the plane up and away from the earth. I did love her despite the jealousy, perhaps all the more so for it, flattered by its furious intensities, titillated by the torments, tears, and tantrums, interpreting suspicions and accusations as coded testimonies of love. Miserable love was thrilling. And the dénouement of the melodramas was always the same: a passionate battle (teeth biting swollen lips, hands tugging sweat-wet hair, nails scratching bristled skin, muscles taut, hearts bursting, and breath on fire) culminating in the mutual victory of simultaneous surrender (with tender touch and a tear or two if not a languid smile). We often slept in the plane, sometimes in hangars, sometimes, when my show was playing the rural halls and cabs, on moors, heaths, or barrens far away from other human beings. There was no more sumptuous a sleep than that which was slept to the sound of rain on the metal skin of the body that protected us. In the morning's gray light, softened by wet windows and lace curtains, I kissed her to lure her out of clouds of sleep, and as her eyes opened, I reassured her with another "I love you," a verbal incantation to ward off jealousies. She hesitated. "Do you that mean that you have a feeling with regard to me arising from a recognition of attractive qualities, or from sympathy, and manifesting as warm affection, attachment, and a desire for proximity? Or, my darling smouse, are you just being religious?"

From 25 and 27

	The Snake and Ladder: the instant I saw the sign, the brightly
67	painted striped serpent entwined through the rigid rungs of the gold-leafed ladder, I had to enter the pub. Buffalo Bill and Geron-

imo were shooting it out for the heart of Matanka Hickok at the Old London Theatre in Oxford on a Friday and Saturday night and in a Sunday matinee. On Saturday afternoon, after a lovers' spat with jealous Billie that culminated in her flying back to London, I visited the Ashmolean Museum to see the snakes and ladders puzzle-game that the Maharaja of Diwanasthan had told me had been unearthed at Mohenjo Daro. That the museum personnel knew of no such antiquity made a drink at the Snake and Ladder invitingly con- solatory. When, standing at the bar, I heard my name called out with consider- able exuberance, I turned to see, much to my astonishment, none other than the Tiger Boy of Alipore in white oxford baggies and a blue blazer. "Hugh," I exclaimed, only to be corrected: "No, no, old chum, call me Puru. I'm not us- ing that absurd pseudo-allegorical cognomen any longer. Let me buy you a whiskey for old times' sake, in honor of Dr. McCloud and the good old days in India. I really couldn't have pulled it off without you," he said, offering me a Players from a silver case. "It was fun, wasn't it?" Eager to hear his story, I was especially interested to find out about Pythia. Puru began by explaining that, during the long voyage from India, she had sulked because her father refused to permit her to disembark in Italy. "Once we had arrived here, McCloud and Wheedle wasted no time in packing us off to Churchill and taking rooms at the posh Hastings Royal Inn. That there was indeed a Blessingham stream reas- sured them that Hastings had spoken through me. Early the first morning there, leading me to the brook and seating me on a blanket, they got down to business. Pythia had come along and each of them was carrying a spade with which to dig up the fortune. While Wheedle, waving his hands about, was muttering, 'Your eyelids are getting heavy,' and counting backwards, I decided to have a bit of fun with them. Once they supposed that I was entranced and that they had recontacted Warren Hastings, I complained a bit about the heat in Kasimbazaar and then, suddenly, midsentence, slipped into Kholo's crass Bengali, and then back into Hastings's English, then into Sharma's chaste di- alect, then back to Hastings for a moment, then Sharma again, back and forth, in and out, just as when the channels on a wireless get crossed and switched. Steadfastly, but with substantial frustration and impatience, Wheedle struggled to tune in on pure Hastings. 'Back, back, farther back,' he whispered to Kholo, desperately trying to contact the political leader of the Raj. My eyes were closed. 'Warren, are you there? It's me, Pinkie. Speak to me.' There was a long silence—oh, what suspense!—and then, opening my eyes, I gazed at Pythia to speak in my finest Hastingsese: 'Marion, my dear, thank God you are here! You surely know how consummately I have adored you all these years and indeed worshipped you as an angel sent from heaven to guide me in what is good and right. As you have ever been my solace, I grieve for the perturbations that my trial required you to endure. You must be assured, my darling, of my whole-hearted striving to secure a means of supporting you after I am gone. What I am about to tell must be guarded in complete confidence: there is some unre-ported money amassed from dabblings in the opium trade, personal profits un-related to the business of the Company or Crown. Since the court has not permitted me to make financial provisions for you, I have sequestered this rev-enue so that, after my demise, you may continue to live in the comfort to which you are so deservedly accustomed. But something shameful must be confessed. Recently, in a weak moment, recovering from Calcutta catarrh and having drunk perhaps a drop too much of medicinal toddy, I fell prey to a groundless fear that you, my angel, after my death, might become the vulner-able target of the subterfuges of venal gentlemen, fortune hunters who would endeavor to seduce you and squander whatever moneys they might wheedle out of you. And so I told Pinkie of the fortune and, foolishly and impulsively, requested him to be its guardian, distributing it to you after my death on the condition of your fidelity in my absence. I beg that you forgive me. Now that I am in my right mind again, I trust that I can trust you, that you would never give yourself to another. I believe in you, my dearest Marion. I do. So please, listen carefully. You must dig up the treasure immediately, before Pinkie has the opportunity to find it. I don't trust Pinkie any longer.' The moment I fell silent, Pythia, referring to me as her 'beloved Warren,' asked where the money was buried. 'I know you remember the spot,' I answered: 'It is that very place near the brook where we made love in England for the first time, in the evening, be-neath the stars, and you said it would be a sacred place for you, eternally re-membered as our secret Eden.' The three of them were panicked. Pythia was their only hope: 'Warren, my darling, my love, my living god,' she tried, 'you must take me there.' I smiled. 'No, no, my dear. I am being followed by Whig spies. You must proceed alone, at night, when no one is about. I know you re-member the place because so many of the loving letters you sent to me from England noted that you were writing from that very spot. You must retrieve the money as soon as possible, move it to a safe place, and tell no one where it is, not even me, just in case I might, in some future moment of weakness, fall into the temptation to speak of it to another.' It was wonderful! They were totally dismayed and utterly devastated. I rose to approach Pythia. 'My darling, let us speak no more of such crass things as lucre. There is no more precious treasure trove than your body, softer, warmer, and richer than any plot of earth. My dearest one, I must have you now, kiss you, caress your naked flesh, and lie in love betwixt your breasts. Now, my beloved.' I reached for Pythia and she was terrified. 'I'm sorry, Warren, I have a headache.' I laughed. 'Ah, to be cured with kisses on your brow!' She screamed, 'Wake him up! Stop him!' Wheedle recited his demesmeric mantra at top speed: 'At the count of three you will wake up; you will feel refreshed and relaxed. One. Two. Three.' He repeated it again and again and with each number I took another lustful step toward Pythia and was about to embrace her when her father lunged in between us to rescue his daughter from being raped by the governor-general of British India. I closed my eyes to kiss Dr. McCloud on the lips. The shock of being knocked to the ground returned Hugh Mann's soul to its rightful carnal abode. It didn't look good for the fortune hunters. They were so desperate that, against the odds, they tried again the next day without any Marion to distract her husband. Once Wheedle had me under, he said it again: 'Warren, it's me. It's me, Pinkie.' I looked at McCloud and then back at Wheedle. 'Judas!' I cried: 'You have betrayed me! How dare you bring Burke with you! Look at him, hoping to destroy me! Why have you done this to me, Pinkie? I would challenge you to a duel and pray that I would die if I were not able to slay you. But, ha ha, no no, the last laugh is on you, Pinkie. Marion has already moved the money and hidden it where neither you, nor Burke, nor any other scoundrel shall ever discover it! Even I do not know its location!' Dropping his spade, his head hanging in sorrow, Dr. McCloud walked slowly back toward the inn. I don't think, however, that I can be held responsible for the subsequent stroke that has rendered him quite pathetic. It's really too bad, he's rather a dear fellow. Fortunately the doctor had retained his family farm in Lancashire, where he is now in Pythia's care. Wheedle, eager to return to India and resume his expedition in search of the Abominable Snowman, brought me here to Oxford and donated me to the Pitt-Rivers Museum of Anthropology as a 'living artifact.' Not wanting to make fool of himself, he told the curator nothing of the experiments in animal magnetism and the supposed empirical proof of transmigration. I was presented simply as a feral boy who had been reared by tigers in the jungles of Bengal. In addition to Dr. McCloud's medical documentation, there were ample newspaper reports to authenticate me. Exhibited in the museum's foyer, I was installed in a little enclosure wherein I could be observed clad in a rabbit-skin loincloth, scratching and sniffing about amidst imitation shrubbery and stuffed tigers realistically posed. I gnawed upon mutton chops and tossed the bones over my shoulder. English propriety required that my toilet be concealed behind the rubber rhododendron bushes upon which were perched several stuffed vultures. Scholars from various faculties of the university came to examine me, to contemplate my physical attributes and behavior, and to empirically test my motor, cognitive, and linguistic aptitudes. Sir Jeremy Bates, Hillcastle Professor of Dogmatic Morality and Eschatology, taking a particular interest in me, convinced the curators of the museum that I should learn to read. As I already read quite well, I was able to display remarkable intellectual talent, getting the hang of both language and literacy in less than a month, at which point the good Professor Bates introduced me to Latin. Because, as a child, I had been present, as you may recall, at Jonathan Blessingham's Latin lessons, I was in a position to flabbergast my master Bates with a swift mastery of the canonical language. When we studied St. Nubes of Apulia's *De Ascensione Inversa,* I demonstrated the extraordinary power of my faculty of memory with recitations: *'Si scalam divinam requiris incipere risu parve angele cognoscere in herba serpentem.'* That I had learned to speak and read both English and Latin so rapidly was sufficient evidence that I could and should be admitted as a student into the University of Oxford. I applied to St. Hugh's, but since it is a woman's college I was denied admission and forced to accept a place at Christ Church, reading theology under the supervision of Professor Bates. That I needed a name (since Major Wheedle had never indicated that I had one) in order to enroll gave me the welcome opportunity to revert to my true and original one: Purushottam. I added Deva as the surname. Oh, but enough about me. What about you, Isaac?" I hadn't gone very far into my story when, hearing that Shula was with me in Oxford playing the part of Matanka Hickok in "Buffalo Bill and Geronimo in Love," Puru interrupted: "Shulamite Levi, my first love! She's here? It's hard to believe. I must see her. Let's have a croquet party! That would be terribly amusing! I do hope it doesn't put her off that I'm civilized now. I don't think women really like that quality in a man."

From 46

68 "Women have always flown," Billie said after a sip of Vin Mariani. She gazed out of the window at the night sky in which she so loved to glide: "We have coursed our way across the firmament for millennia, leaving the earth and its inhabitants behind and below, gone far above the migratory flocks of clouds and birds, disappearing into thin air, soaring and enraptured." She loosened her silk scarf. "Women have flown as witches, by means of secret incantations and magical unguents, upon their brooms or besoms, or on the backs of black goats, and as saints, with their pious prayers and quiet meditations, upon clouds, winds, or on the backs of golden raptors. Don't imagine that I am some sort of delusional believer in the supernatural; but these women, I am amply convinced by their own testaments, experienced, without the aid of a machine, exactly what I have experienced in a plane. They have described with precision all that I myself have felt, all the sensations of soaring and diving, accelerating and gliding, the feel of the moist insides of clouds and the chill thin air of the upper atmosphere, and all that I have seen, the demeanor of a distant earth, the stunning spectacle of its mountains, lakes, and rivers, its farms, villages, and towns. This is not to claim that these women took their bodies with them. No, most likely they did not, nor did they wish to be so bogged down. The body is merely the baggage we are often constrained to take on aerial journeys. Yes, the balloon, kite, dirigible, and airplane are all quite useful for carrying baggage or the bodies of pilot and passengers; but the soul, as every aviator knows, with or without the plane, is the real flier." Her brain fueled with cocaine-laced wine, Billie could soar for hours, expounding the romance of flight. Scornful of the increasing use of airplanes for commercial transport, she felt they should be reserved for play and adventure and to deliver only love letters and declarations of war. She removed her fur flight jacket and unbuttoned the collar stays on her blue broadcloth man's dress shirt. Reclining on the bed in the back of the plane's cabin, she stretched out a leg for me to pull off a soft leather boot. When, the first time I watched her undress, as she unbuttoned the sky-colored shirt and the light of a setting sun through the windshield glinted off the gold charm hanging between cumulus-white breasts, I thought it was a cross. It was only later, sitting up to talk, smoke cigarettes, and drink coca wine, that I noticed that cruciform ornament was an airplane. I laughed. "Oh, I thought that was a cross around your neck, that you were perhaps religious." She answered seriously: "It is a cross. And I am religious. Flight is holy. Prayer is merely one mode of flight and vice versa." She believed it. "Flight is praise, petition, and penance. And it requires faith." One late afternoon, as we sat on the wing of the Junkers, which she had parked for the night in a field near Canterbury, she professed the creed: "Although the founders and first builders of the Church were men, its most passionate mystics and blissful martyrs have been women: St. Teresa of Avila, St. Catherine of Siena, St. Wilhelmina of Apulia, and countless others. So, too, though Wright, Cody, Blériot, and Sikorsky, are the Matthew, Mark, Luke, and John of the flight of heavier-than-air vessels, it has been left to women to reveal the secrets of the sky with love. Aviation is mystic transport and holy ascension. Men are natural inventors, apostles, theologians, and mechanics and have, with masculine skills, taken possession of a feminine earth. But women are the chosen mistresses of the heavens. It is theirs to charm and beguile the bearded gods of ancient pantheons. 'Billie' is short for Wilhelmina, Wilhelmina of Apulia, my patron saint, the most graceful and beatific of aviatrixes. 'Rapture,' she wrote in her *Book of Holy Ascension,* 'begins in awe. A cloud or eagle appears, or an unseen wind or angel is felt, and you are afraid. First there is the delicate touch and then the strong grip as it lifts you, transporting body and spirit higher and higher and, if you do not resist but allow yourself the glory of surrender, the terror passes, you melt, dissolved with joy by the vision of the stretch of earth below and the glimmering of heaven above.' Her rapture," Billie said in a voice dramatically muted by piety, "is holy rape, a reconciliation of horror and delight, the perfection of flight and its meaning." She recounted the hagiographic tale of her tutelary saint, whose image was engraved on a medallion above the altimeter. She was born in Sicily in the early years of the thirteenth century. "If we are to trust her poetry as a reliable source of autobiographical fact, she was a brewer's daughter. Given in marriage to a goat farmer's son at the age of thirteen, she endured all of the catholic miseries of medieval matrimony with resignation, escaping on occasion by means of what she describes in her verse as the 'wings of reverie.' It was at this time that Ulrich von Hohenstaufen, vassal to Frederick II, champion jouster, minnesinger of some repute, and self-proclaimed suitor of Venus, went on a quest to find and win the heart of that goddess of love (undertaken after a revelation of her resurrection from the Mediterranean at a place not far from where Wilhelmina lived her dreary life). The knight saw the girl driving her husband's goats to feed on the grassy hills. Awestruck by the girl's extraordinary beauty, the man dismounted, kneeled before her, offered his glove, and spontaneously composed and recited his famous '*Du bist min, ich bin din, des solt du gewis sin.*'" As I tugged on the legs of her tight jodhpur breeches, she arched her back to set them free and, after another glass of Mariani, continued her chronicle of Wilhelmina. The knight had taken her to the Castel del Monte to present her to Frederick II. Dazzled by her beauty, the Holy Roman Emperor honored her with a seat in the High Areopagitic Court of Ladies, whose function it was to inspire *Frauendienst,* the devotion to women which, according to Frederick himself, was the purest wellspring of poetry. The most noble knights of Christendom were among Wilhelmina's suitors, and many insinuated in their *Tagelieder* that they had been blessed by her fingertips and nourished by her lips in surprise nocturnal visitations. That she had never been observed either leaving the castle at night nor returning before dawn gave rise to rumors that, leaping from the tower, she would fly as if with wings to and from those secret assignations ("just as I flew here from London to be with you, my dear"). Billie's final chapter was more ecclesiastical: In order to understand a vision that had overwhelmed her during vespers, Wilhelmina turned to Bishop Nubes of Apulia, a learned member of Frederick's Council of the Keepers of Holy Tongues. She had, she informed the prelate, witnessed the Assumption of Our Lady of the Immaculate Heart: "She rose from the earth with arms spread, gown billowing, head tilted to the side, radiantly smiling with tears flowing down her cheeks, aglow in the nimbus that transported her higher and higher. As I gazed up at her in wonder, she, bowing her head to look at me, seemed to be signaling with her right hand for me to follow." Billie explained that the bishop, interpreting the vision as a portent, had counseled Wilhelmina to devote the remainder of her life to the fulfillment of that divine call, to renounce the court for the sake of the cloister so that she might, through her meditations, know the mysteries of rapturous flight. "She became, she informs us in her *Book of the Holy Ascension,* a Sister of Sacred Silence. On the day of the feast of the Assumption of the Our Blessed Lady, Wilhelmina's sisters witnessed it (though they could not speak of it because of their vow of silence): she rose slowly from the ground of the cloister garden, higher and higher, disappearing into the clouds, and was never again seen on earth." The autobiographical resonances of the story were apparent: Billie was not exactly the daughter of a brewer, but her father, Sir John Custis, was president of Custis & Custis Fine Ales, Wines, and Spirits. Though her father continued to provide her with financial support, she rarely saw him. After his wife had been committed to an asylum several years earlier, he had taken up with a girl no older than his daughter, of whom Billie did not approve. I supposed that her bouts of exorbitant jealousy had something to do with her feelings for her father. It was for deliverance from the squalid emotional life of the luxuriously appointed Custis home that Billie had consented at an early age to marry the foppish offspring of a member of the House of Lords. The marriage lasted no longer than Wilhelmina's, and though Billie told me nothing of knights who might have courted her or lovers to whom she might have flown for midnight assignations, I suspected that they were legion. The vision of the Assumption seemed comparable to her own transformational witnessing of the flight of Isabel Cody in 1908. I was troubled by the dénouement of the story: that Billie had her own immaculate heart set on setting the records for speed, altitude, and distance at once, on flying faster, higher, and farther than any man or woman, bird or angel, satanic witch or ecstatic saint, made me fear that suicidal impulses were disguised to herself and others as aeronautical adventurousness, that she yearned to disappear into the clouds and "never be seen on earth again." And that made me love her all the more urgently, trying with my body pressed over hers to hold her down upon the earth. I struggled to assuage the dangerous jealousy that seemed somehow connected with that illicit desire for extinction. I wanted her to be more in love with me than she was with death. With the encouragement of cocaine, jealousy would bewitch her: upon awaking from a dream in which she had discovered me in a garden with a naked girl, she was infuriated with me and wrathful of "that redheaded bitch." When I tried to pacify her by saying that I had dreamed that I was with Bachnele Poopik, a fully clothed Lithuanian midget, in the Alhambra Theatre, sweeping the stage under his direction, and by joking that, since I was having more fun in her dream than in my own, I wished she might have sent the girl over, it only fueled her rage. I should have heeded Bachnele Poopik's warning: "Never joke with a woman. When women say they like a sense of humor in man, they don't mean it, at least not in a lover." This was corroborated by a passage in St. Wilhelmina's *Book of the Holy Ascension,* the book Billie gave me as a gift on the feast day of the Assumption: "The Holy Virgin never laughed, for laughter, by aggrandizing the body, traps the spirit and holds us to the earth. The saints and martyrs weep. All tears are holy. There is not laughter in heaven, nor are there any words, not the faintest whispers, nor even prayers, for in heaven there is nothing to pray for. Heaven, I can attest from my transports, is a perfect silence. Was it not because they laughed that certain angels fell to earth?"

<table>
<tr><td>

69

</td><td>

There were the cynics who surmised that it was a lie that he could no longer lie, a joke that he couldn't joke, and a trick that his trick hadn't worked. Whatever the truth, the Great Whydini was, much to the amazement and delight of Professor Wonderful, alive and

</td></tr>
</table>

well (well, almost well) in free residence at Paradise House on Blackfriars Road, a charity hospice for elderly, infirm, or insane variety and music hall performers. Wonderful was offended by the rumors rife in magic circles that the master magician, in his performance of the bullet-catch trick some years earlier in Blackpool, had faked the freak accident because of financial difficulties. It was a symptom of the injury to the performer's brain that his right eye constantly blinked. This uncontrollable spasmodic motion of the ocular muscles was interpreted by some not as a tic but as the wink of complicity that means "just joking." His loss of all sense of humor, another symptom of the trauma, was diagnosed as neurologically linked to his inability to prevaricate or speak foreign languages. "Other than that," Professor Wonderful cheerfully announced, "he is fit as the fiddle." My magician was thrilled to have found his hero, the conjurer who, touring India, had judged the magic contest in which a callow Wonderful had first performed for the public, the prolific author of the books that had given him the confidence to give up rice farming in a Bengal village: *Winning Friends with Magic, Meeting Women with Magic, Bible Tricks and How to Do Them,* and his more theoretical and technical work for specialists, *The False Thumb Tip: Its History, Philosophy, Psychology, and Practical Use.* Ever since arriving in England, Professor Wonderful had been making inquiries to various professional British magic societies in hopes of locating the conjuring celebrity. Upon discovering that he was living in Paradise House, Wonderful had gone to the home to bow down before his idle idol. "So many magicians have copied him," Professor Wonderful informed me, "the Great Howdini, the Great Whendini, and the Great Whatdini." Once he found the Great Whydini, the master was almost all that Wonderful talked about. It was a tragic story: since he could not lie, it was hard for him to make an honest living. And his wife and assistant of over twenty years, the woman whom he had sawed in half and restored so lovingly so many times, had run off with an escape artist, none other than the Great Wheredini. Since the poor man always told the truth, whenever he was addressed as Whydini, he'd confess the true name that he had, for fear of anti-Semites, kept so long a secret: Joseph Lipschitz. "But he will always be a Great Whydini to me," Professor Wonderful said with a sigh and informed me that he had tried to convince the man to return to show business, promising that he would help him, being for him like a Seeing Eye dog for the blind, a lying-mouth man providing patter, jokes, and verbal misdirection. That the Great Whydini was Jewish reaffirmed Professor Wonderful's resolve to convert to Judaism in preparation for his marriage to Shulamite Levi. "Turning this shmuck into a Hebe," Bachnele observed, upon meeting him after the opening night of our short run at the Alhambra, "is going to be a tougher magic trick for Elohim to pull off than that old staff-into-snake routine. Not as big a miracle as the parting of the Red Sea, perhaps, but a lot more pointless." Professor Wonderful had announced his plan to convert to the religion of Israel to Bachnele in order to appeal to the midget, as a future fellow Jew, to arrange a meeting with King George and Queen Mary, who as everyone in variety had heard, had been so impressed with the Brothers Bigger. The reason he needed to talk to the His Majesty, Wonderful confided, was to solicit his assistance with a magic trick by which Professor Wonderful would make a name for himself by disproving the music hall dictum that "magic, like mime, trick cycling, juggling, and striptease, will never work on radio." Professor Wonderful's idea was that Bachnele, using his influence in the entertainment industry, could get him a spot on the *Sunday Variety Hour,* during which he would ask the listening audience to help with a trick by closing their eyes and concentrating; through the power of that collective concentration, they would magically turn off all the electricity in England. When their radios went off, they'd open their eyes to discover the lights out. That's where the king, the only man in the world with the authority to have all electrical circuits in Britain simultaneously closed down for thirty seconds, would come in. And he would do it gladly, Professor Wonderful was certain, because he loved magic and gags and because the trick would demonstrate to his subjects the incredible power the people of England could wield if only they would put their heads together for a common cause. Bachnele warned the magician not to even consider going on radio if he wanted to continue working in music hall. The powerful Variety Artistes' Federation had issued a formal resolution for the boycotting of the BBC on the grounds that the broadcasting of variety entertainment established a context and venue for art and amusement that, in alliance with cinema, threatened the survival of music hall as a living art form. Bachnele shook his head. "Why people would want to listen to a box and not see the entertainer, or go to the cinema and not hear the entertainer, when they can see and hear (and if they want, after the show, even touch and smell) entertainers in a variety theater, I'll never know. But that seems to be the trend. The broadcasters and film producers are trying to do to the music hall in London what the Babylonians and the Romans did to the Temple in Jerusalem. All we can do is pray for the coming of a variety Messiah." That night he invited me to join him at his supper club for more bacon. After commenting over our before-dinner drams of Glentos-sel that he thought I had grown since he had last seen me, he criticized my routine: "The costumes and shooting are good, but it's not funny enough. People pay to laugh. Get more jokes. Whatever you do in life is just what it is; but what happens onstage has to be more than what it is. Onstage you shouldn't be doing something, but showing something. That's why we call it a 'show.' And every good show should have lots of jokes. Well, at least that was, if I remember correctly, the opinion of Rabbi Akiba in the Talmud." The midget stopped to signal for more whiskey and continued as it was brought: "The other thing is your climax. It stinks! Cutting a dame in half and getting two of them undermines the whole appeal of the trick which is, as the Bible says, 'in making whole that which has been rent.' The mystery is not reproduction, but resurrection. Speaking of dames, I hear you're shtooping the famous flygirl. Have you done it up in the sky? The closest I've come to that was in a cabin way up on Mt. Baldy with a Canaanite priestess when we were filming *Torah*. She was a big girl, really big, and I love big women, the bigger the better. Elohim, praised be His name forever and ever, blessed me by making me a midget. Big women love holding a little guy in their arms and having him kiss their tsitkehs. I think that as a midget I bring out something maternal in them, something that gives shtooping a benevolent quality. Ola says that little women are nuts about him, that they love to be bounced on his lap and tickled; he thinks that as a giant he brings out something childlike in them, something that gives sex an innocent quality. So the little dames want Ola, and the big ones want me. And there are some, usually of average size, who want both of the Brothers Bigger, and I mean at the same time!" Hesitating as our mixed grills were set before us, Bachnele suddenly looked uncharacteristically forlorn. "I love Ola," he said and then sighed: "You must understand that. But, listen, bubele, I'm going to confide in you, confess something terrible, tell you something I've never told anyone, well, not anyone except Elohim every Yom Kippur, a few other close friends, and a couple of other people when I was drunk. It's my only regret in life. Well, that's not exactly true either. I also regret that I never shtooped Tivya Rabinowitz when I could have. Sometimes I feel it's eating me up. I can't help feeling guilty even though I know that as Jews we are exonerated of all our sins each year and there have been many Yom Kippurs since it happened. It was during the Durbar of Delhi in Chula Vista. Remember? You had some sort of Indian snake act and I was in the automaton. Okay, let me just say it: I shtooped Skadi Namnlösa. Ola doesn't know. He's my best friend in the world. I wouldn't have done it if I would have known that he was going to be my partner someday. But I couldn't help it. She was so beautifully big, I mean really big! When we can't help ourselves, Rabbi Akiba reminds us, we can't help ourselves. We can only pray that Adonai might forgive us." Taking another bite of bacon, he asked if I believed that God would pardon him. When I told him that I couldn't answer because I didn't believe in God, he laughed. "If there's no God, who can I thank for my success and for getting me membership in a club that won't allow Jews to join? Who can I thank for this bacon? Not the waiter, not you, and certainly not myself! That would be arrogant. And also, if there is no God, who can I ask for forgiveness? And if there's no one to ask, how can there be forgiveness? And if there is no forgiveness, the world is evil. And if the world is evil, how can we sing or dance, joke or laugh? And if we can't sing, dance, joke, and laugh, why should we bother to live?"

From 50

70 "Croquet is one of the most civilized of ludic activities," proclaimed Purushottam Deva, the former Tiger Boy who had once squatted to defecate midgame on the croquet court of the government estate in Alipore. Now dressed to kill in white duck trousers, a pink-rose bow tie, and a cardinal-trim V-neck pullover, he approached his blue ball with composure and grace. The hedges bordering the field of play had been pruned into the shapes of animals. It was to play croquet and other games, both outdoors and in, that we had been invited to spend the weekend in the country at Blessingham Manor. There would a morning of shooting (pheasant), an afternoon of fishing (trout), an evening of formal dining (trout in aspic followed by braised pheasant with chestnuts), as well as a hunt breakfast and garden picnic, a high tea and midnight champagne party during which there would be a talent contest. The croquet match pitted Purushottam as captain of the Indian team (the "Sepoys," made up of himself, Frederick of Diwanasthan, and Shree Karnaghee) against the "Colonialists" with Jonathan "Pinkie" Blessingham as the captain in command of Professor Bates and me. The only reason any of us were really there, I surmised, was to provide Puru with the opportunity to see Shulamite Levi, the Sephardic demimondaine of Sonagacchi who had initiated the lad into the mysteries of human love. He couldn't contact her without me and she wouldn't have come without her fiancé. So, to make a party of it ("a reunion of my Calcutta chums," he said, smiling), Puru invited me to invite them and anyone else "who might amuse us." I brought Billie, Maarnath, Kamadhenuka, and, for old times' sake, Karnaghee and Yogi Shamboo Baba, whom I'd see occasionally when we were in London. Karnaghee took the liberty of inviting the son of the late Maharaja of Diwanasthan, Frederick, who had himself once been a student at Oxford. Puru was happy to have Frederick, an accomplished croquet player, on his team. The Sepoys beat the Colonialists in every contest. Their victory in the hunting and fishing was, however, contested by Professor Bates who did not consider it quite cricket that the Sepoys be permitted to count the fish and fowl brought in by Maarnath. The former snake charmer had scattered chopped-up down from a pillow into the stream and then, when the trout rose to the surface of the water for a nibble on what appeared to be insect life, he used the Enfield Hammerless Takedown 16-gauge double-barreled shotgun that he, like each of us, had been issued for the pheasant shoot, to kill the fish. That the buckshot had blown the trout to smithereens was ruled irrelevant; that the bits and pieces of piscatorial flesh retrieved from the stream with a net weighed in at over seventy pounds gave him credit for having caught forty fish. Lured by the pieces of bread from breakfast that Maarnath scattered in the Blessingham woods, the pheasants were unaware that certain choice morsels contained a treble hook attached to fifty yards of fine linen line that led to a level winding reel on the steel casting rod with which Maarnath pulled them in for beheading. His catch of thirty-two pheasants and forty fish exceeded the collective catch of the Colonialists, who had put their hope for game birds in me as a variety sharpshooter. "It's because I do it on the stage," I apologized, "that I've never developed the skill to hit actual targets with a normal gun. I'm not really a marksman. I merely play one. I'm an entertainer." Frederick, who had come in second to Maarnath in fishing and hunting and had been the croquet champion of the day, consoled me: "In that case, you'll no doubt be triumphant at the talent contest tonight." Informing the young man that I had known his father in India, I offered my condolences. The sole surviving son of the late Maharaja of Diwanasthan was a clean-shaven version of his father, younger of course, more portly and more handsome in a simultaneously distinguished and debauched way, with royally sensual lips and the warm complexion of one who spends long hours in Turkish baths. Boldly dressed in dramatic stripes for the croquet match, a habit that would have seemed unfashionable on most men, his sartorial confidence created the impression that all sophisticated fashion-conscious gentlemen would soon be wearing knee-length striped trousers with fleur-de-lis-embroidered stockings for lawn games. His plaid Bond Street sport-and-field cap suggested that Frederick had inherited his father's passion for hats. He did not, however, inherit much more than that. In his last will and testament, the Maharaja had bequeathed nothing to his son except his collection of erotic miniatures and pornographic photographs. "I don't understand!" Frederick had woefully exclaimed to his father's former guru, in response to which Karnaghee (so he revealed to me) explained, "In death your father is trying to tell you not to be a homosexual. If the Maharaja had been able to imagine that you would marry a woman and produce bull-like sons to perpetuate the royal line of Diwanasthan, he would surely have left you not only his other collections, but also his custom Peerless automobile and Diwanasthan Palace." That the Maharaja had bequeathed nothing to his wives was more comprehensible in that he had naturally assumed that, because they had vowed to immolate themselves upon his funeral pyre, they would have no need for worldly possessions. Though the police had prevented the women's collective suicide, they had, despite the protest of Albert Bannerjee, respectfully allowed for the fulfillment of the Maharaja's wish that his stuffed elephant, the magnificent Bill, be cremated with him. The Maharaja had willed everything, the castle and all its contents, to the Diwanasthani people. The only true living citizens in possession of the passport that entitled one to make a claim to that nationality were the palace servants, Krishna the chauffeur, the blind chief of police, the old man who managed the chai and biscuit stall outside the castle, the farmer who tended the loki and cannabis crops, the crone who kept the shrine of Manasa the snake goddess, and Guru Karnaghee. Following the guru's advice, Frederick had hired Menachem Goldman in Calcutta to wage a legal battle on his behalf. The suit was being filed in cooperation with the London lawyers Meier and Mordecai Goldman, twin cousins of the Calcutta Goldman twins. It was their strategy to argue that Diwanasthan Palace, originally Wankton Castle as purchased, disassembled, shipped to India, and reassembled there by the Maharaja, was a British historical monument and that, as such, it must, in accordance with the statutes of international property law, rightfully be disassembled once more, shipped back home to England, and re-erected in Wanktonshire, where it had originally stood. The sale of its contents would provide the Diwanasthani people with a means to meet their decreed obligation to finance the return and reconstruction of the castle. Mordecai Goldman had worked out a deal with Lord Coke-Wankton (son of the dissolute aristocrat who had sold the castle to the Maharaja in the first place) whereby he would have the opportunity to purchase back the monument that was being returned to his property for an undisclosed but mutually agreed upon sum to be matched by the Royal Historical Society of England and Wales. Since Frederick was, as far as British inheritance law was concerned, the Maharaja's rightful heir outside of Diwanasthani jurisdiction, he would get that money minus the legal fees. It was the first time Frederick had met Puru and he liked him enormously. During the entire weekend, though nothing, to my knowledge, illicit transpired, there was ample erotic intrigue in the air: Billie suspected that I might be attracted to the not unattractive Miss Sylvia Woodlands, who had come with her mother as Lady Blessingham's guest; Professor Wonderful was worried that Shula might have an assignation with Purushottam; and Jonathan feared that Puru might harbor an old desire for the Jewess or a new one for Frederick. At the midnight champagne party, Frederick, with the stroke of a saber, opened a bottle of Château d'Amour 1915, a vintage, he noted, "made all the more luscious by the knowledge that the grapes were picked and stamped by prisoners of war." That was, he modestly announced, his most useful talent. Puru and Jonathan, the self-appointed judges of the contest, nodded their approval. Again we were divided into the Sepoys and the Colonialists and again the Indians won. In addition to Frederick, their team consisted of Karnaghee, Shamboo Baba, Maarnath, Kamadhenuka, and Professor Wonderful. Our team was made up of me (I juggled three empty champagne bottles), Shula Levi (who sang *"Tut, Tut, Tootsie, Salut!"*), Lady Blessingham (singing "La rinocerontessa lasciva," a high-spirited aria from Giacomo Algolagnia's opera *La Bestia a Vapore*), her guest, Lady Woodlands (who recited sonnet forty-three from *Sonnets from the Portuguese*), and her daughter Sylvia (who showed us a watercolor of a dead trout that she had painted that afternoon), Professor Bates (who, boasting that he could spontaneously translate into Latin, Greek, and Hebrew any words given to him by our opponents, was challenged by Frederick with "Toot, toot, Tootsie, goo'bye"), and Billie (who folded a piece of paper into an airplane which she made to loop the loop over our heads only to return to the hand that threw it). For the Sepoys, Maarnath, whose only real talent was snake charming, merely bleated Geronimo's war chant from our variety act. Professor Wonderful turned a cane into a bouquet of paper roses and back again into a cane, which might have been astounding if everyone hadn't already seen it so many times that day. Karnaghee's prediction that there would be another world war in 1939 didn't seem impressive at the time, nor was it at all entertaining. When Kamadhenuka, under the influence of many glasses of champagne, removed her blouse to display eight little breasts, it was more embarrassing than amazing to everyone but Maarnath, who cheered with all the exuberance of love. But the Sepoys were triumphant. The champion of their cause was Shamboo Baba. The fakir stole the show, dazzling one and all and winning the contest for his team hands down by using his yogic powers to lift an iron anvil with his penis. As everyone applauded, Karnaghee intoned, *"Om Shree Shivalingaya namah!* Baba has demonstrated what can be accomplished through asceticism and devotion to Lord Shiva." The Hindu holy man turned to the professor of theology with a challenge that encouraged the Sepoys to gloat over their victory: "Can faith in Jesus Christ enable the Christian to do anything miraculous with a penis?"

To 38

| 71 | While sometimes the game seems more complicated than it is, at other times it is more complicated than it seems. The fun of playing, if not the winning, seems to be or is in determining the connections, imaginary or real, between seeming and being. It was |

my roll, and, in fear of the histrionic mayhem that Billie's jealousy, certain to be aroused by the knowledge that I would be seeing a former lover, would sponsor, I wanted to block her from coming with me to Lancashire or, even more disastrously, from surprising me with a visit during the Blackpool-Preston-Lancaster run of our show. I strategized my move. Knowing that she would be there if she suspected that she was not wanted, a beginner would have tried to trick her by nonchalantly asking her to come along or at least visit in a few days. The more advanced a player became, the more nonchalant the asking would be. But Billie's jealousy, I understood, had made her a keenly concentrated and ferociously competitive player, adept at seeing through strategies and staying a move ahead. Since she knew that I was not a beginner, she'd realize that, by saying I wanted her to come along, I was really trying to prevent it; and so she'd know that it was her best move to come. On that level of play, I reasoned, my best move would thus be to, also nonchalantly, say that I didn't want her along; then she'd reason, I reasoned, that by saying I didn't want her along, I was trying to get her to come along and that, therefore, nothing would be gained from the move, that there was no ground for suspicion or jealousy. But, formidable opponent that she was, she would surely know that I knew that she knew that. And so, knowing that, I reconsidered making the beginner's move, but doing so expertly, with such finesse that it would actually be a highly advanced move that just seemed like a beginner's move; I'd nonchalantly ask her to come along or at least visit in a few days. Nonchalance, as all players of the game know so well, is what separates love's duffers from the champions. Acting nonchalant is, however, different than being nonchalant, more difficult in some ways, easier in others; acting nonchalant requires acting that you're not acting nonchalant, and, obviously, acting like your not acting like you're acting that you're not acting that you're acting, and so on and on depending on the level of play. Very nonchalant, the player must remember, furthermore, is less nonchalant than nonchalant. Love, given the complex interplay of skill, luck, and chance, is a tricky game. I figured that, since Billie was so much more expert at its tactics than I, I could increase my odds of winning by turning it entirely over to chance and hoping for a lucky roll. I reasoned that if I just said that I didn't care one way or the other whether she came along or not, the odds became even that she wouldn't. Just as it doesn't matter how much or how hard you shake the dice cup, it wouldn't matter if I said it very nonchalantly, nonchalantly, non-nonchalantly, or even chalantly. I rolled and lucked out. Billie didn't come to Lancaster. When I landed alone on the doorstep of the farmhouse, Pythia greeted me with a hug that was sufficiently affectionate to simultaneously express friendship and belie any suggestion of erotic inclination. She announced that a month earlier she had married a Mr. Sidney Green, whose framed photograph she was proud to show me. Given her beauty, I was startled by her chosen mate's crooked nose, irregular lips, close-set eyes, numerous moles, and the bald pate with hair from the side pulled and pasted unconvincingly over it. "He makes me completely happy in every way," she sighed. Since Mr. Green was at work and would not be home until evening, I would not have the pleasure of meeting him, as I had to be at the theater by six o'clock. And after the show was not feasible, since they retired early so that Mr. Green could rise before dawn rested for the long daily drive to Preston, where he was employed as a curator at the Lancashire County Zoo. "We met at a meeting of the Browning Society," she reported. "I went along to the monthly gathering in order to inform the members that I had been Elizabeth Barrett in a previous life. Assuming that they would be thrilled by a visit from their esteemed poet, I was appalled by their mocking laughter and a rude request from the president that I not attend the next month's gathering, but that I go to a meeting of a Theosophical Society instead. Even though there were far fewer men than women at the meeting, I had not actually noticed Mr. Green as, due to congenital shyness, he's not a very imposing figure in a group of people. That is not the case, I can assure you, in private intercourse with him or when, at work, he is in a group of animals. At any rate, he wrote me a charming note, apologizing most eloquently for the behavior of the Lancashire Browningites, professing his own confidence in my sincerity, integrity, and probity, and inviting me to tea so that he might learn what it had been like to be Elizabeth Barrett Browning. He had so many questions about her and, of course, about Robert. Although good manners prevented him from asking about intimate details, I sensed a curiosity in that area. But our relations remained formal. I saw him occasionally at his mother's home for tea and not infrequently at the zoo. After discovering my interest in animal behavior, he arranged for me to be admitted at a time when the zoo was closed to the public so that I might witness the insemination of Preston's Rhodesian lioness by a Congolese lion brought up from London. Perhaps it was the spectacle of the visiting cat mounting the local puss, biting her neck, his mane shaking from the powerful pounding of his loins, all enhanced by the sound of roar and growl, that made Mr. Green subsequently a bit more bold in courtship. The lions were necessarily separated before the inevitable postcopulatory shift in instinctual drives, wherein sexual desire turns into aggression. Once he had seen to that, he revealed why he had joined the Browning Society; his mother, impatient as she was that he marry, had suggested that a poetry group would be an ideal hunting ground for respectable candidates for matrimony. I advised him to take his time, to enjoy himself with the ladies for a while before restricting himself with domesticity. He despondently confessed that he was already thirty-four years old and that his mother said that there's something unnatural about a bachelor over thirty. Without conscious encouragement or permission, my brain suddenly did the mathematical calculations—Mr. Green had been born in 1889! I was stunned. Don't you see? He, and not Mumtaz the Indian elephant cow as I had previously suspected, had been Robert Browning, born, I learned by asking the date of his birth, not exactly forty-nine days after the poet's death, but close enough. When I explained all of this to him, he did not laugh at me as others might have done, but rather opened his arms and, with a passion previously uncharacteristic of him, cried out, 'Elizabeth, my darling! Together again at last.' I fell into those arms, overjoyed and transported. 'Robert,' I asked, 'how do I love thee?' He urged me to count the ways. And so, with his mother's blessings, we were married last month. It was sad that Daddy was too sick to celebrate." Since she was still obsessed with reincarnation, it seemed appropriate to inform her that Guru Karnaghee, her former adviser in transmigrational matters, was in England. The mere sound of his name transformed her demeanor. "I am sorry to say that I am all too well aware of that unpleasant fact." Pythia glowered to report that Karnaghee had located the McClouds months earlier and contacted them "in order to try to swindle money out of us with his Hindu humbug. Upon discovering Daddy's condition, he promised that he could restore him from the symptoms of the stroke. Hope made me so weak and trusting that I gave him the money that he claimed would magically contribute to the cure. Of course he was as entirely ineffectual in revitalizing my father as he was successful at filling his own purse. He's a scoundrel. If there's any justice in karma, he'll be a rat in his next life." "Since you no longer believe in Karnaghee's prognosticatory powers and omnivoyance," I teasingly asked, "am I to assume that you no longer want me to kill you in Dallas, Texas, in 1963 so that you can become the president of the United States in your next life?" She took the joke seriously: "That is correct. By that time Sidney will have retired. Presumably his mother and my father will sadly have died by then, and we, with our respective inheritances, shall be living happily in a villa in Tuscany, just as we did years ago when we were the Brownings. And there we shall work out our future lives together." Escorted in to see Dr. McCloud, tucked into bed in a room in which all seven portraits of his wife hung on the walls, I was able to talk to, but not with, him, since the most recent stroke had rendered him incapable of voicing comprehensible syllables. But the look in his eyes indicated recognition and slight tears suggested a longing to ask questions. "He can hear everything you say," Pythia said before leaving us alone. I told him the story of the rescue of Lingnath, assuming that, given his affection for the snake charmer, he would take pleasure in it. I believe that he must have laughed within. After informing him of the passing away of the Maharaja, I told him that Professor Wonderful and Shulamite Levi were with me ("and they're in love"), and that Maarnath the snake charmer was also with me, and that he too was in love. It is always a fine thing to learn that people one likes are in love. The doctor made a gurgling sound. I had to get going in order to be at the theater in time to be Buffalo Bill. Seeing Pythia did not, as Billie would surely have suspected had she known of the rendezvous, resurrect any former desires for her. But that night alone in my room in the cold Lancashire lodge after the show, I did imagine and yearn for intimacies with another girl. I could picture her, even though I had never actually seen her. I knew nothing of her. But I was certain that night that she was waiting somewhere up ahead or climbing some ladder from behind. In an opened door the girl's face was framed and it was so stunningly adorned with natural features that it needed no cosmetics to intoxicate the eye: brandy-brown ringlets, absinthe-green eyes, claret-red lips, and cheeks rosé. Her breath was crème de cassis, her smile eau-de-vie, and with a voice of heady mead she asked for my help. Although I knew that what I roll and where I land is merely a matter of chance, and that whoever she was, whatever she rolled, and wherever she landed, was also just chance, the vividness of the vision tempted me to imagine that somehow my chances and hers might conspire to arrange, as sure as the best of luck or fate, for us to meet in some square ahead. In the meantime, however, I couldn't help missing Billie. I wished that I could have made her accompany me or at least surprise me with a visit. I felt that I had played it all wrong. I should have tried to get her to come along by nonchalantly saying that it would be better if she didn't. No, that would have been a beginner's move, not nearly as cunningly effective as falling to my knees, begging her to, please, please, come with me."

72 "More bacon," Bachnele commanded the waiter and then whispered to me, "Let's eat as much chazer as we can just in case they're starting to suspect that I'm a Yid. *Ess, ess gezundheit!*" The midget and the giant had just returned from Paris, where Les Frères Bigger had played a week at the Folies-Bergère. "The French think it's funny when a man farts; the English think it's funny when a man dresses up as a woman. Oi! Only Hebes and schvartzes know what funny really is." I was eager for news of Angel, Kitty Hawk, Dévoué Rabonnir, Devora Rabinowitz, or whatever she called herself these days, the seraphic girl on the high wire that stretched to the past, who in memory, dream, and imagination could still take my breath away. "She's called Cyranie Sirène, a name to make her memorable in her role as a beautiful bare-breasted mermaid in a submarine revue at the Folies. The French love bare tsitskehs. But who doesn't? It's all very artistic. The French love art, too. It's got symphonic music, live fish, and a dramatic story, based on *Romeo and Juliet,* about the mermaid's ill-fated love affair with a sailor played by some French feygele. There are almost as many homos in France as in England! So the mermaid and her lover, whose parents object to their romance, do an underwater ballet with lots of bubbles coming out of their mouths and then they swim into a cave. Without even wondering how they can hold their breath for so long, the audience imagines what the sailor is doing in there with a girl who's a fish from the waist down. The French love bizarre sex acts. Other than the fact that her fingertips are so wrinkled after every performance, she's pleased with the shtick. It's a living. She's happy. She has a little white poodle. She always wanted a poodle." I wanted to know if she knew he had seen me, if she had asked about me, and if she was in love. "Love?" Bachnele blinked, paused to swallow his bacon, and then grinned. "What do I know? She's living with some alter kaker, a man old enough to be her grandfather, the Marquis d'Échelle, a blind man, no less! Not a Jew, but it could be worse: he's rich! *Angeshtopt mit gelt!* The money's inherited, but he's been successful as a playwright too. Are they in love? Is he shtooping her? Or is it like father and daughter? I don't know. They know and God knows. I don't ask. As long as she's happy, I'm happy. And she's smiling these days, my sweet girl, my rose of Sharon and lily of the valley." When, as we finished the second bottle of claret, Bachnele urged me to accompany him to Hastings House, offering to treat me to the happiness that he swore I'd enjoy there, I declined the invitation. "I don't think I could be pleased by a whore. For me, the pleasure of being with a woman relies on believing that she actually desires me, that she thinks I'm handsome, or funny, or sweet, or smart, that she wants me for who I am, not for my money or, in this case, your money." He laughed dismissively. "If you pay enough, and ask for it, the girl will be happy to desire you for who you are. If that's what you really want. Yeah, she'll even love you for who you pretend to be. I've got the perfect girl for you, a blond-haired octoroon from the Caribbean, a real doll, tall, and big tits too. Her name's Mary, just like the queen and the Virgin. She loves Jews. It won't cost very much for her to think you're handsome, funny, sweet, *and* smart. I'll bet she'll even throw 'wise' into the bargain. Don't be a domkop, come with me." A redundant use of the word "whore" in a reiteration of my disinterest offended him. "Whore!" He repeated it several times, first disdainfully, then affectionately, with amusement, then mockingly with shock, fear, and desire, mustering the full arsenal of his dramaturgical skills to bring out every possible semantic nuance of the syllable. And then he laughed again. "Whore? Every time you walk onstage in that ridiculous Buffalo Bill costume, every time Little Bigger sings and dances, we're no different than any nafkeh in garter belts. They're entertainers like us and we're performers like them. They want what we want: to please people, to get paid a little bit for that, and to give people their money's worth. It's show business!" My swearing that Billie was waiting for me, bolstered by an apology and an agreement that I'd go with him some other night to meet Caribbean Mary, was my only way out. He patted my hand affectionately and we rose from the table. "Take this card. It's the address for Hastings House. Tell the doorman you are a friend of the Bigger Brothers, and then say the password and the door will open. The password this month is 'happiness.'" A distinguished older gentleman stopped us by the cloakroom. "Mr. Bigger! What a delightful surprise! I had the pleasure of seeing you last night at the Palladium. As an aficionado of music hall theater, I can assure you that you and your brother are variety artistes of the highest order. Do permit me to congratulate you. I am particularly partial to comedians. It is only humor that makes life bearable, don't you agree? Yes, if not for jokes, life itself would be a joke, wouldn't it? You told some fine ones last night, very droll indeed. You had me laughing most exuberantly, just the tonic I needed at the close of a dreary day. Speaking of jokes and music halls, have you heard the one about the two Jews who decide to take in a variety show? No? Well, they bought the very cheapest tickets, of course, seats way up in the highest balcony. And one of them, pushing and shoving to get a better view of the stage, accidentally fell over the railing and plummeted to his death. After the performance, the other Jew went to the manager of the theater to demand a refund of the money for his friend's ticket, complaining that 'he had, after all, only seen the beginning of the show.'" Much to my surprise, Bachnele bellowed with laughter: "Damn! That's a good one! Can't wait to pass it along!" Thanks to that gentleman I was able to say yes when, two nights later, as I arrived at the Metropole to get ready for our show, a grinning Eddie Burke asked me if I had "heard the one about the two Jews who decided to take in a variety show." As I applied the pancake that would begin to turn my face into that of Buffalo Bill's look-alike illegitimate son, I imagined the face of Caribbean Mary in my mirror; as she brushed rouge onto her cheeks and mascara into her eyelashes, she winked at me. Simultaneously we adjusted our blond wigs. Sitting next to me at the dressing table, applying the bright red, black, and yellow stripes of his Apache war paint, Maarnath complained to me in a rudimentary English that prevented Kamadhenuka from understanding what he was saying, "Please, sir, you are upsetting my darling and making me most sad by hurting her feelings. Never are you looking at her breasts with admiration when she is changing into her costume! And thus she feels that you, who we must please because you have brought us to bountiful Britain for fame and fortune, are not pleased by her especially numerous breasts." Turning to smile at the girl who stood naked from the waist up behind her beloved snake charmer, I told her in my best Bengali that her unusual array of teats was, in my humble opinion, very impressive indeed: "I greatly admire each and every one of them and you for having them." Maarnath was grateful. "See how she is smiling now!" I painted the rubber mountings of Buffalo Bill's mustache and goatee with spirit gum and set them aside to dry while I prepared my chin and upper lip with the same adhesive. After I had placed his hair on my face, while I was pressing and holding it there for a secure bond, Professor Wonderful told me how handsome I looked: "Just like a real thing!" He smiled grandly. "I am the happy man! Everything is a beautiful! First of the all, I shall be performing Amazing Buried Alive illusion and thusly gleaning an attention of His Majesty King George and a world. Second of the all, I shall be converting to a Jew. Best of the all, I shall be a happily wedded husband of the Shulamite Levi, a queen of the Jews and a most supreme beloved of all my times." "Three minutes," Eddie Burke called with a knock on our door. As I rose to put on my Stetson, fringed jacket, and black holster belt, I told Professor Wonderful how happy I was for him on all three counts, and he in turn asked if I had heard the one about the two Jews who went to the variety show. Responding to Burke's final call ("One minute"), I led my players to the wings from where we watched the final antics of George Strong, whose "Honolulu Lulu, the Rula' of the Hula" female impersonation act had replaced Wilkie Wilde's lampoon of *Salomé*. The latter had had some sort of religious experience during his lewd dance with the ventriloquial head of John the cigarette-smoking Baptist that had inspired him to renounce theater as the dominion of Satan. Mr. Strong, a variety veteran, had patronizingly revealed his "philosophy of comedy" to me: "Anything done badly enough is comic, even comedy." The Merry Muses of Middlesex were milling about in scanty togas, ready to go on, waiting for my act to end even before it had begun. "Aloha!" Honolulu Lulu squealed as the curtain came down and Professor Wonderful stuffed Kamadhenuka into her side of the gaffed box for the dénouement of our routine. "My pappy always said he'd rather manage a million Indians than one woman," I'd drawl once the curtain rose. Since Eddie Burke demanded lots of shooting and very few words, I had only forty-five seconds to say howdy, introduce the three of us to the audience, and to get them to accept the preposterous proposition that we were reenacting an actual scene from history. Whether or not they believed a word I said, they did believe that it actually required some skill for me to hit the exploding whiskey bottles with bullets rapid-fired from my Colt Peacemakers. They loved the noise, smoke, and, much to my amazement, the sawing-a-woman-in-half routine. There was a note from Billie waiting for at me after the show. She explained that she would not be meeting me that night as arranged: "I'm flying up to Manchester to look at a new plane." With some difficulty I found a cab. Arriving at my destination, I knocked on the door, announced the name of the friend who had recommended me, and pronounced the magic word: "Happiness."

73 "You shall be circumcised in the flesh of your foreskins," God proclaimed to Abraham, "both he that is born in your house and he that is bought with your money shall be circumcised." The hallowed commandment was repeated to the proselyte, Professor Wonderful, by Abraham Shoymer, an accountant employed by the Hillcastle Oriental Steam Navigation Company and, according Bachnele, who had solicited his services for the event, "the best mohel in England." The magician's bris was performed and celebrated at the Lance and Grail pub on Wimpole Street, a hangout for variety performers. Although rabbinic opinion on the necessity of a minyan for a circumcision may be divided, Bachnele and Shoymer insisted on one to make it yontifdik. And so ten men with fringed prayer shawls draped over their shoulders gathered around the magician's penis: me, Bachnele, Shmuel Grossman, Getsle and David Kopitsky, Abraham Shoymer, Mordecai Goldman, Joseph "the Great Whydini" Lipschitz, and Father John Rose, who, even though he had converted to Christianity and changed his name from Benjamin Rosenberg, qualified as a Jew by maternal lineage, circumcision, and love of a good time. Pinching the tip of the foreskin, Abraham prayed: *"Baruch ata Adonai . . ."* The guests crowded around behind us, jostling for a good view of the organ about to be marked with the Covenant. "What a groisser putz!" Bachnele whispered to me under the loud cantilation of blessings. "We could sell the foreskin as a leather yarmulke and give the money to the poor! Shoymer's only done babies with tiny little petselehs. I hope he knows how to carve such a big salami." Getsle Kopitsky, cast as the sandek, had the responsibility of holding the convert down in the liturgically designated chair of Elijah in case, unable to endure the torture of initiation into Judaism, the Hindu were to try to escape. Cocaine was applied locally and schnapps provided the more general anesthesia both for the initiate and the audience, the sacramental blood of the grape being reserved for postoperative festivities. Professor Wonderful avowed that he was willing to endure any pain for the sake of the pleasure promised by the marriage to Shula that would transpire once he had become a Jew. Because Lipschitz, as a result of his brain injury, couldn't lie, he, winking like crazy, told the truth: "It's going to hurt like hell. You're nuts to do it. You'll be sorry. It might get infected. You could bleed to death." The former Great Whydini would have been thrown out if his presence hadn't completed the minyan. "Don't listen to him," assured Getsle Kopitsky, tightening his grip on Wonderful's arm: "He's just kidding. It's an old Jewish custom to joke like that. It doesn't hurt a bit. There's nothing more wonderful than a bris, my favorite of all Jewish occasions. You're a lucky man!" As Shoymer made the preliminary incision on the dorsum of the prepuce, forming the two flaps of skin that he then folded away from the glans, Professor Wonderful squeezed his eyes closed and held his breath. The vessels under the skin of his neck were swelling. To calm his trembling fingers, Shoymer paused for a dose of schnapps before trimming the folds of profane preputial flesh from the profusely bleeding penis. No sooner had he sliced into the first fold than a scream, no longer humanly repressible, erupted from Professor Wonderful's throat; the magician had, however, through the power of love mustered sufficient strength to modulate the shriek into a deafening "Shuuuuuuuula!" She smiled happily. No sooner had Kopitsky released him than his body fell limp. More cocaine was administered topically and more schnapps internally before Shoymer daubed the mutilated reproductive organ with powdered coral and styptic tannin to stop the hemorrhaging. "I warned you," a winking Lipschitz shouted, only to be hushed so that we could join in prayer to praise and thank the God of our fathers for giving us, as His chosen people, the commandment of circumcision. Professor Wonderful gulped his wine as soon as it had been blessed and held out his cup for more. Shoymer was pleased to announce the former Hindu's new Jewish name: "Pinchas ben Avraham, 'the dark-complexioned son of the father of a mighty nation.'" And everyone cheered: *"L'chayim!"* After Shoymer warned him not to get an erection for at least a week, there were more *l'chayim*'s. Before we could eat the food that Mary the barmaid and Paul the publican had set out on the bar with sworn oaths as to its kosherness, we were required to bear witness to the immersion of Pinchas ben Avraham that would solemnize his adoption into the family of Abraham, Isaac, and Jacob. One of the reasons for choosing the Lance and Grail, in addition to the bargain price that Paul had given Bachnele, was that it had adjoining quarters with a bathtub. Although it wasn't a real mikvah, the Kopitskys, Bachnele, and Shoymer agreed that as long as it had a little rain from heaven mixed in with the London tap water, it would serve the purpose. Naked and shivering, his blood turning the bathwater as red as God once turned the waters of Egypt, Pinchas ben Avraham made a formal announcement of his acceptance of the yoke of the Law: "I am now the Jewish gent from tip to toe and never eating a pork again. Never! Loving my Torah and my Shulamite night, day, and the in-betweens. *Ameyn.* For my Shula I am happily giving up an end of my lingam, the pork, and what have you. *Ameyn.* And a God is thus granting me the Shula. *Ameyn.*" Offering the neophyte bandages for his wounded penis, a kittel for his naked body, and a yarmulke for his dripping-wet head, Shoymer congratulated him. "Every time you look at your pecker, you will think of God and the Covenant. *Mazel tov!* And now let's eat and drink in the hope of the coming of Messiach." As the guests ate and drank, there were many more *l'chayim*'s and *mazel tov*'s. Unable to eat a bite, Billie took me aside. "That was the most disgusting and barbaric act of savagery that I have ever had the misfortune to witness. No wonder so many people have persecuted the Jews. It's the punishment they deserve for doing that to little boys." She wasn't the only one disturbed by the ritual. Mary the pub girl had fainted during the operation. Father Rose rushed to minister unto her, giving her a dose of the cocaine that had been brought to deaden Wonderful's penis. As she came to, he comforted her: "Our Lord Jesus Christ was circumcised," he explained and, pointing to the cheaply framed and printed portraits of the Knights of the Round Table that decorated the walls of the Lance and Grail, he told her that while those famous knights had searched for the Holy Grail, a lesser known servant of God and king, Sir Glansic, had gone alone on a solitary quest for the divine relic known as Praeputium Christi, the Holy Prepuce. A weak Pinchas Wonderful, propped up in the chair of Elijah and drinking as much wine as was poured for him, accepted congratulations. Shula stood beside him, stroking the hair around his yarmulke with affection: *"Il est un homme gentil, tu sais,"* she smiled tenderly, *"vraiment bienveillant."* Eddie Burke agreed to book Serious Sally, "The Girl Who Never Laughs," to substitute for us so that we could attend both Wonderful's bar mitzvah at a little synagogue in Whitechapel a few days later, and his wedding to Shula at the Kopitsky house in Maidenhead a week after that. I was honored to hold one of the poles of the huppah that slanted down toward the corner that was supported by Bachnele. At the side of his beloved, beneath that canopy, Professor Pinchas ben Avraham Wonderful, with tears in his eyes, took the wine with a trembling hand from Abraham Shoymer, sipped it, and then, raising Shula's veil, placed the cup tenderly to her lips. There was another prayer, a responsive recitation from the Song of Songs, the exchange of rings, another cup of wine, and then Shoymer blessed them: "Praised be Thou, O Lord our God, King of the Universe, Who created a groom and a bride, joy and gladness, mirth and merriment, dancing and delight, love and friendship." After the wineglass had been wrapped in a white cloth and set on the floor, the groom, pausing before crushing it with his heel, said, "This is to remember the sadness during the time of a joy." The sound of breaking glass was the signal to exclaim *"Mazel tov!"* and fill every goblet to the brim. The bride and groom kissed, laughed, cried, kissed again, and then danced to the klezmer melodies of Shecky Shikker and his Shikyingels: "Oh I'm falling, I'm falling, yeah, fa-fa-falling in love. It's appalling but enthralling that I'm falling, falling in love vid you. La-laa-la, la-laa-la, ei! ei! ei!, falling in love vid youuuu!" Shula danced as she had not done since the Ananga Ranga Club days, turning gracefully for her beloved, who, because he could not dance so well himself, subsequently performed magic in her honor. Wrapping the pieces of the wineglass that had been ceremonially broken in a white napkin, he whispered magic words ("I am my beloved's and my beloved is the mine") and then, unwrapping the napkin, he displayed the goblet restored and full to the brim with red wine. He offered it to Shula and she drank. Taking a bow to her, he made a proclamation: "A Judaism is my religion, but my faith is the love, and my only God is the Shula. If the Adonai is seeing her, He will understand the everything." Everyone danced, each man taking a turn with the bride, and each woman a round with the groom. Bachnele, who had danced with every girl and woman at the party with his head nestled into their laps, teased Professor Wonderful by swearing to God that he had received a telegram that afternoon from King George, whom he had personally invited to the event, offering royal congratulations to Mr. and Mrs. Wonderful and extending apologetic regrets that he and Queen Mary would not, because of urgently pressing diplomatic obligations, be able to attend the wedding. "He's also very sorry they couldn't make the bar mitzvah and especially the bris." I believed the magician believed it: extremes of joy, no less than extremes of sorrow, encourage us to believe unbelievable things. Shecky Shikker sang the last song of the evening: *"Toot, toot, Tootsie, geh vek, toot, toot, Tootsie, schrei nikt!"* As I bade the wedding couple good night, the magician, embracing me warmly, whispered in my ear: "I am the happiest person in a world." In less time than it had taken the Hebrew slaves redeemed from Egypt to make their way to Mt. Sinai and receive the Law, the Hindu from Bengal had lived an entire Jewish life: he had been circumcised, become a son of the commandments, and celebrated the covenant of marriage. And a few months later, just prior to the first occurrence of the Days of Awe since his conversion, I was heartbroken to be called to the oldest Jewish cemetery in England to help bear the pall and recite kaddish for Professor Pinchas ben Avraham Wonderful.

74 "Buried Alive Magician Dug Up Dead" was the small headline of the small article in the *Telegraph:* "Mr. Pinchas Wonderful, a magician from Calcutta, India, was discovered dead yesterday upon being disinterred from a grave which he himself dug in Hyde Park a week ago for the performance of the Indian Buried Alive illusion made famous as a religious feat in the Orient by fakirs. Expecting to see the entertainer emerge from his grave alive, many spectators were disappointed. A spokesman for the City of London Ministry of Parks and Gardens denied that, by issuing the magician a permit to perform the illusion in the park, they bore any responsibility for the unfortunate accident. 'The mishap should serve as a warning about the dangers of magic,' the spokesman noted. 'There have been thirteen reported deaths so far this year from magic gone awry.' Memorial services for Mr. Wonderful will be held tomorrow at the Hashkaba Cemetery in Whitechapel." The news item appeared beneath the announcement of another death: "The British expedition for the conquest of Mt. Everest has been terminated, according to its leader, General Bruce. All hopes for the survival of George Mallory and Andrew Irvine, who disappeared in a blizzard on the North Col last week, have been abandoned. In a joint statement, the Royal Geographical Society and the Alpine Club of Great Britain have announced that since no bodies have been recovered it is impossible to determine whether or not Mallory and Irvine reached the summit of the world's highest mountain." With no less dedication than the Himalayan climbers, Professor Wonderful had invested all the money that he and Shula had saved into preparations for the illusion. He had paid dearly for an advertisement that appeared in the *Telegraph* two weeks prior to that newspaper's announcement of his death: "At noon on Sunday, the world-famous Indian magician the great Professor Wonderful will be Buried Alive in Hyde Park near the carousel by the Serpentine. Using the mystic powers of Yoga to give his mind mastery over his matter, the incredible Oriental Illusionist will amazingly retard his respiratory, digestive, circulatory, reproductive, excretory, and other bodily processes to such a degree that he will remain alive, without air, food or anything else, for an entire week. The public, including all esteemed members of the medical, legal, religious, and academic professions, are invited to behold and be inspired by both the breathtaking burial and, one week later at the same locale, the vivacious disinterment. This thrilling miracle, never before witnessed outside the confines of the Mystic East, is being performed free of a charge as a royal salute from a humble representative of Colonial India to Their Imperial Majesties,

King George and Queen Mary." It had been Wonderful's dream that the event would draw sufficient press coverage to attract the attention of the variety-loving royal highnesses, who, he imagined, would then invite him to perform at the upcoming Royal Command Variety and Music Hall Gala Performance at Victoria Palace. Just as Bachnele had lied to Wonderful about the monarch's telegram expressing his regrets about not being able to attend his circumcision, bar mitzvah, and wedding, so too he told Shula that the king and queen had sent their condolences and humbly apologized for not being able to take time out from diplomatic obligations to attend the funeral. Shula wasn't at the cemetery anyway, since it is the custom of Jewish women in North Africa not to attend the burial of a husband. She had, however, anointed the eyelids of the deceased with ashes at the Ekvelt Funeral Home. There she had bid her *"Adieu, mon amour"* to the remains of Professor Wonderful as they were loaded onto the Minerva hearse hired by Jonathan Blessingham at the request of Purushottam Deva. His shroud was the kittel, given to him by Shula, that he had worn at his conversion. Draped over the corpse was a tattered old Lithuanian tallith that had been donated by Bachnele Poopik, who sighed: "It's too big for me anyway." He shook his head. "Oi, oi! Death is a pain in the tooches! Just when you think you're having fun, the Angel of Death rudely interrupts everything and ruins the game." It seemed appropriate that half of the pallbearers were Hindus (Maarnath, Puru, Shamboo, and Karnaghee) and the other half of the team was Jewish (me, Bachnele, Lipschitz, and Getsle Kopitsky, who, after it was over, made a remark that would have seemed like a joke if it hadn't been muttered so woefully: "It was a lot easier to hold him down at his funeral than it was at his bris"). As we bore the coffin, the very box that Professor Wonderful had designed for his Buried Alive illusion, toward the plot, we made the customary seven stops corresponding to the vanities enumerated by Ecclesiastes. "Vanity of vanities, all is vanity," Getsle said at each pausing place: "He who digs a pit falls into it; and a serpent will bite him who breaks through a wall. If the serpent bites before it is charmed, there is no advantage in a charmer." We were followed by a somber cortege of mourners: Eddie Burke, Ola Namnlösa, George Strong, Mimi Nevis, the Muse Erato, Serious Sally, Frederick of Diwanasthan, and Kamadhenuka. Explaining that she didn't "care much for funerals," Billie did not come with me, but offered to fly me at sunset over the cemetery so that I might scatter rose petals from the heavens onto his last resting place as a final homage. Because Shula had asked me so plaintively to deliver the eulogy, I complied as sincerely as I could. "This is the third time I have seen this dear man buried, the second being no more than two weeks ago in Hyde Park, and the first being several years ago in Calcutta. On the prior two occasions, I knew that I would see him again, that the burial was just entertainment, that the magician was offering us a comforting illusion of death being defied. Although sorrow tempts me to give up hope of ever seeing him again after this day, joy, all the delight that was ever broadcast by his irrepressible smile, promises that I will, in fact, see him again. Yes, again and again in memories and the dreams that memory composes. They will take me to this sweet man who yearned with all his heart to enthrall people with the pleasures of a wonder that is the only solace in moments like this. Memory magically grants me a vision: dressed formally in tails and top hat, smiling radiantly, he holds up two gleaming rings, one gold and one silver, before our eyes. 'This is the man,' he says of the one, 'and this is the woman,' he says of the other. Slowly and tenderly he rubs them together, and lightly, with lips puckered as if to kiss, he blows upon them. All at once, to everyone's amazement, the rings are interlinked. Professor Wonderful gazes at the inseparable rings with wonder as if he himself is dazzled by some divine magic that has chosen and blessed him as its outlet into the world. As he hands the joined rings out to be examined, he smiles: 'This is the eternal love.' In paying homage to a man who truly believed in the eternity of love, I cannot do disservice to his memory by doubting that there is such a thing as eternity and that it is not established by the magical power of love." One by one we took turns with the shovel to cover the coffin with earth. *"Yitgadal ve-yitkadash shemay rabba,"* we solemnly recited, in memory of Professor Pinchas ben Avraham Wonderful, in the liturgical unison that is meant to alleviate sorrow no less than it enhances joy at other celebrations: "Glorified and sanctified be the great name of God in the world which He will create anew, and in which the dead will be revived and ushered into everlasting life." Not having been at my father's funeral, I was saying it for him as much as for Wonderful, and for all the dead, who, according to my father, will crawl underground to the Holy Land to be resurrected when the Messiah arrives. I said it for George Washington and Lucy too that day, for I had recently received a letter from my mother reporting that the unfortunate actor had so strongly identified with Othello, the black ram, that he had, in a fit of jealousy, shot his beloved white ewe, Desdemona. Immediately afterwards, putting the hot barrel of the revolver in his mouth, he had blown out his brains to end the intractable misery of love. In the same letter my mother informed me that she had married Hayim Grossman: "Your father was the love of my life. Hayim allows me to continue to feel and give expression to the love that your father taught me was the reason to be and stay alive. Remember to light the Yahrzeit candle for him next month. Don't forget to remember him." More than the sight of the flickering flame of the memorial candle, the smell of Wyoming Willie's Wondrous Hair Pomade made his memory a blessing. While the flame evoked a vision of the fire that had consumed him, the perfume of the brilliantine was his abiding spirit, kept in the tin like a genie in a bottle, ever ready to grant wishes. I missed my father and in doing so remembered once asking him about his own father: "Do you miss him?" He answered with a smile that confessed to no sadness. "I'm a marksman, son, a sharpshooter. And a good marksman never misses anything." "I missed you today," I told Billie as I strapped myself into the seat next to her in the Junkers F-13. Giving her one of the white roses from the offertory bouquet, I told her that, as I watched the coffin disappear beneath shovel after shovelful of earth, I had yearned to keep her warm with my body as she kept me warm with hers, "warm and alive for and because of each other." The funeral had put me in a sentimental mood. Rising from the runway, the plane veered toward the setting sun. "If we could fly a thousand miles per hour," Billie shouted over the roar of the accelerated motor, "we could keep up with the sun. If we had enough fuel, the sunset would last forever. We'd fly in eternity. That's what I want." Tearing the petals from the roses, I made a pile of them in my lap with hopes that by luck or chance a few might not miss the grave of Professor Wonderful. I readied myself to scatter them as Billie, pointing to the cemetery, banked away from the half-set sun toward the dark field of death. I pulled the window open wide enough for my hand to fit through it. "Now," Billie shouted with the certitude of a fighter pilot carrying bombs over an enemy encampment. I released the rose petals. Billie raised the nose up into a sky that in darkening seemed to be stripping off a drape of light to tease us with its stars. Later, as I held Billie in my arms, with closed eyes I could see white petals floating slowly down through the darkness to settle like snow upon a grave. If someone were to behold it, they would surely be amazed by what would seem a miracle, if not a wonderful trick performed by a dead magician.

	"Disappearing Act!" was the medium-sized headline of the
75	medium-sized article in the *Telegraph:* "The body of Mr. Pinchas Wonderful, a magician from Calcutta, India, was discovered missing yesterday from the grave in which it was buried last week in a

Jewish cemetery in Whitechapel. The corpse was being disinterred following the reading of the deceased's last will and testament in which it was indicated that the late magician had wished to be cremated and to have his ashes returned to India for scattering in the Ganges in accordance with Hindu law. Inspector Milton Trout of Scotland Yard's Bureau of Missing Persons announced today that, in an effort to recover the missing dead person, an alert has been sent to medical schools to which the cadaver might be or already have been offered for sale. 'Body snatching,' Inspector Trout noted, 'is a serious crime in this country.'" I could not help but notice the familiar name in another article on the same page, a follow-up story to the report on the ill-fated assault on Mt. Everest: "Major L. A. Wheedle, explorer, cryptozoologist, mesmerist, director of the Pan-American Institute for the Scientific Investigation of the Incredible, and a renowned expert on the elusive Yeti, popularly known in Britain as the 'Abominable Snowman,' revived some hope today for the recovery of Mallory and Irvine. 'I would not be surprised if they were to return alive,' the major announced at a press conference in Sikkim. 'Tibetan lore abounds in accounts of half-frozen Sherpas being found by Yetis who make their homes in caves in the highest and most inaccessible of Himalayan peaks. The hirsute giants have been known to take imperiled humans to their lairs and revive them there with rich Yeti milk while keeping them warm by nestling with them. To my long sustained hope of finding a Yeti, I now add a more urgent hope that a Yeti has found the valiant climbers lost on Everest.'" I was in the midst of reading the article when a knock on the door of my room at the Merry Medusa roused me from bed. As I was expecting Billie, I was startled to see a small man in a big coat, with a small hat on his big head, small eyes on either side of a big nose, and a small mouth that revealed big teeth when he introduced himself as Inspector Trout of Scotland Yard. "Do I have the pleasure of addressing a Mr. Isaac Schlossberg, formerly resident in Calcutta, India? Yes? Would you mind terribly if I came in? Thank you, sir. I do hope you will be able to help clarify a few things. Is my information correct that you were a personal acquaintance of the late Mr. Pinchas Wonderful, a Hindu magician and convert to Judaism whose body is currently missing from its grave, and that you did graciously help to bear the pall at his funeral. Yes? Very good. I have, sir, in my possession, retrieved from Scotland Yard files, a curious letter written some time ago in India, signed with your name and addressed to a Mr. Menachem Goldman, Esq., a lawyer in Calcutta. Permit me to read it aloud. 'I am guilty: I stole the brain of the Jewish criminal and snatched the body of the Hindu snake charmer.' Now, I must ask you, sir, what are we to make of this? I am quite certain that you can explain the relationship between the two missing Hindu cadavers. Coincidences always intrigue me. It would be terribly helpful if you could do so in person at Scotland Yard. Please, sir, do feel free to dress before we leave." Without taking his eyes off me, he backed up to the door and opened it, and three uniformed policemen entered. "It's a bit chilly out today, sir. I would suggest that you wear something warm." After I had put on Buffalo Bill's fringed leather jacket, I was, despite my alarmed protests, handcuffed. "It's just a precaution, sir. Nothing to worry about. I'm certain we'll have everything cleared up in no time." I was taken to the Uxbridge jail, where, after being relieved of the contents of my pockets and of my belt in case I should try to hang myself, I was confined to a holding cell furnished with a metal bench, a toilet, and a framed photograph of King George. After several hours there, I was photographed, fingerprinted, and escorted into an interrogation questioning room. "You could expedite matters substantially, sir," Inspector Trout said, "and avoid further inconvenience by simply informing us of the location of the body of Mr. Wonderful." I pleaded my innocence. Billie had come to the Merry Medusa for me as expected, and, upon learning from the desk clerk that I had been taken to jail, had followed to post bail for my release. It was, however, to no avail, since, given the bizarre nature of my crime, I had been placed under psychiatric observation. She had immediately solicited the legal services of Mordecai Goldman, whom she had met at the missing corpse's circumcision. When he appeared in my cell the next day, I told him the full story of the redemption of Lingnath the snake charmer, and explained that I had written the incriminating letter to his cousin in order to protect my collaborators from prosecution and to abort any suspicion that Lingnath might be alive. The lawyer shook his head grimly. "I would suggest that you tell the truth about India. I shall then argue that all evidence that you stole the body of Professor Wonderful is circumstantial. I'm confident that if you do as I advise, you will be free by Yom Kippur, unless, of course, they find the magician's body and some evidence to link you to it. If they can prove that you did do it, we can enter a plea of insanity. There won't any jail time, just a spell in a psychiatric institution. It won't be so bad. It's not like the old Bedlam these days." But a confession of what had happened in India could mean that Lingnath would be sought by police in Calcutta, rearrested, and sent back to prison for murder. As I wasn't used to having moral dilemmas, I needed to think about what to do. In the meantime Goldman was at least able to convince the examining psychiatrist to grant permission for Billie to see me. "Oh, Isaac, it's hard to believe you'd do such a strange thing," she said sighing. "I didn't do it!" I insisted, and she assured me that she believed me in the same way, with the same tone of voice, as she had said she believed me when I told her for the first time that I loved her. I didn't know whether to believe her or not. She had brought a copy of the *Telegraph* in which there was a story about me: "Mr. Isaac Schlossberg, a Jewish variety cowboy from America, is being held at Uxbridge jail on suspicion of stealing the body of Mr. Pinchas Wonderful, a Hindu magician from Calcutta, India, from a Jewish cemetery. Mr. Schlossberg, who spent several years in India with Hindu fakirs and snake charmers, confessed to grave robbing and stealing human brains in Calcutta." The story of my imprisonment was next to an item about someone luckier than I: "Mr. Adolf Hitler, a prominent representative of Germany's National Socialist Labour Party, was released from prison in Bavaria today for good behavior after serving two of the five years of his sentence. A prison spokesman noted that Mr. Hitler was an exemplary prisoner: 'disciplined, neat in his habits, cooperative, modest, and always courteous to prison guards.'" The next day, my fourth in jail, Shmuel Grossman, now my stepuncle, visited to disclose in whispers that he was working on a plan for my escape: "First we'll get you transferred to the psychiatric hospital. It will be easy to sneak you out of there." Once that was accomplished he would take me with him to the Soviet Union, where, safe from fascist, capitalist, and colonialist despots, I could be truly free. "My friend Trotsky can arrange for you to do your Buffalo Bill routine for the Central Committee." "But Shmuel," I insisted once more, "I didn't do it." His eyes were on fire. "Of course you didn't. Anti-Semites took the body. The desecration of our graveyards was common in the Pale of Settlement, and we'd be accused of their crimes. They'd say we were making golems. Remember what happened to me in Florida! Ten years in prison for being a Jew! The Jew is never innocent in a capitalist society." The next day, my fifth in confinement, Inspector Trout appeared in my cell. "Good afternoon, Mr. Schlossberg, you are quite free to leave whenever you wish. I do hope your incarceration has not been too terribly inconvenient." He handed me a copy of the morning *Telegraph* open to its latest story about Professor Wonderful. "Magician Resurrected!" was the large headline of the large article. "Professor Pinchas Wonderful, a magician from Calcutta, India, amazed the audience at the Alhambra Theatre last night and established a place for himself among variety immortals by returning from the dead." I soon learned that my former spot on the program, right before Mnemosyne and Her Muses, Shula, billing herself as Shuladevi, Nautch Girl of Hindustan, had danced to the strains of the sitar onto the stage upon which there was a coffin on display beneath a projected lantern slide of a smiling Professor Wonderful standing in that same coffin in Hyde Park. As the slides changed to illustrate the story for those who might not have read about it in the *Telegraph,* Eddie Burke narrated: "The great magician, performing the famous Indian Buried Alive illusion, was, according to plan, inhumed near the Serpentine in Hyde Park. Next slide, please. Something went wrong. A terrible accident! Upon being disinterred, the magician was discovered to be dead. Next slide. Funeral rites were performed and Professor Wonderful was reburied in a cemetery in Whitechapel. Next. The subsequent reading of his will revealed that he had wished to be cremated so that his ashes could be scattered in the sacred waters of the Ganges in India. Next. Upon being exhumed for that purpose, his body was found missing." At that point Shula opened the coffin, the very box that I had helped carry at the magician's funeral, to show that it was empty, and then she turned it in a circle to dispel any suspicion of trapdoors. "In Hindustan," Burke announced, "they believe that the dead can be brought back to life through the magic power of love. We shall test that tonight!" As the coffin was closed, the music surged and Shula sang: "I am dying from the pain of separation and only you can save me. Return to me, my beloved, before it is too late." Her French accent made it exotic. When Shula suddenly opened the coffin, out popped a happily waving and bowing Professor Wonderful, resurrected by the power of love. Everyone cheered. Shula then took his place in the coffin and, after the cover was closed and immediately reopened, she appeared to have disappeared. "I must bring my beloved back from a death as she did for me," the magician proclaimed. Climbing into the coffin after her, he disappeared once more. But then, almost instantaneously, Shuladevi and Professor Wonderful, now dressed as bride and groom, marched down the aisle from the back of the theater to the stage to the sound of Mendelssohn's Wedding March. The audience stood to applaud magic and love. The next day, Professor Wonderful received an invitation from Buckingham Palace to perform at the Christmas Royal Command Variety Performance at the Palladium.

To 11

76

"Mr. Adolf Hitler, released from prison in Bavaria on Monday, announced, in an interview in *Der Stürmer,* that he plans to rebuild the Nazi Party," the article in the *Telegraph* explained. "Questioned about the origins of his political ideas, Mr. Hitler recalled a school excursion from his hometown of Linz to Vienna to see Buffalo Bill's Wild West show in 1899. 'As the orchestra played the overture to *Parzival,* Colonel Cody galloped into the stadium in complete control of his white stallion, so magnificent with its long flowing mane. The colonel's blond hair fluttered in the breeze and the gold buttons on his uniform gleamed gloriously. Buffalo Bill's masterful demonstrations of both marksmanship and horsemanship were, for me as an impressionable ten-year-old, a revelation of the true and perfect manhood to which I aspired. While the other boys were merely entertained by a showman, I was profoundly inspired by a man of mythic might.'" I was in the midst of reading the article when a knock on the door of my room at the Merry Medusa roused me from bed. As I was expecting Billie, I was startled to see a stranger's face. The natural features needed no cosmetics to intoxicate the eye of any man: brandy-brown ringlets, absinthe-green eyes, claret-red lips, and cheeks rosé. Her breath was crème de cassis, her smile eau-de-vie, and her voice was mead. "My name is Eve Kopitsky, Getsle Kopitsky's youngest daughter. I saw you at the wedding of that Jewish Hindu magician at our house. My father said you're an entertainer, so I hope you can help me. I want to be a stage actress like Sarah Bernhardt. When I was ten years old, Papa took me to see her at the Palladium on her Farewell Tour. She was a Jew too. I could act in motion pictures if my voice isn't sweet enough for the stage, or on the wireless if I'm not pretty enough. I want to make people cry and laugh. I really can act. Listen. 'Give me my Romeo: and when he shall die, take him and cut him out in little stars and he will make the face of heaven so fine that all the world will be in love with night and . . .'" In fear that Billie might suddenly arrive and make a scene over the discovery of the spirituous girl reciting lush poetry in my doorway, I stopped her. "You're a great actress. And yes, I want to help you. But right now I'm terribly busy. Meet me tomorrow, no, not tomorrow, day after tomorrow at noon, no, not noon, at three o'clock at Piccadilly Circus, yes, by the statue of Eros. Okay?" As thrilled as if she really had her foot in the door to British theater, she sighed that parting was such sweet sorrow, that she'd say good-bye till it be the day after tomorrow. On the condition that she didn't have to go to the theater, Billie had agreed to fly me to Oxford to find Professor Wonderful, who was performing magic in Eddie Burke's variety revue at the

New London Theatre. Remembering me as Buffalo Bill's illegitimate son, a janitor admitted me into the theater through the back entrance. I made my way straight to the door of the dressing room that had once been mine and, without knocking, threw it open, much to the surprise of both the magician, who was grandly smiling at himself in the mirror, and the magician's assistant, who was rolling a net stocking up a leg extended into the air. *"Isaac, mon chéri! Quel plaisir!"* Shula exclaimed as, without the slightest dent in his smile, Professor Wonderful turned to greet me as if ignorant of the suffering he had caused me. "I am a highly happy and honored by your presence for a great tonight. Shalom! Namaskar! Bonjour! You shall witness a Zig-Zag Lady, Disappearing Maharani, Sawing-Nautch-Girl-in-Half, and what have you with the Oriental flair, performed in your behalf." I interrupted. "I want to kill you. I hesitate only because, after spending five days in jail because of you, I know that prison does not suit me. But at least wishing to see you dead and buried for the last time is, I'm happy to say, not a crime." Seemingly stunned that I was even the slightest bit upset by my incarceration, not to mention the fact that he had usurped my place in the show, the magician told me to "kindly calm your down." In an effort to rescue her husband, Shula, insisting that he had meant me no harm, supplicated my forgiveness: *"Sois un petit peu bienveillant, mon chéri."* Professor Wonderful added, "I do not know what my blessed wife is uttering for I have not yet learned a fluent French, but I agree one hundred and one percent if not more." He hesitated before whispering, "Please, we are the friends. Forgive. It was the show business! I am forgiving in the India when you forget to dig me up. Please. For a friendship. " Since I couldn't kill him, I figured I could try to forgive him a little bit and still hate him a lot. Shula informed me that Kamadhenuka and Maarnath were in Oxford, and that she was working the St. Giles Fair as a medical curiosity. Maarnath was her agent and manager. I left the magician and his wife without confessing to any forgiveness. As I pushed through the crowd in St. Giles in search of my snakeless snake charmer, a banner caught my eye: "Lazarus Lycophron, Automatic Anagrammatician." A girl in a toga was making the pitch, promising that if you told Lycophron your name he would reveal all the anagrams it contained in less than a minute. The game was that you had to pay him a penny per anagram. Figuring that it wouldn't cost me more than a shilling, I stepped up and as soon as I said "Isaac Schlossberg," she punched the clock: "A hog's scarce bliss," he, closing his eyes, began automatically and seemingly unthinkingly: "So crass, I belch gas. Carcass: big loss, eh? Go basic: crash less. I bless cargo's cash. Gas is a cross belch. So glib, caress cash. Basic ogress-clash. Bliss: a gross cache." With each anagram his assistant dropped a slug into a metal bowl: "Chisel a gross scab. I bless hog-carcass. Gosh, a scarce bliss. Search basic gloss." Only fifteen seconds into the minute and slugs were already threatening to fill the bowl: "Access or big slash. Ah, be classic gross. Bless his cargo sac. Choice: brass? glass? Chose gas-car bliss. Classic ogress: bah! Brag: he's so classic." I was still thinking about the hog's scarce bliss and he was speeding up, firing anagrams faster than I could figure out what they meant or remember if he was repeating himself: "Gross: slice Casbah. I scorch glass base. Loss? search big sac. Obsess: garlic? cash? Oh, caress big class. Orchis-abscess, gal? Slosh! I grab access. So, bless cigar cash. Sleigh across scab." By the end of the sixty seconds I owed him almost three pounds and paid it, although I felt it was cheating to count "Gosh, a scribe-class" and "Gosh, ascribe class" as two. But it's a pleasure for one raised in carny to be bilked by a talented con. I asked the assistant if she knew where I could find the girl with eight breasts. "Such a lovely girl," she said, "and a very popular attraction, quite the little star. I can tell you, those titties are the real thing. King George's personal physician came 'imself to examine 'er and could 'ardly believe 'is eyes. They got a tent down past the Mt. Everest 'Elter-Skelter, next to Mamoo the Amazin' Oriental Snake Boy. She's from India. They got a lot of amazin' things over there, you know." Before going to Kamadhenuka's tent I had to see Mamoo. As his keeper, wearing what was supposed to be some sort of Indian royal robe and a pink silk turban that clashed with his red beard and freckled Irish face, poked the python's body with a cane, the boy flicked his tongue, rolled his eyes, drew back his lips to show his fangs, and hissed. A young man next to me demanded his money back: "This is the most stupid, inane, transparent, and pointless illusion that I've ever seen. It would be obvious to an idiot that there's a hole in the table out of which that terrible little actor has stuck his face and into which that snake's head has been crammed. How dare you charge us for such a pathetic display." Nonchalantly tossing the heckler a coin, the showman eyed him as he left so that he'd be sure to recognize him if he ever ran into him on the street. If that happened he'd probably beat the man up and get his money back with interest. Kamadhenuka was being shown by a man calling himself Dr. Morgagni who wore a round throat mirror on a band across his forehead, a stethoscope around his neck, and rubber gloves on his hands. After ten or so customers, all men over the age of eighteen, had been lured into the tent with me among them, he introduced the girl as "one of the most curious specimens of womanhood ever beheld by man." With all the bravado of Sarah Bernhardt making an entrance onto the stage at the Palladium, a beaming Kamadhenuka emerged from behind the soiled canvas curtain at the back of the tent wearing a salwar kameez that concealed what the rubes had paid to see. "A single pair of mammary glands," the doctor began, "the usual number in man and ape, is the least number normally found in any mammal. The largest number of breasts is found in certain insectivora, in whom there are as many as thirty pairs." After dragging out the spiel to intensify curiosity, he finally, while maintaining a clinical tone, asked Kamadhenuka to remove her blouse. As she did so, the nipples in her otherwise normal armpits were momentarily revealed. The other six nipples, however, remained concealed by the three brassieres that she was demurely wearing. "While supernumerary mammae are found in all races, they are more common in the darker women of the Orient," he continued, giving social significance to anatomy. Suddenly noticing me, Kamadhenuka's proud smile became even more enthusiastic. Once her audience of inspectors (trying to keep their disappointment over not seeing more nipples to themselves so that their curiosity would seem more scientific than prurient) had dispersed, I went around to the back of the tent where Kamadhenuka greeted me first with a proper Indian anjali and then with an uncontainably sloppy European hug. "Breasts growing," she said in English. "Baby coming!" I asked the doctor, who was changing into farmer's overalls to display his five-legged pig, where Maarnath was. "Drinking, no doubt. But stick around, he'll run out of money and be back to get some from his wife." While I waited for the snake charmer, Kamadhenuka reverted to Bengali to tell me that they had heard from Maarnath's wife in India and that she was proud of his success as an American Indian on the British stage. The inebriated snake charmer finally appeared and, overjoyed to find me in the tent, threw his arms around me. He proclaimed that he had been confident that I would be released from the prison, where Wonderful had told him I was incarcerated, because he had prayed to Lord Shiva to that end and even fasted for an entire day to ensure the granting of that boon. He told me that he loved me so much that, if their baby was a boy, he would name him after me. Touched by his affection, I replied, "I hope your little Isaac will grow up to be healthy and happy and live a long life." "No, no," Maarnath frowned. "Not Isaac. He will be called Buffalo Bill Junior, since you will always be Buffalo Bill to us!"

77

"I'm sick of Buffalo Bill," I told Eddie Burke. "Me too," he said, "but for British audiences Buffalo Bill's Wild West show *is* America, and I need something American. So if you want to work for me again, think up a new routine for the old scout, something with a sexy girl and lots of shooting in it." And so I got dressed to kill in a blond wig and goatee, fringed buckskins, a black Stetson, and thigh-high Sears & Roebuck boots. Simultaneously fast-drawing both of his Colt .45-caliber six-guns pistols, Buffalo Bill fired—*Ka-bamm! Ka-bamm!*—and the two whiskey bottles on the bar were blown to smithereens. "That ain't nothin', Bill," said Jessica James. "Watch this!" The Dakota desperada, gunslinging outlawess, stagecoach robberette, who was enough wild woman to strike terror and lust, if not awe and adoration, into the heart of any cowpoke on the range, was played by Eve Kopitsky. Her chamois skirt was cut high enough to show off her fancy-top Lone Star red leather boots with their silver spurs. A heart was embroidered on her holster. The Wild West routine began with Jessica leaning on the bar of the Badlands Saloon, drinking shots of bourbon whiskey. "Howdy, folks," I'd say, "I'm mighty happy to be over here in England to show you good people some American-style shootin'." And then I'd tell them the tale of Jessica James: "When Buffalo Bill warned her to stay away from the Badlands Bank and get out of town before sundown, Miss Jessie just laughed in his face, sayin' she didn't have to listen to any man 'cause she could shoot better than any gunslinger, outlaw, or lawman in the West." Because we were only allotted five minutes for the entire routine, I had to keep the story short to get us to the shooting contest as quickly as possible without compromising the evocation of the Wild West mood. Eddie Burke had warned, "Three hundred seconds, not three hundred and one. And remember, more bullets than words. I want to hear guns, not mouths, going off." After Jessica James drew her Peacemaker and shot one, two, three bottles off the bar, an undaunted Colonel Cody took three bottles himself and juggled them, and in the midst of a cascade, one was tossed out and up to be blown to bits. And then another, then the third, and the muzzle of my .45 was smoking. Jessica turned her back on the four bottles on the bar across the stage, drew her pistol with one hand and held up a mirror with the other. No sooner had the crack shot blown the four bottles away than she demurely powdered her nose in the mirror. One minute to go and not a second to lose: removing his Stetson, Buffalo Bill, after tying a black silk blindfold over his eyes, asked Jessica to make sure he couldn't see a thing. A lone whiskey bottle stood on the bar. It would have been impressive enough if the great American would have simply hit it, but that wouldn't have been show business. Fast-drawing both six-guns at the same time, he emptied them with rapid fire and all twelve of the bottles on the shelf behind the bar exploded. "Well, folks, Buffalo Bill's won," Jessica conceded as she poured us each a drink from the lone bottle on the bar and raised her shot glass in a toast: "Here's to Colonel Buffalo Bill Cody, the fastest, slickest, sharpest gun in the West." Burke approved and audiences were sufficiently entertained. Eve Kopitsky did it perfectly for four months, in about a hundred performances, until our London debut at the New Oxford Theatre, our biggest crowd to date. Her proud parents were there with the Shoymers. Maybe Eve did it for them. She raised the whiskey glass, but did not make the toast. "O serpent heart," she began, "hid with a flow'ring face! Did ever a dragon keep so fair a cave? Beautiful tyrant! Fiend angelical!" And as if possessed by the ghost of tragic Juliet, Jessica James continued as the curtain came down between us and a baffled audience: "Dove-feathered raven! wolfish-ravening lamb! Despised substance of divinest show!" Burke fired us on the spot. As Professor Wonderful and Shula took their places by the coffin on the stage for the curtain to rise again, an upset me asked an unrepentant her why she had done it. Eve answered with a question: "Do you still love me?" I hesitated before answering, remembering how, months before, at our first meeting by the statue of Eros in Piccadilly Circus, she had startled me with a similar question: "Are you going to love me?" I had hesitated then, too, avoiding an answer by telling her that I needed an actress for a dramatic vignette in a variety show. After listening to the story of Buffalo Bill and Jessica James, she frowned. "I don't think I can play the part. I've never fired a gun in my life. But even if I could shoot, the story's not very dramatic. What about love? Bill and Jessica should be in love. Audiences like love. And death. Good drama has death in it. Love and death like in *Romeo and Juliet*. Audiences love to cry. Or, if you don't want it to be a tragedy, it should at least be a comedy. It doesn't really matter which it is, comedy or tragedy, but the hero and heroine absolutely must be in love." I assured her that she would be able to shoot, since we used charge-gaffed bottles. "That's where your dramatic talent comes in, acting like you're a markswoman even though you're not. I agree with you about the need for love. Again, that's where your theatrical talent could make the show. Even though our characters don't say or do anything to indicate their passion for one another, you'll make the audience feel Jessica's love for Buffalo Bill. That's the art of acting." Eve's acting was clearly quite good enough, judging from Billie's enraged reaction to our premier performance: "That little Jewish strumpet is in love with you. I can tell it just by the way she looks at you onstage." Billie distrusted Eve despite my vehement, and I thought brilliantly acted, protests that I had no interest in any intimacy with the girl, that our relationship was purely professional, that I needed her because I couldn't work the routine, the only one I had, without a girl to play the part. I swore on my life that there was nothing going on between me and the actress. "Her father was a friend of my father. She's like a family member. I go to synagogue with them sometimes." "I have to go to synagogue" was the excuse used on many a Friday night and Saturday morning to cover my illicit trysts with Eve Kopitsky. It was, in fact, on Rosh Hashanah that I did first make love with her. At our initial meeting by the statue of Eros, she had told me that her father had rented rooms for the family at a hotel in Whitechapel so that they could walk to the synagogue on the Days of Awe. "I'll have my own room," she said and I interpreted her words with all the rigor and faith of a Cabalistic exegete mining meanings from the depths of the Torah. The hope of embracing Eve inspired me to go to the synagogue for Rosh Hashanah more than any promise of the Messiah's coming could have done. Sitting between Professor Wonderful and Bachncle, in the same row as Mordecai Goldman, Abe Shomyer, Getsle Kopitsky, and Joseph Lipschitz, I turned, as the shofar was blown, to look for Eve among the women in the gallery. "Rosh Hashanah is my favorite holiday," she said later that night as, wrapped in a white bed sheet, she welcomed me into her room, candlelit and fragrant with figs and pomegranates, "because it celebrates the birthday of Eve. And the days and nights between Rosh Hashanah and Yom Kippur mark the period during which she was not ashamed of her nakedness." As the sheet fell to the floor Eve exposed Eve, the Mate of Man. Her nakedness was an esoteric midrash on the story of creation, revealing that, in the garden that was her true home, Woman experienced in every part of her body the pleasure that is now felt only in the genitals. And the intelligence that is now only in the brain was in every part of her body too. And the feelings of the heart, that, too, the same thing: every part of her, every fiber and cell of her flesh, was alive with pleasure, wisdom, and love. She led me through the wilds of a nocturnal pasture toward the western horizon's distant light, closer and closer to the source of splendor. I trembled before the radiant spectacle of the spinning sword of fire wielded by the fiercely laughing cherubim who guards the gateway to the forbidden garden of delight. "Nakedness makes us invisible," she whispered, pulling me by the hand past the guard and into the garden. "But we must leave before dawn." She took me to the tree with its graceful trunk and supple limbs, deeply rooted, yet to bear fruit but laden with heavy night-blooming flowers, darkly whorled with seminal dewdrops on swollen luminescent petal lips, fused and exuding rich perfumes as irresistible invitations into the deep darkness of fleshy carpal. She touched the stamen, blew loose pollen with honeyed breath, and I whispered, "Bear tempting fruit for me to eat." There was a serpent in the tree: it's variegated scales formed dusky reticulated patterns on its heavily sinuous, constricting, coiling, tapering body. The head was human and the face was mine. The next time I made love to Eve was in the same room on Yom Kippur and in the morning, to the melody of the Kol Nidre. Hungry from the fast, I sought absolution and deliverance from an unwelcome guilt; since I was not married to Billie, it was not adultery, but it was infidelity. Is that a sin? Wondering whether my father had ever been unfaithful to my mother, I remembered listening to him talking over such matters with Jake Grossman: "Adultery," he said, attributing his insights to the Talmud, "means sleeping with another man's wife, trespassing on his property. It is not infidelity to your own wife. Wandering on free land, although you have property of your own, is not a sin." Jake Grossman had wholeheartedly agreed. During the recitation of *Avinu Malkenu,* I transferred the guilt from myself to Billie as Aaron did the sins of Israel onto the head of a trembling goat: her jealousy had driven me into Eve's garden. "She mustn't know," I told Eve, in fear equally of both the pain I'd cause Billie and the anger she'd direct at me. "And I won't tell my parents, either," Eve promised. "They'd be very upset. Yes, it must be secret." Illicit love is for thrill seekers; it's drama, and so my actress took to her part in it as to the role of Juliet. I'm sure the Kopitskys were actually well aware, and not upset at all, of their daughter's intimacy with me, since without the slightest hesitation they let her go on the road with the show. Mrs. Kopitsky told her little Sarah Bernhardt to eat kosher and keep the Sabbath. The latter she always did for the joy of reading Adam's words over Eve: "This is now bone of my bones, flesh of my flesh." While we stood in the wings, right after being fired by Burke, as the curtain rose in front Professor Wonderful and Shula, Eve, after my long hesitation, repeated her question: "Do you still love me?"

78 "Do you want to go high, or fast, or far? That's the question that aviators, more than everybody else, must answer," Billie remarked as we walked along the runway at the dawn of a misty day toward the hangar where her new plane was ready to fly. "I've set my heart on distance." By soaring to a height of 13,950 feet in August of 1922, she had held the altitude record for women pilots until Amelia Earhart flew five feet higher in October of that year, setting a record that was broken two weeks later by Baroness Gertrude von Hohenstaufen with a new record that was broken after yet another week by Paris bluestocking Comtesse Seraphita de la Mettrie. Altitude records were continually broken, and soon, Billie explained, fliers would hit the ceiling. "And in any case, I've set altitude once already. Now the other two. First distance and then speed, and finally, someday, all three at once. Higher, faster, and farther than anyone else, man or woman, before me." Although speed was tempting (particularly to one addicted to cocainized wine), it meant flying short distances at low altitudes in a small monoplane, and for the time being, Billie wanted an aircraft large enough to sleep, eat, and make love in, a plane that could take her anywhere in the world, from England to the Antipodes, from pole to pole, from the Dead Sea to the Tibetan plateaus. It was not so much to claim the American prize of $25,000 for being the first aviator to cross the Atlantic as to demonstrate that "women are the chosen mistresses of the sky, the dominatrixes of heaven," that Billie, just recently the beneficiary of a generous bequest from her suddenly dead father, had purchased the Grafenberg-Dominion I.M.2, christened *The Spirit of St. Wilhelmina,* powered by a single Kegel-Whirlwind 200-horsepower air-cooled radial engine and fitted with extra fuel tanks and customized wing struts, which, in conjunction with the elegant airfoil contour of its fuselage, would give my beloved the superior lift, thrust, and distance needed for the transatlantic journey. The wheels could be replaced with pontoons for a sea landing in case of emergency. She reckoned she could cross the ocean east to west in less than thirty-six hours, despite the west-to-east headwinds that had less intrepid male contestants hoping to fly from America to Europe. Vin Mariani would keep her awake over the Atlantic. Except for the medallion of the saint above the altimeter, the cabin had not yet been personalized. "This time I want a more cloistral decor, something evocative of Wilhelmina's cell." Strapping myself into my seat, I thanked her for consenting to fly me to Lancashire to attend the funeral of Dr. Anthony McCloud. "As men and women of faith, let us reflect upon the mystery of death and the blessing that our love bestows upon the deceased," the newly appointed young country vicar began. "Today we honor Dr. Anthony McCloud, and, each of us sadly remembering him with love in our own way, we pray that he will have everlasting life and that he will be waiting for us to join him in glory on high." I left Billie's side to take my turn in the formal offering of condolences to Pythia, who stood in between her homely husband and the mother from whom he had inherited his looks. In front of me in line, Puru, the former Tiger Boy, was eulogizing: "Dr. McCloud civilized me, transforming an unruly, filthy savage into what I am today. He should have won the Nobel Prize for his work with poisonous snakes and me." When it was my turn, I wanted to kiss Pythia's tear-wet cheeks, but because the black veil over her face made such solace awkward, I merely raised her warm hands up to my lips. With their fragrance evoking musky midnights in Alipore, I whispered sadly, "I'm so sorry." She whispered back angrily, "Get him out of here! I do not want him here! I will not speak to that scoundrel!" She was referring to Karnaghee, who had queued up behind Professor Wonderful and Shula. When I tried to accommodate her by asking the guru to step out of the line with me, he refused to budge. "I must inform her that I have consulted the astrological charts, made all the complex calculations, and determined that her good father will soon be reborn in Tibet and become the next Dalai Lama." I overheard Professor Wonderful's strange condolences: "I was buried like this not long ago, and look what has happened to the me." He actually meant well, but it was, despite the sadness he surely felt, difficult for the magician to modulate the exhilaration that he was feeling after his performance for the royal family. It had been a sufficiently grand success to allow him to buy his way out of his contract with Eddie Burke and secure booking on an all-European tour. Karnaghee was gloating no less than Wonderful: he had reinstated his family name, Dayal, and authored as Dayal Karnaghee an inspirational book, *Thinking of Positive Power*, published by the International Vedanta Society. It had sold hundreds of thousands of copies. With the success of his international bestseller, Dayal Karnaghee had earned sufficient religious status and money to open his own ashram in Kensington where people came to hear his profound philosophical disquistions and to witness Shamboo Baba's miraculous demonstrations of Linga Yoga. "While people are most in awe of anvil lifting, they also enjoy seeing the Vajroli Mudra wherein, after constricting his bladder, the adept Shamboo immerses his divine lingam of Shiva into a vessel of water, and then, after sucking the water into his bladder through his urethra, urinates for the sake of purification. He then does the same with milk, then honey, and mercury. I give a spiritual commentary, ornamented with Sanskrit pearls of wisdom, explaining that the mastery of this particular yogic feat allows the celibate holy man to enjoy sexual intercourse, after the culmination of which he recovers his chastity by sucking the emitted semen back into his own body, thus showing the secret of having a cake and eating it too." Speaking of cake, all of us except Karnaghee and Shamboo were invited by Pythia McCloud-Green to proceed from the grave site to the chapel for "father's favorite angel food cake." Although I felt compelled to accept the invitation in order to offer further, less formal, condolences to Pythia, Billie insisted that we leave. I supposed that, since her own father had so recently died, it was perhaps death that was upsetting her. But love turned out to be the culprit. No sooner had *The Spirit of St. Wilhelmina* begun her ascent than my aviatrix asked about Pythia: "What's going on between the two of you? In the way in which you held her hands and kissed them there was far more desire apparent than condolence. And there were tears in her eyes as she looked through that veil at you. She's in love with you. What's going on? Tell me the truth." Taking umbrage at her accusations, I shouted to be heard over the noise of the engine: "She was crying because her father just died." Resolutely refusing to allow her jealousy to put me on the defensive, I played offense in the game: "Okay, here's the truth: yes, she was a lover a long time ago in India, but that's over. She's married now, and now I love you. Surely you don't expect me to have never been with another woman before you?" After a gulp of her bittersweet Vin Mariani straight from the bottle, Billie was, as the plane soared higher, faster, and farther, yelling: "I knew it! I knew you fucked her! It was obvious. And while that may have been before you knew me, you were reliving it as you kissed her hands. I could tell! That was an unforgivable infidelity. And that little bitch, that Jewish slut, Jessica, or Eve, or whatever her name is, I know you're fucking her too. I know it. I can tell. I hate you. Get out of my plane, you fucking profligate bastard." I denied the clandestine affair with Eve vehemently. It had, after all, ended. It wasn't, I must confess, because I didn't still love Eve or she me, but a motion picture director in the audience for our performance on the night we were fired had approached her to offer her the part of the heroine in a version of *Romeo and Juliet* that he was going to film. That sexual intimacy with him was a condition of the casting gave Eve no choice but to end our liaison: "We have to put art before our own individual needs to love and be loved, because art re-creates and redefines, enriches, purifies, and perpetuates love, establishing it as a sensibility and an ideal in which all human beings are invited to participate and find fulfillment. By playing Juliet, I shall give more to humanity than I could ever give you by merely playing myself." In her excitement over the prospects of being a motion picture star, she actually believed it. "After we finish the film, we're going to perform the play on the BBC so that moviegoers will have the opportunity to hear what they've seen." I swore to Billie that I had never even been slightly attracted to Eve. "There's no cause for jealousy. That's the truth!"

Taking another swig of the wine that fueled her mind to fly faster than the aircraft that contained us, she screamed: "I hate you, you fucking bastard. I can't believe you've been lusting after that pathetic little Hebrew whore." Begging her to relent, I invoked true love by paraphrasing the vicar's recitation from Paul's letter to the Corinthians that we had heard at Dr. McCloud's funeral: "Love is kind, generous, forgiving, and devoid of envy, possessiveness, anger, and jealousy. It rejoiceth in truth." She interrupted: "I hate you. Fuck you, you cheating, dirty Jew." We were still gaining altitude and speed. Letting go of the stick and releasing the clasp on her safety belt, Billie turned in her seat to reach back and pull a parachute pack up, forward, and into my lap. She then produced a Luger from under her seat and pointed it at my heart: "Put on the parachute and get out of my plane." With no intention of actually jumping, I slipped my arms through the straps of the parachute harness and buckled the belt of it, figuring that if she thought I was really going to jump, she'd calm down. "Okay, I'll go. But would you mind explaining how I open the chute?" "That's for you to figure out, you philandering little son-of-a-bitch," she screamed. "Get out! Or I'll shoot you." Desperate for a better strategy, I tried a new move: "Would you marry me, my darling? I love you and want you to be my bride. I want us to celebrate our honeymoon right here in this plane, flying across the Atlantic together as husband and wife." *Ka-bamm!* The sudden sound of gunshot startled me and the sight of a bullet hole in the door of the plane, indicating that she had only missed me by a few inches, made the point. Sliding the door back and edging out of my seat into the opening, I was holding on for dear life in a hope that Billie was bluffing. I waited for her to ask me to sit back down. The gun went off again. The crack-*ka-bamm!* and bright flash of it so shocked me that I lost my grip. As I screamed "I love you," I realized that I was falling from the heavens down toward a distant earth.

79

"Oh I'm falling, I'm falling, yeah, fa-fa-falling in love. It's appalling but enthralling that I'm falling, falling in love vid you. La-laa-la, la-laa-la, *ei! ei! ei!* falling in love vid youuuu!" I had forgotten about the silly vaud ditty that Shecky Shikker had swingingly belted out in a Yiddisher accent at Wonderful's wedding until the white silk parachute opened and, because I wasn't harnessed in quite right, almost ripped my arms out of their sockets. "Oh I'm falling, I'm falling," I sang beneath the aeronautic huppah as I descended from the heavens happy that I was probably going to survive the fall: "Yeah, fa-fa-falling in love." The earth below seemed a huge game board, its edges extending beyond the horizon, its squares made up of fields crossed by straight ladders of railway and snakes of winding road. My life was patterned by love into rows of those squares, a game and story back into which I was falling, where, I wasn't sure. As *The Spirit of St. Wilhelmina* disappeared into the far sky and the growl of her engine faded beneath a *shhhh* of high wind, I kept singing: "La-laa-la, la-laa-la, *ei! ei! ei!* falling in love vid youuuu." I was not singing to Billie, but to a girl whom I did not yet know, whom I had never seen, whose features were yet to be imagined, whose body was yet to be fashioned out of my rib, bone of my bone, flesh of my flesh, dream of my dreams, a girl in a square below and ahead, unaware that I was up above her, fa-fa-falling to her in love. She did not yet know that she was waiting for me. She was number ten, I mused, in love's ten-in-one. "The lady of the East can see and hear what's in the future, all that is in store for you," I heard from high above: "She often talks of love." Transported by erotic ballyhoo, I saw the portraits of the girls on the banner line and their eyes followed me down to earth. "All ten ladies of love, all for the price of one. Let them tease and please you, daze and amaze you. Come on in. Don't be afraid of love!" Floating into a wayward cloud, my face washed and eyes closed by its mist, I counted each tableau vivant: one, Angel; two, Carmen Zambra; three, the nameless girl that Jesus brought to me; four, Pythia McCloud; five, Nagini; six, Billie Custis; seven, Eve Kopitsky; eight, Mary the Caribbean; nine, Sylvia Woodlands; and ten, a girl yet to be known. The girls formed a chorus: "Oh he's falling, he's falling, yeah, fa-fa-falling in love." Whenever I fall, there's that preposterously tempting illusion that it's meant to be, that love is more than a game of chance. An annoyed flock of geese in V-formation honked avian complaints about my trespass in their sky. A gust of wind lifted me, then held me suspended between heaven and earth and turned me, and I could see a distant village in which, I mused, Sylvia Woodlands might be having a picnic by herself, champagne and strawberries that might be shared with someone who dropped in. My sudden landing would surprise her: "Mind if I join you, Miss Woodlands? Remember me?" I'd ask as I folded up my parachute. "We met on the croquet square at Blessingham Manor." For fear of arousing Billie's jealousy that weekend, I had pretended hardly to notice her. But I had a sure feeling that if I had been free to speak with her at greater length, I would have invited her to see my show, and after the last curtain she'd come backstage, where I'd amaze her with wild tales of the Wild West. I'd invite her for supper. We'd eat a little but drink, talk, laugh, and flirt a lot, and then, too tipsy to make it home, she would come back to my room and no sooner would I have closed the door than she would have pressed her body against mine, opening her mouth hungrily as my hands scouted for the stays and buttons of her clothes. Fingers furrowed fields of flesh below, plowing deeper and deeper, inside, outside, rising, falling, swaying and floating slowly, emerging from a cloud, slowly down to earth, afraid to land, swinging in the harness of the parachute again, rocking to and fro in a sky resonant with airy sighs, windy whimpers, and faint gusts of "I love you, I love you." If only I had had the courage to speak to her that weekend at Blessingham Manor, if only we had not merely passed each other but actually landed on a square together, it might have been forever. Now she'd ask what I'm writing. "It's about you, Sylvia," I'd say, lifting my pen from this sheet of paper to look at her: "I'm trying to write about love." She'd touch my hand and smile. "I have always felt that we were destined to be together. I have loved you ever since the day I first saw you on the croquet court." She repeats it, "I love you," again, and then, upon returning to this page, floating back down to earth, I recognize the accent. It's not Sylvia's voice. "Bachnele already paid me," Mary the Caribbean said as I retrieved my wallet from the trousers on the chair, waiting to walk away with me. "It's his treat and he gave me an extra fiver to say 'I love you.' I said I'd throw that in for free. I mean it's just three little words. But he insisted. He's such a sweetheart and a gentleman. All the girls here love him. And not just because he's a midget. He's got other qualities, too." I didn't feel that Bachnele had gotten his money's worth; she did say "I love you," but not very convincingly. Not like Eve Kopitsky, who could say "I love you" more eloquently than any other player in the game: "My bounty, Isaac, is as boundless as the sea, my love as deep; the more I give to thee, the more I have, for both are infinite." Wondering, since her love was so infinite, whether if she had been sleeping with other men whenever I was with Billie, I had sat up in bed to ask her point-blank. "Well, sometimes," she admitted, "but that doesn't mean I don't love you. I mean if a man really wants me, it's pretty hard to say no, especially if he's handsome, or intelligent, or kind, or sweet, or Jewish. I love being loved and desire to be desired. I can't help it and don't think I should be ashamed of it. I love being kissed and hugged and told that I'm beautiful. What girl doesn't? But, as I said, it doesn't mean that I don't love you. I do. I really do. Listen: 'This bud of love, by summer's ripening breath, may prove a beauteous flower when we next meet.' I love the way Shakespeare was so good at putting into words exactly what I feel." Still floating, unable to do anything to determine where I was going or know where or when I'd land, I knew, as fewer and fewer of the squares became visible, only that I was coming closer and closer to the earth. "It's appalling but enthralling that I'm falling, falling in love vid you. La-laa-la, la-laa-la, *ei! ei! ei!* falling in love vid youuuu!" I tried to make the "you" any woman but Billie, whose jealousy I had too long mistaken for love. But the harder I tried not to think of her, the more she intruded, and upon entering my mind she was furious to find Sylvia, Mary, and Eve there in her sky: "Just as I suspected!" Would Billie wonder, I wondered, what had happened to me? Would she give that second bullet a second thought and fear that she might have killed me? Every lover, I reckoned as another gust swept me sideways across the sky, in some way tries to kill the beloved at least a little bit. While lust unabashedly longs for life, love secretly yearns for death as the only eternity there can ever be. Lust, by nature honest, laughs at the solemn duplicities of love. I could understand why I had loved Angel, Nagini, and Pythia, but not why I loved the ever-jealous Billie. I didn't want to, but the harder I tried not to, the more I did and the more I did, the harder I tried not to. Lust, delighting in the present, declares itself and takes what it wants; love, clinging to the past and worried about the future, pretends, sulks, and finagles. Plotting its revenge, love reminded me that I knew enough about stage makeup to create the illusion of a wound on my breast. "Do it, go to Billie and remove a blood-stained bandage to display the marks of love's martyrdom and tell her, 'The bullet just missed my heart.'" It was tempting to try to take advantage of the fact that she had almost killed me. In a well-intentioned seduction, the lover too often attempts to make the beloved feel guilty, imagining that guilt will weaken and bind the beloved. But in the end, the beloved makes the lover feel guilty for trying to make the beloved feel guilty. Where lust is by nature innocent and pure, love seems always smudged with guilt and confusion. Because I loved her, Billie's suspicions and jealousy made me reward her with a solicitousness that made her all the more suspicious and jealous, which made me (because I loved her) want to not love her, which made me feel guilty, which made me angry, which made me feel even more guilty, which made me (because I loved her) want to punish her by doing something to give a cause to the guilt that I was in my innocence causelessly feeling (because I loved her). Where lust, ever sure of itself, always affirms itself, love is always anxious and eager to undermine itself. I hoped to purify lust, to purge it of the messiness of love before landing back on earth. Had Billie really loved me? Had Pythia really loved me? I remembered that she had, on occasion, said "I love you," but she took the power out of the words by uttering them cheerfully. There must be a bit of sorrow, fear, pain, or at least a little worry in the phrase to make it a convincing expression of love. Pythia's "I love you" was like a kiss on the cheek, an endearment, a sweet nothing, a salutation: "Good-bye, darling. I do love you. See you tomorrow." Had Nagini really loved me? I had taught her to say the English words and when she did pronounce them, it always made her laugh. She had never said: *"Aami tomaake bhaalo baashi."* Why? Was that too sad to say in her mother tongue? I was close enough to the earth to see the thatched roofs of the farmhouses and the spire of a village church. I could distinguish between the cows and sheep beneath me and couldn't see more than four squares. "Oh I'm falling, I'm falling, yeah, fa-fa-falling in love." I was singing to Angel. Had she really loved me? I could see her: as clouds passed behind her, her white lace costume she would disappear and then reappear before the blue of sky. As the earth came closer still I could hear her, too: "Let's try not to be sad. Let's drink to us and to first love. Please, Isaac, don't make it difficult. Let's drink to the future too, to the true love that each of us, somewhere, someday, will surely find." Where, I wondered, as my feet touched the earth, was the girl whom I did not yet know, number ten, the one who did not yet know that she was waiting for me?

80 An unlucky roll landed me, several months later, in the Soviet Union, where I was always cold, usually anxious, and often drunk. I was in a dark square on the edge of the checkered game board, repeatedly missing my turn, constantly passed over by the tokens of friends, strangers, and ghosts. Occasionally players would stop in my square, and, until their turn came to roll again, they'd reveal ups and downs with stories of the ladders they had struggled to climb and the serpents that had bitten them. Since I was out of work in London when I received the invitational letter, Shmuel Grossman's salutary slogan, "Workers of the World Unite," did not seem to apply. But the old family friend was eager for me to join him in Leningrad (chosen as his new home for its previous name, St. Petersburg). He was exultant in his trust in the promises of a glorious life that had been made by the leaders of the Communist Party. Shmuel, who had written to Trotsky from prison in Florida, was finally introduced to his hero at a rally in Leningrad by none other than Jesus Estafar, who had been performing his "Pancho Villa: My Father, the Revolutionary!" act with the Leningrad State Circus ever since breaking from Jake Grossman during the *Last of the Wild Redskins* Soviet run. Shmuel assured me that, with the combined influential powers of Trotsky and Jesus I would have no trouble getting work with the circus, juggling, shooting, "or anything else you can do that is funny or in any other way serves the proletariat." Even if the border patrol hadn't confiscated my gaffed guns and trickshot ammunition, even if Jesus and Trotsky had fallen on their knees to beg on my behalf, I wouldn't have been able to perform with the Leningrad Circus: they already had Señor Pancho Villa Junior's sharpshooting act; my juggling was pitiful in comparison to their Stavrogin, who could juggle seven live trout; I couldn't walk a high wire without a very long balancing pole or mechanic; I didn't know enough Russian to tell a joke; and I was neither sufficiently anguished nor merry enough to be a clown. But Jesus saved me. Remembering my Swami Balakrishna act, he found work for me with the avant-garde Chushka Animal Theater doing a Futurist snake-charming routine. Because of my ignorance of Russian political history, I did not understand any of the supposedly hilarious references, gestural or verbal, of the allegorical and socialistically satirical snake number, which had been written for me by Dmitri Balaganshchik, who was respected in Russian variety circles as the "world's greatest living author of revolutionary comedy sketches for animals." As I recited lines, which I had memorized without understanding, I never knew who or what I or my snakes were supposed to represent, or why the tab got so many laughs. It seemed to prove George Strong's hypothesis that anything done badly enough is comedy. Although reason had urged me to leave the Soviet Union as soon as I could, love held me back. I could not help falling for Zinaida Shigalova the moment I saw her somersaulting above me at the Leningrad State Circus. I was dazzled by her high swing, fluid twists, and smooth returns, bewitched by each break and lift, every split, planch, and bird-nest. Jesus Estafar introduced me to her after the show. *"Razreshitie mne predstavit' vam Isaak,"* he said in perfect Russian: *"On v glubokom odinochestve."* Although I vehemently denied that what I thought that meant was true, she didn't believe me, took pity on me, and invited me to her room, where we smoked Balkan cigarettes, drank Ukrainian vodka, and had Siberian sexual relations (that is, without removing our coats, scarves, stockings, or gloves because of the cold). Afterwards I sang "Oh I'm falling, I'm falling, yeah, fa-fa-falling in love," and she lit another cigarette, poured two more glasses of vodka, and happily announced: "My first American! My first, unless you count Mexico as America. I like it that you're an American. It's exotic like chewing gum. And one of my heroes, Buffalo Bill Cody, was from America." I couldn't believe it: it was if the Wild West scout was tailing me. When I told her that I had performed as Buffalo Bill in England, she didn't believe me. And it was hard for me to believe her explanation of her admiration for the American celebrity. As a child, before the Revolution, she had lived in Prokovskoe, a small town in Siberia on the banks of the Tura. Booking agents for the Buffalo Bill Wild West show had recruited there four Cossacks, the Oblakov Brothers, to perform with the Rough Riders of the World in America. Returning to Prokovskoe after Buffalo Bill's death, they, unlike the majority of Cossacks, fought with the Bolsheviks against Karensky's provisional government. Victory rewarded them with official positions in the new Bolshevik regime. Innokenty Oblakov, the oldest of the brothers, given leadership of Prokovskoe, established there the Buffalo Billshevik School for the Circus Arts, where Zinaida had trained as a trapeze flyer. After demolishing the statue in the town square of Grigori Efimovich Rasputin (until then the only native of Prokovskoe to have made a name for himself) and replacing it with one of Buffalo Bill, Comrade Oblakov officially changed the name of the town to Codigrad. Buffalo Bill, Zinaida sincerely believed, had been a socialist. It should not have been surprising to me, given his political proclivities and experience in animal theater, that Nagendra Bannerjee would show up at the Chushka. That his show, a parodic political history of the first quarter of the twentieth century, starring a Russian wolfhound, German shepherd, English sheepdog, French poodle, and a Chinese chow, was hailed as a work of genius in a review in *Izvestiya* made Nagendra proud to boast that he had, "in all modesty, put India on the map of revolutionary animal comedy." Zinaida, who had never before met a man from India, so enjoyed the canine revue that she invited Nagendra to accompany her to Leningrad's zoo, which, since the Bolsheviks had freed all the creatures from its cages, remained open and free of charge to the public as a monument to the liberation of the oppressed. She didn't return home for several days. During my second year in Leningrad, Zinaida gave birth prematurely to a boy who did not have the strength to survive long enough on this earth to be circumcised. As Nagendra was quite darkly complexioned and the baby was very fair, I reckoned that the child might have been my son and thus the inheritor of the Hebrew verse *"Tzechok asah li Elohim kol-hashomea yitzachak-li."* At the beginning of my third year in Leningrad, Shmuel Grossman, who had been translating Russian propaganda into English, Yiddish, and Hebrew for the People's Bureau of Information, was arrested when the secret police discovered that he had been found guilty of espionage as a German agent in a city in Florida, significantly in their minds, named St. Petersburg. He was tried, convicted, and sentenced to one hundred years of hard labor in a Siberian rehabilitation camp. Having recently been expelled from the Communist Party, Trotsky could do nothing to help him. When, shortly thereafter, Trotsky was expelled from the Soviet Union for ignoring Stalin's order to abstain from political activity, Jesus Estafar convinced him to accompany him to Mexico where he would be safe. At the same time, after OGPU agents saw my inane snake act at the Chushka, I was arrested along with a Kulak and his dancing bear during a sweep to purge Soviet theater of its eccentricities and require all performing animals "to truthfully and historically represent reality in its revolutionary development and to serve the ideological transformation of the working animal in the spirit of socialism." I was, however, more lucky with my dice than either Shmuel or Trotsky were with theirs. After only two days in jail I was released into the custody of Professor Vladimir Yesnovitch, who, having arranged passage for me to Finland, took me to the Leningrad railway station. Ignoring my questions as to how he had known where I was, and how he was able to free me, he asked me to remove my glove so that he could see if there was any change in the scar on my hand. "Slowly," he said, "slowly it is going away." I had to leave in a hurry with only a moment to kiss my beloved Zinaida good-bye. As my train pulled out she sang: *"Toot, toot, Tootsya, do svidaniya! Toot, toot, Tootsya, ne plakai!"* Although mail had been sporadic during the dreary years that were, despite days and nights with Zinaida, wasted in the Soviet Union, news of birth, marriage, and death seems to have a way of getting through. I have no idea how Pythia had known to write to me care of the Chushka to announce that she, like my Zinaida, had given birth to a boy. Before naming him, she had scoured the obituaries in papers from around the world to discover who, by dying forty-nine days before her son was born, was a candidate for being reincarnated in her offspring. "All the evidence," she noted, "points to Rudolph Valentino." I learned in a letter from Professor Wonderful (written to ask me to perform the impossible trick of arranging for him to do a magical tour of the Soviet Union) that Kamadhenuka had given birth to triplet girls; three hungry infants posed fewer problems for her than they would have caused a woman with only two breasts. Eve Kopitsky had, Wonderful further reported, married the director of the silent motion picture in which she had played Juliet. She soon left him, however, for the chief of programme coordination at the BBC, whom she subsequently abandoned to have an affair with a married Scottish scientist named John Logie Baird. She had met Baird at a party in London celebrating the first successful transmission of his new invention, an electronic machine he called "television." After Mr. Baird, returning to his right mind, terminated his scandalous liaison with Eve, she, in turn, returned to her husband and starred in his new *Romeo and Juliet*, remade to capitalize on the new talkie technology. Lady Blessingham, Professor Wonderful's letter continued, was accidentally shot in the head during a weekend pheasant hunt at Blessingham Manor by Professor Bates, whose drunkenness had allowed his myopia to convince him that the figure walking toward him in the woods was a bear armed with a rifle. The magician also informed me that the Great Whydini ("being unable to tell the lie") had committed suicide, and that Yogi Shamboo Baba had died after jumping off the roof of the Dayal Karnaghee Ashram in Kensington in an effort to demonstrate to the public the fact that yogic practices could give the adept (provided he had remained celibate and vegetarian for one lunar year) the power to fly. His death aroused suspicions in the skeptical that the fakir must have secretly either broken his vow of celibacy or had a bite of meat. And occasional letters from my mother, always assuring me of the happiness of her married life with Hayim Grossman, kept me up to date on who had died in America: Al Alighieri, Jr., Conway Conwell, Beryl Grossman, Colonel Charles Bladud, and a Schlossberg cousin in Milwaukee. I also heard that Billie Custis had disappeared over the North Atlantic in her *Spirit of St. Wilhelmina* just forty-nine days prior to Charles Lindbergh's successful flight from New York to Paris.

|81| "*The Spirit of St. Louis* had been sighted over Ireland," Angel (with Napoleon, her white toy poodle, cuddled in her arms and licking her fingers) recollected as we sat next to each other on the stone steps leading up to Montmartre on the night that *Paris-Soir* headlines blaring the kidnapping of the twenty-month-old Lindbergh baby in New Jersey bumped the announcement of Adolf Hitler's acceptance of the chancellorship of Germany to page two. "Everyone in Paris was enthralled in their impatience for the glorious moment when the wheels of Lindbergh's plane finally and officially touched the earth. There was an electrifying excitement crackling in the air, a contagious jubilation like nothing else since Armistice. The arrival of the Messiah couldn't have caused a greater stir. My friend, the aviator Reynard Faucon, insisted that I go along with him to Le Bourget, where the American pilot was awaited with open arms and hearts by fifty thousand ready-to-get-drunk Parisians. We readied ourselves for the historic moment with little French and American flags to wave and champagne to drink straight from the bottle. At the first faint sound of the plane, still invisible in the darkness and in clouds that seemed to have gathered just to greet the aviator, corks could be heard prematurely popping. Hundreds of searchlights, followed by thousands of binoculars and opera glasses, scanned the night, and then, when suddenly the silver plane, so sleek and graceful, appeared low in the spotlit field of sky, heading straight for us, even before the wheels made contact with the runway, the cheers doubled in volume, a tumultuous din reverberating with screams, hollers, laughter, hoots, and hoorays: '*Il est arrivé! Vive l'Américain! Bravo, Lindy, bravo!*' Hats were thrown into the air and flags were waved above the mass of merged bodies that was irrepressibly swept up and away into an unimpedable wave that crashed into the steel restraining fence. It crumpled like chicken wire under hurried feet as the crowd spread across the field. Bolting from my side, Reynard disappeared into the tidal swell of celebrants. The plane was still taxiing when the throng engulfed it like ants swarming around an injured dragonfly. They grabbed on to the wings, rudder, elevators, any part of the machine that they could reach. I was certain that many of them would be trampled to death, that others would be sliced up by the rotating propeller, and that still more would die of such intensely overwhelming delight. The cockpit was sealed and dark and people were ripping patches of the doped fabric from the plane's outer skin. Any piece of the aircraft that would come loose in their hungry hands would be transubstantiated into the flesh of Charles Lindbergh. Had there been any fuel left in the tank, the worshippers would have surely drunk it

as sacramental blood. Hands, prying open the door, reached to pull the pilot out. There he was! *Ecce homo!* Hosanna! The crowd hoisted the hero up and passed him across an ecstatic surge of bodies. For Reynard, as an aviator who had once had his own dreams of being the first man to cross the Atlantic, it was as if Lindbergh had done it for him. The American aviator was a god who had just established the divine standard of perfection. He had not merely crossed the Atlantic; he had done it poetically. Reynard appeared two days later with an unbelievable story. He said that he had been close to the plane, swept away by the crowd that had been carrying the aviator above their heads. When the body of his hero passed close by, he couldn't help but reach out to touch the living idol. He closed his hand, tugged, and, to his utter astonishment, discovered that he was holding by its strap the leather helmet fitted with the very goggles through which Lindbergh had looked down at his now-vanquished foe, the Atlantic Ocean. Thrilled with the trophy, Reynard couldn't resist trying it on. It fit! And all of a sudden, he saw eyes turn on him and heard cries of *"C'est lui! C'est Lindy!"* He was lifted up onto the shoulders of worshippers. They carried him to the Cadillac Phaeton that was waiting to take Lindbergh to the American embassy. Reynard swore that, as soon as he realized what was happening, he began shouting, *"Non! Je ne suis pas Charlie. Je m'appelle Faucon! Ce n'est pas lui! C'est moi, Reynard Faucon!"* But no one could hear him over the cheering, and even if they had been able to hear, they would not have wanted to doubt that they had the real Lindbergh in their arms. If they had heard him, they would have been impressed that Lindy spoke French so well for an American and would probably have attributed the denial of who he was to the great modesty for which Lindbergh was famous. The mistake was understandable, since Reynard was not only wearing the flier's helmet and goggles, but an aviator's jacket, his own but not so different from Lindbergh's. And he's tall and slim like the American, with that same sweet boyish quality. Although Reynard claimed that he was still denying that he had just crossed the Atlantic as the car pulled out and headed toward the city, he confessed to the illicit pleasure that the mistake afforded him. All along the route, the people who were waving their flags, throwing kisses, and cheering allowed Reynard to know what it was like to be Charles Lindbergh and to understand the joy of such glorious accomplishment. Not wanting to disappoint anyone, he waved back on Lindbergh's behalf. A band was playing 'The Star-Spangled Banner' as he was greeted by Ambassador Myron Herrick at the embassy. Being ignorant of French, Herrick did not understand Reynard's disclosure of his true identity. After pinning a medal on the Frenchman, he read a patriotic speech about the American pioneer spirit to journalists assembled from around the world. With the microphones before Reynard, the ambassador wrapped his arm around the hero to say, 'We know you haven't slept for a long time, Mr. Lindbergh, but the world is waiting to hear. What does it feel like to be the first man to fly across the Atlantic?' When Reynard answered, '*Pardonnez-moi, monsieur, mais je ne comprends pas anglais,*' it occurred to several of the journalists that it was strange that a homespun regular guy from rural Minnesota didn't speak English. The truth was realized and Reynard was punched in the mouth by the irate ambassador. As he was being carted out of the embassy to jail, Lindbergh, who had been hiding from the mob of celebrants in an airplane hangar back at Le Bourget, arrived. Reynard waved to the aviator, and, he proudly told me, his hero waved back. After two days he was released because, although the authorities knew that he was guilty of something, they couldn't find a crime in the French penal code that actually described what he had done. Beaming with delight, Reynard came straight to my place. 'Every woman in Paris is dreaming of making love to Lindy,' he said, 'and you have been chosen! Embrace me, my darling! I need a woman after such a long time alone over the Atlantic.' Reynard was helping me with French at the time and I liked him. After all, he looked a little bit like Lindbergh. But I broke it off when I discovered that I was sleeping not only with Reynard but, unbeknownst to me for over a month, with his two brothers as well. The Faucon triplets were trying to put one over on me. And they couldn't understand why it should upset me, since I was 'getting three,' as one of them pointed out to me, 'for the price of one.' But I was furious and a little sad. The misery of former love affairs always seems so silly in retrospect. As I look back on it now, it was really quite amusing, and they didn't mean me any harm. One of them protested, '*Mais notre chérie, nous t'adorons également tous les trois.*' I just didn't get the joke at the time. I should have had a better sense of humor." As she talked, I held her hand in mine, gazing at the profile of the face that was looking out, over and across Paris toward an illuminated Eiffel Tower in the distance. Paris had sophisticated Angel. The fragrance of the hair in which my face had been buried years before beckoned me back into it. Thirty or forty steps below us, penumbral lovers were embracing. I leaned closer still, bringing my lips near to her ear to whisper that I had missed her. Napoleon growled and, withdrawing her hand from mine, Angel stopped her story: "Please, Isaac, don't start again. I don't want to make love with you. Please, don't insist upon it, because you know I love you and so would have to do anything you asked of me. But if you really do love me you won't ask for that. If you truly love me, you'll be kind, you won't complicate my life. Remember the game we used to play? I still have it! Snakes and ladders? It's just like that: to make love with a former lover is to land on a snake head. Back you go! It was nice to be in that square the first time, when you were on your way up, but to go back there again is something else." I had caught up with her on the board of a game we had started as children, but she was about to land on a ladder and leave me behind once more. After having been Kitty Hawk and then Cyranie Sirène at the Folies-Bergère, she would be Dévoué Rabonnir again, but this time as a real actress in a real play in a real theater. She would star in the Marquis d'Échelle's *La Jouissance de Cléopâtre*, soon to open at the Théâtre Sarah Bernhardt. Even if she wouldn't make love with me again, she swore that we would be friends forever, and as a gesture of that friendship she found me a room at the Villa Borghese and promised to take me to the Folies-Bergère to introduce me to Derval and ask him to give me a job as a translator there. "There are performers from so many countries who can't speak to each other," she explained, "so they need translators roaming about backstage before and during the show to help. I hope you remember all those languages your father made you study as a child." I said that I remembered some of them: "But, my Angel, most of my childhood memory is taken up by you. Higher and higher you climb the hundred-rung ladder, and with each successive step, a delicate foot presses down upon my heart to make it beat, and I fear that when you reach the top my heart will stop."

82 *La Folie d'Amour* was the most beautiful thing I had ever seen. It was as if every theatrical event I had ever witnessed or been a part of, every attempt to entertain, amuse, astonish, or delight, had, through the power of art and the grace of money, been perfected. Women were the scenery: brightly illuminated, suspended from ropes or wires, rising and falling, trapezing to and fro, appearing and disappearing; by prop, set, cosmetics, costume, and nudity, women were made more splendidly erotic than women of flesh and blood have the right to be in a world wherein men are mortal. There were stars in my eyes: Mistinguett, Maurice Chevalier, Pepita Perez, Lola Lolini, and Les Sexy Gals Américaines. I took sentimental pleasure in Draupadi, l'Idole des Indes, la Charmeuse des Serpents Féroces, naked except for the snakes draped and writhing around her neck and arms, and the jungle-flowered cache-sexe precariously secured by a delicate vine. *"J'ai des enlacements libertins,"* she sang, *"je suis le serpentin."* After her a man in jodhpur pants and patent-leather boots cracked a whip to make tigresses sing and dance for him; the cats were lithe chorines with naked breasts, furry paws, and curling tails. I was relieved that there was no Buffalo Bill in "L'Ouest Sauvage," a number in which bare-chested cowboys in ten-gallon hats and fringed chaps that exposed their buttocks, shooting pistols and spinning lariats while chorally yahooing, rounded up bare-bosomed Indian maidens in war-bonnets and fluttering eagle-feather skirts. I had never expected to see some-one on the stage there whom I knew: but, oh, the moment I saw her, I was cer-tain to my utter astonishment that, yes, it was she, performing before my very eyes after I had I thought that I would never see her again. It was she! Shakun-tala, the albino brown bear who had been kidnapped in Port Said, playing the polar bear, Nanooki, walking a slack rope above dancing Eskimo women, nat-urally bare-breasted despite the arctic chill. Warmed only by the fur haloes around their shining faces, they sang a hot ditty about rubbing noses in an igloo on a frosty six-month-long winter night. Shakuntala got all the laughs. "The slack rope for comedy," Angel commented, "the tightrope for beauty." After the final curtain, Angel, taking my hand and pushing against the flow of the crowd, pulled me through a forbidden door into a labyrinth of hallways in which anyone who did not know their way would surely have been forever lost. We emerged from the dark maze into an electrified fluctuous jungle of cables, pulleys, and swings, rolling tormentors, flats, teasers, and drops, curtains rising and falling. Everything was moving. Amidst this fantastic flora, a fervent fauna darted, dodged, shoved, rushed, or stopped momentarily to catch a breath and rest in the ruckus: dancers, acrobats, and workmen, stars, chorines (many still bare-breasted, a few completely naked), jugglers, magicians, animals, and others unidentifiable, pulling costumes off or clothing on as they careened through narrow spaces, up and down tortuous passages, over and across moving sets, laughing, gabbing, shouting or silent, an argument or a tear or two here or there, hectically bustling through the densely packed backstage tohu-bohu. And after having witnessed the perfection of design and order onstage, the illusion that was both the product and source of this chaos, it seemed that, though unperceivable to the naked eye, there was a pattern and plan here, a determinant logos informing this pandemonial brouhaha. We shoved our way to the office of the great Derval, where I waited outside while Angel went in to speak on my behalf. There was a sign above the door: *"Il faut donner à rêver et à rire."* Suddenly I saw her: pulled along by a chain attached to a ring in her nose, the albino funambulist seemed to recognize my voice when I called out "Shakuntala!" She turned to look at me. That I rushed toward the bear, reaching to touch her, infuriated her harried trainer. *"Viens Nanooki, ma chérie,"* he coaxed as I tried to explain to him that I had known her in India. Denying that it was possible, insisting that he had captured her himself near the North Pole, he pulled her away and out of sight into the blustering squall. I had to be happy for Shakuntala, since Angel had said that every female entertainer in the world dreams of playing the Folies-Bergère. Shakuntala had made it. Emerging from the office with an apology, Angel explained that Derval had decided not to hire any more translators. "The men," he had complained, "spend all their time trying to seduce the performers, never translating for the ones they do not find attractive. The homos are worse than the heteros. And the women are as bad as the men. It's better if people don't understand each other." The backstage adventure was not, however, in any way a waste of time as Angel offered to introduce me to the Idol of the Indies, Draupadi Padoux. "I shared a dressing room with her and Les Papillons Folichons, formerly the Kelly Twins from Philadelphia," Angel told me. "Padi's not really an Indian princess, so don't try to talk to her in Hindu or whatever it is they speak over there. She's from Reims and has never even visited India. But she did once have a lover who said he was a maharaja. He had probably never been to India either." Rising from her dressing table to greet Angel with a kiss on each cheek, Mademoiselle Padoux, after politely extending her hand to me, hardly acknowledged my presence. As she finished dressing, Angel told her about her new play. Pulling a silver fox coat over her shoulders, the snake charmer invited Angel to join her at the Séraphin Serpentin in Montparnasse. Angel declined: "No, no, sweetheart, I don't go there anymore. And it's so late. Time for me to be in bed. But take Isaac. He's new to Paris. It will amuse him. It's okay, you can trust him. He won't be a problem." "Why not?" she said to Angel and "Come along, monsieur" to me. A Minerva Landaulet, manned by a White Russian chauffeur whom she addressed as *"mon petit tsar,"* had been waiting in the rain. I told her in French how much I had enjoyed her performance and then, hoping to establish some common ground, if not a complicity, between us, explained that, like her, I had once played an Indian snake charmer and, I added, had spent several years in India, where I had known real snake charmers. She turned away from the rain-wet window through which she had been gazing at the diffused lights of the city to look at me and respond in English: "Am I not a *real* snake charmer?" Switching to English myself, I apologized: "Of course you are. I'm sorry. By 'vrai' I didn't mean 'real' or 'true,' but rather 'traditional,' hereditarily a snake charmer." She turned again to the window and was silent once more. A gold key on the end of a gold chain, entwined snakelike through the fingers of her suede-gloved hand, swung like the pendulum of an impertinent clock counting the seconds. As I can never help but do during moments of silence in the company of a woman with whom I would like to be intimate, I nervously babbled: "In India, only men charm snakes because there it is the female of the species that is most feared. She wraps around the male and constricts him in her coils before the fatal bite. I suppose that here in Europe the snake charmer is usually female because we think of serpents as male. He burrows. We recall the serpent in Eden." Again she turned and spoke in English: "Oh, you're an intellectual! Paris already has too many intellectuals. In any case, the serpent in Eden was female. Look at the depiction in stone on the portal of the Virgin at Notre-Dame. It was the Protestants who turned the beguiling temptress into the satanic tempter." I was at least pleased to have enticed her into conversation and smiled to playfully accuse her of being an intellectual too. "Not at all," she said. "And we're here. Come along, and on the inside, not so much blah blah blah. Only say what must be said." Draupadi opened the door with her gold key and was greeted by a person whose age and gender were impossible to discern. Standing next to a gold-leafed Buddha that was taller than him/her, he/she, with red-glossed lips, darkened eyes, white-powdered skin, and short black hair brilliantined straight back, was dressed in a scarlet silk Chinese robe that was embroidered with dragons in silver thread. After I had been introduced with Angel's words ("He's new to Paris. It's okay. La Sirène says that he won't be a problem"), we were handed black silk kimonos. I followed my cool charmer down a hallway dark and silent except for the fleeting glimmers of lamplights and an occasional cough or sigh in the chambers we passed. My host slipped through a curtain of strung glass beads into a room furnished with three low divans, each covered with lushly brocaded covers of satin and velvet and strewn with tasseled silk pillows of green, gold, and burgundy. Two women reclined on one and, on another, a lone man; all three dreamers had long smoldering pipes in laxly curled fingers. Next to each sofa was a low black lacquered table upon which there was a dragon-and-cloud-embossed box. The androgyne came in after us, carrying a tray set with two silver needles, two black pipes filigreed with gold, and a delicate celadon jar. Placing it on our table, he/she ceremonially presented the oil lamp with a languorous smile and whispered: *"Le keden."* Over its flame Draupadi held a globule of opium that she had rolled between her fingertips and impaled on the end of a needle, signaling me with a nod to follow suit. Then reclining, with her head nestled into a green pillow, she took a deep puff and, closing her eyes, rested the precious pipe across her lap. Lying on my side next to her, I stared at her face and listened to her breathing. Her eyes did not open until her hands were ready to relight the pipe. I smoked with her, and, watching curls of fragrant vapors rise, I was slowly tugged and lulled into dreaming awake and drifting, enveloped in stuporous reveries, witnessing the raptures of voluptuous phantoms and listening to lachrymose whimperings. Floating, floating. I saw myself in a small boat cadently rocking through splashing foam across undulant swellings of a dark oceanic wilderness. Farther and farther out to sea I drifted toward Omou Pan. There was a storm in which I was tossed about and I felt seasick. All of a sudden I was wet, and, awakened by harsh cold, I sat up shivering and alone. Finding the androgyne sleeping at the feet of the Buddha, I tried to shake him/her into sufficient consciousness to tell me where Mademoiselle Padoux had gone. Mascaraed eyes opened and glossed lips yawned before speaking. Draupadi had left an hour or so earlier to be on time for matins at Notre-Dame de Paris. *"Elle est très pieuse, vous savez,"* he said solemnly and then she laughed: "She's Jesus Christ's secret little coquette."

83

Against a darkness of predawn heavens, there was a darker darkness of the silhouettes of the gargoyles of Our Lady of Paris. Under their gaze I waited for five consecutive nights for her to come in hunger for the taste of sacrifice. It was all that was left for me to do after the failure of every other attempt to find her: my note, accompanied by a sentimentally red rose, was unanswered; the paunchy old man at the backstage door, like the forbidding cherubim spinning a flaming sword at the eastern gate of Eden to keep the fallen out, laughed at all pleas for entry into the hallowed dressing rooms of the Folies-Bergère. If I waited in front of the theater on the rue Richer, whether before or after the show, it seemed that she must have arrived or left by the back, or by the front if I waited at the back. I couldn't get into the Séraphin Serpentin without a gold key and Angel, swearing that she didn't have a home address for Draupadi, counseled me to relinquish my fascination: "To make love to a dancer from the Folies is the naughty dream, if not religious aspiration, of princes, potentates, premiers, and presidents. The girls, you must realize, are lavishly courted by Arabian sheiks, Greek shipping magnates, Indian maharajas, Nobel laureates, Oxford dons, Catholic bishops, Zulu chieftains, Chinese warlords, and Hollywood movie stars. And these men are driven to the maddest extravagances of courtship. There was an infamous soubrette, also a snake dancer, at the end of the last century, Emilienie Bombance, who was wooed (you'll love this story and I swear it's true) by none other than good old Buffalo Bill Cody! Persistently begging for her affections, he offered her things that would have bankrupt him had she surrendered to his advances. But she told him that there was only one thing that would win her over: one night of *l'amour sauvage* with Geronimo, the Apache Wildcat. When Geronimo refused to come to Paris for that purpose, an infuriated Buffalo Bill used his influence with Brigadier General Miles of the United States Cavalry to have the Indian imprisoned at Fort De Leon in Florida. To this day, slang among the Folies girls for a man who makes a fool of himself in wooing them is '*un bouffalobil*'; and a man who rejects a Folies girl is '*un géronimo.*' So, please, my darling, don't make a *bouffalobil* of yourself: *il faut géronimer!*" Finally, on my fifth vigil, as the cathedral bells announced the dawn of Assumption Day, she appeared and surprised me by not being surprised to see me. Touching a suede-gloved finger to my overeager lips to quell my absurdly zealous professions of joy, she asked me not to follow her into the cathedral: "You may wait here for me if you wish. I'll not be long. But do not come in." I obeyed. Emerging from Notre-Dame, she invited me to accompany her:

"Take my arm in yours and walk with me. But don't speak. Don't dispel the light or disturb the peace. Don't disrupt the feeling of love." She said nothing until we were inside the apartment on the third floor of a building near the Place de la Concorde. As she removed her gloves, hat, scarf, and fur coat, she asked me to be seated. I couldn't restrain myself from relating the lengths to which I had gone to locate her. Silently fixed on me, wide brown eyes made me feel so foolish that I stopped my ridiculous blathering and solemnly apologized for being such a *bouffalobil*. As she left the room, she invited me to make myself comfortable. It's wise to be a fool with women, I realized, as long as you can impress them that you truly know what an idiot you are. Rather than opening the dark burgundy velvet drapes to let in the day, she had lit votive candles to illuminate the chamber with a more sacerdotal light. The elegantly appointed room, blatantly implying a wealthy patron, made me feel so out of place that in her absence I rehearsed another apology (more impressively urbane), another confession (more touchingly humiliating), and contemplated my geronimization. It seems unjust that the more you desire a woman, the more it must seem that you don't. Like the many thousands of people who had been diverted at the Folies-Bergère that year, I had seen Draupadi naked, and, like all of the men who were blessed by that vision, I was dazzled. Flowing tresses, jingling bangles and anklets, bare breasts and thighs brightly lit, dancing lithe and languorous, she was dressed only in serpents. Behind her the chorus of women snake charmers with their hypnotic flutes dictated the bends, bows, and pirouettes of the enchanted vipers that were men in scaled leotards. Her nudity onstage was an adornment, a dramatic interpretation of nakedness. It was a costume disguising natural nudity as the exotic nakedness of the primordial Woman. She was bare but not exposed, disrobed but in no way dismantled. And the snakes, descendants of the antediluvian serpent who gave human beings their knowledge of nakedness, made her nudity all the more dangerously beautiful. She returned in a white silk peignoir and a black cashmere fichu beneath which the fold of a scarlet satin foulard was just barely visible to the naked eye. The robe suggested pale skin, the shawl soft dark down, and the glimmer of shiny scarlet evoked moist flesh. Clothing thus intimated intimate regions. Garments, I discovered in the time that we were together, were always worn during lovemaking. In private, I was not permitted to see the nakedness that was uncovered on the stage each night; but I was allowed to search for it and a deeper nakedness with touch (my fingers slithering beneath silk like serpents under leaves), and to taste it through the fabric (leaving round wet lip prints behind, formed where they had discovered the nipple-jewels through the gown), to smell it through the perfume (where my nose had breathed through the soft shawl). And I could hear nakedness in ardent breathing occasionally punctuated by faint sighs. Once we were lovers, she insisted that I not come into the theater, explaining that she didn't like to perform when there were men with whom she was intimate in the audience. She also told me not to enter the cathedral, that she couldn't genuflect in the presence of human lovers. It was lewdly exhibitionistic in her mind to be watched in communion with Christ, incorporating His flesh into herself, "devouring Him so that He can consume me." When invited, I would wait for her outside the theater to go with her to the Séraphin Serpentin, where I'd carefully limit my intake of opium so that I wouldn't be too stupefied to accompany her to the Passion-carved portals of Our Lady of Paris. Her visits to the opium den were in no way a moral contradiction of her piety. There was nothing in the Bible, she reminded me, against opium: "What is more spiritual than peaceful dreams and visions?" As mysteriously as bread was the flesh of Christ and wine His blood, so the smoke of opium was divine breath and holy spirit. And also by invitation, I'd wait outside Notre-Dame at dawn to walk her home. Since she worked every night and slept every afternoon, lovemaking always took place in the morning. And then I'd be dismissed. During the several years I spent as her lover, I never saw her eat. If the choice had been mine, I would have watched her dance each night, pray each morning, eat and sleep each afternoon, but a condition of loving her was that I be *"sur demande,"* available two or three times a week at most. She did not care to know what I did when I was not waiting for her, and I don't know if she had other lovers. She told me about a priest in Reims where she was born and had taken her first communion, been confirmed, and studied ballet. He was, she avowed, very pious, maintaining his vows with faith. It touched her that he had never touched her, never so much as shaken her hand. "Whenever he looked at me, I knew that he saw through all concealments to a nakedness that no other man has ever seen. His eyes opened my eyes to love." She felt, she said, that if she were to actually show him her naked flesh, it would blind him; if she were to kiss his lips, he would suffocate; if she were to touch him, her fingers would scorch his skin like branding irons. After lovemaking, since she was invariably clothed, I'd be as self-conscious of my nakedness as Adam must have been after succumbing to the temptations of Eve. Naked women could be beautiful because their most intimate parts remained mysterious, concealed within them; but as a man I felt crudely exposed and so would cover my crotch with a pillow, sheet, or piece of clothing. Padi made me constantly aware of nakedness. I began to look at all women I met in terms of the degree to which, whether dressed or undressed, they were naked. I remembered women in terms of that nakedness. Eve Kopitsky was aroused by her own nakedness, as dependent upon its display for pleasure in lovemaking as Padi was on her robes, shawls, and scarves. Zinaida had, I recollected, like Padi, always worn something during lovemaking, at least wool stockings and a wool sweater, but only because of the Leningrad cold; I'm sure she would have loved to lie naked on a beach in the South Pacific. Billie never took off her necklace, the gold airplane that looked like a cross. And Nagini could not, of course, remove her ornaments, the tattooed bracelets of serpents; she bathed in her sari and used it to cover herself after union, for in her world, little girls were always naked, women never. Mary the Caribbean, if I remember rightly, wore a lavender satin sash around her waist, a wig of curly blond tresses, and black silk stockings. Because animals are naked, Pythia, after our first encounter, always removed everything, even her hairpins, for intercourse. And there was that girl whose name I can't remember, the one whom Jesus brought to me. I could still see the fleecy golden pubic hair and the large pale nipples, but nothing else; memory had covered up the rest of her. Although I never had the opportunity to even talk with Sylvia Woodlands, let alone make love to her, I could imagine her nakedness clearly and in great detail: the little circle of bumps around the edge of the rosy nipples, the auburn hairs, the recesses of the belly button, a mole here, a few freckles there, the rough elbow of a smooth bare arm, and the trembling turn open of a soft thigh. Although I know I must have seen my mother undressed when I was a child, I have no recollection of it. I do, however, remember the naked body of the mermaid who drowned in the tank in which her daughter and the snake boy so often bathed together. And I shall always remember the perfect nakedness of Angel as she rolled over on the grass beneath the eucalyptus trees in the clearing beyond the orange groves near Chula Vista. That was when I told her that I would always love her and that I was not afraid to die.

84

"It's a tale of violent death, tragic love, savage jealousy, and bestial rage," Padi answered, shaking her head and shivering her shoulders to express, by theatrical convention, the horror. I had merely asked if she had, by any chance, ever heard of an entertainer named Tara, "a tiger tamer from America, where she was known as Leona Wilder. I met her in Calcutta, where she purchased two Bengal tigers to bring here to Paris, to perform in a revue at the Folies-Bergère." "Heard of her?" Padi asked as she sat up in bed to begin the story: "Everyone in Paris had heard about 'Tara Tata, la Belle Dompteuse des Tigres,' an exotic number, well received not only by the public, but by the critics as well, characterized in *Paris-Soir* as *'une allégorie d'amour.'* I didn't know her personally because I was then just beginning at the Folies and she was a star with her own private dressing room. But I watched her perform many times and was inspired by her to develop my own animal act. I'd use snakes rather than tigers, however, because they are much less dangerous and they only eat once a month. It was breathtaking to see Tara with those huge and frightening cats, naked except for the thigh-high boots, the straps around her wrists, neck, waist, and the little wrap around her hips, all tiger skin. And when the petite lady cracked her whip there wasn't a man in the house who wasn't eager to be tamed. Shere Khan, the male tiger, ten feet from peg to peg and five hundred pounds of lithe and deadly power, behaved like a pussy cat with her, licking her face with his enormous tongue, purring and rolling over so that she could scratch his stomach. As he danced for her and she for him in time to the music, the audience could believe that even the most dangerously ferocious of beasts will become gentle under the sway of a lady's affections. Ah, but in a gold-gilded cage onstage there was Shere Khan's mate, the terrible Mohini, growling to bare her sharp teeth, banging furiously against the bars, roaring with exceptional rage when Tara fondled Shere Khan. Then the beautiful Tara would challenge the female feline with a mocking laugh: *'Alors, ma rivale jalouse, venez! Êtes-vous assez féroce pour être l'amante de mon cher Shère?'* The audience would gasp with anxious awe when Tara threw open the cage door and Mohini leapt out, growling, flashing her dagger-teeth and extending her razor-claws, placing herself between Tara and Shere Khan, ready to pounce upon her rival in love. Calm and graceful, without a trace of fear, Tara snapped her whip, fired her pistol in the air, and stepped toward the roaring tigress, hissing like a cat herself. Another crack of the whip, another hiss or two, a long stare deep into the tiger eyes, and Mohini would back down. Then, just when you thought she was subdued, suddenly, she'd lunge again, swinging a deadly paw at Tara's face. But the tamer, too quick and agile for the cat, ducked unshaken, cracked the whip again, and with another pistol shot, another sharp hiss and deep gaze, she stepped closer in. Cowering under the threats of the courageous tamer, the tigress would lie down in surrender. Tara would then pet Mohini to solemnize the truce, and Shere Khan, relieved that his mate and tamer had settled their differences, would join them for the grand bow. Maurice Chevalier sang a song about her, 'Taratata! Tara Tata tâteras ta tarte-tatin!' and 'une tataratarine' became Parisian argot for both a powerful, sexually beguiling woman and a fig dessert. Tara fascinated men and she inspired women by allowing them to imagine that as long as a woman had courage, she would be triumphant in love, at least if, in addition to courage, she had large bare breasts, a pistol, and a whip." "What happened to her?" was the obvious question and Padi was ready to answer: "Feral beasts can hardly be expected to distinguish between life and imitations of it, between reality and art. The tigers couldn't be blamed. Wild animals can never be tamed, but only trained with reward and punishment to behave in ways that appear tame. One day, while Tara was rehearsing with Mohini, the tigress suddenly, unexpectedly, and for no apparent cause, attacked, really attacked, and with one bite of her powerful jaws and a fierce twist of her head, tore Tara's arm right out of its socket. Tara's husband, unusually devoted to his wife for an Englishman, heroically rushing into the cage, picked up Tara's pistol and aimed it at the head of the beast that was devouring his wife's arm. He fired repeatedly but to no avail, since it was loaded with blanks. Seeing his beloved Mohini assaulted by a rival male, Shere Khan instinctually pounced from behind and ripped the screeching man into shreds of meat. As Tara, her shoulder gushing blood, struggled to crawl out of the cage, the two tigers calmly consumed her husband's flesh. Everything had been eaten by the time police marksmen arrived to discharge their automatic rifles through the bars of the training cage into the man-eating couple. Without her two tigers and one of her arms, Tara no longer had a spot at the Folies-Bergère. But animal trainers never know when to quit. After she was released from the hospital, she had another tiger shipped from India, and now she's performing in Grand Guignol sketches at the Théâtre du Maldoror in Pigalle. As I prefer beauty and the sublime to horror and the macabre, I've not gone out of my way to see it, but I hear from others with stronger stomachs and better senses of humor than I that she reenacts, much to the thrill of die-hard guignolers, the attack of Mohini." While Padi was dancing with serpents on the stage of the Folies-Bergère that night, I was sitting in the audience at the Maldoror watching *La Belle Dompteuse des Tigres*. After the tiger had ripped Tara's arm out of its socket and the house doctor had to be called to revive a man in the third row who had fainted,

I ducked out to find my way around to the back of the theater, where I was able to enter an unlocked door without having to talk my way past anyone. Guessing that the sign *"Cave Felem!"* marked Tara's dressing room, I knocked, heard an *"Entrez,"* and opened the door to behold the one-armed woman in a pink satin kimono sitting at her mirror with a tiger dozing at her feet. She didn't recognize me. "It's me, Isaac Schlossberg. Remember? I met you in India. I was at your wedding at Diwanasthan Palace. I was heartbroken to hear about Colonel Coffin-White. He was a great game hunter. His passing is a sad loss." She spoke cordially: "This is my Shankar. Come closer and pet him so that he knows you don't mean him any harm. He won't bite you. He's been castrated, declawed, and he's an opium addict. Scratch behind his ears." As I complied, I remarked that I had been impressed by his acting. "That's not acting," she noted, explaining that Shankar had learned, through reward (horse offal) and punishment (the same electric collar she had used on the feral boy in Alipore), to obediently take his dinner, a leg of lamb larded with blood packets, disguised as a human arm and attached to Tara, each night onstage. "Why are you here?" she asked. "Is it that, after hearing that Francis is gone, you thought that you might be able to have your way with me? Did you think that, since I'm missing an arm and a husband, I would be desperate for a man and thus easily seduced?" Utterly shocked, I vehemently denied the ridiculous accusation, apologized for disturbing her, and said that I would leave. "No, no," she insisted with a softening of her glower. "It's all right. It's just that it happens so often that men who have seen the act fall in love with me. Many guignolers fantasize about intimate relations with a woman who is missing a limb. I've come to expect it. Sit down on the divan and have a brandy with me. How did you like the show?" It seemed to please her that I told her that I loved it (which felt strange to say since I was referring to the spectacle of her being mauled and mutilated). Shankar opened his eyes, looked around for a moment, and then went back to sleep. She rose from her chair to sit next to me. "Yes, I remember now, you were at the boat to see us off. That was sweet of you." She extended her single arm to show me the ruby bracelet that the Maharaja of Diwanasthan had given her as a wedding gift. "It was found in Mohini's upper intestine," she remarked, moving her hand toward my face. That she began to stroke my hair the same gently reassuring way in which she had been petting Shankar when I came in made me nervous. All of a sudden she grasped my hair, tugged on it to pull my face toward hers, and utterly shocked me by kissing me with an open mouth. She nibbled on my lower lip, made me flinch with a hard bite, and, as I tried to rise, pushed me down, turned and, with her pink silk dressing gown parting like a stage curtain, straddled me as she ravenously kissed me. Through scary panting and wild moans, she whispered, "My darling, I've been waiting. Don't make me wait any longer." Because I had absolutely no desire to make love to her, I was surprised and then relieved that I was somehow vaguely able to do what she wanted me to do. Shankar, I noticed in the midst of it, had awakened to watch us without much interest. Gaily announcing that love always made her hungry for *choucroute garnie,* she invited me to Le Cochon Enchâiné. Although I still did not find her sexually alluring and would certainly never allow what had happened to happen again, I was pleased that I had apparently made her at least a little bit happy. And I was grateful for the meal and touched when she asked me to give her a helping hand with a knife to cut the large slice of ham that was draped over her pile of sauerkraut. During dinner I told her about some of the things that had happened in India after she left, and then explained that I was looking for work: "I'm quite experienced at handling snakes. And it occurred to me tonight during your show that a snake act could do well at the Théâtre du Maldoror. I'm sure audiences would enjoy seeing me strangled by a python or bitten by a cobra." Dropping her fork, she glared at me icily: "Oh, so that's why you came and fawned over me, pretending to be smitten. That's why you seduced me, just so that I would get you a job! You were just preying upon a helpless maimed widow for your own ends! I had imagined it was love! But no, damn you, all you think about is yourself!" I was even more shocked by this verbal outburst than I had been by her carnal advances a few hours earlier. Who has seduced whom, it seems, even in the most inconsequential of erotic interactions, is always up for grabs. There was, no matter how hard I tried, no way of convincing her that the accusations were false. But then her grimace gave way to a condescending laugh. "Okay, my disarming little gigolo, have what you want. Unlike you, I try to be generous and kind. I'll introduce you to Madame Diotime, the proprietor of the Théâtre du Maldoror. But it is the last thing I shall ever do for you. Our love affair is over. I cannot love a man who thinks only of himself."

To 47

85	The table was cluttered. There were body parts, fashioned of plaster, rubber, and animal flesh, that looked passably human: twisted arms with hands clenched talonlike, a rigid leg with a muddy shoe on the foot, and the head of a man whose mouth was hideously

contorted into a silent scream beneath a peppery mustache; his carroty hair stood on end and he was missing an ear. There were plenty of bones, two human skulls, a monkey's, a dog's, and an owl's, a baker's dozen eyeballs, a couple of tongues, a few penises, a brain in a glass jar and a heart in another. There was a fantastic array of weaponry: pistols, daggers, stilettos, razors, brass knuckles, blackjacks, cleavers, axes, hooks, and picks; medical and dental equipment galore (hypodermic needles, scalpels, forceps, trepans, and surgical saws). There were piles of bloody bandages, jars of chemicals, and an ashtray into which Madame Diotime snuffed out a Gitanes Maïs without taking her diagnostically probing eyes off me. Rather than voicing the obvious ("Why do you want to work in Grand Guignol? How can you contribute to the theater of terror, rage, revulsion, abjection, and cruelty? Have you had any experience?"), she silently waited for answers. When I began in French (*"Je connais très bien les moeurs des serpents et . . ."*), she shushed me: "Your accent makes it unpleasant for me to listen. English, please." Starting over ("I've had a lot of experience with snakes and I have a few ideas for plays"), I proceeded to tell her about my upbringing in carnival, sideshow, and vaudeville and I showed her the snakebite scar on my hand. Cigarette smoke, but no words, came from her mouth. Fearing that my time was running out, I sensed that, if I had any hope of being hired, I needed to intrigue her with characters and plots. "I am writing a piece called *Samoo le Serpent-Garçon*. A mad scientist, Dr. Bungarus, after decapitating both a small boy and a huge snake, grafts the boy's head onto the body of the snake. I haven't quite figured out why he does so, but I do know how to rig the operating table for the illusion. After chopping up the boy's body and incinerating it in the laboratory furnace, he notices the head of the snake on the floor and stoops to pick it up. Suddenly the jaws of the severed head open and clamp onto the hand of Dr. Bungarus, who then falls over and writhes about on the stage, convulsing from the effects of the deadly venom, as the snake with the head of the boy laughs and howls: *Vive la justice!* No? Okay, I have another idea, *Les Yeux de la Vipère,* in which a mad herpetologist, Dr. Antoine Denuage, who has been injecting himself with venom to build up an immunity to snakebite, uses serpents to kill people whom he then dissects to study the effects of the various poisons on the nervous system. He has a beautiful daughter who goes so insane that she imagines she's the poetess Elizabeth Barrett Browning." Diotime stopped me. "Write out the scripts. I'll stage one of them and let the audience decide your fate. But I must advise you: for someone as young as yourself, a profession in Grand Guignol is perhaps not such a good idea. Audiences are already dwindling because of the competition of the cinema. At first, with the silents, it was not such a problem, but once the screams of film actors could be heard, it was a blow. And soon, when they film motion pictures in color, with blood flowing as crimson as ours, well, then I'm not sure what will happen. The Grand Guignol theater on rue Gilles de Rais has already turned into a cinema. Perhaps you should consider a career in films." Confessing that I had already acted in motion pictures, that I had been young George Washington, Warren Hastings, and several biblical characters and that I had been decapitated by Cleopatra, "not, of course, all in the same film," I assured Madame Diotime that I wanted to appear, as the French idiom has it, "in flesh and bone." "Our goal," she explained, "is to create a divertissement that makes every member of the audience want to escape from the theater. I would like to bolt and lock the exits, to hear them begging us to stop the show and open the doors, pleading to purchase tickets for release." Madame Diotime assessed the success of each performance on the basis of the number of people in the audience who vomited, convulsed, or fainted. The occasional heart attack was a triumph to be celebrated with champagne after the show. That I had spent some time in India intrigued her. "Everyone is fascinated by the sinister Oriental," she remarked, "their grotesque gods, macabre rites, and exquisite tortures. I shall expect you to use your experiences in the East to come up with some disgusting plots and grisly characters." She had herself authored and directed several horror plays set in India. One of them, *L'Honneur,* was currently being staged, giving me an immediate opportunity to learn from the master. I watched every performance of it that week, taking special note of her use of history, exotic settings, body parts, and stage blood. Act I: Colonel Reading and his beautiful daughter, Mr. Blue and his new bride, and young Private Wright are trapped in a bungalow that is surrounded by fanatical sepoys. Private Wright courageously volunteers to go for help. No sooner has he left the bungalow, however, than there are prolonged, bloodcurdling screams from offstage. His severed head, with a note nailed to the pate that insults the British Crown, is then tossed onstage through the window. Act II: In panic, Mr. and Mrs. Blue, despite Colonel Reading's attempt to stop them, run out the door and there are more bloodcurdling screams. Mr. Blue, blood dripping from the socket in his face from which an eye had been gouged, his feet and hands amputated and the four stumps profusely bleeding, crawls back to report the sexual atrocities that the sepoys have wreaked on his wife before cutting off her breasts and disemboweling her. He dies. Act III: Pounding on the bolted door, the sepoys continue to insult the Crown. Colonel Reading's daughter, fearing that she is about to be raped, pleads with her father to kill her. Out of love for her, he fires his pistol into the center of her forehead. Holding her dead body in his arms, her brains oozing out of the hole in her skull, the colonel hears the bugle that signals the arrival of the Bengal Lancers, who, to the tune of "Hail Britannia," slaughter the sepoys. More bloodcurdling screams. Entering the bungalow in victory, the Lancer commander discovers that Colonel Reading has gone insane. "Yes," I told Diotime, "the play is remarkable. *Absolument shakespearien!* if you'll pardon my French. It inspired me to finish my scripts." After reading them, and choosing *Le Serpent-Garçon,* she edited it extensively. I was cast as Dr. Bungarus and Gilles, a precocious ten-year-old who, conveniently for his theatrical career, looked no older than six or seven, was the boy whom I would decapitate. Counting on charming Draupadi Padoux to lend me a python until I could order a troupe of ophidian actors from Bannerjee Brothers Menagerie in Calcutta, I assured Madame Diotime that I had the perfect snake to play the part of the snake. As we discussed the technical procedures that would be used for the decapitations, I realized just what an artist Madame Diotime was. She designed all the illusions herself, constructing the knives with the blood in their handles, both stilettos with retractable blades for stabbing and butcher knives with extendible blades that had curves concealed them for simulated slicing. She sculpted superb stumps and fashioned sensational scars. She was especially proud of her blood, a rich soup of glycerin, cochineal, lac, and a secret syrup that would, after gushing in floods and spurts of glistening scarlet from hidden bulbs on the bodies of victims, congeal and darken like real blood under the stage lights. Madame Diotime was a genius. Perhaps that was what made her so powerfully attractive. In her presence, or in afterthoughts, one could not help but be fascinated by her strange beauty, and yet in photographs, I noticed, she was actually rather homely with harsh features and signs of age. It was, I believe, in addition to her artistic genius, her complete confidence in her carnality and a belief in her own beauty that made her such a ravishingly alluring woman in person and in memory. I thought her hair was blond, and yet, one day as I fished a strand of it out of a bowl of blood she had mixed for me, I realized that it was really gray. She appeared majestically tall and yet whenever I stood close to her I would be reminded that she was quite petite. When dressed in men's clothes, as she often was, she paradoxically appeared all the more feminine. And vice versa. She entertained lovers of both genders and of all ages and races. She would inevitably tire of them after a few weeks and dismiss them. But they always accepted rejection with gratitude for having had the opportunity, no matter how fleeting, of an intimacy with her.

Monsieur Becque was the exception. Formally a chef with a restaurant of his own on the rue Villon, he had been sent to prison for killing a customer who had had the gall to criticize first his *quenelles de poissons* and then to complain about the main course, his *cervelles en matelote;* that might have been tolerable, but when the finicky client deemed the chef's *pouding de cabinet* inedible, Becque rushed from the kitchen with a revolver and shot the man in the mouth. Because the court deemed the murder *"un crime passionnel,"* Becque was sentenced to only two years in prison, where, given his professional background, he was assigned to the kitchen. During a fight with the prison's head cook over the proper method for heating a *sauce diable aux anchois,* he suffered the loss of an eye when the cook plunged a citrus stripper into his face. One of the conditions of his parole had been that he swear before God that he would never cook again. Upon meeting Monsieur Becque at a bal-musette on the rue Bombance and accepting his invitation to dance a java, Madame Diotime was captivated by his eye, which, because of the way it rolled about in its socket, was obviously made of glass. She hired him on the spot to play the countless characters in her dramas who had an eye gouged out onstage. Before each performance, his prosthetic eye would be replaced with a goat eye supplied free of charge by a neighborhood butcher, who was a constant lover of theater and a former lover of Madame Diotime's. The sight of a knife (as I witnessed during his performance as Oedipus in Madame Diotime's delightful comic farce, *La Foutaise en Maternelle*) inserted slowly into the eyeball, with the milky vitreous ooze dripping down the blade, enhanced by the champagne-cork sound that the eye made when popped from its socket, was spectacular. Secretly—given the conditions of his release from prison—he would sometimes cook for Madame Diotime, and on one of those occasions, to celebrate the signing of my contract, I was invited to join them for dinner. Her worktable, cleared of the clutter of body parts, weapons, and medical equipment, was set for the feast. As Becque held a gleaming carving knife over his *porc grand-mère,* I praised, with an enthusiasm that I hoped concealed my anxiety, the *museau de cochon* with which we had started. Filling our glasses with champagne, he smiled, raised his coupe, and, wishing me all the best in my new career of entertaining people with atrocity, perversion, filth, injustice, degradation, lust, and violent death, toasted: *"A votre santé!"*

86 "'I act according to the intention of the Almighty Creator,' Germany's chancellor, Adolf Hitler, said in a speech at an anti-Jewish rally in Munich yesterday," reported *Paris-Soir:* "'By fighting the Jews I do battle for the Lord.' An inspired crowd responded with jubilant cries of *'Heil Hitler'* and *'Jude verrecke.'* In an interview following the rally, the chancellor made a candid prophecy: 'In years to come I shall be honored in all lands as the hero who had the will, courage, and strength to exterminate the Jewish pest from the world once and for all.'" Angel snatched the paper out of my hands. "You shouldn't read that nonsense," she said as, removing her gloves and nestling Napoleon comfortably in her lap, she seated herself next to me at the table on the terrace of Le Jeu de Scène, a café conveniently close to the Théâtre Sarah Bernhardt, where she was in rehearsal. "The news is just bad melodrama, not even good farce, not in the least bit entertaining. Terrible plots, predictable characters, and the same old depressing themes. The Marquis says that one of the benefits of his blindness is that he is no longer tempted to read either the newspaper or the Bible." Everything the Marquis d'Échelle said was, as far as Angel was concerned, at once profoundly amusing and subtly wise. Bachnele had told me about him in London: "An alter kaker, old enough to be her grandfather, a blind man, no less! Not a Jew, but it could be worse: he's rich! The money's inherited, but he's made a few bucks as a playwright too. Artsy stuff, the kind of plays that people think are good just because they don't understand them." The Marquis had gone, so Angel's version of the love story went, once upon a time to the Folies-Bergère. The curtain rose to reveal the great tank of water in which La Sirène performed her piscatory ballet, her mermaid tail rhythmically waving as she somersaulted and pirouetted amidst a school of gracefully circling rays. The Marquis turned to his escort, a model whose nakedness was famed in Paris for having transformed more than one painter into an artist: "I have never seen a more beautiful girl." The word "seen" was stressed. The Marquis could, Angel told me as if she believed that such a thing was possible, see her without seeing her. He gazed at her by feeling the feeling in the room, sensing her beauty through a subtle reading of the sounds in the hall as symptomatic of enthrallment: whispers, silences, shuffling, soft breathing, muffled gasps, hushed sighs, the way the orchestra played (how fast, slow, loud, soft, excitedly, calmly), and other noises unnoticed by those distracted by sight. "He can see many things," Angel swore, "to which we are completely blind." The artist's model had been dispatched to bring Angel to his home the next day. "He asked me to undress and since he was blind I saw no reason not to do so. 'Nakedness modulates a woman's voice,' he said, 'and allows her to speak more openly and honestly.' The Marquis has seen through me." The love affair made no sense to me: she obviously knows, I reflected during her tediously adoring panegyric, that the old man can't appreciate her beauty, unable as he is to perceive the curve of her brow, slope of her neck, or roundness of her breast. Even if he has traced the contours with his fingertips, he's ignorant of the heavenly blue of her eyes, gingery gold of her hair, creamy pallor of her belly, and rosy blush of her cheek. And Angel, I knew, had always loved to be seen. I pitied the blind Marquis d'Échelle for not being able to behold her nakedness, resented him for depriving her of the glory of revealing it, and envied him for not having to be the victim of memories of its bewitching beauty. Memory teased me with the voyeuristic pleasures to which I had become addicted: the little girl on the high wire, too far away to be touched, heard, or smelled, but perfectly placed for the eyes; the young woman on the screen, offering Cleopatra to no other sense but sight; at the Paradisio and the Breakers, dancing with veils flourishing around her. The Marquis could only try to imagine what I had seen. Angel lit a small cigar. "My newest affectation," she said laughing. "The Marquis smokes them." She never actually referred to him as her "lover," but rather as her "teacher" or even "master," her "benefactor" or even "savior." When she first met him, he was staging a play that he himself had written: *Les Rêveries Érotiques de Tiresius.* "Do you know the story?" she asked. "The blind seer? The man who, because he separated two copulating snakes and killed the female, became a woman, and then, seven years later, by separating another pair of love-entwined serpents and killing the male, became a man once more?" I said that, yes, I knew the fable well, lying in order not to have to hear about it. But she gave a detailed account of the Marquis's rendition of it anyway. "Oh," I commented, "it's a comic farce." That angered her: "You wouldn't understand. He's an artist, you're just an entertainer. And, in any case, you mustn't insult him again. If you do, I'll stop loving you." I fought back, impulsively arguing that if she really did love me, as she said she did, she would make love with me. "I won't make love with you," she countered, "precisely because I do love you." The game was on and I wanted to win. "Oh, I see: if I insult him again, you'll stop loving me. And, if I understand the rules correctly, you will then, because you no longer love me, make love with me once more? Okay. In that case the Marquis d'Échelle is a dirty old man and a hack writer. Let's fuck." She ducked my jab, parried with a smile, and thrust with "I can't help loving you, Isaac. I'll always love you, my first love. I know that we'll be friends forever." I fought back. "Do you have sex with him?" She dismissed my question by laughing. Napoleon was licking her fingers. Before I could make another move she laughed again. Laughter is always sure to give a player the edge, and, personally, I consider it cheating. But Angel always had been a cheater. When as children we played our game of snakes and ladders, she'd wait and watch for me to turn my head away from the board even for a split second to seize the opportunity to push her token forward a square or even up a row. If I accused her of doing so, she would just laugh, then as always. After doing the outside free show on the wire, Angel would often sell the ten-in-one tickets for my father, and no one ever suspected the sweet little Angel of shortchanging: out loud the child would count the money carefully, then count the change into her hand, then palming a coin or two, turn over what seemed like the right change into the hand of the mark, misdirecting with a polite "Here's your ticket, sir. Thank you. Enjoy the show. Next, please." It wasn't cheating, but acting, just another demonstration of her mastery of one of the sundry entertainment arts. Angel laughed again. "Let's not fight anymore," she insisted. "You know I love you, and I know you love me. My play is opening in less than a month and Consuela's coming all the way from California for it. She's bringing her husband, Siegel. Did you know they got married? Bachnele's coming from London. I can't wait to meet his bride and see the new baby. They're arriving a week early so that we can celebrate Pesach together, just like in the old days. You will come to the seder, won't you? If you don't, I won't love you anymore." She had won the round of the game and was happily smiling. Her childhood dreams had come true: she lived in Paris and she was about to again play the Queen of the Nile. *La Jouissance de Cléopâtre* had been written expressly for her by the Marquis d'Échelle. I had had no interest in meeting the man, but Angel insisted on it. I could not see him any better than he could see me during any of our few encounters, since they always took place in his completely darkened library. At our first meeting, as I ran my fingers along the spines of books in shelves that I could not see, he said it was a pleasure to meet the young man whom Angel had loved since childhood. "First passions set the scene for future acts of truer love. I must confess that I am relieved that I am myself no longer young. During my youth, I would fall wholeheartedly in love with any and every woman who was at all beautiful to behold. Do you know that inclination? Love is, after all, a sense of irresistible beauty, a response to it and appreciation of it. I am, alas, a Platonist. Blindness has allowed me to more easily be willing to begin the arduous climb up the philosopher's ladder of Eros, from the low rungs of youth toward higher rungs from which the spirit beholds an eternal beauty beyond both light and darkness, a pure beauty that is not dependent upon ephemeral forms. To envision that most true and perfect beauty is to be wholly absorbed by it. And that absorption, the complete fulfillment of love, is immortality." Like so many Frenchmen, he fancied himself a philosopher of love, and Angel believed that what he said was profound. Although I didn't under-stand what on earth he was talking about, I supposed that it might have sounded truer, or at least more poetic, in French. And I wondered whether it meant that, because he was on such a high spiritual rung of the ladder of love, he had transcended the transient pleasures of physical intimacy with Angel's ephemeral form. "So," I couldn't restrain myself from asking Angel again that afternoon as we sat together on the terrace of Le Jeu de Scène, "do you actu-ally sleep with him? And I don't mean 'sleep' in the literal sense. What I mean is, do you actually make love with him? And I don't mean 'make love' in a philo-sophical sense. What I mean is, does he fuck you? And I don't mean 'fuck' in an expletory sense. What I mean is, do you do *it* with each other?" Angel laughed again, stood up, tucked Napoleon under her arm, tousled my hair, kissed me on the cheek, and said, "I don't know what you mean by *it*." Out loud she counted out the money for our coffee into one hand, then turned over what seemed like the right amount into my hand, misdirected me with a "Good-bye, my darling," and left for rehearsal. I continued reading the newspaper that she had snatched from me a half hour earlier: "Stormtroopers, marching into Ho-henstaufen on Friday evening, dragged the Jews of the township from their homes and beat them. On Saturday morning there were reports that ten of the Jews had died. The survivors were taken into protective custody at a camp near the picturesque upper Bavarian town of Dachau."

From 18

|87| "Consider your life," Madame Diotime advised. "Look for the horrors beneath the plain surfaces of quotidian experience. Let memory provide the characters, and imagination generate gruesomely terrifying situations into which to put those beings. When they discover themselves brought to life in horrible predicaments, they will come up with the dialogue and construct the plots for you. Let them suffer. And then laugh at their misery." Grand Guignol productions at Madame Diotime's Théâtre du Maldoror by convention alternated the macabre with the farcical: "First there should be hot-blooded screams, all the stimulating thrill of terror; and then coldhearted laughter, all the dangerous relief of humor. The subsequent terror will be all the more terrible to those who, in the throes of laughter, have let down their guard. The more you can scare them, the more easily you will be able to make them laugh, and the more they have laughed, the more easy it will be to frighten them. That's the art of Grand Guignol." Like every other American in Paris at the time who couldn't either paint or play jazz, I wanted to write, and Madame Diotime encouraged the endeavor. Following her counsel, I composed horror plays and comic farces featuring characters who had played parts in my own life. "Even the most innocent scenes from real life," she explained, "have dread, disgust, and depravity embedded somewhere in them. Extract from your past all the filth and gore that at the time you might not have noticed, all the madness from what seemed normal, and all the fright in what seemed safe. And then reconsider the terror and realize how ridiculous, how absolutely comical, it is, and write a farce." Since comedy is more difficult than horror, I started with the latter. It was at once a rendition of Buffalo Bill's Wild West classic, "Attack on a Settler's Cabin," and an adaptation of Madame Diotime's own *L'Honneur* (retitled *L'Honneur Américain*). I substituted savage Apaches for Madame Diotime's fanatical sepoys, and in place of her commander of the Bengal Lancers, I had Buffalo Bill leading the United States Cavalry all too late to the rescue. The head of Private Wright was not merely severed from his body but also scalped, and the note nailed to it, signed by Geronimo, insulted the president of United States. Since Madame Diotime had reminded me on several occasions that my plays, whether comedy or horror, should have lots of sex in them ("sex and death for horror, sex and love for comedy"), I expanded Mr. Blue's account of the sexual atrocities endured by Mrs. Blue in the Apache camp. A hundred Indians raped her. Encouraged by Madame Diotime to write more about the American West, I presented her next with *Le Tirailleur.* Act I: A cowboy named Wyoming Warren

has married Frisco Fanny, a beautiful dance hall girl. After Apaches kidnap Fanny and rape her, Warren comes to her rescue. In single-handed battle with the Indians, his eye (because Monsieur Becque would play the part) is put out by an arrow. Not letting that stop him, the cowboy kills the entire tribe of Indians and scalps their chief (yelling, "This scalp for Custer!"). Act II: Some years later, famous for his exploits against the redskins, Warren has been hired by a traveling Wild West revue as a one-eyed marksman. He is demonstrating his skill at tomahawk throwing, when he slips and (because Tara would be cast) accidentally chops off one of Fanny's arms. In the comic version of the same play, *Le Tirailleur Malgré Lui,* Fanny runs away with the Indians because her husband doesn't satisfy her sexually. The Indian chief, unable to endure the nagging white woman's sexual insatiability, forcibly returns her to Warren. But, because the cowboy doesn't want his wife back, he fights with the Indian, and when he appears the scalp him, the Indian yells, "Give me back my toupee!" Disgusted with both of them, Fanny runs away to join a Wild West revue. To celebrate being rid of her, Wyoming Warren and the Indian chief open a bottle of champagne and the popping cork puts out Wyoming Warren's eye. *Exeunt omnes.* Madame Diotime liked it, but it upset Tara. "What about Fanny's arm? She doesn't lose her arm in the farce! How can I play the part? Other than tiger taming, losing an arm is my only talent." Tara's theatrical reenactments of her real-life loss of her arm to a tiger soon, much to the dire disappointment of her fans, came to an end with the untimely death of Shankar. That he had suffered his heart attack onstage, however, was some consolation. "That is the dream of every true entertainer," Tara sniffled, "to die on the boards." In attempting to arrange a fitting funeral for Shankar, Tara had been humiliatingly laughed at by the directors of all the cemeteries in Paris. With genuine sympathy for the bereft woman, Madame Diotime, however, found a suitable grave for the animal in the garden of an ex-lover and cat fancier with a house in Versailles. Having had no body to inhume after her husband had been eaten made it all the more meaningful to Tara that she should bury Shankar in style. Despite the misunderstanding between Tara and me at our initial meeting in Paris, she had remained civil, though aloof, during the time we worked together at the Maldoror. "Grief over the loss of a loved one," she said as she handed me the engraved invitation to the funeral, "encourages us to forgive those for whom we have felt enmity, even if they have wronged us. Death reminds us of the vanity of holding a grudge." As she could not find a real cleric willing to perform the obsequies for the deceased feline, Monsieur Becque, dressed ecclesiastically in the very vestments that he wore onstage as the psychopathic priest in *Les Curées du Curé,* agreed to play the part. With his false eye rolling about in its socket, the actor recited an obsequy of his own composition: *"Shankar était gentil toute sa vie / Mais maintenant il est parti vers l'infini / Le tigre est dans les cieux / Nous espérons qu'il est heureux."* Too heartbroken to continue her work on the stage, Tara returned to the United States. Because Madame Diotime paid by the play, I turned out as many as I could as quickly as I could, ever looking back over my life for inspiration. In my *Le Charmeur des Serpents*, Lingnath, plotting with Mrs. Sassoon, really did use poisonous snakes to kill Godfrey Sassoon so that he and Mrs. Sassoon could be lovers and run off together to Hawaii. The snake charmer does not realize that, because he himself has been bitten so many times over the years, his bodily fluids are highly toxic; and thus Mrs. Sassoon dies a grisly death in the Hindu's arms as result of kissing him. In despair Lingnath tries to kill himself by allowing his deadly snakes to bite him; but because of the immunity to venom that he has unknowingly developed, his attempts at suicide fail and he goes mad. In *Le Neurologue Anglais,* a Dr. Adderson is conducting psychosurgical experiments on convicted murderers to determine what areas of the brain are responsible for both sociopathological behavior and love. After removing a portion of the postcentral gyrus from the brain of a psychopathic murderer, he implants it in the head of a poodle. The dog bites him and Dr. Adderson dies of rabies. If Tara had not retired, Dr. Adderson would have had a fiancée whose arm was ripped off by the mad poodle. I continued to draw upon material from my own life: *L'Hypnotiseur* (in which Major Wheedle, unable to bring Pythia McCloud out of a mesmeric trance, is murdered by her), *L'Enfant Sauvage* (in which Hugh Mann mauls Dr. McCloud and eats his heart), *Le Taxiderme* (in which Albert Bannerjee kidnaps beautiful women in order to kill, stuff, mount, and pose them in imitation of nudes from famous works of art), *Le Maharaja* (in which an Indian potentate offers his ten wives to be sacrificed to Kali in a ritual meant to revive sexual potency), and *Le Prestidigitateur* (in which a magician accidentally saws his wife in half while trying to perform the famous trick). My personal favorite was the semi-autobiographical *Le Guignolier,* in which a writer-actor in Grand Guignol theater, having so lost his mind from working in the genre that he is unable to distinguish between art and life, hires people off the streets to act in his plays and actually murders them onstage. Just as the members of the fictional audience in the play imagine that the players are just pretending to die, so members of the real audience of the play would hopefully fear that it all might actually be real. "Is this a horror piece or a comic farce?" Madame Diotime asked after reading the script. "Try to distinguish more clearly between the two sentiments." Confessing that *Le Guignolier* was not supposed to be funny, I explained that I would be pleased if it were, since, despite what I had learned years before from George Strong (that "anything done badly enough is comic"), I was struggling with comedy: "It's so much harder than horror." Madame Diotime explained to me that if I ever found it difficult to turn a macabre tale comic, I should merely have my characters break wind. "Farting is always funny. It is the secret ingredient of great comedy." She elaborated on her theory of the genre in specific terms: "Cuckoldry, impotence, nymphomania, satyriasis, gluttony, and sloth are comic. Foreigners, drunkards, and prudes are funny as are very fat people and stutterers. Misers and priests are both amusing (particularly if they fart), so are midgets and dwarfs, but since they tend to be expensive, I avoid them as characters. Although the penis is much funnier than the vagina, the vagina is comic if it belongs to a nun, whore, old wife, or young virgin, or if it itches. Everything that itches is funny. It's funnier when a woman farts than when a man does. Baldness is funny, but psoriasis, festering carbuncles, scabs, scabies, and other dermatological anomalies aren't. Diarrhea and constipation are hilarious as is everything else that relates to the bowels. Gonorrhea is funnier than syphilis, but not anywhere near as good for a laugh as crab lice. Pubic hair is funny, especially if just one of them is found somewhere it's not expected to be. God the Father is funnier than either Jesus Christ or the Holy Spirit. Flowers aren't very funny, but fruit is, as is any vegetable that reminds the audience of a penis. Jews are funny when they are in love, girls are funny when they are not. Dogs are funnier than cats and homosexuals are funny unless they are pedophiles. Snakes are never funny, piglets always are. Snakes, however, frighten people and fear is killingly funny. Devils are funny if they are red and have little horns and a goatee. Angels are not particularly comical— well, not unless they fart. Tears are funnier than laughter." Madame Diotime sighed and then laughed. "And horror is funnier than comedy."

The first cup had been filled. After reciting the blessing, Bachnele dedicated the offering to Angel's mother: "Tivya Rabinowitz, who lives in our memory, nourished there with our love." That the toast brought tears to the eyes of Consuela Heimenhoff suggested that, even after many years and all that she had done for Angel, the lingerie heiress still felt guilty for running Tivya over with her Peerless. Throughout the evening Consuela repeatedly and unabashedly announced, "I love Jews!" Over the bitter herbs she explained that "even though my family came from Germany, I've always loved Jews. I never knew I was one, however, until just a few weeks ago, when I read Chancellor Adolf Hitler's official declaration in *Reader's Digest* that anyone who has one Jewish grandparent is a Jew. Well, my mother's mother was a Jew, of course not a practicing one. She celebrated Easter rather than Passover and sang Handel's *Messiah* in a Lutheran choir each year during the Christmas season. But 'born a Jew, always a Jew,' as they say. Naturally the Heimenhoffs kept it a secret. But I'm not ashamed. No, not at all, I think it's actually rather exciting. And it's just as well that I am a Jew because that *Reader's Digest* article, the one about Mr. Hitler, further reported that in Nuremberg a non-Jewish woman who had married a Jew was arrested, tried, and convicted for 'racial defilement.' I wouldn't want to be accused of that!" She turned to her husband: "Darling, could you pass me some of the unleavened bread that your ancestors and mine on my grandmother's side of the family used to eat in the wilderness?" Siegel reminded her to call them "matzahs." Bachnele had brought the symbolic bread with him from London, along with Haggadahs, yarmulkes, his wife, Thalia, and their new baby, Moshe. After Consuela's proclamation of Jewish ancestry, Thalia frowned. "I guess I'm the only Gentile here. Please don't hold it against me. At least I'm not Egyptian." Professor Wonderful consoled the very tall former Muse of Comedy: "Don't worry about being the goy as we Jews are saying. I was one once myself." It was serendipitous that the magician was there with Shula. Just a week before, while waiting for Padi at midnight outside the Folies-Bergère, I had seen his name on the poster for a new show: *La Folie de la Magie*. I took the liberty of inviting the Wonderfuls to join us. After his success at the Royal Command Performance, his *Magic of India* had been booked for an all-European tour that included, before the Paris engagement, runs in Rome, Vienna, and Berlin. "We were in Germany when the boycott of Jewish shops started," Shula dolefully recounted. "No one knew that we're Jewish, so we weren't harassed. In fact, we were treated very well. Helmut Schreiber, Hitler's favorite magician, was our host. Schreiber does an Indian magic show himself, wearing a turban, Oriental robes, and slippers with curled toes, and billing himself as Kala Nag, 'the Black Snake.' He informed us that Hitler loves magic. 'The Führer subscribes,' he said, 'to the dictum and principle that is the very basis of our art: *mundus vult decipi.*' He offered to introduce us to the German chancellor and even to arrange for us to perform for him." Moshe was crying so feverishly that we could hardly hear what Shula was saying. When Thalia raised her blouse to present a huge breastful of milk to the infant, Bachnele insisted that she anoint the nipple with Pesach wine. "He's beautiful," Angel told the mother. "It's so good to have a baby boy with us, one named Moshe no less, to remind us of the little Moshe in the basket among the reeds of the Nile." Thalia noted that she wished that she had had a baby girl. "And I was hoping for a midget," Bachnele added, "a chip off the block, like father like son. But we love him anyway, and there's always the next time." "As the maror reminds us of the bitterness the Israelites experienced in Egypt," Siegel declared, "so let the beautiful breast of Thalia Poopik remind us that the Lord promised us a land of milk and honey." We dribbled drops from the second cup of wine into our plates as a symbol of blood with the recitation of each of the ten plagues which "the Holy One, praised be He, brought upon our enemies." After we had thanked God for smiting the firstborn children of Egypt, Bachnele professed his faith that "our God will do to Hitler just what he did to that shmuck Pharaoh." Before we drank the wine, Bachnele dedicated the offering to the memories of Abraham Schlossberg and Jake Grossman. *"V'hi she-amdah la-avotaynu v'lan,"* he recited. "In every generation do enemies rise up against us, seeking to destroy us. But the Holy One, praised be He, always delivers us from their hands." We had said more blessings, eaten more matzah, and filled the third glass of wine, when Siegel announced that Bachnele, who had been so re-markable as a three-foot-tall Pharaoh in *Torah,* would be returning with him to California to play none other than Adolf Hitler in Siegel's newest motion picture project, *The Little Dictator,* a satirical depiction of current events in Europe. "After seeing my film," the director promised, "nobody in the world is going to be able to take that Nazi seriously. What better use could there be of my talent as a director, not to mention Bachnele's as an actor, than to save the Jews of Germany? I've always wanted to make a comedy. I don't want audiences to as-sume that, just because it's a Joseph Siegel film, it's only going to be all the pow-erful and profound stuff about life and death. Everybody likes a good laugh once in a while. The Passover should remind us of that. The great Hillel used to have the priests of the Second Temple in Jerusalem roaring with laughter over his zany ideas for new sandwiches." After we had eaten the most famous of Hillel's sandwiches, Angel notified the hotel bellhop that we were ready for the meal to be served. Although the Marquis d'Échelles was not present, he had, out of his devotion to Angel, graciously made the arrangements for the ceremonial supper, reserving the room for us at the Hôtel Drumont, ordering kosher wine from the Rothschild estate, and paying the bill in advance. *"Qu'est-ce que c'est?"* an obviously disconcerted hostess asked the waiter, pointing at the plate that he had set before her. *"Une spécialité de la maison, absolument délicieuse!"* he answered: *"Jambon braisé Esterhazy,* 'am braised in wine wiz zee cream and zee truffle sauce." *"Quelle catastrophe!"* Angel exclaimed. "Even if we could eat ham, we can't mix meat and dairy products, at least not on the Passover." Offering to take the food away, the indifferent waiter noted that, because the kitchen had just closed, no other meal could be served that evening. Siegel proposed that we vote on whether or not to eat the nonkosher food. Everyone but Professor Wonderful, it turned out, was in favor of consuming it. The magician consented to go along with the majority, however, "not because I want to eat a pig, but because the Jew must stick together." Consuela justified her vote by again citing the article she had read in *Reader's Digest:* "Because Adolf Hitler doesn't eat ham," she said, "I think we should." And so we did. Bachnele emended the customary grace after the meal in which we thanked God for providing us with our food "even if it was chazer. *Deigeh nisht!* We'll atone on Yom Kippur." Then, after reciting the blessing over the third glass of wine, Bachnele dedicated the offering to Angel's success in *La Jouissance de Cléopâtre.* The actress declared that such things were not worthy of divine blessing, that we should drink instead to the deliverance of the Jews from the oppression they were facing in Germany. We drank the third glass, filled the forth, set out the cup of Elijah, and I opened the door for the entry of the prophet who announces the coming of the Messiah. The manager of the Hôtel Drumont entered in Elijah's place. "I apologize for the problem with the menu," he said in perfect English. "I hope that you will trust that our chef, being entirely ignorant of the dietary restrictions of the Hebrews, did not prepare the meal as an intentional act of anti-Semitism. This hotel has a long history of service to the Jews. Sarah Bernhardt once stayed here and, subsequent to his release from Devil's Island, Alfred Dreyfus celebrated his being awarded the Cross of the Legion of Honor in our dining room. Major Dreyfus himself ordered the *jambon braisé Esterhazy.* When asked why he, as a Jew, had ordered ham, Dreyfus explained, 'The Emperor Napoleon granted freedom to the Jews on the condition that they swear their loyalty to France. I eat this pork as an expression of that loyalty. *Vive le jambon!'* " Declining our invitation to join us for the last glass of wine, the manager closed the door that had been opened for the immortal wanderer behind him. "Hitler," Consuela Heimenhoff informed us, "still maintains that Dreyfus was guilty. That's what the article in *Reader's*

Digest said. He's got proof of a Jewish conspiracy, previously suppressed information on how the Jews were able to make the guilty seem innocent and the innocent seem guilty. I forget the details, but Hitler explained it all in a speech in Nuremberg. He also warned the German people that Jewish men, being lustful by nature, will do anything to have sexual relations with Aryan women." "I can't speak for all Jews," Bachnele commented, "but I know he's right when it comes to me." "Hitler, shitler," Professor Wonderful exclaimed: "Hitler is the shmuck!" Despite his conversion and the fact that he had gone to great pains to memorize the Four Questions for our celebration that night of the Angel of Death's passing over our dwellings, no one at the seder really took Professor Wonderful's Judaism very seriously. Even Shula, the woman for whose sake he had converted, seemed a little embarrassed when he recited the *"Borai pri hagophens"* louder than anyone else: "We are a chosen peoples!" he declared with a grand smile after each blessing. "Even though I attended his bris, bar mitzvah, kiddushin, and his Jewish funeral," Bachnele whispered to me, "it's hard for me to think of this Hindu kishef-macher as a Yid." Professor Wonderful had the same problem with the Nazis several years later. After being arrested by officers of the German occupation army, Shulamite Levi (I was to learn in a woeful letter from Padi) was loaded aboard a deportation train that took her from Paris to Auschwitz. Professor Wonderful had appealed to German officials to book him on a train with the same destination so that he could be with his wife. "I am the Jew!" he insisted: "I will proudly display a circumcision for the proof!" The Nazis laughed at his plea. *"Du bist kein Jude,"* one of them joked: *"Du bist ein Arier!"* It was late. We had recited a psalm proclaiming our trust that the Lord, the God of Abraham, Isaac, and Jacob, would bless us and protect us from our enemies forever. We drank the last cup of wine and said good night.

89 *Le Fromage Humain* was the title of my newest Grand Guignol composition. "An insane dairy farmer," I explained to Madame Diotime, "kidnaps nursing mothers, takes them to his dairy, confines them in pillories in his barn, where he attaches the suction cups of electric milking machines to their breasts, and, with rennet from the stomachs of their disemboweled babies, makes human cheese." Stopping me before I could get to the most appealingly appalling and distinctively disgusting parts, the impressaria of the Maldoror deemed my creation "too intellectual." Madame Diotime was more pleased with my *La Cléopâtre de Paris*, written in the hope of capitalizing on the popular success of the Marquis d'Échelle's *La Jouissance de Cléopâtre* in which a Jewish girl from America had become a sensation as the beloved of Caesar and Antony. The drama critic for *Paris-Soir* declared Angel the reincarnation of the illustrious femme fatale: *"Elle exprimait tout—la volupté du cœur, la passion mystérieuse, la promesse d'un amour inconnu, délicieux, atroce et exquis!"* The play had run to full houses three nights a week for several years at the Théâtre Sarah Bernhardt. Characterizing Dévoué Rabonnir as "la nouvelle Sarah," a critic for *Le Figaro* raved that the actress defined the legendary seductress of the Nile in ways that offered audiences a new understanding not only of the character, but of Woman herself. The production only closed in Paris when Angel accepted an invitation to perform with the Old Vic in London, not in the Marquis's *La Jouissance de Cléopâtre* but in Shakespeare's *Antony and Cleopatra* with Cedric Hardwicke as Antony. A critic for the *Telegraph* hailed Angel as "America's gift to the British stage. Miss Rabonnir *is* the Queen of Egypt." Another lucky ladder, I conceded, taking her to the top of the board. The Marquis did not accompany his protégée to England, since, so she told me as a testimonial to the purity of his love, he felt that he had done all that he could do for her. I was on the platform at the Gare d'Orsay to see her off. "I remember the day you came to say good-bye to me in Los Angeles when we were kids," Angel said. "Do you remember?" She laughed. "I have a surprise for you!" She handed me a wrapped package, which upon opening I discovered to be the game of snakes and ladders that I had given to her years before. She kissed me on the cheek and then once again a train took her from me, transporting her to some place where undoubtedly "she would catch another Antony in her strong coil of grace." In my version of the Cleopatra story, the Egyptian beauty was a contemporary vamp who had fled to Paris from Cairo after having used her wiles and charms to embezzle a fortune out of a love-crazed King Faud. "She has taken an apartment in the Place de la Concorde from the window of which she can see Cleopatra's Needle. The bewitching noctambulist goes each night to the bal-musettes to invite fresh prey to that apartment, which she has decorated as an Egyptian harem room. Our ravishingly beautiful praying mantis plies her quarry with opiated wine as she dances for him in Oriental veils. 'Take off your clothes and crawl into my bed,' she orders as she begins to slowly remove her own diaphanous garments. Little does her aroused pickup know that there's a poisonous snake in the bed. The good part is when the victim leaps out of the bed with the mouth of a deadly serpent clamped to his naked leg. A rubber snake will seem real, since the audience will have noticed her hiding a real snake in the bed earlier on. My Cleopatra experiences sexual pleasure from watching men die." Monsieur Becque interrupted: "It would be more entertaining if she experimented, using different methods of killing each man: not only a snake, but also scorpions, poison, acid, guns, knives, of course, and people are crazy about strangulation, bludgeoning, and dismemberment. "Okay," I conceded, "but in the final act, I need a snake. My vamp kills herself by holding a deadly asp to her breast." When Monsieur Becque wanted to know why she committed suicide, I stated the obvious: "Because she is Cleopatra." In that case, he wondered, where did Caesar and Antony come in? "King Faud is my Caesar," I explained, "and Antony is a gangster from Chicago named Tony. After falling desperately in love with him, Cleopatra stops murdering men in order to marry Tony and go to America with him. But before her dreams come true, Tony is gunned down by a cop named Octave." Given the recent success of other theatrical versions of the escapades of Cleopatra, Madame Diotime surmised that the play might have some popular appeal. "You can play Octave," she said to Becque. "We'll take the usual advantage of your eye by having Tony gouge it out before you shoot him. Isaac, as an American you're perfect for Tony, and I have just the girl to be theater's newest Cleopatra. She came to see me a few days ago looking for work. Her name is Fatima and she's a real Arab." It wasn't until after the play had run for several weeks that, fatigued by the energy it took to sustain the role of Fatima while playing the part of Cleopatra, she confessed in English that she was in fact from Philadelphia and that her real name was Amy Berkowitz. She had run away to Paris, she further divulged, in search of love, fun, and "la vie de Bohême." She wasn't a very good actress but could speak French with an Arabic accent, and she was pretty enough with her large searching dark eyes and delicate aquiline nose. She was happy to have a job in the theater, even if it meant strangling, poisoning, stabbing, bludgeoning, and shooting men each night and then applying a snake to her naked breast. "Before this I was working as an artist's model. The pay's okay, but it's boring to sit still for so long. Killing guys is a lot more fun." Informing her that I was an artist myself, I asked whether she would pose for the portrait that I wanted to make of Cleopatra, *La Reine Déshabillée*. She named her price and we had a deal. As we entered my room in the Villa Borghese, she asked where my paints and brushes were. "You don't even have an easel, a smock, or beret! You said you're a painter. You're not! You're a liar!" Insulted by the accusation, I corrected her. "I did not say I'm a painter; I said I'm an artist. And I am. I'm a writer, a literary artist. Let me remind you that I am responsible for *La Cléopâtre de Paris*. I said I wanted you to pose for my portrait of the nude Cleopatra, which I do. That the portrait is in words is merely a question of the medium of artistic expression and should not concern you as the model. If you would please undress, I'll get down to work." She complied, and after posing her in royal languor, I picked up my notebook and pen to begin the composition. I had to keep reminding her to be still. At one point she rose, came over, and, standing behind me with her hand on my shoulder to read what I had written, offered a critique. "It's not a very good likeness. 'Large searching dark eyes and delicate aquiline nose'? My eyes are hazel and 'aquiline' is so overused on noses. There's not enough roundness to the breast or curve to the neck. The whole thing needs highlighting, you know, some 'very's here and there, and some shading too, here, like this: 'Very large hazel eyes ever searching in hopes that there is something to be seen.' Isn't that better? My eyes should follow the reader around the room. Did you know that I've posed for Picasso? I'm not wild about his paintings, but he does serve his models wine. Don't you have any wine?" I set the portrait down to pour us each a drink. "I don't sleep with the artists for whom I pose, not even Picasso, because my mother told me that it's professionally unethical. Let me set up a still life for you, some wine bottles and fruit and a few flowers. That's what you can write about if you want to make love to me." That I was in love with Padi didn't trouble Amy, and it didn't bother me that she was in love with a musician named Léon who had enlisted in the French army to play the ophicleide in a military band. Padi, after all, worked every night and slept every afternoon, and Léon was often out of Paris on maneuvers near the Maginot Line, rehearsing battle tunes in case Hitler were to attack France. When Léon had first warned her that a German invasion was inevitable and suggested that it would be advisable for her to return to the United States, Amy had suspected that he was just trying to get rid of her. In the end, however, Hitler was not to blame for her hasty departure; when her mother died of a heart attack, her father pleaded with her to return to Philadelphia. Monsieur Becque invited me into his dressing room, where, after offering me a glass of wine to ease the sadness I was feeling over the loss of Amy, he showed me a flyer reporting that, due to the German annexation of Austria, and, just that week, Bohemia and Moravia, vast numbers of Austrian and Czech Jews were being deported to concentration camps. "In the manner of the mother of Moses who hid her child in the bulrushes thousands of years ago," the flyer read, "many Jewish women have now hidden their infants. A large number of motherless newborns are thus starving in the German occupied states. Mothers of the babies of France, you are called upon to save the lives of the innocent with donations of milk. Breast pumps will be provided and the milk will be collected by appointment. Milk is Life! Milk is Freedom! Give Milk!" When Becque asked my opinion, I told him that, as a Jew, I thought it was very noble. He laughed. "Noble? Hardly, but hopefully profitable! I'm working with a *fromagère* in Picardie. Human cheese! I will collect the milk and my friend will produce the delicacy. It will be expensive because quantities will be limited. After all, it takes more than ten gallons of milk to make only one pound of cheese. But that will only increase its appeal amongst connoisseurs. Because I am an honest man, I felt I had to tell you. You deserve some percentage of the profits for coming up with the idea in the first place, and all the more if you assist me in collecting the milk and selling the cheese. *Vive le fromage humain!*"

90 In September of 1939, I received four letters from women, all of which were about Hitler and each of which urged me to return to the United States. I couldn't figure out how Pythia, isolated as she was in her Tuscan villa, had known to write to me care of the Théâtre du Maldoror. Much to my pleasure, she addressed me as "My dearest one." I paused to indulge in the sweetness of a memory of her in a yellow day dress, poised in the tête-à-tête in the card room of the house in India. "I have something to tell you, something important, and very serious," she began. "There was a gala celebration here in the Piazza San Foutini just over a week ago, on April 20, a government sponsored celebration of the fiftieth birthday of Adolf Hitler, staged as a demonstration of Italian support for an Italo-German alliance. There was German wine, food, and music. But my husband and I hardly took part in the festivities since Mr. Green, while not averse to a good Gewürztraminer, has an antipathy to both bratwurst and the flügelhorn. I didn't think much about the event, as political celebrations are not uncommon here these days. But then yesterday, April 28, it was my husband's fiftieth birthday. We celebrated quietly at home by having Sidney's favorite, a scrumptious English steak-and-kidney pie. It was just the two of us and our darling Rudolph, who, by the way, already at his tender age adores the cinema, which comes as no surprise, given his previous incarnation. After tucking Rudolph in, I retired to my bed and Mr. Green was already sleeping soundly in his. It was not his snoring that kept me awake that night, but something else. Restlessly I tossed and turned. And then it struck me! I was, as dear Robert once wrote, 'stung by the splendor of a sudden thought.' Oh the incredible truth! Rising from bed, I hurried to the study, where, pacing about and trembling with excitement, I tried to comprehend its meaning and implications. It was clear. Robert Browning died on March the 2nd, 1889, fifty-seven days before the birth of Mr. Green. The numbers have always been somewhat troublesome to me because, as we know from the expert testimony of Tibetan lamas, Pythagoreans, Theosophists, and others well versed in the dynamics of metempsychosis, it takes forty-nine days for the soul of the deceased to reincarnate. Well, it's so obvious! Adolf Hitler was born exactly forty-nine days after Robert's death! Do you understand? Chancellor Hitler, and not Mr. Green, was my beloved spouse eighty years ago when I was the poetess Elizabeth Barrett Browning. And Robert is, in keeping with promises made to me upon my deathbed, searching for me now. This explains why the chancellor (who, by the way, is a staunch believer in transmigration) has not yet married. Deep within his soul, he knows that he has yet to find the woman with whom he is fated to be reunited by the power of love. I remember, my dear Isaac, that when you came to visit us in Lancashire, you seemed a bit skeptical that Mr. Green had previously been Mr. Browning. You suspected! Thus I turn to you now. Who else would understand my predicament? Surely you must see the awkwardness of the situation. I have, since marrying Mr. Green, become fond of him. But although our marriage has been a pleasant one, it has been devoid of the ecstatic passion one would expect Elizabeth and Robert to enjoy in their transmigrational reunion. Obviously the fact that I am both married and British makes the situation difficult. But I am confident that I am meant to be with the Führer and that once he finds me, takes me in his arms, and hears me count the ways in which I have eternally loved him ('freely, purely, and with passion put to use in my old griefs'), he'll give up all this political tomfoolery with which he has been so preoccupied lately and settle down with me. Realizing, upon hearing the sonnets I composed for him, that he was once Robert Browning, he will surely devote himself entirely to recapturing the joys of union with his beloved. Love shall redeem Europe and, indeed, all the world! As a man of Hebrew descent you have perhaps been disturbed by Hitler's stance on the Jewish question. Let me explain his anti-Semitic tendencies. They are the result of an unfortunate incident that occurred in London in 1846. Robert had commissioned a Jewish tailor with a shop on Wimpole Street to fit him with a suit for our wedding. The tailor promised that the outfit would be finished in time for the marriage ceremony, and indeed it was ready just hours before the event. But, much to our horror, the legs of the trousers and sleeves of the jacket were so short, the waist so large and coattails so long that Robert, upon dressing and looking at himself in the mirror, lost his temper and cursed the tailor: 'I'll kill that damn Jew for this!' Once Elizabeth and Robert are reunited, I shall remind the Führer of the fact that, while he did indeed look like an absolute clown in his wedding outfit, the marriage itself turned out to be a joyous one. In remembrance of our connubial blessings, Mr. Hitler will surely forgive the Jews for making him look so absurd at his wedding. So you see, it is not merely to satisfy the imperatives of my own destiny, but also to save Jewish lives, that I must contact my Adolf. I have written to him, this very morning, care of the Reichskanzlei in Berlin. Whilst I hope and pray that my message reaches him posthaste, I fear delays, for he is moving about so much these days. If I am unable to consummate my reunion with Robert's soul in Adolf's body soon, I'd suggest that you consider returning to America. From the sorts of rumors that one heard during the Führer's birthday celebration, I'd guess that it might be a bit tough for you Jews here in Europe in the near future. My dear Isaac, my ever faithful friend, I must ask for your advice in respect to all of this. What should I tell Mr. Green? I fear that it might upset Sidney to learn that he has, in fact, never been Robert Browning and that I must leave him to be with Adolf Hitler. I do hope that he understands and does not make a fuss over custody of our beloved Rudolph. I'll write again soon, hopefully from the Berghof. In the meantime, hugs and kisses! Your loving Pythia." Angel's letter, posted from London on the day the German army launched its initial attack on Poland, had arrived a few days before Pythia's. "I'm very annoyed with Hitler!" she began. "How terrible it is! How tragic! War with Germany is forthcoming and that means that the Old Vic will close and that *Antony and Cleopatra* will be kaput. With most young British men fighting on the continent and everyone in England obsessed with the war effort, no one will be going to the theater. Not even Shakespeare can compete with Hitler! How can that nasty little anti-Semite do this to me? Just when I finally become a real star of real theater, that damn Nazi has to ruin my career. You know that I generally like most people and I'm not one to hold a grudge, but I can honestly say that I really do hate Adolf Hitler. Imagine what will happen if, as he has sworn to do, he actually conquers Europe and occupies Britain. I'll be cast as Margaret in Goethe's *Faust*! And Napoleon will be forced to play Mephistopheles. I don't like the part or the play, and I don't want to have to learn German. I've landed on a snake. It's swallowing me, and down I go. I don't like it, but I feel that I must go home. You too, Isaac. Yes, I think both of us must go back." I was surprised to get a letter from Amy Berkowitz. She was working as an artist's model again, posing for a painter in New York named Edward Hopper, who, she wrote, "makes me look very lonely and melancholy when in fact I'm neither. But I guess that's what art's supposed to do." Hitler was introduced into the letter in an effort to encourage me to return to the United States. She promised that I could stay in her apartment on Hester Street. "Léon has written to tell me that war between France and Germany is certain. He says that he wants to be on the front, playing his ophicleide for the troops when it begins. That may be fine for him, but you're an American. On the radio tonight, President Roosevelt reassured the nation that America will never go to war. So come home. It's not safe for you there, nor for any other Jew. Come home." My mother reiterated those sentiments in a letter that, like all her correspondence, contained news of all the people who had died since her previous letter. It was so long since I had seen my mother that I no longer knew any of the deceased. She had a new life with her husband, Hayim Grossman, in Miami. She wrote that she had just seen Bachnele Poopik's lampoon of Hitler in Joseph Siegel's *The Little Dictator*: "He was so funny that I am sure Hitler would, if he were to ever see the movie, want to kill Bachnele. Speaking of Hitler, Hayim says it's dangerous for you to be Europe. He also says he can get you a good job if you come home. I haven't seen your sweet face in such a long time, my son, my darling Isaac. It's been far too long. So, please, please come home." I probably wouldn't have paid any attention to Pythia, Angel, Amy, or even my mother if it hadn't been for Madame Diotime. I was sitting in front of the mirror in my dressing room applying the makeup for *Le Gynécologiste Allemand* in which, as the diabolical lead, I tortured and murdered pregnant women. After removing the living fetuses from their wombs, I placed them in alembics and, with a variety of experimental nutrients, worked to cultivate a race of physically perfect and intellectually advanced human beings. Standing behind me so that she could see my face in the mirror, Madame Diotime spoke: "Tonight is the last. I'm closing the Maldoror." I turned to ask why. "I can't keep up with the competition," she said: "Hitler is so much better at Grand Guignol than I. There is no future. Go home." Three days later, always one to try to please the women in my life, I kissed both Madame Diotime and Draupadi Padoux good-bye and left for America.

<table>
<tr><td>**91**</td><td>"Imagine a land of fun, a prosperous nation in which work is play and laughter is the national anthem." It might have been the voice of God for all the hope it offered those visitors to the New York World's Fair of 1939 in Flushing Meadow Park who had the pa-</td></tr>
</table>

tience to stand in line for General Motors' Futurama. The Voice promised votaries of progress a homeland for their descendants in an American Zion overflowing with the milk of science and the honey of technology. Comfortably seated on armchair-clouds, we were borne by conveyor belt westward through spacious skies, from sea to shining sea, over a sprawling model of tomorrow's holy land, "the United States of America at the dawn of a glorious new millennium, a mere two generations from now." As we crossed fruited plains and amber waves of grain, looking down at the orderly cities, connected by superhighways, in which our children's children thrived, the narrative eased us into a future present tense: "In the year 2000 men and women are handsome and vigorous, their children adorable and well behaved." The Voice was good-humored: "Although Shirley Temple is seventy-two years old, she's as cute as ever, thanks to rapid developments in pharmacology, cosmetology, reconstructive surgery, and the nutritional sciences." Little Miss Temple was singing "Come On, Get Happy" as I learned that by the beginning of the twenty-first century man will have played golf on the moon. "Television broadcasting has been perfected. Every American family has at least one receiver. In the comfort of our own homes we watch motion pictures, variety, game shows, and news events as they happen; we attend a sports event, cheering for our favorite team, and then, with the mere push of an electronic button, we're at a church service giving thanks to God for all the blessings of modern life!" There was the prophecy of "electrocomputators" with television screens and typewriter keyboards, a machine no larger than a notebook allowing us "to process data, find and store information on any subject, and communicate instantaneously with others all around the world. While the kids use them to do their homework and play thrilling games, Mom finds a new recipe for a dinner that's both healthy and delicious and even does some shopping. After checking in at the office on his Electrocomp, Dad sneaks a visit to a peep show in the privacy of his workshop. Yes, the future is bright." As we glided over the purple mountain majesty of a beautiful, cheerful, and hygienic America, the Voice was reassuring. Amy Berkowitz, with whom I was staying, had insisted that I experience Futurama. She had seen it more than ten times herself and, as an employee of the fair, had free passes. In addition to those tickets and vouchers for meals at both Eat-O-Rama and Tastes of Tomorrow, she made good money, considering that she worked only three hours a day. Amy was one of eight girls, all of them certified as "genuine professional artists' models," who did rotating shifts as the Female of the Future in the Crystal Gazing Palace. As a recording of "America the Beautiful," sung by the Boy Scouts of America Glee Club, softly played, an elevator delivered Amy to a mirrored butte, beneath a mirrored ceiling and surrounded by mirrored panels, upon which she'd discard a hooded mirror-sequined cape to reveal the neonatural nakedness of tomorrow. Her G-string was embroidered with an electron orbiting a proton, her pasties were silver stars, and her earrings flashing lights. The mirrors multiplied her into a spectacular illusion of one hundred identically perfect beauties, simultaneously viewed from every angle, and dancing in precise synchronization to "O beautiful, O beautiful, God shed his grace on thee!" The sovereign Voice glossed the spectacle: "The Female of the Future is not only beautiful—she has a college education, knows how to drive a car, and even change a flat tire." Amy Berkowitz curtsied, put her cape back on, and, as the elevator lowered her out of sight, waved good-bye to the ten rows of dazed gazers in the gallery. "I wish the future was here now," Amy, as if indoctrinated by the transcendent Voice, sighed. "But then, I guess, it wouldn't be the future." I was with her when the sad news came from Paris that her paramour had died on the battlefield. Léon was one of the first official casualties after the French declaration of war against Germany. It happened in the Saarland, just over the German frontier. After ignoring repeated orders to stop playing the Marseillaise on his ophicleide, he had been shot by a member of his own military unit. Taking refuge in my arms, Amy wept. "I loved Léon," she whimpered, "even though he wasn't a very good musician." I kissed the tear from her cheek and tremble from her lip. After having gazed at her as the centiform Female of the Future, it was impossible in the darkness of her room not to imagine that I was making love to one hundred women at once. I was engulfed in a swarm of naked bodies, undulating in precise synchronization and moaning in harmony. As I fancied she was the hundred women on the mirrored stage, she may well have been imagining that I was the hundreds of men who, in the darkness of the Crystal Palace, beheld her nudity each day, the thousands each week, the millions who would ultimately come to the World's Fair, be dazzled by her centuplicated beauty, and dream of her, the future perfect, for the rest of their lives. I was each and every one of them as they burst out of me, racing against each other, fighting for dear life, squirming their way through the aperture into the pulsing cervical canal, swimming desperately, frantically seeking the humid fallopian tunnel to the egg—the single, lonely ovum that longed to absorb the one most powerful amongst them. It was that egg that made the woman drop her cape and dance alluringly for the men hidden in the darkness. I imagined the Voice: "Having ejaculated, the Man of Tomorrow withdraws from the Vagina of the Future, rolls over, and, just as he has done for centuries, wonders if he has satisfied her. Some things never change." Amy wanted to know if I thought it was dirty. "Yes," I sighed happily. "No, not that. My show. The Crystal Gazing Palace. My father is coming to New York and, well, if the show is obscene, I don't want him to see it. But I do want him to come if it's art or if it's science." I told her it was both. The Conwell All-American League of Decency, supported by various church groups, censuring the World's Fair generally as a menace to morals, had singled out the Crystal Gazing Palace as particularly depraved. Erotic displays were defended on both aesthetic and scientific grounds: "Goddesses of Olympus" in the Greek Pavilion was definitely art, and "Darwin's Eve," an exhibition in the African Pavilion of dusky women with large bare breasts, was anthropology. Technology legitimated the sex in "Mr. Electro's Pleasure Garden," where a shiny metallic robot, surrounded by flamboyantly dancing near-naked women, depicted a future in which even electronic automatons will have fun. The nudity in "Fashions of the Future" was explained by the Voice: "By the beginning of the twenty-first century, through Eugenic selection and Electrocomputatortional bioregeneration, the bodies of Americans will be perfectly designed and beautiful to behold. Self-regulating air-conditioning and heating devices will maintain agreeable temperatures while cellophane and tecca fabrics allow Americans of the tomorrow to display their fit, firm forms in even the coldest of weather." The exhibition was sponsored by the North American Eugenics Society under the auspices of the United States Department of Immigration with additional support from Tootsie Roll, Sears & Roebuck, Dr. Scholl's, and Borden's Milk. Elsie the Cow mooed beneath a diagrammatic history of the reproductive technology that had made her America's champion milk producer. The society also sponsored an exhibit of skulls from around the world. The crania of Negroes, American Indians, Filipinos, Orientals, Arabs, Jews, and Caucasians, accompanied by specimen jars containing exemplary samples of the fetuses, brains, hearts, and reproductive organs of each of those races, demonstrated the "gradual disappearance of Neanderthaloid traits in man's climb up the evolutionary ladder toward the twenty-first century." I headed for the Tibetan exposition, near the Perisphere, in front of which I was to meet Amy after her matinee performance. I went with her to the fair to indulge myself in those attractions that seemed to represent scenes from my own life, for all its fun and unpredictability, its vulgarity and sweetness, ups and downs, all its snakes and ladders. I visited Great Britain, France, the Soviet Union, and India; I reenacted memories in the Aerial Joyride, the Life Savers Candy Parachute Jump, the Aquacade,

Midget Town, the Reptile House, the Wild West, and the Sharpshooting Gallery. Emerging from the Hall of Aviation, I wished with all my heart that, through some technological miracle, I could contact my father. "There's a photograph of you in the Pioneers of Flight exhibit!" I'd say. "Yes, it's really you. And yes, you do look very handsome in your aviator's jacket, standing by *Amuriel* with a happy smile on your face." Yes, it would be nice if, in the future, science could provide a way for us to telephone the dead. The American Telephone and Telegraph exhibition did at least promise that by the beginning of the twenty-first century there would be small wireless telephones with which, according to the Voice, "people will even be able to make calls from their automobiles!" In a promotion meant to encourage Americans to have telephones installed at home, there was a bank of them that anyone could use to call anywhere in the world and talk for three minutes free of charge. Courteously smiling "Alexander Graham Belles," dressed scantily in the spirit of the fair, were on duty to find the number of anyone who had a telephone and to connect the call. Although she hadn't heard my voice in twenty years, and even though all I said was "Hello," she knew immediately who it was: *"Mein zeese nishumule!"* she laughed with delight. "My Isaac, my darling, my son! I miss you. Come to see me. Please. You must. I love you."

92 *"Baruch ata Adonai,"* she began once more with sure fingers covering quivering eyelids, a creamy white fringed silk shawl draped over her dyed strawberry hair. Soft smiles concealed any wistfulness that might have been felt over the passing of time. Surely she remembered. "We're born and we die," my father would say on Friday nights, "but the Sabbath persists and remains the same forever. We're here to fleetingly delight in its eternity." When the actress opened her eyes, her tears were as believable as her smiles. As the shawl slipped down into folds upon her shoulders, what remained of my father within me, using my eyes to see her, saw that she was still beautiful. Candlelight glowed in the diamonds in her earlobes as she waved her hands in magical circles of grace over the white tapers in the antique silver holders. My mother spread the light of creation and warmth of love around the room, through the house, out into the world, and up into the night, as she recited words that I had heard each Friday night of my childhood. With no less art than that with which she had played Fatima el-Fatiha the Danseuse of the Desert, Jezebel the Vixenish Votaress of Baal, Maharanee Mayadevee the Mystic Mentaliste of Mysore, Deer Heart the Renegade Apache Squaw, Madame Endor the Merry Medium of Manasseh, and Sarah Schlossberg the Immigrant Jewish Bride of Avraham ben Menachem, she was now, on a stage that was a grand antebellum mansion on the north bank of the Miami River where it flows into Biscayne Bay, acting the part of Mrs. Hayim Grossman, treasurer of Southern Florida's Sisterhood of Irgun, member of the board of directors of the Dade County Jewish Orphanage, patron of the Everglades Opera, and genteel hostess to the many Jewish and Italian businessmen who came to visit her husband. We drank Sabbath wine, and then, just as she did when we were on the road in Wyoming Willie's ten-in-one, she held my cheeks in warm hands, kissed my forehead, told me that she loved me, and lit a Camel cigarette. That my memories of my mother were exclusively dramatic vignettes, visions of parts she had played, was no betrayal of the human being. She loved the characters she and my father had invented, each one a facet of the precious gem that was her true self. Receiving money from her by Western Union each month in Paris, I had pictured her in the role of the self-sacrificial Jewish mother scrimping to help her beloved son, a part she could have played in a shaytl and tichl while braiding challa and stirring a pot of cholent. I was surprised by the luxury in which she now lived and pleased by the pleasure it seemed to give her. "Money is a blessing," she said. "'Wealth and riches,' King David sang, 'shall be in the house of the man who delighteth in the commandments of the Lord.' Don't listen to anyone who says that money doesn't make a person happy or that wealth doesn't mean anything. Rich people claim that in hopes that it will discourage the poor from trying to take their money away from them; and the poor try to believe it in order not to be all the more miserable for their poverty. It's a lot of fun to be wealthy." Every Sunday morning my mother would sit in her garden of roses to drink champagne and read the newspapers. Joining her there, I noticed the headline "Hitler in Paris." As she poured a glass of wine for me, I told her about the photograph of her first husband in the Hall of Aviation at the World's Fair, and she smiled. "He was a good man, crazy and sweet, his warm heart brimming over with love, and . . . well, we had fun." We drank to the memory of Abraham Schlossberg. "With the Nazis in France," she sighed, "champagne's going to be difficult to get. Thank God Hayim has the ways and means—he's active in the wine, beer, and spirits trade." Genuinely proud of her second husband's success, she spoke admiringly of his humble beginnings in business in the 1920s with a conviction that being a bootlegger had been a pious act of service to the Jewish community and to the God of Israel, who had created and sanctified the fruit of the vine. Prohibition, she believed, had been an attempt on the part of anti-Semites to prevent Jews from celebrating their religion. "There can be no Shabbis and thus no Jewish life, no Pesach, Purim, or Sukkot, no brises, bar mitzvahs, nor Jewish weddings, without wine. Long before President Hoover, the wicked King Antiochus imposed a Prohibition law on the Jews. Republicans! And as the Maccabees fought against their oppressors, so Hayim and his associates rose up against the enemies of Israel." Hayim had risked imprisonment to smuggle wine and schnapps into America from Cuba and the Bahamas so, she believed, that Jews could keep the Sabbath holy and maintain the covenant. Hayim and his partners (Toots Goldman in Milwaukee and Mack Silverman in St. Louis, and the younger ones, Meyer "The Hammer" Lansky in New York and Benjamin "Bugsy" Siegel in California) were, in my mother's theatrical imagination, no less pious than the Maccabees, the five sons of an American Mattathias known to the FBI as Arnold Rothstein. After the repeal of Prohibition, the modern Maccabees continued their holy struggle by donating proceeds from gambling, narcotics, prostitution, and extortion to Jewish charities. Hayim Grossman made sure that a substantial percentage of the profits from Hialeah Park Racetrack, the Melkart Dog Track, and the Ponce de Leon Jai Alai Fronton went to support efforts for the establishment of a Jewish state in Palestine. As the Hasmonean heroes of Jerusalem plotted the death of King Demetrius of Syria, so Lansky, Siegel, Silverman, Goldman, and Grossman—"May their names be recorded in the Book of Life!"—were planning to kill Hitler. For the love of her husband, my mother, believing that the assassination would, like the drowning of Pharaoh and his armies in the Red Sea, be a fulfillment of God's will, overlooked the fiscal motivations behind the plot: because Hitler was sending so many Eastern European Jews to concentration camps, American Jewish gangsters were losing their heroin suppliers, and the Italians were taking over the drug trade. But as Judah Maccabee had made a treaty of alliance between the nation of Israel and the Roman republic, so Meyer Lansky forged a coalition between the Jewish syndicate and the Italian Mafia. "In this very house," my mother said cheerfully, "Lucky Luciano ate potato latkes last Chanukah." After refilling my glass of champagne, she startled me by bluntly asking if I was happy. "Of course I'm happy," I told her: "I've always been happy. It's chronic with me." "Are you so happy because you aren't married," she asked, "or are you not married because you're so happy." I had to think about it. "I probably would have married Angel years ago if child marriage had been legal in America as it was in India. I don't know. I've been in love a lot, but it just never works out." My mother believed that the reason her marriage to my father had been such a sweet one was that it had been arranged by a shadchen. If not for that matchmaker in the Pale of Settlement, she noted, I would never have been born. "Matchmakers see who should be together. Never mind want to be together. While lovers are blinded by present pleasures, matchmakers have their eyes on future fulfillment." She couldn't help playing the part: "I've got the perfect girl for you. Bunny Gotlober. Remember her? Moshe and Tsipi's daughter. She was still just a little girl when you left for India. But, oh, she's grown up into a fine young woman, beautiful, with green eyes and a curvaceous figure. She's intelligent, kind, generous, warmhearted, and goodhumored. She's working as a nurse in Los Angeles. If you ever get out to the West Coast, you should look her up." I heard the voice of Maharanee Mayadevee the Mystic Mentaliste of Mysore: "I predict that someday you'll marry Bunny Gotlober." The clairvoyant did not, however, reveal what she knew was in my immediate future, the fact that I was about to leave Miami. That was disclosed to me several days later by Hayim as we sat together in his private box at the Ponce de Leon Jai Alai Fronton. He told me whom to bet on in each match, and I doubted that it was by clairvoyance that I won every time. Even though Grossman was a criminal, because he loved my mother so much and seemed to be making her so happy it was difficult not to like him. I hadn't seen him since my bar mitzvah and I still remembered how energetically he had danced and, as I watched the women watch him, how much he amused them. Hayim wrapped his arm around my shoulder after the final jai alai match and said: "Listen, son, I love your mother. I'd do anything for her. Anything. And she wants me to help you out. And it's not just for her. It's for Abe too. He'd want me to help his son." I insisted that I didn't need any help, that I was fine and content with my life. He corrected me: "No, son, you're lost. You're forty years old and you still haven't accomplished anything. You need to do something important. Your problem is that you have no aspirations." When I insisted that I did, he demanded specifics. "To be the first man to climb Mt. Everest," I answered without thinking, and then rattled off whatever came to mind: "or capture an Abominable Snowman, or assassinate Hitler, or write a book." Hayim stopped me there. "Listen, son, a Jew needs two things: love, not just a woman to fuck, but a wife who cares for him and makes a nice home for him; and work, not just a job to make money, but a profession by which to define and distinguish himself. You've got neither. That's what's troubling your mother. She's got the love problem solved. She's got a wife for you named Gotlober. She wants me to take care of the profession. 'Isaac's a wonderful actor,' she says to me. 'Can you help him with that?' Can Hayim Grossman help? You can bet on it, son. Anything to make your mother happy. Anything. So I've arranged it with my associates. You're going out to Hollywood to star in a motion picture. And you know who's going to get the Academy Award next year for best actor? I'll tell you who—you, Isaac Schlossberg! Yeah, you, your mother's son! If the Syndicate can decide who wins the Kentucky Derby, the World Series, the Miss America Pageant, and the gubernatorial elections of Florida, New York, Illinois, and California, it shouldn't be much too tough to determine what actor gets that schlock little statue of Oscar. It's going to make your mother very happy, and when she's happy, I'm happy. And when Jews are happy, God's happy. What more could we ask for? So I've got an airplane ticket for you, and Ben (don't ever call him 'Bugsy') Siegel will take care of everything in Los Angeles. What happens now is up to Siegel."

93

"*The Fountain of Youth,*" Bugsy Siegel, sitting next to me in the back of limousine that had picked me up at the airport, said. "That's the title of the motion picture and it was my idea—the fuckin' *Fountain of Youth*. And you're Ponce de Leon." The gangster lived up to his reputation as the most handsome and best-dressed killer in the underworld; frosty blue eyes stunned and froze you as a slyly smoldering smile disarmed and melted you. The suave mobster elaborated: "So Meyer and I are in Miami for a meeting, staying with Hayim and your ma (not a bad-lookin' tomato for her age), and we keep seeing this name—fuckin' Ponce de Leon this and fuckin' Ponce de Leon that: Ponce de Leon Municipal Swimming Pool, Ponce de Leon Mechanical College for Colored People, Ponce de Leon Sanitarium, Ponce de Leon Jai Alai Fronton, not to mention cocktail lounges, restaurants, motor hotels, a movie theater and a burlesque house. 'Who the fuck is Ponce de Leon?' I ask, and Hayim tells me: 'The fantazyor who discovered Florida. He came over from Spain looking for the Fountain of Youth. If you drank from it, so the legend went, you'd stay young forever.' So I get to thinking out loud: 'Wouldn't it be something if there really was a Fountain of Youth and this Ponce de Leon actually found it, but didn't tell anybody because he wanted to keep it for himself, and he's still alive today, looking as young as ever.' Meyer pipes in: 'You're dreamin', bubee. It's a goddamn fantasy. Like the Land of Oz. You been out in Hollywood too long. There's no Yellow Brick Road and there sure ain't no Fountain of Youth.' That's when I get the brilliant idea—a movie about Ponce de Leon called *The Fountain of Youth* in which the asshole actually finds the fuckin' fountain and he's been alive for five hundred years! Imagine all the dames he's fucked, not to mention all that he must know about history! So I tell them the idea, and 'You're a genius, Ben,' Hayim says to me. And he says he's got the perfect guy to write the script and direct it, a friend of his—Joe Siegel, the shmuck who made *The Little Dictator,* that stupid movie about Hitler with the midget. Personally, I don't like Siegel. He's not related to me, even though he spells his name just like me. He's a fuckin' drug addict. I've warned him: 'Stay away from the happy powder while you're directing my movie, or I'll put a bullet in your fuckin' brain.' I'm only using him because Hayim believes in him and wants him for the job and we, my colleagues and I, try to respect each other's wishes. We're meshpucha. To make a long story short, we encourage our investors to put up the bankroll and we go into production. Siegel casts some Mexican to play Ponce de Leon. But two days into the picture and the fuckin' spic vanishes into thin air! That's when Hayim calls to tell me that he's got someone to take the wetback's place. That's you, Schlossberg! I was going to offer the part to my favorite actor, Moe Howard—he's a genius. But Hayim says he wants you, that it means a lot to him, and, like I said, we're meshpucha." Dropping me off at the Garden of Osiris, the gangster handed me the script with the advice to have my lines memorized by morning. "We've got to get back on schedule or heads are going to roll." "Samoo the Amazing Snake Boy of Hindustan," the other Siegel, who had been waiting for me on the set, roared as he threw his arms around me: "One of the ten players in my first motion picture, *Wyoming Willie's Wonders of the World.* And here we are working together again! Talk about mazel! We've done a lot of great work together, but my *Fountain of Youth* is going to take the cake. The picture's got it all: love, sex, adventure, political intrigue, war, history, violence, tragedy, humor, and, best of all, it's got a profound message. Because you're the star now, I've reworked the original script, making Ponce de Leon a Hebe who came to the New World to escape the Inquisition. It's kind of a parable about Jews today. Everything always works out for the best. You're a much better actor than Valentine Rudolfo anyway. You more than compensate for his so-called disappearance." As if trying to keep it a secret, the director lowered his voice to tell the story of the previous Ponce de Leon, Valentine Rudolfo, my old friend Jesus Estafar: "It's unbelievable, but true. I'm sure you heard about Trotsky, that Russian Jewish Commie who was recently assassinated in Mexico? There was an ice pick in his brain. The newspapers insinuated that the hit had been personally ordered by Stalin and that it was carried out with the aid of high officials in the Third International and the support of the Mexican Communist Party. That's what people, both us and the Commies, want to believe because it makes a kind of sense, and sense is always reassuring. But I'll tell you what really happened. After being thrown out of the Soviet Union, Trotsky was still denouncing Stalin. So there were threats. Rudolfo had met Trotsky in the Soviet Union when the actor was doing his *Pancho Villa: My Father the Revolutionary!* He was trying to be nice; he invited the pinko to hide from Soviet henchmen at his family house in Coyoacan. In the meantime, hearing about my *Fountain of Youth,* Rudolfo telephoned me long distance to ask if he could audition for the lead. Why not? He had been a passable Angel of Death in *Torah,* and he wasn't too bad as Antony in *Cleopatra.* And being a Mexican, I figured, is almost like being a Spaniard. So I brought him up for a screen test, and since he looked better than Caesar Romero in the conquistador helmet, I cast him. But just two days after we had started shooting, he showed up at my door in the middle of the night, short of breath and shaking in terror, to tell me that he had to get out of town as soon as possible, that he had to go into hiding, and that he needed my help. He knew he could trust me to keep a secret. According to him, Stalin wasn't behind the assassination of Trotsky after all. No, it was one of Pancho Villa's real sons who, after seeing a revival of *Pancho Villa: My Father the Revolutionary!* in Dallas, was so offended by the impostor's ridiculous portrayal of his father that he recruited a few members of the old Villa gang to terminate Rudolfo's acting career. After the hit men discovered that the man they had bumped off was not Valentine Rudolfo, but rather his incognito houseguest, none other than Leon Trotsky, they delivered a message to Ponce de Leon's dressing room here at the studio, pinning it to the wall with an ice pick: *'La próxima vez no la pifiamos,'* it said. *'¡Eres hombre muerto, cabrón!'* So I let him hide at the house for a couple of days while I got the stuff I needed from the studio costume and makeup departments to disguise him with payes, a beard, a shtrayml, and a long coat, as a Hasid. I advised him that if anyone approached him on the street or tried to speak to him to just say *'A gezunt ahf dein kop'* and keep moving like he's late for shul, but to not actually go near a synagogue because they might need him for a minyan and, for God's sake, when he went to a restaurant, not to order pork. So now he's the wandering Jew and you're Ponce de Leon! And I'm glad it's you. I was worried because that thug Bugsy wanted to give the part to Moe Howard. Thank God Moe couldn't do it; he had just started shooting a new Stooges movie. I don't like Siegel. He's not related to me even though he spells his name just like mine. He's been a real buttinski on the casting. Mostly for the female parts. Bugsy shtooped every actress who auditioned. Women will tell you they love men who are sweet, kind, intelligent, and have a good sense of humor. But it's not true. They like mean, tough, heartless bastards like Siegel, especially if he's handsome and has a big schlong. No woman can resist Bugsy Siegel. He could shtoop Eleanor Roosevelt if he wanted to. Maybe he already has. You know who actually has shtooped Eleanor Roosevelt? You'll never believe it. Don't tell a soul. It's a secret. Bachnele Poopik! I'm not kidding. And he shtooped the queen of England too. That's what I've heard. And the word is that, while he was making *The Wizard of Oz*, the little Litvak banged both the Wicked Witch of the West and the Good Witch of the East." Bachnele Poopik, who was currently starring in *Joe White and the Seven Amazons,* a movie based on the Snow White fairy tale, swore the gossip wasn't true: "Siegel's a coke addict. You can't believe a word he says." The midget testified that he loved his wife, Thalia the tall Muse of Comedy, as if love was a guarantee of fidelity. All I could see was his little feet above me. His calves faded into the steam that rose to billow and hover in sultry clouds against the white tiled ceiling of the steam room at the Hebron Hills Country Club. Bachnele was naked on the hottest top tier of the benched walls of the bath, while I, overwhelmed by the nebulous wet swelter, crouched near the cooler floor, wrapped in a soaking wet white terry towel. The hot fog condensed on my skin, mixing with perspiration to run down my face, chest, and arms, down my legs and between my toes into rivulets that formed evaporating puddles on the squares of white tile. "When we first came to America," the diminutive actor reminisced, "most of us lived in tenements without baths or heat. So the neighborhood shvitzbod, especially in winter, was where the men would come to get clean and warm together. We'd shmooz, and there's something about a steam bath that, just as it drains the sweat out of you, also draws out the truth. Not like shul, where we prayed, or at the landsmanshaftens where we bullshitted. No, the shvitz was like a mikva for the men, a place where you were purified." The truth that the steam brought out of Bachnele was that he had never been happier in his life. "It's the happiness that comes with true love," he said, quoting the Ketuvim: "A good wife is more precious than jewels; the husband who entrusts his heart to her has no lack of fortune. She fears not the snows of tomorrow and she laughs at the times to come." He adored his wife and loved little Moshe, his three-year-old son who was already taller than him. Bachnele believed he had been born under an auspicious sign, that he was lucky to be a midget. Because of it people noticed him; and because of that he had been successful in show business; and because of that he was attractive to women; and because of that Thalia had married him; and because of that he had a son; and because of that he was a happy man. "Luck," he said, "created us and gave us dominion over the earth. Luck chose us, the Jews, as its people, delivered us from Egypt, and wrought miracles for our forefathers in the days of old. Luck rules the universe. Praised be luck forever and ever. *Amein*." When he stopped, I looked up only to discover that he had disappeared into the roiling white cloud bank of heated mist above me. It was silent except for the steady hiss of the steam. The midget seemed truly to have vanished.

To 65
From 28

94 *The Fountain of Youth: The True Story of Ponce de Leon.* There were ten stories from the four-hundred-year-long life of the Jew who discovered Florida. The opening shot was a closeup of his face. Only when Ponce de Leon reaches into it with a cup, does the audience realize that the image is a reflection in water. Cut to medium shot: dressed in a white linen suit, pink silk shirt, and a Panama hat, Ponce de Leon drinks from the Fountain of Youth and lights a cigarette. Voice-over: "Some folks say smoking is bad for you, but I've been smoking for over four hundred years and I feel great." Each historical vignette from my very long life ended with a return to the modern set, where Ponce would say something that the Eagle Studio Thrillharmonic Orchestra tried to invest with profundity: "Staying young for four centuries is great. Don't listen to anyone who tries to convince you that to live forever would be a burden. Eternal youth is even better than it sounds." The first flashback was set in Castille during the Spanish Inquisition and was a commentary on current events in Europe (King Ferdinand had the distinctive Hitler mustache on his lip). Queen Isabella was portrayed by Debbie Rabonnir, who, in hopes of returning to the British stage before she was too old to play Cleopatra again, was once more waiting for a war in Europe to end. "Youth!" the Queen confides, "I have more gold than I need. I want eternal youth! If you can find the legendary fountain for me, Ponce, it shall be our secret. And when Ferdinand has grown old and dies, you and I, still as young as we are now, shall be married and you can be the king of Spain." Ponce suspects, however, that once he has located the fountain for the Queen, she will have him executed just as she has ordered the death of Señora Endora, La Bruja Marrana. After the Jewish sorceress had, in royal psychic consultation, revealed to the Queen the existence of a Fountain of Youth in the New World, Isabella condemns the witch to be burned at the stake so that she couldn't tell anyone else about it. Moments before her execution, Señora Endora warns Ponce de Leon (one of the many illegitimate sons of Count Jaime El Pedazo de Pelotudo Ponce de Leon) never to reveal his origins: he is a Jew because his mother, none other than Señora Endora herself, is a Jew, and to be Jewish is as dangerous then as now. Ponce's second flashback is of the Culosa Indians welcoming him and his men to Miami Beach. Worshipping the god Camoo, a serpent with a human head, the Culosas ritually drink sacramental water from the holy fountain, which in their mythology sprang from Camoo's burrow. The waters have kept the men potent, the women fertile, and everyone young and handsome. In return for bottles of Jerez Brandy and a conquistador helmet,

Chief Chupa, the Culosa king (played by Lucky Luciano's nephew Cazzo), is happy to give Ponce cigars, gourds of the magical water from his fountain, and unlimited access to native girls, whose beauty has been so perfectly preserved by that libation. Ponce warns the chieftain: "Once word gets out about your rejuvenating fountain, beautiful women, aromatic cigars, and sandy beaches, the Europeans will come and take it all away from you." Ponce and Chupa devise a plan to prevent that: in the middle of the night, after slitting the throats of the Spaniards, the noble savages return the dead bodies to their ship, a caravel bearing the name *Isabella*. One of the sailors is decapitated and dressed in Ponce's distinctive uniform and the real Captain de Leon falsifies the ship's log: "La Miami de la Florida (24°46' north latitude, 80°12' west longitude): the land is unarable, the women ugly, and the putrid waters of a spring we had hoped might be the legendary Fountain of Youth are mephitic, causing diarrhea and dementia. Hurricanes ravage the coast and the savages are bloodthirsty. I pray to the Lord Almighty that we shall soon be delivered from the infernal place named Miami, the Culosa word for 'snake cloaca.'" With her anchor lines cut, the *Isabella* drifts out to sea, where the strong current of the Gulf Stream delivers her into the hands of new explorers. While the body of the fake Ponce de Leon decomposes in a tomb in Puerto Rico's Cathedral of San Juan, the body of the real Ponce de Leon remains young in Miami, drinking and smoking with Chief Chupa and making love with nubile Indian ingenues for the next forty years. His third flashback is of the slaughter of innocents. Ponce is ready for the inevitable Spanish conquest of Florida. Before the soldiers come ashore he removes his alligator-skin loincloth and shell ornaments; and by the time all the Culosas have been slain, posing as Father Ponce, he is wearing the black robe of an evangelical Franciscan priest whom Chief Chupa had killed and eaten a few years earlier. "I have prayed to Our Lord Jesus Christ for deliverance," Father Ponce tells his redeemers as a preface to lies about being sent to Miami by the pope to save the souls of heathens. Not only have the savage Culosas supposedly tortured and castrated him, they have desecrated his baptismal font by urinating in it. Putting their Carib slaves at his disposal, the pious Spaniards help Ponce build a church around the holy fountain. Believing that he is a eunuch, the bishop of Cuba doesn't worry about sending the beautiful Sor Conchita de la Cruz (played by Debbie Rabonnir) to start a school in Ponce's parish for Indian children. Isolated as they are from monastic authority, the nun, soon discovering that through a miracle of God Ponce's testicles have grown back, becomes his paramour. So madly in love is he with her that, wishing to remain young together always, Ponce rashly divulges the secret of the fountain to her. "Love longs for eternity," Ponce de Leon says with tears in his eyes. When Joseph Siegel learned that Shirley Temple still owed Eagle Pictures one song from an unfinished film she had made there at the beginning of her career, the director immediately wrote her into the script: So thirsty is Ponce's beloved Sister Conchita for youth that she sneaks drinks behind his back, guzzling so much of the rejuvenating waters that, instead of merely remaining youthful, she actually becomes younger and younger until she is young enough to be played by Shirley Temple. The diminutive star wears a petite nun's habit in her song-and-tap-dance number "You're Only as Old as You Think You Are." The cute little bride of Christ continues to tipple so voraciously from the Fountain of Youth that she turns into a baby. Crawling up onto the edge of the fountain to slake her thirst, the infant nun falls in and disappears. In Ponce's fourth flashback as reflected off the surface of the waters of the Fountain of Youth, when the British, under the command of Colonel Nigel Hathaway, take Miami from the Spanish at the Battle of La Almeja Barretosa, he pretends to be an Anglican deacon who has been forced by Spanish papists to convert to Catholicism. Guinevere Hathaway, the colonel's beautiful wife, bored with life in the colony, announcing that interior decorating is one of her hobbies, offers to convert Ponce's Catholic chapel into a Protestant one. Bewitched by the charming Guinevere, Ponce falls under the tumultuous sway of adulterous love. Once again passion longs for eternity, and again Ponce foolhardily reveals the secret of the fountain. Exulting in the prospect of perpetual youth, Mrs. Hathaway takes another illicit lover, a dashing young English slaver named Bob. Guinevere, made as much the fool by love as Reverend Ponce, discloses the secret to her handsome swain. After murdering the colonel and Mrs. Hathaway, swashbuckling Bob, wanting the fountain for himself and not imagining that an Anglican deacon might be a skilled swordsman, attacks Ponce. Sending Bob to hell in a duel reminiscent of that between Errol Flynn and Basil Rathbone in *Captain Blood,* Ponce vows never to again trust anyone with whom he is in love. And so, in memories five and six, spanning another century of American history, it becomes poignant: Ponce keeps falling in love with young women, deeply and truly in love, but as the objects of his affections, each in turn, grow older and older while he remains ever youthful, he necessarily has to contrive some reason to terminate the affair lest they find out about the fountain. It is even more painful for him to renounce his love for each aging woman than it was for any of them to accept abandonment. "Is the wilting rose not all the more beautiful for her transience?" Ponce wonders. In segment six, Ponce de Leon, having fallen in love with a Jewess, divulges his Marrano heritage, demolishes the Anglican church, and builds Miami's first synagogue, Temple Lekh Teda, on the holy land where he had been living for three hundred years. Because Meyer Lansky thought there should be a musical number in the film, the seventh section of the motion picture, tracing Florida's history from the antebellum days through the Civil War and Reconstruction, featured a fantastically choreographed sequence in which the actresses who had been Culosa maidens, now lavishly dressed as Southern belles, sing and dance Stephen Foster numbers and then, in bathing suits, dive into a colossal Fountain of Youth to perform a spectacularly synchronized water ballet. Lansky tapped his feet during the rushes and, applauding exuberantly when it was over, declared, "A hell of a lot better than *Gone With the* fuckin' *Wind!*" In segment eight, a cinematic chronicle of the development of Miami Beach into a tourist mecca, there is a snazzy nightclub, horse track, jai alai fronton, and golf course. Dressed in a full tuxedo, Ponce de Leon takes leave from the rabbinate to dance the lindy with his latest love interest (played by Bugsy Siegel's latest love interest). Disillusioned with high society and wild parties, Ponce returns to the rabbinate for flashback nine, in which an increase in the creative involvement of the producers was apparent: When the members of the congregation of Temple Lekh Teda are deprived by Prohibition of the kosher wine necessary for their adherence to the covenant, they appeal to a group of freedom fighters from New York. The gangsters did the casting: Errol Flynn as Benjamin Siegel ("Although I'm better-looking than him," Siegel boasted), Clark Gable as Meyer Lansky ("Although he's better looking than me," Lansky admitted), and Zeppo Marx as Hayim Grossman ("Because he's a Jew," Hayim explained, "and because he deserves a chance to do something without his brothers stealing the show"). When I suggested that it might be difficult to get Flynn or Gable, Bugsy scoffed: "I give them a choice: 'You can be in the motion picture or you can have a bullet in your fuckin' brain.'" It didn't come to that: The Prohibition sequence was never filmed; nor was the climax of the motion picture, in which a hurricane would, in devastating Miami, destroy the Fountain of Youth forever. Joseph Siegel's razing of Miami promised to put David Selznick's burning of Atlanta to shame. But it never happened. The director was discovered lying on the floor of his trailer at Eagle Studios. Someone had, as they say "put a bullet in his fuckin' brain." There was more surprise than terror in the director's eyes.

"Vanity of vanities," said Rabbi Solomon Brodsky, his head covered with a tallith as he posed reverently by the closed casket, within which lay Joseph Siegel, on the chapel stage of Hollywood's Hebron Cemetery. He recited the monologue of Koheleth as a finale to the first act of the obsequial drama: "The dead are more fortunate in death than the living are to be alive. And better off than both is the yet unborn who hath not yet witnessed the evil there is under the sun." There was a small cast of mourners: a veiled Consuela Heimenhoff-Siegel comforted by Angel; my mother with her husband, Hayim; a weeping Cazzo Luciano; and two smiling Calusa maidens; there was a conquistador, a boom boy, and a grip, as well as Colonel and Mrs. Hathaway, Carmen Zambra and her three daughters, and, at the back of the room, keeping to himself, a davening Hasid in a long coat and strayml who made me wonder, "Could it be Jesus Estafar?" The entr'acte featured a cortege in solemn procession behind a slow hearse. Act II was set at the grave site. So that the burial itself didn't undermine the dramatic impact of the funeral by lasting too long, rather than taking the time to fill the grave, the coffin was merely covered with a blanket of simulated grass after each of the mourners had ceremonially shoveled a clod of dirt onto it. Cemetery gardeners would finish the job. As a transition into Act III, Brodsky reverted to Ecclesiastes: "'Go now, and eat thy bread with joy and drink thy wine with a merry heart under the sun.' Let me add that there are sandwiches and cakes as well as bread, and schnapps and highballs as well as wine; and you don't have to stand under the sun because we've reserved the Arnold Rothstein Memorial Reception Hall." My mother led me to a nearby grave marked "Abraham Schlossberg. Avraham ben Menachem. 1873–1920. Husband and Father. In Loving Memory." Although his body had been cremated in the explosion of the airplane that crashed to earth long ago, his charred bones had been gathered for burial in Hebron Cemetery. Having picked up two pebbles, one for the widow and one for the son, Abraham's wife directed me to place mine next to hers on the tombstone as a notice to all that, even twenty years after his death, the deceased had not been forgotten by the living. The rabbi waited for us to join the party and then recited the counsel that King Lemuel had been given by his mother: "Give strong drink unto him that is ready to perish, and wine to those who grieve. Let them drink and forget their sorrow and think no more of their losses." Raising his glass, the rabbi made the toast: "Let us now drink to the memory of the deceased." And then there was the surprise ending to the drama, a special event to allay our grief: Although Shirley Temple had been unable to attend either the chapel service or the burial, she arrived with her mother and a bodyguard in the nick of time for the finale. "In memory of Uncle Joe," she announced with characteristic sweetness from the dais, "I'd like to sing a little song. It was his favorite in the whole wide world. Golly, I hope I can sing loud enough for him to hear it all the way up in heaven." The little girl began to tap and croon: "Toot, toot, Tootsie, goo'bye. Toot, toot, Tootsie, don't cry." Sidling up next to me, Rabbi Brodsky asked in a whisper whether I reckoned that Temple was a Jewish name. As Shirley curtsied to the applause of the bereaved, Cazzo Luciano, drying his tears with a wet cocktail napkin, took me aside to invite me to an upcoming Italian funeral (whose had yet to be determined), promising that Catholics put on a better show than Jews: "Who the fuck cares about Shirley Temple anyway? Enrico Caruso sang at my old man's funeral." Despite the mafioso's assessment, a few mourners did seem to care about the child star: Carmen Zambra, her three daughters, two Calusa maidens, the boom boy, a cemetery gardener, and Rabbi Brodsky stood in line for her autograph. I remembered Carmen well: the sound of her voice ("What do you think? I mean about first love and all that?"), the shine of the unbuttoned buttons on her red-and-black-striped shirt, the smell of horses and hay, the closed eyes and glistening tears on flushed cheeks. But she did not seem to know who I was. "Were we friends?" she asked with a polite smile. Asking Carmen to excuse us, Angel took my hand to lead me outside. "I need to talk to you. Let's find someplace where we can be alone." I was pulled across a landscape of graves toward a small whitewashed shed set apart from the plots and several hundred yards from the reception hall. "Your mother told me that you're getting married," Angel said without looking at me, "to some nurse named Kitty, or Bunny, or Bambi, or something like that. Well, my darling Isaac, congratulations. I'm happy for you, of course, delighted that you've found someone to love for the rest of your life. But I must say that, well, quite frankly, I'm a bit surprised." I followed her through the open door of the shed and, seating myself next to her, amidst casket winches, pall pulleys, and grave markers, on the same sort of platform that had just been used to lower the director's coffin into its final resting place, I insisted that the marriage was merely my mother's whim and certainly not my plan: "I hardly know her." The air in the cramped grounds-keeping shack was headily scented with fertilizer, mulch, herbicides, pesticides, and Angel's French lilac perfume. As I leaned close, bringing my lips near her ear to whisper if not kiss, I suspected that she would withdraw from me as she had done whenever I had mustered the same boldness in Paris. Instead she turned her face to me, and as her eyes closed her lips parted. Reclining against a rolled blanket of simulated grass, she permitted me to lift the hem of her black silk mourning dress. Anxiously I touched her. I

388

feared that it was only because she felt that she was losing me that she gave herself to me. I recalled the words of Koheleth: "More bitter than death is a woman whose heart is a snare and whose hands are bonds." The breath that was her life was sweet enough to mask all the bitterness of death, and her binding hands were tender enough in their caresses to inspire surrender to the snares of desire and fetters of love. "Whoso pleaseth God shall escape her," saith the preacher, "but the sinner shall be taken by her." I wished that I could believe in God just so that I might, in defiance of Him, become a great enough sinner to be taken by Angel and inhumed in her forever. "We'll always know each other," she said softly as she rose to straighten her dress: "I feel it. Always." Angel smiled. "I must get back to Consuela. She needs me. It's a sad time. Let's go separately so no one suspects." Standing in the doorway of the shed to watch her walking quickly back to the reception hall, I wondered whether what had just happened meant anything, not only to her, not only to me, but anything at all. Meandering after her, in no hurry to get to the hall, not wanting to talk or listen to anyone, I stopped to sit on a large roll of simulated-grass grave covering, left no doubt by a negligent gardener by an old grave. There was a tombstone. I read the inscription "Minka Wiseman, 1899–1918." If only I had met the young girl before going to India, I mused, it might have all been different. She might have come with me or I might have stayed with her, and then—oh, the splendid "perhaps" of chance—she might still be alive. Or if not, at least the words "Mistress and Helpmate, In Loving Memory" would be engraved upon the headstone. With closed eyes I could see her eyes opening with ghostly desire, full lips trembling with phantasmal love, golden ringlets falling carelessly on pale white shoulders. I heard the lost girl softly humming a mysterious melody from the square outside the grave, and I could smell her in the faint scent of floral offerings wilting on a nearby grave. I began, for the first time in a long time, to cry. I wept not for Joseph Siegel, nor even for my father, but for Minka Wiseman, trying in tears to remember a soul never known, to recollect a body never seen and a voice never heard. With my face buried in my hands, slumped over in sadness and longing, I sobbed. An arm wrapped around my shoulder and a hand rested on my knee. Hayim Grossman was trying to console me: "Like the song says, 'Don't cry, Tootsie.' At least not for Siegel. He was a shmuck. Listen to me, son. I'm risking my life by talking to you like this, by telling you what I'm going to tell you. It's because I love your mother and would do anything to make her happy. She loves you, and if anything bad were ever to happen to you, she'd be unhappy, and when she's unhappy, I'm unhappy. And when Jews are unhappy, God's unhappy. What could be worse than that? So listen to me, son: you've got to get out of town. You've got to hide. Siegel's going to kill you." Looking up at him in hopes that I'd see the grin of joking, I saw a serious frown: "They don't call him 'Bugsy' for nothing. Listen. Joe was fudging the budget of the movie, embezzling money and, well, the syndicate doesn't tolerate dishonesty. There's got to be justice. When he was questioned about the missing cash, he claimed his star, Ponce de Leon, which is to say, you, Isaac Schlossberg, had demanded more and more money. He swore he gave most of the cash to you. I told you not to cry over Siegel. I told you he was a shmuck. Personally I know you weren't in on it, but Bugsy doesn't think things through like I do. He figures you had a role in Siegel's scam. All I can say is: get out of town before it's too late, son. And don't tell anyone where you're going, not even your mother." Taking the threat seriously enough to leave the cemetery without returning to the reception hall to say good-bye, I hesitated only long enough to find a pebble to set upon Minka Wiseman's tombstone. The taxi waited outside the Garden of Osiris while I grabbed the few belongings I needed and then it took me to San Pedro, where I hid in a room at the Spouter Inn until there was an ocean liner to take me away forever. In hopes that he'd talk to Bugsy, I wrote a letter to Cazzo Luciano informing him that I was leaving for Palestine "to join a Zionist assault company, the Palmach, to fight the enemies of Israel—Nazis, Arabs, Italians, and, in light of their latest White Paper, the British. Please, dear Cazzo, convey my warmest wishes to Ben Siegel. He's such a snazzy dresser and a brilliant mind, a real inspiration to me both as a Jew and a human being." I wrote to my mother to try to convince her not to worry about me even if she didn't hear from me for a while. In a letter to Angel, I told her that I loved her, had always loved her, and would always love her. "Always." I was confident that she would understand that there was something truthful about the lie since she had, herself, said the same thing to me. It was, in fact, the very last thing Devora Rabinowitz ever said to me. She had said it at the funeral, after making love with me, as she turned to walk away from me and across the field of graves.

96 Unaware that rolls of dice and sea would ever return me to these volcanic islands in the middle of nowhere, I had had no inclination years ago to linger long enough in Honolulu to make a square of it. This time I traveled here under the assumed name of Isaac Codee. Excitedly giggling black-haired children, wiry and wet, dove from the landing dock into the shimmering aquamarine of Honolulu harbor for coins tossed for luck or amusement by voyagers on the decks, and full-bodied women, smiling sunshine, in flowered muumuus, with floral leis banding their heads and hanging around their necks, were lined up to kiss our cheeks, garland us with flowers, and say, "Aloha." Skirted in lava-lavas and bare-chested, the hefty Happy Hawaiians of Halehalakahiki chanted "Honolulu Lula, the Rula' of the Hula," and *"E haole hupo loa, hele aku."* Passing through a grove of coconut palms, my taxi pulled into the pink porte-cochere of the pink hotel, and as the doorman, costumed as a maharaja with a pink turban and cummerbund, opened the car door, girls in grass skirts and coconut-shell brassieres, with fragrant pink flower necklaces, bracelets, and anklets, began to sing "Toot, toot, Tootsie, aloha." The taxi driver said "aloha" to bid me good-bye at the same moment that the maharaja said "aloha" to greet me. And "aloha" said the Filipino dressed in a Chinese coolie costume who, with my bag in hand, led me under pink archways into expansive pink-marbled halls, pink-pillared and lush with pink-potted ferns, palms, and demure serving girls in pink kimonos who blithely bowed to say "aloha." By the grace of the late Ponce de Leon and Joseph Siegel, I had enough money to reserve a luxury Ali'i suite with a view of the ocean. The bellboy boasted of the famous people who had previously slept in the room: "Fatty Arbuckle, D. W. Griffith, Shirley Temple, Moe Howard, and, just last week, the Japanese ambassador, Kichisaburo Nomura." Lying down on the iron-frame bed and lulled by a rhythmically somnolent *shhhhh* of surf whispered with sunlight through my bamboo-awninged window, I thought of Minka Wiseman and wondered what to do next. It was by chance, I believed, that the first passenger ship out of San Pedro had been bound for Honolulu. Many of the women in the hotel, I soon discovered, had traveled to Hawaii without men in tow. Wearing garlands of pikake and brightly colored dresses, they yearned to laugh innocently and play naughtily, to drink sweet rum drinks and bathe in warm foamy surf. Any man could meet them: On a sprawling seaside lanai they were seated in cane-and-wicker lounge chairs to write a letter beneath a pink canvas umbrella; or they rocked in swinging shaded porch chairs to read a newspaper or a romance or just to look out to sea; they sipped tea in a tropical garden amidst liana-entwined palms, monkey-pod, and banyan, voluptuous growths of ti, hibiscus, gardenia, and seemingly antediluvial halekonia. The women sipped zombies or royal pink ladies in the Coconut Grove Ona Mau Bar, and they lounged barefoot at the Beachcombers' Beachside Bar, wearing sunglasses and sun hats to imbibe Buster the bar boy's aloha rum punch from coconut-shell goblets. In formal attire they might dine on green-turtle soup Kamehameha in the Captain Cook Room, or gather in the Sugar Cane Ball Room for concerts by the Royal Hawaiian Orchestra. They flocked to the Merry Moe of Maui Luau Lollapalooza on Sundays. They would shyly emerge from pink cabanas to recline on pink towels spread out for them by a beach boy on clean sand beneath green palm-frond parasols. They rubbed their bodies with fragrant oils. I watched one of them pull a white rubber bathing cap over her sandy-colored hair as she strode toward the waters of the Pacific. After testing the temperature with a pointed toe, she dove into a wave, disappeared for a few moments, came up for air, gasped, and laughed with pleasure. Her Cestus bathing suit wetly revealing, the pretty girl emerged from the warm splashes of spume like Venus born from a mythic sea. She pulled off the tight bathing cap and shook her hair loose. All you had to do to meet a fe-male visitor to these islands was to say "aloha," and she'd be sure to say it back, and then one of you would say, "It means hello, good-bye, and I love you." And then you'd laugh and make a date to swim, play table tennis, drink rum or eat poi, watch the sun rise or set, visit a pineapple cannery or enjoy some other manner of foreplay. "Aloha," Miss Sandy Sanders, the bather with the sandy hair, whose trip to Hawaii had been the prize for winning the Miss Wyoming Junior Roundup Queen Contest, whispered as I opened my eyes in the morn-ing. "Let's order breakfast in bed like movie stars," she said with all the effusive enthusiasm one would expect from an eighteen-year-old Wyoming girl chap-eroned only by an alcoholic grandmother (herself a former Roundup Queen). She smiled between bites of papaya: "I can't believe I lost my virginity in the same bed in which Shirley Temple once slept." When Sandy and I stopped at the Beachcombers' Beachside Bar for a matutinal aloha rum punch before go-ing for a swim, Buster the bartender told us about the deaf blind man who was enthroned in a low pink canvas lounger on the beach in front of the Royal Hawaiian Hotel each morning. "That's him," Buster said, "over there with the two wahines. Go on over and have a look. The girls like to show him off. He's kind of a tourist attraction here. Quite a joker. He's the happiest guy in the world." Since he hadn't heard any new jokes since the World War, Larry Littler told the same ones that I had heard on the deck of the *Alexandria* years before, and the punch lines still caused him to convulse with laughter. Introducing my-self to his two nurses, the gaunt Michiko Murasaki and the corpulent Wahanui

Wong-Wichsenheimer, I explained that I had met the Littler family on the boat that had brought Larry to Hawaii. I took his hand in mine in hopes, unlikely as they were, that he might remember me by my handshake. "Oh, you must be new here," he said cheerfully. "You're going to love it. It's heaven." Michiko explained that he didn't mean "like heaven," but that he actually thought he was in heaven. Neurosurgeons at Hickok Military Hospital had successfully removed the bullet that had been in his brain since the Battle Champs-Labitte; but ever since the operation Larry believed that he was dead: "He thinks God has brought him up to heaven as a reward for killing so many Germans during the war in Europe." Wahanui elaborated: "The operation caused other damage too. Now, not only can he not see or hear, he can't smell or taste either. Touch is the only sense that's left." No sooner had Larry recovered from laughing over a joke he had told about a rabbi and priest who had gone to a brothel together than he began one about a nymphomaniac who was being interviewed by St. Peter at the Pearly Gates. As Michiko massaged his shoulders with coconut oil, Wahanui inserted the end of a straw into his mouth so that he could drink rum from a hollowed-out pineapple. Even if he couldn't taste it, she said, he relished its effects. "Thank you, God, thank you!" Larry exclaimed, sifting sand through his fingers and digging into it with his toes: "Thanks for letting me into heaven. It's so peaceful and comfortable, and nobody tells you what to do. But you know what I like best about it? Having sex every day with angels. Thank you, dear God." Sandy said that her heart went out to the poor fellow. "No," Michiko insisted, "he's very, very happy." "And," Wahanui added, "he's the best lover a girl could ever imagine. My only worry is that maybe there really is a heaven. What if he dies and goes there, and it isn't as good as this?" Sandy and I visited Larry again the next morning to listen to him tell more jokes to God. A man about my own age, wearing a flower-print aloha shirt with matching aloha shorts, carrying a ukulele in one hand and an aloha rum punch in the other, sauntered over. "Aloha," he cheerfully said. "I see you've met my pal Larry and the ladies. We go back a long way. We came over on the boat together, him and me, years ago and have been chums ever since, although I don't know if he actually knows who I am." I, however, did know exactly who he was. Yes, I remembered Morris Mendelssohn, who had since become Merry Moe of Maui, singing emcee at the Royal Hawaiian Luau Lollapalooza each Sunday afternoon and cantor at Temple Beth Aloha each Saturday morning. Some months later Moe filled me in on Larry: "The girls used to be hookers. But Larry's father, who had made plenty of money in the Alaska gold mines, hired them to take care of his son in perpetuity. His parents have both passed away, and he thinks the reason that they're not around is that they're still down on earth." Just after dawn, standing in the pink porte-cochere to bid good-bye to Sandy, I draped a flower lei around her neck using the cover of Hawaiian ceremony to kiss her cheek without compromising the propriety imposed by the presence of her hungover grandmother. "It was fun to meet you, Mr. Codee. If you ever get to Wyoming, give us a holler." She stepped into the taxi, closed the door, leaned out of the window, and, as the car pulled away, shouted, "Aloha." Even though it was still early in the morning, bathers had already begun to gather on the beach. Beachboys were arranging the palm-frond parasols, Buster was opening the beach bar, and Michiko and Wahanui had just set Larry up for the day. I swam out toward a girl who was floating on her back. "Aloha," I said and when, after her "aloha," she told me that she was on her honeymoon, I said "aloha" again and submerged to swim under and past her. I was still underwater when I heard the rumbling. Coming up for breath, I saw the flash of hellish fire. I heard the furious boom and fulminant peal, and felt it, the shake and roll of the incendiary percussive barrage. There was more fire up the coast, explosive flare and flash, detonation after detonation as fierce brushes of flame blackwashed the sky with soot and cinder. There was the growing growl and roar of planes, glide- and dive-bombing, soaring and strafing. With the screams and howls of air-raid sirens, ambulances, fire engines, and police cars, frantic bathers were swimming to shore as fast as they could and everyone on the beach was running for dear life. Oily black clouds, spackled with the radiant red of antiaircraft fire, curled out of the harbor. Aerial shrapnel pelted the earth like brimstone upon Sodom. By the time I reached the shore, everyone had fled to shelter. Buster, Michiko, and Wahanui had disappeared, and only Larry Littler, unable to hear the terrible anthem of bombs bursting in air, to see the rockets' red glare, or to smell the smoke and sulfur, was left grinning on the beach. "So a minister walks up to a prostitute and . . ." Kneeling down next to him, I draped a pink Royal Hawaiian beach towel over our heads as if that would protect us, and as he continued the joke, I held his hand in mine. Finally calming down after uproariously and convulsively laughing over his punch line, he sighed. "Oh God, dear Lord, thanks again for bringing me here. Heaven's even better than they told us it would be in church. I don't know what I did to deserve it."

From 31

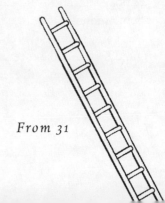

97 I've been stranded here, one of the few temperate places on earth where there are no snakes, since the bombing of Pearl Harbor. When the Royal Hawaiian was patriotically surrendered to the United States Navy Department of Recreation, Amusement, and Morale as a rest and relaxation station for submarine officers and servicemen, nonmilitary guests were turned out. The good news was that the military governor of the Territory of Hawaii had, after extensive deliberations, decided not to camouflage the building, but to leave it as cheerfully pink as ever. Although I had to evacuate my luxurious Ali'i suite, I was, thanks to Merry Moe of Maui, able to secure a small room, formerly a large closet in what had been a grounds maintenance building in the Royal Hawaiian's coconut palm grove. It has been my home for the last three years, and it is where I sit right now writing on a large square of newsprint by the light of rationed kerosene. It's how I entertain myself. Once Moe learned that I had had experience in vaudeville, music hall, variety theater, and the movies, that I can juggle, sharpshoot, and do a few magic tricks, he hired me to replace the three Japanese comic tumblers in his Luau Lollapalooza, who were arrested on suspicion of treason. We entertain the troops on the weekends at the Royal and the Moana and during the week at Pearl Harbor and Hickok Air Force Base. There are also U.S.O. functions at Princess Papuli Palace and Hale Haole. Due to blackout and curfew regulations, the shows are over thirty minutes before sundown. Because everyone in Hawaii was, at the beginning of the war, required by martial law to register and carry an identification card (both so that bodies could be identified after bombings and so that potential enemy spies and saboteurs could be singled out), I reverted to my true name. I did so with some confidence that, given World War II, Bugsy Siegel was probably more interested in killing Adolf Hitler, Benito Mussolini, and Hideki Tojo than Isaac Schlossberg. Becoming myself again in real life, I have nevertheless adopted the stage name Professor Leroy Lestrange for the Luau Lollapalooza. With a gimmicked slate and the one-ahead method that I learned from my mother, I do a mentalism routine. With closed eyes and fingertips touching my temples, I say, "Yes, yes, it's coming in clear now. Premier Tojo!" The troops cheer when I reveal his thoughts in an exaggerated Japanese accent: "Ah so! Yanks too damn tough for us Japs! Kicking our yerrow asses!" Then juggling models of Japanese fighter planes, after a bit of patriotic patter, I throw them one at a time into the air, quick-draw my U.S. Army revolver, and, using bullets gimmicked with spread shot, blow them out of the sky to the cry of "Remember Pearl Harbor!" With gas masks on their laps, our boys whistle, stamp their feet, clap their hands, and then spread two fingers into a sign of victory. There are illusions: Zig-Zag Jap, Vanishing Nip, Sawing Hirohito in Half, Levitating American Airmen, and then the climax of the show, the Miraculous Missing-in-Action Box, which allows the audience to imagine that boys lost on Bataan, Buna Beach, Okinawa, or Kiribati might someday reappear. Because Honolulu is the casualty evacuation center for the Pacific, lots of the members of my audience sit in wheelchairs and have missing limbs; many are drunk and, in the midst of their laughter over my routine, on the verge of tears. They ache for the touch of a wife or sweetheart back home, a nurse, volunteer war bond salesgirl, a U.S.O. hula dancer, Hollywood ingenue, a Wac, Wave, or Spar. Since the men outnumber the women by about three hundred to one, the prostitutes, vending that tender touch and a moment or so of solace that might almost seem like love, are devoting long hours to the war effort. There's something about curfews, blackouts, restricted liquor, rationed food, air raids, bomb shelters, gas masks, and a sense of impending death that make people amorous. In light of the ratio of men to women, I consider it a lucky throw of the die that I've found Norabelle Roth, daughter of Lieutenant Commander Gilbert Roth of the United States Navy. She's only half my age, but as fun as fun can be under martial law, and beautiful in her sarong dress and matching bolero jacket with its silk-screened tumescent red and fleshy yellow anthuriums. She often comes from the base to swim in the mornings. Before going into the ocean, we usually sit for a while with Larry Littler by the wall of coiled barbed wire that has been stretched along Waikiki Beach to prevent an invasion by sea. Larry recognizes my handshake now. "Did I ever tell you the one about the nymphomaniac who dies and comes up to heaven?" Norabelle laughs at his jokes, if not his laughter. It's hard not to delight in his peculiar cheer, uncompromised as it is by war, death, and losses of love, by the sorts of realities that are seen or heard these days. Although he doesn't know it, he is now married to Wahanui. The disappearance of Michiko after the bombing of Pearl Harbor made the marriage feasible. The fact that matrimony has rendered Wahanui Larry's sole beneficiary might have some suspecting that she married him for his substantial trust fund. But anyone who has ever watched her massage his body with coconut oil, or heard her tell people how sweet he is, is convinced of the genuineness of her love. She uses the monthly stipend to buy war bonds for her country and Hawaiian shirts for her husband. Although he can't see the hula girls, outrigger canoes, palm trees, pineapples, fish, and tropical flowers that emblazon the new shirts, he smiles with the pleasure of feeling the softness of the cotton blends, rayon, crepe de chine, and silk. Each morning Wahanui drapes a fresh dew-moist ginger lei around her husband's neck and kisses his cheeks. For the wedding she dressed Larry in a black silk shirt decorated with bright birds of paradise that matched her muumuu. Since Larry had no idea what was going on, the radiantly blushing bride had to say "he will" on his behalf when the minister asked if he would take her to have and to hold as his lawfully wedded wife until death did them part. Wedding guests included me and Moe, Wahanui's three sisters, Haunani, Heidi, and Hee Hing, and their seven boyfriends (two privates, an ensign, an apprentice seaman, a midshipman, a sergeant, and a corporal). Even though Larry couldn't hear it, Moe arranged for the Happy Hawaiians of Halehalakahiki to play the "Hawaiian Wedding Song," and even though the groom couldn't taste it, to go with the pineapple wedding cake that Wahanui herself had baked, Buster provided French champagne, Château d'Amour, served in ginger-ale bottles because of the liquor restrictions that have been imposed on us by the war. We were cheerfully drunk when Buster confided that he had a key to the lock on the door to the Royal Hawaiian's secret wine cellar that had been sealed under martial law. Even as the war ended his career as a bartender, it put Buster in the new business of selling fine wines from that secret cache to commissioned officers of the United States armed forces. He also makes money from the sales of morphine, a substantial stock of which serendipitously came into his possession when a package sent to the Waikiki Red Cross Emergency Station was inadvertently delivered to his door. In addition to providing our GIs with liquor and drugs, Buster knows how to sneak call girls into the Royal Hawaiian, thus sparing the more preoccupied and discreet submarine officers the inconvenience and embarrassment of a trip to the red-light district downtown. Any of the girls who happen to spend the entire night at the hotel are likely to show up in the morning to sit with Larry on the beach. One of the regulars, a cute blonde from Bellingham called "Honolulu Lulu," told me just the other day how much she envies Wahanui for "landing a swell guy like Larry." And I envy him for having found in silent darkness a woman like Mrs. Wahanui Wong-Wichsenheimer-Littler. She sings him to sleep each night and he hears the songs, she assures me, by feeling the melody in the ways in which she holds him, pressing on the high notes, stroking on the low. Reclining against her breast, he feels the rhythm of the music in her breathing. Today I envy him for all that he cannot hear or see, for all that he cannot know, because today I received a very sad letter from my mother. I hadn't written to her during my first month in Hawaii, but now, no longer afraid of Siegel, I write each Sabbath and telephone once a month. Since it is illegal to speak a foreign language during a long distance call, I've had to ask my mother not to call me *"mein zeese nishumule"* over the phone, explaining to her that it might sound like a Nazi secret code-phrase to government monitors. As ever, her letters report the deaths of loved ones, friends, and acquaintances: Ola Namnlösa, Leona "Tara Tigresse"

Wilder, Tubs Shortman, and Jake Grossman. And then there was Bachnele Poopik: "He lived a long time for a midget," she wrote; "they don't have much of a life expectancy." Yesterday the news in the *Honolulu Star* was that Adolf Hitler has committed suicide. And today the news in the letter from my mother is that Devora Rabinowitz has died of cancer. The little girl in white lace who once climbed the high ladder to walk the wire across the sky, has fallen. I remember: Angel's hair around my face as she bowed over me in love; the banded scarlet king slithering through her fingers, taking pleasure in the warmth of her hand; her smile as she sat upon her throne on the golden burnished barge with its purple sails and silver oars. And I remember playing snakes and ladders with her. I still have the game that my father gave to me in square 1, that I gave to Angel in square 10, and that she gave back to me in square 89. Early in the war, with nothing else to do one night, thinking of Angel, I got out the game and, just for a laugh and old times' sake, I thought I might play it solitaire. The board evoked stories of love and death and trying to have a good time anyway. Staring at the ten rows of ten squares each, crisscrossed as they are by the snakes of memory and ladders of longing, I saw my life organized in terms of it. If square 1 is the Dead Sea, I mused, must not square 100 be Mt. Everest? Then my life might be, by the grace of chance, luck, or fate, a book of holy ascension from the lowest place on earth to the highest. With a sense of that and time to kill until the war is over, I started writing this, and I have been working on it on and off ever since. I realize that, in order to win the game, I ought to try, as mad as the idea seems, to climb Mt. Everest. It's an adventure worthy of Wyoming Willie. Opening my tin of his Wondrous Hair Pomade and taking a whiff, I am reminded that I write this in memory of my father and for the sake of a child—Nora told me today that she's pregnant. Holding the die in my hand, I'm ready to play. Once the war is over, I'm hoping to climb to the summit of Mt. Everest, to marry, and to have a son to whom I can entrust the Hebrew words that Avraham ben Menachem taught to me. "God made laughter for me so that whoever hears my laughter will laugh with me." I want it to end happily ever after. So now I'll roll the die, and let's see what happens.

98 Dearest Nora: It will not be surprising that I am writing to you on this sheet of newsprint if curiosity has compelled you to open the Sears & Roebuck boot box which I left behind, if you have already looked at some of the ninety-seven squares of my life that are its contents. After reading this letter, fold it in half and in half again and add it to the box. There is actually no reason for you to read the other squares until all one hundred are done, until I have stood higher on this earth and closer to heaven than any other human being before me. Now that the war is over, I fear that others might beat me to it. Mr. S—— was on the ship from Honolulu to Singapore; but, still, I refuse to let him enter and play in this game. I ran into an old friend, a herpetologist named Vladimir Yesnovitch, on the boat from Singapore to Calcutta. Until he took my hand in his to examine it, I had almost forgotten about the scar that was left on it by the fangs of a harlequin that, by biting me, made me think I was going to die so many squares back. Professor Yesnovitch smiled to observe that the scar is almost completely gone. I said good-bye to him on the dock in Calcutta where I was greeted by Kumar Bannerjee, another friend from the past whom you'll remember if you have read very much of what I have written. He was sorely disappointed that I would be staying at the Tollygunge Players' Club rather than at his home in Blacktown. And I was sorry that I would not have the opportunity to see his brothers, Nagendra or Ganesh, again. Nagendra, secretary-treasurer of the Communist Cricket Club of Calcutta, was in jail for sneaking into the grounds of the Victoria Memorial and defiling the monumental statue of the empress of India with a bucket of fecal matter. Ganesh was in the Soviet Union selling Indian wildlife to the Leningrad State Circus, which was soon to be rebuilt after the heavy bombing that killed all of its animals during the siege of the city when the Germans mistook the circus for the Soviet Central Intelligence building. The passing away of Mother Bannerjee has left Albert despondent over the refusal of Calcutta's Municipal Department of Death Disposal Services to issue him an embalming permit. The innovative taxidermist had long dreamed of some day stuffing and mounting his mother. And, in spite of the hallowed Hindu injunction of cremation, she was in favor of Albert's plan. On her deathbed she had agreed to sing "Jai Hind" into the microphone of a tape-recording device that would be implanted in her bosom. Albert was going to wire three of the extended fingers on her right hand as switches to play, pause, and rewind the song. Although I wasn't able to see Maithun Wadsworth Tagore in Calcutta, I was pleased by Kumar's account of his professional success: Maithun was in Hollywood, hired by Mack Silverman, the new head of Eagle Studio, to collaborate on the script for *The Charge of the Stooge Brigade,* in which the Three Stooges, after being sprayed with water from an elephant's trunk, chased by a tiger, and frightened by cobras, narrowly escape from the Thugees who attempt to sacrifice them to the bloodthirsty goddess Kali. Ganesh, Kumar reported, had supplied Eagle with the elephant, tiger, and a snake charmer from Mayapur to handle his collection of defanged cobras. Although none of the snake charmers in Mayapur recognized me, I was welcomed hospitably enough and directed to sit on a charpoy, drink chai, and smoke a chillum. I inquired about Lingnath and his daughter Nagini, a woman with tattooed serpents around her wrists, their heads resting on the backs of her hands. A young boy had begun to play the *bin* for my pleasure and I could hear the giggling of the girls who peered at us through cracks in walls. Smiling generously, a handsome young fellow approached. Barefoot and shirtless, he wore only a black lungi and orange turban. He was adorned with gold earrings and rosaries of snake vertebrae and the eyes of Rudra around his neck, and there was a jewel as dark red as a clot of blood in the ring on his finger. Salaaming, he introduced himself as "Bolon Nath Sapera." "Nagini Saperin?" I asked. "Lingnath and Nagini. My friends. Here?" Seemingly pleased, the young man answered, "Lingnath grandfather. Nagini mother. Bolon son." With his large dark searching eyes, delicate features, and bewitching smile, he resembled his mother but was lighter complexioned. The child who had been playing the *bin* handed it to Bolon, who took it up and swayed as he played upon it with all the abandon of his ancestors. Another boy began to drum, another to dance, and another to sing: *"Sapere bin baja de re calungi tere sath."* "Play your *bin* for me, O snake charmer, and I'll walk away with you." At the end of the song, Bolon lit the chillum. When I asked where I might find his mother, he shrugged his shoulders, exhaled ganja smoke, and informed me that she had died while giving birth to him. Since he himself had never known her, he was always happy to meet someone who had. He wondered what I had to say about her, and I told him that she was a good woman. My sadness over not being able to see Nagini was at least somewhat assuaged by the surprising delight of once again shaking the hand of the irrepressible Professor Pinchas ben Abraham Wonderful. He had returned to India after the war, billing himself as "International Maharaja of Magnificent Magic and World Famous for Buried Alive," and, given the prestige accrued by his success abroad, he was prospering with his traveling show. He announced that he was engaged to a Bengali Hindu girl from his own farming village and that the marriage would take place as soon as he could get the approval for her conversion to Judaism from the director of the All-India Rabbinate in Cochin. It was difficult, Professor Wonderful said, to explain to the girl and her family what Judaism was. But they didn't really care: By becoming a Jewess, she would marry an internationally renowned entertainer rather than an unknown local farmer. The magician assured me that this second marriage in no way compromised an enduring love for Shula. He had courageously, although unsuccessfully, attempted to avenge her death in a concentration camp by assassinating Hitler. "I wrote to the friend and colleague Helmut Schreiber, Hitler's favorite magician, offering to do the free performance of my magic for Führer in celebration of the Aryan Unity as the hope that Germans would win a war and liberate my India from the British." Schreiber arranged Wonderful's visit from occupied Paris to Berlin so that he could join the team of German, Austrian, and Polish magicians scheduled to perform at Hitler's upcoming surprise birthday party. Professor Wonderful was thoroughly searched and his magic equipment examined by S.S. officers before he was admitted to the Reichskanzlei, where the party was being thrown for the dictator. The plot had been simple enough: Professor Wonderful would perform routines from his usual repertoire of illusions and then, for his finale, with a smile and a wink, he would invite the Führer himself to lie down in the sawing-a-lady-in-half box and announce, "I shall now demonstrate to a world that our Führer is an indestructible." That would surely get the birthday boy into the box. Once he had Hitler there, the magician would actually saw him in half. When Wonderful exclaimed, "Whoops! I goofed!" and everyone realized that the magician had blundered and that their leader was dead, Professor Wonderful, he had himself been well aware, would probably have been executed. "It would have been worth a revenge for an extermination of my love, the Shulamite Levi. I would be proud to die the death, giving my life to save a world from the Nazi." Unfortunately when Hitler was invited into the box, he declined, commanding Eva Braun to lie down in it in his place. Unwilling to either kill a woman or risk being executed for doing so, the magician performed the illusion in the usual way, seeming to saw Fräulein Braun in half and then reassembling her unharmed. With an appreciative *Ausgezeichnet!* the Führer stood to excuse himself from the party, announcing that he was going to his bunker to issue an order for the German Army to occupy Hungary and round up the Jews there for deportation to Auschwitz. After hearing about his past plan to assassinate Hitler, I told Professor Wonderful about my present one to climb Mt. Everest. Slapping me on the back, he assured me of his confidence in me, musing that the only reason no one had yet been successful in making it to the top was that up until now no Jew had tried to do it. He escorted me to the office of the Royal Mountaineering, Trekking, and Hiking Club in Chowringhee to obtain information on Himalayan climbing. I was advised there to come here to Gangtok in order to contact a Sherpa named Khram Nag

Gyatso, who would be able to give me mountain climbing lessons and arrange all the necessary guides, porters, and pack charges for the proposed expedition. I was warned, however, that more difficult than making it to the summit of Everest would be getting permission from the Dalai Lama to enter Tibet and set foot upon sacred Chomolungma, Goddess Mother of the World. Having advised me to enter the Himalayan kingdom, like many a sahib before me, disguised as a Buddhist monk, Khram Nag has, after several days of rigorous haggling, already made arrangements to purchase from the lamas of Enchey Monastery the ochre and vermilion robes that are characteristic of the Nyingmapa order, together with such accessories as prayer wheels, rosaries, and vajra liturgical scepters. Khram Nag, a Bhotia in his mid-twenties and in fine shape, the youngest son of Milarepa Nag Gyatso (one of the bearer-guides on the Royal Geographical Society's reconnaissance expedition of 1921), has been teaching me the fundamentals of mountain climbing. In the evenings I drink tomba, a milky fermented millet libation, with Khram Nag and his father. They are pleased that I have brought plenty of American cigarettes and whiskey with me; there's nothing quite like a shot of bourbon to warm the bones on a freezing Himalayan night. We plan to take the drink and the smokes, concealed in the ornamental cabinets in which Buddhist scriptures are traditionally transported, with us into Tibet and up Everest, but we cannot bring oxygen cylinders, crampons, ropes, climbing ladders, or any other alpine equipment that might, by belying our ecclesiastical disguises, reveal our true purpose to soldiers on the other side of the Tibetan border. Khram Nag assures me, however, that the lamas of Rongbuk Monastery at the base of Everest will be happy to rent out mountaineering equipment that has been left behind in failed attempts to conquer the mountain. And so tomorrow we set out northward through the Tista gorge toward Lachung, where, after resting for a night, we will change into the robes of Buddhist pilgrims to venture into the Forbidden Kingdom. Once there, if we are stopped by guard patrols and I am questioned, lest it be discovered that I do not belong there, I will not speak. Khram Nag Gyatso will inform anyone who cares to know that, intent upon deliverance from this world, I have taken a solemn vow of silence.

To 36

Have I told you, my dearest, that I was born, so my father swore to his God, in the deepest exposed depression on earth, on the shores of the Dead Sea, at the darkest hour of the darkest night of the last year of the last century? And now, as the longest, lightest day of this year approaches, I am ready to make my way through the clouds to the top of the highest peak on earth, to finish this game so that I might play another. I can clearly see my notorious destination ten thousand feet above me. The haughty pyramidal face of the recalcitrant goddess condescendingly gazes back at me in silence. From the sublimely brazen peak, her topknot, a streaming white plume several miles long, twists and curls eastward as an undulate serpent of cloud in the stark blue field of a heavenly oblivion. We made good time, considering the obstacles; only three weeks from Gangtok to the monastery, from where I write to you for the last time before setting out tomorrow at dawn. The border seemed imaginary as not a soul was there to stop us. High and higher we climbed through pine and rhododendron, and then down into valleys carpeted with pink geranium, coral potentilla, and crimson primula. There were huge velvety orchids, striped sticky purple and blotched phosphorescent black, bristly snake-vines with fast-clutching tendrils, ravenously gaping flytraps, sharp-needled cacti, and steaming sulfur pools in which I would have bathed had Khram Nag not warned me that the simmering dark waters were toxic. Then we'd struggle up again through magnolia forests so suffused with cloud that Khram Nag would disappear, reappear, and vanish again before my eyes. I could hear his breathing and the ghostly scuffling of unseen animals: the skittish snow leopard, red panda, and Himalayan bear. Emerging from mountainous mists, we found ourselves on a vast glacial moraine, surrounded by monstrous hummocks of scarred stone, snowy parapets and barren precipices of coal-black and chalk-white rock streaked with gold and striated with silver. We'd pass grazing herds of wild asses, blue goats, and insouciant yaks foraging for the summer highland grass that sprouts somehow in the crevices of the cold scree. Twisted seracs of murky ice loomed larger and larger along the way. Mossy cairns with rough weather-worn Tibetan inscriptions and ragged red, black, and yellow prayer flags were occasional markers of human presence. Whitewashed pawn-shaped chortens, more and more frequent the higher we forged, intimated the proximity of Rongbuk. I heard the voice before I saw the lama on the granite ledge above us: *"Guten Tag,"* he shouted, *"möchten Sie etwas trinken?"* My laughter made him ask, *"Ist mein Deutsch so beschissen?"* "No, no," I assured him. "Your German may be perfectly fluent, but it startled me. I speak English." Peering down at us through sunglasses, he was lackadaisically spinning a prayer wheel. "Despite your robes," he said, "I knew that you were not pilgrims. You do not walk like men who are celibate. And you, sir," he said pointing directly at me, "as your gait is so characteristically Occidental, I assumed that you were German in that, for the past few years, with the exception of my old friend the renowned Major Wheedle, all the foreign visitors to Rongbuk have been German." Making his way with ease and grace down the precarious talus slope, the spry old cleric introduced himself as Kushog Doubtub Gylatsap, high regent to the supreme abbot of the monastery. He informed us that if we were there in search of the elusive Abominable Snowman, he could, for a mere two hundred rupees per snapshot, pose for us in a very realistic Yeti costume. When I explained that it was our object to climb Everest, he cordially invited us to make ourselves comfortable in the visitor's quarters until the supreme abbot, whose permission and blessing were required to set foot on the mountain, would receive us. Dinner was brought to us and, as we had eaten only Borden's Beef Lozenges and Tootsie Rolls for the past few weeks, the hot meal of fried kiang lung and *Gerstensalat mit Yakwurst,* washed down with mulled qingke wine, was a welcome gastronomic novelty. The sausage did not, however, agree with Khram Nag. That he began to suffer from dysentery made the three-day wait for an audience with His Holiness, Rinpoche Trindzin Padmasambhava Pheesha Sanyen, all the more interminable for him. But I was happy to have a straw bed by a yak-dung fire and a warm Himalayan bearskin blanket under which I have been able to sleep soundly to the soporific drone of rumbling kettle drums, grumbling deep-toned trumpets, and the monotonously repetitious mumbling of *"Om mani padme hum."* The stone floor of our room is strewn with dry straw and the ceiling is caked with soot. Illuminated by yak-butter lamps, there is a photograph on the wall of Adolf Hitler. The regent inquired if we did not think it remarkable that the German eyes would follow you if you walked around the room. When I asked if he had heard the news of Hitler's death, the lama laughed. "No, no, he is quite alive and residing here in Tibet." The most adept of astrologers, diviners, and necromancers had confirmed that, forty-nine days after entering the Bardo in his bunker in Berlin and passing through various transitional states of postmortem consciousness, Hitler had been reborn as a Drogpa Tibetan boy in a manger in Geje: "Now a year old, the former Führer is being raised as a Tulku in the royal palace of Lhasa so that he can protect Tibet in the future from the menace of Chinese communism." After the three days of waiting to see the supreme abbott we had to endure an additional two hours in the low antechamber of the high audience hall. "Waiting," Khram Nag grumbled, "is easy for monks, accustomed as they are to meditating. Meditation is, after all, just intense waiting." The white walls of the waiting room are decorated with ten gold-leafed ladders, each with a painted serpent of a different hue entwined in its ten rungs. The regent has explained the iconography: "The ladders represent the ten classes of sentient beings from the insects to the gods; the rungs of the ladders represent the ten steps from the lowest hell up to the highest heaven. The last rung is the step into nirvana, which is freedom from rebirth and deliverance from all worlds. Nirvana is extinction. It is nothing, perfectly, purely, and splendidly nothing. The ten serpents are the primary sentiments that are characteristic of consciousness: love, sorrow, mirth, fear, disgust, courage, anger, wonder, pity, and serenity." When the doors to the audience hall were slowly opened, we were ordered to our knees to crawl into the room to make humble obeisance to the supreme abbot, who sat upon a throne, the feet of the legs of which were human skulls. Slowly raising my head to look at him, I was startled by his physical immaturity; he could not have been much older than Shirley Temple. Wearing sunglasses, a gold crown encrusted with lapis lazuli, turquoise, and coral, and a scarlet silk robe embroidered with silver threads in serpentine designs and holding a scepter topped with another human skull, he indifferently recited Tibetan homilies. Later, back in our quarters, I asked Khram Nag what the venerable child had said. "The usual nonsense," my friend, grumpy from dysentery, said as he shrugged. "The center is everywhere. All things return to their source. Everything is an illusion. He says that life is like a game. But that's obvious, isn't it? Life is like a game because anyone who has ever invented a game has tried his damnedest to make it like life. Why would any one listen to the supreme abbot? He's just a kid. What does he know? What does anyone know? All the religions of the world are foolish. They entertain us at their best and delude us at their worst." Whether he knew anything or not, the abbot did have the power invested in him by the Dalai Lama to decide whether or not we were permitted onto Everest. When he asked me directly, with the regent interpreting, why I wanted to scale his beloved Chomolungma, I announced that, having been born at the Dead Sea, the lowest place on earth, it was natural for me to want to visit the highest place. The boy said something to the regent, which Khram Nag paraphrased in a whisper: "Having been born at the highest place on earth, he now wants to visit the Dead Sea someday." I was granted permission to make the ascent. Khram Nag's dysentery has so worsened that he insists on returning to Gangtok. I'll send this square with him to be mailed from there. And the next square, the vision from the highest place on earth, the last rung of the ladder, I shall deliver in person. Initially, Khram Nag's decision to go home to Sikkim seemed a serpent in this square, threatening to take me back, for I was afraid to try the ascent alone. But the regent, speaking for the supreme abbot, assures me that I can do it. When he swore that it is easy, I had to ask why, then, has no one yet accomplished it? He laughed. "Many of the monks have been to the top many times. I must warn you, however, not to let your expectations get too high: there's nothing up there." But what, I asked, of all the foreigners who have tried and failed? Again he laughed. "No, no, many have been to the top. The Italian Jesuit priest, Hypolito Defideri da Pistoia, climbed the mountain over two hundred years ago. Before him there was Pir Abdul Khus Mahmud, and after him Comte Boniface de la Mettrie. There were others before them. And after them, most recently, Mallory and Irvine, with the permission of the previous rinpoche, made it to the summit." He explained why those two perished on the way down, and why we have not heard of previous successes of both Tibetans and foreigners: "Chomolungma, the Great Eternal Goddess Mother of the World, the Perfection of Woman, will give Herself to any man She loves. But She loves only him who so truly loves Her that he is willing to give his life for Her, and to remain faithful to Her after the ascent. She will not tolerate cads who brag to others that She has given herself, or men who, after their intimacies with Her, imagine that they have seduced and conquered Her, when it is She who has seduced and conquered them. That was, no doubt, the fatal mistake of Mallory and Irvine. You have not heard of the other men who have been allowed to reach Her exalted summit and return, because Chomolungma demands discretion in matters of love." The regent assures me that, as long as I love Her with all my heart, and promise not to speak of conquest, She will guide me with the wind that is Her voice to the highest of heights. Although I do not, he adds, require oxygen cylinders, crampons, ropes, or any other equipment, he has given me a gift: a pickax with a ladder engraved upon its wooden handle and a snake entwined through its ten rungs. I have carved my initials on the handle for good luck. To-morrow morning Khram Nag leaves for Gangtok and I set out up the face of the Eternal Goddess. Once I have been to the highest place on earth, once the game is won, there will be nothing left to say.

To 2

100

ENDGAME

While editing this manuscript, I could not help but occasionally wonder how much of it is true, which events actually happened and which characters are real. Was the author documenting his own life or fabricating a new one? Why did he write this? And for whom was he writing—himself, my mother, me, or strangers who might happen to have the opportunity and inclination to read it?

During the past year, in doing a bit of library research on Wild West shows, fairs, vaudeville, early cinema, British music hall and variety, the Folies-Bergère and Grand Guignol (and spending a week in Philadelphia, rummaging the archives of the Worden Museum of American Popular Entertainments), I did discover occasional references to an Isaac Schlossberg. But nothing significant was unearthed. Although I did not find any record of a Wyoming Willie, there was both a Montana Mike and a Nevada Ned with traveling ten-in-one shows during the early years of the twentieth century. And though Edward Burke's *Encyclopaedia of Modern British Theatre* makes no mention of Deborah Rabonnir, there was an American actress named Delilah Rubin who played Cleopatra in London in the years prior to World War II.

Although I do not believe in anything supernatural, neither in God nor in an afterlife, and certainly not in reincarnation, I was, nevertheless, startled by the information that Isaac Schlossberg apparently died on June 21, 1946, because I was, really and truly, but no doubt coincidentally, born forty-nine days later, on August 8 of that year. The fact that forty-nine days is, as the manuscript repeatedly mentions, the period designated by Tibetans as the time it takes for the spirit of a deceased person to enter a new body during the rebirth process, is at once amusing and eerie to me. I struggled, while working on this book, to understand the nature and meaning of my relationship to the author.

That struggle led to thoughts of Khram Nag Gyatso, the last known person ever to see my father. I wondered if, by chance, the Sherpa might possibly still be alive. If so, I supposed, he might be able to clarify a few things about the climb up Mt. Everest.

Impulsively, just over a month ago, after finishing my part of the work on this book, I telephoned a number listed in the Lonely Planet's guide to India for the Sikkim Tourist Information Center in Gangtok. I asked whoever it was who answered if he knew of a Sherpa named Khram Nag Gyatso. The distant voice suggested that I contact Tommy Trungpa's Tantric Treks, Sikkim's oldest tour operation, a firm for which most of the Sherpa guides of the area have worked at some time or another. The manager of T.T.T.T. politely referred me to the Hotel Shangri-La. An elderly Mr. Gyatso was known to occasionally appear in the hotel's bar, the Lost Horizon Lounge. Then telephoning that hotel, I spoke with a harried desk clerk, who, before abruptly hanging up on me, snapped, "Yes, yes, he is often present. Come here if you wish to meet him." I rang up again to leave my telephone number and a message for the Sherpa to contact the son of Isaac Schlossberg. And then again, after a wait of several days, I called to ask if my message had been delivered. "Yes, yes," the clerk, seemingly annoyed with me, barked. "He knows everything. As I have already said, sir, come here if you wish to meet him." Again he hung up on me. Further attempts to contact Khram Nag Gyatso by mail sent to him c/o the Shangri-La brought no results.

After several weeks of trying not to think about the prospect of meeting my father's final friend, curiosity got the better of good judgment, and I booked a flight to Calcutta. After stopping briefly in Los Angeles to see my mother, I went on to spend a few days in Honolulu, where I visited the Kamehameha Hawaiian Historical Society. I found nothing more substantial in the society's archives than a menu-program for the 1944 season of Happy Harry of Halelolo's Royal Hawaiian U.S.O. Luau Lollapalooza upon which a Professor Leroy Lestrange was billed as a "magician and mind reader."

As I'm not much of an adventurous traveler myself, I found India trying. Call me squeamish, but I preferred the white sands of Waikiki to the black hole of Calcutta, the dismal city where I was stranded for three days while waiting for a government permit to travel to Sikkim, and then for a flight to Bagdogra Airfield in Northern Bengal. Though fearful of leaving the poolside bar of the Taj Bengal, I mustered just enough courage, given the time that I had, to do a little field research. It was disappointing that the only thing that the only person who would talk to me at the Tollygunge Players' Club said was "I'm sorry, sir, information about the club's history is reserved exclusively for club members." There was, I discovered, no longer an Ananga Ranga Club in Sonagacchi, and there must have been a thousand Bannerjees in the telephone directory, not a single one of whom appeared to have either a menagerie or a taxidermy business. I did, however, get the chance to watch an elderly snake charmer with betel-stained teeth, an orange turban, and a black lungi perform on the street outside the Taj. He offered to stage a fight between a cobra and a mongoose for me: "In secret. Private. Very illegal and thrill-packed. One thousand rupees only. Even the life of a snake is not cheap. You will be happy. No? Okay, photograph of a python around your neck. Very beautiful. Everyone in America will love you with a snake. One thousand rupees only. No? Okay, what do you want?" I wanted to escape Calcutta and to meet Khram Nag Gyatso.

The six-hour taxi ride from Bagdogra to Gangtok along high mountain roads precariously rimming sheer drops into deep abysses made me question the value of the quest. In genuine terror I ordered the wild-eyed and whiskey-breathed driver to slow down. "No, sir," he shouted. "Any slower and we'll never get there." I corrected him: "No, no, sir, any faster and we'll never get there." Glowering into the rearview mirror, he mocked me: "Very funny joke, sir. I understand. Yes, I have heard that one before. I enjoy laughter as much as the next man. I am no stick-on-the-mud."

I tried to ignore his incessant chatter, his repeated declarations that Sikkim is heaven on earth ("but even better"), and his persistent offers to get me a much cheaper hotel than the Shangri-La ("the Bardo hostel") and to book a ten-day trek for me through the Himalayas ("even into government-forbidden areas"). He wanted to sell me a shawl or a carpet, hashish or heroin, a girl or a boy, or anything else "in India or the world," that I might want to purchase at a special discount bargain price offered to me, his "brother from America." All I wanted was for the ride to come to an end. When it finally did, and after being outrageously overcharged for it, I checked into the dilapidated Hotel Shangri-La.

Retiring to my room (which had identical views of the Kanchenjunga range through the single unwashed window and on the grimy 1991 calendar that hung on the wall next to that window), I discovered that it was impossible to shower, since the hotel plumbing was being fixed. Filthy as I was, I went to the Lost Horizon Lounge. The bartender, identifiable as a Sikh by his turban and beard, dressed in a black bow tie and maroon waistcoat with the words "Playboy Club" over the familiar bunny logo embroidered on the pocket, shook me the Lost Horizon's special Yetini cocktail, as he happily welcomed me to "heaven on earth" and offered to arrange a trek for me.

When I asked him about Khram Nag Gyatso, he was reassuring: "Oh yes, he'll be here. He is our only regular customer." After waiting at the Shangri-La for three miserable days, primarily for the Sherpa and secondarily for the plumbing to be fixed, I was on the verge of giving up when a purposeful nod and wink from the bartender indicated that the person entering the lounge was none other than Khram Nag Gyatso. I felt his hand on my shoulder: "Good evening, Mr. Isaac Schlossberg, Junior," he said, laughing, as he sat down next to me. "They told me you were here a few days ago. It is such a pleasure to meet the son of my best friend, the one and only Isaac Schlossberg!"

Expecting someone who looked like the Dalai Lama in climbing boots and a yak-fur parka, I was surprised at the sight of the old man wearing a Yankees baseball cap on backwards, a Disneyland sweatshirt, rose-tinted sunglasses, and obviously counterfeit Nike running shoes.

"Although I am Isaac Schlossberg's biological son," I explained, "my name is Lee Siegel."

"You look exactly like him anyway," he said, beaming. "And I suppose you have many of his qualities. You don't happen to have any American cigarettes, do you? Nothing from duty-free? Too bad. Maybe next time. Excuse me, Mr. Singh, I'll have a whiskey straight-up to drink to the memory of Isaac Schlossberg. I'm a little short on cash today, but . . ." The Sherpa and the bartender both looked to me for some word or gesture to indicate that I would pay for the drink to toast my deceased father. I gave the sign and got to the point: "I'm here for the truth. I'd like to know more about a letter that you wrote to your cousin, a lama in Tibet, some years ago in which you confided in him that Tenzing Norgay once confided in you that, when he and Edmund Hillary reached the summit of Everest, they found evidence that my father had already been there."

Changing the direction of the interview, he asked if I was enjoying Sikkim and if I would like for him to arrange a trekking tour for me. "Also you must see the Institute of Tibetology, the Reptile Sanctuary, Royal Do-Drul Chorten, Enchey Monastery, and, of course, the Government of Sikkim Cottage Industries Emporium."

"I'm not here to shop or sight-see," I insisted. "I want to know about Isaac Schlossberg. I've read something that he wrote about himself, a kind of book. You appear as a character in it. My father seems to have been a storyteller and so it's often difficult for me to distinguish his made-up tales from truths about his life. I want information about his assault on Everest. I'd appreciate your help with that."

Khram Nag Gyatso acted as if I had insulted the dead. "Isaac Schlossberg was the most truthful man who ever lived!" He then reverted to telling me about various government-approved treks for which he would happily sign me up. When, after his third drink, he excused himself to go to the lavatory, I didn't bother to warn him about the plumbing.

"The man is a pathological liar," the bartender grumbled in his absence. "Don't believe a word he says."

It seemed reasonable advice and, taking it, I berated myself for having been so foolish as to travel so far in order to meet a man who had nothing meaningful to say. By the time he returned from the toilet, I had paid the bill. I informed him that I was going up to my room to sleep and that I would be leaving for Bagdogra in the morning: "It was a pleasure to meet you, Mr. Gyatso. Good-bye." Although succumbing to his request to buy him another drink ("one for the road in memory of Isaac Schlossberg"), I declined the invitation to sit with him while he drank it.

In the morning, after checking out of the hotel, I stopped by the Lost Horizon to give Mr. Singh an extra tip for his sympathetic company during my visit to Sikkim.

He had a startling tale to tell: "As I said, the Sherpa is a pathological liar. Sitting here at the bar last night after you left, he told me a ridiculous story which no one would believe. But, since it is about you, it might be of some interest. 'This Siegel seems like a nice chap,' he said. 'I feel bad about it. I hate to hide the truth from him, but, I'm sorry, I think I must do what I think his father would want me to do.'"

In the story that the bartender told me that Khram Nag Gyatso had told him, my father, as I already believed, had indeed left Hawaii at the end of World War II and come to Gangtok with the intention of climbing Mt. Everest. But after the prologue, the story was entirely different than anything I might have imagined. "I told Schlossberg," the Sherpa had revealed behind my back, "that a man would have to be crazy to try to climb Chomolungma. It's too difficult and dangerous. It would be suicide. One afternoon I took him for a little hike up to Rumtek to meet a pretty Lepcha girl there who had always had a fancy for foreign fellows. It didn't take any more than the climb up Ranipol Hill for my friend to realize that he was no mountaineer. There was no way he was going anywhere near Mt. Everest. But he was in an awkward situation because he had promised so many people back home that he would be the first man to reach the summit. He had even written some kind of book about his conquest of Chomolungma. And there was another problem: a certain lady in the U.S.A. who was pregnant with his child. Isaac Schlossberg loved her, but he wasn't ready to get married, have a family, and give up his freedom and his adventurous way of life. He was a fun-loving fellow and that rosy-cheeked Lepcha girl was very beautiful and sweet. So he sent some letters to the American lady that would cause her to believe that he had died heroically on Mt. Everest. The Lepcha girl became his mistress and they moved into an old house in Darjeeling. I used to visit them there. He told me more than once that he felt a little sorry about deceiving the American lady and her child. But he consoled himself with the thought that they were better off without a scoundrel like him. Like many other American children born at the time, kids whose fathers had died in the war, his child, he was happy to know, would grow up believing that his father was a hero. The legendary adventures of Isaac Schlossberg would be more inspirational than the ordinary deeds of a real father with human foibles."

I was trembling with confusion, anger, mistrust, and other emotions for which I have no names as the bartender told me what Khram Nag Gyatso had told him. "So what was I to tell the son of Isaac Schlossberg tonight?" my father's friend had asked. "Should I have ruined a good story with the truth?"

I checked back into the hotel to wait for the return of the alcoholic Sherpa. That evening, the moment he entered the lobby, I pounced upon him by surprise, grabbing him by the collar of his Disneyland sweatshirt to choke him as I put it bluntly: "You dirty, fucking liar. I know that he never went to Tibet, that he never even tried to climb the goddamn mountain. I know about the Lepcha girl and his lies. But I want to hear it from your own mouth. Tell me the story. Tell me the truth, or I'm going break your scrawny little neck. And I want to know about the letter to your cousin. The lie about the mountaineering ax on Everest. Why did you write that letter?"

The desk clerk was looking down at the books, trying to ignore the scene as, trembling in terror, Khram Nag Gyatso begged for forgiveness. "Please don't hurt me. Remember, I was a friend of your father." Worn down as I was by my arduous journey, that plea made me want to kill him. I was sickened by the revelation that was the rotten fruit of my pilgrimage.

After repeating an abridged version of the same story that the bartender had told me, he had the nerve to ask if we might go into the Lost Horizon for a drink to help him relax for the telling of the sequel. Perhaps it was because, as someone who has never been a particularly aggressive person, I felt mildly ashamed of my violent outburst that I consented to it.

The Sherpa downed his whiskey and asked Mr. Singh for another. Knowing that Gyatso knew that he must have been the source of my knowledge of the truth, the embarrassed bartender offered the drink to the old man on the house. He listened with me to the outrageous story: "Your dear father and the Lepcha girl lived together for a few years. But she was very young and he was getting older and, well, she ran off with another man, a young fellow from Switzerland who, by the way, successfully climbed Everest with the Swiss expedition of 1956. Your father decided to go to Israel, which had become an independent state, and to live there on some sort of communal farm." Mr. Singh poured another whiskey.

"Why," I demanded, "did you write that fraudulent letter about Tenzing Norgay to your cousin?"

"I'm getting to that. If you want the truth you have to be patient. Not having heard from Isaac for some years, I thought he might be dead. But then, one day about twenty years ago, out of the clear blue sky, he showed up here in Gangtok saying that he needed my help. He was with a woman named Bunny. She was an old friend of his. They had run into each other in Israel. That's where they got married. Not beautiful like his Lepcha girl, but not bad for a wife."

According to the Sherpa's account, Mr. and Mrs. Schlossberg returned to the United States after the Six-Day War in Israel to settle down in California. Late one night, while watching an old B-movie on television, my father recognized the female lead in the film, an actress screen-named Noreen Nash, none other than the daughter of Brigadier General Gilbert Roth of the United States Navy, the girl whom he had left in Hawaii years before. It had not been difficult for him to find out more about the Hollywood actress: she had married Dr. L. E. Siegel, a physician in Beverly Hills, and they had two sons, one of their own and me. Subsequently my biological father, apparently making some effort to learn about his only son, discovered that while my younger brother was a successful doctor like his father, I was struggling as a writer.

"Thus it was to help you," the Sherpa said with a smile, as if what followed would exonerate the author of this book, "that your dear father came here, discussed his plan with me, and dictated the letter to my cousin."

Schlossberg was, it seems, dismayed that either my mother had not tried to get his autobiographical game book of snakes and ladders published or, if she had tried, she had not been successful in finding a publisher for it. Or maybe she had not even read it. But the discovery that Sir Edmund Hillary was not really the first man to reach the summit of Mt. Everest would certainly be big news, and a commercial publisher would surely want to buy the rights to a book that documented that fact and told the story of the man who truly was the first to conquer the tallest mountain in the world. The book would be a best-seller. But interest in the manuscript needed to be aroused.

"He wanted you, his only son and beneficiary," Khram Nag Gyatso said as if I'd be touched, "to have the royalties from the memoirs of Isaac Schlossberg. I came up with the idea of sending the letter in question to my cousin, Zabs-Dkar Khedrup, both because he has a very big mouth and because of a fight that he had with Tenzing Norgay when they were kids in school together. Khedrup, whose father forced him to become a Buddhist monk, had always been jealous of his classmate, the climber who went on to become an international celebrity. I told Isaac that he'd certainly blab the story and that coming from him, a Buddhist lama, the story would be indisputable. But, unfortunately, Khedrup was arrested in Lhasa by the Chinese army and disappeared before he had the opportunity to discredit Norgay. I never saw your father again. But he wrote to me from California in '89. I still have the letter, if you'd like to see it."

Written in the same hand that I knew so well, the hand that once scrawled this book of lies, the letter informed the Sherpa that he was alive and well and "just finishing play in another game, and having as good a time as any ninety-year-old could possibly imagine. My life has always been a lot of fun."

The return address on the envelope (upon which his name appeared as "Isaac Codee") indicated that he was living in Santa Culebra, California. It took a week to get there from Gangtok, Sikkim.

The small Spanish-style home was occupied by a retired couple from Philadelphia who explained that they had bought the house a few years earlier from a widow, a Mrs. Bunny Codee. They suggested that, if she was still alive, I might be able to find her at the Zechut Avot Jewish Home for the Elderly in Santa Monica. They knew nothing about her husband.

After telling the receptionist at the old folks home that I was Bunny Gotlober-Codee's stepson, I was shown to her room. The little girl who had asked the Four Questions of Passover at the seder in a tent outside the fairgrounds during the California run of the Durbar of Delhi of 1915 was now a very old woman. She was toothless, and there were only a few wisps of white hair remaining on her spotted pate. Gray-blue eyes stared at me through the drooped and wrinkled flaps of eyelid as I introduced myself.

"I didn't know that my Isaac has a little boy," she faintly muttered. "Maybe I did and just forgot. I don't know. Are you my son too? You sure do look like your father. Just like when I married him." She hesitated, looked suddenly frightened, and asked, "Is he dead?"

"No, he's doing just fine," a nurse, entering the room, said in a voice that was as jolly sweet as it was booming loud for the almost deaf old woman. "He sends his love to you, honey. He says you'll be together soon." At a normal volume she confided in me, "I tell them that, the ones that miss their dead spouses. It makes them happy."

As she checked the bedpan, set the clock to the right time, and then sorted the medications on the side table, I asked if she knew anything about Mr. Codee.

"Not much. I heard he was some sort of ghostwriter, you know, one of those people who writes books that other people publish under their own names. Ghostwriting! It doesn't seem honest, does it? I mean you read an autobiography, a book that someone is supposed to have written about himself, and it turns out that someone else wrote it!"

I drove from the old folks home to my mother's house. Appalled by the revelation that the author of this book had never even attempted to climb the world's highest mountain, that he no more died on Mt. Everest than he was born at the Dead Sea, I felt that my mother also ought to know the truth. I hoped that she wouldn't be too upset or feel betrayed. She took it in good spirits. The story even seemed to amuse her.

My major concern at the time, however, was not my mother, but my publisher. Since the manuscript for this book had been accepted on account of its significance as a historical document, written as it supposedly was by the first man to successfully climb Mt. Everest, I feared that publication would be canceled. Compelled by what I consider the importance of truth, I telephoned my editor to confess my father's sin.

"It's already in page proofs," he said, and there was a disconcerting silence.

I apologized.

"Well," the editor finally sighed, "I suppose we could release it as a novel."